10634905

NORFOLK LIBRARY
AND INFORMATION SERVICE

... ... the University
Missouri in 1970 with a BA in Creative Writing
and Literature. Following a career in publishing
she became an editor with TSR in 1983 and now
lives with her husband and two cats in Lake
Geneva, Wisconsin.

TRACY HICKMAN worked as a supermarket boy,
a movie projectionist and a theatre manager before
landing a job with TSR. That job led to his
association with Margaret Weis and the creation
of the *Dragonlance* chronicles. He currently lives in
Utah with his wife Laura and their four children.

Voyager

MARGARET WEIS &
TRACY HICKMAN

WELL OF DARKNESS

The Sovereign Stone Trilogy
BOOK 1

HarperCollins*Publishers*

Voyager
An Imprint of HarperCollins*Publishers*
77–85 Fulham Palace Road,
Hammersmith, London W6 8JB

www.voyager-books.com

This paperback edition 2001
4

First published in Great Britain by *Voyager* 2000

Copyright © Margaret Weis and Tracy Hickman 2000

The Authors assert the moral right to
be identified as the authors of this work

ISBN 0 00 648614 2

Typeset in Plantin Light by
Palimpsest Book Production Limited,
Polmont, Stirlingshire

Printed in Great Britain by
Clays Ltd, St Ives plc

ACKNOWLEDGMENTS

For years, ever since we first worked on the Dragonlance project together, we have been telling stories to fantasy artist Larry Elmore. Then one day, Larry Elmore told us a story. He told us a story about a wondrous realm where paladins of good, wearing magical silver armor, fight vampyric paladins, whose cursed armor is dark as the bottom of a well of darkness. In this world, dragons battle huge creatures known as bahk. Elves live lives dedicated to honor and the sword. Orken sail the seas in pirate ships. Dwarves ride shaggy ponies across vast plains. Humans build castles of rainbows. Wizards draw magic from the air and the ground, from fire and water and the darkness of the Void.

We were entranced with this world of Larry Elmore's creation. We wanted to meet the people who lived there and share their lives and their adventures with those of you who also enjoy exploring strange and mysterious and wonderful realms of fantasy. We are pleased to bring Larry Elmore's vision to life in this first book of the Sovereign Stone trilogy.

And for those who would like to find their own adventures in this realm, we invite you to play the Sovereign Stone role-playing game, created by Lester Smith and Don Perrin.

In conclusion, all of us who have been involved in this project want to thank you, Larry, for creating this world and for inviting us to go adventuring in it with you.

– Margaret Weis and Tracy Hickman

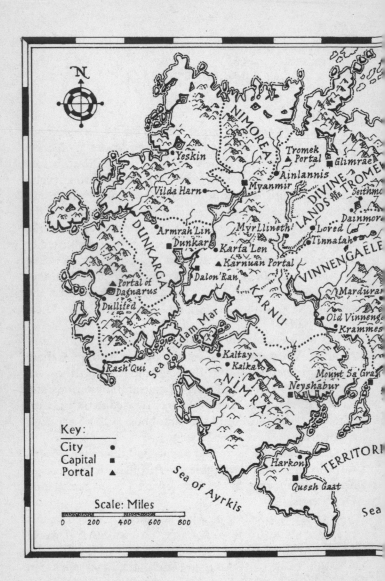

PART
ONE

ONE

———◆◆◆———

The Whipping Boy

THE BOY GAZED UP AT THE CASTLE. ITS shining white marble walls were wet with the spray from the seven waterfalls that flowed on either side of it, four to the north and three to south, and glistened in the early-morning sun. Rainbows shimmered and danced around the castle walls. The peasants believed the rainbows were fine cloth spun by fairies, and more than one silly lad had gone to his death in the tumbling water trying to snag them.

The boy knew better. He knew that rainbows were not substantial, being made of nothing more than sunlight and water. Only that which exists in both the darkness and in the light is real. The boy had been taught to believe only in what was real and substantial.

The boy looked at the castle without much feeling, good or bad, nothing but a sort of uncaring fatalism that is often seen in ill-used dogs. Not that the boy had been particularly ill-used in his life, if to be ignored is not to be ill-used. He was about to leave his parents and his home and enter into a new life and by rights he should have felt sad, homesick, frightened, and trepidatious. He felt none of those: only tired, from the long walk, and uncomfortably warm and itchy in his new woolen stockings.

He and his father stood before the gate set in a high outer wall. Beyond the gate was a courtyard and beyond the courtyard myriad steps leading up into the castle, which had been built against a cliff. The castle looked out to the west, gazing out over Lake Ildurel, its back planted solidly against the rocks to the east. Its very topmost turrets were level with the River Hammerclaw, which flowed from east to west and whose rushing water, tumbling over the cliff face, created the rainbows.

The castle walls were white marble – the boy had once seen a representation of the castle at a feast, made of sugar lumps – and it was several stories tall. How many stories the boy could not count because the castle roamed all over the cliff face. So many turrets jutted off every which way, so many battlements slanted off in such different directions, and so many small lead-paned glass windows winked in the sunlight that the sight confused him. He had wanted to play with the sugar castle, and his mother had told him he might, but the next morning he found it had been eaten by mice.

The boy gazed, awed, at this castle, which was not made of sugar and not likely to be eaten by mice or even dragons. One wing of the castle caught his eye. This was a wing to the east, overlooking the four waterfalls. Atop it was a turret larger than all the rest, with a balcony that stretched around it. That was the King's Walk, said his father. King Tamaros, blessed of the gods, was the only person permitted to walk that balcony.

The King must be able to see the whole world from there, the boy thought. Or if not the whole world, then at least the entire great city of Vinnengael. The boy could practically see the whole city himself, just standing on the palace steps.

Vinnengael was built on three levels, the lowest level

being even with the lake, which stretched to the horizon, its distant shore just barely visible from the King's Walk. The second level of the city was built atop a cliff that rose up from the first level. The third level was built atop another cliff, which rose from the second. The palace stood on the third level. Across from the palace, behind the boy and across a vast marble courtyard, was the Temple of the Magi.

Temple and palace, the heart of the kingdom and its head, were the only two major structures standing on the third level. Soldiers' barracks occupied the north; the barracks were attached to the palace. To the south, built on a jutting rock groin, were the elegant houses of the foreign ambassadors.

The men-at-arms guarding the outer gate gave the boy's father a bored glance as the two of them passed through. The boy craned his neck to gaze up at the huge portcullis, with its rows of grim teeth. He would have liked to stop, hoping to see some blood, for he was well acquainted with the tale of Nathan of Neyshabur, one of the heroes of Vinnengael, who had ordered the portcullis to be lowered though he himself was standing beneath it, fending off the kingdom's enemies, refusing to give ground though the wicked teeth thundered down upon him. Nathan of Neyshabur had lived and died several hundred years ago, when the city and the castle, but not the rainbows, were young. It was therefore unlikely that his blood would still be dripping from the portcullis, but the boy felt disappointed, nonetheless.

His father yanked at the boy's mantle and demanded to know what he thought he was doing, gawking like an ork during festival time, and hustled the boy along.

They walked across a vast courtyard and entered the castle proper, where the boy was immediately lost. His father knew the way well, however, being one of the King's courtiers, and he led the boy up marble stairs and down marble halls and around marble statues and past marble columns until they reached an antechamber, where the father shoved the boy down onto a carved wood chair and summoned a servant.

The boy gazed at the high ceilings, stained with soot from the winter fires, and at the wall opposite, where hung a tapestry that depicted long-bodied, long-snouted, long-eared dogs that resembled no known dog then living and people all turned sideways hunting a stag which, by its expression, appeared to be enjoying it all immensely though it had six arrows in it.

A man entered the antechamber, a youngish, bad-tempered, grim-looking man clad in a high-collared tunic, buttoned down the front, of rich design, with long flowing sleeves. His legs, visible from the calf down, were thick and bulky, his ankles being nearly as wide as his feet. His hose were of different colors, one red and the other blue to match the red-and-blue design in the tunic. His drab hair was combed back in the current fashion among humans and curled around the neck; he was clean-shaven.

The boy's father was dressed in a similar manner, though he wore a surcoat over his tunic, and his colors were green and blue. The boy was dressed the same as his father, except that his mantle and hood covered his clothes, for the season was late autumn and the air was chill. The man conferred briefly with the boy's father, then turned his gaze upon the boy.

'What did you say his name was?'

'Gareth, Lord Chamberlain.'

The chamberlain sniffed. 'I do not know when I have seen an uglier child.'

'Any child would appear ugly compared to His Highness,' said the boy's father.

'True, m'lord,' said the chamberlain. 'But this one appears to have worked at it 'specially.'

6

'His Highness and my son are the same age to the day, born the very same night. Her Majesty wished –'

'Yes, yes. I am familiar with Her Majesty's wishes,' said the chamberlain, rolling his eyes and tucking his thumbs in his wide leather belt to indicate that he thought Her Majesty's wishes a crockful of crap. He frowned down at the boy. 'Well, there's no help for it, I suppose. As if I didn't have enough trouble. Where are the rest of the lad's clothes? You don't expect us to clothe him, I assume.'

'My retainer is bringing them around the back,' said the boy's father with a hint of frost. 'Surely, *you* didn't expect us to cart them through the streets.'

The two men regarded each other with ice-rimed stares, then the chamberlain placed his thick leg and pointed shoe in front of the other leg and bowed from the waist. 'Your servant, sir.'

The boy's father also 'made a leg' as the saying went, his hands at his waist so that the surcoat did not fall forward and pick up dirt from the floor. '*Your* servant, sir.'

The boy stood in his hood and mantle, hot and itchy, and stared at the stag with the six arrows sticking out of its side, kicking up its heels and looking very merry.

'Come with me, then, Gareth,' said the chamberlain in resigned tones. 'Say good-bye to your father,' he added indifferently.

Gareth bowed to his father in a courtly manner, as he had been taught. His father gave the boy a hurried blessing and left quickly, to attend His Majesty. Neither father nor son was saddened at this parting. It had been a six-month since the boy had last seen his father, as it was. The fact that the boy was now a member of the court meant that he would likely see his noble parents more often than at any other time in his childhood.

The chamberlain laid a heavy hand upon the boy's shoulder and steered him through the palace rooms.

'These are the private quarters for the royal family,'

explained the chamberlain in sonorous tones. 'They will be your home, too, from this day forward. To be chosen as the prince's whipping boy is a high honor. I trust you are sensible of it.'

Gareth was not sensible of much of anything at the moment, except the man's heavy hand pressing him into the marble floor and making his shoulder ache exceedingly.

'The position was much coveted,' the chamberlain continued, his words pressing down on the boy with as much weight as his hand. 'Many fine lads were put forward as candidates, lads of sixteen and some even older. Much coveted,' he repeated.

Gareth knew this to be true. His father and his mother and even Nanny had ground the fact into him over and over, until it seemed a part of his flesh, like the charcoal ground into the smithy's hands. The whipping boy bore the prince's punishment, because the prince, chosen by the gods, could never be touched in anger by mortal hands. The whipping boy also served as companion to the young prince, and was educated alongside the prince. Since the two would grow up together, the whipping boy and his family must naturally profit from such an arrangement.

Gareth was also well aware that he had not merited this honor. His father was a lord, but not a very important lord; his mother one of the Queen's ladies-in-waiting. The coincidence of the boy's birth being on the same night as that of the young prince was all that had recommended him.

Her Majesty the Queen came from Dunkarga, a kingdom to the west. It seemed that the people of Dunkarga held the belief that the stars affected their lives. Gareth knew this was nonsense; his father had told him as much. How could far-distant, coldly sparkling objects, as big as motes of dust, have an effect on mankind? But Gareth's parents had been quick to take advantage of the fact that Queen Emillia believed that the stars took an interest in her.

Hearing of the search for a whipping boy, Gareth's mother had hinted to the Queen that only a child born under the same stars as the prince should be considered worthy of sharing the prince's destiny. The Queen was quite taken with this notion and called for the royal astrologer, whom she had brought with her from Dunkarga. His hand fingering the coins in his purse deposited by Gareth's father, the royal astrologer solemnly confirmed that this was indeed the case. Gareth being the only child of noble blood born that night (his father had checked to make certain), he was chosen.

At the age of nine, Gareth was to take his place at court and start upon the performance of his new duties, which would be to bear the punishment for the prince's infractions. As they walked through the palace, Gareth recalled the story, which his mother often told, of how the Queen – on hearing that one of her ladies-in-waiting was also in labor and about to give birth – had ordered that his mother's legs be tied together, so that no other child should precede her son in anything. His mother's pains had fortunately stopped – scared out of her, likely enough – or it was probable that Gareth would not be walking the palace halls this moment. His mother's labor having started up again after the prince's arrival, Gareth was born three hours later. His first cries were drowned out by the explosions of the celebratory fireworks.

Gareth's mother had handed him off to a wet nurse the very night he was born, so that, after her lying-in period, she could return to her duties as lady-in-waiting. He was raised at his father's country estate, brought up mostly by servants, who had either indulged the boy or neglected him as the whim took them.

Thus in his fourth year, Gareth's parents, on one of their rare visits to their son, were dismayed to find their child a spoiled brat, a little hooligan, as dirty and uneducated as any peasant child of similar years. Gareth's father sent for his own former nursemaid, who had retired to help her husband make cloth. Now a widow, she was glad to hand over the business to her grown sons and enter, once again, a noble household.

She took Gareth in hand and taught him to read and write and provided him with the manners he would need when he was old enough to take his place at court. Gareth missed Nanny at that moment far more than he missed either his father or his mother. Her task done, she had been sent back to her family.

'Do you say your prayers, Master Gareth?' the chamberlain asked suddenly.

'I do, my lord,' Gareth replied in a small voice, the first words he had spoken.

'Then say them, now, young sir. Pray to the gods that His Highness takes a liking to you, for if he does not, Her Majesty will be rid of you, stars or no stars.'

Gareth peered out from under the folds of his hood, looked again at the soot-stained ceiling. The gods were somewhere up there, beyond the soot and the marble. Like the rainbows, the gods could not be touched. Gareth didn't think they would be much interested in him. Besides, his only prayer at that moment would have been to go back home, which would have made his parents exceedingly angry, and so Gareth considered it better not to pray at all.

The palace was a grand confusion to Gareth. He seemed to have been walking through it for most of his life; though it was probably only an hour since he had entered the main gate. He would come to love the palace, love its cool, serene beauty, love its mysterious alcoves and secret passages, but that would happen much later, after he'd recovered from homesickness and the fear of sleeping in a strange place, and after he'd learned his way around, which took him almost a year. For now, the palace was immense, cold and empty corridors that led to immense, cold rooms filled with massive, heavy furniture, everything tinged with the scent of woodsmoke.

'His Highness is here, in the playroom,' said the chamberlain.

Two guards – the prince's bodyguards – flanked a large wooden door. Gareth had seen the King's Guard only on parade days and then only from a distance. Clad in their shining plate armor and chain mail, they appeared enormous in his sight, ferocious beings, who inspected him thoroughly from top to toe, searching him for weapons, thrusting their hands beneath his velvet doublet and even peering at the insides of his small shoes.

Gareth held still and meekly submitted to the indignity. Somewhere in the past some rival chieftain had sent in his young son, armed with a dagger, to stab the royal heir.

'He's clean,' said the guard, and opened the door.

The chamberlain nodded and, grabbing Gareth again by the shoulder, ushered him into the playroom. As they were walking across the threshold, the chamberlain leaned over to whisper harshly, 'Don't touch any of His Highness's toys. Don't look at any of His Highness's books. Don't fidget, don't pick your nose, don't gape or pass wind or stare out the window. Don't speak unless you are spoken to. Do not sit in the prince's presence, never turn your back upon him, for that is a terrible insult. If you must use the privies, ask His Highness's permission to be excused. When you are whipped, scream loudly and cry a great deal in order to impress upon His Highness how much the beating hurts him.'

The numbness, which had carried Gareth this far, gave way to despair. If the gods had been anywhere near at the time, Gareth would have prayed – not to leave the palace, for it seemed hopeless to him that he should ever find his way out – but to simply die on the spot.

11

He could not look at any of the wonders around him – marvelous toys, from all parts of Loerem. He took no interest in the shelves of books, though he loved reading and had read over and over all two of his father's books – given to his father as gifts, he had never been known to look at them. Gareth did not even see His Highness, for the whipping boy's eyes were filled with tears and it was all he could do to stumble alongside the chamberlain and not fall over any of the clutter that filled the playroom.

The chamberlain's hand shoved Gareth into the floor.

'His Royal Highness, Dagnarus, Prince of Vinnengael.'

Gareth sank to his knees, mindful of his father's teaching. He had an impression of somebody coming up to take a look at him, as one inspects a pig at market.

'Leave us,' said a voice, imperious, even then.

Gareth thought, of course, that the prince meant him. He was only too glad to comply. Leaping to his feet, he was ready to bolt. A hand – his hand, the prince's hand – grabbed hold of his sleeve, however, and held him fast.

'I said leave us,' the prince repeated, and Gareth understood that the prince was speaking to the chamberlain.

'But, Your Highness, you know nothing of this boy –'

'Are you forcing me to give you an order three times?' the prince asked with an edge to his tone that made Gareth shiver.

'As Your Highness commands,' said the chamberlain, bowing very low and backing out of the room. Not an easy feat, considering the floor was littered with hobby-horses and toy ships and chariots and child-size shields and spears.

He shut the door, and Gareth was alone with his prince.

Blinking back his tears, he saw him, and, in that moment, he feared him.

The two boys were equal in height then, though Dagnarus would be taller when he came to manhood. He was large-boned, whereas Gareth was slimmer, and so the prince seemed bigger to the whipping boy. The prince's auburn hair – the color of the leaves of the sugar maple in the autumn – was thick and heavy and cropped close around his face in the fashion of the time. His skin was pale with a smattering of freckles over his nose, the only flaw to his flawless complexion.

His eyes were green, flecked with gold, large and brilliant, framed by russet eyelashes that made it seem as if they were gilded with burnished gold. He was dressed in a green doublet and hose that brought out the red of his hair and deepened the green of his eyes. He was well formed, strongly built, with remarkable strength – for a child – in his hands.

The green eyes went over every inch of the whipping boy, inspecting him much more thoroughly than the guards outside the door. Gareth remembered everything he *wasn't* supposed to do, but no one had told him yet what he was to do. Unhappy, uncomfortable, overawed, humiliated, he cowered before this calm, self-possessed, beautiful child and, seeing his inadequacies reflected in those wonderful eyes, wished again that he might die.

'What is your name, boy?' Dagnarus asked, and though the voice was still imperious, it was not unkind.

Gareth could not answer for the tears in his throat.

'Are you mute or deaf, boy?' the prince demanded. He was not impatient or sarcastic, merely requiring information.

Gareth shook his head and managed to blurt out his name. With what little courage he had left, he lifted his head and peeped at the prince warily.

Reaching out his hand, Dagnarus touched Gareth's face, rubbed his cheek. He drew his hand back, looked at his fingers, and looked back at the whipping boy.

'It doesn't come off,' the prince said.

'No, Your – Your Highness,' Gareth stammered. 'I was born with it. A curse.'

13

Other children of Gareth's acquaintance had either mocked him or run from him. Dagnarus did neither. He would never run from anything. And he would always look a truth in the face, no matter how ugly.

'A curse?' Dagnarus repeated.

The green eyes brightened. The prince drew Gareth over to a pair of chairs, made to child size, which stood beside a child-size table. Several books had been shoved off the table, to make room for a miniature catapult, carved of wood, with which he had been firing peas over a wall made of blocks. Gareth's gaze went hungrily to the books. Dagnarus's gaze went proudly to the catapult.

In that moment, the two were defined.

Dagnarus sat down. Mindful of his instructions, Gareth remained standing.

'Tell me of the curse,' Dagnarus ordered. He never made a request, everything was a command.

Shyly, Gareth began, 'Yes, Your Highness. It seems that when my mother was –'

'Why don't you sit?' the prince interrupted.

'I was told not to, Your Highness,' Gareth said, feeling his marred face burn.

'Who told you? That great idiot?' The prince dismissed the chamberlain with a snort. 'Ignore him. I always do. Sit down in that chair.'

'Yes, Your Highness.' Timidly, Gareth sat down. 'It seems that when my mother was –'

'And you must not call me "Your Highness,"' said the prince.

Gareth looked at him helplessly.

'You must call me Dagnarus,' the prince said. He put his hand on Gareth's, and added, 'You will be my friend.'

In that moment, Gareth loved him, as he had never before loved anyone or anything.

'Now.' Dagnarus settled back, folded his arms across his chest. 'Tell me of this curse.'

14

'It was when my mother was carrying me in her belly,' Gareth said. This story was another one of his earliest recollections, and he knew it by rote. He spoke at first shyly and hesitantly, but, finding an interested listener, he gathered more confidence and was eventually talking quite volubly. 'She was in the marketplace, on an errand for the Queen, your mother, and there was a beggar woman sitting on the corner. She asked my mother for a coin for food. My mother had no coins to give; the only money she carried belonged to the Queen. My mother said as much and was walking on when the beggar woman cursed her. I kicked in my mother's belly very hard and my mother knew then that the beggar woman was a witch and that her curse had struck me.

'My mother summoned the city guards, and they arrested the witch. She was tied hand and foot and thrown into the river, where she floated a long time, which my mother says proved that she was a witch. The people threw rocks at the witch, and eventually she sank. The midwife said my mother was to drink rose hip tea, to wash off the curse, but it didn't work. I was born with this on my face.'

The large purplish blotch surrounded Gareth's left eye, crawled up onto his forehead and down onto his left cheek. His nondescript brown hair was cut into bangs across his forehead, to hide that portion of the mark, but there was no hiding the mark around his eye or on his cheek.

He could not recall the number of potions and ointments, salves and creams the servants used at his mother's behest to try to rid his face of the curse. And although several took off his skin, they had done nothing to remove the mark. One enterprising serving lass had even tried sanding it off. Fortunately, Nanny had heard his shrieks and come to his rescue.

'Do people make sport of you?' Dagnarus asked, staring at the mark.

Usually Gareth didn't like to be stared at, but the prince

wasn't like the rest, he wasn't mocking or sniggering. Dagnarus was merely curious.

'Sometimes, Your Highness,' Gareth admitted.

'They won't do so anymore,' Dagnarus stated with finality. 'I shall order them not to. If anyone does, you must tell me immediately. I will have the person executed.'

The prince was showing off. Gareth was not completely ignorant of the ways of the court, and even he knew that a nine-year-old prince did not possess life-and-death power over others. But Gareth was touched and pleased, if not with the sentiment, then with the feeling that at least now he mattered to someone.

'Thank you, Your Highness, but it's not important, and I wouldn't want anyone to be beheaded because –'

'Yes, yes.' Dagnarus waved his hand.

He had a short attention span and, although he would listen well to something in which he was interested, he would cut off impatiently any conversation that he found boring.

'I don't like the name "Gareth,"' he announced.

'I am sorry, Your High –'

The prince lifted his chin, stared.

'Dag . . . narus,' Gareth said. He left a pause between the syllables, for he was truly afraid that the prince would change his mind and order him to return to the formal appellation.

Dagnarus smiled. The smile brought out the gold flecks in his green eyes, made the eyes sparkle like topaz and emerald.

'I will call you Patch,' he said.

Gareth bowed his head. The moment was solemn as a christening.

'You understand your duties, Patch? You are to be whipped when they want to punish me.' The prince turned to his toys, caused the arm of the catapult to move up and down by pressing on it with his finger.

'You know that, don't you, Patch?' he reiterated. 'They told you that?'

'Yes, Dagnarus,' Gareth replied, a little uncomfortable with his new name.

'They hit you because no ordinary mortal dares lay hands upon his king. They think that if they beat you, I will feel remorseful, and I won't disobey them anymore. That's what they think.'

He frowned, the green eyes darkened. The gold glints disappeared like jewels sinking beneath the surface of still water. He joggled the catapult, rolled it about on its small wooden wheels.

'It won't work,' he said, and his voice was stern. 'I tell you that right now, Patch. I will be sorry to see you beaten, of course, but there are things that they want to try to make me do that *I will not do*.'

The green eyes, looking at Gareth, were dark and still. 'Not if they were to kill you for it, Patch.'

This statement was different from the former boast. This was spoken in a strange, unchildlike voice, a voice without innocence, a voice that knew the meaning of what he said.

'You can leave, if you want to, Patch,' Dagnarus added. 'You won't get into trouble over it. I'll tell the Queen, my mother' – he said this word with a slight curl of his lip – 'that I didn't want you. I don't need a companion.'

Gareth looked around the room, and he didn't see the wonderful toys, or the books, or the guards at the open door, keeping watch to see that the whipping boy didn't strangle His Highness, or the servants lurking about, waiting to satisfy His Highness's least desire. Gareth saw the prince's loneliness, stark and bare as a bone. He saw it as a mirror reflecting his own loneliness. He saw the stag with the arrows, leaping merrily.

'If they want to whip me, Dagnarus,' Gareth said shyly, 'they're going to have to catch me first.'

17

The golden jewels sparkled, the green eyes glittered, and the prince laughed out loud. So boisterous was his laughter that the chamberlain, who had been skulking about in the hall, hoping for a fight to break out that he might be the one to tell Her Majesty that he, the chamberlain, had been against this from the start, thrust his head inside the door.

'Did we summon you? Get out of here, you old fart!' Dagnarus shouted, and threw a wooden block at him.

Emboldened, Gareth tossed a block at the chamberlain as well. His aim fell quite short, for his throw was meek and halfhearted. Dagnarus's block was thrown with much more accuracy and skill and missed the man only because the chamberlain had the good sense to slam shut the door.

Dagnarus opened one of the books, a large, leather-bound volume with gold leaf on the cover. The pages were vellum, trimmed in gold. Timidly, Gareth admired the book. He gazed in wonder and awe at one of the illustrations within – a knight in fabulous armor battling a dragon out of Nanny's bedtime tales. He recognized a book written by the magi, who keep a record of great deeds done by heroes of the past and use them as teaching tools.

'Do you want to read this story?' Gareth asked with wistful longing.

'No.' Dagnarus scoffed. Closing the book impatiently, he stacked another volume on top of it. 'This shall be our fortress.' He positioned the catapult in front of it and prepared to fire. 'We are going to play at war.'

TWO

——————◆-◆-◆——————

The Lesser Guardian

THE ELVES HAVE A LEGEND THAT RELATES
how, at the beginning of time, the flutter of
a butterfly's wings caused the air currents to
expand out like ripples in the water, gaining in strength and
potency until eventually the whispering flutter built into a
tempest that laid waste to a city a thousand miles away. If
this legend is true – and the elves reverence the butterfly
on its account – then perhaps the sound of the marble flung
from the prince's toy catapult, smashing into tiny soldiers,
was magnified in the ears of the Shield of the Divine, so
that he heard the boom of war and smelled the blood of
thousands.

He reflected on war as he scattered bread crumbs to the
golden-scaled fish, whose thrashings as they fought for
the food disturbed the tranquillity of the ornamental pond.
The Shield was fond of the tranquillity, but he also took
pleasure in watching the fish fight over the bread crumbs,
one reason he fed them himself instead of consigning such
a mundane task to his servants.

Fish fed, the Shield held out his hands. A servant bearing
a bowl of fresh water and a towel stepped forward. The
Shield washed the crumbs from his hands, dried them

on the towel, and spoke to another servant. 'I will hold audience in the cedar grove this afternoon. Has Silwyth of House Kinnoth arrived?'

The servant bowed. 'Yes, Shield. He awaits your pleasure.'

'He will take wine with me in the cedar grove,' the Shield decided. 'Produce him at the prescribed hour.'

The servant bowed again and departed, backing out of the august presence. The nobles, three of them this day, who had been given audience by the ornamental pond, glanced at each other. Silwyth of the House Kinnoth – the Shield's own house – had been nothing more than a small fish in the pond before this. Though he held the rank of Lesser Guardian of the Eastern Forest, a rank and title granted to him by the Divine, and though he was a cousin to the Shield, the Shield had many cousins, and there were many Lesser Guardians. The taking of wine in the cedar grove had just elevated Silwyth's status from small fish to large.

The servant, who was one of the house servants, carried the message to a servant who was outside the house and who carried it to Silwyth, who had not yet entered the house but who was waiting in the fourth terrace above the gatehouse. Since Silwyth had been accorded the honor of taking wine with the Shield, and thereby accorded the honor of entering the house, the servant requested that Silwyth accompany him to the ninth terrace above the gatehouse, the terrace closest to the house.

Silwyth received the news of his audience and of his relocation to the higher terrace in silence, with outward calm, though within him his heart reveled. Elves are taught from an early age to keep their emotions concealed, that they might not disturb or offend or intrude upon the lives of others. This custom makes the elves appear cold and unfeeling to humans, who let their emotions run amuck, doing all sorts of harm. The elves believe that it is wrong to invade the life of another even by the look upon one's face, thereby to force someone to share in one's joy or sorrow, elation or despair. Only those closest and most intimate with an elf – the partner of the soul, for example, or one's honored parents – may choose to take upon themselves the burden of a shared life.

The reason for such control and discipline is simple – survival. Elven lives span three hundred years or longer. Their cities are few and densely populated. Elves are not adventurous; they rarely roam far from their homes and their ancestral advisors and will do so only if they have an excellent reason. They are the very antithesis of the dwarves, who never stay in one place longer than two days. As little as they understand humans, elves understand dwarves still less.

The birth rate is high among elves, the death rate low (unless some or all of the seven great houses are at war). Elven families remain together, and thus elven households and elven cities are crowded. An elf lives almost continuously in the sight, sound, and smell of many other elves. Only by maintaining the strictest discipline and control on themselves do the elves manage to survive in such crowded conditions, their sanity intact.

A human entering an elven household marvels at the tranquillity, the quiet, the peace, and is astounded to hear that there may be thirty elves sharing that single tiny abode, including great-great-grandparents, great-grandparents, grandparents, parents, children, children's children, to say nothing of the servants, the Honored Ancestor, the aunts and uncles and cousins. By contrast, an elf visiting a human household is overwhelmed by the noise, the stench, the confusion, and is similarly astounded to find that only a few people – parents, a child, and perhaps a servant or two – occupy the dwelling.

The higher ranking the elf, the larger the dwelling place, though the size of the house is offset by the fact that more of his relatives are probably living there, as well as the Elders of the House and their immediate families and any visiting nobility. Guests are usually accommodated in guesthouses, located near the gatehouse, which is where Silwyth had spent the night of his arrival. His family's home was north of Lovod, the Shield's city. Silwyth had traveled a day and a night, changing horses on the road, in order to answer the Shield's summons.

Silwyth climbed the innumerable flagstone steps leading from the fourth garden up to the ninth, restraining his eagerness in order to maintain the correct distance between himself and the servant. The gardens were built in terraces along the sloping face of a mountain. Ornamental shrubs and ponds surrounded small tinkling fountains. Orchids and roses and trailing vines covered stone archways. Paths led between carefully carved hedges and into shady grottoes. The gardens, exceedingly beautiful, served several functional purposes as well. They informed the visitor that the man who owned the gardens was prosperous and powerful, since he could afford the labor required to tend them, while their beauty helped the visitor forget that he was climbing a thousand stairs up the side of a mountain in order to reach the main house. If he was fortunate enough to reach the main house. Many visitors to the Shield never moved past the fourth garden, some never saw anything beyond the first. Silwyth was being greatly honored.

The gardens also served a military function, defending the house from attack. Silwyth, a soldier himself, could not see the deadly traps, cunningly concealed by the plantings, but he knew they were there. He noted that the narrow stairs – too narrow for more than one person to pass at a time – twisted and turned among the gardens, and that these stairs, cut into the hillside, were the only way to reach the house. Any army attempting to climb the rock-strewn face of the mountain would be spread out across the mountainside, hampered by the rocks and the loose soil, and would be easy targets for the Shield's expert bowmen.

Passing one of the shady grottoes, overhung with fragrant tube-flowers, Silwyth noted the grating concealed in the stone floor – the entrance to one of many underground tunnels that undoubtedly led from the house and into the garden. Armed troops could travel secretly and, unseen beneath the ground, burst out at any point.

The Shield was well protected and, by all accounts, he needed the protection. House Kinnoth was playing a dangerous game.

Arriving at the entrance to the ninth garden, the servant paused to give Silwyth time to appreciate the beauty and permit that beauty to influence his soul. Knowing that the soul must be fed, as well as the body, in order to maintain the proper balance essential to good health, Silwyth thrust all thoughts of a worldly nature from his mind and allowed his soul to roam freely about the lovely garden.

The servant stood quietly at the garden's entrance, waiting as Silwyth walked the carefully laid-out path that wound among the various plantings, each group of plants speaking to a different part of the soul, each fragrance stimulating a different part of the body. When Silwyth had completed the walk, the servant bowed and asked if the Honored Guest would care for refreshment.

Here was another mark of his increased status with the Shield. Silwyth had not been offered so much as a cup of water in the fourth garden. He accepted, for to refuse would be to give offense. The servant departed. Silwyth sat down on a smooth rock ledge overhanging a lily-strewn pond. Several fish swam by, hoping for crumbs.

From there, Silwyth had an excellent view of the Shield's house, one of several he owned. Though this was one of the lesser dwellings, it was the Shield's favorite, by all accounts. His main dwelling was a large castle in the city of Lovod, a city that had been ruled by House Kinnoth since the Father and Mother had placed their children upon the earth.

The main house was built of wood, armored by clay, raised high upon a stone base made of huge blocks of granite. The house was three stories in height, its design graceful and pleasing to the eye, as well as utilitarian. The armory was built next to the house, attached by a walled-in corridor. A granite wall surrounded the house, which could be reached only by circuitous paths built between the wall and the front entrance. The castle in the city was built in similar fashion, although on a much grander scale, and was even more heavily fortified. The Shield and his family lived in this house most of the year, occupying the castle only in times of war.

Silwyth took care that his gaze did not rest too long upon the house and its defenses. Anyone watching him – and he was certain he was being watched – might suspect him of trying to find a way to defeat those defenses. Silwyth's gaze accorded the house the admiration it was due, then returned to the garden. He was rewarded for his politeness. Another guest occupied the garden – a lady.

He had not noticed her during his soul-soothing walk; she walked in another part of the garden, separated from his by a stream of water that flowed in a gentle, well-disciplined manner along a stone waterway. An arched bridge, crossing over the stream, led to the other part of the garden. The servant had brought him to this side of the bridge, deliberately keeping the two guests separate. The lady strolled the paths, admiring the flowers, occasionally touching one with her hand. Her maidservant accompanied her, keeping the correct distance between them, as was proper.

Silwyth rose to his feet and moved out into the open, letting himself be seen, so that the unknown woman would not think he was spying upon her. The maidservant saw him, drew her mistress's attention to him. The lady glanced in his direction, made a formal bow. Silwyth returned the bow, pressing his hands together and raising them to his forehead, for though he did not recognize the woman, he recognized by the pattern of the fabric of her sumptuous robes that she was the wife of one of the Guardians of the Eastern Wood. As such, she was higher rank than Silwyth, who was a Lesser Guardian. Her husband must be visiting the Shield. Silwyth wondered why she walked in the ninth garden above the gatehouse when, by rights, she should have been walking in the house-gardens.

The servant returned, bearing jasmine tea and a plate of sugared rose hips. At the same time, a servant entered the lady's side of the garden, bearing a teapot and a plate. Elves consider that to eat or drink in the presence of another without offering to share is extremely impolite. Thus, unlike humans, elven servants do not wait upon their masters during mealtime, but are dismissed to take their own sustenance. The greatest insult one elf can offer another is to eat something in that elf's presence without extending an invitation to join in the meal. The great war between the Houses of Trovale and Wyval, which lasted five hundred years, was initiated when the lord of House Trovale ate a pomegranate in the face of the lord of House Wyval.

In this instance, however, the garden provided many secluded areas where two elves who were strangers to each other might take their refreshment in privacy, if they chose. The decision was up to the lady, because of her higher rank.

She glanced in Silwyth's direction, said something to her servant. The maidservant crossed over the bridge, approached Silwyth, her eyes cast down. She bowed three times, very low.

'Honored Stranger, my mistress requires me to say that the garden is too beautiful for two eyes and one mouth

25

to do it justice. Four eyes and two mouths could better express their appreciation of such wonders. She asks if you would honor the garden by joining her.'

'I honor the garden and I honor Her Ladyship,' Silwyth replied, and crossed the bridge, following after the maid-servant.

Reaching the other side, he bowed once, advanced several steps, bowed again, advanced again, and came to within ten paces of the lady. There he stopped and bowed yet a third time. Straightening, he said, 'I am Silwyth of House Kinnoth, Lesser Guardian of the Eastern Forest. I thank you for the honor you do me. My house and I are at your service.'

The lady was gazing up at a cuckoo, perched high in a tree, his inane call sounding discordant over the soft murmured plashing of the fountain's water. Hearing Silwyth's voice, she lowered her gaze and turned her head to look upon him.

'I am Lady Valura, of the House Mabreton.'

That much Silwyth knew, by the symbol of the Mabretons embroidered in her gown. Again he wondered why she was there, when her husband must be inside the house.

The lady took her seat at a small table the servants had placed next to a pond. The servants arranged the teapots and the plates, then departed. Silwyth, moving to take his seat only after the lady was herself seated, saw two warriors clad in the colors of the Mabretons standing in the shadows of a grotto. Servants were bringing the warriors tea, as well, which they could enjoy and still keep close watch upon their charge.

Given the lady's youth and beauty – she was one of the most beautiful women Silwyth had ever seen – he was not surprised that her husband should put a guard over such a treasure. His next words were spoken in perfect sincerity.

'The garden is indeed beautiful, Lady, but the addition

of the flower of the Mabretons has enhanced its beauty one hundredfold.'

Lady Valura inclined her head politely. No blush stained the orchid-petal softness of her cheek, no smile of pleasure touched her carnelian lips. She was accustomed to compliments and bored by them.

'You have an audience with the Shield, Lord Silwyth?' she asked, indicating with a gesture that he should pour the tea. Had Silwyth been of higher rank, she herself would have acted as hostess.

'To my honor, Lady. I am to take wine with the Shield in the cedar grove.'

Lady Valura raised a delicate eyebrow, regarded him with more respect.

'You will meet my husband there. Lord Mabreton is also taking wine with the Shield in the cedar grove.'

'Your Ladyship is wise, then, to take advantage of the warmth and beauty of the day to walk in the garden, instead of being cooped up within four walls; no disparagement to the magnificence of the house, which is, I am certain, quite commodious and comfortable.'

Now the lady's lips turned upward, and warmth lit the green eyes from within so that Silwyth was reminded of the sun shining through green leaves. She sipped her tea and bit into a rose hip, then said, 'In other words, Lord Silwyth of House Kinnoth, you are wondering why I am waiting for my husband in the garden outside the house instead of in the gardens within.' She ignored Silwyth's polite protest, adding, 'I am the daughter of Anock of House Llywer.'

Silwyth bowed in understanding. He should have known this by the tattoo markings around her eyes, a tattoo that resembles a mask, but which denotes an elf's ancestry. He had been so taken by the lady's beauty, he had not studied the details of the tattoo. The wife of the Shield was Hira of House Tanath. House Tanath and House Llywer

27

had been warring on and off for several hundred years, and though the two were nominally at peace now, they remained acknowledged enemies. A daughter of House Llywer could not enter the house of a daughter of House Tanath without losing face, nor could the daughter of House Tanath very well entertain her enemy. But since the wife of such a high-ranking nobleman could not be left to languish in the gatehouse, the ninth garden was the compromise.

Should the houses go to war again, Lord Mabreton might be in a sad situation, torn between duty to his family and, by extension, his wife's family, and duty to the Shield, who would face a similar problem. The Shield must recognize this, and so he was doing his best to keep the two sides from going to war.

'Ordinarily, I remain at home when my husband has an audience with the Shield, but we travel from here to Glymrae, there to enter the Portal and journey to Vinnengael, where my husband accepts a post as ambassador. He felt uneasy about leaving me alone in our camp and insisted that I accompany him.'

'Have you ever traveled one of the Portals, my lady?' Silwyth asked.

'I have not, my lord. Have you?'

Neither elf, it seemed, had ever entered the magical Portal, nor had been to the celebrated city of Vinnengael. Both had heard stories and compared their information. They discussed traveling through the Portals – magical tunnels constructed by the magi of Vinnengael which permitted the elves to reach that city in a journey of one day, as opposed to a journey of six months.

'I have heard that being inside the Portal itself is quite unremarkable,' said Valura. 'The magi have caused it to look like any tunnel dug through a mountain, instead of a tunnel that has been carved through time and space. You are surrounded by gray walls that are smooth as marble, a gray ceiling, and a gray floor upon which one walks with ease. The temperature is neither hot nor cold. The journey takes half a day and, from what I hear, is boring in the extreme. Nothing to see, nothing to do. I must say that I am disappointed. I was hoping for some excitement.'

So life with Lord Mabreton was not exciting. But perhaps she had not meant that the way it sounded. Whether she had or she hadn't, Silwyth pretended he had not heard this statement, which could be taken as highly insulting to her lord. Silwyth did store it away in his memory, however, as one that might someday be put to future use.

'It stands to reason, however, Lady Valura,' he said smoothly, 'that the Portal should be made as ordinary in appearance as possible. Think of the traders and merchants who must pass through it many times. If doing so was frightening or even uncomfortable, they might not be so ready to make the journey.'

'I have found that people will endure great hardship in quest of profit, Lord Silwyth,' said Lady Valura. 'However, I do see your point. I will forgo my excitement so that the peddler may bring his shoes into the markets of Vinnengael without suffering undue distress.'

Their talk turned from the Portal to the realm of the humans. There, at least, Lady Valura was certain of finding excitement, though not perhaps the type she relished. She recounted stories of how truly dreadful life among humans could be, with their crude behavior, odious practices, and boorish manners.

'I plan to have as little to do with them as possible,' said Lady Valura. 'We are not even to live in Vinnengael. I refused to do so. Lord Mabreton has built a home for me in an isolated, forested area of land on the River Hammerclaw, as far from the human city as is practicable. My lord will use this home as his own retreat, when the vagaries of the humans become too much for him to bear.'

Silwyth offered the proper commiserations, though his words were not particularly heartfelt. In truth, he could not sympathize overmuch with the lady. He was one of those rare elves who enjoyed traveling; he enjoyed new experiences and would have given a large portion of his not-inconsiderable wealth to be able to journey to Vinnengael, of whose wonders he'd heard much. As it was, he was tied to home. He could not leave his family without permission, permission his father would never grant. Duty to the family overrode all individual wants and needs. Duty to the Shield would take precedence, however. Not even his father could dispute such an order. Silwyth had been dropping hints in the right ears that he would be interested in accepting any assignment the Shield might have to offer.

The teapots were dry. The soldiers were rattling their swords in their sheaths, indicating that in their estimation the meeting between their mistress and the handsome young stranger had gone on long enough.

Silwyth himself recognized that it was time to take his leave. He rose, bowed, thanked the lady for her generosity in sharing her repast with him. He asked if there was anything he could do to serve her. She replied no, dismissed him with a languishing wave of her hand, which plainly said, 'You have amused me for an hour. Now I find you boring. You cannot leave fast enough to suit me.'

Silwyth made his departure, backing away from her until a suitable distance had been reached whereby he could turn his back on her without offending her. He crossed over the bridge and, as one is encouraged to do when in a garden, spent a pleasant two hours looking into himself, evaluating the garden of his inner dwelling place, uprooting weeds and nurturing those plants that seemed to him to be most valuable. There, in his inner garden, he planted a flower in honor of the beauty of the Lady Valura.

The shadows of night crept into the garden. The birds were singing their sleep songs and the night-blooming flowers were starting to open their petals and send forth their haunting fragrance when a servant arrived to say that the Shield was taking wine in the cedar grove and that he asked Silwyth to join him.

Silwyth followed the servant up the covered walkways leading to the house. The sound of bells rang in the air; wind chimes hung from every corner of the overhanging roof. The elves hold the wind sacred, magic comes from the wind, and so they believe that wind chimes sing with the voice of the gods.

Silwyth entered the house, walked past the guards, who accorded him the respect due his rank, neither more nor less. Inside the house, he was left in the interior hallway until the mistress of the house could be apprised of his presence and grant her permission for him to enter. This she did, without bothering to come see him herself; he was only a Lesser Guardian. He made the customary polite inquiries as to her health and happiness and, receiving satisfactory answers as to both, was taken to the Shrine of the Honored Ancestor.

Every elven household has an ancestral advisor, ancestors who have agreed to forgo resting in the eternal garden of the Mother and Father in order to remain with their kin, offering counsel and advice. Since the Father and Mother make their will known through the Honored Ancestor, their counsel and advice, however unpleasant both may be, are ignored only at great peril.

Every house sets up a shrine to the Honored Ancestor. In the poorer homes, this shrine may be quite simple, consisting of a table, an incense burner, a small silver bell, and the ever-present gift of fresh flowers placed upon a table. Or the shrine might be elaborate, as was the shrine in the House of the Shield, which took up an entire room. The room was filled with objects that had been owned by the Honored Ancestor – painted screens, hand-decorated fans, even her clothes and her shoes, and a set of mah-jongg, her favorite game. She often played a game or two with the Shield in the evening.

Silwyth rang the small bell to make known his presence, made his reverence, and was about to take his leave when he saw a woman of stately mien, clad in the colors of the House, regarding him from the rear of the shrine. Awed, he recognized the Honored Ancestor herself.

Astonished and highly gratified at the honor done him, Silwyth made his lowest and most reverential formal bow, hands crossed over his breast, remaining in that position for the count of thirty heartbeats. He lifted his head to find the Honored Ancestor regarding him with favor. She smiled and inclined her head to him. Then she disappeared.

The servant who was accompanying Silwyth saw this, of course, though he made no mention of the fact; servant and guest did not indulge in idle chatter. However, on arriving at the cedar grove, the servant whispered into the ear of the Shield's own personal manservant, who whispered into the ear of his master, who looked upon Silwyth with heightened interest.

Elves prefer, when at all possible, to live out of doors. A dwelling is a place where one takes shelter from the elements and one's enemies. If neither the weather nor a rival house threatens, an elf works, plays, loves, sleeps, and eats out of doors. There are much more elaborate furnishings outside the house, therefore, than there are within. The Shield's sleeping bowers – kept secret and hidden away beneath night-blossoming trees – his private and formal dining areas, the kitchens, the play areas for the children, his nine audience chambers, and the family gathering areas were all located outside, arranged in various parts of the extensive house-garden area. Most of these had ornate latticework walls built around them and were covered over with canopies of leaves which sheltered the elves from all but the most torrential rains.

The choice of audience chambers the Shield used was dependent on several factors: time of day, importance of the meeting, and, above all, the honor that the Shield wished to accord to a visitor. The lowest of these was the fish pond, which was used in the morning for routine business of the House. The most elevated of these was the cedar grove.

Simple, elegant, impressive. Those were the impressions Silwyth received when he entered the grove. Cedar trees five deep formed a circle around a patio of polished white rock, upon which was placed a semicircle of ornately carved wooden chairs, painted and heavily lacquered both for beauty and to withstand exposure to the elements. The cedar trees had been cut and trained over the centuries to grow to the same height, their lower limbs trimmed so that all presented the same expanse of trunk. The limbs and leaves formed a broad ribbon of green above, the trunks and the shadows formed a ribbon of brown below.

Silwyth stood in the shade of the outermost rank of cedar trees, waiting the Shield's pleasure. Silwyth did not wait long. No sooner had the manservant announced Silwyth's arrival than the Shield himself rose and walked through the cedars to welcome his guest – a very great honor.

Silwyth bowed, one hand pressed over his heart, in homage to the Shield.

The Shield returned the gesture with a bow studied in its minuscule degree of inclination, which indicated a polite acknowledgment of Silwyth's rank and standing with perhaps just a bit something extra.

'The servant tells me that our Honored Ancestor, the Lady Amwath, has done you great honor, Lesser Guardian.'

'Unworthy as I am, Shield of the Divine,' Silwyth

said humbly, 'the Lady Amwath, your honored mother, did acknowledge me and seemed pleased to receive my heartfelt reverence.'

'My honored mother always did have an eye for a good-looking young man,' said the Shield with a chuckle.

Silwyth was considerably shocked by what might be considered the son's disrespectful attitude, but then he recalled having heard that the Lady Amwath, who had been widowed at an early age, had been known for her independence, her keen grasp of politics, her vaunting ambition, and her lusty enjoyment of life. Her skill and maneuvering had brought about her son's rise to the exalted post of Shield of the Divine, which meant he was the second most powerful man in the elven realm. The fact that the Shield was determined to be the first most powerful was an open secret.

Not knowing what reply to make to such a statement, Silwyth bowed again, thus saving himself from having to speak. One other man sat in the chairs of the cedar grove – Lord Mabreton, husband to the Lady Valura.

The Shield escorted Silwyth into the grove. Lord Mabreton rose to his feet. The Lesser Guardian bowed to the Guardian, who returned the bow with respect. Silwyth had never met Lord Mabreton, who was not Silwyth's liege lord, but came from a different part of the realm. Silwyth's lord, the guardian to whom Silwyth owed allegiance, was Lord Dunath. Lord Dunath was getting on in years, however, being almost two hundred and seventy-five. A frail old man, his body nothing more than sticks of bone covered by taut, smooth skin, he spent nearly all of his time with his brush and his ink, composing long poems about the glorious days of his youth.

Silwyth regarded Lord Mabreton with a curiosity enhanced by having just recently met the lord's beautiful wife. Most elven marriages are marriages of convenience, arranged before the children are even born. In many instances, the married couple actually come to love each other. Silwyth guessed immediately that this was not the case with Lord and Lady Mabreton.

The lord was older than the lady by a good one hundred years; this must be his second or maybe even third marriage. He was tall and powerfully built, with cold, dull eyes and the sort of mouth that never laughed unless it laughed at the misfortune of another. Thickbodied, thickheaded, as the saying went; just the sort to be insanely jealous of a wife whose beauty he undoubtedly prized only as a trophy. Silwyth immediately disliked the man.

The Shield invited the gentlemen to be seated. He placed Lord Mabreton on his right hand and Silwyth on his left, in a chair that was one removed from the Shield. Leaving the chair vacant was a mark of respect to the absent Lord Dunath.

The servants brought jugs of white wine that had been cooling in bowls of snow, carried down from the mountain peak. Plates of other delicacies were passed, fruit and breads and sugared wafers, all quite delicious. The servants placed the food and wine on a table, which they had carried in for the purpose, then – as was customary – they left. Silwyth, as the youngest and the lowest ranked, poured the wine for his elders and his betters.

No business is discussed with the wine. Only certain topics are permissible. These include the praising of the house and grounds of the host, the praising of the family of the host, who in return praises the families of his guests. The praises take the form of storytelling. Elves are passionately fond of stories, particularly stories dealing with the glories of their ancestors, and they relate these with relish at any given opportunity. The goal of every elf living is to do something so brave, so honorable, so renowned that the story will be one his descendants can relate with pride.

Lord Mabreton began by telling the well-known story

about Lady Amwath's courage in battling the assassins who had just murdered her husband. Silwyth, who had studied up on stories about the Shield's family prior to coming, on the off chance that he might actually be asked to relate one, had originally selected this story, then rejected it, as being the one best known and therefore most likely to be related.

Silwyth was glad he had chosen another story and was rehearsing it in his mind, when the half of his brain that was listening to Lord Mabreton realized that the man was making a dreadful mistake.

Thinking to flatter the Shield, who had been in his mother's womb at the time of the attack, Lord Mabreton hinted that it was the Shield himself who lent his mother the courage to kill the two assassins. A weak woman, he concluded, could have never been so courageous on her own.

The Shield received the praise-story with due courtesy, replied with a story designed to honor Lord Mabreton. Silwyth alone had seen the angry tapping of the Shield's sandaled foot beneath the embroidered hem of his robe. The Shield was quite proud of his mother. Silwyth guessed that Lord Mabreton's consequence had fallen.

How far? Silwyth wondered. And what will this do for me?

Silwyth's turn to tell his story came. He had been diligent in his research and recited a story he had heard from his own ancestral advisor – his long-dead grandfather. A rather ill-tempered ghost, Silwyth's grandfather was not one to hang about playing mah-jongg. He was jealous of the living and was constantly meddling in their affairs, bringing proclamations from the gods on an average of three times daily. The Father and Mother, it seemed, took a great interest in petty household concerns, for that was about all the ancestral advisor ever seemed to discuss. He was a keen supporter of the Shield and his house, however, and had agreed to provide Silwyth with a praise-story after only a modicum of bitter complaining that no one ever listened to him.

The Shield was pleased, though no one but Silwyth could have told. Certainly not the obtuse Lord Mabreton, who paid no attention to Silwyth's recitation, but slumped in his chair, half-asleep from the wine, impatient to end the ceremonial part of the meeting and get on to business. The Shield's foot did not tap once, however. His keen eyes, fixed on Silwyth, did not waver.

'I had not heard that story before, Lesser Guardian,' said the Shield when Silwyth was finished. 'I thank you for telling it. I trust you will tell it again many times in my hearing.'

Silwyth realized the implications of such a statement and thrilled to hear it; perhaps he was to be made a part of the Shield's own personal retinue. Lord Mabreton stifled a yawn.

The servants returned after the lapse of the time pre-scribed for the drinking of the wine to clear away the jug, the bowl of snow, the empty food trays. Now it was time for business. Lord Mabreton came fully alert. The Shield beckoned to his personal assistant, who had arrived with the departure of the wine. The assistant came forward, handed the Shield two scrolls, one tied with a dark green ribbon, the other tied with a paler green ribbon. The dark green went to Lord Mabreton, the Guardian; the paler went to Silwyth, the Lesser Guardian.

Both men unrolled their scrolls and read the orders, which came from the Divine's own brush. The orders were expressed in the form of elaborate poems, whose intent lay couched somewhere in the flowery phrasing. Silwyth affected to read the document with polite attention. The real orders would come from the mouth of the Shield.

Perusal concluded, Silwyth looked up. The Shield was staring out into the cedars, a line of concentrated thought deepening upon his brow. The Shield was one hundred and fifty, the prime of life for an elf. He was known to be a fierce and courageous warrior, intensely ambitious, fond of the power he held and determined to keep it. Rumors had been circulating for a year that the Divine was jealous of the Shield's power, which – because the Shield controlled a mighty army – was greater than the Divine's own power. The Divine was doing all he could to build up alliances among the other houses, perhaps even plotting to overthrow the current Shield and set up one upon whose loyalty he could depend.

The Shield turned his thoughtful gaze to Silwyth, who met and held it. There was a time for humility and a time to reveal one's inner strength. The Shield seemed pleased with what he saw, for he nodded once, slightly.

'Lord Mabreton,' said the Shield, turning away, 'you are hereby ordered by the Divine, Master of Us All' – this said with a slight curl of the lip – 'to travel to the human royal city of Vinnengael, there to take your post as ambassador.'

Lord Mabreton expressed his joy and gratification and willingness to obey an order that obviously came as no surprise to him, since he and his wife and their retinue were already well on their journey.

The Shield turned to Silwyth. 'You, Lesser Guardian, Silwyth of House Kinnoth, will accompany Lord Mabreton. You are very fortunate, young sir. Your request to study in the Great Library of King Tamaros has been granted.'

So that was what that meandering poem was about. Silwyth had been unable to fathom it, especially as he had made no such request. He expressed his heartfelt gratitude to the Shield and to Lord Mabreton for permitting him to travel in such exalted company.

By the scowl on the lord's face, this was the first Lord Mabreton had heard he and his wife were to have a traveling companion, a young and handsome traveling companion. He dared not argue with the Shield, but he thought enough of himself not to bother to conceal his displeasure – another mistake. Business concluded, the Shield rose in the gesture of dismissal.

Lord Mabreton and Silwyth made their farewells, gave their thanks for the honor done to them in being admitted into the presence of one so mighty. The Shield added his own compliments. Turning to Silwyth, the Shield very slightly lowered his eyelids, lifted one eyebrow.

Silwyth and Lord Mabreton backed their way across the white rock and into the cedars, where – having taken the requisite number of steps – they could turn without their backsides giving offense.

'I suppose we will have to delay our departure, so that you, sir, can return to your house and pack,' were the first ungracious words out of Lord Mabreton's mouth, as they followed one of the servants through the gardens.

Silwyth was angered; the tone might have been used to a peasant, not another lord. He knew better than to reveal his anger. Lord Mabreton might be trying to goad him into an argument in the hopes of persuading the Shield to change his orders.

'I am accustomed to traveling lightly. I have with me what I need for the journey. I will cause you no delay, my lord,' Silwyth replied and, taking a misstep on a loose piece of flagstone, he lost his footing and fell to the ground.

Embarrassed, Silwyth staggered hastily to his feet. He made a gallant attempt to continue on, but found he had injured his ankle and could not place his weight upon it. Biting his lip against the pain, he sat down upon a stone bench.

'Well, what have you done to yourself?' Lord Mabreton demanded, stopping, glaring.

'Only a turned ankle, my lord,' said Silwyth. 'Please,

continue on your way. I will remain here a few moments to allow the pain to subside.'

'I've seen men make less fuss about an arrow in the gut,' Lord Mabreton sneered. 'Now we shall have to haul about a cripple. I take my leave of you, sir. I trust you will not meet with any further mishaps!'

He marched off, muttering to himself and trampling the flowers.

Silwyth remained behind, seated upon the bench. The servants, solicitous and concerned, brought him steaming water with oil of eucalyptus to bathe his injured ankle and cloths to bind it. This he did, most solemnly, sitting upon the bench and waiting. He would stay there for an hour, until darkness fell. If he had misread the signal, no harm would be done.

Silwyth had only just bound up his ankle when the Shield appeared.

'I hear you slipped on a loose flagstone, my lord,' said the Shield. 'I am sorry to have been the cause of your injury. The flagstone will be repaired immediately, the caretaker suitably punished.'

'He should not be punished on my account, my lord,' Silwyth protested humbly. 'The flagstone was not loose. It was my fault. I was not watching where I was going.'

The Shield sat down upon the bench beside Silwyth, who was glad of the dusk, for he felt that he could not properly contain his elation.

'Well, it was a lucky accident,' said the Shield, with the slightest hint of a chuckle in his voice. 'I was wanting to have a chance to speak to you privately. I have been making inquiries about you, Lesser Guardian. People say you are a man of intelligence.'

Silwyth made a seated bow.

'I can see for myself that you are a man of penetration, discretion, and quick wit,' the Shield added dryly. 'It has also been reported that you get along well with humans.'

He gazed at Silwyth speculatively, inviting elaboration.

'One of the family's holdings lies on the border of Tromek and Vinnengael, my lord. A human village is located not far from our dwelling place. There is some interaction between the humans and the elves who live in the vicinity; some of the humans have worked for my family. Laborers, of course; they are not permitted to enter the house.'

The Shield nodded in understanding. Such a lumbering, chaotic force would disturb the carefully modulated tranquillity of an elven household for a month.

'The truth is, my lord . . .' Silwyth paused, hesitant to make his startling confession, a confession that might either promote him in the eyes of his mighty lord or damn him utterly.

'Speak freely, Lesser Guardian.' The Shield encouraged him. 'By the way, I am sorry I forgot. Does your ankle pain you?' The Shield's voice had a sly edge.

'Not much, my lord,' said Silwyth, able to smile now that the darkness concealed his features. 'Since you ask me to speak freely, my lord, I must tell you that I have come to enjoy being around humans. Certainly they have many faults: they are uncouth, they smell bad, they are insensitive to the ways of nature, they laugh too much and too loudly. But I find that I admire their energy. Being around them stirs my mind, sets it to thinking and creating. Too often, I feel like this fish pond, my lord. My thoughts placid and unmoving, stir only at the very bottom, rise up only at feeding time. The humans are a raging river, into which I plunge and feel the exhilaration of being tossed and tumbled, swept along on the rushing current.'

Silwyth halted, alarmed at himself. He had been carried away by his enthusiasm. The Shield would not want to hear of the inner feelings of a Lesser Guardian. Silwyth lowered his head and, clasping his hands in his lap, awaited the just rebuke.

'Yes,' said the Shield. 'I was right. You are the man for the job.'

'My lord?' Silwyth looked up, pleased and delighted.

'How much do you know of the current political situation?' the Shield asked, casting the Lesser Guardian an intense, penetrating glance that cut through the night's shadows. 'Of the problems arising between the Divine and me?'

'I know that you are loyal to the Divine, Your Honor, and that the Divine trusts you as his Shield,' said Silwyth.

'I see you are a diplomat as well,' the Shield said wryly. 'Suffice it to say, Lesser Guardian, that it is my considered opinion that the Divine seeks to increase his power by seizing some of mine. Instead of being content to issue edicts and pass judgments on land disputes and marriage contracts, he defies tradition by wanting to become involved in the collecting of taxes and, what is far worse, the waging of war.

'To this end' – the Shield laid his hand upon Silwyth's forearm, a mark of great distinction, which caused Silwyth's frame to tremble with the honor – 'to this end, the Divine has sent to me, stating that it is his considered opinion that *his* soldiers will be assigned to guard the Portal entrance. The soldiers of our house, House Kinnoth, those who currently guard the Portal entrance, those who have guarded it since the inception of the Portal, are to be reassigned.'

Silwyth was shocked. He found it hard to believe that the Divine had actually had the temerity to make such a demand of the Shield. It was a grave affront, an insult. Silwyth wondered that they were not already at war.

'The Divine rescinded the order, soon after he made it.' The Shield answered Silwyth's unspoken thought. 'He realized he had gone too far. But he has not given up the idea. This Lord Mabreton, whom you met here tonight, is one of the hands of the Divine.

'You,' said the Shield, tightening his grip on Silwyth's forearm, 'will be *my* hand.'

'My lord, I am unworthy of such honor.' Silwyth made the requisite response.

'You are worthy, Silwyth,' said the Shield, further honoring the guardian by using his name. 'I have watched you for a long while, keeping you in mind for just such an assignment.'

'What does Your Lordship require me to do?'

'Lord Mabreton's task and the task of the other elven ambassadors to the humans will be to convince King Tamaros that the Divine is well within his rights to take control of the Portal. King Tamaros is wise for a human. He will not want to get involved in what he knows are elven affairs. The Divine plans to manipulate King Tamaros into sending *human* soldiers to guard the elven entrance to the Portal.'

'Is the Divine mad?' Silwyth forgot himself, spoke out freely and too loudly.

A glance from the Shield counseled Silwyth to lower his voice. The servants had been sent away, but almost certainly some in the Shield's household were paid spies and might be skulking about in the shadows. The Shield would know who these people were, of course, and would be watching them, intercepting their communications. But still, wisdom lay in discretion.

'No, the Divine is quite cunning, in fact,' said the Shield. 'If Tamaros believes that an elven war will be a threat to Vinnengael – if he thinks, for example, that I have designs upon the Portal because I want to use it to send my troops to make war upon him – then he will have no choice but to order human soldiers to guard the entrance. When you and I and the people of House Kinnoth are refused admittance, when our merchants cannot travel to Vinnengael to sell their wares, when our coffers run dry, the Divine can say to us without losing face that it is the humans who seek to weaken us.'

'Does the Divine want a war with the humans, my lord?'

'He would like to see House Kinnoth go to war against the humans, yes, Lesser Guardian. With our house diminished, he could seize the power we now wield.'

'And what makes him think human armies would distinguish between our two houses, my lord?'

'Precisely,' said the Shield. 'Humans are like fleas. Once they invade your dwelling, it is difficult to rid yourself of them. The Divine does not see this. He is a man who cannot see beyond the tip of his own nose.'

'What is your will for me, my lord?' Silwyth asked, his blood thrilling.

'You will have no official rank, of course. You travel as a scholar and as such you will present yourself. Tamaros is a scholar; he will take you to his heart, provide you with access to his great library, which is in the castle proper. Ingratiate yourself to him, Silwyth. Make yourself a pleasant companion, earn his trust. And if ever the opportunity arises for you to enter the King's household, seize it with both hands. Thus you will keep me informed of all that the Divine's representatives do and say, and, with luck and skill, you will be able to insinuate yourself into a position to thwart them.'

'My joy at having earned your trust, my lord, lies beyond my ability to express it,' said Silwyth, rising to his feet and bowing so low that his forehead nearly touched his knees.

'Yes, I see that your joy acts like a tonic. It is capable of healing a sprained ankle.' The Shield smiled broadly. Rising, he extended his arm to Silwyth. 'Come, Lesser Guardian. I fancy the ankle pains you a great deal. Accept my arm. I will escort you to the house. You will limp on that ankle for a few days, I should think.'

'You are right, my lord. The pain is excruciating. I thank Your Lordship for the help.'

With the Shield's assistance, the Lesser Guardian limped through the garden and into the house, where the Shield's lady-wife honored him with a sleeping roll for the night.

Silwyth was still limping the next day when he joined Lord Mabreton and the Lady Valura at the entrance to the Portal that led to the city of Vinnengael.

THREE

The Reading Lesson

LIFE IN THE PALACE WAS FAR DIFFERENT from the life Gareth had known, a life which, for the most part, had been spent wandering around the empty rooms of his parents' house, staring enviously out the window at the rough-and-tumble play of the peasant children or holding Nanny's yarn as she wound it into a great ball. Weeks passed while Gareth tried to learn to understand his altered circumstances and adapt to them. His problems were enhanced by the fact that no one took the time to explain to him what he was supposed to do and how he was supposed to act. They expected him to absorb it, as a plant absorbs sunlight.

The beatings he suffered were on his own account, therefore, and not on his master's. As it happened, Dagnarus – normally a sullen and rebellious student – was particularly well behaved during those early days of Gareth's arrival, and Evaristo, the prince's long-suffering tutor, took pride in the fact that his idea of procuring a whipping boy was a grand success. Dagnarus's behavior had improved because he did not want to see his new little friend hurt. That was Evaristo's fond notion and one he imparted to Their Majesties. It was some time before they were all disabused, Gareth included.

The first few nights, alone in his little closet that was just off the prince's enormous bedchamber, Gareth cried himself to sleep. Stiff and sore from the beatings meant to teach him courtly behavior, he longed for home and Nanny with a longing he seriously thought he might die of. Home had been dull and lonely, sterile and cold, but it was familiar. He knew what was expected of him there.

Not much. He was, after all, a child.

In the palace, Gareth was no longer a child. He was considered an adult, albeit one built on a slightly smaller scale. He was expected to act like an adult, not a child. To be just, the beatings that the chamberlain and the tutor administered were not meant to torture Gareth. They were meant to help him, at age nine, reach adult maturity in the shortest time possible.

Gareth's first beating came on the first morning of his arrival.

The whipping boy's duties included attending His Highness every morning upon His Highness's rising. At home, Gareth had been used to sleeping as long as he wanted – the more time he spent in bed, the less time the servants had to deal with him. He considered it cruel in the extreme to be turned out of his warm bed at what Gareth considered an ungodly hour. Prince Dagnarus despised lying abed. He was up early, in order to miss nothing of the day, and he would go to bed late, to miss nothing of the night.

A long night of shooting peas over the walls of the book fortress, combined with the excitement and tension of the day, left Gareth sleeping soundly through the ringing of the bell that summoned the servants to His Highness's bedchamber. The flat of a servant's hand on Gareth's bare bottom roused him from his slumbers. The servant threw the boy's clothes on him so fast that his smalls were all bunched up under his woolen hose and his tunic was on backwards. The servant sent him off to the chamberlain, who grabbed the sleep-drugged child, shook him into wakefulness, and hustled him into the royal bedchamber.

Gareth stood next to the servants, watching while His Highness dined in bed, drinking hot chocolate and eating warm sugar buns that smelled heavenly to the boy, for in the excitement yesterday, no one had remembered to feed Gareth. His stomach rumbled loudly in the silent bedchamber, causing a servant to whip around and, with astonishing swiftness, rap Gareth on the head.

Winking his eyes from the pain, Gareth tried to stop smelling the chocolate. To distract himself, he looked around the bedchamber, with its enormous carved wooden bed surrounded by heavy velvet curtains, the wooden chests and wardrobes filled with clothes, the prince's pointed-toed shoes lined up in a row, the tapestries which had purportedly been sewn by the Queen's own hands.

Dagnarus sat propped up by a mound of pillows. Across the bed was a velvet throw decorated with the family crest of two griffins holding the sun, done in golden thread. He ate the sugar bun quickly, yet neatly and with grace, and drank the chocolate. He submitted to having his face and hands washed and his hair combed. Then the prince climbed out of bed.

Despite his best efforts, sleep crept over Gareth.

He yawned, a wide, gaping yawn that cracked his jaws.

The chamberlain, with cool aplomb, turned around and slapped the boy across the face with such force that his blow sent the child tumbling into a wardrobe.

The prince glanced at the whipping boy, then glanced away. Gareth, nursing his bruised and stinging cheek, hoped the prince would reprimand the chamberlain for his cruelty, but the boy's hopes were dashed. Dagnarus said nothing. He retired to the privy attached to the bedchamber, there to perform his morning ablutions.

Because of its proximity to the river, the palace was furnished with fresh, running water, which circulated throughout the palace by means of a system of ingenious waterwheels and channels. Gareth had never seen anything like it. He had always used the outdoor privies at his own house and he couldn't help feeling that emptying one's waste inside the palace walls was filthy and indecent. The child found it difficult to overcome this feeling and it had caused him great distress his first night there until he discovered that he could sneak away to use the servants' privies, which were located behind a wall of the courtyard outside.

His Highness returned and proceeded to allow the servants to dress him. Gareth stood still as a rabbit with the hounds around, afraid to breathe, lest he do it wrong.

After the prince was dressed, Dagnarus left to pay his respects to his father, King Tamaros, who was also an early riser. Gareth was whisked back to his closet, fed a leftover sugar bun tossed to him by a servant, and drank a cup of thin milk. He was then marched off to the playroom, there to await His Highness.

Dagnarus soon returned. 'Well, thank goodness, that's over,' he announced, settling down eagerly in front of the catapult. 'You've no idea what a chore that is – bidding good morning every morning to my father.'

Gareth edged his chair closer to the prince, hoping that His Highness would see the bruise upon his cheek and feel some pity. He was doomed to disappointment. Dagnarus's attention was concentrated solely upon his war engine.

Gareth was curious. 'Why? Is he horrid to you?'

'What a dolt you are!' exclaimed Dagnarus, casting Gareth a scornful glance. 'Of course he's not horrid to me. My father is never horrid to anyone, not even to those that deserve it. It's boring, that's all. The same thing, every day. He and my brother sit in that room with their books and their papers and their advisors, mulling over this treaty and worrying over that tax when there's lots more interesting things they could be doing.'

'My father says that Vinnengael is the center of the world,' Gareth said, having only a vague idea what that truly meant. 'I suppose there's a lot of work for your father to do to manage it.'

'He could leave it to others,' Dagnarus said. 'He's king, after all.' Tiring of the catapult, the prince shoved it petulantly to one side. He fidgeted around the playroom, scoffed at the idea of reading a book, and dragged Gareth over to the large sandbox, which took up at least a quarter of the room. There the prince began to arrange tiny soldiers made of lead into formation at one side of the box.

'Sit down, Patch. You will be the general of the opposing army.'

'I saw your brother once, during a parade,' Gareth said, dutifully taking his place at the opposite end of the sandbox, though he had no idea what he was supposed to do with the opposing army. He stared at the tiny lead figures with some perplexity, afraid to touch them. They seemed very fragile. 'He is a great deal older than you, isn't he?'

'Twelve years older,' said Dagnarus. 'He's my half brother, really.' He added, with a careless air, 'He hates me.'

'What?' Gareth looked up, startled.

'It's true. He hates me. He's jealous of me.'

'Why?'

'Because I'm Father's favorite.'

Gareth believed the prince. At that time, Gareth would have believed the prince if he had told him that the castle was likely to fly off its foundation and go whizzing around among the waterfalls.

The chamberlain flung open the door. 'Your Highness, your tutor, Evaristo, is without.'

Dagnarus made a face, rolled his eyes, and sighed.

'Send him in,' said the prince, continuing to arrange his soldiers.

'He hit me very hard,' Gareth said, sniveling a little, and giving the chamberlain a baleful glance, hoping to elicit some sympathy.

'He's an old fart. I shall be glad when Mother gets rid of him. As for hitting you' – Dagnarus shrugged – 'you deserved it. You must never gape in my presence, Patch. It is disrespectful.'

Gareth swallowed his sniffles. 'What's your tutor like?' he asked, changing the subject. 'Is he mean?'

'Bah! The man's a soft fool. Schooling's a waste of time anyway. I learn ten times more from Captain Argot than I do from that ninny Evaristo. Usually I don't even bother to be here when he comes.' Dagnarus glanced up from his soldiers. 'I'm only here because if I wasn't here . . .' He paused, frowned, and knocked over a stand of soldiers with a flick of his finger.

'If you weren't here, they'd beat me,' said Gareth, warmed by what he thought was the prince's compassion.

'That's not it!' Dagnarus scoffed. 'It's your duty to be beaten, after all. It's just . . .' His gaze focused, frowning, on his soldiers. 'I don't want them to send you away,' he said in a low voice.

'Revered Magus Evaristo,' announced the chamberlain.

Dagnarus scowled. Gareth glanced up with trepidation, fearful that here was new torment. His fears dissolved when he saw the smiling-eyed young man who entered the room.

Evaristo was thirty, though his thin face and cheerful countenance made him appear younger. He wore the habit of his order, the brown robes of the Order of Knowledge, and the symbol of his order – a golden key around his neck. Over his robes he wore a red scapular, which only magi may wear and which sets them apart in a crowd. He carried several large books in his hands.

Evaristo appeared considerably startled to see the prince.

'Your Highness, your presence here is a pleasant surprise,' said Evaristo. 'To what do I owe this great honor?'

Dagnarus glowered, the green eyes sparked. Obviously, he did not like to be teased. Jumping to his feet, he glared at the tutor.

'You should not speak to me in that tone! I am your prince.'

'You are an ignorant little boy who pays no attention to his studies and who will grow up to be an ignorant man,' said Evaristo calmly. Ignoring Dagnarus's anger-flushed face, the tutor smiled down at Gareth. 'And this must be the whipping boy.'

'My name is Gareth,' he said, bowing low.

'Your coming has made a difference already, Gareth,' said Evaristo, placing his books upon the table and arranging chairs around it. 'It has been many days since His Highness deigned to attend class.'

Evaristo was moving chairs and so he did not see the slight, mocking smile touch Dagnarus's lips. Gareth saw it and understood it immediately. Though he had known Dagnarus less than a day, Gareth knew him better than did Evaristo. Dagnarus would be here this morning, to make certain that his new companion would not be considered a failure and whisked away.

As for Gareth, he considered beatings a fair trade in exchange for education. Learning to read and to write had been among the happiest moments in the home that was already starting to fade from his memory, as a dream that seems so clear on waking, yet dissipates with the day's events.

Evaristo was a wise man, a patient man, an excellent teacher to a pupil who wanted to learn. He worked with Gareth for an hour that first day – during which time Dagnarus kicked the table leg or used his quill pen to draw, on the leaves of the rare books, crude pictures of soldiers running each other through with gigantic swords.

Eventually, growing bored, the prince left his chair and roamed over to stare longingly out the window, to where the soldiers were drilling in the courtyard. After their drill was ended, he amused himself by dropping bits of tile, pried loose from a window, down onto the pavement far below, watching them smash into pieces, startling unwary pedestrians.

Evaristo, gratified to find someone who appreciated him, paid little attention to the prince. Gareth, after his initial shyness, was eager to win his teacher's approval.

Gareth read every text handed to him, beginning with the primers Nanny had given him to occupy himself so that he wouldn't bother her during her nap time, and finishing with one of the books he had so coveted yesterday.

The book had been written by the Head of the Order of Knowledge, known as the Librarian, especially for the young prince's edification. The book was one of a set that gave detailed accounts of each of the major and minor races living in the known world. The race Gareth read about that day was the orken.

He had seen orken lumbering about the marketplace on those days when he had been permitted to accompany the menservants on their errands. The orken lived on the waterfront, on the shores of Lake Ildurel, a lake so huge that it had tides, like a sea. The orken were themselves a seafaring race, and plied the boats that sailed from the lake to the true ocean, the Sea of Ayrkis. Only a few orken lived in Vinnengael; their homeland was far to the south, although their true homeland might be considered the sea.

Orken are taller than humans, with massive chests and thick necks, arms, and thighs. Their clothes are loose-fitting and comfortable, consisting of trousers and shirts with open necks and long, flowing sleeves. They rarely wear cloaks even in the coldest, most inclement weather, for their skin is tough, and they are impervious to the cold.

Most orken, male and female alike, are sailors. The orken homeland consists of villages and cities built along the seacoast; no orken live in the interior. Orken are traders and fishermen in their own minds, pirates in the minds of others. They are considered slow and stupid by humans and elves.

Gareth's interest in the orken overcame his shyness at reading in front of the prince and the tutor. The boy first located the orken homeland on a map, then he started reading about their history, stumbling over the crude-sounding names of the orken cities, names such as Quash'Gaat and Kallka. Enthralled, he read on and on until he felt eyes upon him.

Gareth looked up to find Dagnarus had turned from the window. He was staring at the boy with such a hostile aspect that Gareth's flow of words stopped as swiftly as if the prince had popped a cork into his mouth.

'Your Highness,' said Evaristo, into the sudden silence, 'Gareth has read this passage well, but with some difficulty. Perhaps Your Highness would like to read it correctly.'

To Gareth's astonishment, Dagnarus cast Evaristo a look of such black malevolence and hatred that the boy would not have been surprised to hear the prince order the tutor beheaded on the spot. Evaristo was unperturbed.

'Your Highness?'

Dagnarus's back stiffened. He turned away from his tutor, stared out the window.

'I do not choose to read,' he said in a stone-cold voice. His neck was red, a pinkish red contrasted against the smoky red of his hair.

'Very well, Your Highness,' said Evaristo. 'Gareth, please continue.'

Flustered and upset, fearful that the prince would hate him, Gareth lowered his head over the book and mumbled something to the effect that the words were too difficult. He could not continue.

Evaristo merely smiled, said only that perhaps a night's sleep would restore his memory. Setting the ork book aside, Evaristo asked Gareth what he intended to do with himself when he came to manhood.

The boy had never given the matter any thought. He was still so shaken by the book incident that he could make no reply, but sat staring down at his hands.

'Your father is Lord of Walraith, I believe,' said Evaristo. 'Perhaps you intend to be nothing more than lord of the manor.'

'The estate is my mother's, and it is entailed,' Gareth said, not looking up. 'Upon her death, it goes to a cousin.'

He was not quite clear what this meant. All he knew was that his mother and father never ceased complaining at the unfairness of it all and had handed over a considerable amount of their fortune to lawyers in an effort to free themselves.

'I see. That is why you were brought to the royal court. Well, then, you will need a trade, an occupation. One suitable to your standing, of course. Perhaps you might consider becoming one of us, Gareth,' Evaristo continued. 'A magus. Provided that you have the necessary aptitude for magic.'

Dagnarus whipped around at this and fixed his green eyes upon the boy.

Gareth looked to the prince for approval, doubting he would receive it. He was astonished, therefore, to see Dagnarus nod emphatically and form the words, 'Take it!' with his mouth.

'I should like that of all things, Revered Magus,' Gareth said, adding hurriedly, 'but I will not leave His Highness.'

Evaristo glanced again at Dagnarus, and seemed pleased to note the bond between them. 'Don't worry, Gareth. Formal training of a magus does not begin until you are twelve years of age. At that time, you must enter the Temple as a novice. However, that day is a long way off.'

No more was said upon the subject.

'And so you are going to be a magus,' said Dagnarus, returning to the sandbox after Evaristo had departed.

'If that is what Your Highness wants me to do,' Gareth said meekly.

'I do. But you must promise me that you'll end up smarter than Evaristo if you study to be a magus. That nattering old ninny!' Dagnarus squatted by his sandbox, quite disgusted.

The toy soldiers had been painted with a fine eye for detail. Gathering up his nerve to touch them, Gareth picked up a miniature chariot and was amazed to discover that the wheels actually spun.

'They used to be enchanted,' Dagnarus said off-handedly.

'Really?' Gareth nearly dropped the chariot.

'Yes. When I said the word "march," the soldiers would march about and the horses would pull the chariot back and forth. My uncle made them – my mother's brother. He's a sorcerer in Dunkarga. But Evaristo lifted the enchantment.'

'Why?' Gareth was disappointed and tried to imagine the tiny soldiers marching across the sandbox, the little chariot dashing about madly.

'He says that magic is serious. It's not meant to entertain small children. We shouldn't meddle with it. He's an old killjoy, like all priests.'

'If that's the way you feel about magi, why do you want me to become one?' Gareth wondered.

'Because you will be *my* magus, of course,' said Dagnarus. 'You will keep an eye on the other magi for me and tell me of any who appear to be growing too strong. Magi are very powerful, you know. What with their magic and all, I was thinking of becoming one myself, but I can't do that and be king at the same time. Your being one will work out much better.'

Gareth had never been at court, but he was a child of the court, so to speak. The royal family and their gossip and intrigue were meat and drink to his parents. Though only nine, Gareth knew quite well that Dagnarus was second in line for the throne, that his elder brother, Helmos, was crown prince and would succeed his father, King Tamaros. Since Tamaros came of a long-lived family – his mother had seen her ninetieth year – his death wasn't expected anytime soon. Only by the gravest mischance would Dagnarus ever gain the throne, so Gareth's parents had said.

He had brains enough not to repeat this.

'When do you think you'll be king?' Gareth asked instead.

'When I'm ready,' Dagnarus replied.

Placing the chariot and its rider at the head of his army, he gave it a push that sent the chariot spinning down the sand hill, careening madly toward the miniature enemy.

They played in the sandbox until the servants arrived with supper.

The boy and the prince ate their supper in the play-room. They ate plain fare, for it was well-known that young stomachs could not digest rich food. The rabbit stew wasn't as good as Nanny's, who put garlic in hers. Gareth mentioned that to the prince, who said he would speak to the chamberlain with instructions to the cook. They sopped up the gravy with bread. After supper, the chamberlain came in to say that Her Majesty wanted to see her son and meet the whipping boy.

Dagnarus made a face, but he said nothing. He sub-mitted to having his hair combed and his mouth wiped, though he rebelled at the idea of changing his hose, which were dirty at the knees from crawling around the sandbox.

He and Gareth – who was reduced to a state of almost pitiable terror at the thought of meeting the Queen – accompanied the chamberlain through the castle's corridors to Her Majesty's quarters.

'Suppose she doesn't like me,' Gareth whispered to Dagnarus as they passed a row of armored knights standing still as death in the corridor.

Even in his trepidation, Gareth thought how terribly uncomfortable it must be for these knights, accoutered as they were in full plate and chain mail, to stand at attention like that and never move. He could not see that they even breathed, and he was quite worried about them, fearing that they might have smothered beneath those heavy helms. He said so to the prince.

'You are such a child!' Dagnarus said, hitting Gareth in the arm. 'The suits of armor are empty. They're only placed there for show. There are no knights inside.' Pausing a moment to chuckle, he added, 'What makes you think my mother won't like you?'

'The chamberlain said I was ugly,' Gareth answered.

'He did?' Dagnarus looked displeased.

'What if your mother doesn't think I'm a fit companion?'

'Don't worry, Patch. I like you, and that's the only thing that matters.'

The chamberlain was not permitted to enter the women's apartments, and he transferred custody of the boys to the Mistress of the Wardrobe, a stern-looking woman, who curtsied to the prince, examined Gareth with intense and disapproving scrutiny, and led them in to the Queen.

They entered through ornate, gilt-edged doors and walked into rooms of incredible wonder and beauty. At least that's what Gareth thought then. In later years he would come to see that the furnishings were ostentatious and in poor taste. The smell of perfume was all-pervasive and made him giddy. He sneezed three times, receiving a thwack on the head from the Mistress at each one of his indiscretions. The scent came from oil lamps that burned brightly, illuminating the bedchambers. Though it was daylight outside, the curtains were drawn. Her Majesty found that sunlight was harsh on the eyes and bad for the skin.

The boy and the prince passed through six sets of outer rooms decorated with tapestries and blazing with light from the oil lamps – an amazing display of wealth, for oil was not native to Vinnengael, but had to be shipped from the land of the orken, who trade in whale oil and ambergris.

Her Majesty was in the sitting room off the bedchamber, which Gareth could just glimpse through an open door. She slept alone; the King's bedchamber was in another part of the palace, although the two connected through a private passageway. Gareth's own parents did not sleep together, so this arrangement did not surprise him. Indeed, Gareth thought for years that only the poor slept together, and then because they could not afford better.

Queen Emillia was seated at her dressing table, admiring herself in the mirror while one of her ladies brushed her hair, which was thick and luxuriant, the same color as her son's. At first glimpse she could be termed 'pretty.' A second glance revealed imperfections. She knew how to dress to enhance the looks she had, but there was no denying the fact that her eyes – while a lovely color – were set too close together, above a nose that was overlong and brought to Gareth's mind the noses of the hunting dogs of the tapestry. Her lips tended to pucker, as though she had been constantly eating persimmons. If those lips had smiled, rather than pouted, and if the light in her eyes had been that of intelligence rather than ambition, the aspect of her pinched face would have changed for the better. As it was, her face seemed to be drawn together to form a single point, ending at the tip of her nose.

Completely self-absorbed, she found fault with everything and everyone with two exceptions: her lapdog and her son. She lavished her affection on these two in equal parts, treating them similarly in that she gave them to other people to look after and only took notice of them when they were clean and neat, fed and brushed, and not likely to snap.

Her supporters – and the Queen did have supporters, every person of power has supporters in a royal court, for, as the elves will tell you, the winds of fortune may blow steadily from one direction for years, only to shift around in the night and knock down your house – her supporters said that it was no wonder she was irritable and ill-tempered. Emillia knew quite well that her husband didn't love her. She knew that he didn't even like her very much. Theirs was a political marriage and, from the constant trouble her father – a minor king in Dunkarga – continued to cause, it must have seemed to King Tamaros that he had made what was popularly known as an ork's bargain.

Dagnarus resembled his mother only in the luxuriant red hair. He had inherited his good looks from his father's side of the family and, indeed, was the portrait come to life of his grandfather, painted when he had been crown prince.

'My poppet,' said the Queen, and gave her son her cheek to kiss.

Emillia did not look directly at Dagnarus, but saw him only by reflection. All the time she spoke to her son, she was directing the servant in the arranging of her hair, which would then be adorned by a wimple. She was only twenty-five, had married a man nearly seventy.

Dagnarus kissed his mother with a show of filial affection that sent the ladies-in-waiting cooing and pronouncing him a 'sweet' child.

The Queen's hair was not being done to her satisfaction, apparently. The part was off-center and was giving her a headache. Fuming, she ordered them all away, calling them idiots, and turned at last to fuss with her son. She combed his hair with her fingers, adjusted his tunic, twitched at his belt, and petted him as she might have petted her dog, which was barking at the boys with great ferocity.

Gareth was staring at the dog when he heard his name mentioned. Dagnarus caught hold of Gareth's wrist and dragged his friend forward. The Mistress of the Wardrobe, breathing down the boy's neck, exerted pressure on his shoulder blades, but Gareth had been well schooled. He sank to his knees before Her Majesty and remained there with his head bowed until she should deign to acknowledge his presence.

'Let us see what you look like, child,' said the Queen.

Gareth lifted his face.

Her Majesty's eyes widened. She gave a little gasp of horror and fell back in her chair. Clutching at her son, she dragged him away from the marked child and shielded him as though the mark might be contagious.

Mortified, Gareth covered his face with his hands and wished he might sink through the rug and the marble floor beneath it.

'No! Impossible! Why wasn't I told?' the Queen cried.

The Queen's ladies came fluttering to Her Majesty's aid, bearing water and wine and feather fans to restore her. Gareth could see nothing, but he could hear the rustle of their skirts and smell their perfume as they crowded around the Queen. One of them stepped on him in her eagerness to attend. Another advanced upon Gareth holding a pillowcase in her hand, with the intention of clapping it over his offending head. Gareth heard his own mother's voice crying out that the unfortunate child should be removed immediately.

'No, he shall not,' said Dagnarus.

Wriggling out of his mother's grasp, the prince reached down and took hold of the first part of Gareth that came to hand, which was his hair. Dagnarus hoisted the boy to his feet. Gareth's face burned with shame. He hung his head. Dagnarus took hold of his friend's limp hand and locked his own hand over it like a manacle.

'Patch is my whipping boy, Mother,' said Dagnarus. 'I like him, and I'm keeping him.'

The Queen looked up from amidst the arms of her ladies, where she had taken refuge.

'Dagnarus! Are you . . . certain? . . . Look, look at him.' She gave a wave of her hand in Gareth's direction and averted her eyes.

'I will have this, Mother,' Dagnarus said. 'I want it.'

That was all he had to say to her, then or ever. *I want it.*

The Queen permitted Gareth to kiss her hand, so long as he was careful not to touch his marked cheek against her skin. Gareth's mother, radiant, suggested that the mark might be camouflaged with powder. The Queen was struck by this notion, and Gareth thought for one terrifying moment that they were going to go through with it, but Dagnarus again came to his rescue.

'The mark was put on his face by the gods,' said Dagnarus, adding in all innocence, 'You wouldn't want to insult them by seeming to disrespect them, would you, Mother?'

The Queen's eyelashes fluttered. Like most people of modern thinking in Vinnengael, Queen Emillia did not put much faith in the gods, who for her were far distant. According to her and many members of the royal court, the Revered Magi were closer and able to manifest their power so that one could see it and utilize it. Therefore, people looked to them and their magic for aid rather than to the gods. King Tamaros was the exception. A devout man, he was strong in his faith and it seemed that the gods appreciated this, for Tamaros and – through him – all of Vinnengael had been singularly blessed.

But though Queen Emillia did not think much of the gods herself, she insisted that her child at least appear to worship them. Emillia was no match for her sharp-witted son. He had her backed into a corner, and there was nothing she could do to escape, except to complain again of the headache and say weakly that she was going to return to her bed.

The ladies were dispatched in all directions, some running for water to cool Her Majesty's forehead, others running for poultice of nettle to soothe her eyes. Gareth's mother lifted her gaze to heaven in thanksgiving, then shoved him out of her way as she rustled off to fetch lavender water to chafe Her Majesty's hands.

Dagnarus said graciously that he hoped his mother would be feeling better soon, and he and Gareth left the bedchamber. Dagnarus wore a smile on his lips and kept Gareth's wrist clasped firmly in his hand, as though he dared anyone to try to take his friend away from him.

As for Gareth, it had been on the tip of his tongue to blurt out that it was an old beggar woman who had cursed him, not the gods. He kept silent, however. He was learning to trust Dagnarus, learning to leave everything to his better judgment.

FOUR

Tangled Threads

WHEN THE TUTOR, EVARISTO, HAD ORIGI-nally been appointed three years before to teach the young prince, who was then six, the tutor and his wife rejoiced, thinking their fortunes were made. Evaristo was an ambitious man, fond of his comfort, pleased with his snug house in the city, and hoping to provide a good life for his children. Evaristo knew the reverse all too well.

When he was a youth growing up poor and ignorant in the streets of Dalon'Ren, Evaristo had been a hedge-wizard – as it is known disparagingly in Loerem – an itinerant sorcerer who picks up the crumbs of magic let fall by the gods and uses these to cast spells. There were many hedge-wizards living in Loerem, utilizing their magic with varying degrees of success. Magic, like the sun or the air, the water or the dirt, is available to any man or woman with the skill and the desire to lay claim to it. Some are better than others at using magic, just as some are better stone masons or better lute players. There are those who have a true gift and talent for magic and those who merely dabble in it.

Evaristo was talented at it. Magic proved useful to the

survival of himself and his family, Dalon'Ren being then a town with few laws and even fewer people to uphold those laws. Magic gained Evaristo the respect other boys earned with their fists.

Evaristo might have become one of the feared robber-sorcerers, who roam the woods and prey on travelers, but it was then that the church of Vinnengael, under the auspices of King Tamaros, began to try to impose order upon the ranks of those who lived by the use of magic.

This met with considerable resistance. The rumor went out that the church was planning to arrest all sorcerers and either force them to join the church or forbid them to use their art. Many hedge-wizards fled to the hills, others – like sixteen-year-old Evaristo – prepared to fight. The church, which was then led by Revered High Magus Dominaa, acted wisely. Dominaa sent out the priests with instructions to neither arrest nor intimidate talented wizards, but to do everything in their power to tempt them into adding their talents to the church's vast reservoir of magical power.

Evaristo, who had been living off the crumbs of magic, was shown a grand feast, given a taste of wondrous power he had never even imagined. He was quick to join, one of five who traveled back to Vinnengael with the church's recruiter.

One might have imagined that after a chancy life of scrapping and scrabbling in the streets of Dalon'Ren, Evaristo would have entered into the ranks of the war magi. He thought so himself, at first, but his soul discovered the library, with its shelves of books, its hushed, timeless atmosphere. His soul wanted to remain there, and Evaristo granted his soul's wish. He was admitted into the Order of Knowledge and did so well that he rose rapidly through the ranks and was now spoken of as perhaps one day being made Librarian, Head of the Order.

When the opportunity arose to become the young

prince's tutor it seemed that he had stepped on the turnpike leading directly to this goal. After three years spent enduring the prince's insults and bad behavior, Evaristo realized that he must have missed a signpost somewhere along the way.

'Dagnarus is an intelligent child. It's not like he can't do the work. A waste! A waste!' Evaristo said to his wife in frustration, as they ate their midday meal.

'Poor lad, it's not his fault. I've known stray cats to have a better upbringing,' his wife returned, settling down to dish out the lamb *en casserole*. She was particular about the cooking, never leaving it to servants, as did some other housewives.

'Half the time he doesn't come to the sessions,' Evaristo continued. 'When he does come – which is when the Queen takes it into her head to be concerned over her son's education, a thing she does about once in every six-month, and the boy knows he cannot escape – he is rude to me. He snorts, he kicks the table, he stares out the window, he scribbles in the books. I cannot lay a finger on him, of course. Nor do I think beating him would do any good. This is excellent lamb, my dear.'

'Not much like his brother,' observed the wife.

'True enough.' Evaristo sighed and dunked his bread in the gravy. 'Helmos is a gifted scholar, and that may be part of the problem.' Glancing out the window, which overlooked the street, to make certain that no one was in earshot, Evaristo leaned close to his wife, lowered his voice. 'The one lesson Dagnarus has learned well, a lesson he learned at his mother's knee, is to detest and despise his half brother. What Helmos is, Dagnarus is not – so the child has already determined.'

'You'd think his father the King – may the gods bless him – would take more interest in the boy.'

'King Tamaros wakes early and goes to bed late and still leaves the affairs of state unfinished,' said Evaristo.

'He is a wise man, a great ruler; he has brought peace to the world and prosperity to Vinnengael, but only the gods are perfect, my dear. Only the gods can love that which is not worthy of love, or so we are taught. Sometimes I wonder if even the gods must find it difficult to love our Queen.'

'Hush, dear! Not so loud,' warned his wife. Rising, she went to close the shutters. 'The King's heart may be buried with his first wife, but that doesn't mean he doesn't love the child of his second. Dagnarus is flesh of his flesh, for mercy's sake.'

'Tamaros dotes on the child. He adores the child. But he doesn't love him. And Dagnarus knows it.'

'Poor lad,' said the wife, shaking her head. 'Poor lad. More lamb, my dear?'

Evaristo, in desperation, had come up with the idea of the whipping boy. The tutor was under no illusions. He did not think that Dagnarus would suddenly take to learning in order to spare an underling from being punished. But he might do so because, quite simply, Dagnarus could not bear to be bested at anything.

Evaristo used Gareth to make education a competition, and although Dagnarus saw through the tutor's plan almost immediately, the prince found it galling to know that the whipping boy was better at something than he was. Dagnarus studied grimly, hating every minute of it, and making poor Gareth so nervous in the process – for he was truly afraid the prince would come to hate him along with the books – that Gareth was relieved on those days when Dagnarus could stand the schoolroom no longer and played truant.

A beating, though painful to the boy, was far better than being roasted in the fiery glare of the prince's green eyes. Gareth did not mind Evaristo's beatings, which were halfhearted and given only because Gareth was the whipping boy, after all, and it was expected. Evaristo was careful to leave marks on the backs of Gareth's legs and his buttocks, marks which were exhibited to Dagnarus, by way of making him feel bad. They never did have the desired effect.

'Good to see you are earning your keep, Patch,' Dagnarus would say on his return from his day of freedom. 'I'm doing you a favor,' he would add with a glint of gold in his green eyes. 'If you're not beaten regularly every three-month, the chamberlain will think you an extravagance and turn you out.'

The chamberlain. At least Evaristo seemed sorry to have to beat the boy, and the tutor always apologized very hand-somely afterward. The chamberlain did not apologize, nor was he sorry to beat Gareth. On the contrary, he seemed to enjoy it. Dagnarus hated the man and was always doing or saying something to shame him or ridicule him. The chamberlain did not dare strike the prince, but he could take out his ire and frustrations on Gareth.

To give Dagnarus credit, when he saw that the beatings were becoming more severe – the man broke Gareth's nose, on one occasion – the prince ceased his tormenting and began to work actively for the chamberlain's removal. This took some time, for Queen Emillia liked the man, who came from her homeland of Dunkarga. Dagnarus had his way, however, as he always did. The hunt for a new chamberlain began and ended with an elf named Silwyth.

Silwyth had come to the royal court of Vinnengael only a few months earlier to further his education. He was about one hundred years old, which made him the equivalent of a thirty-year-old human. Dagnarus and Gareth had heard rumors of the elf's appointment, and neither of the boys was pleased. They had seen him around the court and knew him to be cold and reserved, polite and correct, and highly disciplined, as are all elves. He looked a hopeless bore.

As it turned out, these very boring qualities were the reason for his selection. Silwyth was chosen by the King himself this time, not the Queen, following an unfortunate incident involving the prince.

An important visitor had come to court, one of the monks of the Monastery of the Keepers of Times. These monks are among the most revered people in all of Loerem. They devote their lives to recording history upon their bodies, tattooing events on their skin as they occur. When they die, they leave their bodies in the monastery as a permanent record of events. Held sacred by every race in the world, the monks are always accorded the very highest honors in any kingdom they visit. King Tamaros and the monk were walking through the palace when, on rounding a corner, they came upon Dagnarus and Gareth playing stickball.

An unlucky hit by Dagnarus sent the ball – a bundle of rags tied together with twine – hurtling past the monk's ear, narrowly missing striking the monk in the head.

Dagnarus realized that he'd gone too far. He could be charming when he chose, and he apologized to the monk most graciously.

The monk, whose robes had embroidered on them the green body of the Earth Dragon, making him a high-ranking Keeper of the Past, was very good-natured about the incident. He said something to the effect that 'boys will be boys, even if the boy is a prince.' King Tamaros added his own apology and looked very grave as he led his guest away. The next day, Silwyth was appointed Master of the Prince's Bedchamber.

The boys first met Silwyth when their tutoring session had ended for the day. The servants were clearing off their supper dishes when he entered, escorted by the King's own chamberlain. Silwyth was tall and straight-backed, his face pale and impassive. He wore traditional eleven clothing – silk long trousers which covered the legs (elves consider it immodest to reveal the leg, even under hose) and gathered at the ankles. Over those he wore a long silk tunic, embroidered with hand-screened images of birds and flowers. His almond-shaped eyes were dark brown, his hair jet-black, worn smoothed back, clubbed at the nape of the neck.

He bowed to the prince, but his bow was not servile. It was the bow of an equal, of one gentleman to another. Dagnarus was quick to notice and quick to take offense. He cast Gareth a glance that said, 'We shall make short work of this fellow.'

Gareth sighed. The elf's arms, though thin, were well muscled.

The King's chamberlain performed the introductions, which were lengthy. First he introduced the prince, with all his names and titles. Then the chamberlain named the elf, the elf's house, his father and his grandfather and his grandfather's father.

'Whose service were you in before you came here?' Dagnarus asked, as if he were interviewing candidates for the position of stable hand.

The King's chamberlain clucked his tongue reprovingly, but the prince ignored him.

'I serve the Father and the Mother, Your Highness,' replied the elf. 'After them the Divine and after him the Shield of the Divine. After him, I serve –'

'I don't mean that,' Dagnarus snapped. 'I meant whose service. Where were you a servant before you came to Vinnengael?'

'I am not a servant, Your Highness. I am a Lesser Guardian of the Eastern Wood, a rank that is equivalent to that of a count in Your Highness's court.'

'A count?' Dagnarus was surprised. He thought the elf was lying. 'Then why would you want to act as my chamberlain?'

'I have great esteem for your father, King Tamaros,'

replied Silwyth, bowing as he pronounced the name. 'I am pleased to serve him and his son in any capacity.'

This wasn't really an answer, but it was all the prince was likely to get; that much was obvious. Elves are known to be skilled at keeping their true motives secret.

'You will call me Dagnarus,' said the prince, after a pause to digest this information. 'And this is Patch.'

'The whipping boy,' said the King's chamberlain, with a sniff.

Silwyth made no comment. He repeated their names with a bow for each of them.

'*You* must not call him Patch,' Dagnarus continued petulantly, but only after the King's chamberlain was well out of hearing. 'I am the only one who may call him that. *You* must call him Gareth.'

Dagnarus said the 'you' with a sneering emphasis that was quite insulting. Gareth blushed for the prince's bad manners. Silwyth merely bowed again and accepted the correction.

Dagnarus turned away, his lip curled in derision. This elf offered no challenge; it was all too easy.

The boys started to leave, for the afternoon stretched ahead of them and Dagnarus had arranged with a King's guardsman to teach one of the prince's dogs to hunt.

'Where are you going, Your Highness?' asked Silwyth.

Dagnarus tossed the bit of information to him as he might have tossed a bone to that same young dog.

'The training of the dog must wait, Your Highness,' said Silwyth, speaking respectfully. 'His Majesty is holding a levee this afternoon. You should be in attendance. I have laid out your best clothes.'

'Don't be ridiculous,' Dagnarus scoffed. 'You can't expect me to waste my afternoon sitting around listening to a bunch of peasants do nothing but whine, bicker, and pass gas.'

'Your brother, Helmos, will be there,' said Silwyth. He

71

appeared, on second thought, to reconsider. 'But perhaps I was mistaken in thinking Your Highness might want to attend. I see that you are too young to be taking an interest in the workings of the kingdom. You would probably find the talk above your level of understanding. I will put your clothes away.'

'Wait!' Dagnarus ordered angrily, as the elf was leaving. 'Why should I take an interest in the King's business when I can do nothing to affect his policies?'

'Can you not, Your Highness?' asked Silwyth with an arch of a black eyebrow.

Dagnarus took his meaning immediately and was struck by the notion. It was true that Silwyth himself would not have been standing there if the prince had not worked actively for the removal of his predecessor. In those few words, Silwyth opened up an entire new play-yard for Dagnarus, the play-yard of court intrigue and politics. The prince's cheeks flushed with pleasure and anticipation; the dog was forgotten.

'I will attend the levee,' said Dagnarus. He hesitated a moment, then asked, 'Do I need the King's permission?'

'I have already obtained permission for Your Highness to attend,' said Silwyth.

Dagnarus was inclined to be angry at the elf for taking such a liberty, as well as anticipating the prince's decision, but, with uncharacteristic self-control, he swallowed his ire.

'Patch, run and tell Argot that I cannot come today.'

The prince left for his bedchamber, with Silwyth in attendance.

Gareth departed on his errand, glad to be excused from the hunting, for the boy disliked the society of the soldiers, finding them rough and crude and a little frightening. But the men had been Dagnarus's companions practically since the day he was old enough to beg them for rides upon their warhorses, and he spent every free hour he could find with them.

As for Captain Argot, people asked him if he did not find it irksome to have a nine-year-old underfoot, even though he was the prince. So Argot did at first. Not only was the small child a nuisance, but Argot lived in terror that the prince might be hurt or killed and that would be the end of the captain's career and possibly his life. Argot tried as best he could, with as much diplomacy as possible, to discourage Dagnarus from hanging around the barracks.

Eventually Argot, who was a good commander and a good man, realized that this was one battle he was going to lose. As often as he hauled the prince – dirty and smelling of horse – back to the palace, just as often did the prince sneak out again. The soldiers were becoming accustomed to having the prince around. They were flattered by his attentions and more than willing to make a soldier of the boy, especially as his older brother had a weak stomach for warfare – or so rumor had it. Argot requested a private meeting with the King to discuss the matter. The captain approached the situation thusly: if Dagnarus was going to handle the weapons and ride the horses, he should be trained in their use.

Queen Emillia would have taken to her bed for a month had she seen her son, stripped to his waist, riding bareback on a gigantic stallion, brandishing a small sword which the men had made 'specially for him, and screaming the war paean. The fawning courtiers, who were so busy passing on all sorts of other damaging gossip about members of the court, did not tell Her Majesty what her son was doing for recreation. The reason they did not was because Emillia had a bad habit of taking out her ire on the one who brought her information she didn't want to hear.

As to why Tamaros would encourage his younger son's interest in a military life, that is easily answered. The second son – the son who is not king – must find something

73

to do with himself. The only two career paths open to a man who will most likely be a prince all his life are that of magus and soldier.

It was obvious to everyone – even his mother – that Dagnarus would never be a scholar. Soldiering was, therefore, the obvious choice. Tamaros planned for the day when his two sons would rule Vinnengael; one son the wise and just king, the other son the people's trusted guardian.

As Evaristo had told his wife, only the gods are perfect.

Gareth knew his way around the palace fairly well, by now – the private quarters, that is. He had no business in the public part and so rarely went there. The one time he had ventured into the rooms where the King and Queen held audience, he hadn't liked it. Courtiers like his father stood about in knots whispering and murmuring, or laughing boisterously, all of them hoping for a chance to catch the King's eye.

Dagnarus and Gareth were free to roam the private quarters, and the boys flattered themselves that they knew it better than anyone else, having discovered several secret passages which they fondly believed were known to them alone. In truth, the passages were part of the castle's defenses, should it ever come under attack, and were well known to all the castle's inhabitants. The boys used these narrow hallways and hidden doors to play at war themselves and to spy upon the maidservants while they were undressing.

One of these corridors provided a shortcut from the upper levels of the palace down to the courtyard and thence to the barracks. Here Gareth found Argot, who had the prince's dog on a lead and was scratching the animal behind the ears.

Gareth told the captain the prince would not be able to hunt that afternoon. Argot nodded and without a word handed over the dog to another soldier, who led the animal back to the stables and turned him loose. The dog gleefully rejoined its fellows and dashed off to chase rats.

Gareth liked Argot, who was not rough and loud and vulgar as were most of the other soldiers. He was young for a captain, being only twenty-eight, but he was well trained in his profession, well suited to command. Argot took his duties seriously, seldom smiled, and never spoke unless he had something to say. He did not ask why the prince could not come, but Gareth was bursting with his news and eager to tell.

'His Highness has gone to attend the King's levee,' he said, swelling with borrowed importance.

'Hunh,' grunted another soldier, an old grizzled veteran who had so many battle scars twining his body that he looked like a gnarled old tree. 'The King'll be turning the boy into another bloody book-reading clerk, just like his brother.'

Argot cast the man a sharp glance. 'Mind what you say, Barr. Small vessels hold lots of water, and they have been known to crack and spill their contents.'

Gareth imagined naively that the captain was referring to a bucket of water standing nearby, which he'd put out for the dog, and so he paid no attention to this statement.

'The whole bloody court knows it,' muttered the veteran, but he looked uneasy and glared at the boy, who had no idea what he had done to offend him.

'Dagnarus doesn't like to read books,' Gareth said, thinking that somehow the soldier was disparaging the prince.

'Don't mind Barr; he's in a bad temper over a wench who spit in his eye last night,' Argot said, adding unexpectedly, 'I have no duty today, and my horse needs exercising. Since His Highness cannot come, perhaps you would like to learn to ride, Gareth.'

The boy was amazed and vastly pleased. It was many years before he realized, looking back on the incident, that Argot was hoping to distract the child, induce him to forget Barr's unfortunate remark. At the time, Gareth thought only that Argot was being unusually kind. The captain led his big warhorse out of the stables and tossed a blanket over the horse's broad back. Lifting Gareth, he settled the boy on the horse and told him to grip with his legs. Argot kept hold of the reins.

Gareth stared down from what seemed to him an immense height, half-fearful and wholly thrilled. Reaching out timidly, he patted the horse on its gray-spotted neck. The horse was accustomed to the weight of Argot, in his full battle armor, and made no more of the child than if he'd been one of the flies buzzing around its ears. The horse swiveled a bored eye at Gareth, shook its neck, then nuzzled Argot, hoping for an apple.

Argot led the horse with the boy astride out into the yard in front of the stables. They walked around slowly and with every moment that passed, Gareth's fear eased. He wound his hands in the horse's gray mane and once even dared kick the horse in the flanks with his heels – not very hard, the horse probably didn't even feel it. But in that moment the boy saw himself a warrior.

Argot walked the horse around the courtyard for about ten minutes. Gareth's backside soon started to hurt where it bumped painfully against the horse's spine, and his thighs ached, but he would not say a word of complaint or ask to be taken off, not for all the silver tams in the kingdom.

Argot praised the boy, saying that he sat a horse well, and was telling how his own father had taught him to ride before he could even say the word 'horse,' when a soldier, out of breath, came clattering into the courtyard, shouting for the captain.

'Here!' Argot waved his arm.

'Captain,' the soldier cried, saluting. 'We have caught Shakur!'

Argot stopped walking and so did the horse. Argot spoke a word of command and the horse froze in place, standing stock-still in the yard, with the boy on his back, while Argot went over to speak to the soldier.

'He fought like a demon, sir,' the soldier continued. 'Hanuit may lose his arm over it. They've carried him to the healers.'

'What of Shakur?' Argot demanded. 'Is he dead?'

'No, Captain.' The soldier grinned. 'Though Hanuit had his revenge on him. We followed your orders and took the bastard alive. They're bringing him here now.'

A troop of soldiers entered, their armor clashing and rattling. Two of them carried between them a man whose arms had been bound behind his back with bowstrings. Gareth could not distinguish any features on the man's face for the blood that covered it. All Gareth could see were two eyes, black and malevolent, above a gruesome wound. The man was lucky he still had two eyes. The sword slash had barely missed the right one. His cheek was laid open from the right cheekbone beneath the eye, his nose was sliced almost in half. The wound continued down the left cheek to the jaw, baring bone and cartilage to view.

He was a man of average height and no very great girth, but inordinately strong. His arms were lumpy with muscle, his thighs bulged, his calves were bigger around than Gareth. Sinews, tendons, and blood vessels formed tree-branch patterns beneath his brown, suntanned skin. His hair was shaved close to his head, as was the fashion of many of the soldiers, to make it easier to deal with lice, and for coolness beneath their heavy helms. His brows were black, as was his short-cropped beard. His face was dirty and seamed with licentious living.

He did not come tamely, but fought his captors every step, planting his feet and refusing to move. The skin on his upper arms was cut and bleeding. His body gleamed with sweat. The men dragging him along were also hot and sweaty, covered with his blood, and seemed worn-out from their efforts.

But there was an air of grim triumph about them when they brought the man before their captain. The prisoner ceased to struggle. He stood staring at Argot with a defiant leer made hideous by the terrible wound.

Flies buzzed around the prisoner, drawn by the blood. Gareth was frightened and sickened, but horribly fascinated at the same time. Part of him wanted to run away, but part didn't, which was good, because he wasn't going anywhere. He could not dismount the horse without help, and Argot had forgotten the child's existence.

'Shakur,' said Argot, his voice grating, 'you are accused of thievery, lying, and desertion. I won't ask how you plead, for you'd only lie, and the very fact that you were captured five miles outside of the city limits is proof that you are a deserter. Still, I will give you a chance to speak in your own defense.'

Shakur laughed and spit in Argot's face.

One of the soldiers holding Shakur drove a fist into his stomach, doubling him over. The other drew a knife and, grabbing hold of Shakur's head, bent it backward, exposing the man's throat.

'Let me finish what Hanuit started, Captain,' the soldier begged, brandishing the knife.

Shakur held still, made no protest, showed not the least fear.

'No!' Argot was stern. 'The King alone may sentence a man to death. Take this wretch to the dungeons, there to await His Majesty's pleasure. Send one of the healers to see to his face.'

Argot rounded on his heel, turning his back on the man to show his disgust. The soldier, grumbling, thrust his knife back into its sheath on his belt.

Shakur's arm muscles bulged, he gave a grunt and a shudder. The bowstrings that held his arms pinned behind him popped loose like so much silken thread. He knocked one soldier to the ground with the back of his hand, felled the other with a blow from his fist. Shakur lunged straight at Gareth.

The deserter did not want the boy. He wanted the horse.

Terrified, Gareth kicked at the man with his feet, acting more out of panic than bravery. The child was nothing but an annoyance to Shakur, however. Grabbing the boy by the leg, Shakur heaved Gareth up off the horse's back and sent him flipping head over heels into the air.

Had Gareth fallen on the hard-packed ground, he would have ended his days as whipping boy by breaking his neck. As it was, he landed in a hayrick. His body smashed the flimsy wooden manger to splinters, but the hay cushioned his fall. Dizzy and breathless, he lay amidst the ruins, shocked nearly out of his wits and amazed that he was not dead.

Shakur leapt on the horse's back and drove his heels into the animal's flanks. The captain's horse was a battle-tested war mount trained to respond to an unfamiliar rider. Argot whistled in a certain way. The horse heard the command to rear, which is one of the first a warrior teaches his mount, and stood up on its hind legs to try to throw off the unwanted rider.

Shakur wrapped his arms around the horse's neck, nearly strangling the beast, and fought grimly to hang on. The horse was prepared for this maneuver, however. Lowering its head, it kicked with its back hooves. Then the horse reared up on its front legs again, shaking its head and baring its teeth, and finally succeeded in throwing the man.

Shakur landed on his back in the dust, where he immediately curled himself into a ball to escape the slashing hooves. Only another whistled command from Argot – a command given in no great hurry – saved Shakur from being trampled.

The horse cantered to Argot's side, where it stood glaring and snorting and stamping a forefoot. Soldiers had come running from all directions by then. Several of them picked up Shakur, who had finally had the fight knocked out of him, and hauled him away. More soldiers helped their fallen comrades, one of whom lay unconscious for three days from Shakur's blow.

Argot cast Gareth a glance. Seeing that the boy was alive and breathing, the warrior went to his horse. Argot made certain the animal had suffered no harm, then he ordered one of the stable hands to return the horse to its stall. After that he came over to see about the child.

Gareth bore the man no grudge for the delay. The horse was a valuable animal. He was only a boy, and the whipping boy at that. Embarrassed and feeling guilty, as if somehow it had all been his fault, Gareth tried to sit up.

Argot shook his head and ordered him to lie still. Bending down, he felt him all over for broken bones.

'Does your head hurt? Is there a ringing in your ears?' he asked, peering into his eyes. 'Do you see two of me? What is your name?'

'No, sir,' the child said, blinking back tears at the kindness in the man's voice. 'Gareth, sir.'

'You'll do,' Argot said, and smiled. He helped the boy to his feet and brushed the hay and wood splinters from his clothes. 'That was a brave thing you did, lad. Kicking at that bastard like that. He might have torn off your leg.'

'I did not mean to be brave, sir,' Gareth said, trying hard not to cry with all of the soldiers standing around, staring at him. 'I was only frightened.'

'Well, lad,' said Argot, 'and what do you think bravery is?' He rested his hand upon his shoulder. 'We'll make a soldier of you yet.'

'Thank you, sir, but I'd rather not,' Gareth said earnestly.

Argot laughed and clapped the boy on the back.

'You are a stout fellow. The prince is lucky in his choice of a friend. You are welcome to come along with the prince anytime, and I will continue our riding lessons.'

Gareth thanked him politely, though he privately resolved that if he never came near a horse again in his life it would be too soon. He asked anxiously what would become of Shakur.

'If the gods are just, he'll rot in the dungeons and be eaten by rats,' said Argot.

After the incident, Gareth limped back to the palace, his limbs stiffening, and hid himself in his dark closet, to nurse his wounds and have his cry in private. There, Silwyth found the boy. The elf did not say a word, but stripped off Gareth's clothes, bathed his scratches, removed a wood splinter or two, and washed his face, which was covered with dirt and slobber.

Dagnarus appeared in the doorway. Silwyth faded back into the darkness.

'So, Patch,' the prince said in a stern voice, 'I hear you have been having adventures without me.'

Gareth truly thought the prince was angry. Ducking his head, he said he was sorry, he never intended such a thing, which was certainly the truth, and he hoped with all his heart that an adventure never befell him again, which was also the truth.

To Gareth's surprise, Dagnarus started to laugh. He was in an excellent humor and, bounding into the room, flung his arms around his friend and gave him a hug, which made Gareth wince.

'Argot told me the whole story, Patch. I am proud of you. I should have liked to have seen it!' The prince regarded the boy with undisguised envy. 'It's too bad we can't split ourselves in twain and be two places at once.'

Gareth agreed that this was a shame and asked if His Highness had enjoyed the levee.

'No,' Dagnarus said, pacing about the small room, for he could never stand still. 'It was boring and stupid. I do not know how my father stands it. Listening to these wretches whining and complaining about the King's decrees. One even had the nerve to say to the King's teeth that he thought my father had passed a bad law.'

'What did the King do?' Gareth asked, shocked.

'He listened to the fool, and said he would take the matter under advisement. I would have had him whipped down the palace steps,' said Dagnarus, frowning. 'When I am King I will make what laws I choose, and no one will dare criticize them.'

He came and sat down on the bed beside Gareth, his green eyes shining with excitement in the light of the oil lamp Silwyth had placed upon a shelf.

'And do you know what else I learned, Patch,' Dagnarus said. 'A king does not need to be educated! He has advisors, Patch! People who tell him whatever it is he must know.' He put his hand on Gareth's shoulder. 'You will be my advisor, Patch, so you must study very hard.'

Three days later, they heard news that Shakur had escaped.

Gareth lived for days after that in unreasoning terror, imagining that the convict would seek his revenge upon him. Countless times the boy woke up in cold sweat in the night, imagining the man with a knife in his hand, ready to slit his throat.

'Don't be silly, Patch,' Dagnarus said scornfully, when the boy ventured to relate his fears. 'The man is long gone. Why should he risk being thrown back into the dungeon over you?'

That made sense, and Gareth ceased to worry about Shakur. As for Evaristo, his hopes of turning the prince into a scholar (and thereby gaining rich reward himself) were dashed. His Highness was rarely in the schoolroom after that and, eventually, Evaristo quit beating the whipping boy, seeing that it did no good.

FIVE

Royal Audience

A WEEK AFTER GARETH'S ADVENTURE, SILWYTH woke the child earlier than usual, which was already early enough.

'What is it?' Gareth grumbled, shivering in the cold of the morning. The palace, with its massive stone walls and stone floors, was cool on the hottest days, and this was the middle of winter, when the wind raced down from the mountaintops, carrying the snow with it. 'Why do I have to get up now?'

'You are to have an audience with the King,' said Silwyth.

The boy went colder than the stone floor on which his bare feet shivered, and he was wide-awake in a moment.

'He's . . . he's going to get rid of me,' Gareth said, quaking, his teeth chattering.

'Don't be silly,' Silwyth said. 'He has heard of your bravery and would like to do you honor. Eat your breakfast.'

'I'm not hungry.' Gareth couldn't have swallowed a mouthful. 'And I wasn't all that brave,' he added, squirming as Silwyth rolled up the woolen hose, preparatory to sliding them over the child's skinny legs.

'I trust you will *not* say that to His Majesty,' Silwyth admonished.

'Oh, no!' Gareth cried, terrified at the thought. 'I won't be expected to say anything to him, will I?'

'You are not mute, child, nor are you a barbarian. You will be expected to carry on a conversation like a civilized person.'

A conversation with the King! The boy couldn't imagine such a thing, and he was even more frightened than he would have been had he been told that His Majesty was planning to cut off his head.

'Stop shaking,' Silwyth ordered sternly.

'What do I talk about?' Gareth quavered.

'His Majesty will guide the conversation, asking you questions, and you will answer them. Do not speak until he speaks to you. Reply politely and graciously, but concisely. Speak out clearly, holding your head up. Don't stare down at your feet and mumble as you did the other day when Crown Prince Helmos came into the schoolroom.

'Bow low on entering, then stand erect. If you are fortunate enough that His Majesty beckons for you to come near him, walk forward to within two paces of him, bow again, and stand still. Do not fidget or tug at your clothes. Keep an eye on His Highness. Dagnarus will alert you if you are doing something wrong.'

'He will be with me?' Gareth said, cheering up.

'Certainly. You are to accompany the prince on his morning visit.'

The boy was vastly relieved. He had envisioned himself called to a formal audience in the Great Hall, and the prospect of meeting and chatting with the King by himself with crowds of courtiers snickering behind their hands was terrifying. If Dagnarus was with Gareth, he felt he could handle anything, from escaped prisoners to conversing with the King, Dagnarus's father.

Gareth felt so much better he was actually hungry again,

but Silwyth refused to allow him to eat anything, for fear he might spill crumbs on his good tunic. He did permit the child to drink some milk, so that his stomach wouldn't make unseemly sounds. He held the cup to Gareth's lips, first draping him with the blanket and warning him not to dribble.

Gareth attended the prince at his rising. Dagnarus smiled at his friend, pleased with the honor being accorded him. The attendant lords, who were always hanging about the prince, currying his favor, were much more respectful to the whipping boy, and he understood, to his confusion, that this audience had improved his standing.

His newfound courage seemed to ooze right out of his soft leather slippers, however, as he accompanied Dagnarus to his father's study. The prince laughed at his fears.

'My father is pleased with you,' he said. 'Don't be nervous. No one can possibly be afraid of him.'

'How did he come to hear of what I did?' Gareth wondered.

Dagnarus shrugged. 'How does he come to hear of anything that happens in the kingdom? He listens.'

Gareth considered this. It was true that King Tamaros knew all there was to know about what happened in his court, in his kingdom, and in the world. Only the monks of Dragon Mountain and the all-seeing gods were said to know more. As it happened, Captain Argot had reported the story of Shakur's capture to his friends and, pleased with Gareth's courage, Argot had included the boy's part. The captain's friends had spread the tale, and one of the courtiers, always hoping to ingratiate himself with the King, had told His Majesty of the bravery of the prince's friend, implying, of course, that the prince was the one responsible.

Snow had fallen in the night – a heavy, wet snow, for which the farmers were grateful – and the morning was cloudy and cold. A gray day outside meant a gloomy day inside the castle's stone walls, for the windows, long and narrow in order to foil possible attackers, did not admit much light even on the brightest days.

One of the servants walked before the boys, carrying a lighted flambeau. The castle was silent, the thick walls deadened noise and not many of the castle's denizens were yet awake. The servants were up, of course, and they scuttled here and there, more silent than the mice, who could always be heard scratching and skittering. The few lords whom His Majesty permitted to attend him in his bedchamber had gone to their own breakfasts. The Queen and her retinue would not rise for many hours yet.

The prince and the boy passed the stands of armor. The flambeau's light threw the shadows of the armor back against the walls; the fire shone bright in the metal helms. The shadows moved as the candle flame moved, and it seemed to Gareth's startled gaze that an army of flame and darkness was emerging from the walls. Startled and dismayed, he cringed when Dagnarus laughed boisterously, pointing out the phenomenon of the shadowed knights to Silwyth. The prince's laughter seemed as sacrilegious as laughing in the Temple.

The candlelight continued on before them, and the moment the light was withdrawn, the shadows disappeared. The dark army vanished. The armor went back to being just armor – dust-covered and starting to rust in places.

The two continued on past the Queen's chambers, which Gareth could have found had he been blind, owing to the constant reek of perfume, and entered the King's chambers. The boy had never before been in that part of the castle.

Though awed, he felt considerably more at ease there, mainly because the halls were much lighter and smelled of leather and ink and vellum. He peeped inside a half-opened door and found the great library.

'Stop gaping, Gareth. You look like a peasant,' Silwyth ordered, laying a remonstrating hand upon the boy's shoulder.

Gareth's mouth snapped shut, but he continued to gape, if only inwardly. He had never seen so many books in his life; shelf upon shelf, entire rooms that had been transformed into libraries to house the King's books. Only the Temple of the Magi held a larger collection.

Eager and nervous as he was for his approaching audience, Gareth could not help but slow his steps and gaze with longing into the rooms. The servant had doused the candles as they entered that part of the castle, for no fire was ever permitted anywhere near the Royal Library.

Early as it was, scholars were already seated at the long tables that ran down the center of the room, heads bent over the books. The morning sun had yet to reach the room, but the readers were able to see quite clearly by means of stone-light – smooth, round river rocks heated magically until they glowed with a soft yellow light. The rocks were placed on stands, which could be moved from table to table by the scholars. Gareth was impressed. Magi charge dearly to cast such a spell, which involves an immense transference of magic from the earth into the rock. His family had one stone-light in their house, and it was lit only on special occasions. Here there must have been twenty, and they were lit every day.

Though there was a preponderance of humans, all races were represented. Gareth was surprised to see a gray-bearded dwarf among them – dwarves are not scholars. Few dwarves can read and write their own language, much less the languages of others. The dwarf stood up to retrieve another book, and Gareth saw that one of the dwarf's legs was shrunken and deformed. He was one of the Unhorsed, a dwarf who can no longer ride and would therefore be a burden upon his clan. The Unhorsed choose to sacrifice themselves for the sake of the clan by living in permanent dwellings, where they set up forges for blacksmithing and markets for trade. Though revered by their people for their sacrifice, the Unhorsed are also pitied by their fellow dwarves. This dwarf was of high rank among his people, and had been invited to Vinnengael by King Tamaros, to learn the human language and to add to the magi's knowledge of the dwarves.

'Come along, Patch,' said Dagnarus, irritated. 'Whatever are you gawking at? It's only a bunch of books.'

The two boys entered King Tamaros's study, his favorite room in a palace of well over two hundred rooms. It was the very room Gareth had noted on his first day of arrival, the room in the large turret with the massive windows, surrounded by the balcony known as the King's Walk.

Gareth could understand why Tamaros loved the room. It could have been tapestried by books. Located high in a square tower that jutted out from the castle proper, the room had four windows – large, square-cut windows, which each faced one of the cardinal directions. The view from any direction was magnificent, showing the mountains to the north, the prairie lands to the south, the River Hammerclaw to the east, Lake Ildurel to the west. The boy had never before realized the world was so vast.

The view helped to relieve him somewhat of his crushing disappointment. There was only one person in the room, and that was Dagnarus's half brother, Helmos.

'Where is my father?' Dagnarus demanded. 'Why isn't he here? He was to have given audience to my friend, Gareth.'

Gareth had seen the crown prince before, but generally only from a distance, as he rode by in a parade or stood upon a balcony or strode past them in the corridors.

The one time Helmos had come into the schoolroom, Gareth had been too overwhelmed and shy even to look at the man.

The two brothers were not close. Considering the difference in their ages, this was not surprising, but the matter went deeper than that. Their interests and tastes were completely dissimilar; and though each son was stamped with his father's image, each seemed to have inherited features denied the other. Dagnarus had his father's firm mouth and strong chin; Helmos had his father's penetrating eyes and slow, warm smile.

'His Majesty was called away on a matter of extreme urgency,' said Helmos, looking up from his work. 'He left his regrets and his wish that the audience should be held at another time.'

Pigs' bladders are often filled with air and given to small children to use as balls. When stuck with a pin, the bladders deflate. Gareth knew how they felt: excitement, fear, and anticipation whistled out of him.

Dagnarus frowned, displeased. He wanted this, and he couldn't imagine anything could be important enough to interfere with his desires.

'This will not do. Where is my father?' he demanded.

'He is meeting with the elven ambassadors,' Helmos said quietly. 'They came through the Portal this morning, bearing news of great import. His Majesty is not to be disturbed.'

Dagnarus had that stubborn look about him, as if he meant to run off and interrupt the meeting anyway. Silwyth clicked his tongue. Helmos looked grave.

'Please, Dagnarus,' Gareth whispered, feeling his face so flushed it was a wonder blood didn't leak out his ears. 'It's all right. I don't mind. Truly I don't. I'll meet His Majesty another time.'

Helmos, at twenty-two years of age, was a compassionate man, a sensitive man. Many people, unable to see beneath the unassuming manner to his heart, thought him a weak man. One of these was his own brother.

Helmos saw Gareth's deep disappointment, his unhappiness, and his embarrassment, which Dagnarus, with his obstinacy, was only making worse.

'I know that meeting me is not nearly so wonderful as meeting our father,' Helmos said, 'but I would be interested to hear the tale of Gareth's bravery myself.'

Helmos smiled at the boy, a warm smile that came straight from some place of goodness within him, and lit the dreary day brighter than the sun. He put Gareth in a chair at his table and seated himself opposite the child, as if the whipping boy were his equal. Helmos made no mention of the cursed mark upon Gareth's face. His eyes did not avoid it, however. He saw it, acknowledged it, and thereafter thought no more of it.

Gareth's gaze strayed to the book Helmos had been perusing, and he saw to his astonishment that it was written in a foreign language. He recalled hearing that Helmos spoke elven fluently, as well as dwarven. He also spoke many of the varied human dialects, and a smattering of orken.

Dagnarus posted himself behind Gareth and, giving his friend a jab with a finger between his shoulder blades, started him talking. At first, Gareth stared down at the table, fearful of lifting his eyes, and mumbled into the high collar of his tunic. Helmos listened intently; his questions were knowledgeable. He proved that he was interested in what the boy was saying and gradually, Gareth forgot himself and began talking to the man freely and easily, without restraint.

'And you did not run, not even when this deserter came right at you,' Helmos said, regarding him with approval.

'I couldn't very well run, Your Highness,' Gareth replied, bound to be truthful. 'I was on the horse. And 'it was a very *tall* horse, Your Highness,' he added with a shiver at the memory.

'You could have jumped off,' Helmos pointed out. 'You chose to stay and confront your enemy.'

'He kicked the man,' said Dagnarus, supporting his friend with admirable loyalty. 'And beat him with his fists.'

Gareth shook his head. 'I don't remember kicking him. Or if I did, it was only out of panic. A rat will fight a lion, they say, if the lion has the rat cornered.'

'Let us say that in this instance, the lion fought the rat,' said Helmos.

Gareth didn't take his meaning, at first, then he saw the man's blue eyes, their smiling warmth, and he understood the compliment. The man's smile permeated the boy. Gareth had never felt so happy, so proud, so accepted. He did not think it possible for his happiness to increase, but it did the very next moment.

'Gareth,' Helmos said, speaking to the boy as if he were an adult and not a child of nine, 'it is my great honor to have been nominated for the exalted post of Dominion Lord. It is my privilege to invite those of acknowledged bravery and honor to attend the feast that will be held prior to my entrance into the Temple for the testing. Prince Dagnarus will attend, of course, and I would like you to be there, as well. If you would like to come,' he added, always modest and self-deprecating.

The court had been talking of nothing else for weeks. To become a Dominion Lord was a high honor, an honor one worked a lifetime to achieve. It might have been expected that the envious would whisper that Helmos had been chosen only because he was the King's son, but such was the high regard in which the crown prince was held that not even the most jaded courtier muttered. Simply because he was nominated did not mean he would be chosen. Helmos would have to undergo rigorous tests

– tests in honor, in chivalry, in knowledge, and in wisdom. The other Dominion Lords would judge these tests and then vote on his worthiness. But there were few who doubted that Helmos would pass.

King Tamaros was understandably proud. The feast was to be a splendid one, a feast the like of which no one had ever before seen. No expense was being spared. Gareth's parents were to attend, but they would never have considered bringing their son. Gareth had hoped Dagnarus might be able to sneak back some of the sweet-meats from the banquet. That had been his dearest wish. Now he was being offered a place at the table.

Gareth stared at the crown prince blankly, struck dumb by the honor. Pent-up tension, nervousness, and, above all, the knowledge of the man's understanding and kindness, welled up inside the child and flowed out his eyes.

Helmos pretended that he didn't notice that the child was sobbing. The crown prince began to talk to Dagnarus about his dog, giving Gareth time to pull himself together and to wipe his nose on his sleeve.

Dagnarus boasted of the dog and his abilities for some time. The polite conversation between the brothers lagged a bit, then Helmos said, 'And how did you like attending the King's levee?'

It was a harmless question, Helmos meant nothing by it, but Dagnarus tensed, regarded his brother suspiciously.

'I liked it.' Dagnarus spoke defiantly, as if daring Helmos to say otherwise. 'Why? Did you think I wouldn't? Did you think I had no business being there?' He bristled, his eyes sparked.

'I thought only that it might be tedious for you,' Helmos answered, with a wry smile. 'I find it so, sometimes. The suitors can be extremely long-winded.'

Dagnarus relaxed, though his skin twitched, like that of a dog who realizes that what it took for a foe is a friend.

'Yes, I thought some of them incredibly stupid,' he said

bluntly. 'I do not know how our father puts up with them. Some had no reason to be there at all. Our father is too lenient, sometimes.' Dagnarus stood with his hands clasped behind his back, his feet apart, frowning at the memory.

'Indeed?' Helmos was interested. 'What ruling did you take exception to?'

'That business about the Trevinici,' Dagnarus replied. 'The ones who had encroached upon royal lands. The fault was theirs. Our father did wrong to give credence to them by listening to their silly arguments.'

'What would you have done?' Helmos asked.

'Sent in my army to drive them off,' Dagnarus answered, with a shrug.

'The Trevinici had no knowledge that they were trespassing,' said Helmos quietly. 'They are a warrior people and, mistaking our intentions, would have fought to defend themselves. Many on both sides would have died. It was much better for our father to invite them here to talk, to explain to them that they are camping on land that belongs to the crown, and ask them to leave it in peace.'

'They thought him weak,' said Dagnarus impatiently. 'I saw them sneer when they left, and they laughed.' His frown deepened. 'They were laughing at our father. They are barbarians. Armed might is all they understand.'

'If they do not leave, our father will speak to them again. Eventually, they will come to understand and respect his commands.'

Dagnarus snorted. 'They will mock him and laugh at his commands. They will poach the King's animals and cut down the King's trees. And when more of their kind see that we do nothing to stop them, they will move in, too. You might as well announce that the royal lands are open to anyone who wants to squat there.'

'Who has been saying such things?' Helmos asked, frowning in his turn.

Though only nine, Dagnarus had been fed intrigue with his mother's milk. He shrugged, and said casually, 'Oh, I've heard it around. No one that I can recall.'

Helmos disliked confrontation. He changed subjects, continuing to talk of the Trevinici, but focusing on the odd symbiotic relationship they had with a group of nonhumans known as the Pecwae. Helmos spoke at some length, giving Dagnarus time to calm down, and finished his discourse by showing the children a piece of the marvelous and magical turquoise jewelry the Pecwae make.

While Dagnarus and Gareth were eagerly examining the ring of sky-blue stone and wondering what magic it might perform, Helmos cast an oblique glance at Silwyth, who had been standing all this time in an inconspicuous corner of the room.

Silwyth understood the signal. Advancing, he bowed and reminded Dagnarus that the hour was nearing when they should have their session with the tutor. Dagnarus and Helmos bid each other good day with distant cordiality. Gareth had recovered himself sufficiently to be able to thank Helmos for his kind attention and to assure him that nothing in the world could make him happier than attending the feast.

Helmos smiled before returning to his book.

Dagnarus and Gareth left, shepherded by the silent Silwyth. They passed the Royal Library again, and Gareth gazed at the books with intense longing.

Dagnarus paid no attention. He was deep in thought, his brow furrowed. When he reached the stand of armored knights, he said, 'Silwyth, what would the Shield of the Divine do if he found these barbarians camped upon his land?'

'The Shield would put them to the sword, every one of them,' Silwyth answered, quite calmly.

'But why?' Gareth asked, speaking with unusual spirit. He had just found a hero to worship in Helmos and thought he needed to come to his defense. 'What harm do they do? The King only loses a few deer and a couple of old trees. His Majesty has thousands of deer and millions of trees.'

'That is not the point,' said Silwyth. 'The Trevinici are nothing. His Highness was correct in what he told the crown prince. It is the other kings who will see this and say, "Ah, if the barbarians have taken this illegally and not suffered, then why am I not able to do the same?"'

'Precisely,' said Dagnarus, triumphant. 'Have a fun day with Evaristo, Patch.'

Vaulting over the balustrade, he was off down the staircase before Silwyth could grab him.

In the playroom, alone with the tutor, Gareth related most of the details of his visit to Evaristo, adding the discussion between the two princes.

'His Majesty was quite right to deal with these barbarians mercifully,' Evaristo maintained. 'Many lives would have been lost otherwise, as Helmos wisely said.'

'Silwyth told Dagnarus that this means other kings will see us as weak and take advantage of us,' Gareth argued. 'He says the elves would have put the Trevinici to the sword.'

'To serve as an example, no doubt,' said Evaristo, sniffing. He did not like Silwyth, nor did he like the influence he saw the elf exerting over the young prince. 'That is typical of elven thinking. They are a people in love with warfare and their own unbending notions of honor. They respect nothing but a sword thwack to the head. His Majesty showed true wisdom in this decision. All men should honor him for it. To grant mercy where none is expected or deserved is a sign of strength, not weakness.'

'Tell me about the Dominion Lords,' Gareth begged. 'Tell me about the ceremony of Transfiguration.'

Evaristo complied, seeing that his young pupil was much

too excited to pay attention to multiplication tables, which had been the chosen course of study that day.

'To understand the reason the Dominion Lords came into being, you must first understand why and how the magical Portals were created,' said Evaristo. 'Do you know anything of that, Gareth?'

'My nanny took me once to visit a friend who worked in one of the elven households. I saw the entrance to the Portal that goes to the land of the elves, but I did not go inside it. Nanny said that the gods made the Portals and gave them to King Tamaros as a reward for being wise and good and trying to convince people to get along with each other. There are four Portals: one leading to the elven lands, one leading to the dwarven lands, and one to the orken. The last one is in the Temple, and it leads to the gods.' Seeing his tutor frowning, Gareth faltered. 'Isn't that right?'

'You are right in that there are four Portals. I see that I will have to clear up some of your misconceptions. I do not know how these stories get started,' Evaristo muttered.

'King Tamaros was thirty-five years of age and already, by the grace of the gods, he had become High King, which means that he is king above many lesser kings. Not only that, but even then, young as he was, he was honored throughout Loerem as the greatest ruler Vinnengael has ever known.'

Gareth nodded to show that he was listening and paying close attention. Evaristo, pleased at the boy's interest, proceeded, expanding warmly upon the subject, which was one of his favorites.

'Tamaros had managed to unite the kingdoms of the humans – the Dunkargans and the Nimrans – which had never been done before. He did this not through war, but through peaceful negotiation. He built roads and opened trade routes that benefited all. Seeing that the opening of roads and trade routes helped ally the previously warring kingdoms of humans, Tamaros determined that opening trade routes to the realms of the other races might help unite the continent.

'But the continent is vast. It takes a dwarf a year of hard traveling overland to reach Vinnengael from Saumel, the City of the Unhorsed. It takes the elves nearly as long and the way is dangerous for them, passing through human lands as they must. The orken and their ships must journey many weeks at sea, through perilous storms and chancy winds to reach Vinnengael. Thus few humans ever saw an elf or a dwarf or an ork, few came to know them, and therefore no one trusted them.

'Tamaros summoned the heads of the Orders of Magi and asked them to devise a means by which people could be magically transported from a central location in their individual homelands to Vinnengael. And send people from Vinnengael to visit the homelands of other races.

'The answer was, of course, the Portals. The idea came from the great magus Petra Petar, the Seneschal. It is his office that is responsible for the care and regulation of the land, for the growing of crops, the altering of weather, the building of roads. He and his people are much traveled, and he had also been thinking that easier means of transportation overland could be devised. He presented Tamaros his ideas on the Portals. Tamaros was pleased and ordered the magi to begin work to build them.

'The Portals were not created overnight, Gareth,' Evaristo said, and he looked off into the distance with a sigh. 'The head of my Order – that of teaching – was involved in the work, as were the heads of all the Orders. I was one of her assistants – low-ranking, then, more dogsbody than anything else – and I worked sometimes far into the night, for it was our given task to research the old texts for clues on how such Portals might be created.'

'And how was that?' Gareth interrupted excitedly.

'Child, child,' Evaristo chided. He turned to the very

last part of the book on mathematics, exhibited a problem whose myriad numbers covered two entire pages and lapped over onto a third. 'Can you understand that equation?'

'No, Master,' said Gareth, looking daunted. He had advanced only as far as the six-times, having become mired in the vagaries of the sevens.

'The magic used to create the Portals is far, far more complex. I could not begin to explain it.'

'I'll understand when I'm older,' Gareth said gloomily.

Evaristo smiled wryly. 'We adults do say that a lot, don't we? Well, how shall I put this? You have seen the drill the stonecutter uses to bore into the marble? Think of all the elemental magicks coming together, spinning round and round faster and faster until, like the stonecutter's tool, they spin so fast that they bored right through solid matter, forming a hole in both the material part of the world and the temporal.'

'A hole,' said Gareth, musing. 'But isn't that the . . . the Void?' He lowered his voice, pronounced the awful word with a pleasantly satisfying feeling of dread.

'Hush, Gareth!' Evaristo frowned. 'Do not speak that word lightly! Of course, it was *not* Void magic! As if the Revered Magi would countenance such a wicked thing. The Void destroys, it does not create. Now, where was I?' He looked exceedingly cross.

'You were telling me about the Dominion Lords, Master,' Gareth said meekly.

Evaristo's face cleared. 'Yes, so I was. That is a much more suitable topic for discussion. King Tamaros, for his part, was beginning to see that the creation of the Portals had the potential to bring about peace and also, at the same time, the potential for war on a very drastic scale. The elves were already suspicious of our motives. They became convinced that the only reason the Portals were being built was so that the humans could sweep in and take control of elven lands. Tamaros spent two years in negotiations, trying to persuade the Divine that the Portals would be used only for peaceful purposes. He promised that each of the races could put guards and guard gates on their ends of the Portals. He promised that no human should come through without first obtaining permission from the Keeper of the Portals.

'All these things he promised, but how was he to make certain that his promises were kept? Already, hundreds of people were clamoring for permission to use the Portals, and they had not yet even been built. King Tamaros knew that while some of these people had honorable intentions, many others were scoundrels and crooks. How was our King to guarantee that those who entered the Portals would observe our laws, once they were beyond our control?

'As always, when confronted with a problem, King Tamaros turned to the gods. He left his palace, entered the Temple, there to fast and pray. He stayed in the Temple for nine days and nine nights, sleeping on the stone floor of a small cell, eating nothing, drinking only water. I was privileged to be one of those attending him at that time,' said Evaristo.

'I can still see him, dressed in plain robes, robes plainer than those of the lowest novice, for he was not one of the magi and would never pretend otherwise. His long hair fell unbound over his shoulders. His chin was unshaven, which was unusual for him, and his beard was flaxen and shimmered in the candlelight. The fasting had not left him gaunt, but had brought out the fine bone structure of his face. I placed the water jug I had brought on the floor beside him. I spoke to him and asked if there was anything I could do for him.

'He did not see me or hear me, and I knew he walked with the gods. I withdrew in silence. The next day, Tamaros left the Temple and revealed the will of the gods.

'Ten humans would be chosen to travel through the Portals. These ten would be our ambassadors to other races. They would live among the other races and learn their ways. They would be responsible for any others who entered the Portals and watch over those who came and went after them.'

'The Dominion Lords,' Gareth cried, in sudden understanding.

'Yes, and those duties were their first,' said Evaristo. 'Since that time, their power has grown, as has their responsibility. King Tamaros searched the human kingdoms for those most worthy of this honor. He set high standards for the Dominion Lords – the person must be well educated; must be able to speak at least two other languages besides his or her own; must be trained in combat, in order to defend the weak; must be skilled in diplomacy; must be caring and compassionate, strong and courageous.

'When finally ten candidates were chosen, King Tamaros presented them to the gods. It was then, for the first time, the Transfiguration – the Miracle of the Armor – occurred, and King Tamaros was given to know that his choices were wise and pleased the gods.'

'I'll get to see the Transfiguration, won't I, Evaristo?' Gareth asked eagerly, not as much interested in the religious aspects of the ceremony as he was in the spectacle.

'Please the gods, you will see it,' Evaristo replied somberly, with a note of rebuke. 'This is a very serious ceremony, Gareth, and one that is not to be undertaken with a light heart. The Transfiguration takes its toll on the mind and the body. One candidate did not survive, but fell down dead upon the altar. The armor and her body had fused as one and could not be separated.'

'Did that mean the gods didn't like her, Master?' Gareth asked.

'At first, some thought that was the reason. But then

the Revered High Magus pointed out that the gods had given the lady the blessed armor. The ruling was made that the lady's spirit had accepted the gods' gift, but her mortal body was not strong enough to bear it. She was buried where she fell, before the altar. All candidates since then kneel upon her resting place and she is always in their prayers and their thoughts. Some term her the Eleventh Dominion Lord, the Lord of Ghosts.'

Gareth was owl-eyed with wonder and sick with worry. 'That won't happen to Helmos, will it, Revered Magus?'

'We pray to the gods that it does not,' Evaristo answered solemnly, then, seeing the boy was pale and unhappy, the tutor added more cheerfully, 'Helmos is young and strong and eminently worthy. He will spend a week in the Temple preparing himself for the ordeal, performing what are known as the Seven Preparations. He will be fine.'

Gareth always said his prayers at night, for Nanny had told him the story of a boy who did not and who had been eaten by bears. But he usually recited them in haste so that he did not have to kneel long on the cold stone floor. That night, Gareth added Helmos to his prayers and emphasized to the gods most specifically that they were to take good care of him.

Gareth did not mention his newfound hero to Dagnarus. He did not discuss Helmos with Dagnarus at all, unless the prince brought up the subject, which he did only rarely. Instinct or childish intuition or simply the fact that Gareth had come to know Dagnarus well during these past few months gave the whipping boy to know that he was supposed to have only one hero, and that hero was Dagnarus.

SIX

Crown Prince, Lord of Ghosts

EVARISTO WAS NOT OVERLY SORRY TO LOSE Dagnarus as a pupil. At first, the tutor had been worried, even frightened, that he might be in trouble with not only the royal family but his own superiors for failing in his assigned task. But as time passed, and no one said a word of fault or blame, Evaristo relaxed and gave himself to the enjoyment of teaching the one pupil he had left – Gareth.

When his superiors required him to report on his progress, Evaristo was honest about his failure. He did, however, take care to lay the blame on the prince's chamberlain, Silwyth. It was the tutor's considered opinion that the elf was responsible for the prince's truancy. Evaristo stated that the elf was not a suitable mentor for the young prince; the tutor advised that the elf be removed from his post.

He discussed the matter with his wife, the next morning, as he was preparing to depart for the castle.

'Was that wise, my dear?' asked his wife. 'Was that prudent? The king himself made the decision to place this elf in that position.'

'I am playing politics,' Evaristo replied. 'You should see the Librarian's face when I mention a word against

Silwyth. The woman loses so much color that you'd think her throat had been cut. The situation is very delicate. There has been a shift in power among the elves. I am not clear as to details – elven politics are always so murky and bloody, one doesn't want to hear about them for fear of ruining one's dinner. But as I understand it, the previous Shield of the Divine, who had ruled for only about a hundred years, was deposed by the current Shield, presumably because the former Shield approved the creation of the Portal leading from Vinnengael to Kar-Khitai. The former Shield requested death and his request was granted –'

'How very dreadful!' exclaimed his wife.

'I told you, my dear, elven politics.' Evaristo sighed. 'At any rate, the current Shield is now threatening to shut down the elves' side of the Portal. Ambassadors are shuttling to and fro between the King and the Shield. Of course, it's all about trade concessions. The elves have no intention of closing their side of the Portal. They're objecting to the tariff charged for eleven merchants to bring their goods to market. That's all it is.'

'This poor elf lost his life over a tariff?' the wife asked, dismayed.

'No, no. That was just part of it. It had something to do with the ancestral advisor – the family ghost, you know. The current Shield's ancestral advisor advised him to challenge the former Shield or something like that.'

'Ghosts acting as advisors, my dear?' His wife was growing increasingly bewildered.

Evaristo smiled fondly at his wife. 'I see that I shall have to teach you a complete course in elven ways and mores, my dear. Every elven household is quite dependent on its resident ghost. But I am late for my lessons with Gareth. What a sweet child he is, docile and sensitive. He will make an excellent magus. I almost wish he was not quite as good friends with the prince. Still, Gareth is young yet, and

Dagnarus's influence over him will undoubtedly lessen with time. I am pleased beyond measure that Gareth admires Helmos. A far more suitable role model.'

'I am sure he is, but what has this to do with the chamberlain?'

Evaristo did not hear. He was heading out the door. His wife pursued him.

'We were talking of Silwyth,' she said, gently prodding.

'Oh, yes. Sorry, my dear, I was distracted.' Evaristo halted, reached for his hood. An icy sleet of a freakish spring cold snap was falling. 'The King does not want to offend the elves in any way, shape, or form, and thus Silwyth's reign as chamberlain is assured, despite the fact that he encourages the young prince to escape the classroom and hang about with the soldiers.' Evaristo gave his wife a kiss on the cheek. 'No one dares breathe a word against the elf, and, therefore, no one dares blame me for failing in my duties to the prince, for if they do, I will say in public what I have hitherto been saying in private.'

'I don't like this, Evaristo,' said his wife, detaining him with a loving hand. 'All know that elves will resort to anything – poison, a knife in the back. No job is worth that, even if it is in the royal court. Tell the Librarian you want to be reassigned.'

'Thank you for your care, beloved. Unfortunately, no job pays so well as this one. Besides, I am in no danger.' Evaristo smiled wryly. 'Silwyth has won. His influence over the prince is assured. I am not a threat. And, as it is, no one is thinking of anything else except Helmos's Transfiguration.'

'You did remember to bespeak good seats for us, didn't you, my dear?' his wife asked anxiously.

'I did.' Evaristo lingered, putting off going outside as long as possible. 'Did I tell you that Helmos invited the child Gareth to attend the feast? What a generous, noble man our crown prince is! Gareth is so excited the only way I could get him to study at all yesterday was to have him read the Histories of the Dominion Lords. That calmed him down, I can tell you. Hard to believe that a topic so interesting could be written so as to put one to sleep. But that's Septimus Grubb for you. Ah, well, I must be off.'

Throwing his hood over his head, Evaristo braved the storm, slipping and sliding perilously on the slick cobblestones.

Gareth was not the only person excited about the up-coming ritual. A Dominion Lord had not been chosen for twenty-five years. Those who had witnessed the last ceremony were suddenly in great demand for their recollections and spoke of little else. Court seamstresses and tailors were working by lamplight to answer the need for fine new clothing. The city itself was to be dressed for the occasion. Dignitaries and guests were traveling to Vinnengael from all parts of the world, including one of the monks from the Monastery of the Keepers of Time on Dragon Mountain.

Buildings were being painted and repaired, streets swept, flowers planted. Shops were to close for the Day of Transfiguration; the taverns, too, though not without a fight between the Innkeepers Guild and the Lord Mayor of Vinnengael. The innkeepers maintained that all their guests would be thirsty after a hard day of cheering and hand-clapping and wanted the taverns open. The Lord Mayor replied that it would be difficult enough to control the excitement of the populace without half the populace being sozzled. The innkeepers at last agreed to close, on the condition that they be allowed to add an additional halfpenny tax to the cost of each room to make up the loss and that they be allowed to open an hour early the following day.

106

Everyone in Vinnengael was caught up in a pleasant and excited bustle with the exception of the Revered Magi. As Evaristo had tried to impress upon Gareth, the Transfiguration of a Dominion Lord is a sacred and solemn ceremony, one that they take extremely seriously. The day after his feast, Helmos would enter the Temple of the Magi to begin the Seven Preparations. At that time, the Temple would be closed to outsiders, the only exception being the Hall of the Healers.

The other Dominion Lords would accompany Helmos to the Temple, where he would be tested, questioned, and judged on his performance of the seven rituals. If at any point any one of the other Dominion Lords found fault with the candidate, he or she could bring the concerns to King Tamaros, who would review the candidacy. The other Dominion Lords were said to be well pleased with Helmos. There was no thought of contesting his nomination; no one feared that he would fail.

Evaristo refused to answer Gareth's questions concerning the Seven Preparations themselves, saying that these were sacred to the magi and secret and that the boy would learn about them when and if he was found suitable for acceptance into their exalted ranks.

There were only five Dominion Lords at the time of Helmos's nomination. The Lord of Strength, Lord of Courage, Lord of Knowledge, Lord of Honor, and Lord of Justice. Those ranks that were vacant were Lord of Chivalry, Lord of Gallantry, Lord of Diplomacy, Lord of Thought, and Lord of Beasts.

'Each of the Dominion Lords is gifted magically by the gods, a gift that will enhance the performance of the lord's duties,' said Evaristo, after he had made Gareth memorize all ten duties and the names of those who had been so honored.

Gareth had good reason to know this for a fact, for once, walking through the market with Nanny, he had seen the Lord of Strength lift a cart loaded with building blocks off an injured dog. He had used nothing but his bare hands and the gift of the gods, according to Nanny. The boy had been awed at the sight of the knight, resplendent in his tunic bearing the symbol of the Dominion Lords – two blue griffons bearing a golden disk.

'And I suppose the Lord of Courage is courageous.' Gareth had never met the Lady Mary of Krammes, but he had heard stories of her valor.

'Not only is she courageous,' said Evaristo, 'but she has the ability to inspire courage in others.'

'What about the rest? What does the Lord of Knowledge do? Does he know everything there is to know?'

'That would make him a god. No, Gareth, the Lord of Knowledge is able to see into another's heart and know his true motivations. The Lord of Beasts has the gift of being able to communicate with animals.'

'Why is there no Lord of War?' he asked, running through the list.

'A Dominion Lord's duty is to promote peace, Gareth,' said Evaristo, smiling. 'We have no need for a Lord of War.'

'Dagnarus will be sadly disappointed,' Gareth said. 'He plans on being the Lord of War when it is his time to be made a Dominion Lord.'

Evaristo's smile vanished. He looked exceedingly grim. Plucking the list from the boy's hand, the tutor tucked it into a large portfolio, which he carried with him from the Temple. 'Come, Gareth, we have spent enough time on Dominion Lords. For their sake, we have neglected the dwarves. Explain to me what you have learned about the Unhorsed.'

That night, the feast was held in honor of Helmos. The food was plentiful and lavish. The wine flowed. The courtiers gushed. The King was proud. The Queen, fancying herself slighted, was petulant and sulky. Gareth was entranced, so thrilled and awed he was unable to eat. He spent the evening staring with adoring eyes at his hero, who seemed surrounded by a golden glow. Helmos appeared set apart from the rest, exalted, as if he were already inside the Temple, with the gods.

Dagnarus was bored, or so he maintained. When the two boys were led away to bed – right when the party was starting to grow boisterous – Dagnarus paused a moment, jerking away from Silwyth's guiding hand, to look back at his elder brother.

'I will have this,' he said.

'Gods willing,' said Silwyth.

Dagnarus flashed a green-eyed, fire-eyed glance at him and smiled.

After His Highness was safely tucked away for the night, Silwyth sat up late in his room in the palace, a room in which he always felt stifled, for the windows were nothing more than thin slits in the massive walls. The elf longed for his bed in the woods of his home, longed to breathe deeply of crisp, cool, pine-scented air. Oftentimes he woke in the night from a terrifying dream in which he was being suffocated.

Taking advantage of the fact that most of the castle's inhabitants were in a state of pleasant inebriation and he was not likely to be summoned to attend the prince at this late hour, Silwyth took out brush and ink and composed a poem to be carried to the Shield. The poem was long and filled with symbolism, images of rainbows in the waterfalls, eagles soaring above the palace walls, silvery fish rising to the surface of the lake. Any human reading it – any human who happened to be able to translate the elven language – would have dozed off from sheer boredom. The Shield, upon reading it, would see beneath the flowers, the stems, and the leaves to the poem's roots, its true meaning.

As per your orders, I have insinuated myself into the King's household. I am chamberlain to his younger son, a froward boy, who at the age of nine, is ambitious; quick to learn, but impatient of study; fearless, willful, comely. A dangerous combination, especially for a human. He may be of use to us in the future. I view him as one might a charmed viper. So long as the music plays and the charm holds, he will be tractable. If the music ever ceases, he will rise up and strike.

As to Lord Mabreton, he is all you could ever hope him to be. Relations between his faction and the humans are deteriorating rapidly. Lady Mabreton remains in seclusion in her distant dwelling on the River Hammerclaw. She has not yet put in an appearance at court, for which we must be grateful. The song of her beauty would drown out the braying of her donkey of a husband.

The King's elder son, Helmos, is to be made a Dominion Lord. The Divine's influence grows weaker. We should be prepared to act.

Placing the final brushstroke, Silwyth summoned one of his servants, a man of his own household, who had traveled to Vinnengael with his master. Silwyth handed the poem, rolled into a compact scroll and tucked neatly into a carved bone scrollcase, to the servant.

'Take this to the Shield of the Divine. Here is money for the Portal and my authorization to enter it. No eyes except those of the Shield may rest upon this document. If you are in danger of being captured by the enemies of the Shield – be they human or elven – you will first destroy the document and then destroy yourself.'

The servant bowed to indicate he understood and was willing to accept the duty imposed upon him. He thrust the scrollcase into his tunic, where it rested against his heart. Bowing again, he took his leave.

Silwyth, his own duty done, did not bother to go to bed. He went to stand by the window that looked down upon the courtyard below, empty but for the castle guard.

War will suit me very well, Silwyth thought, watching the soldiers mark their rounds. The first human soldiers that come through the Portal will prove the downfall of the Divine and the rise of the Shield. And when the Shield ascends, so do I.

The sun's rays, struggling to creep into the elf's pinched windows, brought to mind the view of the dawn that was his on rising from his bed in his own home.

Tears stung Silwyth's eyes; he wept unashamed.

SEVEN

The Burning Lake

THE NEXT MORNING, HELMOS ENTERED THE temple to undergo the Seven Preparations. The fortnight during which he was gone was the longest in Gareth's life. The day on which Silwyth came to tell Prince Dagnarus that his brother, Crown Prince Helmos, had been chosen by the Council of Dominion Lords to be a Dominion Lord, that he was the first ever to have received a unanimous vote, was a golden day in Gareth's existence, never mind that Dagnarus was in a bad mood and punched Gareth in the face over nothing, splitting open his lip.

The morning of the ceremony of Transfiguration, Gareth was awake before Silwyth summoned him. Awake and already half-dressed in the new clothes which his parents had purchased for him. This was a day of firsts. The boy's first time to see the Miracle of Transfiguration, his first time to enter the Temple of the Magi, his first short tunic. Putting on the short tunic, tugging it over his new, parti-colored hose, Gareth felt six feet tall already. Silwyth pinned on the child's cape and arranged his hair under his cap.

Dagnarus proved unusually querulous and difficult.

Ordinarily, he was wide-awake, the first out of bed, teasing the attendant lords, who stood around his bed blinking sleepily and stifling their yawns in their sleeves. This day, the prince slept late, or pretended to. The lords stood about in their finery, watching the sun rise, fidgeting and looking increasingly grim. Gareth was in a panic, fearing that he might miss the ceremony, though it was at least six hours away.

Silwyth took matters in hand. He opened the windows, letting in the fresh air and the light of a truly remarkable and glorious sunrise. Gareth stared in wonder at the bright bands of red streaking across the sky, deepening to purple, flaring to orange and then to gold, and he was thrilled for Helmos, to have this good omen.

Silwyth opened the bed curtains, saying, as he did so, 'His Highness rings, gentlemen. Let us attend him.'

Quite the contrary, His Highness hadn't rung. The small silver bell stood on the nightstand; Dagnarus glared at Silwyth from the pillows.

'Good morning, Your Highness,' said the chamberlain. 'I wish you joy of this day. You have slept somewhat past your time, undoubtedly by reason of excitement for your honored brother. This does you much credit, Your Highness. A lesser prince might feel jealous over the attention paid to an elder sibling. A truly great prince will feel that the honor attending his brother reflects well upon himself.'

To give Dagnarus credit, he had probably not realized until that moment that he *was* jealous of Helmos, not until Silwyth pointed it out. The feeling was only natural. Dagnarus was the spoiled and petted child, the younger, the darling. Yet Helmos was the child beloved.

King Tamaros could not love Dagnarus as he loved the only child born to himself and the woman he would think of to his dying day as his one, true wife. Being a kindly man, Tamaros felt guilty that he could not love

113

his younger son. He wanted to love Dagnarus, he tried hard to love him. His efforts were plain for all to see and unfortunately took the form of indulgence. Tamaros never scolded Dagnarus, or spoke harshly to him or denied him anything he wanted, except the one thing he wanted most – his father's true affection. As for Dagnarus, he was always striving to win the love that dangled before him like the carrot hanging just out of reach of the donkey chained to the waterwheel.

Having had his faults pointed out to him, albeit subtly, Dagnarus altered his behavior. In an instant, he changed from sulking child to gracious prince. He apologized to the lords for having kept them waiting and then magnanimously dismissed them from his service that morning, saying that he knew they would want to be arraying themselves in their finery. The lords were pleased and left him with many wishes for joy on this day and presents to mark the occasion. Gareth stayed. Dagnarus had given the boy a look that meant he wished him to remain.

Dagnarus was also to wear the short tunic, which pleased him and put him in a better humor. Unlike most small boys, the prince enjoyed dressing up. He knew that fine clothes enhanced his beauty and, even at that early age, he understood the power his good looks gave him over others.

While he ate and dressed, the two boys discussed the events of the day, badgering Silwyth with questions.

'Why isn't my father a Dominion Lord, Silwyth?' Dagnarus asked.

'Your father is blessed above all men in being given the gift of creating the Dominion Lords. It would be unseemly in him to bestow such a gift upon himself, just as it would be unseemly for Your Highness to buy yourself a gift.'

Silwyth placed a golden circlet upon Dagnarus's brow and said that it was time to attend his father and mother.

'Why are no elves Dominion Lords, Silwyth?' Dagnarus wondered, as they were making ready to depart.

'That is a very good question, Your Highness,' said Silwyth. Neither his face nor his voice betrayed any emotion, yet his customary coolness warmed with ire; a flicker of flame burned in his dark, slanted eyes. 'I believe that certain people have been asking His Majesty the very same thing.'

Dagnarus and Gareth exchanged glances, but they had no time then to discuss this ominous statement or what it might mean, for the prince was led away to attend to his duties. Gareth went to meet his parents.

His mother cried when she saw him in his short tunic and said that she had lost her baby.

The Temple of the Magi was an enormous building located on the same level as the palace. A vast open square separated the Temple from the palace. Decorated with reflecting pools and fountains, flowers and trees in stone urns, the Temple was a sprawling complex of many buildings, including the Hall of the Healers, the University, where those students training to be magi were housed and where they studied, and the chambers and offices of the ten High Magi themselves, with their attendant scribes and secretaries and servants.

The centerpiece of the Temple was an immense amphitheater under a high-domed roof. The amphitheater was used for various purposes. Religious ceremonies for the holidays were held there. The heads of the guilds met there once a month to discuss business. There the people could come and commune with the gods, place flowers on the altars, light candles for their prayers to be answered. On that day the ceremony of Transfiguration would be held there.

Emerging from the palace in company with his parents, Gareth gazed down upon the usually empty square, now a veritable sea of bodies. The entire population of Vinnengael was in attendance, for the gates to the third level had been thrown open wide, in joy of the occasion, and those who lived on the first level, down by the waterfront, or on the second level by the marketplace, were permitted to enter the royal city. Many people had traveled from Dunkarga, not only to see the parade, which would be all they would see of the ceremony, but to sell their goods at the fair being held in Helmos's honor.

Captain Argot cantered past on his warhorse. Both man and horse looked stern, for he and his soldiers were charged with keeping the crowd, which must have numbered in the tens of thousands, under control. Soldiers lined the route from the palace to the Temple, standing foot to foot, arms locked together, forming a living wall behind which the people surged and heaved, all eager to catch a glimpse of the royal procession. Other soldiers stood in a triangle-shaped formation upon the palace stairs. They carried huge bronze shields and, in case the crowd became unruly, the soldiers would form a wedge of bronze that could cleave through the melee with ease.

Gareth's family took their places with the rest of the nobles, for they were to march in the parade. His Majesty's chamberlain was sorting them into a line according to rank and standing; Gareth's family was near the front, which suited him fine, although it annoyed his father. The higher the rank, the nearer the end of the line. This meant that they would reach the Temple stairs first, however, and Gareth would have a chance to see the rest of the procession.

Indeed, no one wanted to march in front. The chamberlain was having a difficult time of it, arguing, persuading, cajoling, bullying, shouting himself hoarse. Places in line had been settled in advance, but the plans had fallen apart at the last moment, when one noble had fancied himself

116

insulted. The chamberlain had made the mistake of moving him to the rear and now the rest were demanding that they be moved as well.

Gareth paid no attention to the arguing. He was watching Captain Argot, and thinking of the time he had ridden on that very horse. The captain was yelling down to his men, something having to do with orken. Several of the soldiers shook their heads; they appeared worried. Gareth was panicked, fearful that the orken might be going to cause trouble, then he realized, after a moment's inspection, that there weren't any orken. This was unusual, for orken love celebrations and parades and can always be seen in the crowd, standing head and shoulders above everyone else, their mouths agape with the wonder of the spectacle.

Argot leaned down from his horse to speak to his men, and Gareth listened intently, for Dagnarus would be interested and eager to hear what was afoot. He was always interested in anything involving the soldiers.

'They're not plotting something, do you think?' Argot shouted, to be heard above the noise.

'No, Captain!' roared one of his lieutenants, moving closer to be heard. 'Their shamans said that the omens were bad.'

Argot smiled grimly. 'What was it – a flock of geese flying north from south, instead of south to north?'

The soldier chuckled. 'Something like that, Captain. Did you see the sunrise this morning, sir?'

'Yes, more's the pity,' said Argot. 'I haven't been to bed for two nights running. I must admit it was remarkably beautiful, the gods shedding their blessing on the occasion.'

'Well, the orken thought it remarkably frightening,' said the lieutenant. 'Lake Ildurel turned red – red as fire. The orken who were out in their boats for the early-morning fishing began to bellow and howl like the water *was* on

117

fire, begging those ashore to come rescue them. Not an oar would any ork put in the water, though, until the red had disappeared. The fish they caught they threw back overboard, saying the catch was cursed. Now they're all shut up in their houses, quivering in every limb.'

'Praise to the gods,' said Argot, with a relieved sigh. 'At least that's one worry we won't have this day.'

He rode off to deal with the next crisis – a woman shrieking that her jewels had been snatched.

The matter of precedence having been settled – not at all to Gareth's father's satisfaction – they once more took their places in line.

The nobles walked amidst the throng of cheering people, whose laughing, grinning faces were an odd contrast to the faces of the soldiers, who looked particularly dour and grim.

The people were happy and good-natured; life was good in Vinnengael then. The poor were well cared for by the Church; the prosperous middle class paid taxes, but did not feel themselves overburdened. The wealthy contributed to the general good and lived at their ease.

Behind the nobles came the ambassadors from the other realms – a majority of elves, a single dwarf, no orken. Because of the bad omen, not even the orken ambassador could be persuaded to march, though Gareth would later hear that King Tamaros himself had sent a kindly and reassuring message. After the ambassadors was a pause, to heighten anticipation. The crowd grew hushed, breathless with excitement.

By this time, Gareth's family had arrived at the Temple steps. The guild head, the minor lords, the landed nobles, and the ambassadors lined the stairs, awaiting the King's arrival.

A blast of trumpets marked the start of the royal procession. First came the royal standard-bearers, then the trumpeters, their instruments gleaming in the sun. Then came the ten High Magi, each denoted by the varying colors of the chasuble, worn over the white and gold-embroidered alb, common to all members of the priesthood.

After the magi came the kings of other human lands, riding in their horse-drawn chariots, accompanied by their knights. Behind them was the Queen and her court, she being borne along in a litter carried by four enormous men. She was flanked by the Mistress of the Wardrobe and other royal ladies-in-waiting, who were scattering petals from roses that had been grown indoors during the winter in anticipation of this day. The Queen's father, Olgaf, King of Dunkarga, had been invited to attend the ceremony, but he had declined; an insult that had sent ripples of indignation through the court.

Gareth looked closely at the Queen's litter, for that was where Dagnarus usually rode, alongside his mother. The prince's accustomed place was vacant, however, and Gareth was worried for fear that perhaps the prince had taken it into his head to refuse to attend. Then the cheers (halfhearted) that had greeted Her Majesty died away, replaced by a murmur and a soft sighing among the crowd.

Dagnarus walked behind his mother's litter, keeping a good distance back of it, keeping another good distance between himself and the King's retinue, which was following along behind. The prince walked alone on the rose-strewn road, waving his hand graciously to the crowd. His red hair shone like fire in the sun and would have sent the orken running, had any been there to observe it. He walked tall and straight and he was so regal for his age and so beautiful that the women cooed over him like doves.

Behind the prince rode the five Dominion Lords, each on a magnificent steed. Their armor – different for each lord and representing something of the character of the lord –

was polished silver and gleamed in the sunshine so that it was almost painful to look upon their brilliance.

The Dominion Lords escorted Helmos's horse, riderless, which was led by one of the prince's knights. The sight gave Gareth a pang, for a riderless horse is always present in a soldier's funeral procession, and he feared for a terrifying moment that something had happened to Helmos. Logic prevailed. It occurred to the boy that if such had been the case, the horse would have been draped in black, whereas for this parade the horse was garlanded in flowers, destined to bear his rider in triumph when the ceremony was concluded.

As for Helmos, he was inside the Temple, kept in sacred isolation, his time spent in prayer for the ceremony to come.

Following along after Helmos's horse were the King's Knights, twenty of them, in full regalia, riding matching black steeds and carrying their shields.

And then the cheers mounted until they must have deafened the gods.

King Tamaros appeared, riding in a chariot of gold and silver, drawn by four white horses. He drove the chariot himself, handling the warhorses with skill and ease. He was nearly lost to view in a blizzard of spring blossoms thrown by the crowd for luck. Crushed flowers were inches deep after he had passed; their perfume lingered in the air for days after.

Tamaros dismounted his chariot at the Temple stairs. The magi lined the stairs and bowed as he passed. Queen Emillia greeted him prettily with a kiss, which pleased the crowd. Dagnarus bowed to his father, which pleased the crowd still more. The Most Revered High Magus escorted the royal family into the Temple. The Dominion Lords followed, and the rest of the crowd came after in descending order. There were so many people that Gareth worried he might not get a seat, but his father said that seats were reserved for them and that there would be room even for some carefully selected common people to view the ceremony.

At last Gareth made his way into the Temple. Walking out of the bright, warm sunlight into dark, cool shadow, he was temporarily blinded and even slightly chilled, for he had been sweating beneath his heavy clothes and, in the coolness, the perspiration set him to shivering. Outside he had experienced the joy and excitement of the parade. Inside, all was quiet. The noise of the crowd was shut out when the great doors boomed closed, and he was forcibly reminded of the solemnity and gravity of the ceremony. The people around him were solemn and hushed; if they spoke at all it was only in whispers. He felt nervous, subdued, stifled.

The story of the Lord of Ghosts came to Gareth's mind, and he glanced about fearfully, wondering if she were in attendance.

The ceremony of Transfiguration of a Dominion Lord took place in the great amphitheater of the Temple of the Magi. This was the first time Gareth had been inside the amphitheater, and he was overcome with awe and wonder. The theater was built to resemble a compass, with each of the four cardinal points being dedicated to the element it represented. North was Earth, the most important to the humans, for all human magic flowed from that source. The altar to the gods stood at the north end of the theater.

People moved quickly to take their places, stumbling over each other in the semidarkness, with whispered apologies. The gaiety of the parade still lingered with some; Gareth heard smothered laughter among the nobility; while the gallery that held the common people was alive with excitement – exclamations of awe, wonder, and good-natured grumbles as they jostled for a better view. But eventually the reverent atmosphere of the Temple's interior, enhanced by the beneficent faces of the gods

121

gazing down upon them all, began to affect the crowd. People hushed and fell silent.

Queen Emillia and Dagnarus entered, escorted by His Majesty's knights. They took places of honor in the very front row of seats, facing the altar, which was raised on a stage.

Gareth stood up to catch a glimpse of Dagnarus. The prince looked pale and unusually solemn; the reverential nature of this ceremony had finally impressed him. His head lifted when he felt the eyes of the crowd upon him; as he gazed out upon that sea of expectant faces with calm dignity, murmurs of admiration rippled through the audience. Gareth's mother twitched at his tunic, told him to sit down and behave himself. Gareth sat down reluctantly, but he discovered that by scooting over close to his mother and peering out between the shoulders of the people in front of him, he had a good view of the prince.

The ten High Magi and the Most Revered High Magus filed in and took their places on the stage in high-backed carved wooden chairs ranged alongside the altar, five on either side, facing the audience. Then came the Dominion Lords, who formed a guard of honor around the altar. Last entered King Tamaros. He sat on one side of the altar, opposite the Most Revered High Magus.

All was in readiness. The crowd was silent. No person coughed, no child whimpered. The High Magus, who was then the great wizard, Reinholt of Amrah'Lin, rose to his feet. He bowed to King Tamaros, then spoke in low, solemn tones.

'Let the candidate be brought forward.'

Two Dominion Lords left their posts and walked to a back alcove, shrouded in deep shadow.

A door opened, emitting a bar of light. Silhouetted against the light was Helmos, a figure of darkness. He didn't remain in darkness long, for the light of the candles on the altar illuminated him as he took a step forward. The

Dominion Lords shut the door behind him. That door led to the interior of the Temple, where Helmos had completed his Seven Preparations and spent the night in the sacred Portal of the Gods.

Helmos came forward and the crowd breathed a sigh, all of the people as one.

He had always been comely, but his days of prayer and now the prospect of the completion of this honor, which had been his one goal since he could first speak of it, made him radiant. Clad in plain white robes, he shone with an inner light that seemed to lift the oppressive darkness of the Temple's interior and bring the sun among them. Helmos was not excited, he was not afraid. He was not among the people at all, but was walking with the gods. He had no more knowledge the people were there than if they had all been as small as the rats that lived in the Temple and had been displaced at the crowd's arrival and could be heard (and occasionally felt) scrambling to find their holes.

His honor guard escorted Helmos to a place before the altar, a marble edifice devoid of decoration, covered now with a white cloth of finest linen, which had been sewn by his mother during her lying-in, in anticipation of this glorious day. As he came to stand before the altar, Helmos reached out his hands. Clasping his father's hand in his right, Helmos placed his left hand upon the cloth. Both his parents were with him in that moment.

Gareth's mother found and held his hand tightly. She was weeping silently, as was nearly everyone in the theater. His father wiped his eyes and put his arm around his wife and child. They were more a family in that instant than they ever were before or after.

King Tamaros bowed his head, quite overcome.

Queen Emillia gave a loud, gushy sob and clutched at Dagnarus. He sat bolt upright, rigid, refusing to look at her or acknowledge her. His face was pinched, his gaze fixed on his brother. Gareth could tell that the prince's very soul was consumed with envy.

Helmos lifted his head. He stepped back from the altar.

'I am ready, Most Revered High Magus,' he said.

Two Dominion Lords came forward, removed the white cloth from the altar, and reverentially folded it and handed it to one of the magi to hold. The High Magus sat down in a chair placed behind the altar. Two of the magi brought forth a scroll of fine vellum, wrapped around rods of solid gold. Unrolling the vellum, they spread it out before the High Magus. He was given a brush and a small jar of lamb's blood. He dipped the brush in the ink and held it on the parchment. When the time came, the High Magus would be imbued with the presence of the gods and would write down upon the parchment the title Helmos would take as Dominion Lord, whether it be Lord of Chivalry, Lord of Justice, or whatever the gods chose for him.

The High Magus being ready, he said, 'Let the Miracle of Transfiguration commence.'

Helmos knelt before the altar. King Tamaros came forward, rested both hands upon his son's bowed head, and called for the gods to bless this man and grant to him the wisdom and the power accorded to a Dominion Lord. In return Tamaros asked Helmos if he was willing to dedicate his life to the service of others, willing to sacrifice his life if need arose.

'The gods please, I am,' Helmos replied simply.

Tamaros stepped back from the altar.

Helmos turned and faced the audience. His eyes gazed straight ahead into the smoke-tinged darkness of the amphitheater. Where his soul looked, no one knew. Crossing his hands over his breast, he waited.

People stared in rapt fascination. Gareth held his breath, for fear that even a small involuntary movement on his part must have a negative effect. He had heard descriptions of the Miracle, but no one and nothing had prepared him for what he was to witness. It is doubtful if anything could have.

'The Miracle of the Armor commences,' the High Magus announced.

A spasm of pain contorted Helmos's face.

'What's happening?' Gareth whispered frantically, sliding from side to side on the bench, trying desperately to see.

'His feet,' said his father in a voice his son didn't recognize. 'Look at his feet, Gareth.'

Helmos's bare feet and legs were as white as the marble of the altar. Or rather, they were marble. He was being turned to stone.

A shudder shivered through the boy. 'It's killing him!' Gareth whimpered.

'No,' said his father. 'This is the Miracle.'

'Don't look, Gareth!' his mother hissed urgently. She held her hands over her eyes, but he noticed that she was peeping out through her fingers.

Gareth wanted to close his eyes, for the sight of Helmos's agony was terrible. But he kept them open, as a tribute to his hero. If Helmos could endure this pain, the child could endure the pain of watching him suffer.

Gasps and murmurs and one loud, awestruck, 'Gods help him!' from the commons' gallery swept through the crowd.

Gareth shifted his gaze from Helmos for only a moment, and that was to look at Dagnarus.

He was very pale; his eyes were round, but wide-open. He sat very still.

Helmos kept his eyes on his father the entire time, drawing strength from love. Tamaros did not flinch, or cast down his gaze. He smiled at his son reassuringly, his faith in the gods unshaken, and gave his son the support he needed to endure the agony. The Transfiguration was

125

swift, thank the gods. It was over in less than a minute, though it seemed to Gareth to take several lifetimes.

The body of the young man was white marble beneath the cloth robe, stone cold, rigid, immovable. Thus appear the carven figures of the kings and queens, the noble knights and lady wives, and honored magi which adorn the coffins that rest in the Hall of Eternity, far beneath the Temple.

The stone eyes remained fixed on Tamaros. Helmos's last sight was that of his father's loving face, still smiling, though streaked with tears.

Rising to his feet, Tamaros walked over and laid his hand upon the cold edifice that had been his son.

'Oh, gods of Earth and Sea, Fire and Air, bless this, thy servant.'

Tamaros stepped back.

The stone figure of Helmos began to glow; orange at first, then red as molten magma. The light illuminated the Temple. The heat from the stone figure radiated outward until some in the first rows were forced to avert their faces.

Not Dagnarus. He had not moved since the ceremony began. His lips were slightly parted, drinking in all he saw, making it a part of his very being.

The light given off by the stone grew increasingly bright. Now it shone with a blue-white brilliance that was painful to the eyes. Gareth blinked constantly, wiped away tears, but continued to watch.

The white-hot rock began to alter shape.

As a smith makes armor from only the finest, strongest metal, so the gods make the armor of a Dominion Lord from the finest and strongest within the candidate. The armor of a Dominion Lord comes from the heart and from the soul. The gods give the armor physical form, using what is within the body to shield the body. From that moment on, the Dominion Lord has only to call upon the armor to protect him and it will do so.

The armor is magical, a gift from the gods, and therefore invulnerable, impervious to attack from ordinary weapons. The armor of each Dominion Lord is different and unique from the armor of any other Dominion Lord, for the armor is forged from the different strengths of each person.

'Forged from the strengths, it protects the weakest parts until those can be transformed into strengths,' was how Evaristo later explained it.

The radiance was like the sun's reflection shining from a thousand mirrors and so dazzled the eyes that the audience was effectively blinded. Gareth was forced to close his eyes, but the light continued to beam through the lids; he saw it shine yellow, through a red web of his own blood vessels.

And then the light died. And then he could see.

The Miracle of the Armor was complete. A helm of wondrous beauty covered Helmos's head. The sides of the helm were formed in the shape of the silver wings of a swan, the crest of the helm was the graceful swan's neck and proud head.

Helmos's hand moved, lifted to his face. A collective sigh breathed through the audience, for this was a sign – the first sign – that he was alive. Tamaros was the only one of all those in attendance who did not appear vastly relieved. His faith had never wavered.

Helmos raised the visor of his shining helm, revealing his face, a face imbued with awe. As he slowly descended from whatever blessed realm he had traversed and became aware of his return to more mundane surroundings, he saw his father, whose face was suffused with pride. The son's awe melted into joy.

The two clasped hands. The audience, tension eased, gave a thunderous cheer, which reverberated off the high-domed ceiling, shook the walls, caused the candles to flicker, and boomed against the altar with the force of a tidal wave.

King Tamaros presented Helmos to the people, who responded with another deafening roar. Gareth clapped until his hands stung; his father shouted himself hoarse, and his mother waved her handkerchief as did all the ladies, making it seem as if a flock of white birds were fluttering through the Temple.

King Tamaros raised his hand, and the cheering ceased. The people settled back down into their seats, for the second part of the ceremony was about to commence. The King and Helmos both turned to face the altar, where sat the High Magus. He had not joined in the celebration; nor had any of the other magi, being intent upon their communion with the gods.

The High Magus sat with eyes closed. The audience rustled and shuffled, coughed and whispered, and eventually lapsed once more into reverential silence – a silence that was slightly tinged with impatience – for the main spectacle was over. This was only the formal presentation of the title, which most had determined would be Lord of Justice. Everyone was eager to move on to the many parties being held in the new Dominion Lord's honor.

The High Magus, his eyes tightly closed, stretched forth his hand. One of the other magi assisted the High Magus to dip the brush into the lamb's blood. The High Magus put the brush to the vellum. Holding his hand still, he allowed the gods to guide it. Gareth could see red letters flow from the brush, but he was too far away to read them; nor could he have read them, since from the child's vantage point, the writing was upside down. But he saw and everyone watching saw the magi who had assisted the High Magus stare at the words written in blood, give a perceptible start, and take an involuntary step backward.

The other magi now craned their heads to see, and they appeared shocked and troubled, looked to each other or to the King. Tamaros's position was much like Gareth's; he was viewing the words from the top down and could not make out what they were. He felt and saw the unease of the magi. All of the audience could sense it, and began to murmur in doubt and foreboding. King Tamaros stolidly kept his place at the head of the altar, standing beside his son, though he must have longed to rush around and see for himself what had everyone so upset.

The High Magus was completely unconscious that he was writing anything disturbing. He opened his eyes, smiled at King Tamaros and at Helmos and then, quite confidently, looked down at the vellum. His own astonishment and shock were evident to every person in the Hall. There are some who whispered later that he must have known what he was writing; some even went so far as to say that he wrote what he did on purpose, that it was politically motivated.

'If so, then he must be a consummate actor,' a bitter Evaristo told Gareth later. 'Even to the point of causing his complexion to drain of blood, for he went so pale that if the Lord of Ghosts was truly in attendance, she must have thought she had discovered a companion.'

Bracing himself, the High Magus rose to his feet and, first casting a look at Tamaros, a look that was eloquent and speaking, the High Magus turned the scroll for the King to read and then read it himself in a loud, almost defiant voice.

'It is my duty' – he should have said 'pleasure' but he had sense enough to alter it at the last moment – 'to present to the people of Vinnengael their new Dominion Lord, chosen by the gods as the Lord of Sorrows.'

Lord of Sorrows.

Dismayed, Gareth thought immediately of the orken and their bad omen, of the sea in flames. He held more respect for them and their beliefs from then on.

A murmur, low and thrumming, rippled through the

audience. They didn't like it; they wanted it explained. Gareth's father, brow furrowed, was talking to his neighbor. Gareth's mother, fanning herself with the handkerchief, was talking breathlessly to her neighbor. Gareth looked at Dagnarus, to see his reaction, but Silwyth was bending down to speak to the prince at that moment and hid him from his friend's view. King Tamaros was highly displeased, his anger obvious in his scowl, his clenched fist, and in his stance, which was hunch-shouldered, like a fierce old owl.

'It is the will of the gods,' continued the High Magus in his defensive tone, adding sternly, 'We question their will only at our own great peril.'

'Yes, but what does it mean?' the King demanded, angry not at the High Magus, but at the gods. The King was frustrated, hurt in his pride. The father was frightened.

The High Magus took his time delivering the answer. While he considered, Gareth looked at the person everyone seemed to have forgotten: Helmos.

He had stood through all this turmoil steadfast and calm and radiant, still with the gods, perhaps. Whatever fears and foreboding everyone else was feeling left him untouched. His armor protected him from more than arrows and sword strikes. The shining armor was an outward symbol of his faith and its luster remained undimmed. He knew what the gods meant and intended. He knew it for himself and that was all that mattered. The rest of the world would discover the answer in time. Or not.

'I believe that what the gods are saying, Your Majesty' – the High Magus spoke hesitantly, feeling his way – 'is that your son, Helmos, will be the Dominion Lord who will take the sorrows of the people upon himself, make their pain his pain, stand between them and evil.'

A soft sigh went through the Temple. Helmos nodded

once, slightly, almost imperceptibly. Yes, the High Magus had got it right.

King Tamaros looked stunned, then his face flushed. He was embarrassed. He turned to Helmos.

'Forgive me, my son.' Tamaros raised his gaze to the heavens. 'Gods, forgive me! For a moment, my faith wavered. But you understand, you who are all-wise, all-knowing. I am a father.'

He wept unashamedly, and there was not a dry eye in the Temple. Gareth's mother sobbed into her handkerchief and, feeling for his hand, squeezed it hard. His father sniffed and snorted and looked as if he knew just how Tamaros felt. Gareth's parents never loved him half so well as they did upon that day, and he loved them at that moment. They all came to their senses after it was over, but for a time, the magic lingered.

In the midst of the weeping, Dagnarus rose from his seat and ascended the stage. He strode forward, oblivious to the raised eyebrows of the magi, and went to stand before Helmos. The prince held out his hand.

'Let me be the first to congratulate you, brother,' he said in his clear voice.

This was not a planned part of the ceremony: that was obvious from the troubled glances flitting among the magi. But Dagnarus's words and actions pleased King Tamaros, who was feeling loving to all the world just then. Dagnarus was a beautiful child, standing in the altar-light, his red hair glowing like flame. He was respectful and admiring of his brother, gazing up at him with the reverent awe one might expect of a child his age.

Helmos clasped his younger brother's hand. King Tamaros rested one hand upon Dagnarus's head, the other upon Helmos's shoulder, linking the two in kinship's bond.

The High Magus made a small, oblique gesture. One of the magi skimmed silently forward, rolled up the vellum in

131

haste, and removed it from the altar. This done, the High Magus relaxed. He was all smiles and shed his blessing upon the crowd.

Helmos left the amphitheater to cheers from the crowd. Clad in his wondrous swan armor, proud and handsome, he rode down the rose-covered street.

Lord of Sorrows.

EIGHT

Star Brothers

S HORTLY AFTER HELMOS'S TRANSFIGURATION, the royal court celebrated Dagnarus's tenth birthday. The prince's birthday was celebrated with elaborate festivities, though Gareth was told that the party was not as spectacular as it had been in years past. Missing were the elven fireworks displays. The elves did not send Dagnarus a present that year either, nor did he receive the customary gifts from the dwarves and the orken. Their ambassadors did not attend the party.

King Tamaros looked somber and preoccupied, as did Helmos and the King's advisors. They were halfway through the feast – which consisted of roast calves' heads, gilded and silvered, and a whole roast sheep, among other delicacies – when a page slipped into the hall. Coming to the King, the page whispered in his ear. King Tamaros looked alarmed and grim. Rising to his feet, he beckoned to Helmos and to two of his advisors. Leaning down, Tamaros gave Dagnarus a kiss on the cheek.

'You will find your present from me in the stable, son,' said the King.

'Thank you, Father,' said Dagnarus, his eyes shining.

Tamaros and his retinue departed. Once they were

gone, there was a general run on the door by the remaining lords, departing in haste to find out what was going on.

Queen Emillia was incensed over this 'slight,' as she termed it, and, after His Majesty left, her shrill voice could be heard above the revelry, whining and complaining about His Majesty's selfishness. One of the returning nobles eventually informed Her Majesty that the King had been called away because all the ambassadors from the other races and the ambassador from the King of Dunkarga were threatening to leave the court that very night. King Tamaros had gone to try to placate them.

Even Queen Emillia had brains enough to realize that this was serious, particularly as it appeared her own father was involved, and so she silenced her complaints, to the great relief of those seated around her.

Gareth feared Dagnarus might be upset at his father's sudden and abrupt departure, but, on the contrary, the prince's spirits were as high as his friend had ever seen them. Dagnarus talked with animation, teasing one of the lords to tell him what this wonderful present in the stable might be and pretending to be frightfully disappointed when told it was nothing but a bale of moldy hay.

'What does this mean, about the ambassadors?' Gareth leaned over to ask during a lull in the conversation.

'It means war,' said Dagnarus, his eyes gleaming red in the firelight.

'War!' Gareth was shocked.

He wanted to ask more, but Dagnarus was too much in demand. A steady stream of courtiers came to the table to offer their felicitations, each making certain that the prince knew how much his gift had cost and how much more valuable that gift was over another. Soon, the jugglers and the minstrels came dancing in, and the boys had no more chance to talk.

Nor did Gareth have the opportunity to question the prince the next morning. Dagnarus was up before the sun, eager to begin the day and see his new horse. Gareth rose with reluctance, groggy and stupid from the revelries of the night before. His head throbbed. Only the finest wine was served at the King's table, and, even watered, as they gave it to the boys, it was still potent. Gareth came more fully alert when he entered Dagnarus's apartment. The lords in attendance spoke together in low mutterings, glancing askance at Silwyth, whose calm, placid face registered no more emotion than did the cloudless sky outside the window.

'What news of the ambassadors?' Dagnarus asked from his bed, where he sat, drinking chocolate.

'They are still in Vinnengael this morning, Your Highness,' answered one of the lords. Gareth never did know all their names; they were nothing to the boy but an assortment of faces, like pastries at the banquet – each one different but all cut from the same sugary dough. 'It is said that the King, your honored father, spent all night attempting to convince them not to leave.'

'The elves are the most ntentious,' said another, and bowed in the general direction of Silwyth. 'Your pardon, sir.'

Silwyth, who was laying out the prince's clothes, acknowledged this with a slight inclination of his head, but did not look at the lord. Dagnarus glanced at Silwyth and smiled slightly. Silwyth's almond eyes slid over those of the prince, and Gareth guessed that Dagnarus knew more about what was transpiring from his chamberlain than from any of the gossipy noblemen.

Gareth hoped to question the prince, but when he went to look for him, before his tutoring session, Dagnarus was gone – off to the stables to look at his present, a magnificent stallion.

The prince's playroom had become increasingly Gareth's playroom, or rather his schoolroom. Evaristo entered, also looking a bit draggled. As a mark of courtesy, he had been invited to the prince's party, although Silwyth had so arranged it that the tutor sat at the very lowest table. Evaristo had been so pleased at the invitation, which he had not expected, that he took no offense. Though he winced at the light, he was in a good mood and, seating himself at the table, opened the first book of the lesson. The tutor no longer looked for Dagnarus. He would have been astonished past measure if the prince had walked in.

'Master,' Gareth said anxiously, 'Dagnarus says that there is to be a war. Is that true?'

Evaristo looked startled; adults are always startled to find that children take an interest in what are considered to be adult affairs. But he believed in giving truthful answers to such questions. He was not one who talked down to children or tried to shield them from unpleasant subjects. He did pause to choose his words carefully.

'King Tamaros is a wise man,' Evaristo said at last. 'It is to be hoped that in this case wisdom will prevail over folly.'

'Whose folly?' Gareth asked.

Evaristo was grave. He studied the boy, considering how much he was likely to understand.

'Did Prince Dagnarus discuss this with you, Gareth?'

'He hasn't yet, but he will,' he answered, which was no more than the truth. Dagnarus discussed everything with his friend. 'I'm to be his advisor when he's King, you know. And he wants me to have practice.'

Evaristo sighed, displeased, though not at his pupil. 'I wish His Highness would not speak so. It will make people think he wishes harm to befall his brother, for that is what must happen if the younger son is to be King. Of course, I'm certain he doesn't mean such a thing, but it doesn't sound proper to those who don't know him.'

Gareth, who did know him, kept silent.

'Very well, then, Gareth,' Evaristo continued, 'I will tell you what is happening. I will tell you the truth, though if certain people were to catch wind of what I say, I would be in serious trouble.'

Court intrigue. It salted the food, watered the wine, sugared the fruit. Gareth had dined on it since the first day of his arrival. He promised Evaristo solemnly that he would never tell a soul except Dagnarus. The boy felt honor-bound to mention this.

'I am certain His Highness already knows much of what I am about to say,' Evaristo replied in wry tones. 'The folly started with Queen Emillia's father, King Olgaf of Dunkarga. Olgaf is a grasping, covetous, discontented man, ruler of a grasping, covetous, and discontented kingdom. The people of Dunkarga have always envied Vinnengael its wealth and beauty and power, all of which they want for themselves. They could achieve it, if they worked at it, but they don't want to work. They want someone to hand them the prize.

'They want the Portals,' he said. 'Or rather, they don't necessarily want the responsibility of the Portals, they want the wealth the Portals bring. As you know, for we have worked out the sums, Vinnengael takes a percentage of all goods brought through the Portals for trade. That is only right, for there is great expense involved in maintaining and guarding the Portals, regulating who enters and who leaves. The percentage we charge is fair, and the merchants do such a prosperous business that they are happy to pay it. No one is complaining about the fees or the taxes. King Olgaf has more sense than to make those an issue, though that is where the heart of the matter lies for him.'

'Is Dunkarga a poor country, then?' Gareth asked.

'If they are, it is their own fault,' Evaristo returned snappishly. 'King Tamaros was quite willing to share the wealth with his poorer neighbor. He reduced the fees Dunkarga's merchants paid to bring their goods to the Vinnengael markets to almost nothing. He encouraged the dwarven, elven, and orken traders to travel to Dunkarga to sell their wares. A few did, but they didn't stay long. Dunkarga proved inhospitable to those of other races. Two elves were beaten, a dwarf was driven out of town. They nearly hanged one of the orken merchants for cheating. King Olgaf did nothing to stop this or to try to change his people's isolationist attitudes, which are merely a reflection of his own. He wants to reap the fruit without first sowing the seed.

'The one task Olgaf labors well at is stirring up strife. If he spent one-tenth the energy helping his own kingdom as he spends in causing trouble for others, Dunkarga would be a mighty power.'

Evaristo sighed and shook his head, crossed his arms over his chest, and gazed severely out the window in the direction of Dunkarga, which lay on Vinnengael's western border. 'He is a clever old hyena, I'll say that much for him. He has a nose for weakness, knows where and how to strike in order to inflict the most damage.

'First he decided that the easiest and quickest way to get hold of some of Vinnengael's fabled riches was to make his daughter Queen. I recall well when he first sent his couriers to court with the offer. King Tamaros turned them down summarily. The King dearly loved his first wife, the mother of Helmos.

'Alas,' Evaristo continued with a sad and pensive air, 'it is a fact of life that the blessing the gods grant with one hand they take away with the other. An accident, a senseless accident, ended the Queen's life. A snake startled the horse she was riding. She was thrown from the saddle. Her back was broken. The healers could do nothing to save her.

'Queen Portia had not been dead a year before King Olgaf began his machinations, urging Tamaros to remarry. Well, he has achieved his goal. His daughter is Queen, but that hasn't gained him much.

'So Olgaf is left to fret and stew and do what he can to raise Dunkarga in people's estimation. And the only way this mean-spirited and narrow-minded fool can seem to do that is by tearing down Vinnengael. Thus he undermines Tamaros's work whenever he can, either by planting suspicions and doubts in the minds of the elves and the dwarves and the orken, or encouraging those doubts already in place. This business, now, is all Olgaf's doing. He put forward the name of an elf to be Dominion Lord.'

Gareth recalled Dagnarus asking of Silwyth, *Why are no elves Dominion Lords?* And Silwyth's answer. *That is a very good question, Your Highness. I believe that certain people have been asking His Majesty the very same thing.*

'Tamaros explained to the elves that the gods had not granted him power over them. It was not his place to intercede with the gods on behalf of the elves. He did not want to be seen to be meddling in elven affairs – all of which one would think the elves would be glad to hear. Olgaf twisted the King's words, however, and now the very fact that Tamaros has quite wisely refused to intercede with the gods on behalf of the elves has been upended to make it appear that he is preventing the gods from granting gifts to the elves.'

'What will the King do?'

'I don't know, Gareth,' said Evaristo. 'The elves have not declared war, yet, mind you. And the fact that His Majesty has persuaded their foremost ambassador, Lord Mabreton, to remain at court is an excellent sign.'

'Then you don't think there will be war?' Gareth asked hopefully.

'The gods willing, no,' said Evaristo.

'The gods willing, yes,' said Dagnarus, over supper.

He was flushed and hot, scratched and bruised, and smelled strongly of horse, but Gareth had never seen the prince in a better mood. He did not want to talk about the war, not yet, though it was much on Gareth's mind. Dagnarus was more interested in describing his horse, claiming it to be the most wondrous horse ever born.

'It is of dwarven stock, and everyone knows that their horses are the finest and strongest in the world. Of course, this horse was bred to be bigger than dwarven ponies, in order to carry a human, but it is the heart and the blood of a horse that count, and those come from the dwarven side, so Dunner says.'

'Dunner?' Gareth asked, thinking the name sounded familiar.

'Do you remember that dwarf we saw in the Royal Library? The one reading the book? That is Dunner. He is one of the Unhorsed, which means he can't ride anymore. But he likes to be around horses, and when he is finished with his studies, he spends most of his time in the stables. He was there this morning, specifically to look at my horse, because he had heard it was such a magnificent animal.' Dagnarus fairly glowed with pride.

'Dunner is going to help me train the horse for battle the way the dwarves train their horses. And he is going to teach me to shoot an arrow from horseback. None of our soldiers can do that, not even Argot. The dwarves can rain down arrows on an enemy, slaying hundreds before the enemy can get close enough to fight back. And their ponies wheel in every direction at just a single whistled command. They can travel miles and miles without resting. A dwarven chief once rode two hundred miles in a day and night, changing horses only once. That is how they plan to conquer the world.'

'Do they?' Gareth was alarmed. He began to see himself ringed round with enemies.

'That's what Dunner says.' Dagnarus winked. 'I didn't contradict him, though of course we know better. Still, when I am Lord of Battle, I will make my knights learn to fight using bow and arrow from horseback. I plan to start right away. Training for it, that is. Dunner says I must learn to ride using the strength of my legs alone to hold me in the saddle. That frees my hands to hold the bow.'

Gareth regarded his friend in admiration and awe. 'Do you dare?'

'Well, of course!' Dagnarus said, adding casually, 'I tried it today. Not on my horse, he's not broken yet, but on one of the stable ponies. I fell off six times, but Dunner says that I have a knack for it, and I'll soon improve. I stayed on a whole three minutes the last time.'

Gareth could only shake his head. He was preoccupied, still fretting. 'Evaristo says that there won't be a war. Your father convinced the elven ambassador to stay and keep talking.'

'Evaristo is behind on his court gossip,' said Dagnarus dryly. 'It is not only the elves who are threatening to go to war now; it is the dwarves and the orken as well.'

'What?' Gareth was appalled. 'When? How did that happen?'

'It seems that someone – no one knows who – sent anonymous messages to both the dwarven ambassador and the orken, telling them that the King was granting concessions to the elves in return for the elves aiding Vinnengael in a war against the dwarves and orken. A dwarven army now camps outside their end of the Portal, threatening to seize it. We have sent soldiers to hold it open. The orken rioted in the streets of Vinnengael today. Didn't you hear about that?'

'No. I didn't hear anything,' said Gareth miserably.

'If you would take your nose out of a book now and then, you might smell something,' said Dagnarus. He glanced around. 'More stew, Silwyth. I'm starving.'

Silently, the elf glided forward from his accustomed place, which was always as near to a window as he could manage. He ladled stew from the pot and placed the bowl in front of the prince.

Gareth sighed. It was all very well for the prince to skip his lessons, run off to talk to Unhorsed dwarves, and gallop about on ponies. The whipping boy did not have that luxury. Gareth said nothing however. Dagnarus would never understand.

Silwyth, his task done, faded back to take up his watchful stance by the window.

'The soldiers quelled the riot,' the prince was saying. 'But not without a few cracked heads – that's what Argot said. The soldiers are patrolling the town. And we've sealed off *our* end of the Portals. Argot says he doesn't want to wake up to find an army of orken and dwarves come thundering through.'

'Is your father going to join with the elves and go to war?' Gareth asked.

'Don't be ridiculous. You know my father.' Dagnarus snorted. 'He would never do such a thing. Though it is an interesting idea . . .' He paused, musing, while he chewed on a mouthful of lamb.

'But if we know that your father, the King, wouldn't do anything so underhanded, then surely the dwarves and the orken must know the same thing,' Gareth said, after a moment's thought.

'The well-fed dog eats tamely from one's hand,' observed Silwyth suddenly from the window. 'The starving dog will bite off that hand. That is an elven saying.'

'What does he mean?' Gareth asked in a whisper. 'Is he calling your father a starving dog?'

'Who knows?' Dagnarus returned. He hadn't been paying attention. 'The elves have a saying for everything.'

'Do you really think there will be a war?' Gareth persisted, unhappily.

'What else can my father do except go to war?' Dagnarus mopped up the rest of the stew with a bit of bread. 'He cannot allow the Portals to remain closed. Trade would suffer. The merchants would be up in arms. Dunner says that the entire economy of Vinnengael might collapse and leave us as poor as Dunkarga.'

'But it's all a lie,' said Gareth, bewildered. 'The King will just tell them that it was a lie and then they'll understand.'

'*You* don't understand, Patch,' said Dagnarus, regarding his friend with kindly pity. 'Silwyth explained it to me. They don't *want* to understand.'

The prince glanced over his shoulder at the elf. 'I won't need you anymore this afternoon, Silwyth. I'm going to stay here and play with Patch.'

Gareth was startled; Dagnarus had not played in the playroom for several months. He almost said something, but Dagnarus – turning his head – gave his friend a wink. Gareth kept silent.

Silwyth bowed and left the room, saying he would be back in time to assist the prince in dressing for dinner, which he was to eat with his mother that night.

'What do you want to play?' Gareth asked, hoping to take his mind off the lunacies of the adult world.

'Nothing,' said Dagnarus. 'The King and Helmos and the other Dominion Lords are with the ambassadors right now.' He took hold of Gareth's hand. 'Come with me. I've found a place where we can listen to what they're saying.'

Gareth hung back. 'Are you crazy? What if we're caught?'

'Pooh! They won't do anything to me,' Dagnarus returned.

'Not to you, but they'll murder me!' Gareth protested.

'No they won't. I won't let them. Besides, we're not going to get caught. This is a *great* hiding place. Don't be such a girl, Patch!'

Gareth could not, of course, allow himself to be a

'girl.' The enormity of daring to spy on the King made Gareth's knees go wobbly and his insides quiver, but, upon reflection, the feeling wasn't unpleasant. It beat spending another dreary, lonely afternoon by himself in the playroom.

'I'll go,' he said stoutly.

'Good man!' said Dagnarus, pleased.

NINE

Dunner of the Unhorsed

THE KING HAD ASKED THE AMBASSADORS TO meet with him one hour past the sun's zenith. It was that time already, and the dwarf was late. Dunner did not hurry. Although known around the court as the ambassador from the dwarven nation, Dunner was not truly the ambassador. He was the advisor to the ambassador, sent to Vinnengael by Chief Clan Chief Rolf Swiftmane, nominal ruler of the dwarven clans. (Nominal because dwarves' loyalty to their own clans takes precedence over loyalty to all the clans, and they generally agree to abide by a Chief Clan Chief's decision only after their own clan chiefs have approved it first.)

The true ambassador had arrived yesterday through the Portal and would leave today, perhaps immediately if war was declared. In that instance, Dunner would leave as well. He supposed he should be thankful to be returning to his homeland, and in a way he was. In another way, he wasn't.

Dunner limped through the castle corridors, moving slowly, his twisted limb causing him considerable pain. Rain would fall tomorrow and probably the day after, to judge by the aching, which was always worst before a storm. The dwarf did not mind being late. The dwarven ambassador – a fierce chieftain named Begaf Hoofthunder – would most assuredly be late. He would arrive at the castle sometime before sun's downing, but just exactly when was open to question.

Dwarves take a very relaxed view of time. They cannot understand human and elven obsession with hours and minutes. A dwarf divides a day into three parts – sun arise, sun's zenith, sun's downing. These events mark his days, and he observes them only because at sun arise he wakes and breaks camp, at sun's zenith he pauses a short while to rest his horse, at sun's downing he makes camp and sleeps. He keeps no regular mealtime. Indeed, dwarves scorn humans and elves who, the dwarves say, 'look at a time piece to know when they're hungry.' A dwarf eats when his stomach tells him to eat. As for night, what use is keeping time in the dark, when all one does is sleep?

Dunner had been forced to learn to live by human time, mostly because that was the only way he ever got anything to eat. He had nearly starved upon first arriving at the castle. A dwarf seeking a substantial meal in midafternoon was out of luck. The cook, who was busy cleaning up after dinner and starting preparations for the evening meal, refused to allow the dwarf so much as a bowl of stew. Dunner took to carrying bread and cheese in his pockets, while he trained his stomach to regulate its needs by the chiming of the castle's time pieces, some run by water, others by magic.

'There's Dunner! Hello, Dunner!'

Dunner turned his head to see the young prince, Dagnarus, and his companion, the whipping boy (another strange human concept), running through the corridor. The prince waved his hand in a friendly manner, but he did not stop. The whipping boy – Dunner did not know the child's name – waved, too, mostly in confusion, and trailed along after his prince.

Dunner had seen the prince take several nasty falls from his horse that very morning. Now the dwarf watched the child run with easy strides through the corridor and envied the prince his youth and resilience. A fall from his horse when he was a child had ended Dunner's days as a rider. To be blunt, the fall, which had shattered the bones in his left leg, had ended his days as a dwarf. The break had been treated in dwarven fashion – the leg wrapped tightly in cotton bindings and left to mend on its own. During the healing time, Dunner was hauled about on a mobile litter – a piece of canvas attached to two wooden poles strapped to the back of his mother's horse. The poles jounced over the ground, sending flashes of pain through the child with every bump.

When the bindings were removed, the bones had knit together, but in all the wrong places, leaving Dunner with a twisted limb and the inability to ride a horse longer than a few miles at a stretch. The clan chief, having determined that Dunner would slow up the tribe, pronounced Dunner one of the Unhorsed. Dunner's parents took the boy to the City of the Unhorsed, apprenticed him to a professional scribe – a dwarf with a broken back – who wrote messages when dwarves, most of whom are illiterate, needed to communicate with the outside world.

Dunner never saw his parents again. The clan occasionally came to the City of the Unhorsed, but his parents never bothered to look for him, nor did he search them out. Though the Unhorsed were publicly honored for their work, in reality he was an embarrassment to his family, a shame to his clan. Had he returned to his tribe, they would have received him with aloof politeness, just as they would have received an ork, or a very well respected human.

Dunner became much attached to the scribe, a kindly woman who had paid the orken – a race ingenious with their hands – to devise a chair on wheels, which she used to help her move around her house. The scribe was gentle with the boy during those first few lonely days when he thought he should die from missing his family and from being imprisoned in one place, never to leave. He had hoped he would die, in fact, but his body had perversely kept on living.

In time, he learned to bear his fate, as the scribe taught him he must or end up like one of the mad dwarves. This threat impressed Dunner, for he had seen the mad dwarves on occasion and was determined never to fall into that pitiful and disgusting condition. Several of the mad dwarves lived in the City of the Unhorsed. Shunned by the other dwarves, the mad dwarves were ragged and unkempt. They survived by stealing food and living off scraps and offal. They contributed nothing to dwarven society and were therefore viewed as the most lowly of the low, even lower than convicted criminals, who at least paid for their crimes by volunteering to work in the iron mines.

Dunner learned to bear the longing that burned in his blood every sun arise, the longing to leap on one's pony and ride off into the new day. He learned to grit his teeth against the longing, as he gritted his teeth against the pain of his deformed leg. Neither the longing nor the pain ever left him. His heart had died within him. He would never enjoy life, but at least he could tolerate living, mainly by being useful to his people.

His work saved him. He proved a quick student and was soon able to read and write Fringrese, the dwarven language, better than his teacher. An elderly dwarf, she looked forward to escaping her unfortunate state in death, and was glad to turn over more and more of the work to Dunner. Having learned to write Fringrese and feeling the need to try to fill the emptiness in his breast, he decided that the best way to do that was to stuff his head with knowledge. He did some scribe work for several dwarven merchants, also among the Unhorsed, who traded with the orken seafarers. Most dwarves can speak a smattering of orken, enough to deal and barter, which was all that they needed. Too often, however, Dunner saw that the deals they made weren't very profitable, not as profitable as they could have been, mainly because they didn't understand the orken, who have their own way of handling customers.

Dunner began to study not only the orken language, but also orken ways. He learned, for example, that you never closed a deal with an ork on the night of a waning moon, for an ork believed that deals made in moonlight are only good for the length of time that particular moon stays around. Once the moon is gone, the ork feels perfectly free to break the deal, take back his merchandise – never mind that you have paid for it – and resell his goods during the next lunar cycle. Dunner learned to make deals with orken only under new moons, and then to sell the merchandise as quickly as possible. Either that or hide it until the orken traders set sail.

Soon, Dunner was much in demand among the dwarven merchants, who lauded his skills and spread the word that he increased their profits. The orken preferred doing business with a dwarf who understood them, instead of one who followed them around shrieking at the top of his lungs that he'd been swindled.

The elderly scribe eventually died, which meant that her spirit had entered the body of a wolf and would roam free forever and so Dunner could not grieve for her. Envy her, but not grieve. Shortly after he took over the business, the human king sent ambassadors into the dwarven lands to tell them about the Portals. Of course, the Chief Clan Chief of the dwarves was nowhere in the vicinity and so could not make a decision. His absence angered the humans, who had sent messages giving their scheduled date of arrival, expecting the Chief Clan Chief to meet them. That date meant nothing to the Chief Clan Chief, nothing to any of the dwarves.

In order to placate the humans, the dwarves sent for Dunner. He would take down the information and relate it to the Chief Clan Chief sometime in the next few years, whenever he happened to drop by.

The humans had no choice but to make do with this. Dunner had no knowledge at all of the human language but one of the humans spoke a little dwarven and another a little orken. Dunner was a quick learner and by the time the humans left, he had acquired a fair knowledge of both them and their language. He also saw how the Portals might prove to be immensely beneficial; not only would they fatten dwarven saddle-bags and fill dwarven coffers, but they would provide a simple way to fulfill dwarven destiny, which was to rule all of Loerem.

Dunner took the matter to the dwarven merchants of the City of the Unhorsed. He urged them to agree to the building of the Portal on a strictly temporary basis, subject to the approval of the Chief Clan Chief. That way, Dunner argued, the Portal could be tested and the Chief Clan Chief provided with all the information requisite to making a decision.

Dwarven merchants had traveled to human and elven lands prior to this, but the journey could take years and though the money made was considerable – dwarven metalwork was highly prized – the profits barely paid for the time and effort, not to mention the danger. The Portal would reduce the travel time to Vinnengael from one year to less than a sun's cycle. The dwarves could continue to charge the same high prices for their goods, without having to incur half the expense. Profits would leap higher than young colts.

The dwarven merchants immediately approved the building of the Portal. When the human magi arrived, Dunner was the dwarf responsible for arbitrating between them and the dwarves as to location and the hundreds of other minor quibbles that seemed likely to turn into major battles, owing to simple misunderstandings of each other's ways. When the Portal was completed and the first dwarven wagons rolled through on their way to Vinnengael, the magi invited Dunner to come with them, to present him to King Tamaros as the dwarf who had been responsible for bringing this about.

Tamaros invited Dunner to live in the castle, to help with the continued negotiations. The Unhorsed agreed that they needed one of their own in Vinnengael to deal with the unreasonable and irrational humans, and Dunner was the obvious choice. He bore this burden as he had learned to bear the others. He had not thought he could possibly grow more unhappy. He had learned differently.

He had lived in Vinnengael for many years now, with only two rays of sunshine breaking through the prison house, which was how he viewed the castle. The first had been the Great Library. Reading of other lands and other people, learning their histories, their ways, their secrets, helped Dunner forget the pain in both his leg and his soul. The second was the young prince.

Dunner had never been around children. The Unhorsed rarely marry, unless it is to one of themselves, and in that instance any child born to them is considered to be Unhorsed, as well. The child may attempt to return to the tribe, but will probably be rejected. Dunner was one who never married. He saw no reason to share his own great unhappiness with another equally unhappy dwarven female. He had fathered no children. No child had ever looked up to him, admired him, listened to his stories, wanted to learn from him. And then he had come across Dagnarus endeavoring to break his horse and going about it in typical human fashion.

Watching the prince and his friend dash down the corridor, Dunner wondered what they were up to. Mischief, no doubt. It was well-known that Tamaros could not control his younger son; his mother Emillia didn't even bother to try. The only person who seemed to be able to do anything with the prince was his eleven chamberlain, a sly and sneaky bastard to Dunner's mind, but then he had about as much use for elves as he had for horseflies. Dunner more than half suspected the elf of having sent the anonymous communiqué, which had them all teetering on the brink of war. But the dwarf could not prove his suspicions, admittedly based on nothing more than having seen the elf almost smile when he thought no one was looking. Everyone else in the court was blaming King Olgaf. To Dunner's mind, Olgaf wasn't smart enough to have thought this one up.

As for Dagnarus, Dunner could see the good potential in the boy rotting away, like apples in a barrel stored in a dark and forgotten corner. Well, no matter what happened to the prince in the future, Dunner would at least see to it that this was one human who could ride a horse.

After a wrong turning that nearly brought him into the Queen's chambers, from which Dunner retreated with painful speed, he was later still. He continually lost his bearings in the castle, could never learn his way around any building, where every wall that walled him in looked like every other wall.

He finally arrived at the council chambers to discover that, to no one's surprise, the dwarven ambassador had not yet put in an appearance. Dunner checked to see if Tamaros had at least sent someone to fetch the dwarf and his retinue. On being assured that he had, Dunner found a short-legged chair and relapsed thankfully into it.

King Tamaros was not in the room. In order to offend no one by being seen to be chatting privately with anyone, the King would stay away until all parties were assembled. His elder son, Helmos, was in attendance, acting as host prior to his father's appearance. Helmos was now endeavoring to appease Lord Mabreton, who had taken umbrage at the fact that the dwarves were late.

At the sight of Dunner, Helmos excused himself politely and advanced on Dunner with a warm smile. Dunner started to stand up in respect, but Helmos shook his head.

'No, my friend. Keep your seat. No formality between us. It is good to see you. I am glad you could come.'

'I am honored to have been asked, Your Highness,' said Dunner.

He was fond of Helmos, more fond of the young human than he had been fond of anyone in his lifetime, with the possible exception of the scribe. The two shook hands warmly, ignoring Lord Mabreton, who stated loudly in elven that since a dwarf, any dwarf was present, they should carry on with the meeting.

'I wish you joy of your betrothal, my lord,' added Dunner, gazing intently at Helmos and saddened by what he saw.

The prince looked worn-out. He must have slept but little these past few days, if at all. He also looked dazed and bewildered. He and his father had been struck from behind, the blow completely unexpected. One minute they had been on the verge of making peace with the elves, the next minute they were on the verge of war with everyone.

Lord of Sorrows. What a dreadful appellation to bestow on any young man – human or not. Dunner could have kicked those magi who had cast a cloud over the prince's bright hopes around the castle courtyard. In vain had the tutor Evaristo, another of Dunner's friends, argued that it was the gods themselves who had thus named Helmos. Dunner didn't believe a bit of it. Dunner had ceased believing in gods in his childhood, when he had prayed and prayed to them to heal his leg and let him ride again and they had not listened.

At least the mention of his engagement brought a smile to the young man's wan face, gray with exhaustion and worry, and light to his eyes.

'Thank you, Dunner. It is what I have longed for ever since we were children. I asked Anna when she was ten years old if she would marry me.'

'And what was her answer?' Dunner asked, encouraging the prince to talk of pleasant subjects.

'She said that she hated all boys,' Helmos replied, smiling at the memory. 'And then she hit me with a stick.'

'I'll wager she did not hit you this time around,' said the dwarf.

'No, she did not.' Helmos laughed, which caused Lord Mabreton to glower, thinking that the dwarf was gaining some sort of political advantage.

'When is the wedding?'

'Within the month,' said Helmos, growing more somber. He glanced sidelong at the elf lord, who was walking up and down the room, making a great show of his indignation. 'The gods willing.'

Meaning that the wedding would be held if Vinnengael was not at war.

'Thank goodness the marriage ceremony is sacred and private,' Helmos added wryly. 'I've had enough of public spectacle.'

At that moment, the orken ambassador – the chieftain of the orken living in Vinnengael – arrived. Dunner had smelled him long before he saw him; he must have just come from off his fishing vessel. The dwarven ambassador entered on the ork's heels, glaring and angry at being summoned. The smell of horse mingled with the smell of fish. The aromatic oils burning in the lamps made an attempt to override both, but were not having much success.

Helmos welcomed the ork and the dwarf in their own languages. He knew the Captain, as the orken call their chieftain, from previous visits and asked politely about the fishing, which was far from good, the ork said. But they always said that, for a shortage of fish meant they could drive up the price of the catch they took to market.

Dunner made his obeisance to the dwarven ambassador, herded him toward a chair when the ambassador would have squatted on the floor, as if he were home in his tent, and hinted that it was inappropriate – not to mention insulting to the human king – to have brought along twelve bodyguards.

Dunner was negotiating the bodyguards from twelve down to four, these to sit on the floor in the back of the council chamber, when a distraught retainer entered the room, went straight to Helmos, and said something in a low voice. Helmos looked alarmed, then grave. He gave orders to the retainer, then, excusing himself to his guests and asking them to take some refreshment in his absence, he left the room in haste.

All assembled announced loudly that they found this suspicious and were inclined to be insulted. The elf lord refused to eat or drink in the house of his enemy, for, he announced, that would make him lose face. The ork Captain and the dwarves had no such scruples, however. The twelve bodyguards made short work of the fruit, bread, cheese, and wine that had been placed on the table. What they could not eat, they stuffed down their trousers to munch on later.

The retainer returned, announced, 'King Olgaf of Dunkarga,' and retired.

A short man, wizened, with a pinch-penny face, a whining voice, and a mouth that was twisted as if it were always tasting something bad, entered the council chamber.

'Ah, so that's it,' Dunner growled to himself. 'More mischief.'

He mentally apologized to the elf Silwyth for suspecting

him. Dunner knew now who had sent the anonymous communiqué, or at least, if he had not sent it, he had been in on the sending. The capital city of Dunkarga was a journey of several weeks away. The council meeting had been called the day before yesterday, and even if Olgaf had been invited, he could never have arrived in time. He must have known that such an assembly would be held and how better to know it than by instigating it.

Dunner did not like Olgaf, did not trust him. Just then, for example, Olgaf was walking toward the dwarven ambassador with an ingratiating smile, when Dunner knew for a fact that Olgaf had ordered his soldiers to get rid of any dwarf who dared wag his beard in Dunkarga. All dwarves were to be escorted to the border and given a beating to remind them not to return.

Dunner advised his ambassador of this, speaking in dwarven. He was sorry to have to do it, for doing so would add more fuel to the fire and strengthen the ambassador's dislike and distrust of all humans, including King Tamaros. But Dunner could not stand by and watch Olgaf make a fool of the dwarves.

The result was that the ambassador pulled his beard at Olgaf – a dreadful insult, had the human only known, and announced that the twelve bodyguards would be staying. Olgaf didn't understand the insult, but he knew by the dwarf's irate tone that friendly overtures were unwelcome.

Olgaf gave Dunner a look that was like a blow and turned his false flattery to Lord Mabreton, who was charmed to discover that, at last, here was a human who appreciated him.

Helmos returned. He made a reverence to King Olgaf as was due a relative, even though it was only by marriage. Helmos's bow definitely suffered from frostbite.

'Helmos!' Olgaf was in excellent spirits. He reeked of those excellent spirits, in fact. 'Joy on your engagement, nephew! I've seen the wench. A fine furrow to plow, as no doubt you already know!' He gave a lecherous wink.

Helmos paled with anger. The remark would have been considered unseemly in a barracks. The elf lord, who spoke adequate human when he wanted, puzzled out the idiom, understood it, and was appalled. He, at least, had some sense of decorum. Lord Mabreton stepped away from Olgaf, as he would have stepped back from treading on a viper. The ork Captain appeared bored; he spoke good human but took it all quite literally, as orken will. He thought they were discussing farming, a subject in which he was not the least interested. Dunner translated for his ambassador, who, having never heard of a plow or a furrow, couldn't make sense of it and put it down to one more example of human stupidity. Dunner didn't bother to correct him.

Helmos was a gentle man, slow to anger, but this gross insult to his beloved touched him deeply, as Olgaf well knew. The crown prince was trembling with rage and the need to control himself. Olgaf opened his mouth again, intending to further provoke the young man, hoping for a quarrel or even a blow, which would have left the council meeting in shambles. Before Olgaf could spout his next poisonous gibe, King Tamaros entered.

He came without ceremony, sweeping into the room with a dignity and majesty that made Olgaf seem, by contrast, a malignant and evil imp. Tamaros rested his hand lightly, briefly, compassionately, and warningly on his son's shoulder as he passed him, reminding Helmos that to quarrel with such a being would gain nothing, only demean himself. Helmos drew in a deep breath and went to stand behind one of the high-backed chairs placed in a circle, so that the council members could face each other and none took precedence. They did not sit at a table, for that would have meant that the dwarves' chins would be resting on the board, while the legs of the orken would be constantly bumping and jouncing it.

Accompanying the King were those other Dominion Lords who had traveled to the lands of the other races and could add their own counsel, aid the King's decision. Reinholt, the Most Revered High Magus, was not present, a politic move, since the elves and the dwarves, though admitting the necessity of magic, viewed magic-users of any race with the deepest suspicion.

King Tamaros said words of welcome to all present, speaking to the foreigners in their own tongue and making inquiries that indicated that he knew well what was transpiring in their lands. He even welcomed Olgaf, saying that Emillia was always pleased when her father came to visit. A lie, since father and daughter, being very much alike, couldn't stand each other.

The formalities attended to, King Tamaros took his place in his chair at the north part of the circle. The Dominion Lords flanked the King. Helmos sat opposite His Majesty. If this were a human time piece, he would have been sitting at six o'clock. Olgaf was placed at three, the ambassadors opposite him. The twelve dwarven bodyguards squatted at the far end of the chamber, where they were joined – discreetly – by several of the castle guard.

'We thank you all for coming,' said King Tamaros. The old man looked worn and tired, but there was a calm about him, a confidence, which spread over the hurt feelings and wounded egos like a soothing balm. 'We could say that this was all a misunderstanding. Or we could say that it was not a misunderstanding at all. We could say that you were duped, fed false information.'

Olgaf's face grew more pinched, as if someone had his nose in a vice. His mouth curled into a sneer.

'We could tell you that this was an attempt to trick you into declaring war,' Tamaros continued, 'a war that would cost countless lives, leave our children orphans, the peace of Loerem in ruin and shambles. We could tell you this and we would be telling you no more than the truth. But we will not.'

Tamaros paused, gazed at each of the ambassadors intently, holding their eyes, staring into each soul, searching, probing, sifting. The elf lord, the ork Captain, the dwarven ambassador met his gaze and returned it steadily. Olgaf shifted his eyes sideways and muttered something to the effect that his wineglass was empty.

'We will not,' the King repeated. 'Instead, we will say that we have read over the lists of grievances you have presented to us . . .'

The dwarven ambassador appeared quite astonished at this. He had sent no list. He could not write. Dunner leaned over to whisper that he had taken it upon himself to submit a list of dwarven concerns. This was fine with the ambassador. He didn't even ask to see the list, which he could not have read anyway, and he trusted Dunner. Such was the respect in which the Unhorsed were held.

Tamaros waited patiently until the dwarves had ceased their whispered consultation, then went on.

'We have read over your grievances and we say that you are right.'

This was met with astonished silence.

'The Portals are a gift from the gods and belong rightfully to us all. We should all share in the control of the Portals, in the responsibility of maintaining them, and therefore we should all share in the wealth. How is that to be accomplished?' Tamaros shook his head. 'We do not know. We do not have the answer.'

The ambassadors looked grim; they thought he was stalling.

'And that is why,' Tamaros continued, his voice a little louder, overriding their doubts, 'we are taking this matter directly to the gods. This night, I will enter the Temple. I ask that you give me two-and-seventy hours, during which

159

time you will take no action. Nor will we. I will fast and pray and ask the gods for guidance. I know that each of you will be wanting to do the same. Therefore, any of you who would like to come with me to the Temple, to the Portal of the Gods, are welcome.'

Well done, old man, said Dunner to himself, barely able to keep from laughing as he translated Tamaros's words. The look on King Olgaf's face alone was worth the price of admission. He had come there hoping to foment discord, come there to start a war, from which he intended to profit. Instead he was left with the prospect of a seventy-two-hour fast and prayer session.

'Does he mean it?' the dwarven ambassador demanded, regarding Tamaros doubtfully.

'He means it,' Dunner replied. He might not believe in the gods, but he had come to believe in King Tamaros.

The others were considering, turning over the proposal as a jewel in their minds. They were unable to find a single flaw, though it was obvious from the expression on Olgaf's face that he was hammering at it with all his might. At length, after more discussion, all agreed to it, some more grudgingly than others. They would each speak to the gods on their own behalf – the orken Captain would have his shaman read the omens – and then they would return.

All except the dwarven ambassador, who – once he was made to understand how many sunrises seventy-two hours encompassed – looked horrified and said he could not possibly stay in this prison for that length of time. He agreed to let Dunner the Unhorsed represent the dwarves.

King Olgaf said nothing, made no promise to consult the gods or even to return in seventy-two hours. He cast King Tamaros a look of inveterate hatred, a look so malevolent that Dunner was sorry to have intercepted it and rubbed a turquoise stone, a Pecwae gem, worn on a fine silver chain, in order to protect himself from any spillover of evil.

The meeting was adjourned. Dunner, one of the last to leave, limped out of the council chamber and into the corridor, where he was almost run down by the young prince Dagnarus. The prince appeared out of nowhere, accompanied by his friend, the whipping boy. Dunner wondered what in the name of the Wolfgod could have brought the two boys to this part of the castle.

'Move along, will you? You're in my way. Oh, sorry, Dunner. I didn't see it was you,' Dagnarus muttered. He was clearly in a bad mood, appeared put out, as if his dearest wish had just been denied. Gareth, on the other hand, looked vastly relieved.

'Will you be training your horse for battle tomorrow, Your Highness?' Dunner asked.

'Why should I? What's the use?' the boy replied dispiritedly. He wandered off disconsolately down the hall, the whipping boy tailing dutifully behind.

The next person Dunner encountered was Silwyth. He, too, had no business being in this portion of the castle at this time of day.

'If you're searching for His Highness, Chamberlain,' said Dunner, 'he went off in that direction.'

Silwyth walked past without replying. He didn't even seem to hear. Though elves pride themselves on revealing nothing of their emotions on their faces, this elf apparently wasn't bothering. He looked extremely glum.

TEN

The Portal of the Gods

T HE PORTAL OF THE GODS HAD BEEN CREATED by the magi along with the other three Portals at the insistence of King Tamaros. Some of his advisors had been much opposed to it, believing that the less direct communication people had with the gods the better.

Tamaros's idea had been to open the Portal up to anyone who wanted to communicate with the gods. His advisors had nearly leapt down his throat at this suggestion; did he actually want the meanest beggar in Vinnengael to be able to come in and demand the gods knew what? How were people to respect the King's laws if they had the idea that they could go over his head if they were dissatisfied?

Tamaros insisted and the Portal was built in the Temple of the Magi for any to use. Few did. Life was good. The people were content. Let the gods stay in heaven. They weren't needed on earth. Thus, the Portal was little visited.

Those who saw the Portal of the Gods – and there were few, for it was located in an isolated and out-of-the-way portion of the Temple – were disappointed. Expecting a magnificent room with a high-domed ceiling filled with sunlight, they saw only a small cell, reminiscent of a novice's cell. They looked around askance, feeling privately that they'd been cheated.

It was Tamaros himself who had determined how the Portal should appear. He came before the gods in humility, one of their children, not a king, and thus he came to them in a room not much larger than a closet. The Portal was situated in the quietest part of the building, a part that seemed to use silence for mortar to hold the stones together.

Though all knew of the Portal's existence, few in the Temple knew where to find it. Tamaros turned off a main corridor and walked into what appeared to be a blind wall. Angling to his left, he found a small corridor, barely wide enough for an ordinary-sized man to fit between the walls without turning sideways. This corridor was quite long, at least fifty paces. At the end were two steps that went down and two more that went up, and then there was a door. Opening the door led him into a small and windowless closet.

This closet did not appear on any of the plans used in the building's construction. Prior to the gods' blessing, this little cell was known jocularly as Petra's Folly, Petra being the name of the chief builder. The story went that Petra had realized at the last moment that his plans were incorrect, that he was going to have space left over, and that he'd tossed in this closet in order to fit in all the rest of the pieces of the gigantic puzzle that was the Temple of the Magi.

The chief builder always denied this vehemently. He had been inspired to add the closet, he said, having seen it in a vision. Nobody believed him, naturally, until the day when the other three Portals were created. On that day, King Tamaros had walked straight to this tiny closet, though he had never been there before, and announced that this was the Portal of the Gods. Petra was exonerated. He was regarded with awe by family and friends and never quite trusted from that day on.

The rector of the Temple school was honored to escort the King to the Portal. He removed the wizard lock that guarded the door. The servants entered from time to time to clean the small room, sweep the floor, dust the altar, and make certain mice were not nesting in the mattress, but otherwise the room was kept sacrosanct.

The rector, asking the King's pardon, preceded His Majesty into the cell, looked it over carefully to make certain all was neat and proper. Tamaros endured this delay patiently. Time always seemed to slow for him when he entered the Portal. In the palace, the minutes poured past him in a rushing torrent. The moment he entered the Portal, the torrent slowed until it seemed he could delineate each separate drop as it fell into the dark pool of the irrecoverable past.

The room smelled of candle wax and old roses. One of the servants had scattered rose petals over the bed linen. The rector frowned at such frivolity, but Tamaros was pleased. The smell of roses always brought his loved wife to mind. Novices entered behind the rector. One carried a jug of water for the King's refreshment. One held a chamber pot and laving dish for his ablutions. These they set down with utmost care, trembling with mortal dread at being so near their King, and fearful of making an unseemly racket. Tamaros gazed upon the young people with such a benign and kindly eye that they were warmed and comforted and asked for his blessing as if he had been their own father.

And then they were gone, a flock of lambs herded to the door by the shepherding rector, who lit thick beeswax candles and asked if there was anything else the King desired. Upon being told that there wasn't, the rector closed the door. Tamaros locked the door from the inside, using a magical key provided by the Most Revered

High Magus Reinholt, a key that would enchant the door, keep it locked until Tamaros himself opened it.

The King spent long moments standing in the center of the small room, allowing time to slow still further until finally the seconds ceased to drop. The pool became still and placid, its surface not marred by a single ripple.

The peace, the quiet entered the King's heart and his soul. He sat down upon the bed and looked around the small cell with fondness and affection, as a man looks around his home after returning from a long and dangerous journey.

'I would be glad to stay here for the rest of my days,' Tamaros said, his gaze lingering on the altar, which was very plain and simple, a square table made of rosewood, with symbols representative of the four elements carved at each of the four cardinal points.

A noble family had donated the altar from its own private chapel, which was being redecorated in the modern style. The altar – centuries old, perhaps – had been crudely carved by a craftsman with more love than skill. The nobleman had spoken of the altar disparagingly, had considered chopping it up for firewood, but had then reflected that perhaps this might offend the gods. The magi had accepted the gift, treated the altar with the reverence it was due, polishing it with fine oils and giving it a place of honor in the main sanctuary. Tamaros, coming to see it, had felt strangely drawn to it. He had requested it be moved to the Portal, where it fit as if it had been made to order.

A dish of oil stood next to the altar, along with a soft white cloth. Tamaros knelt before the altar. Dipping the cloth in the scented oil, he began to polish the altar wood, his first offering to the gods. As he worked, the worries and anxieties, the petty quarrels, the serious intrigues, the grabs for power, the betrayals, the disappointments flowed from him into the cloth and were rubbed into the wood. The wood absorbed them, as it absorbed the sweet oil.

Tamaros rose from his task, refreshed and cleansed, the cares of the world no longer soiling his soul.

What would they do if I refused to come out? he found himself thinking, and he smiled to imagine his old friend Reinholt's consternation. The thought was tempting, very tempting. He could abdicate the throne in favor of his elder son. Helmos would make a good king.

Would make. He was too young yet for such heavy responsibility. And yet, Tamaros reminded himself, you were King when you were barely older than Helmos.

Tamaros allowed himself to dream, all the while knowing it was nothing but a dream. He would never abdicate, would never do that to his people, would never do that to his sons. How could anyone count upon the crown if it were seen to be nothing more than a hat to be put on or thrown off at a whim? He would bear this burden until the day the gods released him, permitted him to join his beloved, who waited for him in the rose-colored dawn of a new life.

Tamaros felt a great weariness. Between conferences with ambassadors and meetings with his advisors, he had not slept well for months. He lay down upon the bed, luxuriated in the fact that for a few days at least no one would disturb his rest.

He sank beneath a still pool covered over with rose petals.

The small child sat in an enormous chair at an enormous table, waiting for something. He was not quite sure what. He had been deposited there, in the chair, and ordered vaguely to behave, whatever that meant. The table was loaded with food and drink, all he wanted. Some of the most delicious tidbits, however, were too far for him to reach. He stood up in the chair and climbed onto the table, in an attempt to secure the sweetmeats, but they still remained – inexplicably – beyond his grasp.

His parents were there somewhere. He caught glimpses of them occasionally, as they hurried past, in and out of the room, loving, in a vague and preoccupied way. They were extraordinarily beautiful, his parents. Or at least so he imagined. He could never truly see them as they came and went, with barely a glance for him.

They never said a word when he stood on the chair or climbed upon the table, though he might well have tumbled down and cracked his head. He returned to the huge chair – his feet didn't touch the floor – and thought that he should ask his parents to give him the longed-for confection. He knew that if he had it in his possession, it would make him happy. He would never want anything else. He said as much to his parents, the next time they passed by, in a rustle of silk and lace and jewels, smelling of rosewater.

To his awe and delight, they stopped and gazed down upon him from their great height.

'You are a good child. We take pleasure in pleasing you. But are you certain this is what you want?'

'Yes, yes, I am certain!' he cried, and wriggled in the too-large chair.

'It is sweet upon the outside, but bitter to the taste in the center. Do you still want it?'

'Yes, I want it!' He would avoid the center, never come near it.

'There is a reason it has been placed out of your reach. It may be too rich for you to digest just now. With work, you could reach it yourself.'

'I tried! I cannot! I have earned it! Why do you show it to me if you will not let me have it? It's not fair!'

His parents hesitated, considered.

'It is true you are one of our favored children. You have always been good and obedient. Very well. The sweet shall be yours. If you would heed our caution, we advise you to lock it away and not indulge yourself in it just yet.'

167

He promised he should do as they wished, but even as he took hold of the wonderful sweetmeat, he realized he was hungry, so very hungry. Empty and hollow inside. Only this could satisfy him.

His parents lingered, an air of anxiety about them. He had what he wanted and that was enough. Eventually, they departed. He was barely aware of their going. He held the treat in his hands and gazed at it with delight, thinking how all the other children would love him for this and do him honor.

Tamaros woke slowly, woke from a dream that had been both immensely satisfying and vaguely disquieting. He sat up in bed – somewhat surprised to find that he *was* in bed and not in a tall chair. Stupid with the heavy sleep, he sat in the darkness, unable to see, not quite comprehending where he was. The sleep fog gradually dissipated, the dream receded, and he knew, he remembered.

Effectively blind, he rose to his feet and groped through the darkness. The cell was small, there was not much furniture – a chair, a writing desk, the altar. He knew where each piece stood in relation to the others and so found his way to the desk with relative ease. His hands located the candle in its stand, found the tinder and flint beside it.

The candle flame had drowned in its own wax, apparently. The candle had not been out long, the wax was still semiliquid and warm to the touch. He cut a small channel in the side of the candle to allow the wax to drain, then lit the candle. The flame burned clearly, brightly.

The flickering flame was reflected four times in a lustrous diamond pyramid, constructed of four triangles whose base formed a quadrangle at the bottom, came together in a point at the top. The pyramid was large, the base approximately the length of Tamaros's hand. The diamond pyramid stood as tall as a hand and a half. It had been carved from a single stone.

No one could have entered the Portal. Only he could unlock the magic enchantment protecting the door. And, in any case, no one would have dared disturb the King in his sacred meditations. Tamaros gazed at the diamond in reverent awe. The diamond was a gift from the gods, as in his dream. He touched the diamond gingerly with a trembling finger.

The stone was smooth, hard, cold as ice to the touch, without flaw. As he touched it, images formed in his mind, images of an elf holding a segment of the pyramid, a dwarf holding another segment, an ork holding yet another segment, and a human – himself – holding the last. He saw elves, orken, dwarves each undergoing the Transfiguration. He saw the four quarters of the diamond pyramid separate, then come together, united, to form a perfect, flawless structure.

'Sweet outside, bitter in the center.'

The warning voices echoed from his dream. Tamaros tried to understand, but he could not. The diamond was whole and at the same time it was segmented, each segment equal, none receiving a larger share than any other.

Tamaros sank to his knees and with glad tears coursing down his cheeks, he thanked the gods. He spent the next two days in prayer and thanksgiving, and when he emerged from the Portal, he bore in his hands the diamond pyramid, which he called the Sovereign Stone, for it came from the gods, sovereign rulers of them all.

By the Sovereign Stone's grace, each race would have the right to create Dominion Lords of that race. These Dominion Lords, the most wise and learned of every race, would unite to ensure that the continent of Loerem would always be at peace.

As to the 'bitter' inside, there was no 'inside' that Tamaros could see. When the time came, the pyramid would split into four equal quarters, leaving nothing in the center.

ELEVEN

Children Should be Neither Seen nor Heard

NEWS OF THE SOVEREIGN STONE WHISPERED
through the palace before Tamaros ever left the
Temple. Following a day of prayerful thanksgiving, the King sent word that a meeting of the Dominion
Lords, the heads of the orders of the Revered Magi, and
the ambassadors of the other races was to be convened that
very night. The Dominion Lords and the ambassadors or
their representatives came in haste, the magi gathered. The
conclave was held in a meeting room in the Temple. All
waited in eager expectation for the King. Those who had
seen him when he emerged from the Portal reported that he
seemed to have shed twenty years of worry and anxiety.

He had placed the sacred diamond in a velvet bag,
keeping it from the eyes of the curious. Bearing the
gemstone, King Tamaros entered the meeting room. So
radiant did he look, so exalted, and, at the same time,
humble, that the men and women in attendance smiled
with joy and began to applaud, certain that whatever had
pleased their King and given him back his youthful vigor
and health must be to their liking.

Tamaros placed the velvet bag containing the Sovereign
Stone upon the table.

'A gift from the gods,' he said simply, and, opening the bag, removed the diamond. 'The Sovereign Stone.'

All exclaimed over its beauty, but, when Tamaros proceeded to tell them of its use as he understood it from the gods, the smiles began to slip away.

The diamond pyramid gleamed brightly in the light of the oil lamps but not brightly enough to hide from Tamaros the fact that the gods' gift was not being welcomed with universal rejoicing, as he had thought it surely must. He gazed at the people gathered around the table, those whom he considered his friends, his most trusted advisors, and he saw doubt, uncertainty, and, in some cases, outright dismay.

'What is this?' he demanded, and his voice rose in his anger and disappointment, carrying quite clearly to those who had gathered outside the sealed meeting room, unabashedly eavesdropping. On hearing the King's voice shake with anger, the curious – mostly young acolytes and novices – looked guilty and hurried away. Others – mainly the lay servants, who were there because they knew they would be well paid for their information – put their ears more closely to the cracks in the woodwork.

After a half hour of listening to the conversation inside the meeting room the spies ran off to make their reports. So it was that Silwyth heard exactly what had transpired in that meeting, from a young woman in his pay. The first moment he could snatch from the prince's presence, he returned to his room, where he wrote a hurried letter to the Shield of the Divine, a letter that left the palace on its way to the elven Portal before Tamaros and the Sovereign Stone ever left the meeting room.

The letter was brief and closed with this:

Lord Mabreton is already talking of the elves refusing to accept the Sovereign Stone, for, he says, what need do the elves have of it? If the stone was truly good and powerful, our own ancestors would have brought it to the Divine. We do not need to accept alms from the humans.

My lord, fearing that this may also be your response, I beg you to consider this: perhaps the gods have given the stone to the humans in order that it may be kept out of the hands of the Divine! He should accept it. But he should not receive it. Please think on this, my lord, and send me your instructions.

'Where have you been?' Dagnarus demanded, giving the elf a sharp look when Silwyth entered his room later that evening. 'I wanted you.'

'I was taken with a sudden indisposition, Your Highness,' Silwyth replied. 'I beg your forgiveness.'

'I was most seriously annoyed by your leaving,' said Dagnarus coolly, who guessed that something was going on.

'I am sorry to have upset Your Highness. In return, perhaps you would like to hear news of your honored father. News that you will find to be of interest, for Your Highness knows well that I am no tongue-wagging gossip.'

'I know that well, Chamberlain,' said Dagnarus gravely, for Silwyth spoke the truth. The elf never gossiped or spread rumors. The information he brought the prince on a consistent basis was always accurate.

'A diamond that big must be very valuable,' said Dagnarus.

'Indeed, Your Highness,' said Silwyth.

The prince and his chamberlain were not the only people in the palace talking of the Sovereign Stone. Dunner had attended the meeting and reported to the dwarven ambassador, who had – after all – been persuaded to stay the seventy-two hours, provided he and his twelve bodyguards were not forced to remain 'imprisoned' in the castle. The dwarves pitched their tents on the plains outside the city, changing their location every day.

Dunner was enthusiastic over the idea of dwarven Dominion Lords. He described the ceremony of Transfiguration, which he had seen Helmos undergo and which had profoundly impressed him.

It did not impress the ambassador.

'Bah!' he said scornfully. 'This stone is worthless to us. As if any dwarf would permit himself to be turned into solid rock! And all for what? To earn some sort of magical power? Our wizards have too much magic as it is, in my opinion. No dwarf would do such a mad thing.'

'I'm not so sure,' said Dunner, looking down at his twisted leg as he tried to rub away the incessant pain. 'I'm not so sure. I think we should accept it.'

The orken Captain heard the news on his boat, while he was out fishing, one of his people having swum out to inform him. The Captain listened, nodded once, and said laconically, 'Bring me the rock.'

The ork obeyed. He went directly to the palace, where one of King Tamaros's courtiers spent a very bad twenty minutes attempting to make the ork understand that the orken portion of the Sovereign Stone would be turned over to the very highest personage in the orken hierarchy, during a most elaborate ceremony designed to honor the gods and not before.

'Ceremony!' The Captain grunted in displeasure when the ork returned empty-handed. 'Why bother with another ass-numbing ceremony? No need to bore the gods with long-winded talk. The gods have done what the King wanted. The gods have given him this rock. What more is there to say to them?'

A great deal more to say apparently. The meeting of the magi and the Dominion Lords and the King continued far into the night.

The Dominion Lords backed Tamaros, arguing that

the creation of their elven, orken, and dwarven counter-parts would ensure the peaceful coexistence of the races. This would prove the humans' good faith, prove that the humans trusted the other races to act in good faith themselves, create staunch allies, secure the Portals.

The magi worried that some evil person – ork, elf, dwarf – would gain the immense power of a Dominion Lord.

'We will provide guidelines,' said Tamaros, 'suggesting what they should look for in a candidate. But these are only guidelines, not mandatory rules. The Sovereign Stone itself – being a gift of the gods – will reject any candidate for Dominion Lord deemed unsuitable.'

'Is the stone a gift from *all* the gods, Your Majesty?' asked the Librarian, known to be of a philosophical bent, laying emphasis upon the adjective.

'Why do you ask?' demanded the King warily. He knew better than just to answer yea or nay, since neither one was likely to be right according to the philosophical mind.

'Evil *does* exist in the world, Your Majesty,' the Librarian answered without answering.

'Evil exists in the Void, in absence of the gods,' the King countered.

'The Sovereign Stone fills up the Void,' said Helmos, growing angered. His father had been elated by the gift of the Sovereign Stone. He had brought it to them expecting the same elation, and Helmos could see that his father was deeply hurt by what he considered unreasonable doubts and far-fetched suspicions. 'Where there was nothing before to unite the races, now there is something.'

'I only thought it right to mention it, Your Majesty,' said the Librarian meekly. 'My apologies if I have offended.'

'Your Majesty,' said the Most Revered High Magus, 'you have honored us by seeking our advice. Surely, then, it is our duty to ask hard questions, difficult questions, questions you may not like to hear. But it is better to ask them now and to be satisfied with the answers, than to wish later to our great sorrow we had asked them. I believe I may safely speak for us all when I say that we honor the gods for their gift and we honor even more the man whom the gods have chosen to honor.'

Tamaros bowed his head.

'But I must say that I find this vision of the gods disturbing,' said the High Magus gravely. 'As you have related the meeting, we must believe that the gods are selfish, uncaring parents, who view us as small children, unworthy of their time. Is that true?'

'I have accurately described what the gods gave me to see,' Tamaros said stiffly. 'I am certain the learned' – he cast a cold glance at the Librarian, who quailed beneath it – 'will debate the interpretation for centuries to come.'

'Still, Your Majesty,' said Reinholt sternly, 'in a matter this important, I feel I must ask this question, as painful as it may be. Was it the gods you saw as uncaring parents? Or yourself?'

The other magi were aghast. None could believe that even a man as highly placed as the Revered High Magus had dared ask such a question. Tamaros apparently could not believe it either. The King was outraged. He had never been so furious. He took great care to control himself for the moment, however. His rage was visible only in a sharply indrawn breath, the sudden extreme pallor that swept over his face, and the glitter of his eyes.

No one knew where to look. They could not look at the King. They did not want to look at the High Magus. They dared not look at each other, for fear that exchanged glances might be taken for complicity. They stared at the floor, therefore, or the wall or the ceiling. None looked at Helmos, or they would have seen him troubled, saddened.

When Tamaros spoke, his voice was dangerously calm. 'Thank you, Revered Magus. And you are right to ask questions. With the Sovereign Stone as with all gifts of the gods, we must have faith in the gods to guide us along the right path.'

There was no doubt in anyone's mind that the meeting was adjourned. They were all glad to leave. Everyone had noticed, though they did not dare mention it, that Tamaros had not answered the question.

The Most Revered High Magus bowed before the King – a formal bow that was meant to remind His Majesty that although he was political leader of his people, Reinholt was the spiritual leader and that he felt himself duty-bound. The Dominion Lords departed, after receiving the King's warm and personal thanks for allying themselves with him.

Helmos remained with his father, who had not only gained back the twenty years he had shed but appeared to have added twenty more.

Haggard, gray with fatigue – the arguments had been long and wearing – Tamaros stood before the altar and gazed lovingly at the Sovereign Stone, loath to leave it, even to go to his well-earned rest.

'Why can't they understand?' the King demanded queru-lously. 'I cannot live forever. Perhaps, my son, you may be granted the gift of continuing to create Dominion Lords. Perhaps you may not. And after you, who knows? The Sovereign Stone ensures that the power of the Dominion Lords for good will continue. And now that power will extend into the other races. I am convinced that this stone' – he placed his hand reverently upon it – 'will bring peace to the world forever.'

His son rested a loving hand upon Tamaros's thin shoulder. 'They are good people, Father. Dedicated and loyal. Yet, their minds are limited sometimes by petty cares and concerns. They see no farther than the tips of their own noses. You see the beautiful vista that lies before us.'

'And yet,' Tamaros said, not hearing his son, regarding

the Sovereign Stone with a gaze that was now troubled, 'and yet, I wonder. The gods told me . . .' He paused, uneasy, unsettled. 'The gods told me: "It is sweet upon the outside, but bitter to the taste in the center." And "It may be too rich for you to digest just now." What do you suppose that means?'

'The Sovereign Stone would be too rich for one,' said Helmos, after a moment's thought. 'Yet, shared, the dish becomes exquisite. I believe that, again, the gods are telling you to share this gift.'

Tamaros laid his own hand upon his son's. 'You are a good son, Helmos. A good son, a good man. The ceremony of the gifting of the Sovereign Stone will be the grandest ceremony the world has ever seen. A joyous day, it will mark a turning point in the history of the world.'

The King began to make preparations for the ceremony. One of the earliest decisions he made was that his younger son, Dagnarus, would be an important part of the ceremony. The prince, a child, representing all the world's children, would carry the Sovereign Stone from the altar to the King, who would then separate the stone into its four equal parts and distribute them to the representatives of each of the races.

Tamaros made this decision for several reasons – Dagnarus was a beautiful child, he was not intimidated by crowds, he knew the importance and value of royal ceremony. Those were the practical reasons for the decision to choose the prince. The other reasons were less tangible, felt, but not admitted. Truth be told, the words of the High Magus had disturbed Tamaros deeply. If Reinholt was saying such things, others were thinking them. Tamaros included Dagnarus in the ceremony out of defiance. He would show the world that he loved his children. Both his children.

Dagnarus was immensely pleased to be playing such an

important role. The only fly in the honey for the prince was that now he had little time to spend with his new horse. He had to rehearse his part over and over again, something he found tedious in the extreme. When he wasn't rehearsing, he was being measured for new clothes, which was even worse. Much as he loved finery, he detested having to stand perfectly still for the measurements. Since Queen Emillia was in charge, the clothes, when finished, were not right. The cloak was either too long or too short, the dalmatic was either too tight or too loose, his hat too large or too small and so Dagnarus was continually being hauled into Her Majesty's chambers for measuring, while women with pins in their mouths fussed over him and mumbled.

'Dagnarus!' Gareth grabbed hold of the prince as he was about to round a corner. 'Look! Coming down the hall! Mistress Florence!'

Mistress Florence was in charge of the Queen's dress-making and hence was now in charge of Dagnarus's ceremonial finery. She had a determined look on her face and a tape measure in her hand.

'This way!' said Dagnarus, who had been setting out to search for Dunner, hoping to persuade the dwarf to teach more horsemanship.

The boys ducked behind a convenient column, held their breaths until the seamstress scurried past them on her way to the prince's chambers.

'She won't find Silwyth there,' Dagnarus whispered. 'And Evaristo's gone for the day.'

'Which means she'll come searching for you. Hurry up!'

The boys sprinted down the hall.

'How do you know Silwyth isn't there?' Gareth asked. 'Where else would he be?'

'On one of his mysterious errands,' said Dagnarus. 'He always leaves when we're out of the way.'

'Does he?' Gareth wondered. 'He's always there when we come back.'

'That's how I know,' Dagnarus said with a wink. 'He's too punctual. It means he's doing something behind our backs and taking care not to get caught. That and I saw him – No, this route, down the stairs.'

'I thought you said we should find Dunner in the Great Library. This isn't the way.'

'The other way will take us too close to my mother. Down the stairs, down the hall, down a corridor, up the stairs, and we come by the Great Library from the opposite direction.'

Slowing his pace, Gareth worked out this route in his head. 'But that will take us into His Majesty's quarters. That's near the council chamber. We're not allowed to play there.'

'We're not *playing*,' said Dagnarus, casting his friend a scathing glance. 'I never play. Not anymore. Besides, no one will be there this time of day. My father and Helmos will be preparing for this afternoon's levee.'

The boys climbed the broad stairs, rounded a corner, and saw what appeared to be an army of elves, wearing their bright-colored lacquered armor and armed with swords and spears, marching down the hallway.

'Gods save us!' Gareth gasped.

There was nowhere to hide, no long tapestries or stands of armor, no wide columns or friendly alcoves. Dagnarus wiggled the handle of a nearby door, found it unlatched. Pushing open the door, he dragged his friend inside the room and partially shut the door behind them, leaving it slightly ajar. Putting his eye to the crack, he peered out.

'Is it war?' Gareth asked, his voice quavering. 'Are they coming to kill us?'

'Don't be silly,' Dagnarus returned, irritated at his friend's thickheadedness. 'They're wearing their ceremonial armor and there's only twenty or thirty of them. They've come for the Sovereign Stone ceremony, of course. There's Lord Mabreton arriving to meet them.'

'Oh,' said Gareth, feeling stupid. 'Who is it, then?'

'I don't know.' Dagnarus frowned. 'Come to think of it, it *is* odd that they should be here. Their king – what do they call him?'

'The Divine,' said Gareth.

'Right. The Divine sent word to my father saying that Lord Mabreton would be the elf chosen to receive their portion of the Sovereign Stone. Now all these other elves have arrived. I wonder why.'

'Perhaps they're here to guard the stone on its way back to the elven lands,' Gareth suggested.

Dagnarus opened the door another inch, to Gareth's terror. 'Lord Mabreton doesn't look at all pleased to see them. Here's luck! They're stopping right in front of us! Now we'll find out what's going on. I'll be the one to tell Silwyth news for a change, instead of the other way around. Whoever this elf is, he's important. You speak elven.' Dagnarus motioned his friend over to the door. 'Tell me what they're saying.'

'I don't speak *that* much elven,' Gareth protested in a whisper, but Dagnarus only scowled at him and gestured angrily at the door. Gareth sighed, knelt on the floor, and peeped warily out into the hall.

Dagnarus was right. Lord Mabreton regarded the arriving elven contingent with ire and displeasure, both emotions recorded on his face. He managed to smooth them away, but with visible effort. Crossing his hands over his chest, he bowed as the other elves approached.

The elf in the lead – a large man of middle years – did not wear armor, but was dressed in rich, brocade robes, thick and so covered with jewels and embroidery that the robes might well have served as armor. He walked ahead of his retainers, came to a halt in the middle of the corridor. The elf made no sign that the boys could see, but the retainers accompanying him halted as one, acting on some unspoken command. The elf in the lead advanced toward Lord Mabreton, stopped only when he was practically standing on the lord's toes. He was too close. Elven protocol required that a respectful distance be maintained between persons unless one or another had issued an invitation to cross the invisible barrier. One of the elves would have to step back.

The two stared at each other. The strange elf crossed his arms over his chest. Lord Mabreton lowered his gaze and fell back a pace, though he did so with an insipid coldness not lost on either the other elf or the two unseen spectators.

'Shield of the Divine,' said Lord Mabreton, looking uneasy, 'I am sorry I was not on hand at the Portal to greet you, my lord, but I was only now informed you had arrived. We are always honored by your presence, but we cannot but wonder why you have chosen to come to Vinnengael at this time.'

'I have come to see the ceremony,' said the Shield in mild tones. 'A ceremony in which, I understand, you are playing an important part.'

Lord Mabreton's uneasiness increased, though he attempted to hide it. His gaze slid out from under the intense gaze of the Shield. He cast darting glances up and down the corridor, which was empty, except for the elves.

'An unimportant part in an unimportant ceremony, my lord,' Lord Mabreton said in deprecating tones. 'The Divine has asked me to represent our people. The ceremony is scheduled to be held seven days from now. I am certain you will find the wait fatiguing, cooped up as you and your retinue would be in this dank castle. I offer my own house for your lordship's stay –'

'A house that is indeed very fine, also very far from Vinnengael,' said the Shield. 'I stopped at your house,

Lord Mabreton, on my way here. My soldiers find it most commodious. Your beautiful wife is a gracious hostess.'

Lord Mabreton flushed in anger. He made an involuntary movement with his hand, a movement that caused every guard in the Shield's troop to place his hand upon his sword hilt with a precision that made Dagnarus nod in critical approval.

The blood left Lord Mabreton's face in a rush, replaced by a sick pallor. Slowly he lowered his hands, held them, trembling, at his sides.

The guards kept their hands upon their swords. They stood at rigid attention, taking note of everything from the sweat beading Lord Mabreton's brow to a cat slinking through the corridor, searching for a mouse.

The Lord seemed to be struggling to find something to say to this. The Shield saved him the bother.

'I am certain the Divine is right now composing a poem intended to inform me of the gift of the Sovereign Stone, a poem that will explain its powers, among which, as I understand it, is the power to create elven Dominion Lords. Such a wonderful gift from the gods deserves a poem of magnificence. No doubt the Divine will spend months working on it,' the Shield added dryly. 'Months during which he has the Sovereign Stone in his possession. Months during which he will create his own Dominion Lords.'

'He is the Divine,' said Lord Mabreton, blustering, his anger overtaking him. 'And I am the representative of the Divine! The Sovereign Stone is his by right!'

'I am the Shield of the Divine,' said the Shield, his voice glinting with a dangerous edge. 'The protector of the Divine. The Sovereign Stone comes to me by right. You must step aside.'

He advanced forward. 'Or be pushed.'

Lord Mabreton lost his senses. Enraged, he shouted, 'Do you dare to threaten me? I am a Guardian. A loyal servant to the Divine. You dare not touch me! Not without bringing your own House crashing down around your ears!'

Dagnarus punched Gareth on the shoulder. 'Look! Silwyth!'

'I see,' Gareth whispered, rubbing the bruise.

Silwyth had rounded the corner at the far end of the corridor. He walked up behind Lord Mabreton, who, intent upon the Shield, did not see the chamberlain or hear his soft-footed approach. Silwyth came to within five or six paces of Lord Mabreton and then halted, watching the Shield.

The Shield of the Divine folded his arms across his chest, gazed coldly at Lord Mabreton, then gave an almost imperceptible nod.

'You are right, Lord Mabreton,' said the Shield in a mild and conciliatory tone. 'I dare not touch you.'

Silwyth glided up behind Lord Mabreton. Silwyth's hand jerked. The boys saw a flash of light glinting off steel.

Lord Mabreton looked immensely surprised, then shocked. He gave a grunt, his knees buckled. In one smooth gesture, Silwyth withdrew the knife from Lord Mabreton's back and caught the man in his arms, preventing him from falling to the floor.

So swiftly, so silently, so smoothly was the murder accomplished that neither boy realized immediately what he had just seen.

At a gesture from the Shield, one of his bodyguard lifted Lord Mabreton's body and slung it over his shoulder. The lord's head and arms dangled down the guard's back. The guard wrapped his arm securely around the lord's legs.

The lord's eyes, wide-open and unmoving, stared straight at the boys. An expression of astonishment was frozen upon the man's features. A trickle of blood drooled from the gaping mouth.

'He's . . . he's dead!' Gareth gasped with horror.

The Shield glanced around. 'What was that?'

Dagnarus clapped his hand over his friend's mouth. 'Silence!' the prince whispered with dire urgency in Gareth's ear.

Gareth, shivering, nodded. The boys remained crouched behind the partially open door, not moving a muscle, not even daring to breathe.

'Only that, my lord.' One of the guards pointed.

The cat pounced, held a mouse beneath her paw.

'Ah, the hunter's reward,' said the Shield, smiling.

Silwyth wiped the blood from his knife with a white cloth, tucked the knife and the bloodstained cloth into his long flowing sleeve. Artfully, he arranged Lord Mabreton's clothing so that the bloodstain on the back was not visible.

'What do you intend to do with the body, my lord?' Silwyth asked.

'I will have it sent back to our homeland, where he can be given a proper burial. I will do his family no insult. I will not give his ancestors cause to haunt me or his House cause to rise up against me.'

'Yet they will see that he died of a knife wound in the back, my lord,' Silwyth observed.

'True.' The Shield turned to the guard carrying the body. 'When you are safely out of the palace, thrust your sword into the body from the front. Lord Mabreton died doing his duty, misguided though that duty was. We will grant him a soldier's death, that his family may receive him with honor.'

The guard bowed his head to indicate he understood.

'You, Silwyth, will have to show the guard the way out of this impossible place,' said the Shield.

'Yes, my lord. I will show him a passage that leads beneath the waterfalls and from there out by a secret route I have discovered. If anyone stops us, I will say that the lord is drunk. It would not be the first time.' He hesitated, glanced at the Shield as if he would say something more, then lowered his gaze.

'Speak, Silwyth,' said the Shield, smiling expansively. 'You have done me great service this day. I owe you an impertinent question or two.'

'I was wondering . . . Lady Mabreton . . .' Silwyth seemed embarrassed.

'The beautiful Lady Mabreton.' The Shield rested his hand upon Silwyth's shoulder. 'Lord Mabreton has an unmarried brother – recently widowed, I understand – who will no doubt be glad to take the lady for his wife. Do not worry. She will not be made to pay for her husband's follies.'

Silwyth nodded, relieved.

'She will accompany the body home,' the Shield continued. 'I spoke with her last night. The sudden death of her husband will come as no great surprise to her. Nor do I think she will be overwhelmed with grief. And now, I am already late for an appointment to meet His Majesty. I trust I will see you again during my visit, Silwyth?'

'If my duty to the young prince permits, my lord.' Silwyth bowed.

The Shield continued on down the corridor, accompanied by his guards. Silwyth went in the opposite direction, guiding the guard who bore Lord Mabreton's body.

'Silwyth murdered that man!' Gareth gasped, when the corridor was completely empty, when the last footfall could no longer be heard. 'He stabbed him – in the back! I saw his face!' He shuddered and put his hands before his eyes, to shut out the dreadful sight. 'I saw his face!'

'Stop it! You're behaving like some silly chambermaid screeching over a rat,' Dagnarus scolded. He pinched his friend's arm, hard. 'Put your head between your legs. You'll feel better. How I wish I understood elven,' he added, frustrated. 'What was that all about? What were they saying?'

'I don't know,' Gareth mumbled. 'I don't feel good.'

'Tell me, damn it!' Dagnarus gave Gareth a shake that forced him to lift his head. 'Tell me what they said.'

Dagnarus's face was pale, the green eyes burned, burned through the sick feeling in Gareth's stomach, burned through the shock and the horror.

'Tell me, Patch,' Dagnarus commanded. His voice was steady, he exerted a calming influence.

Gareth obeyed, as he was accustomed to obey.

'It was about the Sovereign Stone,' he answered, his voice shaking. 'The Divine wanted it for himself, I guess. This man is the Shield of the Divine and he thinks the stone should belong to him. The lord said that it belonged to the Divine and then . . . then . . .' Gareth gulped.

'So Silwyth works for the Shield,' Dagnarus muttered.

'Your father's going to be furious when he hears,' Gareth pointed out. 'He thought the Sovereign Stone was going to bring peace. Instead, this . . .'

'My father must never know about it,' Dagnarus said firmly. 'You will never tell anyone what we saw today. If you do, Patch' – the prince paused, searching his mind for the most dire threat he could find – 'if you do, I'll have you kicked out. I'll say you stole from me. I'll have your parents kicked out of court, too. Your family will be ruined. You'll be begging in the streets!'

Gareth stared, horror-numbed.

'I'll do it!' Dagnarus said in a tone that left no doubt. 'You know I can. You know I will. Promise me, Patch. Promise me that you will tell no one what we saw here today.'

'But, the man was murdered . . .'

'It's none of our concern. Promise me, Patch! Promise!'

'I promise,' Gareth said thickly.

'That's good.' Dagnarus petted his friend, as if rewarding an obedient dog. 'That's good. The news would have hurt and worried my father terribly. You wouldn't want that, would you?'

Gareth shook his head. He knew full well that Dagnarus wasn't the least bit concerned about hurting his father. This was something else, something Gareth didn't understand or want to understand.

'How will we face Silwyth?' Gareth asked miserably. 'How can I let him touch me after . . . after that.'

'Don't be silly!' Dagnarus said scornfully. 'Argot's killed hundreds of men, and you don't mind if he touches you.'

'It's not the same,' Gareth argued. 'He killed men in war.'

'This is war, Patch. Just a different kind of war. An elf kind of war. Come on. We're late as it is. Dunner will be wondering what happened to us.'

'Why are you staring at me, Gareth?' Silwyth asked that night, as he served the boys their dinner of rabbit *en casserole* and bread. 'Does my face suddenly displease you?'

Dagnarus kicked Gareth beneath the table.

Gareth lowered his head, stared instead at the meal, which he could not eat. He couldn't help himself. He had seen Silwyth kill a man in cold blood. Even an elf, Gareth thought, should show some residue of emotion after committing a deed as heinous as that. But Silwyth was as unruffled and unperturbed as ever. Dagnarus glared at his friend, reminding him of his promise. Gareth, pleading illness, went early to his bed.

But he could not sleep. Through his closed eyelids, he saw the face of the dying elf. He saw Silwyth's face, impassive, uncaring, as he plunged the knife into the man's back. In the next room, in Dagnarus's bedchamber, Gareth heard Silwyth's voice, calm, smooth, speaking to the prince, making him ready for bed.

Shivering in the darkness, Gareth wished the voices to be silent. But then he realized that if the voices fell silent, he would be utterly alone with the ghostly face of the dead elf. Gareth crept from his bed and pressed his body against the door. He could not enter the prince's chamber, not without arousing Dagnarus's scorn and perhaps even his anger. But Gareth needed to be as close as possible to the living, in order to banish the dead.

The prince was in his bed and Silwyth was pausing as he always did before leaving the prince for the night. The elf held a candle in his hand preparatory to withdrawing. Gareth could see the light beneath his door.

'Will there be anything else I may do for His Highness?' Silwyth asked, as he always asked.

'I hear that Lord Mabreton has left the court. Isn't his departure rather sudden and unexpected?' Dagnarus asked.

Gareth shuddered at the prince's temerity. He opened the door a crack, fearful that Silwyth – who had already committed one murder that day – might decide to compound it by murdering the prince.

Silwyth did not immediately answer. He gazed at Dagnarus, who met the elf's gaze, held it, sent it back.

'Not quite unexpected,' said Silwyth, breaking the long silence. 'He was given a choice, and he made it.' He paused another moment, then said, 'I wondered why Gareth looked at me so strangely at dinner, as if I might devour him. You two saw what happened?'

Dagnarus nodded. Gareth shut his eyes, fearing the worst.

Silwyth held the candle steady. The flame never wavered. 'Did you understand what you saw, Your Highness?'

'Not completely,' Dagnarus admitted. 'Patch doesn't speak elven all that well. I know that the Shield wanted to be the one to take the Sovereign Stone and that Lord Mabreton wanted to take it himself. Why did he have to die? Why didn't he just leave when the Shield wanted him to? Why didn't the Shield let him leave?'

'If he had left the palace without the Sovereign Stone, Lord Mabreton would have failed in his duty to the Divine. He would have lost face. He would have been forced to return home dishonored. In order to regain his honor, he and his House would have declared war upon the Shield and his House. The Divine, in order to avenge the insult given to his servant, Lord Mabreton, would have taken sides against the Shield. The elven nation would have been plunged into civil war. It is conceivable that because of the Portals, Vinnengael itself could have been drawn into the war. No one wins a civil war, Your Highness. The loss of life would have been incalculable.'

'My father believes the Sovereign Stone will bring peace to the world,' said Dagnarus. 'Yet one person has already died because of it.'

'The stone *has* brought peace, Your Highness. War has been averted. Peace will be maintained. The death of one has saved the lives of many. The lord's spirit will understand that, when he goes to join his ancestors. Do you plan to tell the King?'

Silwyth asked this quite casually, either certain of the answer or prepared to deal with any eventuality.

Dagnarus shook his head. 'No. I've told Patch to keep silent, as well. No matter what you say, my father would not understand. He would be distressed. He was already angry at the Revered Magi. He said if there was any more trouble or dissent over it, he would lock the Sovereign Stone away and never use it. And that would be a pity,' Dagnarus concluded softly. 'Have you seen the Sovereign Stone, Silwyth?'

'No, Your Highness, I have not had the honor,' Silwyth replied.

'I have,' said Dagnarus.

Gareth listened closely. The prince had said nothing to him of this. He'd said nothing to anyone.

'My father permitted me to hold it one day when we were practicing for the ceremony. I could feel the power within it, Silwyth. The diamond made my skin prickle the way you feel lightning about to strike near you. The hair on my arms rose, and my body tingled all over. It was frightening and thrilling, all at the same time.'

'You felt the power of the gods, Your Highness,' said Silwyth.

'Yes, I know. Such power should not be wasted. What will the elves do with their piece of the stone, Silwyth?'

'The Shield will take it to keep in the name of the Divine. The Shield will make Dominion Lords, who will act in the name of the Divine to keep the elven nation safe and who will work with your people, Your Highness, to promote the good of both great nations.'

'What will the dwarves and the orken do with their share of the stone, do you suppose?' Dagnarus mused.

'I have no idea, Your Highness,' Silwyth said disdainfully. 'Whatever they do, I cannot see that it will be of much importance to us.'

'I will ask Dunner,' said Dagnarus. Yawning, he snuggled down into his soft pillows. 'I will go to sleep now.'

'May Your Highness sleep well,' Silwyth said. He withdrew toward the door, taking the light with him.

'Silwyth,' Dagnarus called, as the elf had his hand upon the door handle.

'Yes, Your Highness?'

'My brother will inherit that power, won't he? He will inherit our part of the Sovereign Stone.'

'Yes, Your Highness. When he becomes King.'

Silwyth waited for Dagnarus to respond, but the prince was silent. Thinking that his charge had fallen asleep, Silwyth withdrew, softly shut the door, leaving the prince in darkness.

Dagnarus sighed, a sigh of frustration, a sigh of longing.

Once the brighter candlelight was withdrawn, moonlight was able to enter, stealing through the window like a ghost of the sun. Gareth, peeping through the door, could see the prince lying on his back in his bed, arms beneath his head, staring, frowning, into the moonlit darkness.

Gareth crept softly back to his own bed, wishing in his heart he had never heard that sigh. He lay down, afraid to close his eyes, fearful he would see once again the face of the dead elf.

But Lord Mabreton must have gone to his ancestors. He must have been rewarded for doing his duty, because Gareth never saw the elf's face again.

TWELVE

The Well of Darkness

EVARISTO WAS CONCERNED ABOUT HIS PUPIL the next day. Normally cheerful and eager to learn, Gareth was silent and preoccupied. He kept glancing sidelong at the door, and – when Evaristo proposed that they study the elven custom of ancestor-worship – Gareth shook his head violently and refused to open the book.

At length, Evaristo decided that Gareth was jealous of the attention being lavished upon Dagnarus, who was, of course, not there. The prince had gone to feed and water his horse, for Dunner had told him that performing such menial tasks for the animal, tasks usually left to stable hands, would create a bond of affection between horse and master.

It is only natural that the child feels neglected, thought Evaristo, who knew Gareth's parents. Adding to the child's jealousy at being left out was the bustle and turmoil and excitement pervading the palace, with dignitaries from all parts of Loerem arriving daily, celebratory parties every night.

The boy was probably dyspeptic, as well as envious. The ceremony was in six days' time, and Evaristo would be heartily glad when the ceremony was over and they could settle back down to normal. Meanwhile, he tried to think of something to do to win back the attention of his pupil.

'Gareth,' said Evaristo, and was startled to see the boy jump in his chair.

'Yes, Master?' Gareth lifted a wan face.

'Let us abandon our lessons today.' Evaristo slammed shut his book and shoved it to the center of the table. 'There are too many distractions. Neither of us can concentrate.'

'I am sorry, Master,' Gareth said. 'It's just –' He hesitated, looking at Evaristo doubtfully.

'Just what, Gareth?'

'Nothing.' Gareth sighed deeply.

Evaristo waited, but the boy remained silent.

It would do him good to talk about his feelings, Evaristo thought. But he must choose the time. Forced confidences would cause the boy to come to resent him.

'How would you like to spend the morning in the Royal Library?' Evaristo asked.

'Truly, Master?'

'Yes, truly,' Evaristo said, well pleased with the success of his suggestion.

Gareth's face had regained its color, his eyes brightened. He jumped to his feet energetically. 'May we go now?'

'Yes, at once. You know that there are rules to be followed,' Evaristo said, as the two walked through the corridors, usually empty, but now crawling with servants and bodyguards, dressmakers and cooks, scribes and secretaries and the occasional dignified personage, holding himself or herself aloof from it all.

'Yes, Master,' said Gareth, trying to maintain the dignity suitable to the occasion.

'You do not speak,' said Evaristo. 'That is the number one rule, and any infraction thereof will result in your being escorted out. If you have a question or you want information, you go to the head librarian, write your question upon a board placed there for the purpose, and receive your answer.'

Evaristo looked severe. 'It is commonly a joke among the novices to sneak up and write "Fire!" upon the board, but I trust you will not be tempted to emulate them.'

'No, Master, of course not,' said Gareth, shocked.

'Good.' Evaristo nodded with approval. 'The head librarian knows the location and contents of every book. That is his job. The books are grouped by category, all very ordered and logical, though it might not seem so at first. For example, you might expect to find a book on shipbuilding among the category for the orken, but such books have their own section. If, however, a book on orken superstitions happens to have a chapter on shipbuilding, you would find that in a different location. And if the book is written in the orken language and not the human, it would be in another location altogether.

'Don't worry,' said Evaristo, resting his hand upon his pupil's shoulder. Gareth was looking stunned, as if he were being pelted with rocks. 'It sounds very confusing, I know, but you will soon become accustomed to it. For today, walk around, familiarize yourself with the rooms. Be careful not to disturb anyone reading, although I do not believe there will be many in the Royal Library this day. Everyone is preparing for the ceremony. If you find a book you would like to read, remove it carefully from the shelf. Place one of the wooden blocks you will see stacked about the room on the shelf to hold the book's place. Carry the book to the head librarian, that he may see the title. Thus he knows who has the volume, in case anyone else requests it.'

The Royal Library was practically deserted. Not even Dunner was there. The head librarian, seated at a great podium, with the large blackboard on a stand next to him, frowned at the sight of a child entering his sanctum.

Evaristo wrote 'Scholar' upon the board. The librarian, who was a small and wizened man with a remarkably large head, undoubtedly to accommodate all the knowledge, gave an abrupt nod and went back to the volume he was perusing.

Evaristo selected a volume for himself and Gareth was left to gaze around in awe.

The peacefulness, the tranquillity spread like oil over his disturbed soul. The very air, smelling of leather and vellum and ink, seemed to be saturated with knowledge. Gareth had the feeling that he could absorb wisdom through his pores simply by standing in this wonderful place. Shelf after shelf was filled with books of every size and shape and description, all very confusing and overwhelming. The shelves reached to the ceiling, which was extremely high. A carved wooden ladder that rolled along the floor on well-greased, silent wheels permitted the dedicated scholar to reach the books on the topmost shelves.

Gareth did not know where to start. Conscious of the head librarian's distrusting gaze fixed upon him, Gareth wandered down the first row of shelves, reading the spines of the leather-bound volumes. So flustered and excited was he at first that he could not make sense of the titles. At length, he calmed down and the words on the spines came to have meaning for him. He was in a section devoted to books written in dwarven, apparently. He knew a smattering of the language, and could puzzle out the words on some of the books, but not on others.

It occurred to him that he might find a book on horses. He would read up on the subject and be able to amaze and impress Dagnarus with his knowledge. Gareth searched eagerly among the books. Dwarves have a great many words for 'horse,' but Gareth couldn't find a single book spine that used any of them. These seemed to all be about 'iron,' for he saw that particular word many times over.

The books about horses must be in another section, he realized.

He could, of course, go ask for the information, but every time he glanced up, the head librarian was staring at him with disapprobation, as if certain beyond doubt that here was a boy who would write 'Fire!' on the board. Gareth lacked the courage to brave the bulbous-headed librarian, and so he decided to try to find the books on his own. Logic seemed to dictate that they would be among the books on the dwarves. Gareth wandered down one aisle and up the next without finding a single one.

The dwarven books – astonishing how many books there were, from a race who, for the most part, had no use for such things – continued into the next room. Gareth followed the trail gladly, relieved to be away from the gimlet-eyed gaze of the head librarian.

Bookshelves filled this room completely. The reading tables were all located in the main room, where the librarian could keep an eye on the readers. Gareth came to the end of the dwarven books without finding a thing on horses, although he might have had better luck if he had not been too intimidated to actually remove a volume from the shelf. He would ask Evaristo the next time they came. For today, he gave himself up to the pleasant task of wandering among the stacks, happy in the mere possession, like a miser among his gold.

He did not notice the passage of time. He went from room to room, his hands clasped behind his back, looking at the titles at eye level and making mental notes of books he would like to read the next time he returned. The list grew until it seemed likely he would have material enough to keep him occupied into adulthood. He realized, with a thrill, that he had entered a room of books devoted to the study of magic.

There were no spellbooks in the room. Those were kept in the Temple of the Magi. But there were scholarly treatises on the magicks of all the races, their practice, their components, their nature.

In only two years, Gareth thought, I will be coming to this room on my own assigned studies. He imagined himself going directly to the book he wanted, removing it, and taking it to the head librarian, who would be suitably impressed by the young scholar's acumen.

Gareth indulged himself in this fantasy as he walked up and down the aisles. At length even this happy fantasy waned. He was tired and his neck ached from being tilted back to gaze at titles above him, titles that were starting to blur together. It was time to go back to Evaristo and yet, Gareth thought with a pang, he had not even so much as touched a single book.

He reached the end of an aisle and there, at the end of the very bottom shelf, in a shadowed corner, lay a slim volume bound in plain binding, much covered with dust. It had tipped over – being the last of a row – and lay on its side. The book seemed shabby and innocuous, obviously a book no one cared about, since they had not bothered to right it. Here was a book he could look at, a book he could pick up and hold and peruse, a book that didn't need a marker to hold its place, a book he didn't need to show the head librarian. Gareth picked up the slim volume, dusted it, sneezed, settled himself cross-legged on the floor – glad of the rest. He opened the book.

It was a disappointment. It was written in Elderspeak – the language of Vinnengael – but it might have been written in some elven subdialect for all he could fathom it. The book had to do with emptiness and death and magic, so far as he could make out, though what any of it had to do with any of the rest of it was beyond his ability to ascertain. Filled with a lot of big words, the book was boring in the extreme. There was only one picture, and it was of four mandalas, representing the four elements. Gareth recognized these because the symbols were quite popular and were used in patterns printed or sewn on cloth, in borders on tapestries, and were often added to the fronts of buildings, for it was believed that they brought luck to the house.

Usually the symbols were arranged in a straight line: an empty circle represented Fire, a circle with a dot in the center was Air, a circle with a line through it horizontally was Water, and a circle with one line running horizontal and another vertical, forming a cross, was Earth. In this book, the circles were not arranged in a straight line, but in opposition to each other. Thus Fire was opposite Water, Air was opposite Earth. In the center was a circle completely dark, so dark that it seemed as if there was a hole in the page. This was labeled 'the Void.' The writer went on to speak of death and blood and the soul and how the power of the elements must pass through the Void and what it meant when they did, none of which Gareth understood.

He knew about the Void, but not much, only that it was like sex – adults talked about it in whispers and frowned if the word was ever brought up in his presence. The Void was very wicked and had something to do with magic and death, but that was all he knew.

Nor did he particularly want to know more. The mention of death brought back full force the horror of the previous day, forgotten in the pleasant surroundings of the library. When a shadow fell over Gareth, he shuddered and knew that the dead elf had returned to demand that the boy speak out against his murder. But it was only Evaristo, come to find him.

Gareth replaced the book on the shelf, standing it upright – he could at least do that much for it, though to his mind it didn't deserve it.

'Time to go,' Evaristo mouthed.

Gareth nodded, ready for his supper. But he felt a sadness as he left the library, glanced back with wistful longing. As he and his tutor encountered a throng of noisy people, he regretted leaving the peace, the solitude.

'Did you enjoy yourself?' Evaristo asked.

'Oh, Master!' was all Gareth could say. 'Enjoy' seemed such a bald and inadequate word. 'When may we go back?'

'Perhaps we will go once a week,' Evaristo replied. Seeing his pupil look cast down, he added, 'We will make a list of questions you have throughout the week, and we will come here to answer them. I will help you find the books you require. What was that book you were looking at in the magic section?'

'I don't know,' Gareth said evasively. He didn't want to talk about the book, was sorry he had picked it up. His hands felt dirty; the dust stuck to his fingers. 'I could read the words, but they didn't make any sense.'

'Yes, I remember how frustrating that can be. Like you, I read as well as any adult when I was your age. Yet the books meant something to adults and nothing at all to me. You can only learn so much from the writing of other people, Gareth. Knowledge comes with experience and with years. You must be patient. You will learn eventually, learn too much, perhaps. Enjoy the innocence of childhood.'

Gareth smiled a little wistfully, and said, 'Yes, Master.'

THIRTEEN

The Gifting of the Sovereign Stone

THE CAPTAIN OF CAPTAINS, HE WAS CALLED. He was the leader of the orken, not only the political leader but the spiritual leader as well. He was old; the ship's bells that marked the watch had rung for him many, many times, so many that he had lost count.

Age was not important to the orken anyway. Only humans and elves bothered to measure off their years, as one measures length with a knotted rope. The orken consider it all nonsense. The cycles of life are far more important to the orken than the constant rising and setting of the sun. Birth, puberty, mating, childbearing, and finally the age of wisdom-sharing. Those are the only knots that count.

Some humans believe mistakenly that orken do not age, since one never sees an elderly, weak and feeble ork, an ork who has fallen into dotage. Orken live and die as do all other races. When an ork feels the feebleness of age setting in, he or she builds a raft, bids farewell to family and friends, and sets out to sea on the last great journey.

The bodies of orken who die at sea or on land are lashed to boards and given to the sea, where the sacred leviathans will make certain that the orken reach their destined location. No orken may be buried on land, and that is one reason orken prefer to live within sight of the sea or at the very least near some great river, which will carry their dead to the sea.

The Captain of Captains was in the Age of Wisdom, that age among the orken when the women no longer have the capability of bearing children and thus may go to sea themselves, the age when orken men lose the hair on their heads and are then granted the privilege of growing a beard. The Captain of Captains had a long full beard, which brushed his massive chest and which he decorated with small shells and beads, braided into the hair.

The Captain of Captains had come to Vinnengael to claim the orken portion of the Sovereign Stone, not because he believed King Tamaros's description of the stone's powers – humans, even the best of them, were notorious liars – but because the Captain suspected a trick.

Somehow, the humans were going to use this stone to attempt to control the orken. The Captain was there to see that this did not happen. He himself would take the human's stone, accept responsibility for the stone. He trusted no one else with the stone, and he didn't even much trust himself. He had given his mate stern orders that the moment he exhibited any strange and inexplicable behavior she was to bash him over the head and send him on the last journey. She would send the stone with him out to sea.

Because of the urgency of the situation, the Captain traveled through the Portal, something he did not ordinarily do. He would have much preferred to sail to Vinnengael in his own ship, but swift though that ship might be, she would never carry him there in time for the ceremony. He found traveling through the Portal cramped, confined, and – being out of sight of any body of water – uncomfortable. He and his crew hastened quickly through the gray rock that wasn't rock, running all the way.

By the time they reached the end, he was sweaty and panting, not from the run, which shouldn't even have had him breathing hard, but from the terrible feeling that the Portal was going to close in on him and digest him, this image coming to him from once having witnessed a snake devouring a rat whole. His crew felt the same. Many were staggering with fear by the time they arrived at Vinnengael.

Fortunately, the omens for the journey had been propitious – the sacred mountain had belched up clouds of steam the day the orken received word of the Sovereign Stone. Long lines of pelicans flying to the north further convinced the shaman that the orken were meant to follow. The Captain reminded his men of these omens to buck up their flagging spirits. This and a fight with the humans when they emerged from the Portal – the Captain told the Portal's keepers that he did not pay a fee, that he never paid fees, and that no human was going to make him pay a fee – did a great deal to improve the Captain's humor.

Human soldiers broke up the altercation. The fee was paid from the coffers of King Tamaros. The human soldiers gave the Captain an escort to the palace.

'Captain of Captains,' said King Tamaros, placing his hands on his hips and giving the short, abrupt nod that was the orken form of greeting. 'Welcome to Vinnengael. Your presence does us much honor.'

The Captain put his hands upon his hips and nodded.

Orken consider the human habit of clasping hands offensive. Orken touch each other only when expressing affection for a mate (and this only after the mating ceremony), when cradling a child (and this only until the child is old enough to move about freely on his own), helping a wounded ork, or fighting a worthy opponent. (Unworthy opponents are killed with weapons.) It is considered a mark

202

of honor for an ork to throttle you with his bare hands, an honor which is unfortunately rather lost upon the victim.

King Tamaros introduced the Shield of the Divine, who was accepting the Sovereign Stone in the name of the Divine. He introduced the dwarven Chief Clan Chief, who had been located and prevailed upon to attend.

The Captain nodded to the elf. The Captain nodded and smiled broadly at the dwarf. Orken like dwarves, considering them the only other race truly worthy of living in the same world as orken. Elves and humans had their place – mainly as a source of revenue. In general, both are considered inferior species who will die out in time, not from any act of aggression, but from their own stupidity.

'My sons, Crown Prince Helmos and Prince Dagnarus.'

The Captain did not nod. He regarded the crown prince with pity and a certain amount of impatience.

'The omens for this human were very bad – the sea catching fire,' the Captain announced. 'Yet you went on to make the man a Dominion Lord, one of your most powerful warriors. Now he is called "Lord of Sorrows." So typically human.' The Captain shook his head.

King Tamaros appeared to have developed a sudden deafness, for he did not seem to hear.

'Orken never know sorrow,' the Captain went on, speaking more loudly. 'Sorrow is curling up and whimpering helplessly when the gods deal you a blow. Better to regain your feet, shake your fist in defiance, and carry on.'

The Captain tapped himself on the chest. 'Among us orken, such an unlucky warrior as this Helmos would have been sent out of the tribe, sent to find a better omen somewhere else.'

Finding that polite deafness would not help, Tamaros tried to turn the subject. 'Prince Helmos has roots,' the King said. 'His roots are here in his homeland.'

'Roots!' The Captain snorted. 'We orken do not have

roots. Nor do you humans. Trees have roots. We have feet and we have them for a reason – choice. A tree has no choice. It must live where its seed falls. Suppose the tree's growth is being stunted by living in the shade of a larger, stronger tree? It cannot move. Suppose it thirsts for water it cannot reach? The tree is doomed. It cannot pick itself up and walk off to find a better location. Yet you humans speak of "roots" as something good, something to be valued.

'Not the orken, nor yet the dwarves,' said the Captain, grinning at Dunner. 'If life is not good where you are, pack up and move. Someplace the sun shines more brightly, the water flows more freely. You need only find it.'

'Perhaps,' said King Tamaros politely. 'But the crown prince has a responsibility to his people. He is destined to be their King.'

'Whale blubber!' said the Captain. 'Let someone else be King. You humans are always wanting to be King. Let someone be King who wants to be King, if that is what will make him happy. Like this young princeling here.

'*You* want to be King, don't you,' said the Captain to Dagnarus. 'None of this sorrowing business for you.'

The orken was following his own trail of thoughts. He said nothing more than what everyone must already know, yet his words sent a ripple of dismay through the room. King Tamaros frowned and looked severe. This had gone far enough.

'Prince Dagnarus is fully aware of the position of the second son, Captain,' said the King in rebuking tones. 'He knows that his elder brother will be King someday, and he gives Helmos his full support.'

The princeling stood with his head down, his eyes demurely lowered as was thought proper with young human children. 'Truly, Captain, I do not want to be King. For that would be to wish some mischance to befall my brother, and that would be terrible. The gods would punish me for such a wicked wish.'

But the Captain wasn't fooled. He'd seen the glint in those green eyes. Lies, all lies, and everyone knew it. Humans lied constantly – to each other and, what was worse, to themselves. Orken never lie. What they say is the truth, for that moment, at least. If circumstances change, a new truth could develop, in which case it may seem that the old truth was a lie, but the orken know the difference. It is not their fault if others do not.

The Captain glanced about the room, which was enclosed, windowless. He could not see outdoors and was beginning to feel stifled. That night the tide would be at its full. Good sailing. He would take advantage of it.

'Give me my portion of the rock, then,' the Captain said. 'Tell me what to do with it, supposing I choose to do anything with it, except toss it to the fish, and I will be on my way. We sail with tonight's tide.'

Again, his words tossed everyone into consternation. The humans were aghast. He could not have the *Sovereign Stone*. It was the Sovereign Stone, not 'a rock.' And what did he mean by 'tossing it to the fish'? This was a sacred treasure! Surely he knew its value!

'How can I? I have not seen it, yet,' the Captain stated, starting to grow angry. 'This rock belongs to the orken, doesn't it? That's what your messenger said. The gods gave it to you humans to give to the orken. And thus the orken may do with it what they choose, and if that means throwing it into the ocean or into the bowels of the sacred mountain, that is what we will do. So, King Tamaros, *if* the rock is ours, then hand it over now.'

The dwarves were laughing, Dunner having translated the ork's words to his chief. The elf, the Shield, stood silent and aloof, looking bored. Ministers and other human minnows swarmed about the Captain, yammering away.

He paid no attention to the small fry. He fixed his gaze upon the King and kept it there.

'Captain,' said King Tamaros, striving for patience, 'the Sovereign Stone indeed belongs to the orken. When you see it and touch it, you will feel its magical power and you will know how to use it to help your people. Since it is a gift from the gods, we must honor the gods with ceremony and prayer, just as you do before you set sail, to assure that the gods grant you a swift and a prosperous voyage.'

The Captain was impressed. He had heard that King Tamaros was a wise human, but he had discounted that until now. He was surprised that Tamaros knew about the orken prayer ceremony, surprised that Tamaros appeared to respect it. The Captain was also surprised to find that what the human said made sense.

'Very well,' said the Captain, grudgingly. 'When is this ceremony?'

'It will be held tomorrow,' said the King. 'In the Temple.'

The Captain frowned. He would miss the tide, but he supposed it could not be helped. There would always be another tide, however; upon that the orken could count.

'I will be there,' he said. 'Provided the omens are good. If not' – he shrugged – 'I will not be there. And now, I need food to fill my belly.'

Once more, ripples marred the surface. Concern on every face, except for those of the dwarves, who were chuckling into their beards. The elf actually permitted himself to think about smiling.

'It is not yet time –' King Tamaros began.

'Bah!' The Captain had had enough.

Already frustrated by the doltishness of humans, he was not going to be starved into the bargain. He turned on his heel and stalked out, intending to return to the orken part of the city, where he would be fed, no matter what time it was.

The next morning, while he was breaking his fast – dining on fish offal soup and hardtack – the Captain sent for the local shaman to read the omens. The shaman came at once, her skin glistening from the rain, for a steady downpour was deluging the city of Vinnengael.

Seating herself without ceremony opposite the Captain, the shaman accepted his offer of soup and ate heartily, with the slurping sounds that indicated her approval of the meal. Shoving her bowl to one side, to indicate she was finished, the shaman, whose name was Morga, began to read the omens.

'There was thunder in the night,' she said. 'That is a bad sign. But the boats that went out fishing this morning returned with an excellent catch – four full barrels. Four dolphins accompanied them, rubbing up against the sides of the boat. An albatross circled the main mast four times. These are all good signs.'

The Captain nodded, to show he was aware of this. 'So what do you think, Shaman? Should I go to the ceremony? Should I receive this rock? I do not like the thunder in the night, nor yet the rain that pours upon us like the gods pumping out their bilge.'

'Thus I read the omens, Captain,' said Morga. 'The thunder and the rain are indeed bad, but, since our catch this day was good, the bad omens are not meant for us. If they had been, we would have cast out our nets and brought them in empty. The omens say you should attend the ceremony. Now, for this rock. It will, so you say, be divided into four parts. We have four dolphins, the four circles of the albatross, the four barrels of fish. The omens say that – *as of now*' – she emphasized the words – 'you should take the fourth part of this rock.'

'As of now?' The Captain regarded her dubiously.

'We must be watchful, Captain,' Morga cautioned. 'The rain continues to fall. The omens are subject to change. We must make certain that the thunder is not meant for us.'

'Of course. You will come with me to the ceremony,' said the Captain.

'Aye, sir,' replied the shaman.

The ceremony was fully as long and as boring as the Captain had expected. Not only that, but he was forced to sit on a raised platform near the altar, which meant that the hundreds of humans who would be on hand to witness the ceremony would stare straight at him. The only entertaining part so far had been an altercation between himself and the magus who was in charge of the ceremony, about whether or not the shaman was to remain at his side.

The magus said that the shaman's presence was not wanted, she was not a dignitary, there weren't enough chairs, and she could not stand, not when the King was seated – all arrant nonsense, of course. The Captain glanced around the stage, spotted a table and a massive oak chair next to it. Since no one was using the chair, he hefted the chair, lugged it across the stage, and plunked it down beside his own chair. Motioning, he ordered the shaman to sit.

The magus nearly fainted. The chair belonged to the Most Revered High Magus! No one else could use it! He must put it back!

The Captain was angry. A chair was a chair. One placed one's ass in it. Was the ass of this magus something special that it required a special chair? Did this magus consider his ass better than the ass of the shaman?

This brought uproarious laughter from the dwarves. Indeed, the dwarven chieftain was forced to retire to the wings of the stage where his bodyguards slapped his back to help him recover his breath. The young princeling grinned and, at a stern glance from an attendant elf lord, ducked his head to hide his grin in his frilled collar.

The Most Revered High Magus arrived on deck.

'The shaman may use my chair and welcome,' Reinholt said graciously. 'I am honored to be able to offer it to her. Another will be brought for me.'

This foolishness settled, the doors were opened and the lords and ladies of the court, plus as many of the common people as could be allowed, filed inside. The building began to stink of humans, and the Captain resigned himself to his fate, pleased that he had thought to rub his own skin with fish oil to obviate the stench.

The Captain dozed through the prayers and the speeches, waking only now and then to glance at the shaman to see if there had been any omens of note. Each time he looked at her, she only shrugged, rolled her eyes, and shook her head. No omens. But then what did one expect, cooped up inside a building, shutting out the natural elements, which spoke clearly to those who knew how to listen. The Captain could hear the rain beating like war drums upon the Temple's roof.

Did the humans really expect the gods to take time off from their work sailing the vessel of the world to listen to all this? With no hand at the wheel, the ship of the world would have wandered aimlessly or run aground or smashed up against a lee shore. The orken know and respect the fact that the gods are busy. When the orken speak to the gods, which they do only by the most dire necessity, they keep it short.

The Captain dozed off again.

He woke to the shaman's elbow digging into his rib cage.

He sat up straight, alert. King Tamaros stood before the altar, where rested the rock, covered by a purple velvet cloth trimmed in gold. The princeling, Dagnarus, stood beside his father at the altar. The King reached out his hand and plucked off the velvet cloth.

The Captain was impressed.

The humans had termed this a 'stone,' which he equated

with 'rock' – a word which seemed to irritate the humans when he used it. A better term would have been 'jewel.' If only the humans had said they were giving him a jewel, he might have taken this matter more seriously.

The Sovereign Stone was truly one of the most beautiful jewels the Captain had seen in his long lifetime. A perfect pyramid, the diamond's smooth sides danced with rainbows.

The shaman sighed and smiled and nodded. So far, the omens were good. Very good.

But still it rained. The Captain remained watchful.

King Tamaros held his hand over the Sovereign Stone. His prayer was short and to the point. The Captain approved it.

'I, Tamaros, King of Vinnengael, call upon the gods to divide this, the Sovereign Stone, that by its division we four races may be one.'

The Captain felt the power of the gods surround the King. Awed, the Captain held his breath. The shaman lowered her head in reverence. There came a sound as of bells chiming, four different notes, all sublime. At each stroke of the bell-like chime, a split occurred in the stone. The pyramid opened, like a flower. Four crystal points glittered in the light of the altar candles.

The audience sighed. Those onstage were overawed, even the elves, who made no attempt to hide their wonder.

King Tamaros offered a prayer of thanksgiving – which the Captain again approved, feeling it was no more than the gods deserved. The king lifted one of the diamond points from the altar and, holding it high, so that all could see, said in a strong voice, 'The gods give this part of the Sovereign Stone to our friends and brothers, the elves.'

He handed the diamond point to the princeling.

Dagnarus's eyes were wide. He was very pale with the solemnity of the ceremony and the weight of his responsibility. Accepting the diamond, he turned, and with slow and solemn step, he carried the diamond to the Shield of the Divine.

So moved was the Shield that, smoothing his robes, he sank to his knees.

'In the name of the Divine, I, the Shield of the Divine, accept the Sovereign Stone. May our ancestors carry our thanks to the gods for this gift.'

The princeling took the next diamond point to the dwarves.

The dwarven chieftain did not kneel. Dwarves bend the knee to no one, not even the gods. The dwarven chief eyed the crystal askance; dwarves are very leery of magic. He wanted it, mainly because the others were each receiving a portion and also because it was his by right. But he was loath to touch it.

The audience began to murmur. The princeling's cheeks flushed red. He glanced at his father from beneath his lashes to see what might be done. The Most Revered High Magus gave a gentle, remonstrative cough, completely lost on the dwarf, who, accustomed to thundering hooves, would react to no less a signal than a horn blast. At length, the dwarf solved the problem by making an abrupt gesture with his hand, a gesture that passed the diamond off to Dunner of the Unhorsed.

Dunner smiled at the princeling; obviously he liked the boy. The Captain noted this and chalked up a mark in the princeling's favor. Dagnarus smiled when he handed the crystal to Dunner, who received it in the name of his chief with a bow of his head and fervent, almost incoherent thanks to the gods. Dunner – the Captain saw – held the diamond tightly, as a drowning ork holds on to the lifeline. A tear trickled down the dwarf's weathered cheek and was lost in his beard. Dunner stared straight ahead, but it was obvious he saw nothing of what was happening. The dwarf chieftain nodded, relieved.

Now it was the turn of the orken. The Captain rose to his feet, a formidable, powerful presence. Dagnarus carried carefully the diamond point, brought it to the Captain, who paid little attention to the human child. The Captain stared intently at the diamond jewel. Unlike the dwarf, the ork longed to pick up the precious object, to claim it in the name of his people, but the question of the bad omens had still not been answered. The rain was falling even harder outside. He looked at the shaman.

She sat in the chair of the Revered High Magus, a tight fit, for she was an orken female of a husky build, and gazed long at the crystal. She could hear the rain, the building seemed to shake with it. At length, lifting her eyes, she looked at the Captain, sighed, and gave a nod.

The Captain took the diamond into his hands.

'Thank you, gods,' he said, and sat down.

Someone in the audience, overwrought, giggled.

The Captain held the jewel gingerly, as he might hold a sea urchin, fearful of hidden barbs. He had felt magic before in holy objects – in the stones thrown forth from the sacred mountain. Such stones are revered by the orken. They are worn as amulets, carried aboard ships, and used in healing. He had never felt the power as strongly as in this wondrous jewel, which sent a tingling sensation – odd but not unpleasant – from his hands through his arms, to his heart and from there to the rest of his body. He felt exhilarated and suffused with energy, uplifted. If he had wished it, he could have flown into the air with the grace of a seabird. Visions raced past the backs of his eyes, too many to comprehend. If he closed his eyes and concentrated, he would be able to distinguish among them, but he couldn't do that yet. He had to watch for the omen, the final omen.

The last portion of the jewel would go to the humans, represented by Crown Prince Helmos, Lord of Sorrows. Dagnarus took the last quarter of the diamond and carried

212

it to his brother. The child was beautiful, the crown prince a comely man. There was little family resemblance in reality, but the audience wished there to be and they cooed and sighed as the brothers stood facing each other. Dagnarus smiled up at his older brother, who smiled down fondly upon him.

Dagnarus lifted the Sovereign Stone. Helmos reached to take hold of it.

No one could say, afterward, what happened. Helmos's palms were wet with sweat, causing the stone to slip. Dagnarus said that his arms were beginning to tire from the strain of being so careful with the diamond, causing his hand to jerk unexpectedly.

No one was to blame, said King Tamaros. It was an accident, nothing more.

As Dagnarus handed his brother the Sovereign Stone and as Helmos reached to take it, the crystal point sliced into his flesh.

The cut was small. Most people in the audience never saw it, never noticed that anything was amiss, for Helmos covered his fumble well, while Dagnarus steadied the diamond to keep it from falling. Several drops of blood stained the jewel, however; blood visible to the Captain and his shaman, if no one else.

Swiftly, under cover of his speech thanking the gods and also thanking King Tamaros, who had interceded with the gods on behalf of all those present, Helmos wiped the blood from the stone on the sleeve of his tunic, where the stain was lost amidst the rich pattern of embroidery. The ceremony proceeded, Helmos saying everything that was gracious and proper. Not even the Most Revered High Magus had noticed the slip.

The shaman had seen it, however. She turned to the Captain, an exultant gleam in her eyes. She nodded vigorously several times and even reached across to clout him violently on the upper forearm, an extremely rare expression acknowledging a victory or some other event worthy of congratulation.

Outside the rain poured down steadily, thunder rolled. The Captain paid the storm scant attention. He could take his quarter of the Sovereign Stone home to the orken land with a clear conscience.

The bad omen had come, but it had come to the humans.

The Captain hoped to leave with the next tide, but there was still the possibility of one more ceremony. He considered trying to avoid it, but the Captain had been present at the incident. By orken law he was a witness and might be called upon to tell what he had seen.

A grand celebration was held in the palace following the Gifting, as it was being called. The Captain and the shaman had little use for human celebrating, which was not celebrating as far as the orken were concerned. Any orken party that did not end with bloodshed and mayhem was considered a dismal failure. The Captain and the shaman were eager to return to their own people, where they could eat a proper meal and fling the empty flagons at the heads of their neighbors. But the Captain had a duty to perform first. He made his way through the crowd – which parted before him with alacrity, the fish oil was ripening – and confronted King Tamaros.

Having no time to waste – the Captain was exceedingly hungry – he grasped hold of the shoulder of a courtier who was monopolizing conversation with the King and flung the man to one side.

'King Tamaros,' the Captain said, his voice cracking among them louder than the thunder, 'when do you kill the boy?'

'What?' King Tamaros stared at the Captain in perplexity. 'What are you talking about, Captain of Captains?'

'The boy.' The Captain jerked a thumb toward the princeling. 'When do you kill him?'

His mother, the Queen, who was seated nearby, gave a scream and clutched the prince, who wriggled, embarrassed, in her grasp. 'The monster!' she cried. 'Call the guards!'

Tamaros cast her a glance, which silenced her, and turned to the Captain.

'You must explain yourself, Captain.'

'When do you kill him?' the ork said for the third time, speaking even more loudly. He had forgotten that the King was deaf. 'Now would be best, but perhaps you want to wait until he has a full belly.'

'Captain, you must be mistaken. I have no intention of killing my son,' said Tamaros.

Humans. A stickler for words.

'Well, the priests, then,' said the Captain impatiently. 'When do *they* kill him? If they want us as witnesses' – he gestured to the shaman and himself – 'then they had best do this fast. I sail with the next tide.'

'No one is going to kill my son,' said King Tamaros, and his voice had a hard edge. He took hold of Dagnarus, who had squirmed out of his mother's grasp. Tamaros encircled the boy protectively with his arm. He had never loved his son as much as he loved him at that moment, or perhaps until that moment he had never before realized how much he did love the child of his old age. 'I don't understand, Captain. How did you conceive such a strange idea?'

'Not a strange idea,' the Captain replied patiently. One had to deal with humans as one dealt with little children. 'The omens for you are very bad. Blood spilt between brothers. You must kill one or the other to ensure stability. I assume that you will kill the younger, who has not yet cost you so much to raise and who is, therefore, of less value to you than the elder.'

'Thank you for your concern, Captain,' said King Tamaros, stiffly polite, his tone formal and cool. 'But we humans are civilized. We do not kill our children.

215

May your voyage be safe and prosperous.' Tamaros turned away.

The Captain regarded the King in astonishment, finding it difficult to believe that even humans could be so obtuse.

'Did you not see the omen?' the Captain cried, but King Tamaros did not appear to hear him.

His Majesty's guards stepped between the King and the Captain, suggesting that it was time the orken left, he'd had as much to drink as was good for him. The Queen was screaming in a shrill voice that she'd never encountered such barbarians and would someone please make these repulsive monsters, who stank of fish, leave her party. Tamaros kept fast hold of Dagnarus, fearful perhaps that the Captain might seize the boy and carry out the death sentence himself.

The Captain had no intention of wasting his time. If the humans chose to ignore the omens, that was their business. The problem was not his. He had the Sovereign Stone, a most precious and holy object. He would return home and begin to study how it might be used to help his people. Shoving the guards out of his way with such force that they smashed a table or two and started all the women screaming in terror, the two orken left the palace.

The moment they walked outdoors the rain ceased, the tattered clouds blew away. The stars, whose bright and steadfast light guide the orken over the ocean by night, guided them unerringly through the confusing levels and streets of Vinnengael, back to the sea.

FOURTEEN

The Bitter Center

THE EARLY-SUMMER RAIN FELL THE NEXT day and the day after that, enclosing the castle in a gray wall of water. Everyone was in an equally gray mood, experiencing the vague and disquieting depression brought about by the fact that the ceremonies were over, the illustrious personages and their entourages had returned to their respective kingdoms, the time of feasting and revelry was at an end. The rain was a presage of the gray monsoon days to come, when the clouds rolled in from the sea and soaked the land. Helmos's wedding was anticipated, but not until fall, so there was nothing to look forward to for a while except more rain.

Dagnarus was in a particularly bad mood, wandering around the castle like a caged animal. The prince was not daunted by the rain, and would have ridden his horse through nothing less than a hurricane gale, but he had no companion and now no horse. Dunner was laid up in bed, unable to walk. His twisted leg hurt abominably in wet weather. Dagnarus's horse had developed a swelling in its left foreleg, which Dunner said was not serious, but which must be rubbed several times daily with liniment, and under no circumstances, was the horse to be ridden.

Dagnarus treated his horse himself, but even he could spend only so much time in the stables. Bored, he would return smelling of manure and wintergreen, to be hustled off to the bath by Silwyth.

The soldiers were out on maneuvers, which took away another of Dagnarus's amusements. He had pleaded to be allowed to go with them but, in this instance, his mother had been unusually firm in her denial and King Tamaros had refused to consider it.

'I find it hellish growing old, Patch,' complained Dagnarus, from the ancient vantage point of his ten years. 'If I were little, I could throw a tantrum and bawl my eyes out and Mother would do anything I asked. I can't do that now.'

'Why not?' Gareth asked.

'Because soldiers don't whine and cry, no matter what happens to them,' Dagnarus returned. 'Not even if they take an arrow in the gut. If I threw a fit, Argot would hear of it, and he'd be disappointed in me. I thought about running away, stowing myself in the supply wagon until they were a long way off, too far to bring me back. But Argot said that would only get *him* into trouble, and so, of course, I couldn't do it.'

Gareth sighed. He had taken a lot of abuse, both verbal and physical, from the prince in the last few days, ever since the ceremony, and wistfully hoped that Dagnarus would find something to occupy his bored mind.

The two were in the playroom. They had finished breakfast; Silwyth was supervising the cleaning of the prince's room and attending to his other chores. Evaristo would arrive soon to begin Gareth's lessons. Gareth wasn't looking forward to the tutor's coming as much as usual. The past two days, Dagnarus had been so bored he'd actually remained in the room with the two of them, mainly for the sake of companionship, not because he had any intention of pursuing his studies. Gareth could take no pleasure in his lessons with the prince seated opposite, moping and scowling and kicking the table leg.

Dagnarus roved about the playroom on a vain quest for something to do. Gareth, sighing again, pulled over a sheet of foolscap and, taking up his pen, began to practice making the graceful letters of the elven alphabet. His hand was wobbly and so, therefore, were the letters. Evaristo was certain to say his writing was a disgrace, but Gareth persevered and was soon so absorbed by his task that he forgot the prince's presence. When Dagnarus spoke from right behind Gareth, the boy was so startled that he dropped the pen, making a large splotch on the paper.

'It's that damn stone, Patch,' said Dagnarus. 'I keep dreaming about it.'

'What stone?' Gareth asked, twisting in his chair.

Dagnarus stood over him, hands curled around the chair's ornately carved back, fingers clenched so tightly the knuckles were white.

'The Sovereign Stone, fool,' Dagnarus said scathingly. 'What other stone is there? I dream of it whenever I go to sleep.' His voice dropped. 'The dreams are very strange, Patch.'

'Scary?' Gareth asked. He had never seen Dagnarus so intense about anything.

'No,' said Dagnarus after a moment's pause. 'In a way, maybe. Disturbing.' He paused again. 'And exciting.' He sat down beside Gareth. 'I don't like the dreams, Patch. They make me feel . . . restless. I can't sit still. I keep thinking I should be doing something, but I don't know what. The dream wants something from me, Patch. And I can't give it. At least, I don't think I can, because I don't understand what it wants. But at the same time – and here's the exciting part, Patch – I know that if I give the dream what it wants, it will give me something back. Something wonderful. Just when I think I have it, I wake up and feel so frustrated I want to hit something.'

Having been on the receiving end of the prince's frustration, Gareth knew Dagnarus was in earnest. So much in earnest that Gareth felt frightened and uncomfortable. He didn't want to hear any more and wished Evaristo would come, but the tutor was late, probably on account of the rain.

Hoping to end the conversation, Gareth picked up his pen, dipped it in the ink, and started to return to his letters. To his astonishment, Dagnarus snatched the pen from his hand, pulled the foolscap over in front of himself.

'Look at this,' he said, drawing with quick, bold strokes, strokes so impatient that the pen spluttered in his hand, the point dug into the paper. 'This idea came to me during the ceremony. I was standing there when my father caused the Sovereign Stone to separate into the four segments. He wasn't looking at it, he was giving thanks to the gods. But I was looking at it, Patch, and this is what I saw.'

Dagnarus had drawn four circles, the four circles that represented the four elements. But he had not drawn them in a straight line, as was customary. He had drawn them in opposition to each other, one at each of the cardinal points. And he had made a black mark in the center, jabbing it so hard with the pen that the point broke.

'That's me,' he said, tossing aside the useless pen and pointing at the center mark with an ink-stained finger. 'That's me, standing in the middle. Do you know what, Patch?' His voice vibrated with excitement. 'If you stand here, in the center of this circle' – he moved his finger to one of the outer mandalas – 'the one that represents Fire, you'd look around you and what would you see?'

He answered his own question. Gareth – staring at the drawing – was incapable of speech.

'You'd see nothing but the circle that surrounds you. Same if you stand in the center of Air and the center of Earth and the center of Water. But if you stand here, in the center of all four circles, where it's empty, what do you see? Every single one of the other circles! And what's interesting is this – no one standing in any of the other circles can see me. Because I'm hidden here.' He stuck the broken pen point into the circle, pressed hard, digging it deeper.

'Give me that!' A hand reached down from above the boys and plucked the foolscap from the table.

Startled, Gareth looked up to see Evaristo bending over them. The tutor's face was livid. He looked angrier than Gareth ever remembered seeing him, angry and disturbed and shaken.

'Who put this idea into your head?' Evaristo demanded, his voice quivering. He glared at Dagnarus. 'Answer me! Who told you about this?' Crumpling the foolscap in his hand, he shook the paper beneath the prince's nose.

Dagnarus's cheeks flushed crimson. He rose slowly and with dignity to his feet, fixed his imperious gaze upon the pale and furious tutor. 'You forget yourself, Magus. How dare you speak to me in that tone? I am your prince.'

Evaristo seethed. For a terrible moment, Gareth thought the tutor might actually seize hold of the prince and shake him. At this tense juncture, Silwyth glided silently into the room, stood silently by, prepared to intervene should it become necessary. The sight of the elf appeared to restore Evaristo to his senses.

He went ashen, even his lips lost their color. He made a mumbled apology. 'I am not well, Your Highness,' he said, and, indeed, his brow was covered with sweat. 'I beg your indulgence. If I might be excused from my duties this day –'

Dagnarus appeared to consider it, then he gave an abrupt nod. 'You may go. And,' he added magnanimously, 'I hope you will soon feel better.'

Evaristo made a faint reply. Still carrying the crumpled foolscap in his fist, he walked unsteadily to the door, exchanging barbed glances with Silwyth on the way out.

'I trust Your Highness has suffered no harm,' said Silwyth, coming forward.

'None at all,' said Dagnarus, smiling impishly. He had enjoyed himself. He might be a prince, but he was also a child, and it was not often that the child, even a prince, could so thoroughly humble and intimidate an adult.

'The tutor carried away a sheet of paper with him. Is it Your Highness's wish that I retrieve it?'

Dagnarus shrugged. 'It was just a scribble. Nothing important. I can't think what could have set the man off. Can you, Patch?'

Gareth made no reply. He stared, as if fascinated, at an ink dot left behind on the table, made when Dagnarus jabbed the pen through the paper.

Dagnarus regarded his friend speculatively, then said abruptly, 'That is all, Silwyth. You may go.'

Silwyth bowed and retired, though slowly and with obvious reluctance.

'Well, Patch, I have earned you a holiday,' Dagnarus said loudly. He was now in an excellent mood. Leaning over, he whispered in Gareth's ear. 'What is it? What's the matter?'

Gareth cast a guarded glance at the door. Moving closer to the prince, Gareth whispered, 'I've seen a drawing like that before!'

'You have?' Dagnarus was disappointed, having fondly imagined he had conceived this idea himself. He frowned. 'Where?'

'The Royal Library,' said Gareth. 'In a book of magic.'

'Magic!' Dagnarus's interest and good humor were restored. 'No wonder Evaristo looked like a bee flew up his ass! What did it say? Tell me, Patch!'

Gareth was sorry to destroy the prince's hopes. 'I don't know,' he said shamefacedly. 'I couldn't understand any of it. The book had a lot about death and emptiness and that picture was in there, too. The book gave me gooseflesh. I wanted to run off and wash my hands. It has something to do with the *Void*.'

He said that last word in a ghastly, impressive whisper, hoping this would discourage the prince. Gareth didn't like the look on Dagnarus's face – eager and excited and intense.

'You must find that book again, Patch. You must show it to me.'

Gareth shook his head. He lowered his gaze to the ink spot on the table. 'I can't,' he lied. 'I don't remember where it is. The library is enormous. You can't imagine how many books. I couldn't take it from the library anyway. They won't allow – Ouch! You're hurting me.'

Gareth tried to break free of the prince's grip, but Dagnarus was strong, stronger than the whipping boy, and had his hand clenched around Gareth's thin arm. 'You will find it,' said Dagnarus. 'You will find it, and you will show it to me.'

The pain was unbearable. Gareth feared the prince might break his arm.

'Yes, Your Highness,' Gareth whimpered, swallowing.

Dagnarus relaxed his grip. 'I'm sorry I hurt you. I didn't mean to, but you mustn't say no to me, Patch. When I tell you to do something, you must do it. Not so much because I'm your prince, but because you're my friend and you love me. Isn't that true, Patch?'

Gareth averted his head, surreptitiously wiped away all trace of his tears, and nodded.

Dagnarus patted his friend on the arm where the white marks of his grasp, now reddening, could be seen quite clearly.

'I'm sorry I hurt you,' he said again.

Evaristo walked bare-headed into the rain without even knowing that he did so, so distraught that he forgot to pull the hood of his cloak over his head. Only when water began

223

to run down the back of his tunic did he think of the hood, and then he discarded the notion. The rain was cooling to his fevered skin, actually felt good. And it brought him to his senses.

Entering the Temple, he paused in the entryway to shake the water from his cloak and to reflect on his actions – past and future. As to the past, he was not particularly proud of that. He had lost his head, admittedly. Hopefully nothing would come of it. As to the future . . .

One of the novices, passing through, saw Evaristo dripping wet and kindly went to fetch him a towel. The tutor mopped his sopping hair, gazed ruefully at the wet cuffs of his robes, the mud-spattered hem, and his generally bedraggled appearance. Not the way most people looked when they requested an audience with the Most Revered High Magus. But then, this was an emergency. At least he'd kept the foolscap dry, tucked safely between the leaves of a book he'd intended to give Gareth.

The Most Revered High Magus was in conference, of course, and could not be disturbed. Evaristo had expected nothing less. He sat in the waiting room, glad for the brief respite, glad to dry off and try to sort out his thoughts. He did not make much headway.

At length, the conference ended. The other magi walked out of the chamber. Several, who knew Evaristo, greeted him pleasantly and would have stayed to talk, but the High Magus's secretary came for him at that moment. His friends gazed after him in wonder and concern. The tutor, they said among themselves, looked extremely ill.

The Most Revered High Magus received his unexpected and unscheduled visitor with cordial politeness, steering Evaristo to a seat by the fire and offering to send his servant for a change of dry clothing. Evaristo was thankful for the attention, but could not spare the time.

'The matter is urgent, High Magus,' he said, 'or I would not have appeared before you in such a state, bringing the wet into your office. I thought you should see this immediately.'

'Yes, Magus,' said Reinholt, looking mystified and somewhat alarmed. He knew Evaristo, not well, but enough to know that the man was not one to jump at shadows. 'What is it?'

Evaristo produced the book, laid it on Reinholt's desk. The book opened of its own accord to the page where he had placed the foolscap. The tutor withdrew the drawing and laid it before the High Magus.

Reinholt frowned. 'I had hoped the old religion was dead. Apparently it has resurfaced. Well, we shall have to deal with it.' He looked up at Evaristo. 'Where did you come by this? Who made this drawing?'

Evaristo drew in a deep breath, let it out along with the responsibility that had lain so heavily upon his shoulders. 'Prince Dagnarus, Your Worship.'

Reinholt stared. His gaze went back to the foolscap, his frown deepened. 'That is not good,' he said, his voice low and troubled. 'That is not good at all. Please, sit down, Evaristo. When did this occur?'

'Just this morning. I came immediately.' Evaristo sank thankfully into a chair opposite the High Magus's desk.

'Tell me exactly what transpired,' said Reinholt in firm tones, intended to calm the distraught tutor. 'But first, how certain are you that the prince drew . . . this.' He waved his hand at the foolscap, loath to name it.

'I am sure,' Evaristo said, sighing. 'I saw him drawing something when I entered the room. I had no intention of surprising him, but he was so absorbed in his work he did not hear me come in. I stood over him and watched him place the point of his pen in the center circle. I heard him say . . .' Evaristo paused, to refresh his memory and to try to calm his shaking voice. '"But if you stand here, in the center of all four circles, where it's empty, what do you see? Every single one of the other circles. And no one standing in any of the other circles can see me. Because I'm hidden here."'

'He said that. You are certain.'

'Yes, Your Worship.'

'And what did you do?'

Evaristo flushed. 'I – I lost my head. "Give me that!" I cried, and I snatched it from his hand. Then I demanded to know how he had come by it, who had showed it to him.'

'His response?' The Most Revered High Magus was quite deeply troubled.

'His Highness, quite rightly, reminded me that I was his subject and that he was not required to answer to me,' Evaristo admitted, ashamed. 'At that point, I pleaded indisposition and begged to be allowed to leave. I came straight here.'

'You did rightly,' said Reinholt.

'I should not have reacted that way,' Evaristo continued, berating himself. 'I made too much of it. I should have treated him as I once treated Gareth saying a naughty word – passed it off as juvenile behavior. That done, I am certain the prince and his young friend would have soon lost interest in it. By my actions, I have given the boys to know that this is important in some way.'

'Admittedly you should have handled the situation in a more rational fashion,' said Reinholt. 'But do not be too hard on yourself, Evaristo. From what he said, His Highness already realizes this to be of importance. How do you think he learned of it? The elf? Silwyth?'

'I do not like Silwyth,' Evaristo said, his voice hardening. 'I am certain that he was mixed up in the sudden disappearance of Lord Mabreton. That is elven politics, however. Lord Mabreton was loyal to the Divine, whereas Silwyth is loyal to the Shield of the Divine. We know that some sort of power struggle is taking place between the two and that, for the moment, the Shield has come out on top. But, much as I dislike and distrust Silwyth, I cannot accuse him of practicing Void magic.'

'What is the basis for your faith in him?' The High Magus did not appear entirely convinced.

'The very fact that Silwyth is a trusted agent of the Shield of the Divine. The elves have no love for Void magic. If anything, they are more set against it than we humans. They revere life, all life, and Void magic requires the sacrifice of life in order to give it power. I believe that if Silwyth had seen that drawing, he would have been more shocked than I was.'

'And he would have found some way to make use of it to the elves' advantage, you can be assured of that. So let us be quite thankful he did not.' Reinholt tapped his hand upon the desk, his gaze going again to the childish scrawl that held such terrible implications. 'If Silwyth did not introduce this to the young prince, then who did?'

'It is hard to tell. His Highness is allowed to run wild. He is friends with that Unhorsed dwarf, Dunner.'

Reinholt shook his head. 'I know Dunner quite well. He would be appalled at this.'

'Then there are the soldiers. The prince spends a great deal of time among them. I suppose one of them could be a practitioner,' Evaristo said doubtfully. 'Theirs is an occupation that deals in death.'

'Perhaps.' Reinholt sat quite still, except for the tapping of a single finger on the table. Evaristo remained silent, his wet robes dripping quietly onto the floor.

'We must know how he came by this. You cannot very well ask His Highness, but I presume you could question his companion, the whipping boy. What is his name?'

'Gareth. This will increase his curiosity, I fear.'

'It cannot be helped.'

'What if he asks questions? Gareth is a bright child.'

'Answer him honestly – nothing good comes of lying.

But be circumspect. Will he tell you the truth, do you think?'

'He is not given to lying normally. But if His Highness orders him to keep silent or to make up some story, Gareth will obey. He idolizes the prince.'

'More's the pity. Well, we must hope for the best. Should we consider taking the elven chamberlain into our confidence? He might have access –'

'Absolutely not, Your Worship,' said Evaristo shortly.

'No, I suppose you are right. The fewer who know of this the better. I need not say that you are to tell no one, not even your wife.'

'I will not speak a word.' Evaristo shivered.

'I have been invited to the palace this evening to dine with His Majesty. You will report to me then. Discreetly, of course. I shall be in the Royal Library prior to the lighting of the candles. Meet me there.'

Evaristo departed on his errand, not at all confident of success. He would have liked to put the task off until the morrow, but the Revered High Magus had said tonight in a tone that left nothing open to argument. Evaristo prayed that he would find Gareth alone. The tutor did not feel equal to coping with His Highness just then.

The gods were either listening or his luck was good. Gareth was by himself in the schoolroom, leaning on a window, his chin resting on his hands, staring out at the rain.

'Gareth.' Evaristo spoke quietly, so as not to startle him. 'May I talk to you for a moment?'

The boy looked up, his face pale, his eyes wary.

'Are you feeling better, Master?' he asked in a small voice.

'I am, thank you,' said Evaristo. He sat down. 'Where is His Highness?'

'With his horse. He has to rub the oil into its leg three times daily.'

Evaristo nodded, relieved. 'I am afraid I frightened you this morning, Gareth. I want to apologize. I didn't mean to do so. The drawing the prince made shocked me.'

'Why, Master?' Gareth wondered. 'What is wrong with it?'

'I will tell you, Gareth, but first I want you to tell me something. Where did the prince first see that drawing? For I assume he copied it from somewhere. A book, perhaps? Did someone in the castle show him?'

'Will that person get into trouble?' Gareth asked in subdued tones.

'Let us say simply that I would like to talk to that person,' Evaristo replied, avoiding a direct answer.

'Well, then . . . nobody showed him the drawing,' Gareth said.

'Indeed?' Evaristo pressed his lips together. He had just noticed the fresh bruise on Gareth's arm. 'Did His Highness order you not to talk about it?'

'No, Master,' said Gareth, meeting his tutor's gaze, not wavering beneath it.

'Gareth,' said Evaristo gently, 'I do not say that you are lying, but I know very well that His Highness did not conceive of this all by himself –'

'But he did, Master!' Gareth protested. 'He said that it came to him when he was holding the Sovereign Stone.'

Evaristo stared at the child. 'He said that. You are telling me the truth, Gareth. This is extremely important. More important than you can possibly imagine.'

'That is the truth, Master,' said Gareth, his lower lip trembling.

'I believe you,' said Evaristo, trying to smile reassuringly. He smoothed the boy's hair with a soothing hand. *I believe you*, he repeated to himself. *The gods help us all!*

'What's the matter, Master?' Gareth asked. 'I don't understand.'

Nothing good comes of lying, the Most Revered High

Magus had said. Yet Evaristo did not see any good coming of telling this child of ten the plain, unadorned truth. Certainly the Most Revered High Magus had not foreseen this situation. Evaristo was on unstable ground. He feared that one false word might send them all tumbling off the precipice. He needed advice. And so, he hedged.

'Do you remember that word you used a while ago, the word I said was not a very nice word and that you were not to use it or words like it? Do you remember that?'

'Yes, Master.'

'Well, this is something like that.'

'It is?' Gareth looked extremely confused.

'You must trust me, Gareth,' said Evaristo, hoping he didn't sound as helpless as he felt. 'There are some things in this life children are not meant to understand. This is one of them.'

'I wish you would tell me, Master,' Gareth said meekly. 'I could try to understand.'

'No,' said Evaristo, making up his mind. 'No, I cannot. Not now. Someday, perhaps, but not now.' He made an attempt to turn the matter with a small pleasantry. 'I trust that this will be like the multiplication tables and His Highness will soon forget all about it, if he has not forgotten it already. He must not consider it to be very important, since he has run off to play with his horse.'

Gareth did not appear convinced. Nor was Evaristo. He could think of nothing more to say, feared that he had said too much already. Taking his leave of the boy, the tutor went to pace up and down an empty hallway until it was time to go to the Great Library.

The Most Revered High Magus was in one of the small reading rooms built off the Royal Library, a room with its own source of stone-light, a room with its own door, which could be shut to ensure a devoted scholar privacy.

'He doesn't want to be disturbed.' The head librarian, eyeing Evaristo with disfavor, wrote upon the board.

'His Worship asked me to meet him here!' Evaristo wrote testily, in no mood to argue. 'Please tell him.'

The head librarian left on his errand, grumbling beneath his breath. He returned, looking disappointed, with the news that the Most Revered High Magus would see the tutor immediately. Evaristo entered the small study room, took his place opposite the table. The Most Revered High Magus was reading a book on Void magic.

'Well?' said Reinholt, his voice hushed.

'It is worse than we thought,' said Evaristo, sinking into the chair. He felt completely wrung out and exhausted. He wondered how he would find the strength to walk home. 'According to Gareth, the idea came into Dagnarus's head during the ceremony, while he was holding the Sovereign Stone.'

The Most Revered High Magus said nothing for long moments. He stared, unseeing, at the book before him. Closing his eyes, he shook his head. Then he sighed, rubbed his eyes. When he spoke, it was more to himself than to Evaristo.

'I advised the King to give me time to study the Sovereign Stone. I urged him to put off the ceremony. The stone is an artifact of the gods. We have no idea what its powers may be – for good or for ill. But His Majesty decided against me. The political situation was volatile, unstable. He hoped that by giving this stone to the other races, as a show of our faith and our trust in them, he would promote peace and goodwill.

'Certainly the granting of the stone has brought about good relations in the short term, but what of the long-term effects? What will happen when the other races begin to create their own Dominion Lords? Will the magic of the stone ensure that these Dominion Lords are men and women devoted to peace? What happens if the stone

231

grants great magical power to someone who is not? His Majesty, who is goodness personified, maintains that the stone itself is good. Who are we to argue with him?

'Now' – Reinholt sighed deeply – 'now we have evidence that the stone is not good. I myself told Tamaros that it was a mistake to allow the prince to handle such an important, powerful artifact. The King would not listen to me. And now . . . now what has he done?'

'I am afraid I do not understand, Your Worship,' Evaristo said. 'What do you fear has happened?'

'Did you see the Sovereign Stone?' Reinholt asked sharply.

'Not very well,' Evaristo replied. 'I am somewhat short-sighted, and I was seated almost in the very back of the gallery.'

'The jewel is formed in the shape of a pyramid, with a four-sided base. When the miracle occurred and the stone separated into four parts, it opened like the petals of a flower. Like this.' Reinholt demonstrated using his hand, clenching it into a fist, then opening the fingers wide. 'As are all objects in this world, the stone is made up of that which can be seen and that which is not seen. What we saw were the four crystal points separating outward. What we did *not* see, because none of us were close enough to see it, was the emptiness left in the center when the stone split apart. None of us, but a ten-year-old child.

'I blame myself,' the Most Revered High Magus said heavily. 'I should have known. I should have foreseen it without studying the artifact. It is logical that the stone should be comprised of all the elements: Earth, Air, Fire, Water, *and* the Void, which is the absence of all. I should have pressed home my arguments. I should have held out against the King. His Majesty would have acceded to my authority if I had remained adamant. My favor with him would have fallen. That was what concerned me. And so I let it go.'

232

Evaristo shifted uncomfortably. He wished he wasn't hearing this. He wished, most earnestly, that he had never become involved. He did not know what to say, was afraid to say anything, for that would remind the High Magus of his presence, yet he was afraid to remain silent, for silence might be mistaken for cunning.

'All of us look into the Void at one time or another, Your Worship,' Evaristo said hesitantly, feeling his way. 'I know that I did when I was young. I was tempted to take that dark path. But when I fully understood the consequences, when I realized what I would be required to sacrifice, I turned away. To give up love, friendship, trust, and regard, to go through life disfigured, shunned and abhorred, reviled and despised. It is a heavy price to pay. It is not surprising that so few choose to pay it. What is surprising is that any choose to pay it at all!'

'And yet, some do,' Reinholt said.

'Dagnarus is only a child, Your Worship. A willful child, granted, a child far too clever for his own good, but a child nonetheless. Today he is interested in this, tomorrow it will be something else. Consider the amount of study required for anyone even to dabble in Void magic. I say this to my own discredit perhaps, Your Worship, but I know for a fact that His Highness has never in his life read a book from the beginning to the end. To give those who do practice this heinous magic some credit, they are self-disciplined, self-denying, wholly devoted to their dark cause to the exclusion of everything else.

'Dagnarus is quite the opposite of this picture. He is self-indulgent, and who can blame him, for both his parents grant his every desire. He loves his pleasures: fine clothes, good food. He is vain of his beauty and we know the curse that falls on those who practice Void magic. And he lacks even the smallest amount of self-discipline. The moment a task becomes too difficult or too onerous for him, he drops it. No, Revered Magus,' said Evaristo, with increasing confidence, 'the prince's very faults protect him from falling to the temptation you fear.'

The Most Revered High Magus regarded Evaristo intently. 'There is something to what you say. You ease my mind wonderfully. Although it seems strange that we should be grateful for a person's failings. Now, the question is, how do we handle this?'

'Are you going to tell the King?' Evaristo ventured.

Reinholt pondered, then shook his head. 'No, I will not tell him. This would worry him unnecessarily. He might mention something to the boy about the matter and it is my belief, bolstered by what you say, that the less we make of this incident the better.'

Evaristo was relieved. Such an interview would have been extremely unpleasant.

'What shall I do, Your Worship? How should this affect my dealings with the prince?'

'Say nothing about it, of course. Let the matter drop. But be watchful. If you see or hear anything more, bring the news to me at once.'

'Of course. But what if the prince asks questions?'

Reinholt smiled. 'Tell him to come here to the Great Library and look up the answers in the books. That should quench his ardor.'

'Indeed it should, Revered Magus,' said Evaristo, smiling, comforted.

The next day seemed to prove Evaristo right. The rain stopped, if only for an afternoon, for dark clouds were already piling up again in the west. But for the moment, the day was glorious, unusually warm and sunny. Prince Dagnarus did not come to the tutoring session. The soldiers had returned from maneuvers, and he was eager to question Argot about how the training had gone. Gareth was still solemn and subdued, but Evaristo considered that natural. He blamed himself. When Gareth asked if they could return to the Royal Library, Evaristo was only too happy to comply, thinking that this treat would take the boy's mind off the unfortunate drawing.

Inside the library, Gareth retraced his steps and found the book without difficulty. He would sometimes ask himself, in later life, if he would have sought out the book had he known the truth. If Evaristo had been honest with him and answered his questions, would Gareth have refused the prince's bidding, no matter how difficult such refusal would have been?

Perhaps. Perhaps not. Gareth could never arrive at a satisfactory conclusion. Certainly Evaristo's evasions had tinged the matter with a titillating air of mystery. And then, too, Gareth, like most children, resented being called a child and told he would understand when he was older. The tutor had made the matter a challenge. Gareth could tell himself this, but he knew the real reason he was stealing the book was because Dagnarus had commanded it. No, that wasn't quite right either. Gareth was stealing the book because Dagnarus wished it.

The whipping boy found the book and, in the silence of the room, where no one walked, no one came, he sat on the floor and began, once again, to look through it. The words that had been so inexplicable seemed to make more sense now, though they would take a great deal of study before he thoroughly understood.

When it was time to leave, it was a simple matter to tuck the slim volume inside his smallclothes, pressed against his stomach, and cover it with his tunic. At that, he was terrified that the librarian, whose eyes seemed capable of seeing through solid marble, would see through the thin fabric and spot the book hidden beneath. The librarian had better things to do with his time than to pay attention to a child. He never bothered to look up, and Gareth walked out of the Royal Library with his prize.

That night, after Silwyth had doused the candle, Dagnarus

sneaked into Gareth's small closet. Dagnarus appropriated the bed. Gareth sat on a small stool, wrapped in a blanket, the book balanced precariously on his knees, the candle in its tall holder on the floor.

'Now,' said Dagnarus, making himself comfortable, leaning up against Gareth's pillow, 'tell me what the book says.'

'Your Highness,' Gareth said, making a last, feeble protest, 'I think you should really read this for yourself.'

'Nonsense, Patch,' said Dagnarus. 'You know how I loathe study. Now read.' He settled back, put his arms behind his head. 'You will explain to me anything I don't understand.'

Opening the book to the first page, Gareth began to read.

'The Magic of the Void, also known as Death Magic . . .'

PART
TWO

ONE

The Lady Valura

'MADAM,' SAID THE MISTRESS OF THE WARD-robe, curtsying to the Queen, 'His Highness requests permission to speak with you.'

'He does?' The Queen looked up from her embroidery, a piece of work she never finished, but liked to hold in her lap. One of her ladies would finish it for her, *put the finishing touches on it*, as the Queen would say, though she had taken only a stitch or two. 'Send His Highness in immediately. No, wait.' Emillia glanced in a mirror, put her hands to her hair. 'I am not prepared to receive him. Inform His Highness that I shall meet him in the solarium in . . .'

'Mother,' came an impatient voice from outside the room, a voice that drew nearer, accompanied by the sound of booted feet. 'I am not one of your courtiers, to be kept waiting.'

Prince Dagnarus entered the room.

The prince had been a beautiful child. Now, at the age of twenty – an age considered by humans to be the age of majority – Dagnarus was a man whose looks, bearing, poise, and demeanor commanded the admiration of all who saw him. Even now, when he had obviously just come from riding, when his auburn hair was wind-blown and tousled, the color high in his sun-browned face, his riding clothes dirt-covered and splattered with mud, he caused those nobles who had spent hours before their mirrors, combing and preening, to regard his good looks with jealous envy.

At the prince's entirely unexpected and unorthodox arrival, the flustered Mistress of the Wardrobe wrung her hands; the ladies-in-waiting flocked together, twittering in pretend consternation and hoping to catch the eye of the handsome prince. Only one of the Queen's ladies continued to calmly ply her needle. She was counting stitches and did not raise her eyes.

The ladies of the court twittered in vain. Although Dagnarus was of marriageable age, none of the yearning noblewomen (or their daughters) had managed to bring a sigh to his lips or a glint to the cool emerald eyes.

'Love weakens a man,' the prince had stated on one occasion when he and his friends were drinking wine and composing sonnets to various ruby lips. 'The sight of the loved face in battle causes the swordsman to hesitate when he should strike. The touch of the loved hand jostles the elbow of the archer and the loved lips bid a commander to retreat when he should be advancing. Thank you, gentlemen, I would sooner drink to the plague as to love.' Saying which, he had thrown his mug into the fire.

The prince had not drunk a toast to love, but he had drunk many to lovemaking. Unbeknownst to anyone else in court, the prince's chamberlain, Silwyth, kept a fund of silver tams ready to ease the pangs of abandoned women. There were any number of redheaded children running about the streets of Vinnengael who could be said to have the blood of kings in their veins.

Dagnarus was not a man to allow animal passions to rule him. He indulged his sexual appetite, but only in order to keep that appetite from interfering with the truly

240

important matters in life. He chose his bedmates wisely, selecting those who were too poor to be a danger to him, and he was honorable enough to leave these women better off, financially, at least, than they were before he dallied with them. He was always coldly honest with them, coldly impersonal in his lovemaking, and it could truthfully be said that none of these women ever languished of love for him at the end of their relationship.

Dagnarus paid scant attention to the simpering ladies-in-waiting. He noticed only one, and that was the one who was not simpering, who did not even look up at his arrival, but continued with her work. Dagnarus was not accustomed to being ignored, and he took this as a challenge. He would make this woman, whoever she was, acknowledge his presence.

'You cruel boy,' his mother berated him in whining tones. 'You have not been to see me for a three-month, and now you break in upon my work and throw my ladies into confusion. Look at you. You have not even bothered to change your clothes, but you come straight to me from the stables. I am extremely ill-used.'

The Queen lifted a lace handkerchief to the corner of her eye. The ladies-in-waiting – all but one – sighed and rustled.

'Come now, Mother,' said Dagnarus in a voice mellow and rich, a voice that he played with the skill of a flutist, 'you know how busy I am. What with my studies and attending the King's levees and taking command of my own regiment, I can barely find hours enough in the day. This leaves me, to my regret, no time for pleasure – for the very great pleasure – Madam, of waiting upon you.'

Dagnarus kissed his mother's hand most contritely, his gaze fixed upon the lady-in-waiting who still refused to leave off her work and give him the admiration that was his due. Dagnarus was starting to feel annoyed. All he could see of her was black hair, smooth and straight, parted in the middle and flowing down her back almost to her waist, and her hands, which were extraordinary for their long, delicate fingers and rosy nails. By the hair coloring, her slender frame and strict discipline, her silken and colorful dress, he knew she was an elf.

'Ah, my child, you work too hard, far too hard,' said his doting mother, who instantly forgave him months of neglect. 'Your brother does not work nearly as hard as you do and yet *he* is to be King,' she added, pouting and bitter.

'Of course, Helmos will be King,' said Dagnarus lightly. 'He deserves it and it will be an honor to serve him.' Leaning near, he whispered, 'Hold your tongue, Mother. You do our cause more harm than good.' Aloud, he added, 'I wish to speak to you, Mother, upon a private matter. Dismiss your ladies.'

It was not the prince's place to command the Queen, but Dagnarus had so long been his mother's master that she obeyed him without question.

'Ladies, leave us,' the Queen ordered. 'I will ring when you are needed.'

The Queen's command could not be disobeyed and obliged the dedicated seamstress to lay down her needle. She rose to her feet with unstudied grace, the grace of a newly blossomed flower lifting its head to the sun, lifting a face whose exquisite beauty was so perfect that anyone seeing her immediately longed to find a flaw, just to make her mortal. Her eyes, almond-shaped and tilted, were unusually large and blue as the air the elves worship. Her lips were full and sensuous, her chin well-shaped but firm, denoting strength of spirit. Lowering her eyes, which seemed to decrease the light in the room to a marked degree, she made her reverence to the Queen and passed coolly by the prince without exhibiting the slightest interest.

'Who was that elf woman who just left?' Dagnarus asked, taking care that his tone should be indifferent. His mother was jealous of his affections and would immediately rid the court of anyone he admired. Though she wanted him to marry, she had determined that he would marry a woman of her choice. So far, those she had presented to him had been ugly as crows. 'I don't recall having seen her before.'

'You would have seen her had you bothered to wait upon me,' said his mother, absorbed with her own grievances. 'She is just arrived at court within the fortnight. Her husband, Lord Mabreton, is the new elven ambassador. There is to be a dinner in his honor this evening. I trust you will attend?'

'If you wish it, Mother,' said the prince, unusually dutiful.

'I do,' said the Queen. 'Helmos will be there, smirking and lording it over everyone. You must be certain to take him down a peg or two.'

As little love as Dagnarus bore his elder brother, not even he could accept the picture of the scholarly, earnest, and modest Helmos 'smirking and gloating.' Dagnarus usually avoided such royal functions if he could, preferring to spend the night drinking and gambling with his friends in the local taverns. His plans changed immediately. He had no objection at all to appearing in his best clothes, seated alongside his father, directly opposite the beguiling Lady Mabreton.

Mabreton. The name had a familiar sound to it. Dagnarus could not recall where he had heard it before. He made a mental note to ask Silwyth, who would know all there was to know about the lady. And her husband.

'What is it you want to talk to me about?' the Queen asked. Eyes narrowed, she regarded her son with suspicion. 'Not about that elf woman, is it?'

'Certainly not, Mother,' Dagnarus said, smiling. 'I only asked because it is right and proper that I know the members of my father's court. Don't you agree?'

The Queen believed him. His tone was nonchalant, his interest in the woman appeared to be only the interest of the moment, quickly forgotten. Dagnarus was adept at dissembling, at hiding his true feelings, at shuffling his mental deck so that the cards he needed were always on the top. No one ever caught him cheating.

He glanced around to make certain that the ladies-in-waiting were not waiting within earshot. Assured that he and his mother were alone, he turned his full attention to the Queen.

'Mother, I have news,' said Dagnarus, sitting in the chair opposite his mother, a chair the lovely Lady Mabreton had just abandoned and that still held her warmth and her perfume. For a moment, the prince had some slight difficulty in banishing her image, but, after only a brief struggle, he succeeded. 'Lord Donnengal is dead.'

The Queen gazed at him stupidly, plied her fan. 'Well, and what is that to me? I never liked the man, for all your father thought so highly of him.'

'Mother,' said Dagnarus impatiently, 'who gives a hang whether you liked him or not? He is dead. Don't you understand what this means?'

The Queen regarded her son doubtfully, wanting to please him, but not certain what he was talking about.

'It means,' said Dagnarus, patiently, 'that there is now an opening among the ranks of the Dominion Lords.'

Emillia's eyes widened. Reaching out her hand, she clutched her son's forearm with such violence that her long nails pierced his flesh. 'It shall be yours! Of course, it shall! How wonderful the ceremony will be. I will have a new gown, of course. The feast will be splendid. We will serve –'

'Mother,' Dagnarus interrupted, his tone cold and biting. He jerked away from her touch. 'Do not have the goose for the feast plucked yet. You know perfectly well that I shall not even be nominated for the post.'

'Well, certainly, you will!' the Queen said angrily. 'Your father cannot deny you this! It is your right!'

'He can deny it and he will,' Dagnarus predicted. 'He does not consider me a suitable candidate. Just because I am no weak-eyed book reader. Just because I sleep through the minstrel's love songs and prefer dicing with my friends than gaping in the face of some old philosopher who yammers on about the deep meaning to be found in the cutting of a nose hair. You may rest assured, Mother, that I will not even merit consideration.'

'You will. I will talk to the King,' said Emillia, rising with a rustle of silk brocade, meaning to leave that moment.

'No, Mother, you will not,' said Dagnarus firmly. He knew well how little love King Tamaros had for his second wife. 'That is why I came to speak to you before –' In his heart he said, *before you do me irreparable harm*, but aloud he finished with, 'before you exert yourself on my behalf.'

His mother was displeased. 'I wonder if you realize how important this is to you,' she said crossly. 'You do not stand a chance of becoming King unless you are a Dominion Lord like your brother.'

'I know the importance, Mother, believe me,' said Dagnarus, his tone dry. *And that is why I choose to handle this myself*, he thought, but did not say. Aloud, he continued, 'As for my becoming King, Dominion Lord or not, it will not happen. At least, not if it depends upon my father. The King will never depose Helmos in my favor.'

'Nonsense. The King adores you –' his mother began.

'Yes,' Dagnarus interrupted with a bitter smile, 'but he does not like me much.'

'I don't know what you are talking about!' the Queen cried, and fumbled for her handkerchief again. 'I am sure you are blaming me. You act as if I would spoil everything for you, when I care about you more than life itself. I don't know how you can be so cruel . . .'

'Stop sniveling, Mother, and listen to me.' Dagnarus was losing patience. 'You will not broach this subject with my father. You will not whine, grizzle, plead, or badger. When he or anyone introduces the subject of my becoming a Dominion Lord, you will behave quite calmly, act as if it is accepted fact. "Certainly my son will be nominated," you will say, looking startled at the very idea that anyone could have doubts. And you will say nothing more. Do you understand? And you will tell my grandfather Olgaf to stay out of this altogether.'

Emillia was a silly, shrewish, vain woman, who had long ago lost all authority or influence she might have held at court. This was not completely her fault. Her father, King Olgaf of Dunkarga, continued to stoke the fire hot beneath the royal pot, keeping the King's soup bubbling in hopes that someday His Majesty would lift the spoon and burn his mouth. Dagnarus needed help from this quarter as much as he needed scorpions in the bed linens.

Emillia did not give way without protesting, with a few squeezed-out tears that her son did not love her, that no one loved her, that her sacrifices were not appreciated, that she was sure she could convince Tamaros to see reason and that poor dear Papa would be only too happy to come to court and insist that Dagnarus be given his rights.

Dagnarus listened to her with as much patience as he could muster, reminding himself that as a soldier he must learn to endure hardship and torment. He knew how to handle Emillia, however; he'd been doing so since he was two years old. He charmed her in one sentence and threatened her in another, until she was not quite certain which was which. Gradually, he persuaded her to his way of thinking.

When the Queen began to conceive of the plan as having been her idea in the first place, Dagnarus knew he had won. He was safe from her machinations. He left her as quickly as he could after that, though he paused in the antechamber, hoping to see Lady Mabreton. He was disappointed. She was not among the ladies moving in haste in response to the Queen's imperious ringing of her bell.

Dagnarus returned to his chambers to bathe and change his clothes and decide on how best to confront his father. King Tamaros had never before denied his youngest son anything, but Dagnarus was less confident in his ability to succeed in this. The nomination of a Dominion Lord was something solemn and sacred to King Tamaros, something to be prayed over and gravely considered. It was not like giving his son a pony. Still, by the end of his bath, Dagnarus thought he had devised the way to approach his father.

'Silwyth,' said Dagnarus, shaking out his wet curls and vigorously toweling himself, 'I want to ask you something.'

'Yes, Your Highness. How may I be of service?'

The elf was laying out the prince's clothes, clothes suitable for an audience with the King, although Dagnarus had made no mention of the fact that he was going to see His Majesty. Silwyth knew. Silwyth always knew. Dagnarus had long given up trying to discover *how* Silwyth knew.

'My mother has a new lady-in-waiting. An elf.'

'That would be Lady Mabreton, Your Highness.'

'Yes, that's the name. Tell me about her, Silwyth,' said Dagnarus. Ordinarily there would be a host of lords assisting the prince to dress, but Dagnarus, having cut his morning amusements short on hearing the news of the death of Lord Donnengal, was alone with his chamberlain.

'She is the wife of Lord Mabreton, a Guardian of the Eastern Wood and a Dominion Lord. He is of the House of Wyval, loyal to the Divine, but not unduly so, if Your Highness takes my meaning. The Shield of the Divine made Mabreton a Dominion Lord, and he is properly grateful.

'Lady Mabreton is a reluctant member of the court. She did not want to come and is said to have adamantly refused to accompany her lord when the subject was first broached. She was made to see that her lord would lose face if she stayed behind, disobeying not only his wishes but those of the Shield. It is said Lord Mabreton threatened her with divorce if she did not come, which would have meant utter disgrace and ruin for herself and her family. I find that rumor difficult to believe, however, since it is obvious to all that Lord Mabreton adores his beautiful wife. It is my guess that her own family were the ones who persuaded her to come, for they are an impoverished House and dependent on her influence. Whatever the reason, she is here in court. Not only that, but she is a lady-in-waiting. I mean no disrespect to the Queen your mother when I say that Lady Mabreton is most unhappy in that position.'

'She is? How interesting.' Dagnarus smiled, well pleased by what he'd heard. 'Tell me, Silwyth. Why is the name Mabreton so familiar to me? Where have I heard it before?'

'You are thinking of the Lord Mabreton who was ambassador when Your Highness was a boy. It was around the time of the gifting of the Sovereign Stone . . .'

The memory came flooding back to Dagnarus, the memory of Silwyth plunging his knife into an elf lord's back.

'By the gods!' Dagnarus looked intently at Silwyth, whose face was calm and composed as ever. 'I know the man you mean! What relation was he to this Lord Mabreton?'

'They were brothers, my lord. The Lady Mabreton was the wife of the first brother. As is elven custom, if another brother is unmarried, he has the option of marrying his brother's widow, should her family deem such a marriage

248

to be of advantage to the lady. In this instance, her family wanted desperately to hang on to the Mabreton family fortune, and so they readily agreed.'

'I see. Why did I never see her when she was at court when I was a child? Not that I would have paid much attention to her, I suppose,' Dagnarus said, grinning as he buckled a jeweled belt around his waist. 'I thought more of my dog than I did women. Still, even a little boy must have noticed such a beautiful creature.'

'I am sure Your Highness would have noticed her,' said Silwyth, and there was something wistful in his voice. 'Our women are famed for their beauty, but hers is beyond compare. She did not come to court then, however. She lived in a house that the first Lord Mabreton had built for her on the shores of the River Hammerclaw. When word of her husband's death reached her, she returned, under the protection of the Shield, to her own family.'

Dagnarus's face darkened. 'Is she still under the Shield's protection?'

Silwyth hesitated, then said, 'No, my lord. She is not. Her family and the family of the Shield's wife are not on good terms, and relations between the two have lately deteriorated. The Shield would not protect her. This is perhaps another reason she thought it expedient to travel to Vinnengael.'

'Excellent. Silwyth, you have caused the sun to shine on my entire day. You've heard the news, of course.' Dagnarus slipped his arms through the sleeves of a richly embroidered and fur-trimmed cloak worn over his short tunic.

'Of Lord Donnengal's passing? Yes, Your Highness. I offer my condolences. He was well-known to you, I believe.'

'Faith, I cared nothing for him one way or the other. What is important is that this leaves a vacancy in the ranks of the human Dominion Lords.'

'Yes, Your Highness, I am aware of that.'

Dagnarus turned, hands on his hips, and regarded Silwyth intently. 'You know I want this. You know I must have it if I am ever to be King. What are my chances? What do you hear?'

'Your Highness might be nominated,' said Silwyth, though he said that doubtfully. 'But the Council of the Dominion Lords will not approve.'

'The vote does not have to be unanimous.'

'True, my lord, but your brother, Helmos, is Head of the Council, and it is doubtful if the other humans would actively oppose him, though some are said to be leaning in your favor.'

'Damn Helmos!' the prince said vehemently. 'Damn him to the Void!'

'Take care, Your Highness. Such sentiments might be overheard.'

'There's no one around but us,' Dagnarus said impatiently, but he lowered his voice. 'What is your advice?'

'You must win the King to your cause, my lord. The other Dominion Lords might well overrule Helmos if they knew that they were acting on the wishes of His Majesty.'

'Exactly my thinking,' said Dagnarus. 'And now, I would like to give a small gift to Lady Mabreton. You know best. What shall it be and how shall it be presented? Jewels? Do elven women like jewels?'

Again Silwyth hesitated, and this time the hesitation was so pronounced that Dagnarus noticed.

'What is it, Silwyth? You look as if you had drunk vinegar. Are you yourself in love with this woman?'

'No, my lord. Far from it,' said Silwyth coolly. 'Elves do not fall in love or, if we do, we do so at our own peril. My marriage is arranged, and when the young woman comes of age in the next fifty years, we will be wed. But the Lady Mabreton is quite beautiful and the one time we met she was extremely kind to me. I would not want to see her hurt.'

'I'm not going to hurt her, Silwyth,' said Dagnarus earnestly. He laid his hand upon the chamberlain's shoulder. 'She refused even to look at me when I saw her with my mother. I only want to win a smile from her. That is all. If she hates humans so much, perhaps I might cause her to change her opinion. Do a service to both our nations.'

'Perhaps, Your Highness.' Despite the prince's wheedling tone, Silwyth did not appear convinced.

'Come, Silwyth,' said Dagnarus. 'You know me. You know that my heart is proof against a woman's wiles. From what you say of this lady, her own heart is not likely to be touched by a mere human. She is unhappy, and who can blame her? Forced to spend her time in the company of my mother! What harm can there be in making her life here a little more pleasant?'

'None at all, my lord.' If Silwyth sighed, he did so inwardly, so the prince could not hear. Silwyth knew well where his loyalties lay. He was not about to jeopardize his position for anything, not even a woman whose lovely flower blossomed in the garden of his mind. As he had told Dagnarus, the Shield would never reach out to protect Lady Mabreton. Silwyth plucked her flower and handed it, though not without the sigh, to the prince.

'As to a gift, elven women consider most jewels to be flashy and ostentatious. However, some are acceptable, these being the diamond, for its purity, the blue topaz and the sapphire, which are favored by the gods of air. However, if Your Lordship does not mind the expense –'

'I don't,' said Dagnarus. 'I have been lucky at the dice lately.'

'Then I suggest a small brooch made of the rare turquoise, which is known for its magical power to protect from harm those who wear it. Such a gift will express your admiration, also your thoughtfulness. It will be a gift she can wear openly, with honor. One that her husband could not fault, nor prevent her from accepting.'

'Excellent. Where do I find this?'

'Turquoise is only to be found among the Pecwae, Your Highness. They are the only ones who know its source. Their jewelry is delicately fashioned, suitable to elven women, and highly prized among our people. If Your Highness likes, I will take it upon myself to go to the market and make the purchase.'

'Yes, do that, Silwyth. Bring the bauble to me, and I will give it to her.'

'Very good, Your Highness.'

'And on your way, stop by the Temple and leave a message for Patch. I wish to speak to him. In fact,' the prince added, struck by a sudden idea, 'I wish to have him present at the banquet. I will secure him an invitation; my father is fond of him and expressed a desire just the other day to see him again. We may be talking late, so make up Patch's old room for him. I presume he can free himself from the clutches of those clucking old hens of magi to spend an evening away from his dank little cell?'

'If Your Highness were to send a written request stating that Master Gareth's presence is required at a function of state, the Master of Students would be bound to accede. Otherwise, I fear obtaining him might be difficult. Novices are required to attend strictly to their studies with no outside distractions.'

'Must the request be written? Well, I suppose it can't be helped.' Dagnarus tugged impatiently on a large signet ring he wore on the first finger of his right hand. 'Here. Compose the letter, sign it for me, and seal it. Instruct Patch to meet me here at the hour the candles are lit. See to it that he has something decent to wear, will you? His shaved head sticking up out of the wide collar of those shabby robes makes him look like a turtle.'

'Yes, Your Highness.' Silwyth accepted the ring.

He had handled the prince's correspondence for many years now, the last ink-blotted and misspelled note the prince had written having been wrung from him by the tutor, Evaristo. The tutor had been dismissed from his duties when the prince was twelve, at the time Gareth, who had been the tutor's only real pupil, had entered the Temple of the Magi to study magic. Tamaros had dismissed the tutor for the prince, having reluctantly come to accept the fact that his youngest son was not and never would be a scholar, though the father continued to hope that, once the wild streak in his nature had been appeased, Dagnarus might at last come to know the rewards of quiet study. A forlorn hope, to say the least.

'I am away to see my father,' said Dagnarus, taking one more critical look at himself in the mirror. 'Wish me luck, Silwyth.'

'I do, indeed, my lord,' said Silwyth. 'You will need it,' he added, but he spoke in elven, a language the prince had never bothered to learn.

TWO

Heart's Desire

'HONORED FATHER, I GIVE YOU GREETING,' said Dagnarus, entering the King's study with a flourish of his cloak which set the papers flying as if stirred by a rising wind.

Crossing over to the King, his cape catching on the corners of books and dragging them askew, his loud footfalls breaking the contemplative silence, his raw, animal spirit seeming to vie with the fire to see which could burn quicker and brighter, Dagnarus shattered the peace of the King's study as effectively as if he had been a crossbow bolt fired through the window. King Tamaros looked up from his work with a welcoming, indulgent, if somewhat trepidatious, smile. Although the sight of his handsome son warmed him like spiced wine, Tamaros was never certain how that wine would go down. At his age, nearing ninety, the King had come to appreciate reliability and stability. Not even Dagnarus's admirers, of which he had many, would have used those two words in connection with the prince.

'Greetings, my son,' said Tamaros, laying aside his work.

The view from the room was spectacular, providing a

scenic vista of the world from each of the cardinal points, encompassing the mountains, the plains, the great city, the magnificent waterfalls with their rainbow scarves, and above all the blue dome of the sky and the radiant sun. The King had entered this room every day for a lifetime of days, but he always paused and gazed in reverent awe, humbled and mindful of the grace of the gods. Dagnarus never spared the world a glance and even complained of the room's brightness.

'How can you read in here, Father? The sunlight is so strong, I am half-blinded.' The prince perched upon the edge of his father's desk, dislodging books and crumpling papers. Composing his face, becoming serious, Dagnarus softened his voice. 'I have sad news, I fear, Father. I wonder if you have heard it.'

'I've heard nothing,' said Tamaros, concerned. He marked his place and shut his book. 'What is it, son?'

'Lord Donnengal is dead,' said Dagnarus in sorrowful, respectful tones. 'I thought you would want to know so that you could extend your condolences to his family. I came as soon as I heard.'

'This is indeed unhappy news,' said Tamaros, truly grieved. 'How did it happen?'

'He was out hunting – a sport in which he took great delight, as you know – and suddenly grabbed his chest, uttered a great cry, and fell off his horse. His squire and his groom did all they could – unlaced his doublet and loosened his girdle, but there was no help for him. His heart had burst, so they say.'

'A hale and hearty man,' said Tamaros. 'A man in the prime of his life.'

'Come now, Father,' said Dagnarus, amused. 'Lord Donnengal was sixty if he was a day.'

'Was he?' Tamaros looked up wistfully. 'I suppose you are right.' He sighed, shook his head. 'Would it not seem that I question the judgment of the gods, I would say that

I have lived too long. Too long. The friends of my youth are dead, and now I throw brands on the funeral pyres of their children.'

Clasping his hands, he bowed his head and whispered a silent prayer for the passing of a well-loved and much-respected friend. Dagnarus, though burning with impatience, had sense enough to hold his tongue, grant his father time to mourn. At length, growing restless, Dagnarus broke the silence.

'I wonder if you realize, Father, that Lord Donnengal's passing leaves a vacancy in the ranks of the Dominion Lords.'

Tamaros glanced up, his prayers interrupted. 'Indeed it does,' he said, adding with a hint of rebuke, '*In due time*, we will discuss filling it.'

'Father,' said Dagnarus persuasively, 'it is only right and proper that you nominate me to fill the vacancy.'

'My son,' said Tamaros, regarding Dagnarus with fond sympathy, 'you do not want this.'

'On the contrary, Father,' said Dagnarus, nettled, 'I want it very much. I am of age. The post is mine by right of birth.'

'Birth, title, rank, fortune – none of that plays any part in the selection of a Dominion Lord. The calling comes from the gods without and from a person's heart within. You want it now because you do not understand what becoming a Dominion Lord entails – a life dedicated to the pursuit of peace, for one thing. And you, my son, are a warrior born.'

'A calling you despise!' Dagnarus said, his face darkening with anger.

'Not so, son,' Tamaros said sharply. He might have outlived two generations, but he was not frail and he was not feebleminded. 'Vinnengael is strong because her army is strong. Our neighbors respect us. They know that we will not try to recklessly expand our landholdings at

256

their expense. But they also know that we will defend our borders against any and all incursions, as you yourself are aware, having fought recently in the wars against the elven raiders.'

'I beg your pardon, Father,' said Dagnarus, seeing that he had made a mistake and that fits of temper would not be conducive to his cause. 'I spoke in haste without thinking.'

Unable to sit still any longer, the prince left his place at the edge of Tamaros's desk and began to walk around the room, brooding, his arms clasped across his chest, his head lowered.

'You made Helmos a Dominion Lord,' Dagnarus said, pausing to regard his father with eyes bright as green flame. 'I am as much your son as he is. I have as much right to the honor as he does.' He leaned forward, wheedling. 'How will it look, Father, if by some terrible mischance my brother dies without producing an heir and I ascend to the throne? The people will have no regard for me, because I am not a Dominion Lord like my brother before me. "He is not considered worthy." That is what they will say. That is what they *have* said,' he added pointedly.

'Who?' Tamaros demanded, angered in his turn. 'Who has said such things?'

Dagnarus lowered his gaze; his thick lashes dampened the fire of his eyes. 'I will not name names, Father. I would not have them fall out of your favor because they happened to speak the truth. Neither you nor the magi consider me worthy.'

'Certainly you are worthy,' said Tamaros uneasily, forced to go on the defensive. 'Your bravery and your courage are undisputed. Your deeds in battle are celebrated throughout the realm. Worthiness is not the issue here, my son. Suitability is. By nature and temperament, you are not suited to be a Dominion Lord, Dagnarus. And whether you are a Dominion Lord or not has nothing to do with whether

257

or not you will be a good ruler. Content yourself with being an excellent soldier –'

'And why, Father, may an excellent soldier not be a Dominion Lord?' Dagnarus countered. His face was flushed with the righteousness of his cause, his countenance aflame. In that moment, he was kingly and noble and earnest, and he impressed his father deeply. 'You yourself have said that in order to ensure our peace, we must be prepared to go to war to defend it. The Revered Magi go to battle alongside us, with prayers upon their lips, holding swords as well as spellbooks in their hands. The gods do not turn from them, but support them and bless their cause. There has never been a Lord of Battle among the human Dominion Lords, true, but that does not mean there was never meant to be one. All elven Dominion Lords are warriors.'

Entranced, charmed, Tamaros gave serious consideration to his son's persuasive words.

Dagnarus, seeing his opportunity, pressed home his point. 'At least nominate me, Father. The other Dominion Lords must vote on me, and if they choose not to sanction me, then I will bow to their will and the will of the gods. But you, at least, should be seen to endorse me. Refuse me this, and people will say that I lack your trust and respect.'

Tamaros began to think, uneasily, that Dagnarus had a point. Helmos was over thirty, in excellent health, strong of mind and body, rarely sick. But the ways of the gods are mysterious and capricious. Accidents happen, an accident had claimed Helmos's mother. And as of yet, Helmos and his wife, Anna, had not produced an heir, much as they had wanted and prayed for one. Ten years had passed since their marriage, and still they were barren. There was every possibility Dagnarus might succeed to the throne, and if it was known throughout the court and the kingdom that he had been turned down for the honor of becoming a

Dominion Lord, people would wonder and doubt and perhaps look about for another king.

Civil war – every ruler's greatest fear. Tamaros had been raised on his grandfather's story of the bloody civil war that had nearly proved Vinnengael's downfall. He had heard how the elves and orken and dwarves had taken advantage of the humans' battles to surge across the borders and gobble up great chunks of land, land that had been won back, but only through more blood and toil. Tamaros must do whatever he could to ensure that his kingdom remained intact, peaceful, stable.

Dagnarus is different from his brother, different from the other Dominion Lords, true, but if we are all the same, Tamaros argued to himself, then the world will stagnate. Some must tend the flock, others must butcher them.

'There is a risk, Dagnarus,' said Tamaros, inwardly marveling and rejoicing at his son's beauty, his robust health, his obvious lusty enjoyment of life. 'Becoming a Dominion Lord is dangerous.'

'I am a soldier, Father,' said Dagnarus. 'Risks are a part of my calling.' He was earnest and humble and more markedly beautiful than ever. 'Will you nominate me, Father?'

Tamaros sighed. His heart misgave him, but he could not say no. 'I will, my son.'

'Thank you, Father, for giving me this chance!' Dagnarus was more brilliant than the sun, at that moment, he half blinded – or wholly blinded – his father. 'I will make you proud of me. And now, I will interrupt your work no longer. With your gracious permission, I take my leave.'

Tamaros nodded. Dagnarus departed and Tamaros could hear his son's voice raised in a lilting dance song as he strode down the hallway. Tamaros did not return to his work, but sat staring unseeing at the volume in which he had previously been engrossed.

259

The King was still sitting, staring at the book unseeing, when his other son, his elder son, Helmos, entered.

Quiet, unobtrusive, Helmos came to stand at his father's side. He waited in silence until Tamaros should be aware of his presence.

'I see that you have heard the news, Father,' Helmos said with gentle gravity. 'I am sorry I could not be the one to bring it. I know how deeply Lord Donnengal's death must touch you.'

'Dagnarus came to tell me,' said Tamaros, reaching out his hand to press the hand of his most beloved son.

'Dagnarus!' Helmos frowned.

'He said that he knew the news would grieve me and that I would want to know so that I could send my sympathy to his widow and children.'

'My brother grows very tenderhearted suddenly,' said Helmos, casting a troubled glance at his father.

Tamaros smiled ruefully. 'I am not quite a doddering old fool. Not yet. I know his true motive in telling me. He wants' – Tamaros gazed hard at his son – 'to fill the vacancy left by Lord Donnengal's death. Dagnarus wants to become a Dominion Lord.'

'Impossible,' said Helmos shortly.

'I am not so sure.' Tamaros was thoughtful.

'Father! You can't be serious! I beg your pardon, Father. I meant no disrespect, but Dagnarus is completely unsuitable –'

'That word,' Tamaros interrupted. '"Unsuitable." We mean that he does not conform to our standard of what a Dominion Lord should be. But I wonder – who are we to set standards? Is it not the gods who choose? Perhaps they have chosen him.'

'How, Father?' Helmos asked.

'By putting the desire in his heart,' Tamaros replied.

'My brother is beset by a great many god-given desires, then,' Helmos returned bitterly. He and his adored wife

260

wanted children so badly, and the gods denied them, whereas Dagnarus fathered bastards with the casual ease of a strolling tomcat. 'And he satisfies them all.'

'What are you saying?' Tamaros demanded, angered.

Helmos sighed deeply, sat down across from his father. 'I am saying what I have not wanted to say, what I hoped I would never have to say to you, Father. My brother must not become a Dominion Lord. When I say he is unsuitable, I do not speak idly. He is a wanton wastrel. He spends his nights drinking and carousing with men and women of unseemly character. His by-blows, got on these unfortunate women, could populate a town!'

'Rumor,' said Tamaros, glowering. 'Envious gossip. Perhaps Dagnarus does gamble and drink a bit too much wine now and then, but I enjoyed a game of dice myself when I was young.'

Helmos shook his head. 'He is next door to illiterate, Father. He can barely write his name.'

'He attends the levees,' Tamaros countered. 'Those times I have called upon him for judgment, he has rendered it wisely and justly. His reputation as a soldier and a commander cannot be faulted.'

'He *is* intelligent,' Helmos admitted. 'He has native wit, an earthy common sense. I do not deny that. Nor do I deny that he is courageous and a good leader of men. So let us leave him as that, Father. Let my brother be content with leading our armies. Do not – I repeat – do not, Father, grant him the magical power of a Dominion Lord! I would not think he would want it anyway. The sworn and sacred duty of a Dominion Lord is to preserve peace.'

'True,' said Tamaros. 'That was what was originally intended. Or at least so I thought. Perhaps . . . perhaps I was mistaken.'

Rising to his feet, Tamaros walked over to the eastern side of the room, looked out at the mountains. It was late afternoon. The sun was westering. Its red-gold rays gilded Tamaros's face, illuminated him, as if he had been dipped in gold, a graven image to wisdom and duty, a King whose legacy would extend through time, a godlike King of mythic proportions.

Helmos thought to himself, I will be a good King. Not a great one. He sees that. And though he loves me, I am a disappointment to him. Well, I am what I am. The gods made me. I cannot change.

Tamaros, his hands clasped behind his back, turned to face his son.

'I had hoped that by giving each of the races the Sovereign Stone, we would come together, learn to live together in peace. My hopes proved fruitless. The elves continue to nibble away at our borders, the dwarves have seized and now rule several human settlements, which they claim were built upon their land.'

'The dwarves believe that all of Vinnengael is built upon their land,' Helmos observed dryly.

'True, true, but I had hoped their attitudes would change. It seems that the Sovereign Stone has made the other races bolder and has made us seem weaker. They think that since now they have the Sovereign Stone, they can attack us with impunity. Perhaps we need a Lord of Battle, a Dominion Lord whose sworn oath is not only to preserve the peace but who will do so by means of a sword if that proves necessary.'

'And if we produce a Lord of Battle, what is to prevent the elves and the dwarves and the orken from producing their own Lords of Battle?' Helmos argued with unusual vehemence, rising to face his father. 'No, Father. Do not be disappointed in the Sovereign Stone. Have faith in it, in the gods. You expect too much too quickly, that is all. Your dream of peace will be fulfilled, but it will take time. We are working with the other Dominion Lords to understand each other, to respect each other's beliefs. Only then, when we trust each other, can we begin to work to change those beliefs that block the way of true peace.'

'There is wisdom in what you say, my son, but you are not yet King. I am, and I must do what I think is best for our people, both in the short term and the long.'

The sun dropped beneath the horizon. Shadows crept through the room. The graven image was now that of an old man, bowed with many cares, stooped and worn.

'Tell me that you have not already promised Dagnarus this, Father,' Helmos said quietly.

Tamaros made no reply, but turned his back and stared out the window.

Helmos was silent long moments. The shadows in the room lengthened. One of the servants entered to light the candles. Helmos made a motion with his hand, and the servant silently departed.

'I have never in my life gone against your wishes, Father,' said Helmos at last. 'But I will not side with you on this. I oppose my brother's nomination, and I will do all that I can to block it.'

Tamaros still said nothing, still stared out the window.

'Dagnarus will have no cause to blame you for this, Father,' Helmos added. 'I will take all the blame upon myself. You will let it be known publicly that you support him. He will not love you less for it.'

'You will do what you think is right, as I have taught you,' said Tamaros, but his voice was cold. 'It pains me, though, to see my sons at war.'

Helmos stood quiet, struggling with himself, longing to please his father but unable to do so by going against his own heart. He knew what he might say to clinch his arguments, knew what he might say to discredit his brother utterly, to blast and destroy Dagnarus forever in his father's eyes. But these words were so black, so ugly, so heinous that Helmos could not bring himself to speak them aloud. He truly feared they might shock his

263

father to death. Besides, Helmos lacked proof. His source was untrustworthy, a woman reporting words about Void magic mumbled in sleep, a woman who had come to Helmos seeking money to buy her silence. His father would refuse to believe her wild tale, and Helmos could not very well blame him.

He must carry this burden alone.

'I am sorry, Father,' he said, and left the room.

Tamaros stood for a long time in the darkness, for the servant whose task it was to light the candles had overheard the quarrel between King and crown prince and was too shocked and awed and frightened to reenter.

THREE

The Whipping Boy Grown

GARETH WAS BONE-TIRED.

He had spent all that day, from very early morning until well after dark, at his studies, his proper studies. He had spent half the previous night at his improper studies, his secret studies. He had not meant to stay up so late, but he was on the trail of a discovery that both appalled him and intrigued him, and he could not abandon his pursuit of the knowledge until his eyes had given up on their own, closing despite him.

The morning bell had caught him slumped over his book, stiff in the shoulders and with a painful crick in his neck. He had been dull and stupid in class that day, drawing the ire of his master. Looking forward to his bed, planning to go to sleep early, he was dismayed to receive the prince's summons to attend a banquet and spend the night in the palace.

Gareth thought longingly of refusing, of pleading indisposition, but the Master of Students – who had given Gareth permission to attend the banquet in the palace and who was now regarding the young man with undisguised envy – would think such a refusal extremely strange and might start asking questions. Then, of course, Gareth

265

would have to answer to Dagnarus, who would be furious. The prince was always furious when his will was thwarted.

Gareth attired himself in the court clothes Silwyth had pointedly left in his cell for him, the dalmatic, the long-skirted tunic known as the houppelande, then much in fashion, the woolen hose and cloak and jeweled girdle and leather slippers. He thought, as he was dressing, how uncomfortable and restricting such clothing was after having become accustomed to the freedom of ecclesiastical dress, which, for novices, consisted of a simple brown robe worn over one's small-clothes, shoes, and stockings.

Gareth had no mirror – the magi were supposed to be above such weaknesses as personal vanity – and thus he was not forced to look at himself wearing the cap Silwyth had supplied to cover his shaved head. The large purple patch that had marred his face when he was young had not vanished (as Gareth had secretly hoped it might). He was not a comely youth to begin with. The hat made him look ridiculous. There was no help for it. His Highness had ordered it, and His Highness was always obeyed.

Gareth left the Temple without a word to anyone, though many of the novices were walking about on various errands prior to the hour when they would take their simple meal. He had few friends among the other novices. Reticent and diffident by nature, self-conscious because of his birthmark, Gareth tended to be quiet and withdrawn at school. His reserve caused his fellow students to call him proud, too snobbish to lower himself to be friends with anyone less than a prince. The truth was, he left them alone for their own well-being. Gareth's clandestine studies into the ancient and forbidden religion of Void magic set him apart from the other students – the innocent students. He feared becoming too close to anyone, feared discovery, feared that if he was discovered, then anyone else closely associated with him might be forced to share his fate.

This did not apply to the prince, but then all that Gareth did or was or could be he dedicated to Dagnarus.

The brisk walk to the palace helped to wake the former whipping boy. The guards greeted him with friendly nods and brusque jerks of the head; most had known him since he was a child. He waved off the page who would have shown him through the castle – Gareth knew the way better than the boy. He paused before a mirror to look at himself and, as he had suspected, the hat did indeed make him look a fool.

The banquet room was hot and noisy, blaring with the light and heat from a roaring fire and myriad stone-lights and candles. Gareth made his obligatory reverences to his parents – his father was already in his cups, red-faced and boorish; his mother was intent upon the latest gossip and barely gave her son a glance. The food had not yet been served; the guests stood about talking and drinking spiced wine. Some young people were performing an impromptu round dance in a corner, accompanied by a flutist and a lute player. Gareth made his way through the throng. He could always locate Dagnarus in a crowd. Gareth had simply to find the largest knot of fawning courtiers, and His Highness was certain to be in its center.

Gareth stood on the outskirts of the group, who were laughing uproariously at one of Dagnarus's tales. Happening to catch the prince's eye through an opening between heads, Gareth raised his hand to let Dagnarus know he was there. He expected Dagnarus to respond with nothing more than a slight arch of his eyebrow and was astounded when the prince – bringing his story to a rather abrupt end – surged through the crowd, which parted as a school of fish parts before the shark, and seized upon his friend.

'Patch! I've been waiting for you this hour or more. What makes you so blasted late? Well, never mind.' Dagnarus talked on, not giving Gareth a chance to open his mouth. 'Come with me. I have an errand of the utomost delicacy and importance. Besides, I want you to see her.'

The prince stood on his toes, to peer over the heads of the crowd. Finding that which he sought, he seized hold of the bag sleeve of Gareth's houppelande and dragged him off.

'Make way! Make way!' Dagnarus called, doing a creditable impersonation of a town crier, to everyone's merriment. The prince opened a path for himself, tugging Gareth along in his wake. Unable to see where he was going, Gareth caromed off people left and right, trod on people's feet, knocked ladies' tall hats askew. Emerging hot and flustered and disheveled, Gareth was appalled to find himself in the presence of the King, the crown prince and princess, and an unknown elven couple, all but one of whom were regarding him with amusement. The exception was the elven woman, whose languid gaze noted him, dismissed him, passed over him to stare at the stone wall.

Gareth was accustomed to the ways of elves, having studied them both in books and through Silwyth, the elven chamberlain. He knew the low regard most elves had for humans, and he would have ignored the insult, ignored the woman as far as politeness dictated, but for two things. The first, she was the most extraordinarily beautiful woman Gareth had ever seen in his life, and the second, the look she was giving the stone wall. Her look did not say, as Gareth had expected, 'I find this cold rock more interesting than those who surround me.' Her look was wild and furtive, and said, 'If the gods had pity on me, they would dissolve this rock and let me escape!'

Gareth's attention was drawn away from the woman. He had to doff his cap and bow to the King, who – owing to his age – was seated in a chair, and to Helmos, standing at his father's right hand, and who looked upon Gareth with a warm smile. Gareth averted his eyes in confusion.

His clandestine studies weighed upon him, particularly whenever he was in the company of Helmos, whom he revered and admired more now that he was able to value him with adult understanding. Gareth took the first opportunity to turn from Helmos and his winsome, fragile wife, Anna, to the elven couple.

'Lord and Lady Mabreton, the newly arrived ambassadors,' said Helmos.

At the name 'Mabreton' Gareth was transported in an instant to the scene of the assassination he had witnessed as a child. He stared at the lord in a kind of panic, stories of ghosts coming to mind, until Dagnarus said the word 'brother,' which cleared up the matter immediately.

Still, the shock had been severe. Gareth remained in a sort of daze. Fortunately, he never had much to say and was able to retire into relative obscurity, where he could observe without being called upon to contribute. From his vantage point, he noted that Lord Mabreton, though he bore a strong family resemblance to his late brother, was warmer, more genial and charming than his brother had been. Gareth looked again at Lady Mabreton. She had withdrawn her gaze from the wall but only to stare intently into the warm, bright orb of a stone-light adorning the great oaken table where they were soon to be seated.

Her husband, who appeared quite fond of her, cast her anxious glances and would sometimes pause in the middle of a conversation to ask her in elven if she was warm enough, should she like a cloak or another glass of wine? She replied coolly, in monosyllables, and did not look at him. Gareth gathered by this that she could not speak the human language. No wonder she found the conversation boring. Except that she did not look bored. She looked trapped.

Others came to claim the King's attention. Helmos was required to attend to his father. Dagnarus was able, with adroit tact, to insinuate himself between the elven couple and the King's party, edge them away so that they formed a small group of their own. Gareth, at a commanding glance from Dagnarus, accompanied them, somewhat mystified. Dagnarus had never before evinced the slightest interest in elves, except as enemies across a battlefield. Now he was going out of his way to be charming and winning. He was talking to the lord, but his gaze went continually to the lady, and suddenly Gareth – feeling extremely obtuse for not having thought of this before – understood.

He was appalled. Dagnarus never spoke to Gareth of his love trysts. Gareth had made it clear at the beginning of his friend's sexual exploits (at about the age of fifteen) that he was not interested, wanted to know nothing of them. Gareth had made a few tentative forays into the world of romance, only to find himself pitied and rejected. He had turned his marred face from love forever. He dealt with his own physical needs by paying for them, having found a comfortable, older whore in a well-established house, who, if she mocked him, at least did it behind his back. Gareth had trusted that Dagnarus would have sense enough to keep away from the ladies of the court, unless he actually proposed to marry one of them. And here he found his friend enamored of an elf, a married woman of noble blood. Nothing could be more improper, nothing more dangerous.

And that, Gareth realized in despair, was just what was needed to add spice to Dagnarus's desire.

'Your lady wife does not appear to be enjoying herself, I fear,' said Dagnarus. 'She must consider us boorish dolts.'

'Quite the contrary, Your Highness,' said Lord Mabreton, with another of those fond, anxious glances at his wife. 'Lady Mabreton does not understand your language and thus she finds it tedious. She studies to improve herself, but that must, of necessity, take some time.'

Gareth, who was now watching the lady closely, noted

a glimmer in her blue eyes and a heightened color in her cheeks and guessed that the lady understood far more than she was willing to admit. Probably too proud to let it be known that she spoke Elderspeak, a language the elves consider uncouth and crude.

'My honored mother, the Queen, is deeply worried about your wife,' said Dagnarus. Reaching into a jeweled pouch he wore at his side, he removed a small bundle done up in black-velvet brocade with a purple silken ribbon. 'I took the liberty, therefore, of obtaining a gift my mother hoped might serve to tell Her Ladyship how much we value her presence among us. Would you be so kind as to present this gift to your wife, Lord Mabreton.'

Dagnarus handed the bundle to the lord with a graceful bow. He did not once glance at the lady.

'That is very good of your mother, Your Highness,' said Lord Mabreton, pleased. 'You must present it to her yourself. My dear,' he said tenderly, shifting to elven, 'the prince has a present for you. You will make me exceedingly happy by accepting it.'

Lady Mabreton turned her gaze from the stone-light and looked directly at Dagnarus. Her countenance did not change. Her eyes were placid and still as an ornamental lake. She bowed to him in the elven manner, but she did not accept the gift.

Dagnarus's color rose. He was not accustomed to being treated in such a cavalier fashion. Rather than serve to drive him away, however, her disinterest seemed to captivate him more than ever.

'Shall I unwrap it for Your Ladyship?' Dagnarus said, and, with a graceful flick of his hand, he untied the bow.

The fabric fell away from the object. Silver sparkled, a stone blue as the sky – indeed the Pecwae believe that turquoise comes from little bits of the sky that have tumbled down to earth – made a bright spot of color against the black fabric.

The turquoise stone was large, the largest Gareth had ever seen, and was exquisitely cut into the shape of a lotus blossom, couched in a wonderfully delicate silver-filigree setting. The lady's eyes widened at the sight. Ice maiden though she might be, she was not proof against something so lovely and so valuable. Pecwae jewelry was reputed to be magical.

Dagnarus lifted the pendant from its velvet nest, strung it on the purple ribbon, and held it to the light. The lady could not take her eyes from it. Now her countenance altered expression, now the rose tinged her cheeks, now her eyes were warm and soft. She spoke to her husband, her voice melodious and low.

'Please express my gratitude to the prince. I hesitate to take such an expensive gift –'

'You must take it, Wife,' her husband said, smiling. 'It is from the Queen. Her Highness would be offended otherwise.'

Dagnarus stood watching anxiously, as if he understood her demurs.

'Then,' said the lady, reassured, 'tell Her Majesty that I accept the gift with pleasure.'

Lord Mabreton translated. Dagnarus was ecstatic.

'I ask a favor in return, my lord. Would it be unseemly of me to be allowed to place the stone upon the lady, myself?'

'Certainly not, Your Highness. My dear, His Highness wishes to place the pendant around your neck.'

The lady bowed her head. Dagnarus tied the ends of the ribbon together. Moving close to her, somewhat closer than was absolutely necessary, he lowered the ribbon and the pendant over her head. His hands moved slowly, taking care not to disturb her hair. An astute observer might have seen them tremble slightly.

'May the stone's magic work as its maker intended,' said Dagnarus softly. 'May it keep Your Ladyship safe from harm.'

She lifted her head to regard him, and Gareth saw in that moment that the elf woman understood Elderspeak, if she did not speak it. She knew exactly what the prince had said. Dagnarus's fingers brushed the side of her cheek. The lady's lips parted, her breath came fast. Her cheek was stained with color as if his touch had drawn blood.

Dagnarus's own breathing quickened, his eyes burned with an unnatural luster. The intensity of feeling between the two was so strong that Gareth felt the hair of his arms and neck rise, as though a lightning bolt had struck too near. He thought everyone in the room must notice the blinding flash, particularly Lord Mabreton, but the elf had turned away a moment to respond to another well-wisher. When he turned back, the moment had passed, the bolt had vanished, leaving Gareth waiting nervously for the thunder.

The concussive blast would be delayed, but it would come, Gareth knew with gloomy foreboding. The one comfort he had taken in all Dagnarus's illicit love affairs was that *love* had never been a part of them. Indeed, Dagnarus often made sport of love and lovers, deriding love as an emotion that overthrew rational minds and weakened a man's courage, diluted his ambition.

Now Dagnarus looked dazzled and singed. He who had railed so loudly and so often against love had stepped over its edge and fallen into its chasm with never a cry or backward glance.

Lady Mabreton had lowered her eyes. She was admiring her gift by the time her husband turned to look at her. Dagnarus would have gone on staring at her, thunder-struck, but that Gareth gave his friend a hard poke in the ribs.

Recollecting himself, Dagnarus received the lady's thanks

given through her husband with a smile and a polite rejoinder. The summons to table spared the group an awkward moment of what to say next. Lady Mabreton bowed graciously, and, placing her hand upon her husband's arm, proceeded to a place of honor at the table. She did not look back at the prince.

'She is the most beautiful woman I have ever seen in my life,' Dagnarus said softly, gazing after her. 'I had never imagined such beauty existed!'

'I'm certain *her husband* feels the same,' Gareth said, unhappy, prickly, and sour.

Dagnarus rounded upon his friend. His face pale with fury, his eyes dilated, he struck away Gareth's remonstrating hand.

'Do not lecture me, Patch!' he said. 'Now or ever. Or our friendship is at an end.'

Sweeping his cloak behind him, the prince turned and stalked away from the banquet table, where the guests were just beginning to take their places. At his mother's shrill inquiry to know where he was going, the prince replied brusquely that he was unwell and begged her leave to be excused. His eyes, when he said this, were fixed upon Lady Mabreton, and the lady was aware of that fact, though she attempted to look unconscious of him. Her hand went to the turquoise pendant. She clasped it tightly, perhaps invoking its protective magic.

Pecwae folk magic was strong, Gareth knew from his studies, but he doubted if it was strong enough, doubted if any magic, even that of the most powerful magus, was strong enough to withstand the potent magic of the heart.

Gareth left the hall, as well. No one missed him, and so he was not required to explain himself.

He found Dagnarus where he had guessed he would find him, stretched out on his bed, still in his clothes, his mood dark and lowering. Silwyth moved about the room in silence, folding and putting away Dagnarus's cloak, which had been tossed on the floor, and directing the placement of a collation of cold meats and fruit and bread and jugs of wine, which the servants carried in, deposited, and left. As usual, Silwyth appeared to know everything that had occurred as if he had witnessed it himself.

Gareth came to stand at the end of the bed.

'That hat makes you look a fool,' said Dagnarus.

'I know.' Gareth plucked it off, stuffed the hat under his arm. 'I'm sorry. About what I said.'

'Why?' Dagnarus asked bitterly. 'You only spoke the truth. She is an elf, she is of noble blood, she is the wife of a Dominion Lord, she is a guest in my father's court – how many more reasons can there be for not loving her. Yet I do love her,' he added softly, beneath his breath.

He had taken off his own hat and was absently picking it apart, tearing at the feathers that adorned it and tugging irritably at the delicate stitching.

'Was that the reason you sent for me?' Gareth asked, sitting on the side of the bed.

'Yes,' Dagnarus returned. 'I wanted you to see her. I did not expect to be preached at!'

'I said I was sorry,' Gareth replied. 'I won't preach any more.'

'Good.' Dagnarus sat up, tossed aside the maltreated hat. 'If you promise me that, you may stay and share this supper with me. And you must sleep in your old room. I suppose the Most Revered High Magus can get along without you for a night?'

His eyes flickered, he cast a sidelong glance at Silwyth. Gareth understood that there was business to be discussed, but not in front of the chamberlain.

'If the Most Revered High Magus needs my advice, he knows where to find me,' Gareth said.

'We will serve ourselves, Silwyth,' said Dagnarus. 'You may have the rest of the night to yourself. Oh, by the way, the gift you picked out was perfect. The lady was quite taken with it, wouldn't you agree, Patch?'

'Quite,' said Gareth dryly.

Silwyth bowed. 'I am pleased to have pleased Your Highness.'

'One more thing, Silwyth,' said Dagnarus as the elf was starting to withdraw. 'What is Lady Mabreton's given name?'

'Valura, Your Highness,' said the elf.

'Valura,' Dagnarus repeated, tasting it on his tongue as if it were fine wine. 'And what does that mean in elven?'

'Heart's ease, Your Highness.'

'Heart's ease.' Dagnarus smiled wryly. 'Her parents were sadly mistaken there. That will be all, Silwyth.'

'May I wish you a restful night, Your Highness.'

'You may, though I'm not likely to achieve it,' Dagnarus muttered.

The elf withdrew. The two young men sat down at the table. Gareth ate with hearty appetite, relishing the food which, though certainly not as fine as the feast he might have enjoyed, was much better than the mutton he would have been eating at the Temple. Dagnarus took a few bites, then shoved his plate aside and concentrated on his wine.

'I had one victory today at least,' he said, breaking a long silence. He stared into the wine goblet, swirled the purple liquid in his hand. 'You heard about the death of Lord Donnengal?'

'I did. I wasn't aware that you liked him.'

'I cared nothing about him one way or the other. That wasn't what I meant,' Dagnarus said, impatient with his friend's slowness of thought. 'His death leaves a vacancy among the Dominion Lords.'

'Yes, I suppose it would,' Gareth replied, all unsuspecting. 'Does your father have someone in mind to fill the post?'

'He does,' said Dagnarus. 'Me.'

Gareth had been about to take a sip of wine. He almost dropped the goblet. He stared at his friend.

'You are in earnest.'

'Never more so,' said Dagnarus. 'Why are you surprised? We have talked of this before.'

'And I have always stated my objections. I thought, the last time we spoke on the subject, that I had convinced you.'

'I gave the matter thought,' said Dagnarus, 'and it occurred to me that if I refuse to proceed with this simply because of the danger, then I am a coward. And if I am a coward, then I do not have the right ever again to order another man into battle or any other equally dangerous situation.'

'This is not the same as doing battle,' Gareth cried hotly. 'It is not the same as taking a spear through the heart – a moment's terrible pain and then merciful death. This is Holy Transfiguration, Dagnarus. This could mean your death; yes, but it could mean much worse.'

Dagnarus was scornful. 'I saw the ceremony. I saw my brother undergo it, and it looked unpleasant, true, but nothing I can't endure. I am stronger than he is. The gods made him Lord of Sorrows. They can't do worse than that to me and may do much better.'

Gareth paused before he spoke. The two were alone in the room. With everyone attending the banquet, there should be no one within this part of the castle. Still, Gareth leaned near, so that the breath of his words could be felt upon the prince's cheek, as well as in his ear.

'Helmos had not looked into the Void, Your Highness.'

'So? What of it?' Dagnarus drew back, impatient.

'Helmos had not embraced the Void, my lord,' Gareth continued urgently. 'You have!'

'And so have you, Patch,' Dagnarus said, his voice cold.

'I know,' said Gareth. 'The gods help me, I know.'

'Well, then, explain to me the problem. And why is this the first I've heard of it?'

'Because I have only just entered into studies along these lines, Your Highness. And because I thought you had given up the idea of becoming a Dominion Lord. I saw no need to mention it.'

'Well, and what will happen? Will I sprout horns and a tail?'

'I do not know, my lord,' Gareth said, ignoring the sarcasm. 'I cannot be sure. Nothing like this has ever transpired.'

'Then find out! Meanwhile, I will pursue my course.'

'I will do what I can, Your Highness, but you must remember that I am leading a double life. No one knows I am working in Void magic. I must pursue my studies in the Temple, which are hard enough. These leave me only a limited amount of time in which I may sneak off to study the forbidden texts.'

'Then give up your studies at the Temple! You have said that your magical abilities are far beyond those they are teaching you anyway.'

'I must keep up the pretense or else they would become suspicious. As you say, my masters would be amazed at the magic I can perform.'

Gareth undid the buttons at his neck and breast, spread wide the fabric, laying bare his chest and abdomen.

At the sight, Dagnarus recoiled. Snatching up a handkerchief, he hastily covered his nose and mouth.

'Zounds, Patch! What foul disease have you contracted? And how dare you spread your contagion to me?'

Gareth's skin was covered with boils and pustules, some

278

of them dried, others fresh and oozing, bound with cloth to prevent the pus from seeping through his outer clothing. His expression grim, he peeled back the cloth, biting his lips against the pain as the cloth stuck to the lips of the ulcerations.

'I do not have the plague, Your Highness,' Gareth said. 'Nor am I contagious. You need have no fears on that score.'

'Then what ails you?' Dagnarus demanded, cautiously lowering the handkerchief, yet keeping his distance.

'Void magic,' said Gareth. 'Unlike magic that comes from the gods as a blessing, Void magic comes from the dark parts within us. These pustules are the physical manifestation of my spell-casting. No one knows quite why this occurs. I personally think it is the body's means of rebelling against the Void, of trying to convince my spirit to turn away from the darkness.'

'Cover it back up!' Dagnarus looked away, repulsed. 'The sight makes my skin crawl. I've seen limbs hacked off and never blenched, but I hate disease. You know that. What possessed you to show me?'

'I suffer only what is required of me by the Void,' said Gareth, buttoning his clothes. 'These are the sacrifices I must make to gain my magic.'

'And what is all this supposed to be telling me?' Dagnarus demanded, hurriedly quaffing his wine and refilling the goblet. 'You're not saying I'll break out in pox like that?'

Gareth did not immediately respond. Instead he asked, 'If you are nominated for the post of Dominion Lord, you must take the Seven Preparations. How do you propose to pass them?'

'I don't know.' Dagnarus shrugged. 'I don't know what they entail. Surely they cannot be too difficult. My brother passed them.'

'I have studied them and I know this much – *you* will

not be able to pass them, Your Highness. Not without recourse to the Void,' Gareth concluded.

'Do you have so little faith in me?' Dagnarus asked, with a dangerous glint in his green eyes.

'Will you bind the sores of lepers?' Gareth countered. 'Sores like these I bear?'

'Good gods, no!' Dagnarus grimaced. 'Why should I?'

'To test your compassion. Will you sit for hours with a panel of the Revered Magi, discoursing on the likelihood of the transmogrification of the soul after death?'

'You're making this up!' Dagnarus protested, laughing and tossing off his wine.

'I am perfectly serious, my lord.'

'Well, then, no, I won't. I will give them a lecture on battlefield tactics instead.'

'You have failed two already.'

'I will not fail. If need be, I *will* call upon the Void to assist me,' said Dagnarus carelessly, filling his wine goblet yet again.

'The Void requires payment for its services, Your Highness,' said Gareth, his voice urgent, intense. 'The Void requires sacrifice. Give nothing, and you will get nothing.'

'Then I will give,' said Dagnarus, his brows drawn, his eyes flashing.

'Give what?' Gareth pressed him. 'What will you be willing to give?'

'Whatever it takes, so long as I'm not disfigured,' said Dagnarus, impatient with the discussion. 'I want this, Patch,' he said suddenly, vehemently. 'I cannot achieve the crown unless I am the equal of my brother.'

'You cannot achieve the crown at all while your brother still lives,' Gareth said quietly.

'Accidents happen,' Dagnarus returned. 'A fall from a horse killed his mother. A slip on a wet paving stone. A tumble from his boat. Or he might catch some plague when he's out doing his charitable works. The Void wants a sacrifice. Let it be –'

'Don't say it, Dagnarus!' Gareth sprang to his feet, spilling the wine and knocking his dish from the table. He clapped his hand over the prince's lips. 'For gods' sake, do not say it!'

'Well, I won't,' said Dagnarus, irritably shoving aside Gareth's hand. 'And don't touch me. I'm still not convinced you haven't got the pox. As to what I said, I didn't mean it. I have no great love for my brother, but I wish him no ill. So long as he doesn't oppose me in becoming a Dominion Lord.'

'If he did,' Gareth replied, 'he would do so only out of love for you. As do I.'

'I have doubts about my brother's affection,' said Dagnarus. 'But not yours, Patch.'

'Thank you, Your Highness.' Gareth was drowsy from wine and fatigue. He rubbed his eyes, trying to stop himself from slipping into sleep.

'Go to bed,' Dagnarus ordered, emptying one of the wine jugs and looking for another. 'You are dull company.'

'I'm sorry, Your Highness,' Gareth said. 'But I have not slept much lately.'

Dagnarus regarded him curiously. 'What magic have you been attempting then, to make a leper of yourself?'

Gareth shook his head. 'I will tell you in good time, Your Highness. But it is too soon yet. Too soon.'

Dagnarus shrugged, not particularly interested.

Gareth started for his small closet, off the prince's bedroom.

'She is beautiful, is she not?' Dagnarus said softly, staring into his full goblet.

'Very beautiful,' said Gareth.

Dagnarus smiled into the wine.

Gareth went to his bed with a sigh.

FOUR

Heart's Ease

'A VISIT TWO DAYS IN A ROW, MY SON? AFTER ignoring me for a three-month? What I have done to be so deserving?' Emillia complained. Too much food and too much wine the night before had left her cross and shrewish, ill-tempered with everyone, including her adored son. 'Especially after disgracing me as you did last night.'

'And for that I have come to make my apologies, Madam,' Dagnarus said humbly. 'I was taken extremely unwell. Had I stayed, I would have truly disgraced you, by depositing what I had eaten for dinner upon what we were to eat for supper.'

The Queen was all concern. She gazed up at him anxiously. 'You do look pale. I believe that you are running a fever. Your skin burns to the touch. You should go to the Hospitalers at once and take a physic.'

Dagnarus was pale and burning, but his fever did not come from any malady other than love. He had been waiting for hours, looking forward with impatience to the time when his mother held audience, looking forward to seeing again the beautiful Lady Mabreton, to perhaps win from her a smile or at least a look. But he could not find her. She was not among the ladies-in-waiting who curtsied to him, not among those cleaning up the spilt powder, which the queen had thrown down in a temper, not among those picking up the clothes Her Majesty had tossed about in a fit of pique.

Dagnarus's disappointment was acute. He was astonished and uneasy at the lady's absence. It occurred to him that perhaps his mother had sent the elf woman upon some errand, to fetch more thread or retrieve a dropped handkerchief or search for a lost earring.

'I hope all went well last night,' he said. 'I trust that Lord and Lady Mabreton enjoyed themselves?'

'Oh, who can tell with these elves,' Emillia returned snappishly. 'Ingrates, all of them. I take this woman into my household at your father's wish, mind you, I would have never chosen her for a companion myself, such a sullen, moping creature, who handed me the pearl necklace when I had asked for the ruby. Didn't she, Constance? I said as clearly as I could that I wanted to wear the ruby necklace and she took out the pearl, just to annoy me, I am certain.'

'Mother,' said Dagnarus gently, 'Lady Mabreton does not speak our language.'

'Oh, of course she does,' said the Queen. 'All elves do. They merely pretend that they don't in order to spy upon us. But it doesn't matter now. She is gone and good riddance. I was quite weary of looking at her. Such a mousy, unattractive woman.'

'Gone?' Dagnarus could feel the blood draining from his face, as it emptied from his heart. Certain that his mother's jealous nature could not fail to note such a dramatic change of countenance, he bent down to recover a comb that had fallen from her hair, hiding his face until he could regain mastery of himself.

'What do you mean gone, Mother?' he asked with affected carelessness. 'Through the Portal? Back to her homeland?'

'I don't know where the elf has gone,' said Queen Emillia, turning to her mirror, refreshing herself after her trying morning. 'Nor do I care. Where are you off to now?'

'I am taking your advice, Mother, and going to the Hospitalers,' said Dagnarus. 'I beg that you will excuse me. I am again quite unwell.'

'Perhaps what he has may be catching,' said Emillia, after he had gone. 'Quickly, burn some sage and bring me a clove of garlic to sniff. Quickly, ladies!'

'Silwyth!' Dagnarus shouted. 'Silwyth, where – Oh, there you are. Silwyth, Lady Mabreton is gone!'

'Yes, Your Highness,' replied the elf coolly. 'I was looking for you to inform you of the fact.'

'Where? Why? Has she gone back to her homeland? Is something wrong? Is it her husband?'

'Your Highness, calm yourself,' said Silwyth in a low voice, glancing toward the open door of the prince's bedchamber.

Dagnarus saw the wisdom in this and kept silent, though he seethed with impatience. He poured himself a mug of wine and drank it down. The warm wine was pleasant, seeping through his veins to his heart, replacing the blood he had lost and restoring him to sanity.

Silwyth glanced up and down the hallway, which was fortunately empty at this time of the late morning. He closed the door.

'Tell me,' said Dagnarus. 'Where has she gone?'

'The Lady Mabreton left court early this morning. She has traveled to her house on the shores of the River Hammerclaw.'

'So she has not gone back to Tromek!' Dagnarus sighed in relief so great that he was forced to lean upon the table a moment for support. 'Why did she leave? Was it my mother?'

'I cannot say, Your Highness –'

'No! by the gods!' Dagnarus answered his own question. 'It's me, isn't it? She left because of me! She loves me, and she fears her own heart. Fetch my boots and my cloak –'

'Your Highness,' said Silwyth, rebuking, 'you cannot act in this impetuous manner. Stop and consider. She is escorted by a troop of soldiers, she has her servants with her. You will bring trouble to her if you are indiscreet. You would never rush off to battle in this mad way, Your Highness.'

The last words made sense, penetrated the happy fog surrounding Dagnarus. This was a battle, this was war. The lady was in retreat, had fled before him, which meant that he had found the chink in her armor of ice. His first thought had been to pursue in haste and secure his conquest, but he could see now that this plan was liable to lose him the war. He needed to scout the land, learn the strength of the enemy forces arrayed against him, decide upon a course of action.

'You are right, Silwyth. I need to know the location of this house. I need to know the layout of the house and the grounds, where the guards are liable to be posted, the location of the guardhouse, how many men are with her, and where the servants sleep.' Dagnarus relapsed into gloom. 'An impossible task, I fear.'

'Not so, Your Highness. A servant of the current Lord Mabreton was a servant to the former Lord. He will supply me with the answers to your questions.'

'Won't he be suspicious?'

'Undoubtedly, but he knows how to hold his tongue. He has been doing so for many years now, at the behest of another.'

Dagnarus eyed Silwyth closely, trying to see past the impassive expression on the elf's face. 'You mean that this man is a spy upon his master.'

'Let us say, Your Highness, that this man serves a greater master than Lord Mabreton.'

'He is a spy for the Shield of the Divine. But you said that Lord Mabreton is loyal to the Shield. Why place a spy on him?'

'The Shield rejoices in Lord Mabreton's loyalty, Your Highness. He rejoices in it so much that he never tires of receiving constant proof of it.'

'I see.' Dagnarus grinned. 'I wonder what you have told the Shield about me, Silwyth.'

'I have told him that you are an excellent soldier, a brilliant commander, a poor scholar, and a follower of the Void.'

Dagnarus raised an eyebrow, leaned back in his chair. 'The Void, Silwyth? What are you talking about? That's a religion for sorcerers and witches. A dark and evil religion, if we are to believe half the nonsense the magi preach against it.'

'A religion for a prince, too, Your Highness,' said Silwyth, removing a thick, warm woolen cloak from a trunk and shaking out the wrinkles. He held it to the light to check for moth holes. 'And an aspiring young magus. Do not concern yourself, Your Highness. I, too, know when to hold my tongue. I have said nothing of this to anyone with the exception of the Shield. It is only right that he knows all he can about the man with whom he one day intends to ally.'

'And when is that day?' Dagnarus asked, after a moment.

'The day when Your Highness is King.'

'And when is *that* day?' Dagnarus demanded.

'The day when Your Highness chooses,' Silwyth replied.

Dagnarus was silent, dangerous. 'Supposing what you say is true,' he said at last. 'I don't like anyone holding such power over me, Silwyth.'

'Which is precisely why I informed Your Highness. I have informed you that I know, and I have informed you of what I have done with the knowledge. What Your Highness does with me now is up to Your Highness. I could offer you assurances of my loyalty and my silence, but if Your Highness does not trust me, then such assurances would be meaningless. And if Your Highness does trust me, then he needs no assurance.'

Dagnarus responded with the glimmer of a smile. 'Oh, I trust you, Silwyth. I'll tell you why I trust you. As you recall, I know the truth about what happened to the first Lord Mabreton. My father would not put the lord's murderer to death for the crime, the killer being a member of a foreign government and all, but he would certainly lock up the assassin in the dungeons for a considerable length of time. To be locked up in a dark cell with no glimpse of the outside – sheer torture for an elf. I believe such an elf would find death preferable. Don't you agree, Silwyth?'

'Indeed, Your Highness,' said Silwyth, bowing. 'Your Highness knows my people very well.'

'Carry on, then,' said Dagnarus. 'Go talk to your spy. We've wasted enough time already.'

Cloaked and booted, provided with the information he needed, a map showing the house's location and a diagram of the house itself, both of which he had tucked into his hat, Dagnarus set out upon his journey. He traveled alone. At first, he had considered taking Silwyth; the prince spoke no elven and a translator might prove useful. After further consideration, he had decided that Silwyth should stay behind in order to divert questions about the prince's sudden absence.

Fortunately, Dagnarus was known to be fond of hunting. One of the huntsmen had that very day brought word of a marauding wild boar, which was terrorizing some villagers. Dagnarus let it be known that he intended to slay the beast. He took his bow and arrows and, while waiting for his horse to be saddled and readied, he and Captain

Argot discussed the various methods of killing a boar and whether one should aim for the eye or the throat.

Argot wondered that Dagnarus took no companions with him. Dagnarus admitted that he was in a foul mood, a thoroughly rotten frame of mind, that he would be poor company for any man. He needed solitude and the fever of the hunt to burn away the cobwebs. Argot wished His Highness good fortune and returned to his duties.

Dagnarus galloped off just as evening shadows were snatching away the rainbows from the falls. The way was not far, the road a good one and well maintained. Many nobles and even a few wealthy guildsmen had homes along the riverbank, where they went to escape the heat of the city during the summer. Moonlight lit the road, and though not often given to poetic musings, Dagnarus imagined the road a ribbon of silver unwinding before him, a ribbon that would shortly – he hoped – tie him to the woman he loved.

Two hours' hard riding brought him to the vicinity of the elven house. He had no difficulty finding his way. He could see the tracks made by the elven bodyguard quite clearly in the moonlight. He could even tell where the party left the main highway and entered the side road leading to the house. Dagnarus halted at the highway to tether his horse, for he planned to proceed from there on foot. He concealed the horse in a glade with grass enough for grazing and a stream for drinking, gave the horse a long lead, and continued his journey. First, he refreshed his mind by looking again at the map of the house, though he really had no need to do so, for the house – her house – was etched in fire in his brain.

He moved silently and stealthily through the forest, his bow and arrows slung on his back, his knife in his hand. He did not expect to meet any patrols in the forest; the elf servant had informed Silwyth that the bodyguards kept only leisurely watch whenever the river house was occupied. Still, he would not be caught unawares.

His precautions were needless. He came within sight of the house without meeting anything more formidable than an irate possum, who hissed at him and bared her teeth, before skulking off into the underbrush. Dagnarus was in high spirits; his desire, the thrill and excitement of the adventure proved an intoxicating combination. He wondered amusedly what sort of omen a hissing possum in his path might be. He'd have to remember to ask his orken friends the next time he went fishing.

He settled himself in the shadow of a tree to watch the house, which he could see outlined against the moon-sparkling water of the swift-flowing river. The house was large and splendid, built in the elven style with white-washed walls and red-tile roof, surrounded by a high wooden stockade. The front of the house was dark; no lights shone inside. Torches mounted on posts at set intervals along the stockade blazed in the night. Looking through the gate, which had been left open, Dagnarus could see a densely planted garden of trees and flowers, intended to remind the elven inhabitants of their homeland. As he watched, two elven guards met at the fence's center gate, completing a patrol that would take them around the entire perimeter. He counted no more guards than these two. The watch they kept was nominal.

The servant had said that the guards walked their patrol only once on the hour, testing the padlocks on the gates. The rest of the time, they talked and played at dice at the main gate.

Dagnarus curbed his impatience, inured himself to wait through an entire cycle to see if the elven guard behaved as predicted. Sure enough, the elves squatted down on their haunches, drew a circle in the dirt with their knives, and brought out their dice bags. Dagnarus was forced to sit through several games, watch tams change hands, and listen to their incomprehensible gabble. A bell struck somewhere within the courtyard. The elves rose lazily to their feet, stretched, and left to make their rounds.

Dagnarus timed them, counting to himself, until they returned. He noted that the two ended up on opposite sides of the gate from where they had started, which meant that they had passed each other at the back of the house. Each lock was therefore checked by two different people, a sensible precaution.

Upon their return, the elves knelt and resumed their game. Dagnarus was on his feet, slipping through the forest, heading for the back of the house, before the first die was tossed.

The stockade's wooden poles, planed smooth to form points at the top, rose above Dagnarus, about double his height. He had been warned about the fence and now drew a length of rope from his belt. He tied a loop with a slipknot, as the orken fishermen had taught him, and flung the loop up to the top of the fence. After several tries, he finally caused the loop to slide over one of the fence poles. He pulled the rope taut, then climbed up the rope to the top of the stockade. Balanced precariously, he looked down into the garden. Some sort of thick, tall bush had been planted along the fence row. There was no way to avoid it. He dropped lightly down and landed in the bush with a rustling of leaves and cracking of twigs that he was certain could be heard back in Vinnengael.

He froze, scarcely breathing, waiting for someone to summon the guard. The elf informant had said that often-times his mistress walked the garden in the night, and when she was in the garden, so were her attendants.

No one called out. No one came to see what was sneaking about in the shrubbery. Dagnarus disentangled himself from the bush. Branches plucked at his cloak, leaves crackled underfoot. A twitch on the rope brought it snaking down on top of him. He coiled it up and hid it beneath the bush. Keeping to the shadows created by the flaming torches, he crept through the garden toward the house.

He moved slowly, testing every footfall, skirting ornamental fish ponds and dodging statuary. The garden was immense. He had passed well beyond the light of the torches, was in the moonlight now, and he was rapidly becoming lost and disoriented. He had spotted the house from atop the fence, but had lost sight of it once he dropped down. He had no idea how far he'd traveled or how he would ever find his way back to where he'd stashed the rope. The innumerable paths led nowhere, but meandered and wandered here and there, sometimes going in circles, once dumping him in a grotto, and twice leading to dead ends, where he was apparently supposed to admire some stupid tree.

The servant had not thought to tell him how to make his way through the garden maze. Dagnarus, having no experience of elven gardens, had not thought to ask. Hot and sweating, scratched, and half-suffocated by the perfume of the night-blooming plants, he began to be extremely frustrated. It seemed he might spend the rest of his days wandering about this godsforsaken place.

He had just accidentally stepped into a pond and at the same time narrowly avoided braining himself on a huge bell hanging from a tree limb, when he looked up and saw Lady Mabreton.

She walked in a large cleared area, walked upon a large round patio made of some sort of magical white stone that mimicked the moonlight, for the rock shone beneath her feet with an eerie pale radiance. She was clad in a diaphanous silken robe, her long black hair was undone and hung about her shoulders, falling to her waist. The moonlight from above and below illuminated her body, which was naked beneath her robe. She wore only the turquoise pendant, his pendant, around her neck. He knew then that she loved him and he would be victorious, and he trembled with the enormity of his longing.

She was not at ease. She was not strolling in the garden admiring its beauty. She paced feverishly, her hands clasped tightly together as if in distress, never once looking about her. She murmured to herself something in elven, which Dagnarus could not understand. She was too distraught to have heard the noise he'd made.

Dagnarus stood with one foot in the fish pond, the chill water seeping through his leather boot, and never noticed. His desire was a physical pain of such magnitude it came near stopping his heart. Yet how to win her? How to confront her? What was she to think of a man suddenly rising up out of her garden? She would suspect him of being a thief or worse. She would cry out for the guards.

He considered seizing her from behind, clapping his hand over her mouth, warning her to keep silent. But she would resent such rough treatment, nor could he bring himself – now that he saw her – to touch her unless she consented. He did not want her by force. He wanted her loving and languishing in his arms.

In her restless pacing, she had walked away from him. Now, she turned and was moving back in his direction.

Dagnarus stepped out onto the moonlit patio, his booted feet ringing on the rock. She lifted her head in astonishment, stared at him with wide and fearful eyes.

Dagnarus sank to his knees before her, spread wide his hands, gazed up at her. 'I will not harm you, Valura. I come to you out of love,' he said simply. 'If you choose, summon the guards and have them slay me on the spot.' He did not hope that she understood him, yet surely his gesture was plain.

She stared at him, her breath coming fast, her hands clasped tightly before her. She did not scream for the guards or cry out for her women. She walked toward him, her steps faltering, and reached out a trembling hand.

'I dream,' she said in a hushed whisper, speaking Elderspeak. 'You are not real.'

Joy surged through Dagnarus's heart. He rose to his feet and clasped her hand. At his touch, she gasped, started, and shrank back, tried to pull away. He detained her, clasping her soft and slender hand.

'I am real, Valura. My love for you is real. As real as your love for me.'

'I do not love you!' she cried, turning her head away from him.

'Is that the truth?' he asked, his heart in his voice. He released his hold on her hand. 'Tell me you do not love me. Look at me and say those words, and I will leave and never trouble you again.'

The lady stood long moments in silence, a silence that seemed to last from the beginning of time. He waited patiently, he who had never in his life waited patiently for anything. But he wanted this as he had wanted nothing else in his life.

At length, she raised her head. Her face was wan and pale in the moonlight, her eyes dark and shimmering like the water in the still ponds, her lips so pallid that they almost disappeared. 'To my shame, I love you, Dagnarus,' she said, and a tear slid down her cheek.

She led him to her bed, located in a sumptuously decorated room just off the patio.

'What about the guard? The servants?' he asked in a breathless whisper.

'I have sent the servants to their rest. They will not bother us. You must be gone before the morning, however.'

He stripped off his clothes. She anointed his naked body with fragrant oil, before their lovemaking, an elven ritual that heightened his desire to burning agony, agony that was quenched and then rekindled and quenched again.

When their love was sated, he lay in her arms, his head

upon her breast, his hand idly caressing her skin, not so much to reawaken desire as to renew its memory. She ran her fingers through his hair and kissed his forehead and his eyelids and shivered at his touch.

'It is almost morning, beloved,' she said. 'The servants will be here to dress me. You must leave now and quickly.'

'No,' he said calmly. 'I won't.'

'What?' She paled. 'What are you trying to do to me? You will be my death!'

'I will leave, but only on one condition. That you return this day to the court.'

'No!' Valura shook her head. She sighed and clasped his hands, kissed his fingers. 'No. Do not ask that of me. How could I see you every day and not long to be with you? How could I endure my husband's touch.' She shuddered. 'No, it would be torture. I am better off here. I have known one night of bliss. That will sustain me.'

'But it will not sustain me,' Dagnarus said, gently shoving aside her hair so that she could not hide behind its fragrant curtain. 'I want to see you every day. I want to hear your voice, to touch you, to love you. There are secret passages in the palace, places we may meet and satisfy our desire. Your husband will never know. No one will ever know.'

She shook her head again.

'Very well,' said Dagnarus, his voice harsh. 'Then let your servants find me. Let your guards come and kill me. If I must live without you, then I do not want to live.'

'By the gods, I believe that you are serious,' she said, regarding him in wonder. She struggled a moment within herself, but her want, her desire was as great as his. 'Very well,' she said, lowering her gaze. 'This day, I will return to the court.'

'This night, we'll be together again!' he said, kissing her.

Gently, chidingly, she pushed him away. 'Go now, my love! Quickly!'

'But how do I find my way out?' he asked, putting on his clothes. He had forgotten in his transport of pleasure the garden maze he would have to traverse.

'Follow the stones that are marked with a rose. They will lead you down some stairs, through a tunnel that passes under the stockade. The tunnel leads into the boathouse. Here is the key to the lock of the door. Go through the boathouse and out its door and you will be beyond the stockade. Farewell, my dear one.'

'Until tonight,' he said, and kissed her one more time, then, seeing that the sky was brightening in the east, he left her.

The rose stones were easy to find, led him straight to the stairs. He entered the tunnel, which was cool and dank, and came to the door of the boathouse. He fit the key into the lock, opened the door cautiously to make certain it did not creak. From the safety of the boathouse, he watched the guards walk their rounds and, when they were past, he strolled out in a leisurely manner, cutting through the woods back to where he had left his horse.

Valura lay down in her bed after her lover's departure, her thoughts walking with him every step through the garden. She started in alarm, thinking she heard the creak of the boathouse door on its rusted hinges. She realized it was only her fancy, she could not possibly hear from this distance. Tensely, she waited for the guards to discover him, but the house and the grounds were silent. The hooves of his horse drummed in her blood, and she knew he was safely away.

She snuggled down in the feather bed, wrapping the blankets close around her. His scent was in the bed, on the pillow. She clasped the pillow to her, breathed in his scent, and the remembered thrill of their lovemaking was pleasant agony.

One of the servants came in, intending to open the curtains to let in the sunshine.

'Leave me,' Valura commanded in a low voice. 'I am unwell. Tell the others to stay away.'

The servant bowed, startled, and scurried out.

'What should I do?' Valura asked the shadows.

She knew well what she should do. She should leave this house, leave Vinnengael, return to her husband's house, to her own land, her own people. Closing her eyes, she pictured her husband's house: the rooms clean and empty, devoid of objects that might create clutter; the gardens well laid out, well tended, kept neat and orderly; the wind chimes that were muffled if the wind blew too fiercely, lest their music become wild and discordant. Valura curled her body around the pillow, huddled on herself like an animal who has escaped the snare. She could not go back. If she did, she would die.

She was one of five children, the middle child, the lonely child. The elder two were brothers, much older, and fast friends. The younger two were sisters, much younger, wholly devoted to each other, petted and pampered by her parents. The only asset her parents valued about Valura was her remarkable beauty, and then, like some prized cow, they thought only of how much they could fetch for her at market.

Valura came from a House that was noble but impoverished, a terrible combination, brought about by poor management and misplaced alliances. A family less noble could work to eke out an existence. They would not be burdened with responsibilities to those above and below, responsibilities that were costly.

Even the gods forsook them, for the Honored Ancestor had grown so enraged at the bunglings of his son-in-law that he left his daughter's house and nothing that anyone said or did could induce him to return. Worn and worried with the constant struggle to scratch out an existence, the parents might be forgiven the fact that they waited impatiently for their children to grow and help share the burden. Valura's brothers were to win wealth with their swords. Valura was to win wealth with her face and her body.

On the day when elven custom deemed that she had passed from girlhood to womanhood, Valura was given in marriage to Lord Balor Mabreton. His was a relatively new House with immense wealth, searching for respectability and a noble lineage for his children. Valura was the answer to his prayers. In the latter case, however, he was doomed to disappointment. Valura had no desire to bear children. Pregnancy, with its sickness and its grotesque swelling of the body, and childbirth, with its pain, were abhorrent to her.

She knew the herbs to drink to rid herself of such a burden, and this she had done three times in her first marriage. If her husband had caught her, he had the right, by elven law, to slay her. Fortunately, the first Lord Mabreton was so obtuse that he never thought to question the fact that his lovely wife was apparently barren.

Stifled by the constraints of elven society, by the strictures of duty – duty to family, duty to one's husband, duty to the ancestors, duty to the poor, duty to the rich, duty to the Divine, duty to the Shield of the Divine, Valura saw the years of her life as a prisoner sees the years of his. Everywhere she turned was a wall.

She had not wanted to move to Vinnengael with her first husband, but not for the reasons she gave out. She did not like humans, that was true. She found them crude and loud, violent and capricious. And for the very reasons that she found them so distasteful, she envied them, admired them. Thus she isolated herself from them, lest they contaminate her with their twin diseases of freedom and independence.

Valura had once in her life seen her cell door open. That was with the untimely death of the first Lord Mabreton. She knew well enough that he had been assassinated, the Shield of the Divine had all but told her the truth in order that she should not cause trouble. She had no intention of causing trouble. She would have fallen on her knees and blessed the assassin, if she had known who he was. Her cell door was opened, she felt sunlight warm on her face, and then it slammed shut, trapping her inside.

The younger Lord Mabreton chose to take her as his bride.

If she had known him first, had married him instead of his elder brother, she might have grown to love him. Dalor was kind and gentle. He never forced his attentions upon her, as had her first husband. But Valura had discovered that the only way she could bear the life inside her prison cell was to make certain that if she could not get out, no one else would get in. Her husband was a good man, who loved her and constantly strove to please her, and she pitied him sometimes. Pity was the only soft emotion she could ever feel for him.

Once again, she'd been forced to live among the humans. This time, she could not isolate herself. Her husband would have been willing to allow her to stay in the house on the river, but the Shield had ordered her to serve as one of the Queen's ladies-in-waiting, an onerous task. Valura hated human ladies with a passion and wanted to be like them with an equal passion. The dichotomy of her conflicting emotions made her soul a frantic bird, beating its wings in frustration against the bars of its cage. Soon, it must beat itself to death.

And then Dagnarus had reached out his hand and opened the door. The bird had flown free, and it had flown straight to him.

She had heard of the young prince, heard much of him upon her arrival. The ladies of the court spoke of him constantly, talking aloud about his good looks and his regal demeanor, his stylish dress. They spoke in whispers about his reputed dalliances, seeming shocked, protesting that they should never allow his advances, but simpering and preening the moment he came into view.

Valura wasn't interested. He was a man, and men were hot breath, clumsy fumblings in the darkness, and pain. And always the possibility of the seed taking root inside her and growing into another creature as miserable as she was.

Closing her eyes, she was once again at the banquet. The first she knew of him was his voice, melodious, low, not raucous like so many humans. His hands, she recalled his hands – clean and well kept, with long fingers, rounded at the tips. Strong hands, not soft hands, but callused from the sword. And in those hands, her gift.

Her hand clasped the pendant around her neck. No one had ever given her a gift such as that, a gift for her alone, a gift that was not meant to be shared with her family. Raising her eyes from the gift to the giver, she had seen Dagnarus for the first time. She had seen the admiration in his eyes, but she'd seen admiration in the eyes of men before, and that did not touch her. But when he had hung the pendant around her neck, when his hand had brushed against her cheek, she had seen admiration superseded by love and longing and she had known an equivalent longing, a longing and desire that surprised and frightened her.

Lying awake that night, she had imagined his hands on her body. She had imagined his breath on her lips, and the thought had thrilled her. Disgrace, ruin, death, not only for herself but for her family – such was the penalty for illicit love. She made herself think of all that might happen and, to her dismay, the thoughts did not frighten away the desire but increased it. She fled, thinking that this must end it. He would be offended, would lose interest in her, would forget.

But even far away from him, locked up in her isolated, well-guarded, and protected house, she had known the torment of loving him. Unable to sleep, she had escaped to the garden, to let the autumn wind cool her fevered body, to remonstrate with herself, to slam shut the door on her cell and keep it shut, though the lock was broken.

And then he was there, the embodiment of her dreams and desires, kneeling before her, bold and tender, daring and humble, leaving the choice, the decision to her.

She smiled, kissed the pendant, and gave herself to remembered ecstasy. She would return to Vinnengael. She would walk out the door of her cell and never look behind.

That evening, Silwyth was assisting the prince to dress for dinner. Dagnarus had dismissed the lords usually attendant upon him, bidding them go drink his health and giving them money for the purpose. He was in an excellent mood, said that his hunting had gone exceedingly well. The lordlings were only too happy to obey.

'Your Highness,' said Silwyth, 'I thought perhaps you would like to know that Lady Mabreton has returned to the court.'

Dagnarus's eyes flashed; his hand, lacing his doublet, shook slightly. 'That is excellent news, Silwyth. Thank you. Is there some clever person that you know who might be able to slip a note to Her Ladyship? Manage the task in such a way that no one would see the exchange?'

'I believe I know just such a person, Your Highness,' said Silwyth, his face impassive.

'Good. Here is the note. Oh, and Silwyth, scatter some rose petals on my bed this night, will you? And see to it that I am not disturbed.'

FIVE

The Dark Draught

THE WEATHER, WHICH HAD BEEN UNUSUALLY warm for autumn, changed from calm placidity to howling gale in what seemed a matter of moments. Huge banks of black-green clouds obscured the sun. The leaves that had been skittering down the street in one direction were suddenly lifted in a flurry into the air, whirled about, and sent flying in a direction completely opposite. The wind rose. Rain pelted down with the force of thrown daggers, and sleet rattled on the wooden shake roofs.

The orken, who had read the omens the previous night – flights of seabirds moving inland – had not gone out in their ships at all that day. The humans, who had laughed at orken superstition and taken advantage of the clear, sunny afternoon to try their luck, found themselves in peril, with the seas running high and wild and the wind ripping sailcloth and snapping masts.

'Surely you're not going out on a such a dreadful night as this?' A young female novice stopped to watch Gareth fasten his cloak closely about his body and lift the hood of his cowl up over his head.

'I must, I am afraid,' Gareth replied, struggling with the

clasp of the large pin holding his cloak together. 'The sick I tend do not find themselves better just because the weather has taken a turn for the worse.'

'How very dedicated you are,' said the novice, looking at him with an interest she had never previously shown, though the two had been together in the same classes ever since they were twelve years old. 'Let me help you with that clasp.'

Gareth allowed her to take the pin from him, thrust the pointed end through the thick fabric of his heavy woolen cloak, and fasten it tightly. She was attractive in a brown-eyed, pink-cheeked, winsome way. Her hands lingered to smooth his cloak and fuss with his hood.

'You will be chilled to the bone when you return,' she continued. 'I will be up late with my studies. Often I make myself a honey posset in the middle watches of the night. I could make enough for two, if you have returned by then.'

Part of Gareth wanted very much to say yes, to drink the honey posset, and perhaps to kiss the honey from those inviting lips. And then what? She would slip out of her robes and he would slip out of his. She would see his body covered with oozing sores . . .

'I am sorry,' he said in confusion – he had never truly grown accustomed to lying – 'but I do not know when I will return. Thank you for the kind thought, but, really, it's impossible . . .'

She had gone on, shrugging, not much bothered by his refusal after all. Gareth sighed and went on his way.

The porter, who let him out the door, had to throw his body against it to force it open against the wind's icy blast. He stared at Gareth as one stares at a madman gibbering and dancing in the street.

Outside, the wind struck Gareth a blow that held him in place, unmoving. Lowering his head, he forged on, making his cautious way down the Temple steps, which were slick with sleet and rain. He had nearly reached the bottom when he bumped into someone coming in the opposite direction.

Each man put out his hands to steady the other.

'I beg pardon,' Gareth said, startled by the collision. 'I trust I have not –'

'Gareth!' The man peered at Gareth, but he could not see him well through the darkness and the storm. 'I know your voice. Yes' – the person turned Gareth so that his face was illuminated by the light of a torch, a torch that flared and sputtered in the driving rain – 'it is you.'

'Master Ev-evaristo,' Gareth stammered.

'Just the person I wanted to see.' Evaristo shouted to be heard over the howl of the wind. 'I have tried for two days to have a word with you. Didn't you get my messages? One would think you were deliberately avoiding me!'

Gareth, who had been doing just that, endeavored to make his escape. 'If you will excuse me, Master, I am wanted –'

'No,' said Evaristo, seizing hold of Gareth with a firm grasp. 'I have you now, and I'm not letting you go. Come back inside. What I have to say will only take a moment, then you may be off on whatever errand draws you forth on such a raw night.'

To have fled would have looked extremely suspicious. Gareth could do nothing but accompany his former tutor back into the Temple. The porter, again forced to wrestle with the door and expose himself to the elements, received them with ungracious looks and mutterings.

Evaristo drew Gareth into a quiet alcove. The tutor removed his soaking cloak. Gareth hunched more closely into his, made certain that his hood left his face at least in partial shadow. One of the sores had erupted on his face. His fellow students mistook it for a pimple, but he feared that Evaristo might see it and guess the truth.

303

'What does take you out on such a night?' Evaristo asked cheerfully.

He had changed little in the intervening eight years, grown rounder and more comfortable perhaps. He was a happy man, a contented man, pleased with his wife and his children, pleased with his advancement in the ranks of the magi. He now ran a school for young boys, children of wealthy merchants, and was doing quite well for himself.

Gareth had his lie to hand, recited it glibly enough, recalling with a sinking heart that in the days of his childhood Evaristo had been quick to tell when the whipping boy was prevaricating and when he was telling the truth.

'Fulfilling the requirement for charitable works . . . I tend the sick . . . housebound . . . I fix their meals . . .'

'The trials of the novice,' said Evaristo, smiling. 'How well I remember. I won't keep you from your soup-making.' He peered at Gareth searchingly to try to see through the shadows. 'How have you been? You look pale, as if you had been ill.'

'I am in excellent health, Master,' said Gareth, hugging the shadows close. 'As you say, the trials of a novice . . .'

'Late hours, too much study. You must get more exercise and eat more. You are far too thin.'

'Master –' Gareth began with a hint of impatience.

'I know. You have somewhere else to be. Gareth.' Evaristo grew very serious. Casting a glance about to see that they were alone, the tutor moved a step toward him. 'Gareth, what is this I hear? That Dagnarus is going to be nominated for Dominion Lord?'

Gareth wondered how best to respond to this. His first inclination was to deny knowing anything about it. This he abandoned. Evaristo knew the close relationship between the two young men. He would never believe that Dagnarus had not mentioned something this important to his friend.

'I know that Dagnarus made the request of his father,'

304

Gareth said, cautiously. 'I had not heard that His Majesty agreed.'

'His Majesty has agreed,' Evaristo said grimly. 'His Highness, the crown prince, is violently opposed. The two quarreled . . . The first quarrel ever between the King and his son. This is very bad, Gareth.' Evaristo shook his head, looking somber. 'Very bad.'

'I am sorry to hear of this division,' said Gareth, and this much at least was the truth. 'As you know, Master, I have great respect for His Majesty and great affection for his son – for *both* his sons,' he emphasized. 'But I do not see –'

'You must dissuade Dagnarus from this course of action,' Evaristo said, urgent and intense. Outside, the wind howled, and rain beat against the lead-glass windowpanes as if it, too, wanted to be indoors where it was warm. 'Nothing good can come of it. He has already brought about a rift between the King and the crown prince. This rift will widen. The Dominion Lords themselves are dividing into factions, further complicated by the fact that now the elven and orken and dwarven Dominion Lords are involved. Dagarus must be made to see reason and abandon this!'

'Master,' said Gareth, extremely uncomfortable, 'I do not know why you are telling me –'

'Because you are the only person who has influence over Dagnarus.'

'Hardly, Master,' said Gareth with a rueful smile.

'You do, Gareth, though you may not think so. You know the rituals, you have studied them. You know that he cannot pass them! That he must fail –'

'Then there is no problem,' Gareth interrupted. 'He will fail, and the Council of Dominion Lords will not recommend him for the Transfiguration.'

'It may not be that simple,' said Evaristo, frowning. 'We both know that a candidate may pass all the tests and still not be recommended. Therefore, it stands to reason that a candidate may do the reverse. Admittedly no candidate in the history of the Dominion Lords has failed the tests and been nominated, but Dagnarus has his supporters, notably the Shield of the Divine for the elves and Dunner of the dwarves.'

'And are you so certain Dagnarus will fail, Master?' Gareth asked.

'Aren't you, Gareth?'

Gareth could not lie in response to this, especially since he had said much the same to Dagnarus.

'If he does undergo the Transfiguration, it may cost Dagnarus his life,' Evaristo continued. 'We've had one Dominion Lord die already. That death caused people to question whether or not the Order of Dominion Lords should be maintained or abolished. If the prince were to die – he is immensely popular among the people – if he were to die, his death would create an outcry so strong that the Order of Dominion Lords might not survive it.'

'I am sorry, Master,' Gareth replied reluctantly. 'But I do not agree with you in this. I believe' – the gods help me! he thought – 'that Dagnarus would make an excellent choice for Dominion Lord.'

'You do not mean that, Gareth,' said Evaristo, regarding him sadly. 'I can tell. You never could lie to me.'

But I am lying, Master, said Gareth silently. I am living a lie. I have been ever since that day Dagnarus bid me look into the Void.

Gareth had nothing to say in reply and, seeing no point in continuing such an unsatisfactory interview, he made his excuses and left. Evaristo remained standing in the alcove, glaring after him, disappointed and angry.

It was with relief that Gareth went back out into the storm, braving the porter's baleful look as he once more forced open the door. Nature's wild tumult accorded well with that of his soul. He left the Temple and its environs, exiting the Magi Gate, sliding on the stone bridge, clutching at the barriers that protected pedestrians from tumbling into the chasm below.

He entered the Ambassadorial District, where the ambassadors from the various races kept stately mansions. The only people abroad this night were the city guards, making their rounds. They marched past, hunched and miserable, the rain streaming down their faces, their lips blue and pinched with the cold. They cast him curious glances, wondering what he was doing out, but seeing that he was a magus and judging that his errand, whatever it was, must be urgent, they did not stop him.

Gareth left the Ambassadorial District, descended the long staircase cut into the rock, which took him down the face of Castle Cliff to the Brewery District. The staircase was wet and slippery with sleet, the descent perilous. Gareth halted, shoved up against the cliff face by the howling wind, and considered going back, returning to the warm sanctuary of the Temple. Shivering on the cliff face, his woolen coat sodden and rimed with ice, he realized that he had come too far to give up. It had taken him months of work and sacrifice to obtain his goal. If it could be said of him that wind and rain kept him locked safe and warm in the Temple, he must forfeit all hope of success. The symbolism of his actions did not escape him. He proceeded on, treading with the utmost care.

He had one more level to go, but the stairs leading from Brewery District to the Slaughtering District, known as the Pit, were not so steep, since they were not intended to be used for defensive purposes, to slow advancing armies, but were meant to promote traffic. The Royal Brewhouse, located at the bottom of the street, was ablaze with light; it would take more than a gale to keep its regulars away. Gareth turned his shoulder to the warmth and life, and passed into darkness, both literally and figuratively.

The acrid scent of blood, mixed with the smell of

animals and dung, tinged the air. Not even the torrential downpour could wash it away. He had entered the Slaughtering District, an apt place to live for a follower of Death magic. Gareth could hear the lowing of the cattle awaiting the butcher's ax, the bleating of the sheep. He turned onto the South Highway.

Butchers' stalls, shuttered and closed for the night, lined the street. In the morning, fresh slabs of meat would be laid out on long wooden tables balanced on trestles, chickens would be hanging from their trussed feet on hooks, dogs roaming everywhere, flies thick. He left the main thoroughfare, turned into a back alley, popularly known among the locals as Blood Alley, for when rain fell, the blood from the butchers' shops washed down the alley and into a culvert at the end.

Gareth kept a wary watch as he slipped and slithered on the icy, wet cobblestones. This part of Vinnengael was notorious for thugs, robbers, and pickpockets. Gareth was known there by sight; the person he had come to visit was well-known and thus he was safe from molestation to a certain extent. There might always be some newcomer, however, someone who didn't know the way of things.

The alley was dark in the daytime. At night and in this storm, it was so dark that Gareth kept his shoulder close to the sides of the buildings, feeling his way. Fortunately, he knew the area. Finding the doorway, located almost at the alley's end, he halted, knocked gently on the door three times and then three times more. A voice bid him enter. The door was not locked. There was nothing inside to steal, at least nothing that would have attracted the ordinary sort of thief. Treasures there were within, but only for those who had the understanding of them.

Gareth shoved open the door, swiftly shut it behind him. Even at that, a flurry of sleet gusted inside, and he had to lean against the door to close it.

The room was warm, overly warm. A fire burned

brightly on the hearth. The room smelled of cooked porridge and air that has been breathed too many times. Added to that was the smell of wet sheep, for Gareth's woolen cloak, which he took off and hung near the fire, began to steam in the heat. And underneath those smells, the fetid smell of withering old age, impending death.

'You came,' said a voice, a mere croak, from a mass of blankets and bedding.

'Of course,' said Gareth gently, bending over the bed. 'How are you feeling?'

'How do I ever feel? Bored. Tired. In pain. These festering sores give me no peace! But I think my time will come tonight. I should like that. To know that my soul joins the darkness and the storm, to be borne away on the tearing winds. I would like that.'

Gareth nodded. He made no protest, spoke no lying words of false comfort. The man in the bed wanted to die. He was waiting to die, had been waiting to die for weeks. Had he wanted to live, he could have done so. He had already extended his life beyond a human's allotted years and could have extended it more, but, as he said, he was in pain, and he was bored. Those who knew him knew he was old, probably the oldest person they had ever known. But none knew how old. None knew the truth. Only Gareth knew. Only Gareth had been permitted to share the secret.

Bright eyes looked out of a head that might have been made of polished marble, so tightly and smoothly was the skin stretched over the bones of the skull. No hair remained on the head, not even eyebrows. The head looked dead already, the animate eyes the only signs of life. The blankets were tucked to the chin, for the body could no longer supply its own heat; the old man was perpetually cold. And the blankets concealed the sores, the ulcerations that covered his body. Most were dry, for he had not cast a spell in a long time. But even the dried scars itched and burned, as Gareth had come to know.

Having checked to see that the dying man was as comfortable as possible, Gareth removed a sharp sliver of wood from his cloak. Ordinarily he could not use Fire Magic, which was the province of the dwarves, but Void magic can mimic other magicks if it is used for destruction. The wood burst into flame. Gareth tossed the sliver on the hearth, strengthening the magic, causing the fire, which seemed to consume nothing but the hearthstones, to burn more brightly. This was one of his tasks – he came every three days to replenish the fire.

He asked if the old man had eaten.

'No. Why should I? Neither eaten nor drunk.'

Gareth began to remonstrate, but the old man cut him off.

'I don't need it. I don't suffer for the want of it. This night,' the old man said, looking up intently at Gareth. 'This night will be my last. I know it. We have much to do. I am glad you have come. I was afraid you wouldn't. If you hadn't, I would have waited, but I am glad you came. I will go away with the storm winds.'

'What is it you want me to do, Master?' Gareth asked.

'The books of Void magic. You've taken them.' The old man peered vaguely into the room. 'I can't see.'

'Yes, I have taken them. They are in a safe place. I have a room I rent, not far from here. The books are there.' Gareth was patient. He'd told the old man this before, but knew that it worried him.

'Good,' said the old man, his hands plucking restlessly at the coverlet. 'Good. There is one left. The one I told you to leave with me.'

'Yes, Master,' replied Gareth quietly.

'Tonight,' said the old man, 'I will teach you the spell.'

'Tonight?' Gareth repeated. His hands went cold, a tremor shook him. Outside the wind snuffled at the door and pawed at the windows, like a live thing, trying to break in.

'Yes. Tonight. On your deathbed, you will teach the spell to your apprentice. Thus the knowledge is passed on. You have practiced?'

'Yes, Master.' Gareth unbuttoned his doublet, lifted his shirt, revealed the ulcerations that blossomed like some noxious flower.

'With what result?'

'Success, Master,' Gareth replied. 'The spells worked as required.'

'Good. Good. All that, though, you can do with other magicks. Ordinary magicks. Not as fast, not as easily, but you can do it. This spell tonight, this is the one you can work with Void magic alone. We have spoken of it before. This is the one spell they envy. The one they fear. The one you want.'

Gareth did not reply. He stood near the bed, hands folded, looking down at the bright eyes in the bone-smooth face.

'You have plans for it?' the old man asked.

'Yes, Master.'

'So did I once,' the old man muttered. 'They never came to anything. But then I never had a prince to sponsor me. I would almost be tempted to stay around to see how you manage. Almost. But not quite. See there? I am no longer curious. And when you are no longer curious, why go on? You will do well. You are talented. My most talented pupil. And if you don't.' He shrugged, the coverlets moved. 'Then it won't matter to me.'

He gestured feebly. 'Slide your hand beneath my pillow.'

Gareth did as he was told. Sliding his hand beneath the feather pillow – the weight of the dying man's head was nothing against it – he touched cold steel.

311

'Careful,' said the old man. 'It is sharp. We don't want any unwitting sacrifices, eh?'

Gareth felt gingerly for the hilt, discovered it, clasped it, and drew out the dagger. He gazed at it by the firelight, turning it over carefully in his hand. He had heard the cagey and cunning old man speak of it, but had never seen it. He had not even supposed it to be in the old man's possession, had imagined that he must search for it. He had hoped for direction to the prize. He had not dared to hope for the prize itself.

The dagger was fashioned in the shape of a dragon – the scaled and sharply pointed tail formed the blade, the outstretched wings the handle. The hilt was the dragon's body and the head, with its gaping mouth and sharp teeth, was the pommel. A dagger for ceremony only, it was not meant to be used for everyday butchery. A good thing, because the blade with its fanciful design was awkward and unwieldy and uncomfortable to hold. The serrated edges of the wings poked into the flesh of Gareth's hand, the scales on the hilt were rough to the touch. The dagger had been well cared for, obviously cherished; the steel gleamed brightly in the firelight.

'My gift to you,' said the old man. Even now, now that he was leaving this world, he looked at the blade with a certain covetous longing.

'Thank you, Master,' said Gareth humbly. He regarded the dagger with an odd mixture of repugnance, revulsion, and anticipation. The metal bit his hand, but warmed to his touch.

'Bring the book. Sit near me, and I will tell you what I know of it. You have heard that King Tamaros was given the power to create Dominion Lords by the gods. I was in the Temple at the time, one of the Revered Magi, as are you. Except that I was not a novice. I was old then, though younger than you see me now. They thought I was in my nineties. In fact, with the help of the Void, I was in

312

my second lifetime, closer to one hundred and ninety. They thought me simple, daft. And so I play-acted my role. Stricken with the infirmities of great age, I was pitied and patronized, and I was completely free. I was able to go anywhere, do anything, say anything. They would all shake their heads and smile, and say, "It's only Zober. A harmless old man. Pay him no mind."'

'They make the same mistakes with children,' said Gareth, thinking back to his own childhood, the ease with which he'd roamed the forbidden areas of the Palace, the light punishment he'd received when caught.

'Don't interrupt,' the old man said snappishly. His breathing was rapid and shallow. 'We don't have much time. Tamaros came to the Temple, I knew the King was there to commune with the gods. I knew what he was planning to ask of them – the ability to create Dominion Lords, knights of good who would serve him and Vinnengael. He had discussed the matter beforehand with the Most Revered High Magus, a private, secret discussion I took care to overhear, using the power of the Void to listen through the walls.

'There was a risk to the creation of the Dominion Lords. The Most Revered High Magus knew it, and so did I. What the gods grant with one hand they take away with the other. To have something you must have nothing. There must be dark for there to be light. Tit for tat. The gods would give Tamaros the power to create Dominion Lords, yes. But at the same time the gods would put into the world the power to destroy them.

'Ten Lords of Good.' The old man pointed at the dagger. 'Ten Lords of Evil.'

'By heavens!' said Gareth, awed, staring at the dagger. 'I had no idea it was that . . . that powerful!'

'The High Magus tried to warn Tamaros of this, but the King decided the risk was worth it. The good the Dominion Lords would do would surely outweigh the possibility of evil. He went on to commune with the gods. As he did that, I communed with the Void. The ability to bring about the destruction of the Dominion Lords would be created in the same moment that Tamaros was granted the power to create them. It was up to me to figure out how.

'What a weary time that was. Tamaros fasted and prayed. I fasted myself, locking myself in my cell. I dared not allow myself to be distracted by anything, either food or drink. I dared not sleep. I listened to the darkness, to Tamaros's words on the other side of the darkness, words barely heard, as if I were standing at the bottom of a vast chasm, and he far above me. But I knew. I knew the moment he had received the blessing. In that moment, the curse came into being. But where?

'I opened my eyes and stared about my cell. I searched everywhere, under the bed, amongst my papers. I even thought, in the first frantic transports of excitement, about smashing my writing desk and searching through the wooden scraps. I could sense the Void magic, you see. Like hearing a drip, drip, drip of water in the night and not knowing where it comes from or how to stop it. A little sound, yet how terrible after hours of hearing it pound monotonously into your brain. You cannot sleep. You become obsessed with ending it. I was about to set out in search of it, proceed aimlessly, for I had no idea where to look, when I recollected myself. I calmed down. I had to consider this logically.

'Born of the Void, this object would be found within the Void. I listened to the darkness and let it draw me into it. You will not be able to guess what I found?'

'No, Master,' said Gareth. 'I cannot.'

'A room in the Temple devoted to the Void!' The old man was smug, triumphant, enjoying the shocked look of his young pupil.

'No! Truly? In the Temple? But how –'

'The Temple is old. It was built in the days when Void magic, though not loved, was at least held in respect. And so, yes, there is a room dedicated to the Void. I found it. I marked it. You will find its location there, in the book you hold.

'I walked through the darkness. The sense that I was nearing my object increased with each step – the dripping sound became louder, if you like – and I knew I was on the right trail. I made my way warily, for people often wander about the Temple at night. No one saw me, however. A good thing. So pent-up and overwrought was I that I believe I would have slain any person who had interrupted my search.

'I found the secret room. I found the altar of the Void. But that which I sought was not there! I howled in frustration, not caring if I woke the entire Temple. I thought the Void was playing tricks, luring me on only to laugh at me. But as I placed my hand upon the black altar, the knowledge came to me.

'The object I sought was located in the very center of the Temple. Just as the Void is located in the center of the four elements.'

'The great amphitheater,' said Gareth. 'In the center of the four altars.'

'Yes. And there I went. I had to know exactly where to look. I had to locate the exact center, or at least as close as I could come. Starting at the Altar of the Humans in the front, I walked carefully to the back of the Temple, counting my paces – a weary task – until I came to the Altar of the Elves, which stands opposite. Proceeding to the Altar of the Orken, which is located at a forty-five-degree angle from that of the humans, I walked to the Altar of the Dwarves, counting every step. Imagine my joy to discover that they were equidistant, one from the other. Quickly, I determined where the center should lie. I paced the distance, counting, reciting the numbers aloud so that I should not become confused in my excitement.

'Someone entered, a novice, come to trim the candles.

'"Who is there?" she called out. "Oh, it is you, Revered Magus Zober. What are doing here? You should be in your warm cell. You are shivering. Let me take you –"

'"No, no, no!" I said shrilly, with the unreasonable irascibility of a doddering old man. "Leave me be! I came here to pray!" Inside myself, I was saying over and over the number I had reached, so that I did not have to begin again. The dripping sound thudded in me, like those huge drums the orken beat so that the rowers can keep the time.

'The woman left, finally, and I continued on. I came to the very center of the room and there the drumming was so loud that it seemed to reverberate through my skull and dislodge my brain. I stood in between two rows of the stone benches. I looked down, and there at my feet was this very dagger, lying on the floor, as if someone had dropped it. Which is, at first, what I thought. Picking up the dagger I saw beneath it a black circle embedded in the stone floor. The circle was small, about the size of your index finger, and insignificant. Countless people had trod on it without seeing it. I myself had walked over that very place and never noticed it. I asked about it later, innocently. Why was the circle there? What purpose did it serve?

'I was told that it was placed there by the builder, something to aid him in his measurements. Of course. That is what they *would* say. But you and I – we know the truth. As all the other followers have the representation of their gods in the amphitheater, so do we followers of the Void have ours.

'I brought the dagger to my lips and kissed it and knelt in prayer and thanksgiving upon the black circle. And it was given to me to know how to use this dagger and for what purpose.'

'And that is?' Gareth spoke in a harsh rasp. His mouth

316

had gone dry, his palms were wet. He rubbed them on his robes.

'Slay a man with this dagger,' said the old man, his voice hushed, so hushed Gareth had to lean forward to hear, 'and the corpse becomes yours to command.'

'What would I want with a corpse?' Gareth asked, disgusted and disappointed.

'Not just any corpse. A corpse that walks,' said the old man. 'A corpse that thinks. A corpse that in all ways appears to be alive. The corpse will retain his form so long as he wears the magical armor granted to him by the Void. Does that sound familiar?' The old man cackled.

'But the beauty of this is that as long as he is in that form he must serve the one who wields the dagger. Thus, you see, he becomes the opposite of a Dominion Lord. The Void magic is his to command whenever he wants. Inside the armor, he has the strength of ten, he knows no fear, feels no heat, no cold, never thirsts, never hungers, except for that which keeps him alive.'

'And that is?' Gareth asked hesitantly, horrified, fascinated.

'Souls. The souls of those unfortunate enough to cross his path when he hungers. He feasts upon the dying and they give him life. Thus the creatures are called "Vrykyl," an elven word. It means "eater of the dead."'

Gareth shivered, pulled his robes more closely about him. The dagger was warm in his hand, he held it tightly.

'Are there –' He hesitated, uncertain how to ask, not certain he wanted to know the answer. 'Are you –'

'A Vrykyl? No.' The old man grimaced. 'How could I be? One may not use the dagger upon oneself, any more than Tamaros can make himself a Dominion Lord. Void magic extended my years. Unlike the Vrykyl, such magic cannot extend your youth, cannot give you strength. That's why I lie here like a broken doll,' he said bitterly. 'That's why I quit casting the dratted spell. What's the point? I've done my duty now. And, to answer your other question, no, there are no Vrykyl in existence today. Not for lack of trying.'

The old man grumbled, shifted restlessly beneath the covers. He made a feeble gesture. 'It is all there, in that book. I wrote down everything I know about the dagger and the ceremony required to raise a Vrykyl. The subject must embrace the Void, that is the key. He must be deemed an acceptable candidate. You can't just slip up behind someone and slit his throat and expect him to become a Vrykyl,' the old man said testily, adding in a mutter, 'I know. I tried. It doesn't work. The dagger fell from my hand before I could strike. The dagger chooses its own, you see. Or rather, the Void chooses its own.'

'I see,' said Gareth somberly. He held the dagger to the light, studied the workmanship, marveled at the detail. He would not have been much surprised if it had turned into a real live dragon in his hands.

The old man sighed deeply, as if he had let go of a great burden. He lay back on his pillow, a contented and restful expression on his face.

'And now it is yours, Gareth,' said the old man.

'Yes,' said Gareth.

The old man closed his eyes. His voice was little more than a whispering breath. 'Now it is yours. I have passed it on, as I was required. You, in turn, will pass it on when it is your time to leave this life.'

'Yes,' Gareth said again. He turned the dagger in his hands.

'You know what to do after I am gone.'

'Yes,' Gareth said for the third time.

'It will not be long now. I am tired. So very tired.'

He said nothing more. All Gareth could hear was the rasp of the shallow breathing and the howl and rattle of the storm.

Gareth rose to his feet, stiff from sitting too long without moving. He placed the dagger upon the table, took the book, and, shifting his stool closer to the fire, opened the book and began to read.

Lifting his head, he looked at the marked candle that burned away the hours. He was startled to notice that two had passed. Outside, the storm was lessening, to judge by the sounds. Sleet no longer tapped on the window, the wind no longer beat on the door. To judge by the silence, the old man no longer breathed.

Gareth went to check on him, lifted his wrist. It was cold and limp. The old man was dead.

Drawing the blanket up over the still form, Gareth thought he must feel grief – he had been coming to see the old man in secret for nigh on five years – but he couldn't. He had never really liked the old man, and all Gareth could feel now was a sense of relief. It was over and done. He had the dagger. He had the book that told how to use it. He had the power to bring into the world the antithesis of the Dominion Lords, creatures of immense magic who would slavishly serve the one who wielded the dagger.

Gareth lifted the dagger to the firelight, watched the flames burn in the shining steel blade. He allowed himself to imagine, for one brief moment, that he had a choice. That he could cast away this dark artifact. King Tamaros would die as peacefully as this evil old man. Helmos would be a good and revered and much loved king. The world would totter along in uneasy peace. He pictured this with clarity, tears of longing and regret wet upon his cheek.

He wiped the tears away with his sleeve.

There was no choice. Not really. Not anymore. He had made it long ago.

Gareth picked up the book and thrust it into his pouch. He wrapped the dagger in a bit of cloth he cut from the old man's blanket, placed the dagger inside his pouch along with the book. He looked around the old man's hovel

319

one final time, saw nothing that was of any use. Gareth opened a jar of lamp oil he had bought some days ago for precisely this purpose. He doused the old man's sheets and blankets and bedding with it. A gesture of Gareth's hand brought the flames leaping from the fireplace. The flames seized hungrily upon the soaked linen. The bed exploded in fire.

Gareth left the house quickly, before the smell of burning flesh could reach him. He walked rapidly up the alleyway, keeping to the shadows, though no one in his right mind would have been out at that time of night, in such ferocious weather. Reaching the end of the alley, he looked back to see the flames starting to shoot out of the roof.

He turned onto South Highway. Not a soul was on the street. The storm had raged itself out, but the wind was still high, blowing fierce and cold off the frothy sea. The wind would spread the fire quickly. By the time anyone noticed the flames, the hovel would be completely destroyed, the body burned beyond recognition.

His soul to the Void.

SIX

The Dagger of the Vrykyl

'YOUR HIGHNESS,' SAID SILWYTH QUIETLY, speaking low in the prince's ear, so that the attendant lords could not hear. 'Gareth requests that you meet him in the old playroom this day at the supper hour. He has something of great urgency to impart.'

'Does he, indeed?' said Dagnarus, sipping chocolate.

'You are looking in unusually high spirits this morning, Your Highness,' said one of the fawning lords.

'Thank you, Lord Malroy, I am in an excellent humor. Perhaps because the weather is so fine.'

'Fine weather, Your Highness?' said the lord blankly.

'There was a terrible storm last night, Your Highness,' said Silwyth softly, leaning near to remove the prince's breakfast tray.

Dagnarus had spent the night in Valura's arms, the two of them hidden away in a secret chamber in an interior wing of the castle that housed foreign diplomats, a part of the castle excellently well suited for love trysts, since it was opened only for special functions or celebrations. Dagnarus had not heard the wind, the sleet, the driving rain. Drowned in pleasure, he had heard nothing but the rushing sea of his own blood. The two had separated reluctantly an hour before dawn, she to creep back to the small room in the palace off the Queen's bedchamber (her husband lived alone in their house in the city; Valura having insisted on being near the Queen), he to return by the hidden passages in which he played as a child to his own bedchamber, to be there to greet the attendant lords upon their arrival in the morning.

'Fine weather to me, Lord Malroy,' said Dagnarus, throwing aside the bedclothes. 'I enjoy the rage and clash of the storm. Get rid of them,' he muttered under his breath to Silwyth.

Silwyth shooed the lords, like so many chickens, out of the bedroom. He saw them safely ensconced with their dice in an antechamber, then returned to the prince.

'What is the gossip around the palace, Silwyth?' Dagnarus asked as he prepared for his bath. 'Has anyone said anything?'

'With regard to yourself and the Lady Valura, no, Your Highness. Beyond the fact that Your Highness has been in an unusually good temper lately and that Her Ladyship has been reprimanded for being dull and sleepy in the Queen's presence, nothing untoward has been noticed.'

Dagnarus smiled. 'I shall have to go into a rage about something, I suppose, to save my reputation. But, see here, Silwyth, I am fairly even-tempered, cheerful most of the time, not given to brooding or melancholia or savage outbursts. *I* don't see any change in myself.'

'Love makes even the ugly attractive, Your Highness, and thus it follows that it would make that which is already attractive beautiful.'

'Love.' Dagnarus mused. 'I thought I was immune to that sweet disease. But you are right. I have caught it, and its fever consumes me. I wonder how soon it will wear itself out.'

Silwyth regarded him gravely. 'It will not wear out soon with the Lady Valura, Your Highness. Elven women are not fickle and changeable as are human females. Where an elven woman loves, she carries that love to her death.'

'Really? You astonish me, Silwyth,' Dagnarus said, shrugging. 'I do love Valura intensely now, but no violent emotion ever lasts long with me – be it battle rage or something softer. Still' – he sighed, recalling the transports of their pleasure in the night – 'I cannot imagine *not* loving her. Perhaps my infatuation *will* last, Silwyth, so do away with that supercilious stare and go and heat my bathwater.'

Gareth sat awkwardly in one of the short-legged chairs of the playroom, his knees bent beneath him, practically touching his chin. The playroom was dusty, for it had been long since abandoned. About once a year, the maids would open it and sweep it and brush away the cobwebs, but then it would be shut up again. Gareth had not been in it for many years, ever since the day he'd left to go to the Temple at the age of twelve. He looked about with fond remembrance overshadowed with a kind of horror, as if thinking back on a dream that should have been pleasant but that, on waking, left him ill at ease.

Picking up the old books, stacked neatly on the table, he heard Evaristo's voice lecturing and Dagnarus's petulant voice disparaging, cajoling, haranguing. He could not hear his own voice, Gareth's voice, at all.

He was reading one of the old books when the door was thrown open with a bang, and Dagnarus strolled in.

Gareth glanced up.

'You look terrible,' Dagnarus said cheerfully. Glancing at his face, he grimaced. 'You should do something about that pimple, Patch. Cover it with powder or something.'

Gareth recalled the time the Queen had wanted to cover his birthmark with powder, how Dagnarus had thwarted her by telling her that the gods had marked him. Well, so they had.

'I had no sleep at all last night, Your Highness,' Gareth returned testily, ignoring the remark about the pimple.

'Neither did I,' Dagnarus said with a wink. He stood slapping his gloves in his hand, for he had just come from riding and was still booted and cloaked. 'Why did you choose this dismal place? I spent enough time imprisoned here. I don't suppose you'd like to hear me read again?'

Gareth walked over, looked out the door. Seeing Silwyth hovering in the hallway, Gareth turned.

'May I suggest that you send the elf away, Your Highness,' he said softly.

Dagnarus lifted an eyebrow, but intrigue was welcome as wine to him. Reaching into an inner pocket, he drew out a handkerchief of fine lace and cambric, delicate enough to have been woven by spiders.

'Silwyth. Here is a trifle I discovered in the marketplace. See to it that it finds its way into the proper hands. Do this immediately.'

'What about your supper, Your Highness?'

'I am not hungry,' Dagnarus said. He glanced at Gareth, who shook his head. 'Nor is Gareth. Leave upon your errand. And make certain that you are not seen.'

Silwyth accepted the charge, bowed, and departed. Gareth, keeping watch outside the door, saw the elf pause and linger in the hallway. Gareth stepped outside the door, stood staring coldly at him. Silwyth inclined his head, then was gone. Gareth waited a moment longer, to be certain the elf did not double back. Finally, convinced that he and the prince were truly alone, Gareth shut the door and slid home the bolt.

Dagnarus watched all this in amused astonishment. 'What precautions! One would think we were plotting to rob the royal treasury. We're not, are we?'

'You're in a good mood,' Gareth said accusingly.

'People keep telling me that.' Dagnarus grinned. 'I'll let you in on a secret, my friend. I'm in love.'

Gareth didn't hear him or, if he did, the words meant nothing. He motioned the prince to stand over by the window, as far from the door as possible. Dagnarus, mystified, accompanied him, stood leaning against the window, his arm resting on the sill.

'What is it, Patch? By the gods, you're all of a tremble! Bad news? Has something happened?'

'Give me a minute. Let me collect my thoughts,' Gareth said, endeavoring to calm himself. He stood by the window, his head bowed.

Dagnarus, caught by the dire note in his friend's voice, waited in silence for the requested minute.

'Come, Patch,' he said at last, growing impatient.

Gareth lifted his head and looked earnestly at Dagnarus. 'That which I am about to show you is known to only three men in this world. The first is dead. He died last night. I am the second. He bequeathed this to me. You are the third. I tell you this to impress upon you the gravity and the enormity of what I am about to reveal.'

'Yes, yes. Get on with it,' Dagnarus said, though he was impressed, that much was obvious, despite his flippant tone. 'I promise to behave myself, Master Tutor.'

Gareth smiled fleetingly at this reference to their childhood, but the smile did not last long. He reached beneath his cloak, drew forth a pouch. He placed the pouch upon the table, opened it, spread the pouch's lips wide.

The day outside was gray and chill, with lowering ragged clouds that seemed undecided whether to storm again or not. Silwyth had lit a fire in the playroom to warm it, but he had not brought lights. The fire sputtered desultorily on the hearth; the playroom was as gloomy and gray as the sky outside the window. Dagnarus was dressed in browns and blacks, Gareth in the nondescript gray robes of a novice. The red velvet was the only point of color in the room, and it seemed to blaze like blood on snow. The Dagger of the Vrykyl lay on the velvet, its polished surface reflecting the gray of the sky and the red of its nest.

Dagnarus regarded the dagger disparagingly. He did not move to touch it. 'Faith, it is an ugly thing. Unwieldy, too. No weapons-smith with any sense would forge a dagger such as this.'

'It's a ceremonial dagger, as you know full well, and was never meant to be used in battle. It is an artifact of the Void,' Gareth said, his voice low and fervent.

'Truly?' Dagnarus studied the dagger with more interest. He still did not offer to touch it. 'What does it do?'

'It animates corpses, Your Highness,' said Gareth.

Dagnarus started to laugh. The laughter died on his lips. 'Are you in earnest?' he exclaimed, disbelieving.

'Earnest!' Gareth stared at his friend, appalled. 'Earnest! I was ten years old when you showed me the Void. Ten years old when you made me read the books of Void magic to you! I have lived a lie ever since, I have sacrificed my peace, my happiness . . . and you ask if I am in earnest!'

'You could have turned aside at any time,' said Dagnarus coldly. 'I never forced you to pursue your studies of the Void. Those you took upon yourself.'

'I know,' said Gareth wearily. 'I know what I did. I would do it again . . . perhaps. I'm sorry, Your Highness. Forgive my outburst. I didn't sleep at all. I spent the entire night reading about this dagger.' He nodded at the weapon.

'Tell me again. What does it do?' Dagnarus asked, and his tone was serious, respectful.

'It came into the world at the same time your father was granted power to make Dominion Lords,' Gareth said, guessing this would catch the prince's interest. He was rewarded by a flicker of flame in Dagnarus's green eyes. 'As the King was given the power to create, so there came into being the power to destroy. Whoever wields this dagger may bring into existence the dark opposite of a Dominion Lord, an evil shadow, an undead creature with magical power and extraordinary abilities, a creature who is loyal to the one who wields the dagger. But, whereas the Dominion Lord draws upon his life energies to fuel his magic, the Vrykyl – for that is what such creatures are called – uses death.'

'Vrykyl. The word sounds elvish. What does it mean?'

'It *is* an elven word. It means "eater of the dead."'

Dagnarus grimaced. 'Not particularly appetizing. How does this work? What must one do? What spell must one cast?'

'The spell is bound up in the dagger. Anyone may use it, but that use is not as easy as it might appear,' he added in a cautionary tone, for he had seen Dagnarus's eyes shine with excitement.

'Tell me, Patch,' said Dagnarus, and now he reached out his hand for the dagger.

'First, the dagger itself chooses the victim. The dagger must find the candidate acceptable. Therefore, the victim must be someone who has embraced the Void.'

Dagnarus smiled, and Gareth could guess what the prince was thinking.

'These rules must be adhered to, Your Highness,' he emphasized. 'The old man who passed this on to me attempted to create Vrykyl by cheating. It did not work.'

Dagnarus raised an eyebrow, shrugged. 'Very well. We will follow the rules. It should not be too difficult to find someone who will be acceptable to the dagger. And so it brings the dead to life. Think of the possibilities.'

'It is an unholy life,' Gareth admonished with a shiver. 'A life that the creature must kill to sustain.'

'We kill every day to sustain our lives,' Dagnarus observed.

'I am not talking about chickens,' Gareth returned irritably. 'I am talking about people. A Vrykyl must feed off other people's souls. A Vrykyl is gifted with magical armor, the same as a Dominion Lord, except that this armor is shining black. The armor covers the Vrykyl from head to toe and remains with the Vrykyl until death –'

'I thought you said these Vrykyl were already dead.'

'I am coming to that, Your Highness. The first act a Vrykyl performs, when he is animated, is to forge himself a dagger made of a piece of his own bone. This he can take quite readily, since he does not feel pain nor does he bleed. He can cut off an arm with impunity. The limb is encased by magical armor, and is not really necessary. The armor itself acts as a limb. Once this knife is forged, using the bone as part of the hilt, the Vrykyl may then use this knife to steal the soul of a victim and thus replenish his own life. Without this, the Vrykyl will eventually diminish to his original state. His body will slowly begin to deteriorate during that period until, by the end, anyone who would see the Vrykyl without his armor would see a corpse that has been moldering in the ground for months.'

'You were wise to suggest we skip supper,' Dagnarus said wryly. 'What does a well-fed Vrykyl look like?'

'Whatever he wants,' said Gareth. 'If he was an old man when he died, he could return to what he was in his youth – the picture of vigor and health. The magic of the armor permits him to cast an illusion of any one he has seen.

'Two things only can kill a Vrykyl: the lack of sustenance and weapons that have been blessed by the gods. If, somehow, you could lock up a Vrykyl for six months without giving him a chance to kill, he would perish. Of course, that would be extremely difficult, because a Vrykyl is possessed of unusual strength. I doubt if the dungeon has been built that could contain one. The blessed sword of a Dominion Lord, if it pierces through the armor to touch the dead flesh beneath, will slay the Vrykyl instantly.'

Dagnarus was scarcely listening. Eyes glistening, he

lifted the dagger in his hand and held it to the light of the gray day. He turned it in his hand admiringly.

'Think what this could mean, Patch! I could create armies –'

'*Not* armies,' Gareth corrected. 'The number of Vrykyl is bound up with the number of Dominion Lords. There are only ten Dominion Lords permitted each race, for a total of forty, thus there may be only forty Vrykyl.'

'Well, leaders of armies, then. I would be invincible! My father is High King of the human lands. I could be High King of all lands, everywhere. When I become a Dominion Lord myself –'

'No!' Gareth cried, shocked. He clasped hold of Dagnarus's forearm, gripped it tight. 'No,' he repeated.

'What do you mean?' Dagnarus wrenched his arm loose from Gareth's painful grip. 'Why do you stare at me like that?'

'Don't you see, Your Highness?' Gareth said desperately. 'You don't *have* to become a Dominion Lord now. You don't need it! That's why I did this! That's why I sought this out! For you! You don't have to risk your life –'

'I find your concern for me quite touching, Patch.' Dagnarus spoke in a cold and dangerous tone. 'But also quite insulting. You are convinced that I am going to fail. I remind you that I have never failed at any challenge I have undertaken in my life. I will not fail at this – a thing my brother could do!' His lip curled.

'You cannot be a Dominion Lord, blessed of the gods, and wield this dagger, Your Highness,' said Gareth.

'Well, then, you will create Vrykyl for me.'

'Certainly, Your Highness,' said Gareth, with a bow. 'And they will be loyal to me, for I am the one who will wield the dagger.'

Dagnarus scowled, not accustomed to having his will thwarted. 'The means must be found to get around this!

You will look for a way, Patch. I will find a suitable candidate. We will test this ourselves and see if this dagger does all that you claim.'

'And where will you find a candidate?' Gareth was skeptical. 'One who would openly embrace the Void?'

'I have an idea,' Dagnarus said lightly. He placed the dagger back in the pouch, covered it carefully, and thrust the bundle inside his shirt, next to his skin. 'I will keep this myself, Patch.'

'Certainly,' said Gareth, looking after it with a shudder. 'I am glad to be rid of it. Keep it secret and keep it safe, Your Highness.'

'Never fear. I am used to keeping secrets these days. Unlike you, I find it a pleasant pastime.'

Gareth only shook his head.

Dagnarus regarded his friend in concern, and Gareth saw the pity in the prince's eyes. Gareth couldn't blame him. He must look dreadful, thin and worn and pale, appearing older – far older – than his twenty years. His nails were bitten to the quick, the cuticles ragged and bleeding. His eyes blinked too often, for they burned, and he tried constantly to ease them. His clothes were unkempt, his shoes shabby. And always that terrible mark on his face. Both terrible marks.

'I'm sorry, Patch,' Dagnarus said suddenly, quietly.

'What?' Gareth gazed at the prince in astonishment. He couldn't remember ever hearing Dagnarus apologize to anyone for anything. 'Sorry for what?'

'For neglecting you. You've done all the work while I've had all the fun. You will see.' Reaching out, Dagnarus placed his hands on Gareth's thin shoulders. 'You must lead this double life of yours a short time longer, I fear. Only until I become a Dominion Lord. Then you may leave those doddering old fools in the Temple and come to work for me, as my advisor, as we planned when we were children. When I am King of Vinnengael –'

'Don't say that, Your Highness,' Gareth said miserably. 'Or at least, not King of Vinnengael. Helmos will be King of Vinnengael, a worthy king. You will be King of the elven lands or the dwarves –' He lowered his head, so that the prince should not see his tears.

'When I am King of the elven lands, then,' Dagnarus rephrased in pleasant, conciliatory tones. 'I will make it all up to you. You will live a life of ease. I will build you a castle, procure you a wife. A wife *and* a mistress . . .'

'Thank you, Your Highness,' said Gareth. There wasn't much else to say. A castle, a wife, and a mistress in exchange for his soul. He might have made a worse bargain.

'And now' – Dagnarus put his arm around his whipping boy, steered him toward the door – 'now we will leave this dismal place which always did depress me and we will get you something to eat. No, no arguments. So what if you are late to your classes? I will send Silwyth along to say that I required your presence. Let us go tease the cook for a midday sup, as we used to do when we were boys. What do you say to cold venison pie and fresh goat cheese? Hot crusty bread and new-made ale?'

'It sounds wonderful, Your Highness,' said Gareth, his stomach turning at the mention.

Dagnarus banged open the door, keeping his friend under arrest, as it were, dragging him along.

'Good! We must fatten you up, put some color into those pimpled cheeks. By the way,' Dagnarus added offhandedly, 'did I mention that my nomination for Dominion Lord comes up before the Council this day?'

'I wish you luck, Your Highness,' said Gareth.

'I know you do, Patch,' said Dagnarus with a smile, his grip tightening. 'I know you do.'

SEVEN

The Nomination

THE COUNCIL MEETING FOR THE DOMINION Lords was set for the fourth day of every third month, during which meeting the Dominion Lords would consider all matters brought before them. Attendance was required, though a Dominion Lord could be absent if he or she was involved in a matter deemed to be of sufficient importance to demand said Dominion Lord's presence. Since the number of Dominion Lords fluctuated, it had been decided that the presence of three-fourths the current number of existing Dominion Lords constituted a quorum.

Matters were decided by vote, a two-thirds majority being necessary for truly important issues, such as the selection of a new Dominion Lord. King Tamaros, though not a Dominion Lord himself, was present in an advisory capacity. He had no vote. Other rulers were also invited to attend, particularly if they had grievances or causes they wanted to bring before the Council.

Ten years had passed since the gifting of the Sovereign Stone. The humans had almost their full quotient (nine of ten) of Dominion Lords. The elves had ten, for they had taken to the notion quite readily. The Shield of the Divine, now possessed of the Sovereign Stone, had gained the upper hand in his struggle against the Divine for rulership of the elves. The Divine was still seen by the elves to be their spiritual leader, but all knew (including the Divine himself, to his constant aggravation) who wielded the true power.

Unlike humans, who must voluntarily put themselves forward as candidates for Dominion Lord, the elven Dominion Lords were chosen by the Shield of the Divine. These elves could refuse – the Council required this – but if they did so, they would lose face and also favor with the Shield, both of which were sufficient to cast themselves and their families into disgrace, a disgrace that might last for centuries.

The Shield had built a lovely shrine in which to house the elven portion of the Sovereign Stone. The stone floated on a cushion of sacred air above a white-marble pedestal, fashioned in the shape of a lotus blossom, rising from the center of a large, perfectly round pool of clear blue water in the center of a sunlit garden. The garden was sacrosanct – no one except the Shield of the Divine was permitted to walk there. Guards surrounded the garden day and night. Elven wizards – the Wyred – had enhanced the garden magically, so that any who ventured in without the proper warding amulet (worn by the Shield) would become ensnared in magical traps. One thief had been caught this way. He had slain himself before he could be taken and questioned, but it was well-known that he had been sent by the Divine.

The eleven ceremony to create Dominion Lords was held in secret, not open to the public, as was the ceremony of the humans. Only the family and the Shield and his retinue attended. Because the elves selected had only nominal choice in the matter, one or two were rumored to have died during the Transfiguration. The fact that more did not succumb was due to the wisdom of the Shield, who carefully screened all candidates before making his selection. The ten current elven Dominion Lords were from Houses that were either loyal to the Shield or, as in the case of Lord Mabreton, were from Houses who had not been loyal to the Shield previously but who were now beholden to him. Not one had been turned down by the Council of Dominion Lords. All had been found worthy.

Although pleased to have portions of the Sovereign Stone, neither the dwarves nor the orken had taken full advantage of the ability to create Dominion Lords. The dwarves, ever mistrustful of human motives, feared that by becoming a Dominion Lord, a dwarf would, in some way, become more human. Only one dwarf had volunteered to become a Dominion Lord. This was Dunner, one of the Unhorsed and a dwarf who had lived for many years among humans.

Dunner could not himself explain the motives that had led him to undergo the dangerous Transfiguration. He had too many motives, all thrown together in the same stewpot. First one, then another would bubble to the surface. From a purely selfish viewpoint, he had hoped to heal his twisted leg and free himself of the constant pain, and this he had achieved. He had emerged from the Transfiguration whole and unscarred – to the awe and amazement of all the dwarves who had gathered to see the show and who began at that moment to have second thoughts about the value of becoming a Dominion Lord.

Dunner had hoped that he would once more be able to ride a horse and join his family clan, wherever they might be. He had achieved this goal with the healing of his leg, but now that he was able to ride, he found that he had little desire to do so. A less selfish motive was the fervent desire to help his people play a more important role in a world he believed was being rapidly usurped by elves and humans. He could do this only by being a part of their world, representing the dwarven interests in the court of Vinnengael, and this he did.

Dunner constantly protested the incursion of humans into dwarven territory, constantly defended dwarven attempts to push them back. True, the dwarves believed that one day all the continent of Loerem would be theirs, all other races their subjects, but the dwarves were in no particular hurry to achieve this manifest destiny, and, meanwhile, because of their constant roaming and refusal to settle anywhere, the dwarves were seeing their own lands being nibbled away by human farmers and sheepherders.

Dunner fought a lone and thankless battle, for the dwarven chieftains considered negotiation a sign of weakness. Most never knew the small victories that Dunner single-handedly achieved or how many dwarven and human lives were saved by his tongue rather than their swords and bows. The dwarven chiefs ascribed the peaceful removal of the human settlements as the will of the gods, which – in a way – it was.

The Sovereign Stone was given to Dunner to keep by the Chief Clan Chief. Dunner placed the stone in a small shrine he had built for it in the City of the Unhorsed, where the stone sat for two years, gathering dust, for none of the dwarves was particularly interested in it. Dunner thought sadly that he was the only one of his people who found it truly marvelous, the only one who took time to pay his respects. But then he noticed that someone else was caring for the Sovereign Stone in his absence. On his return, he would find the floor of the shrine swept, the stone free of dust. He wondered who could be tending it and kept secret watch to find out.

To his astonishment, he discovered the stone's guardians were Unhorsed children, neglected and abandoned. As bereft and unhappy as Dunner himself had been when he was a child, these beggar children had come together to found an unofficial band dedicated to the Sovereign Stone.

The children kept the temple clean and polished the stone itself with soft cloths. At first Dunner was inclined to drive them away; he thought they were making a game of it. But as he watched them, he came to see that in joining together to take care of the Sovereign Stone, the children had done something rare for the Unhorsed – they had emerged from isolation, formed friendships and loyalties that spanned clan lines. They had, as it were, developed their own clan around the Sovereign Stone.

Dunner was pleased beyond measure to realize this and was careful to leave the children to themselves, make no fuss over them, draw no attention to them. These children, he guessed, would be the future Dominion Lords. And, for now, he had strength enough to continue on alone.

As to the orken, the Captain of Captains himself had become a Dominion Lord, mainly to acquire the special armor, which he much admired. And he liked the idea of having to pass certain tests in order to achieve Dominion Lord status. A highly competitive race, the orken are quite fond of tests and challenges, puzzles and conundrums. There is a story told that a human king once saved his besieged city by giving the attacking orken a riddle to solve, promising that he would relinquish his city if they came up with the solution. While the orken sat down in front of the city to argue over the matter, the king sent posthaste to a neighbor for reinforcements. When those troops arrived to break the siege, it is further told that the orken refused to quit the field until someone had given them the correct answer, but that is considered the least believable part of the story.

The Captain wanted to devise tests for his people, but wasn't certain what they should entail. He considered the human tests silly. Binding the sores of lepers – what nonsense. No lepers existed among the orken. As a menace to society, they would never have been allowed to live, and the orken were apparently immune to the disease anyway.

The elves refused to divulge the nature of their tests, so they were no help. Dunner – the only dwarf – had elected to take the human tests.

At length, the Captain decided upon tests involving seamanship (most important), combat, and puzzle-solving (to test the mental capacity), courage, and the ability to make a good bargain. Having set the criteria for the tests, the Captain did not feel it would be honorable to determine the nature of the tests he himself would have to pass. He turned to his mate, instructing her to make the tests as challenging for him as possible. This she did. Feeling strongly that the honor of both her mate and herself was at stake, she made the tests so extraordinarily difficult that the poor Captain barely survived, much less passed.

The tribal shaman deemed survival an acceptable score, however, and, thanks to an exceptionally good omen – a strange black cat appearing out of nowhere and jumping into his lap – she granted the Captain the right to become a Dominion Lord. Following the rigorous and near-deadly testing procedure, the Transfiguration in which he turned from flesh to stone and then back to flesh was a minor inconvenience, hardly to be noticed.

So many orken wanted to become Dominion Lords after that – mainly in order to challenge themselves with the tests – that the Captain was hard-pressed to choose among them. Their ranks thinned considerably when the word went out that orken Dominion Lords not only had to interact with humans, but were expected to be nice to them, too.

At the Council meeting at which Dagnarus's nomination would come up for a vote, there were then nine humans, including his brother Helmos; ten elves, including Lord Mabreton; Dunner, representing the dwarves; the Captain and the only two other orken to have survived the testing procedure.

'The ten elven votes are yours, Your Highness, as the

Shield has promised. Dunner will vote for you, of course, no question there. As to the orken – impossible creatures – it is useless to try to predict what they will do. A bug crawling from left to right instead of right to left will change their votes in an instant. As to the humans, there is not a single one currently supporting you.'

'Thanks to my beloved brother,' Dagnarus said.

'You have, therefore, eleven votes in your favor, Your Highness,' said Silwyth, totaling the figures. 'You need seventeen in order to win – six more.'

Dagnarus scowled. Pacing the room, his hands clasped behind his back, he brought to mind the nine humans ranged against him. His brother, Helmos, would never change his vote. As to the others, Dagnarus hardly knew them. He had never paid much attention to them, except to bow to them on state occasions. He seemed to recall, at a banquet, having passed one of them the salt. He had nothing in common with these men and women, who talked of books and music, philosophy, metaphysics, and the nobility of man.

'I *have* heard,' Silwyth added cautiously, noting the prince's dark and brooding expression, 'that three of the human Dominion Lords are wavering in their decision.'

'Come, that's more like it,' said Dagnarus, looking up, hope revived.

'If I might offer a suggestion, Your Highness?'

'Certainly, Silwyth. No one is better at conniving than you elves.'

Silwyth bowed to acknowledge the compliment. 'In your speech to the Council, you should emphasize the fact that your brother's continual carping on Dominion Lords being peace-minded, his refusal to admit a Lord of Battle to enter into consideration, goes against the original intent of the gods in the creation of Dominion Lords.'

'Does it? You amaze me, Silwyth. Go on.'

'Not so amazing, Your Highness. A candidate must

demonstrate proficiency at combat skills in the testing procedure.'

'But from what Gareth tells me, that is all ceremonial. No real fighting goes on,' Dagnarus argued, disdainful.

'Ceremonial or not, the intent is there. But the most telling argument of all, my lord, is the fact that the gods' gift to a Dominion Lord is magical armor. *Armor*, my lord.'

'True!' Dagnarus was struck by this. 'You're right, Silwyth. Magical armor. The gods intend by this –' He paused, eyed the elf.

'The gods intend, Your Highness, for a Dominion Lord to be not only the wise guide for his people but also their protector and defender. That means in war, as well as in peace. You might mention that all of the elven Dominion Lords and three of the orken are trained combatants and military leaders and that, while we hope and trust that our races will forever be at peace, we can never know what the future will hold. It would be inadvisable for the humans to be seen as being weak in this field.'

'And so it seems to me,' said Dagnarus in his Speech of Supplication before the Council, 'that while we hope and trust that our races will forever be at peace, we can never know what the future will hold. Our friends the elves come here with Dominion Lords who are renowned for their courage and skill on the field of battle. Lord Mabreton, for example, is a hero of the Battle of Tessua's Keep.'

A battle that had proved disastrous for the human army, as all the human Dominion Lords seated around the table well remembered. They looked very dour, especially to see the elven Dominion Lords smiling with immense satisfaction – the elves now controlled Tessua's Keep. King Tamaros was gently nodding, Dunner struck his clenched fist upon the table, expressing agreement in the dwarven manner.

Helmos watched all this with grave concern.

Can't you see what he is doing? Helmos asked them silently. Playing upon old fears, reviving old hatreds. Feeding us poison in sweetmeats, poison whose foul taste is masked by this sugar coating. The elves back him. He has made some deal with them, of course. Lord Mabreton speaks of Dagnarus's kindness to his wife, how he made her feel welcome in this strange court. He says that now she is so much at home that she is loath to return to her homeland! He has not heard the whispers about her. The husband is the last to know, they say. I can prove nothing, nor would I, if I had the chance. I can only pray to the gods that my brother does not bring down disgrace upon us all and most especially upon Lady Mabreton, poor woman. What can he be thinking? Doesn't he knew it would mean her death if her infidelity were discovered?

Perhaps he does know. Helmos regarded his brother with sorrow. Perhaps he knows and does not care. So long as his lusts are gratified. And are the other whispers true – that he worships the Void, he and Gareth, for I hear that he has drawn his too-trusting and too-malleable friend down with him. I dare not say anything about that either, for, if it were true, it would break our father's heart.

'I promise I will dedicate myself to the service of our Order,' Dagnarus was concluding humbly, 'and to the service of the peoples of the world.'

He was handsome, well dressed, his hair curled and combed and shining; his body straight and muscular; he was noble and solemn, earnest and sincere. Taking Tamaros's age-wasted hand in his own strong one, Dagnarus bent down on one knee to thank his father for his faith in him and vowed upon all that he held sacred (Which is nothing, thought Helmos, if he worships the Void) that he would make his father proud of him. Tamaros, rising to his feet, laid his hand upon his son's shining head in blessing. Several of the humans wiped their eyes unashamedly.

Dagnarus rose and faced the Council. He bowed again, with graceful humility. The elves applauded in unison with quiet, subdued clapping of their hands. Dunner went around the table to shake Dagnarus by the hand. The human Dominion Lords murmured among themselves, several casting sidelong glances at Helmos and shaking their heads. The Captain of the orken woke up and demanded in a grumbling voice to know when they were going to eat.

Dagnarus departed; he would not be present for the vote, which, the orken were dismayed to hear, would take place before the Council adjourned for dinner.

King Tamaros rose to speak. He was frail and bent, his hair snow-white, his beard gray and grizzled, but he had not failed mentally. Though his body might be preparing for departure from this life, his mind was not. He put forward his youngest son's candidacy in clear, strong terms, impressing everyone on the Council.

Everyone except his eldest and most beloved son.

Helmos and his father had never before disagreed on anything. Helmos held Tamaros in reverent respect, loved his father as he loved few people in this world. But in this, Helmos was going to cross his father. In this, he could not allow his father to prevail. Yet Helmos must fight this battle with both hands fettered; he must fight without wounding either his opponent or innocent bystanders, which meant that his best weapons were useless to him.

'My son Dagnarus is not a scholar,' Tamaros was saying. 'He cares nothing for books. He sees no beauty in art. He grows restless and bored with the minstrel's song. Yet that, I think, should not disqualify him if it does not disqualify others.' Here the king glanced meaningfully at the orken.

'My son Dagnarus is a soldier. He is a born leader. The men who serve under him revere him for his courage, for his good sense, for his care of them. I have spoken to many of the common foot soldiers who have fought

341

with Dagnarus, and they are united in their praise of him. They would follow him anywhere, I believe. Even into the Void itself.'

'Speak no evil!' said the Captain suddenly, in a booming voice, which startled everyone, for they had assumed by the fact that his eyes were closed that he'd drifted off to sleep again. He sat up straight and made the sign against bad omens, as did the other two orken, seated on either side of him.

The human Dominion Lords smiled indulgently, amused and diverted. Tamaros gravely asked pardon, saying he had not meant to offend. He continued on with his praise of Dagnarus. Helmos sat silently, sadly, barely listening, his thoughts on what he must say in rebuttal, on what effect his words would have on his father.

Speech concluded, Tamaros sat down.

The Captain looked up hopefully. 'We shall vote now. And then go eat.'

'Not quite yet, sir,' said Lord Mabreton, who was the newly elected Head of the Council to replace the deceased former head, Lord Donnengal. 'Any who have aught to say against the nomination of Prince Dagnarus may now present their arguments.'

The Captain sighed deeply, placed his massive elbows on the table, and shook his head. 'Let's get on with it, then,' he muttered.

'Is there anyone who would like to speak against the nomination of Prince Dagnarus?' asked Lord Mabreton in a tone indicating he would be extremely shocked if there were.

He was shocked and King Tamaros was displeased when Helmos rose to his feet.

'What I have to say, I say with the greatest reluctance, knowing that my words will anger my King and grieve him. Silence would be easy for me. Acquiescence would be easy. I would do anything for my King, sacrifice

342

anything. I would lay down my life for him and count it a privilege. I would give him anything of mine – anything – except this.'

Helmos's eyes filled with tears. He looked down at his hands, trembling, as they rested on the table. 'Except what he most wants.' This last was said in a husky voice, and Helmos stood a moment, regaining control of himself, before he continued.

The other Dominion Lords watched and waited, moved by Helmos's anguish and the depth of his feeling, if they were not moved by his words.

He lifted his head, his tears dry. 'I argue against the candidacy of Prince Dagnarus. He is most unsuitable to be a Dominion Lord. True, he is, as you say, Father, a good soldier, a charismatic leader of men. I acknowledge this and I say, Let him be a soldier. Let him be a general. Let him lead men in battle. Do not let him lead them in their lives.

'It is true, as he says, that we Dominion Lords are given marvelous, magical, powerful armor. And when we think of armor, we think of battle, of war. And, yes, we fight. We fight every day of our lives – we fight the battle the gods intended us to fight. We fight against ignorance, we fight against prejudice and hatred, we fight against greed and injustice. We fight to bring peace to our peoples. These are the god-given battles that we fight, and thus we wear the armor given us by the gods. Our weapons are not swords. Our weapons are patience, tolerance, under-standing, fortitude, forbearance, mercy, and compassion. Even you must admit, Your Majesty, that none of these, *none* of these' – Helmos laid emphasis upon the word – 'can be said to apply to Prince Dagnarus.

'The gods know that we are imperfect. I do not pretend to possess half the noble attributes I have delineated. But I strive to do so. And so, I think, do we all. Prince Dagnarus is courageous – I am the first to speak that in his favor.

343

He is quick-witted and decisive. The King acknowledges that Prince Dagnarus is not a scholar, and he brushes aside that fact as being irrelevant in our decision-making process, pointing out by implication that others among our ranks are not necessarily scholars.' Helmos looked at the orken, who were watching him, for a change, with close attention.

'Yet, these who may not be able to read words on a page can nevertheless determine their location on the open sea with precision, using instruments and mathematical calculations that are as meaningless to me as the printed word is to them. The fact that Prince Dagnarus chooses not to study, chooses to remain uninformed about the people and the world around him, refuses to invest the time and energy required to improve his mind, indicates to me that he lacks patience, lacks discipline of self.

'Discipline of self. To my mind, therein lies Prince Dagnarus's greatest fault. You may say, and rightly so, that this is a common fault of the young. And, indeed, Prince Dagnarus is very young. Perhaps he may learn, in time, to overcome this fault. But until that time, if such a time comes, I say to this Council that we must vote against him. Prince Dagnarus is not suited to the noble and puissant office of a Dominion Lord. I cast my vote against him, and I urge the other members of the Council to do the same.'

Helmos sat down, pale, but composed. He had done what he believed in his heart to be right. He could even meet his father's frowning gaze with equanimity, though to know his father's anger was directed at him was a blow that drew blood. Helmos had hoped that his words might sway his father, might tear apart the bright and glittering web of charm Dagnarus was able to weave. Helmos saw that he had failed, that Tamaros, though not angry at his elder son, was deeply disappointed in him.

I can say nothing more, Helmos realized, helplessly. I

cannot voice my suspicions, not without ruining too many lives. I must trust in the gods, that they will prevent my brother from becoming a Dominion Lord, even if we allow it.

'Is there anyone else who has aught to say on this matter?' asked Lord Mabreton gravely. His expression was thoughtful. Helmos had given him something to consider, at least.

To everyone's surprise, the Captain rose ponderously to his feet. The ork had never before spoken up in a Council meeting (except to ask when it was time to eat).

'The omens are bad for this one. We' – the Captain nodded at his two cohorts – 'vote no.' Turning to King Tamaros, the ork added, 'I told you. You should have strangled him when he was a pup.'

The ork sat down. He had said all that was necessary to be said. Helmos was grateful for the support, though he had the feeling that the ork had done more harm than good. King Tamaros was angry now, recalling the incident in question, an incident that had been downplayed as a misunderstanding – a rather humorous misunderstanding. Tamaros was not pleased to be reminded of it, nor was he pleased that the unfortunate incident, which had involved the Sovereign Stone, had been brought up before the Council. Several of the Dominion Lords appeared mystified by the ork's blunt statement and were looking to the King for answers.

Lord Mabreton, taking his cue from the irate king, decided to sidestep the issue. 'Are there any more words to be spoken either for or against the nomination of Prince Dagnarus?'

The elf looked at Dunner, who was known to all of them to be the prince's longtime friend. The dwarf sat with head bowed, uncomfortable. He agreed with Tamaros, so far as his praise of Dagnarus, and yet the dwarf found himself agreeing with Helmos, as well. Dunner was sadly torn.

He liked Dagnarus as well as a dwarf could like a human, and he wanted very much to vote for Dagnarus, for the ballot was not secret. The prince would know the names of those who had voted in his favor and those who had not. Dagnarus would never forgive those who had not. Yet Dunner wondered if he could do so with a clear conscience. For the first time in his life, the dwarf wished himself an ork, wished that there was a flight of birds or a swarm of insects to make clear to him what to do.

'It is long past the supper hour,' he said at last, finding something useful in the strange human custom of eating at set times. 'I cannot think over the rumbling in my belly. Let us adjourn for food, then come back and hash this out.'

The Council voted to adjourn and reassemble in two hours. Tamaros remained behind until all had departed, talking pleasantly, answering questions, thanking those who expressed their support. Helmos remained seated. Several of the human Dominion Lords came to him, spoke to him in low tones. He thanked them for their concern, and they, too, departed. Eventually, father and son were alone.

'Father,' Helmos began. 'Please believe –' His words died.

Tamaros rose to his feet. He regarded Helmos with sadness and with pity. 'It had never occurred to me that you could be this jealous of your brother. That you could so completely misunderstand and misrepresent him. The fault is mine. I have failed as a father to both of you.'

'Father!' Helmos stood up. 'Father, please . . .'

Tamaros turned his back and left the room.

When the Council of the Dominion Lords resumed meeting two hours later, the vote was seventeen to six in favor of Dagnarus.

In the end, Dunner voted for his friend.

EIGHT

Shakur

'AH, HERE YOU ARE!'
The loud voice split the quiet of the library, completely unexpected, like a lightning bolt streaking out of a clear blue sky, and therefore twice as startling. Heads bent over books reared up, readers gasped, hands jerked, causing ink bottles to spill and pens to blot. The librarian was on her feet, her face pinched and pale with anger, and then she saw the person responsible. The angry words were too far advanced to be retrieved, but she was able to garble them sufficiently so that she did not reprimand the prince.

Dagnarus brushed aside her incoherent gabblings, strode among the tables, and came to Gareth.

'I've been looking for you everywhere!' Dagnarus stated, as if it were Gareth's fault that he was not where the prince thought he should be.

Gareth had recognized the prince's voice and was already on his feet, feverishly gathering up the books he had been studying, his face and ears hot and crimson with embarrassment. The other scholars dared not show irritation at the prince, but a young Temple novice was fair game, and so they glared angrily at him.

347

'Now look what you've done!' Gareth said to the prince beneath his breath.

'A fox in the chicken coop,' said Dagnarus, glancing around. 'Dull old farts. I daresay most of them haven't felt such excitement in years. Forgive me, Librarian,' he said in meek and mild tones, bending over the librarian's hand and kissing it reverently. 'I did not mean to create such a stir. I am a soldier, not a scholar, and am unaccustomed to being in such silent, solemn, and studious surroundings. I have urgent matters to discuss with my advisor, Gareth. Matters of state. Most important. Do forgive me.'

'Certainly, Your Highness,' said the librarian, much mollified by his words, which he uttered with disarming sincerity. Though she was quite absorbed in her work, to which she was wholly dedicated, his good looks and charming manner made his kiss on her hand very delightful. She blushed with the honor and the attention and cast an oblique glance from under her lowered lashes to make certain the other magi noticed.

The prince departed the library, his fur-lined riding cloak creating a small whirlwind that swept books off tables and sent papers rising into the air. Gareth followed in the path of the storm, which cut a wide swath of destruction before the prince was safely out into the corridor.

'What –' Gareth began.

'Not here,' said Dagnarus, and, grabbing hold of Gareth's sleeve, he dragged his friend off farther down the corridor, into the part of the castle where the empty suits of armor kept their rusting vigil.

'What is it? What's wrong?' Gareth asked.

Dagnarus had evidently come from outdoors – his cheeks were bright from the crisp, cool air, and he still wore his cloak and riding boots.

'I've been hunting,' he said.

'Hunting?' Gareth stared, unable to imagine what this

348

had to do with him. 'Did the hunt go well, Your Highness?'

'Not for game. For a man.'

'Yes?' Gareth was still perplexed.

'A fugitive. You remember that burgher who was stabbed in an alleyway down in the lower city last week?'

'I heard of it, yes. Robbery, I believe?'

'That's what it was meant to look like – purse and jewels stolen. But the sheriff was suspicious. For one thing, the knife blow that killed the man was quick, clean, struck straight to the heart. He died instantly without a cry. Then, the jewels showed up again in the possession of the grieving young widow, who was being comforted for her husband's untimely demise by a very handsome young "cousin."'

'An assassination, then,' said Gareth.

'Exactly. These two, who were lovers, wanted to be rid of the husband, but not his money. So they plotted to kill him. The assassin would steal the jewels, to make it look like robbery, but the greedy little widow couldn't bear the thought of actually parting with them, so she instructed the assassin to bring them back to her. She and her lover were captured, they made a deal with the sheriff to agree to banishment on condition that they stand witness against the assassin. This they've done. He almost eluded us – he's a wicked, cunning rascal – but we tracked him down in the mountains.' Dagnarus grinned, elated with the chase, pleased with the capture.

'I am glad such an evil man has been brought to justice, Your Highness,' said Gareth, 'but what –'

'What has this to do with us?' Dagnarus leaned close. 'I have our candidate. Our first Vrykyl.'

Gareth felt the blood leave his head in a rush, pool somewhere around his gut, which sank with the weight. Light-headed, he stumbled backward, leaned against the wall.

'What's the matter, Patch?' Dagnarus asked, displeased. 'You looked shocked. Don't tell me you weren't expecting this? Here, lower your head before you pass out on me!'

'I *wasn't* expecting this, Your Highness,' Gareth said, doing as he was bid, hanging his head until the blood returned. 'I never supposed . . . not so soon . . .'

'We must seize time by the fetlock, as Dunner would say,' the prince returned. 'I am eager to see if this works. And we may never have a subject more suitable. A trained killer, caught, sentenced to hang next week. We offer to free him if he'll perform a job for us. A job requiring nothing except that he openly embrace the Void. I don't see how this wretch can turn us down.'

Gareth lifted his head. He could see his face, which looked ghastly, reflected in the armor across from him. The disembodied knight seemed to be regarding him with stern disapproval.

'Your Highness, next week you enter the Temple to begin the Seven Preparations. You should be concentrating on this. I gave you the books to study. You must –'

'I looked at them. Boring old tomes. You will study for me, Patch. You will help me through the tests. Come along,' Dagnarus urged, seizing his friend by the hand. 'I want you to see this fellow. You must explain to him what is required; I don't understand it all. Do we have to get something in writing?'

Dagnarus turned on his heel, eager to proceed. Gareth clutched at him in desperation, dragging him back.

'My prince,' Gareth said earnestly, 'consider this well! Where will we do this deed? How are we to break him out of prison? What will happen if we succeed? Where is he to go? What will become of him? This creature will not be some pet snake to which we toss a rat every month or so. He will demand souls, Dagnarus. No,' he said, bowing his head again. 'No, I can't go through with it. Don't ask me . . .'

'You are the only one I *can* ask,' Dagnarus said softly, bitingly. His hand closed painfully over Gareth's thin arm. 'Why did you give me this dagger if you didn't intend for me to use it?'

'I thought . . . You know what I thought,' Gareth replied in despair, not looking up.

'You thought to dissuade me from being a Dominion Lord. But the Council has voted. I am to be one, and there is nothing and no one in this world that will stop me. As to this Vrykyl, he is an experiment. How can I make plans for him if I do not know how this works? Where do we stash him? *If* we succeed – and I have yet to believe it – I will put him up in one of my hired rooms at the Hare and Hound. They know me there and, most important, they know my money. They ask no questions. As for what he will eat . . .' Dagnarus shrugged. 'Beggars abound in Vinnengael. We might even be said to be doing a public service.

'Patch,' Dagnarus continued, his grip tightening. 'Listen to me, Patch. I want this. You cannot refuse me.'

I could, Gareth thought wearily. But you would never forgive me. And I could not live with your hatred, your anger. Face it, Gareth. You made this decision already. You made it when you took the dagger from the old man. You renewed it when you gave the dagger to Dagnarus. All else is just an excuse, an excuse for your weakness, your cowardice. Admit it. You are as interested in the outcome as he is. You want to know if this will work. You want to know if you have the power to raise the dead.

'Very well, Your Highness,' he said.

'Come on!' Dagnarus hustled his friend along, eager as a child to show off a new toy.

'Your Highness!' The gaoler rose to his feet. Extremely surprised, he made a belated bow. 'Revered Magus.' He made another bow, not so low, to Gareth, who kept his face covered with the hood of his cloak. He and the prince

351

had decided that it would be better if no one recognized him. People might start to ask questions.

'How can I be of service to Your Highness?' the gaoler asked, understandably curious.

Tamaros in all his years as King had never visited the dungeons beneath his castle, nor had Helmos, the crown prince. Tamaros sent agents to make certain the prisoners were being treated humanely – their cells clean, decent food, not beaten or tortured for sport. Beyond that, he had little care for them. This was not surprising. The prisoners had forfeited all their rights by breaking the laws the King had established, laws that were just and fair. In making certain that they were not mistreated, Tamaros showed far more consideration for Vinnengael's prisoners than any other ruler had ever done previously.

'That prisoner we brought in today – the assassin. I helped to capture him,' said Dagnarus, smoothing his gloves. 'I have been approached by this Revered Magus, who begs to be allowed to question this man. There is some thought he may be implicated in the strange death of one of their brethren in Neyshabur last year. Since I helped catch the wretch,' Dagnarus added carelessly, 'I feel a certain proprietary interest in him.'

'Of course, Your Highness. I understand completely,' said the gaoler. He began to sort through his collection of cell-door keys, which he kept on a large iron ring. 'I am always pleased to be able to assist the magi. This way.'

They walked along a narrow corridor carved deep inside the cliff upon which the castle stood. The dungeons where the most dangerous, most hardened criminals were kept were far below the main portion of the castle, down almost at sea level. One descended innumerable steps in order to reach them. Cavelike cells, delved out of the same rock, branched off the corridor on either side. The corridor was brightly lit by torches that smoked in the dank air.

The prison had only a small staff of guards to keep

the prisoners in order. There were very few escapes. An escape had first to break out of a wizard-locked door – nearly impossible, even for another wizard. Then he must elude his captors and climb three hundred stairs to reach an exit, an exit that brought him out into the military's barracks.

'Forgive the long walk, Your Highness,' said the gaoler, 'but we have put him off to himself in one of the cells clear in the back. He's a rum one, he is. I doubt Your Highness remembers – you would have been just a child at the time – but the last time he was in here he managed to escape. One of the few who has done it, I'm proud to say.'

Something stirred in the back of Gareth's mind at this, something unpleasant, for he felt his flesh creep. He could not name his fear, however, and finally put it down to the gloomy atmosphere of the prison – the foul smells, the sounds of hacking coughs, the tromping of booted feet behind, for Dagnarus had brought along two of his soldiers. Otherwise there was quiet. Thick stone walls and heavy iron doors, with only a small opening through which the guard could look when making his rounds, deadened all sound. There was no talking, except possibly to oneself, and this did not carry into the hallway. The prisoners, alone in their cells, might have been alone in the world.

'Here it is,' said the gaoler, halting in front of a cell located at the very end of the corridor. He brought forth his keys, which had been enchanted, found the one that fit, inserted it into the lock. There was a flash of light – that was the wizard lock being removed – then a dull click, which took care of the mechanical lock, and the door swung slowly open. Gareth had been holding his breath against the odors of unwashed body, urine, and feces, then realized that he might as well get used to it. They would likely be here for a while. He tried, however, to breathe as little as possible.

'Shakur!' the gaoler called out, 'you got visitors. His Highness himself.'

There was no answer, except for a slight clanking of chains, which might have been made by a restless shifting of position.

'I'll be right out here, Your Highness,' the gaoler continued. 'Best to leave the cell door open.'

'We do not want to keep you from your duties,' Dagnarus said pleasantly. 'This is a private interview.' Leaning near, he added in low, conspiratorial tones, 'Wizard's work. You understand?'

'Yes, Your Highness.' Though the gaoler looked dubious. 'He's a rum'un, Your Highness. Would just as soon slit your throat as spit at you.'

'I am well armed,' said Dagnarus, displaying sword and knife. 'And I have my bodyguards, whom I will post outside the cell door.' He gestured to the two soldiers accompanying him. 'Now you must allow me to conduct this interview as I see fit, otherwise, Sir Gaoler, I will begin to think you question my authority.'

He spoke lightly, but the gaoler saw that he had gone too far. Bowing low, he departed, first admonishing them to 'yell out' if they needed anything.

'Like fresh air,' Dagnarus muttered, wrinkling his nose. 'If I were stuck down here, by the gods, I'd look forward to being hanged, just to have a chance to get outdoors.'

'Do you realize,' said Gareth, looking around with horror and speaking in low, hollow tones, 'that if I were caught practicing Void magic, this is where they would send me.'

'Have you so little faith in me as that?' Dagnarus asked, with a flash in his eye. 'You know I would not permit such a thing.'

'I know you would do everything you possibly could,' Gareth began deprecatingly. 'But –'

'Come on,' Dagnarus interrupted, his voice cold. 'We're wasting time.'

They entered the cell slowly, pausing at the door to allow their eyes to become accustomed to the darkness. Some of the other cells had small windows, hewn out of the rock, but this cell did not. Apparently they feared that the prisoner might find a way to slide out of a hole six inches by six and then make his way down a sheer cliff. For all his trouble, he would end up being battered to death by the waves breaking against the rocks.

It occurred to Gareth that though they could not see the prisoner, he could see them perfectly well. Gareth moved closer to Dagnarus, who had realized the same thing and had his hand on the hilt of his sword.

'Shakur,' Dagnarus said, his voice echoing. 'I am Prince Dagnarus. This is Gareth, my friend and advisor. We have come to speak to you. Gareth, bring a torch and shut the cell door – not all the way, just enough to insure our privacy.'

'I can provide light, Your Highness,' said Gareth coolly, not sorry to show off his magical skills to his friend and to the prisoner. Lifting his hand, he commanded the stone to catch fire, starting a small blaze in the center of the cell, a blaze that seemed to feed off cold rock. He saw, by the light, the skin on the back of his hand ulcerate. He tugged down the sleeve of his robe.

The fire burned brightly, shed light upon the prisoner, who had been lying on a straw mattress on the floor and who now sat up to stare, first at the fire – the making of which caused him to narrow his eyes – then at them. At the sight of the prisoner's face, Gareth shrank backward until he bumped up against the cell wall.

'What is it now?' Dagnarus demanded irritably, turning to glare at his companion.

'I know this man!' Gareth gasped, pointing at Shakur as if there were forty other people in the cell and he must be singled out. 'When I was a child . . . I was with Captain Argot. He set me on his horse. This fellow was caught deserting. He knocked me off and tried to steal the horse! I told you, Your Highness. Surely you remember?'

'No, I don't,' said Dagnarus carelessly, eyeing the prisoner.

'You must! This man's face haunted my dreams for weeks!'

'Perhaps I have some dim recollection,' Dagnarus said impatiently. 'It doesn't matter now, Patch. He's not going to leap at you again. He's chained hand and foot. Come over here. Unless you want to shout our business for all the world to hear.'

Reluctantly, Gareth crept forward, unable to take his eyes off Shakur, who grinned at him wickedly, enjoying his discomfiture.

The man's face – bloody and battered – had been the stuff of nightmares when Gareth had last seen him, years ago. Shakur had not improved since. The terrible wound had healed, but poorly. Half the muscle and meat was missing, leaving a grotesque mass of scar tissue, which had adhered directly to the cheekbone, causing Shakur's face to look shriveled and shrunken. The eyelid drooped, but he had kept the sight of the eye, apparently, for that eye and its twin regarded them through filthy, matted hair with undisguised, if baleful, curiosity.

'Welcome to my humble chambers, Your Highness,' Shakur said, with a sneer. 'You'll pardon me if I don't get up, but I'm chained to the wall. Go ahead. Stare at me all you like. I won't grow prettier.'

'We haven't come to make sport of you,' said Dagnarus, crouching down on his haunches in front of the prisoner, who sat cross-legged on his straw mattress. 'Nor are we here out of puerile or morbid curiosity. We have a proposition for you, Shakur.' Dagnarus lowered his voice. 'A proposition that will permit you to escape the hangman's noose.'

'A job I can do for Your Highness?' Shakur asked, his tone instantly more respectful.

'Yes,' said Dagnarus, 'a job.'

'Who's the mark?' Shakur asked with professional interest.

'All in good time,' Dagnarus replied. 'First a question. What do you know of Void magic, Shakur?'

Shakur glanced at the fire, burning from nothing, then shifted his gaze to the prince. Interest sparked in the cunning eyes. 'What do *you* know of it, Your Highness?'

'Enough,' said Dagnarus. Removing a knife from his boot, he held it in his hands, tapped the point upon his finger. The blade was sharp and rimed with firelight. 'And now that you know my secret, you will not be allowed to live to tell it. Which leads to an interesting choice. I will kill you here and now – I can always tell the gaoler that you jumped me, tried to seize my sword to make good your escape – or you can leave this cell in company with me and my friend and those soldiers.'

'So what is this job?' Shakur repeated, gazing steadily at the prince. 'And what has the Void to do with it?'

'In order for me to trust you, I require that you embrace the Void,' said Dagnarus, toying with the knife. 'Renounce the gods.'

Shakur shrugged. 'I never had much use for the gods. And I doubt they have much use for me. Is that all?'

'Just about. You must prove your worthiness to me by undergoing a small test. You wouldn't mind that, I suppose?'

'What sort of test?' Shakur was suspicious.

'Nothing much. Just swear by an artifact of the Void that you take the Void for your master.'

'That's all?'

'All that is required of you,' said Dagnarus pleasantly.

'And you'll get me out of here? Save me from the hangman?'

'This very moment.'

'What about a sack of silver into the bargain?' Shakur leered.

'Don't push your luck,' Dagnarus answered, amused.

'Well, then I'm your man, Your Highness,' said Shakur, and he held out his manacled hands to be freed.

'Gareth, go tell the gaoler,' Dagnarus ordered.

'Tell him what?' Gareth demanded, dismayed.

'Tell him we require this prisoner for further questioning and that we'll be taking him with us.'

'We'll be the talk of the taverns,' Gareth said, low and urgent. 'The gaoler will tell everyone he knows. Word will get back to the palace. What will we say when someone wants to know why you freed a convicted murderer?'

'You will give the gaoler this.' Dagnarus removed a purse from his belt, handed it to Gareth. 'Tell him that the man this wretch murdered was a friend of mine, that I have sworn revenge. I am sorry to cheat the people out of a hanging, but my honor is at stake. And then you will ask him to keep silent.'

'What if he won't be bribed?'

'It is *not* a bribe. It is recompense for his trouble. By the gods, Patch!' Dagnarus rose to his feet. 'Must I do this myself –'

'No, no,' said Gareth, grabbing the purse. He did not want to be left alone with Shakur. 'I will do it.'

He departed in haste.

'Who is that?' Shakur asked, with a slight curl of his lip.

'My necromancer,' Dagnarus replied coolly.

'He's young.'

'But quite capable.'

Shakur did not appear impressed. 'When is the job, then? Where am I to hide out?'

'I have made all the arrangements. You needn't concern yourself.' Dagnarus cast a glance at the door. 'What is taking so confounded long?'

Shakur gave a practiced twist of his wrist. 'A knife job, I take it?'

Dagnarus turned to look at Shakur. 'Yes. A knife job.' He turned back to staring impatiently at the door.

'You won't think the less of me if I try to escape, will you, Your Highness?' Shakur grinned.

'I couldn't possibly think less of you than I do now,' Dagnarus assured him. 'You may, of course, make the attempt, but my guards are loyal and quite dedicated to me. You must know them, they serve under Captain Argot. You once served under Captain Argot, I believe. His men have no great love for you, Shakur. They would not be sorry for an opportunity to do you harm. Nothing that would affect your usefulness, mind you. Just something extremely unpleasant.'

At the mention of Captain Argot, Shakur's leer and grin vanished, replaced by a sullen doggedness. He said no more. The voice of the gaoler, raised in disbelief, could be heard coming down the corridor.

'Your Highness!' he began to remonstrate the moment he entered the cell.

'Free this man,' said Dagnarus.

'Your Highness, I must protest –'

'Protest, by all means,' Dagnarus said impatiently. 'And when you have finished, free this man into my custody. I will accept full responsibility for him.'

The gaoler did protest, longer than he would have probably done under the circumstances, considering that it was the decision of a prince he protested. Shakur was a notorious killer, a good catch, and the hanging had promised to be extremely entertaining. Not all the prince's silver could quite make up for that. Dagnarus bore the protestations far longer than Gareth supposed the prince would, but eventually his patience wore thin.

'I *will* be obeyed,' he said, at last, glowering, and even the obdurate gaoler knew that any further argument would not only have been useless, it might have been unhealthy.

Dagnarus ordered his soldiers into the cell. The gaoler released Shakur from his chains. The soldiers strapped an iron belt around his waist, from which dangled two sets of manacles – one set for his wrists and another his ankles. The soldiers locked him in with swift efficiency. It was obvious from their looks that they knew Shakur and obvious from his sneer and attempts at bravado that he remembered them.

They marched him off, the gaoler watching after them sadly, shaking his head and muttering, even as he opened the purse to count his coins.

NINE

The Creation of a Vrykyl

A S HE HAD DONE FOR HIS ELDER SON, KING Tamaros held a feast for his younger son the night before his entry into the Temple. The feast was quite splendid, consisting of capons and pigeons, accompanied by sausages, hams, and wild boar, a whole roast sheep, and chickens with sugar and rosewater.

Gareth, invited as an honored guest, remembered with a pang the feast for Helmos, remembered how thrilled he had been to attend, how kind and good Helmos had been to him.

'And this is how I will repay Helmos for his patronage,' Gareth said to himself somberly, toying with his food and staring into his full wine cup. 'This night, I will assist his brother in a ritual that will restore unholy life to the dead.'

'Come, Patch!' cried Dagnarus, turning from his other companions with a rowdy laugh and slapping Gareth on the shoulder. 'No long faces! This is a time of joy! Drink up!'

He poured more wine into the already full cup, causing the blood-red liquid to slosh over the sides. Gareth cast the prince a reproachful glance, which only made Dagnarus laugh more loudly.

The prince was not drunk, or, if he was, he concealed it well. He could drink all night, drink when others were sliding from their chairs and lying under the table, as limp as the barmaid's rag, and still retain his self-possession. It was as if there was some ice-cold part of him that no heat could touch – not the heat of alcohol, not the heat of love. As a last and desperate measure, Gareth had appealed in secret to the Lady Valura, letting her know what he feared might happen if Dagnarus persisted in his determination to become a Dominion Lord.

The Lady Valura knew full well what trials Dagnarus faced. She had watched her own husband undergo the Transfiguration. Terrified for her lover, who – it seemed to her – must be going to his death, Valura spent a night pleading with him to drop this notion. For her sake, he would turn down the nomination.

'If anything happened to you, my love,' she said to him, stroking the auburn hair that rested on her breast, 'I would kill myself.'

His answer was to kiss her and make love to her and, when the candle had burned down to the level which meant that it was near dawn, he rose from their bed and said that he was sorry they could meet no more from this night on – he would be in the Temple, undergoing his Tests, and though he had thought long on the matter, he did not see how he could escape from there to be with her. He was gentle with her, but she could tell he was displeased, even angry, and she fell weeping back among the pillows.

She did not attend the banquet that night; her husband reported that she was not feeling well. She had not risen from her bed all day, had refused food. Dagnarus said what was proper and, though he sometimes glanced with a somber expression at her empty chair, that expression would then harden and he would drink off another cup of wine and laugh more boisterously than ever.

One other person did not attend the banquet – Prince

Helmos. His absence was noted by everyone with astonishment, and by Dagnarus with extreme displeasure. The King did what he could to pass it off, but everyone could see that Tamaros himself was angry – angrier than anyone could remember seeing him in a long time. Two spots of red dotted his sunken cheeks; his eyes glittered like the eyes of a fierce old raptor.

Breaking all custom, he sent his chamberlain to fetch his elder son. The chamberlain returned alone – everyone in the hall watching, knowing what was going on – and bent down to whisper in Tamaros's ear. The red spots in the King's cheeks expanded until the red suffused his entire face. He choked down his rage, however, muttered something to the effect that Helmos was taken ill. Lifting his wine cup, King Tamaros proposed that the assembled company drink to his younger son, Prince Dagnarus.

This the assembled company did, not once, but many times. It was well that Prince Helmos did not attend the feast, for when the King left – somewhat earlier in the evening than was his wont – the party turned riotous. Gareth could feel Helmos there in spirit, however, feel the prince's disappointment and displeasure. This, combined with the thought of what he must do that night, made Gareth physically ill, so that he was forced to rise from the table.

'Where are you going?' Dagnarus demanded, catching hold of Gareth's wrist, squeezing it painfully.

'I am going to make the preparations,' Gareth said in a low voice. 'Meet me in the playroom. You will be ready, Your Highness?' Gareth almost hoped the answer would be no.

'I'll be ready!' Dagnarus said with a grim smile. Raising his wine cup, he made Gareth a mocking toast and quaffed the wine in a gulp.

Sick with nervousness and fear, so ill that he could barely walk, Gareth escaped the feast. He traversed the palace corridors without really paying any attention to where he was going, turning over and over in his mind the appalling crime he and the prince were about to commit. Moving along the corridors, head bowed, Gareth bumped into someone, who had also been walking abstractedly, lost in somber thought.

'I beg your pardon,' Gareth gasped, stumbling. A firm grip steadied him, and looking up, he was shocked and dismayed to find that the person was Prince Helmos.

'Your Highness, forgive me,' Gareth mumbled, and tried to escape.

Helmos kept hold of him, stared at him in the dimly lit corridor. 'Gareth, isn't it? My brother's friend . . .'

Not friend . . . whipping boy . . .

'You are not well,' said Helmos. 'Here, sit down. Let me call someone . . .'

'No, Your Highness, please! I beg of you. It is nothing. A passing indisposition.'

Gareth hardly knew what he was saying. He attempted to fend off the prince's hands, attempted to escape. His knees betrayed him. He tottered unsteadily and had no choice but to yield to the prince's insistence. A low carved wooden bench ran along the wall. Thinking it would be better to sit down before he fell down, Gareth sank onto the bench and drew his hood over his head, both to let the blood flow back and to keep his face concealed from the prince's penetrating gaze.

Gareth hoped fervently – he would have prayed fervently, if he had not been convinced that the gods no longer listened to his prayers – that Helmos would leave him.

'Thank you, Your Highness,' Gareth said. 'I am feeling much better already. Do not let me keep you from your duties.'

'You are worried about him,' said Helmos, sitting down beside Gareth and resting his warm hand over Gareth's cold and trembling one. 'You fear for him. You are a magus, are you not? You know what Dagnarus faces. The tests we require him to pass are difficult. But the true tests come from the gods. If they . . .' He hesitated, realizing where he was going with that thought, thinking how to phrase his words so that he was not unjust to his brother nor sounded mean nor vengeful. 'The gods find fault with all of us,' he amended. 'We are mortal, only the gods themselves are perfect. The gods found my flaws. I was chastened. The pain . . . the pain of the Transfiguration is hard – very hard! – to bear. Faith leads you to endure. I fear . . .'

He knows! Gareth realized, and the knowledge passed through him like the point of a spear. His body shuddered with the blow. Helmos knows that Dagnarus has looked into the Void and embraced it; he knows that I have joined him in that dark emptiness. He will denounce us . . .

Fearful, Gareth raised his head and looked into Helmos's face. Expecting to see him grim and dour and accusing, Gareth saw kindness, pity, compassion . . .

Gareth lowered his head, his eyes filling with tears. Weak, despairing, terrified of himself and the enormity of the crime he was going to commit this night, Gareth longed to confess his guilt, his dreadful sins. No punishment, however severe, not even death, would be as bad as the torment he currently suffered.

'Tell me, Gareth,' Helmos was saying, and it seemed to Gareth that the crown prince spoke from a great distance away, from a place high above Gareth, as if he listened from a well of darkness. 'Don't be silent from misguided loyalty. Speak now and there is yet a chance for salvation, yours and his. You may even save his life. For love of him, Gareth . . .'

For love of him.

Gareth shut his eyes, a suppressed sob convulsed his body. For love of him. I cannot betray him. I dare not.

You are wrong, Helmos. We cannot be saved, either of us. We have drunk too deeply of the darkness.

And, indeed, Gareth could no longer hear the prince's voice, though he knew Helmos was speaking to him. The voice was kind and gentle, but it was too far away. Far, far away.

Gareth regained control of himself. Lifting his head, he looked at Helmos directly. 'You need have no fear for your brother, Prince Helmos.' Gareth spoke steadily, his gaze did not waver. 'He is strong and he is resolute. He looks forward to whatever trials the gods may send him. He asks for nothing more than to prove his worth to you, to his father, to his people.'

Helmos rose to his feet. Gareth expected anger. He saw only disappointment, sadness, and regret.

'Thank you, Your Highness,' Gareth said, lowering his eyes, unable to see that heart-wrenching sorrow. 'Thank you for your concern. I am feeling much better now.'

Helmos remained a moment longer, but Gareth sat quietly, unmoved.

'The gods be with you, Gareth,' said Helmos, and left.

When Gareth could no longer hear the prince's footfalls, when the corridor was dark and empty, he traversed the silent halls until he came to Dagnarus's bedchamber. There, in the privies, Gareth purged his stomach of the bitter bile he had swallowed and felt somewhat better. He made his way to the playroom, where he found Dagnarus, cloaked and booted, his face hidden by a deep cowl, waiting for him impatiently.

'Where have you been?' Dagnarus demanded.

'Talking to your brother,' Gareth replied.

Dagnarus grabbed him roughly by the forearm, jerked him into the light, stared grimly and intently into his face.

'Don't worry,' Gareth replied coldly. 'I said nothing. He cares for you, that's all. He cares about what might happen to you.'

'He had much better look to himself,' said Dagnarus, releasing Gareth and giving him a shove. 'The hour draws near. Let's go.'

The streets were empty in the upper part of the city where the ambassadors resided. The houses were dark and quiet. Most of the ambassadors had been attending Dagnarus's feast and would probably be wondering what had become of the guest of honor. Silwyth was on hand, to make the necessary excuses – the prince had retired early, mindful of his need to be at his best in the morning.

Gareth and the prince left behind the elegant homes of the ambassadors, turned into a mews, traversed the alley until the end. There was a tavern frequented by the hostlers, stableboys, and servants to the ambassadors. The tavern was filled, it being a night when most of the ambassadors were out. Few gave Gareth and Dagnarus so much as a glance when they entered. The regulars were accustomed to keeping one eye shut, as the saying went. Dagnarus cast a glance at the barkeeper, who nodded and jerked his head. Gareth and the prince, hoods pulled low over their faces, climbed the stairs to the second level.

Two soldiers lounged outside a closed door, playing at dice. At the sight of the prince, the soldiers bounded to their feet.

'All well?' Dagnarus asked.

'All is well,' one replied, as the other, removing an iron key from his belt, opened the door.

The room had no windows. The only way in or out was past the guards at the door. Its furnishing consisted of a bed, a table, and two chairs. Seated in one of the chairs was Shakur. He lay sprawled on the table, a wine jug at his side, his hand still clutching a partially filled mug. A frowsy woman, half-unclothed, slept noisily in the bed.

Gareth walked across the room and shook Shakur by the

shoulder. The man's hand dropped from the wine mug, but that was the only response.

'What is this, Your Highness?' Gareth demanded, alarmed. 'He must be conscious! He must know what he is saying!'

'He will,' Dagnarus replied. 'The sleeping potion will wear off soon enough. Sooner than he will wish, undoubtedly. I thought it would be easier walking through the streets without him bleating and creating a ruckus.'

'True,' said Gareth, regarding their prisoner doubtfully. 'If you're sure it will wear off . . .'

'I am sure.' Dagnarus turned to the guards, drew out a purse. 'Here is your pay.'

The two shook their heads. 'It is our duty to serve you, Your Highness.'

'Well, then,' said Dagnarus, smiling, pleased, 'I thank you for your duty and now dismiss you from it.'

The two saluted, but did not immediately leave. 'Do you require our assistance, Your Highness? The wretch is daring and cunning. He has tried to escape us twice, once by playing possum as you see him now.'

Dagnarus walked over, reached down to Shakur's private parts, and gave a squeeze and a twist. Shakur groaned and twitched, but otherwise did not move.

'He would have to be more than human to feign sleep through that,' said Dagnarus to the now grinning soldiers. 'My friend and I can handle him. Thank you again for your service. Tell Captain Argot I said you were to have a week's leave as recompense.'

The soldiers departed.

'What about the woman?' Gareth asked, as they bundled Shakur into the robes of a novice, making certain his hands and feet were securely bound.

'She's been paid,' Dagnarus returned. 'Well paid. She has earned it. You'd think this bastard could have bathed!'

Once Shakur was disguised and trussed, Dagnarus lifted

the drugged man, slung him over a shoulder. Shakur's head and arms, their shackles concealed by the long sleeves of the robes, dangled down behind the prince's back.

'I shall have to burn my clothes after this,' Dagnarus said, grimacing. 'I'll never be able to remove the stench!'

'Hurry, Your Highness,' Gareth said nervously, disapproving of the levity. 'There is not a moment to lose. We must be in the Temple ready to perform the ceremony at one hour past midnight. And it is nearly midnight already.'

The two left the tavern, carrying their burden. They received a few stares from the patrons, but no one said a word. It was none of their concern. Back out into the streets, they looked like revelers carrying home one of their number who had imbibed more than was good for him. They followed a circuitous route to the Temple; coming around to the back.

There was a tradesmen's entrance, with heavy double doors wide enough to accommodate carts loaded with sacks of flour and sides of beef for the kitchen, casks of wine and ale for the cellar. The carts were trundled inside, where they were unloaded, their contents stacked in the large and echoing buttery.

The double doors were locked with a large iron padlock.

'Keep a lookout,' Gareth bid Dagnarus in a whisper. 'There's a watchman. He doesn't usually make his rounds until well after midnight, but sometimes he is early, walking off sleepiness. If you see anyone, summon me. I know what to say to him.'

'What will you say?' Dagnarus inquired. His eyes, by the moonlight, shone brilliantly. The burden he carried was heavy and foul-smelling, but he bore the weight with ease and the smell with only a grimace. He was enjoying himself, enjoying the danger and the intrigue. 'What is our story?'

'I will say that I am helping home a drunken friend and that you agreed to carry him for me. The watchman is a kind man. He is used to such tales and will let us off with only a lecture and a promise to reform.'

'Well, make haste,' said Dagnarus. He dumped Shakur into a corner, wiped his hands, and brushed off his clothing. Shakur stirred and muttered, he was coming out of his drugged sleep. Dagnarus eyed the padlock. 'This seems formidable. Have you the key?'

'No, that never leaves the porter's side. But I have my magic.' Gareth glanced at Shakur with some trepidation. 'Keep close watch. If you see anything amiss, alert me.'

Dagnarus folded his arms, tilted his head back, admiring the stars, and leaned negligently against the wall. Gareth couldn't see the stars, for the blackness that seemed to envelop him, covering him head to toe like a pall. He cast Shakur another worried glance. Seeing him quiet for the moment, Gareth went to work on the lock, an ordinary padlock, to keep out common thieves. Wizard locks were generally used to keep out other wizards, and it was unlikely wizards would be intent upon breaking into the buttery.

Though time was precious and trickling away rapidly, Gareth paused before he set about his task, nerving himself. As does all magic, the use of Void magic demands a toll from the magus who summons it. Other magicks, those of Earth, Fire, Air, and Water, draw upon the elements to power them. The Void demands to be filled and so Void magic demands a portion of the magus's life force, represented by the ulcerations that form on the skin afterward. A Void magic spell mishandled can result in the death of the magus. The aftereffects Gareth would suffer from casting a spell this powerful would be painful, debilitating. But then, the drunkard knows the same when he wakes.

He breathed upon the lock, breathed seven breaths. 'By the Void, I summon air,' he said. 'Destroy this metal.'

The iron padlock was rusty to begin with. The magic merely accelerated the rusting process. He breathed on it again and the iron turned brownish in the moonlight and began flaking away. He was about to breathe upon the lock yet again, but there came no breath. His heartbeat had altered its steady reassuring rhythm, become erratic, painfully erratic. He felt a flash of fear as starbursts tingled on the backs of his eyes. He struggled, fought to breathe, and, finally, was granted a gasp. His heartbeat returned to normal.

Exhausted, shivering, he was forced to lean against the door for one moment, a moment he could ill spare, before he gained strength enough to carry on. Patches of skin on various parts of his body burned and stung. The pustules were forming. Thankful that Dagnarus had not been present to witness his weakness – a weakness the prince would have never understood – Gareth continued to breathe on the lock until there was a pile of shavings at his feet.

He tried the lock, tugging on it, several times, and when – weakened by the spell – the lock gave way, he ended the spell by ceasing to breathe upon it. He did not want the lock to rust away completely. That would have looked suspicious.

'Well done!' said Dagnarus. 'I am impressed. How did you do that?'

'There is no time to lose, Your Highness,' Gareth snapped, still weak and too nervous to feel pleasure at the praise. 'Bring him and follow me.'

Dagnarus's expression darkened; he did not take kindly to being ordered about by an underling.

'Forgive me, Your Highness,' Gareth said. His hands were shaking, he was covered in chill sweat. 'I am not myself . . . This ghastly business . . .'

Without a word, Dagnarus lifted Shakur once again to his shoulder and walked into the storage room. Gareth, with a shivering sigh, shut the door behind them. When the unlocked door was discovered the next morning, it would seem only as if a rusted lock had finally given way.

Once inside the storeroom, Gareth took one of the torches that habitually stood in a barrel near the door. The storeroom was dark, even in the daylight. A word of Void magic caused the torch to light. Holding it aloft, Gareth led Dagnarus, carrying Shakur, into a large tunnel that branched off into several tunnels, running from the buttery to the kitchen, the wine cellars, and the drying rooms. The air was scented with smells of herbs hanging in the drying room, the dark yeasty smell of wine, the faint odor of decay from fowls suspended from hooks. Mice and rats, eating the spilled grain, skittered underfoot.

They entered another tunnel before they reached the kitchen, passing by enormous casks of wine, and from there into another tunnel. Dagnarus was soon lost amid the twists and turns they took, but Gareth kept to his way unerringly. They had been inside the Temple for perhaps fifteen minutes and Shakur was – with unfortunate timing – beginning to awaken, when Gareth brought them to a halt outside a high, arched entryway carved of marble.

Shakur was muttering and grunting and would suddenly lift his head and shout out an incoherent word or two.

'Can't you keep him quiet?' Gareth whispered.

'Not unless I smother him,' Dagnarus said grimly. 'Quit lurching about, you bastard! Besides, I could march an army down here, and no one could hear it.'

'I suppose you're right,' said Gareth, whose guilt magnified the least sound into a yell calculated to wake the slumbering dead.

'Where are we?' Dagnarus asked, staring up at the ornately carved marble entrance.

'The Hall of Eternity,' Gareth replied in a subdued voice. 'The old tombs.'

Thick, soft dust covered the floor, cobwebs trailed

from the ceiling. Figures of carven marble lay at rest upon sepulchers. All lay in the same posture, with eyes closed and their hands folded upon their marble breasts. All were clad in robes, some with ornate vestments and various head coverings, depending on rank and the style of the time. Men and women were entombed there, slept their marble sleep.

'Long, long ago, this is where the Revered High Magi were once buried,' Gareth said softly, passing among the rows of the dead. 'No one is buried here now. It is not considered fashionable since they built the great mausoleum. No one comes here at all anymore, not even to do them honor. Sad, really. Few people know of this hall's existence; only those of us who live within the Void. The altar we seek is connected.'

'Of course it is,' said Dagnarus, and even his ebullient spirits were somewhat subdued, awed by the presence of death. 'It would be. The ideal location.'

'Quite,' said Gareth dryly. 'That was why the altar was built here, back in the days when the practice of Void magic was accepted.'

Dagnarus looked at the silent, peaceful figures, bathed in the torchlight. Dried rose leaves had been scattered over each one, perhaps twenty-five in all. The floor had been swept, the cobwebs brushed away.

'Someone has done them honor,' Dagnarus said quietly. 'Recently, at that.'

Gareth's pale face took on a tinge of color. 'It was only right, Your Highness,' he said. 'I use them, use their spirits to work my magic. I should give them something in return.'

'Propitiate them?'

'That, too,' Gareth muttered. They had walked the length of the hall, arrived at a small door made of iron, which stood at the end.

This door was wizard locked; Gareth had cast a spell

upon it, a spell that only he, with the correct words and proper counterspell, could remove. He placed his hand upon the door handle, muttering and mumbling to himself, while Shakur, lifting his head, gazed around with bleary eyes.

'Where am I?' he demanded.

'In a tomb,' Dagnarus told him. 'Here, stand on your own feet. I'm sick of carrying you.'

'A tomb,' said Shakur, frowning as he took in his surroundings. 'Funny sort of job, to be done in a tomb.'

'Actually quite an appropriate location,' Dagnarus returned.

The iron door opened with a creak of its hinges. Fetid air wafted over them, causing Dagnarus to wrinkle his nose and Shakur to snort in disgust.

Gareth stood to one side. 'Please, enter,' he said.

Shakur did not move. He peered in, trying vainly to see.

'You've had your two days of fun and frolic,' Dagnarus said. 'Time to pay the piper.' He gave Shakur a shove that sent him tumbling headlong to the floor.

Reaching down to lift the manacled felon, Dagnarus picked up Shakur by the back of his shirt collar and dragged him inside the room. Gareth shut the iron door behind them. He looked at Shakur and, turning back to the door, inserted his finger inside the lock, as he might have inserted a key.

'By the Void, I seal this door,' he said. 'To be opened only on my command.'

'What is the matter?' Dagnarus asked, staring at Gareth, who was hunched over like an old man, his face contorted, his arms wrapped around his body as though he were holding his bones and his organs inside his body.

'The penalty I pay for the magic, Your Highness,' Gareth replied after a moment. Drawing in a pain-filled breath, he straightened. 'You may free Shakur of his bonds. His feet at least. He cannot escape.'

Gareth lit thick beeswax candles placed on heavy wrought-iron stands around the room. Dagnarus released the manacles from Shakur's ankles, hauled the felon to his feet.

Shakur stared around through the thatch of matted hair that overhung his hideously scarred face. 'Hey!' he demanded angrily. 'What's going on? Why have you brought me here?'

'Relax,' Dagnarus said impatiently. 'I spoke of requiring an oath from you. This is where you will take it. In this room, you will embrace the Void, as you agreed. Or' – he gave a quick, tight smile – 'back to the hangman.'

The room was large – a man Dagnarus's height could stride thirty long paces across it diagonally. Round in shape, with a high, domed ceiling, the room was empty except for a stone altar carved of smooth black marble, devoid of decoration. The walls and ceiling and floor were made of onyx, polished so that the tiny pinpoint lights of the myriad candles were reflected in the surface, reflected many times over, for the polished walls took one candle flame and made of it a thousand, looking like stars in a cloudless night sky. Such was the illusion that it seemed those standing within the room stood in the emptiness of the night, with the stars above and below them, adrift in darkness.

Dagnarus gazed about, above and below.

'Patch,' he said, and his voice was soft with awe, 'this . . . this is what I saw long ago, when I looked into the center of the Sovereign Stone. I stood alone in the darkness and the stars surrounded me. There is a power in this room, a force.'

'What you feel is the absence of power,' Gareth said, his voice smothered and quiet as if he were in the Royal Library. 'The gods shun this room, they have no authority over it. This room belongs to the Void.'

'Do the Revered Magi know this room exists?' Dagnarus asked.

'They know,' said Gareth dryly.

'Then why do they not destroy it?'

'They cannot. You see the arched ceiling? The weight of the Temple itself rests upon this room. Destroy this room and the entire Temple is weakened. Such was the wisdom of those who built the Temple so many years ago. Water quenches fire, yet man needs both to survive. He needs air to breathe, he needs the earth beneath his feet, he could not live in a world made solely of one or the other. The gods wield power only because there is a place where they wield no power at all. We are given the ability to draw from both. The gods are wise, they do not seek to destroy their opposite, nor does the Void seek to encompass the universe, for then the Void itself would be filled and cease to exist. If all is nothing, then nothing ceases to be anything.'

Dagnarus had no glib rejoinder. He felt himself suspended in time, suspended in the heavens, in a realm where no laws constrained him, no rules bound him. Life was nothing more than a single candle flame. Breathe on it and it would go out, but millions more were left. And he stood in the center, filling the Void, at last.

'All I do is swear some sort of oath?' Shakur asked.

'To the Void,' Dagnarus replied, turning to look upon him.

Shakur nodded slowly. 'I understand,' he said, and he spoke to himself, but the whispered words flitted through the empty air like ghosts. 'I am ready. What do I say?'

'Do you, Shakur, consent to make the Void your master?' Gareth asked. 'To dedicate your life and your soul to the Void?'

'I do,' said Shakur, shrugging.

'This is serious!' Gareth snapped, glowering. 'We must

be certain of your loyalty. We want to know that you mean what you say.'

'I mean it,' Shakur said bluntly. 'I'll tell you why, if you want. I'll tell you my story. I never asked to be born. My mother didn't want me; I interfered with business. She tried to rid herself of me before I was born, but she failed. My father – who was he? I never knew. Some customer who paid a penny for the privilege of creating me.

'I was kicked and slapped when I was small, until my mother discovered I had some worth after all. Some of the men who called on her also took a fancy to boys, you see, and paid her well for my services. In the end, though, the money was mine. She hit me one night in a drunken rage, she and one of her lovers. I grabbed his knife from the belt he'd thrown on the floor and that was the end of my mother. Of all those I have killed, and there have been many and many after that, I still hear her cries.'

Shakur sank to his knees. Raising his head, he fixed the darkness with an unwavering gaze. 'I was born to the Void. The Void is my master. I do so swear, by the blood of my mother that is on my hands.'

The prince was deathly pale, but an exultant fire burned in the depths of the eyes that had lost all color, were no longer emerald, but seemed to have become the darkness, speckled with stars.

Gareth, strangely moved, said quietly, 'I believe he is sincere. See if he is an acceptable candidate.'

'What?' Shakur frowned. 'What do you mean – acceptable candidate? I swore, didn't I?'

Slowly, touched by a reverence he had never before felt in the presence of the gods, Dagnarus drew forth the Dagger of the Vrykyl. Its polished surface reflected the light of the candle flames, so that small streams of fire seemed to course along its surface, as if it had been pulled from a river of flame. The eyes of the carven dragon on the hilt gleamed red in the light and seemed to wink with pleasure.

'Here, what is that?' Shakur demanded.

'The weapon you will use for the job,' said Gareth, licking dry lips.

Shakur gave it a disparaging glance. 'Too fancy, by half. I have my own pigsticker.' He raised his manacled hands. 'I've sworn your blamed oath. Free me!'

'Are there words to speak?' Dagnarus asked softly, gazing at the dagger with awed wonder.

'No,' Gareth replied. 'The magic is within the dagger. Place it on the altar.'

Reverently, gently, Dagnarus set the dagger on the altar.

'I said release me, damn you!' Shakur cried. Lunging to his feet, he reached with his manacled hands for Dagnarus's throat.

'I will,' said Dagnarus.

The dagger flashed in the firelight. Lifting itself from the altar, the dagger struck Shakur in the back, in the rib cage, struck quickly and struck hard. Shakur's head jerked up, he gave a soft grunt. His eyes shifted from Dagnarus, who was watching him with a strange, terrible smile, to Gareth, who watched the life drain out of them.

Shakur fell, face forward, onto the onyx floor, dead.

The next thing Gareth knew, Dagnarus was bending over his friend, a look of concern on his face.

'Patch? What is it? Are you all right? I forgot you're not a soldier, Patch. I should have made you look away. What do we do with him now?' He gazed down at the body with interest and curiosity.

'We must place the body on the altar,' said Gareth, avoiding looking at the corpse.

'You're not well,' said Dagnarus. 'Sit down before you fall down, Patch. You're no use to me unconscious, which you will be if you hit your head on this stone floor. I will do what is necessary.'

Meekly, Gareth accepted the prince's command. There was no chair in the room, no place to sit, but he leaned his back against the cold stone wall, closed his eyes, and drew in several deep breaths. This cleared the dizziness and eased the nausea. He told himself he had done nothing wrong, he had ended an odious life, one that had brought sorrow and grief to many, a life that the man himself had seemed glad to relinquish. When Gareth lifted his head, he was able to regard the body of Shakur, laid out upon the altar, with equanimity.

'Remove the dagger from the body,' Gareth said.

Dagnarus hesitated. 'May I touch it?'

'Yes, it has done its job, accepted the candidate. Now, place the Dagger of the Vrykyl over the heart. The dragon's head toward his head, the crosspiece aligned with the arms, the point toward the legs.'

He watched as Dagnarus was about to relinquish his hold on the dagger. 'Wait!' Gareth cried commandingly.

'What?' Dagnarus looked up, startled.

Gareth did not immediately speak. He looked at Shakur, then turned his gaze to the prince. 'The life essence of this man is now contained inside the dagger. If you want, Your Highness, you may take that life into yourself.'

'What? Become like him?' Dagnarus regarded Shakur with disgust. 'No, thank you!'

'No, Your Highness. That's not how the magic works. According to the book, if you absorb his life essence, you receive only that – his life force. He no longer needs it. His corpse is being sustained by the Void. His life will extend the years of your life. It will give you two lives, as it were.'

'Truly?' Dagnarus appeared dubious.

'The reason I advise this,' Gareth continued, 'is that it will also, to some extent, protect you. In other words, his life's essence will serve as armor to your own. You know, Your Highness, being a soldier, that armor may be pierced, it may be penetrated, it does not make you invulnerable. But it might help you survive –' He saw Dagnarus's brows draw together in displeasure and said no more.

'It might help me survive the tests of a Dominion Lord,' Dagnarus finished for him. 'You still have no faith in me!'

Gareth made no reply. He stood by the altar, looking down at the corpse.

'Still,' said Dagnarus, slowly mastering his anger and regarding the dagger with renewed interest, 'this second life may be worthwhile for other reasons. A general who is not easily killed in battle would have a very great advantage. Think what it would do for the morale of my men to see me rise, hale and hearty, from an apparently mortal wound! I will take the life essence, Patch. What must I do?'

'You must dip the fingers of your left hand into the dead man's blood, bring your fingers to your mouth, and taste of it.'

Dagnarus did as he was told, wiping on his fingers the blood from the dagger – taking great care not to cut himself – and licking the blood from his fingers with a grimace. 'Not the sweetest wine I've ever drunk,' he said. He looked up. 'What now?'

'That is all, Your Highness. Now place the dagger upon the corpse.'

'I don't feel any different,' said Dagnarus, disappointed. 'How do I know if it worked?'

'You will know, Your Highness,' said Gareth softly.

Shrugging, not particularly pleased, Dagnarus laid the dagger upon Shakur's breast, with the dragon's head beneath Shakur's head, the dragon's wings extended like Shakur's arms. This done, Dagnarus stepped back.

Nothing happened.

Dagnarus frowned, his gaze went accusingly to Gareth. 'It's failed!'

Gareth raised his hand, pointed. 'On the contrary. Look, Your Highness.'

Dagnarus looked, and his eyes widened in astonishment.

The Dagger of the Vrykyl was rising slowly in the air, of its own accord. The dagger hovered, suspended above Shakur's breast.

The scales of the dragon, carved into the dagger, took shape and form, became black and glistening as the onyx walls. The scales – hundreds of them – began to rain down on Shakur. Sharp as shards of obsidian, they pierced the dead flesh wherever they touched. Working their way into the flesh, the scales fixed themselves firmly beneath the surface of the skin, then began to expand and grow larger. Black scale flowed into black scale, each one touching another, until Shakur's body was encased in a hard black-scaled shell.

The shell took the form of armor, black, shining armor that appeared to be made of the body's own tendons, ligaments, bones, and muscle. It was as if his skin had been flayed away and the flesh and bone underneath revealed, except that they were hard as stone, black as jet.

His head was covered by a black helm that resembled the dragon's skull of the dagger, adorned with black spiny protrusions.

Shakur moved.

His hand lifted the visor to reveal his face. His eyes opened. The eyes held no life. They were dark and cold, fixed with a glassy stare. He sat upright. The dagger vanished, only to reappear in Dagnarus's hand.

Shakur's helmed head turned toward the dagger. He looked from it to Dagnarus. Climbing down off the altar, Shakur bowed deeply to the prince.

'By the gods!' Dagnarus whispered. 'By the gods, Patch. It worked!'

'The gods had nothing to do with it,' Gareth said bitterly.

'Well, damn them, then!' Dagnarus cried, laughing jubilantly. He thrust the dagger carefully back into its sheath on his belt. 'Who needs them, I say? *I* certainly don't.' He gazed with pride upon Shakur.

Gareth sighed. 'True, Your Highness.'

'Now what do we do with him?' Dagnarus asked, looking Shakur up and down.

'I am yours to command, Your Highness,' said Shakur with another bow.

As Gareth first heard it, the Vrykyl's voice seemed the same as the voice of a living man. But as it continued to speak, Gareth noted that the Vrykyl's words had a hollow, echoing sound to them, as if spoken from the bottom of a dark well.

'Faith, this Vrykyl's certainly more polite,' Dagnarus said.

'He will respond to your commands, Your Highness, and only yours.'

'Does the Vrykyl know anything at all? Or is he a mindless pupet?' Dagnarus asked. 'If such, he'll be of little use.'

'The magical armor grants that a Vrykyl retains all the memories he had when he was alive. He has all the skills – such as they were. In other words, he will be the same bastard he always was, except that he will obey orders. In addition, he is no longer heir to the body's weaknesses. He has no need of *ordinary* food' – Gareth laid emphasis on that – 'no need of sleep. He will never tire or succumb to thirst. He cannot be killed by any ordinary weapon. Only a weapon that is blessed of the gods may pierce his unholy flesh.'

'Yes, yes, I know all this,' Dagnarus said impatiently. 'He must make a knife of his own bone. That is something I do not think either of us needs to witness.'

'The Blood-knife,' said Gareth. 'The Vrykyl slays his victims with it and steals their souls. He will not need to feed for some time yet, and so he does not need the knife, but when he does, when the flesh starts to rot from his bones, when he feels his unnatural strength start to fail him, he will kill the first person he comes upon. Only you and those you designate will be safe from him.'

'He will not turn his victims into more Vrykyl, will he?' Dagnarus demanded, frowning. 'Vrykyl over which I would have no control?'

'No, only the bearer of the Dagger of the Vrykyl has that power. The Blood-knife merely feeds him, Your Highness.'

'That armor is remarkable,' Dagnarus said, regarding the black, glistening armor with admiration. 'But it will be obvious to everyone who sees him that he is no ordinary Vinnegalean. Must he walk about accoutered like that all the time?'

'The Vrykyl possess the skill of disguising themselves, according to the book, but since it is a skill Shakur did not possess before death, it may take him some time to master it,' Gareth replied. 'He has the ability to look like whatever he chooses. He may take on his former appearance –'

'The gods know why he would want to,' Dagnarus interrupted.

'Or he may take on the appearance of a scholarly old gentleman, or perhaps a comely young man. Thus,' Gareth said, with a half sigh, 'thus does he lure his victims to their deaths.'

'You have done well, Patch!' Dagnarus rested his hand upon Gareth's shoulder. 'I am more than pleased. Whatever reward you ask of me, it shall be granted.'

'This is my reward, Your Highness,' said Gareth, watching Shakur, who stood still as one of the empty shells of armored knights standing unending vigil in the castle's corridor. 'To have served you.' He paused a moment, then added in a low voice, 'You will probably be angry with me for saying this, but I ask you once again, Your Highness . . . No, I beg you!'

Gareth sank to his knees before the prince, raised supplicating hands. 'Give up the idea of becoming a Dominion Lord! Listen to me, Dagnarus. Don't turn away. You have what you have always wanted! You have done what your father did; you have created your own Dominion Lord! With that dagger, you can create more until you will have as many Lords serving you as serve your father! *He* is not a Dominion Lord and yet he is King. You do not need to be a Dominion Lord either. The danger is real, more real than you can imagine!'

Reaching down his hand, Dagnarus touched Gareth's hair, stroked it.

Gareth's eyes closed, tears wrung from pain and exhaustion and nervous tension trickled down his cheeks.

'You love me, don't you, Patch?' Dagnarus said softly.

Gareth could not reply, he bowed his head. His tears burned him, but then, so did his love.

'You and Valura. The only two who have ever loved me. The others – my father among them – fear me, admire me.' Dagnarus was silent, thinking, then he said, 'I don't want to be like my father, Patch. I want to be greater than my father. I want him to look at me the way he looks at Helmos. I will be a Dominion Lord, Patch. I will, though it cost me my life.

'And now,' he said with forced gaiety, turning away, 'what do we do with our Vrykyl, here? I cannot have him roaming the streets of Vinnengael. This very morning I enter the Temple to begin the Seven Preparations.'

'We will keep the Vrykyl down here at the bottom of the Temple,' said Gareth. He had made his argument for the last time. He would make it no more. He would do what he could, now, to keep Dagnarus alive.

'Excellent idea! When I have time in between these silly tests, I will come down and start his training!'

'Your Highness!' Gareth was aghast. 'You are supposed to be spending your time in meditation and . . . and . . .'

'And what? Prayer?' Dagnarus was amused. 'Will the gods listen to me, do you suppose?' He turned away. 'Shakur.'

The Vrykyl bowed.

'You will remain here. You will not stir from this place. No one must find you. If by chance someone comes other than Gareth or myself, you have leave to kill them.'

Shakur bowed again. Gareth felt himself shrivel up inside. He knew well enough that there was little likelihood of one of the other magi coming down to this place, but at the thought of what would happen to them if one did . . .

What have I done? he asked himself, his soul writhing in misery. What have I become? I should end this! I should go to Prince Helmos and lay all bare before him, confess my terrible crimes and find ease in punishment and death! I should. But I won't, he realized, with chill realization. I have drunk the water of the well of darkness. I cannot confess my crimes without betraying my prince. He trusts me. Gareth marveled. I know all his secrets. Every one of them. I could ruin him and yet he has never threatened me, never doubted me.

A cynical voice in Gareth's soul whispered that this was because Dagnarus knew that Gareth was his creature. He had seen to that. From childhood up, Gareth had been bound to his prince with bonds of duty, bonds of love. The bonds were made of silken cord, but they were tied tight. Had Gareth ever tried to throw off those bonds, Dagnarus would have cut him loose. There was no mutual affection, only a pride of ownership.

'Come, Patch!' said Dagnarus, throwing his arm around Gareth's shoulder. 'You are dropping with exhaustion.

And I must go to my darling Valura and console her for being gone from her bed for the next seven days.'

'I thought you had quarreled with her,' Gareth said listlessly.

Dagnarus winked. 'I forgave her.'

The two left the altar room. The Vrykyl had laid himself back down upon the altar, to while away the sleepless hours as best he could. He looked very much like one of the carven figures on the tombs.

Gareth was forced to remove the wizard-lock spell he had laid upon the door, in order for Dagnarus to be able to gain access to the altar room. Reversing the spell cost Gareth as much pain as casting it, pain that he contrived to hide from the prince.

Fortunately, Dagnarus was too absorbed in pleasant anticipation of his lover's bed to notice.

TEN

The Seven Preparations

T HE DAY DAWNED BRIGHT AND FAIR. THE
orken took their boats out – the omens had
promised good weather and a fine catch. Helmos,
from his place standing in the enormous window of the
tower room, looked down upon the lake. He could see
their sails, like white birds, skimming over the water en
route to the fishing grounds.

Below him, in the courtyard, the procession to escort
Dagnarus to the Temple wound its way, snakelike, from
the palace. Soldiers of the army of Vinnengael lined the
route, cheering and clashing their swords against their
shields or thumping the hafts of their spears on the
ground. They had not done that for Helmos.

'He has the loyalty of the men, of many of their commanders,' Helmos said to himself, brooding. 'There is no
danger at present. The army remains loyal to my father.
As long as he is King, the army will back him. But what
about me? What happens when *I* am King?'

Helmos pressed his forehead to the glass. Dagnarus,
resplendent in the simple white robes worn by the candidate, walked down the line of cheering men, accompanied
by his father. Tamaros walked slowly – Dagnarus was

forced to reduce his long, impatient stride, measure his steps to his father's – but the King walked without aid of any sort, refusing to use a cane or lean upon his son's arm. The soldiers might have cheered Dagnarus, but they bent their knees in reverence and respect for their King.

'I understand your plan, your wish, Father,' Helmos said, speaking to the old man walking far below, so far that he seemed the size of one of the child Dagnarus's toys. 'I know that you want me to rule in peace, with wisdom and justice, my loyal brother standing at my back, armed with shield and sword to defend the kingdom. A splendid dream. I pray to the gods, for your sake, my father, more than my own, that this dream will come true.

'But I do not think the gods are listening to my prayers,' Helmos added sadly. 'I think it far more likely that my brother, instead of protecting my back, will stab me in it.'

'So melancholy, my lord?' said a sweet voice at his side.

Helmos turned to see his wife, who, with her customary soft and gentle step, had slipped so quietly into the room that he had not heard her. He smiled at her. Reaching out his arm, he gathered her to his side.

'I was, but your face, like the sun, has broken through the clouds that cluster over me, and lifts my gloom.'

Anna looked down upon the scene below and looked back up at her husband. He shared every thought with her, every dream, every wish, every fear. Every fear except one, which he had not named, not even to himself. She knew what he had been thinking as well as if she had heard his words.

'You and your loved father are still estranged?' she asked.

'He has not spoken to me since the day of the Council meeting,' Helmos said heavily. 'He was furious that I did not attend the banquet, but to do so would have been hypocritical. For the same reason, I chose not to join my brother's escort to the Temple this day.'

'The gods will not permit this travesty,' Anna said. 'Dagnarus will never pass the Seven Preparations. You know that, my husband. The Dominion Lords will have no choice but to refuse to accept him, after this.'

'I would like to think so,' said Helmos, 'but I lack your faith, my love.'

She lifted her eyes to him, astonished and troubled.

'I fear there is another force at work here,' Helmos said gravely. 'And if that is true, I do not know what the gods can do against it.'

'I am not certain I understand what you mean,' Anna faltered.

'I have told this to no one,' said Helmos, 'but the burden of secrecy weighs heavily upon my heart –'

'Then you must share that burden, my love,' said Anna firmly, holding fast to him. 'I am strong. I can bear my portion.'

'I know,' he said, kissing her forehead. 'But this is a terrible secret.' He sighed. His gaze went to the procession. Dagnarus had reached the Temple steps, was being welcomed by the Most Revered High Magus. 'I believe that my half brother is a follower of the Void.'

'In the name of the gods, no!' his wife whispered, appalled. 'Oh, my husband! Are you sure?'

'No, I am not sure. I have no proof,' Helmos said, sighing. 'And I dare not accuse him without it. And even if I had proof, I am not sure I would produce it. Such a blow would kill my father.'

'I hope and pray that you are wrong,' Anna said quietly. 'Dagnarus is arrogant and proud, heedless and uncaring, profligate. But surely he is not . . . not evil, not corrupt. And, if he is, the gods must thwart him! They have power over the Void, so we have always been taught.'

'Perhaps they did, once,' said Helmos, speaking reluctantly.

Dagnarus and King Tamaros had entered the Temple.

The crowd lingered outside, cheering and now singing. He turned away from the window, drew his wife with him. He was concerned to see her pale and wan. Her pallor frightened him.

'I have no right to disturb your peace, my dear. We will not speak of such dark matters.'

'We will, my lord,' she said. 'How can I truly be at peace if you are in torment? Tell me your fears, and I will either do what I can to alleviate them or I will stand with you and stare them in the face.'

'You do not know what relief I feel talking to you about this,' said Helmos, giving in. 'Perhaps I am completely wrong. I would like to think so. Yet . . . but you shall hear. In the old days, when my grandfather was yet a boy, using the magic of the Void was an accepted practice.'

'I have heard that this was true,' said Anna. 'I find it difficult to believe.'

'It is true, nonetheless. My studies confirm it, as did those of Reinholt, when I broached the subject with him. There is even, so I understand, rumor that an altar dedicated to the Void is located within the Temple itself. That is only rumor, the magi deny it. And that, I believe, is where we have made our mistake.'

'I do not understand you. How can it be a mistake to renounce this evil worship?'

'The mistake lies not in renouncing it, but in refusing to admit it exists. Instead of keeping the worship of the Void out in the open, where we may watch the weeds as they grow and trim them if necessary, we deny the existence of the weeds and so they flourish without check. Who knows how tall or thick the weed patch has grown? Who knows how far it has spread or what goodness it has choked out? This is one of my fears.

'For the other, I must use a different metaphor. Suppose that the Void is like hot, molten lava, simmering in a volcano. We have said the volcano is dead, but in reality, it is merely dormant. The bubble of lava is covered over by a dark crust. That bubble keeps growing and growing and, when it finally bursts, the eruption will destroy all in its path. I begin to doubt that even the gods can prevent such a catastrophic event.'

'But the gods are all-powerful,' argued his wife.

'True,' Helmos conceded. He was silent a moment, watching the dispersing throng, before adding, 'And they are all-knowing. Their ways are mysterious. What if they are displeased that we ignore the Void, instead of actively fighting against it?'

'How can they be displeased with us?' Anna asked. 'They gave us the Sovereign Stone.'

'You recall my father's visionary encounter with the gods – he is a child seated at a table, the gods are parents too busy to attend to him and so they hand him this treat to quiet him.'

'So it appeared. I read the gods' actions differently,' said his wife. 'No child wants his parents doting upon him every second, hovering over him. They protect him from harm, true, but in so doing they smother him, keep him from growing to his true potential. No one would love a child more than we would,' she added softly, her eyes lowered so that her husband should not see her pain, 'but we would not be with that child every minute of every day, watching his every move, snatching him away from every danger. How could he learn? How could he grow? Though it would be painful for us, we would let him walk on his own, fall down, make his own mistakes, burn his hand in the fire.'

'My dear one!' said Helmos, deeply moved. He held her close, kissed her. 'My own beloved. You are wise. You should be the mother to a dozen children! The fact that you are not is one more reason I doubt the influence of the gods in this world.'

'Do not speak so!' his wife begged. 'Perhaps they are teaching us a lesson.'

'I do not see what lesson they could be trying to teach us by depriving us of a child,' Helmos said testily.

'Patience, perhaps,' said Anna, looking up at him through her tears. 'Fortitude. A test of our love for each other. A test of our faith in them.'

'I *try* to be patient!' Helmos's voice was harsh with his own swallowed tears. 'I try to be faithful. But it is hard! The gods as my witness, it is hard! Especially when I see my brother's whore-got progeny roaming the streets –'

'Hush!' Anna laid her hand over his mouth. 'Hush! Say no more! We will go this day to the Temple and make an offering –'

'*Another* offering,' Helmos interjected bitterly.

'My dear . . .' Anna remonstrated.

'I know. I am sorry. I will make my offering, and I will ask the gods' forgiveness for doubting them.'

Anna kissed him and left to go about her duties, one of which was to pay a visit to the Queen, who was already planning the celebratory party intended to honor her son's ascendance to the rank of Dominion Lord.

Helmos turned again to look out the window. The courtyard was clear of people. The Temple doors had closed upon Dagnarus.

'I will make an offering. I will ask you for a child,' Helmos said, gazing up into the sky, the gods' reputed dwelling place. 'Yet what will be the true prayer of my heart? Which prayer will you answer, if either? Which should I hope you answer, if it comes to a choice? Would I sacrifice one to gain the other? I almost think I might. Do not let my brother become a Dominion Lord!' He raised his hands in his earnest supplication. 'Do not!'

The three Dominion Lords who would be responsible for conducting the Seven Preparations for Dagnarus stood behind the Altar of the Gods in the Temple. Accompanying them were the Most Revered High Magus and the three magi who would be conducting the trials. King Tamaros sat in his high-backed throne near the altar, looking on proudly. A novice, friend of the prince and present at Dagnarus's own request, stood humbly, with head bowed and hands clasped, in the shadows to one side of the candlelit altar.

The Most Revered High Magus spoke the ritual words.

'The gods be witness! One comes before us to undergo the Seven Preparations required of all humans who would rise to the noble and puissant rank of Dominion Lord. Be it known by the candidate that these Seven Preparations have been designed to help us, the Testers, know your true worth. More importantly, the Preparations instruct you, the Candidate, in coming to know yourself.

'These are the Seven Preparations: Strength, Compassion, Wisdom, Endurance, Chivalry, Understanding, Leadership. It is not expected that you will pass all the trials. It may be that those you fail will prove more valuable to you, for we are taught that we learn more by failure than we do by success. The trial itself is more important than the outcome and it is upon that you will be judged.

'If you, Dagnarus, son of Tamaros, accede to these conditions and if you understand what is required of you and if you are prepared to take these Preparations, then come forward to stand before the altar. Stand before the gods and make your pledge to them.'

The Most Revered High Magus spoke severely, far more severely than was his wont. He, too, was troubled by this nomination. He had argued against it with Tamaros long and hard, to the point where the King had let it be known that his friend Reinholt was treading upon very dangerous and unstable ground. The post of Most Revered High Magus was not a royal post, Reinholt was not dependent upon the King for his position, but was chosen by the Council of Magi. However, the Council listened to the King's pleasure, and should the unsteady ground suddenly shift out from beneath his feet, the Most Revered High Magus could well find himself returning to his former position as Caretaker of Portals.

The matter was now out of his hands. The Dominion Lords had voted and the High Magus could not refuse to administer the Preparations once their votes were cast. He had been deeply concerned about the candidate's suitability, for Reinholt was well informed and he had heard some – if not all – of the same dark rumors circulating about Dagnarus that had come to the ears of Helmos. Now, however, as the prince stepped forward, as he knelt before the altar, the Most Revered High Magus was feeling relieved, hoping rumor had been wrong.

Clad in simple white robes, naked beneath them, Dagnarus was a striking figure. He had yearned for this, planned for this, worked for this ever since, as a child, he had witnessed with envy his brother's Transfiguration. To kneel before the altar, to embark upon the Seven Preparations was the culmination of Dagnarus's ambition. He was not humbled with the thought, nor was he impressed with the solemnity, the reverence, and holiness of the moment. He was not fearful. The trials held no mystery for him, although they were supposed to be kept secret from the candidate. Gareth had provided the prince with a detailed account of each one. They had determined between them how best to either pass the trial or else circumvent it.

Dagnarus was impressed with the fact that at last he had achieved his life's goal – the goal for this portion of his life, at least. The knowledge touched him deeply, filled him with immense satisfaction. He was, therefore, in a state of proper reverence, face flushed and eyes shining with what could be taken by those watching him for holy rapture. Only one person there – Gareth, standing in the shadows – knew that, in fact, the prince's eyes shone with exultation at his own crowning achievement.

The Most Revered High Magus saw none of this. He

saw before him a man of considerable personal beauty and undeniable charm, a prince in stature and in mien, kneeling before the gods and committing himself, body and soul, to the Preparations he was about to endure. The Most Revered High Magus saw King Tamaros's pride in his son, saw the tears in the old man's eyes as he gave Dagnarus his blessing, saw Dagnarus accept his father's blessing with every appearance of grateful humility.

'Well, perhaps we have misjudged him,' said Reinholt to himself and to the gods. 'Perhaps this will mark a change in his life. Who among us has not sowed a few wild oats in his youth? We cultivate the bitter harvest and proceed on. We will see how he handles himself during the trials. Those will tell all.'

He said aloud, 'By the law, you, Dagnarus, will undergo the Seven Preparations alone, without any help or assistance from anyone. The Dominion Lords will observe from afar all that transpires: your actions, your inactions, your words, your deeds. By these, you shall be judged. Do you agree to this, Dagnarus, son of Tamaros?'

'I do, Most Revered High Magus,' Dagnarus said humbly.

'The trials will last seven days. Upon the night of the last day, the Council of Dominion Lords will meet and hear the report made by their three witnesses. They will then cast their votes. If the vote is in your favor, the next day you will undergo the Transfiguration.'

Dagnarus drew in a breath at this; his eyes were emeralds ablaze. 'I understand, Most Revered High Magus!'

'If the Council votes against you, do not consider this as an indication that you are an unworthy person or that you have failed your family, your friends, or yourself. By reaching this exalted state, you have already achieved more than most men and women.'

'I *will not fail*!' said Dagnarus vehemently, emphasizing

each word with passionate intensity, the vow accompanied by clenched jaw and clenched fist.

The Most Revered High Magus raised his eyebrows at this. It was proper at this point for the candidate to express his humble thankfulness at being given the opportunity, not his determination to succeed. Dagnarus's pronouncement not to fail spoiled Reinholt's next line, which was a homily on learning from failure. Wisely cutting that line from the text, the Most Revered High Magus skipped to the conclusion, which was to call down the blessing of the gods upon the candidate.

The ceremony was over. The Most Revered High Magus bid Dagnarus rise. The three Dominion Lords came forward, took their places, one on either side of the candidate and one walking behind – a ceremonial escort. With solemn faces, they accompanied Dagnarus to the small cell where he would spend his hours alone, meditating and praying, during the intervals between trials. Here they left him with words of encouragement and good wishes, which he received with gratitude. They shut the cell door behind him.

Looking about the plain and uncomfortable room, Dagnarus sighed and prepared to make the best of it. He threw himself upon the bed. What with creating the Vrykyl and consoling Valura, he had not slept at all last night. He was allowed several hours of prayer before his first trial, however. He intended to take advantage of the leisure time to sleep, and he was just drifting off when a scratching and tapping on the wall woke him.

At first he thought it was mice, but the tapping came at regular intervals from the wall on the side of the cell farthest from the door. Rising, Dagnarus approached the wall, and tapped back. A faint, very faint, voice came to him.

'The cabinet! Go into the cabinet.'

Dagnarus looked around, saw a tall, walk-in cabinet

standing in a corner. Opening the door, he found a clean white robe and a pair of sandals, such as the magi wear in the Temple. He entered the cabinet. A wooden panel about a hand's width in size, located in the back, shifted. Gareth's face appeared in the aperture.

'Quite clever,' said Dagnarus approvingly. 'Did you do this?'

Gareth shook his head. 'No. And keep your voice down! At different times during the year, various magi are supposed to undergo days of prayer and fasting. Those who can't quite manage the fasting portion of the ritual ask their friends to sneak food to them. Most of the cells have these "pantries," as they are known.'

'That's good to know!' Dagnarus grinned. 'I was not looking forward to supper. I can only imagine what "holy" food they'll feed me. Gruel, in all likelihood.'

'You will get no supper, Your Highness,' said Gareth. 'You are supposed to be thriving upon spirit alone.'

'Come, now, this is hard!' Dagnarus protested. 'I did not know that starvation was a part –'

'Listen to me, Your Highness!' Gareth interrupted, cross with nervousness. They were both taking an immense risk, and he wished the prince would be more serious. 'The first of your trials begins this very afternoon. That is what I have come to tell you.'

'This afternoon. Good. I'll be able to take my nap. Which one is it?'

'The Preparation of Compassion. You will be taken to the Hospitalers, to the part where reside those whose conditions are considered hopeless, those whom we cannot heal. There you will minister to their needs – bathe them, bind their sores, rub ointment into the scabrous lesions, clean up their waste –'

Dagnarus frowned, clearly displeased. 'I told you, Patch, I will not do this. I will not breathe their foul contagious air. I will not touch their rotting flesh! You were supposed to find some way out of this, some loophole in the rules through which I might escape.'

'I searched, Your Highness,' Gareth returned. 'I argued against it as best I could, claiming that this was not an appropriate test for you, a soldier, urging that something more martial might be substituted. You must remember I am only in the novitiate, and though I am given special status as your friend, my arguments carry very little weight with the High Magus or the Council. They refused even to consider my proposal. The visit will be horrible, Your Highness, but it will last only a day and a night. As to catching anything, many of the brothers and sisters who work there do so without falling ill . . .'

'Some, perhaps, but not all,' said Dagnarus darkly.

'True, Your Highness.' Gareth fell silent.

'I tell you, Patch,' said Dagnarus, after a pause, 'every man has a horror of something. I have a horror of disease. When I was a little boy, they made me visit my mother, who had taken ill. I still recall it – the healers tiptoeing in and out, filling the already stinking air with noxious smoke, serving up bitter medicines to purge the body's ill humors, pulling leeches out of jars. I could not stomach it, and I screamed and kicked until they were forced to carry me out.'

He was quiet a moment, thoughtful, then he said in a low voice, 'I cannot bear it, Patch. I cannot.'

'Then you will simply say you cannot, Your Highness,' said Gareth crisply, relieved, 'and put an end to this.'

'No,' said Dagnarus stubbornly. 'That I will not do!'

'Then what *will* you do, Your Highness?' Gareth demanded, exasperated.

'I don't know yet,' said Dagnarus. 'I will think of something. At least,' he added glumly, 'if I *do* have to go, I shall not go on an empty stomach. Let me finish my nap, then bring me something to eat.'

*   *   *

The Order of Hospitalers was one of the least respected, most criticized, and undervalued of all the Orders of magi – at least among the human population. Magic, steadfastly reliable in nearly all other circumstances, was unreliable when it came to healing. Theologians had long argued the reason for this. The most cogent argument, the one most people subscribed to, was the one put forth one hundred years ago by Healer Demorah, head of the Order of Hospitalers.

When it comes to healing magic, we are dealing with what might be considered opposing forces. The magic of the healer attempts to act upon a person possessed of his or her own magic. It is natural for a person's own magic to resist magical influences from outside us. This is the gods' way of protecting us from what otherwise might harm us. Thus we are, to a certain extent, naturally resistant to spells cast upon us, spells that might be evil in nature or intent, spells that might force us to do things we are not inclined to do – one reason love potions are not successful unless the person is already so inclined.

The healer is therefore faced with the problem of overcoming a body's inherent distrust of outside magicks, a distrust that may be enhanced by the body's weakened state. We are successful in treating those illnesses and conditions where we can persuade the body's own natural defenses to work with us in helping to cure the person.

The healers combine magic with other methods designed to induce the patient's own internal magic to aid and abet the healing process, not fight it. The healers do this by many means, one of which is to provide a calm and tranquil atmosphere in which the patient can relax and concentrate all his or her energies upon healing. The Hall of the Hospitalers was, therefore, an attractive place. The building, which was part of the Temple complex, was kept spotlessly clean, for the healers had learned that disease appeared to breed and spread in filthy conditions and that rigorous cleanliness of both the body and its environs was conducive to the patient's well-being.

Huge windows in the outer rooms permitted fresh air and sunlight into those areas where patients were convalescent. Interior rooms were kept warm and snug for those patients suffering from chills, pneumonia, sore throats, and colds. The patients and their internal magicks were daily lulled with the soothing music of harp and flute. The fragrances of sweet lavender and pungent sage masked the stench of illness. Carefully prepared medicines and possets, whose properties had been tested and annotated over the years, enhanced the body's own magic powers of healing.

The art of healing was considered the most difficult of all the arts, requiring extra years of study. The healer must be extraordinarily patient, of easygoing temperament, yet quick to think and react in life-threatening situations. The healer must have an extensive knowledge of the practical application of herbs and herb lore, as well as thorough grounding in Earth magic as it applies to both the healing arts and ordinary, everyday life. In ancient times, such magical knowledge had included Void magic, since it was quite possible that the healer might come across a patient who had embraced the Void. That practice had been discontinued for several reasons. Practicing Void magic was illegal, now, and no one would dare admit to it. In addition, the healers had found it difficult to treat practitioners of Void magic, who sap their own life energy in order to work their dark craft. Thus the body's own magic fights stubbornly against the healer.

The Hall of the Hospitalers was a multistoried building, divided into large rooms with beds for many patients. The patients were segregated along the lines of male and female, adults and children, and by race.

Few elves came to the Halls. If elves fell ill, they almost always chose to return to their homeland for treatment.

On the rare occasion when one was brought here in an emergency situation, the elves had their own room which was open to the sky (in clement weather) and filled with trees and plants. Their healers accompanied them, stayed with them, and forbade any outside interference.

Neither the dwarves nor the orken availed themselves of the Hall of Hospitalers, having their own practices for healing magicks, most of which human healers viewed with shock or a shudder, but which seemed to work for the races involved. The orken patients were immediately immersed in seawater, no matter what their malady – one reason why so few orken lived inland and, if they did, lived in places where travel to the sea was no more than a day's journey.

Following the seawater treatment, the patient was taken either to his home or that of the shaman, who attempted to make life intolerable for sickness, which was viewed as a physical entity that had seized hold of the victim. An orken patient was therefore subjected to foul odors, rancid food, hideous masks (worn by the shaman and the victim's relatives, intended to frighten away sickness), and the bleating of a bagpipe, a sound sickness presumably found abhorrent. How orken lived through the cure was a mystery to most humans, but the orken not only lived through it, but apparently thrived on it.

The dwarves' method of practicing the healing arts was not to practice them, or to do so very wantonly and haphazardly. A sick or incapacitated dwarf was a hindrance and a danger to the entire tribe. Most dwarves who fell sick suffered in stoic silence, pretending that they were fine and avoiding the dwarven healer for as long as possible, for most of the time the cure was worse than the illness. It was the responsibility of the dwarven healer to have the dwarf back in the saddle and thus their cures tended to be drastic and unpleasant, though oftentimes effective. Dwarven healers were not chosen for their salubrious temperament, as were humans, but rather for their strength, for dwarven healers were often required to convince a reluctant patient that treatment was necessary. To this end, dwarven healers were almost as skilled in knot-tying as the orken.

Not being one to brood on situations and events over which he had no control, Dagnarus slept away the morning and woke feeling much refreshed. Hearing approaching footsteps, he hastily knelt before the small altar in the cell and assumed an attitude of prayer. He was so deeply sunk in his meditations – his eyes closed, his head bowed, his hands clasped – that the Dominion Lords who came to escort him to the Hall were at first loath to break in on his communion.

They were under time constraints, however – this first trial must be begun this day, and so, after a whispered consultation, one of them stepped into the cell and touched Dagnarus gently upon the shoulder, apologizing most profoundly for disturbing him.

Disappointed that his stratagem had not worked (though he had not really expected it would), Dagnarus let the knight shake him a couple more times, then opened his eyes and gazed up at the man with an expression indicative of one who draws himself away from something inordinately wonderful and beautiful to look upon the ugly and the mundane.

'My lords,' he said respectfully.

'Your Highness,' said Lord Altura in equally respectful tones, pleased by the prince's air of chastened humility, 'it is time for your first trial. You will accompany us.'

'I am ready, my lords,' said Dagnarus, rising to his feet.

He wore the white robes. The other three Dominion Lords wore their full ceremonial armor, as befitted the occasion. Two walked beside him, one behind.

During the walk to the Hospitalers, Dagnarus appraised closely the two knights, one to either side. It was the first time he'd been able to study their armor closely. He was impressed with what he saw. The armor was lightweight, yet strong enough to turn any ordinary weapon, and many magical ones. The different pieces of the armor: the greaves and shin guards and ornately designed breastplate, the helm and the mailed gloves, were not donned in pieces, but appeared on the body by the will of the Dominion Lord, who touched a pendant and invoked the gods. The armor would also appear of its own accord, if the Lord was threatened.

Dagnarus's longing to obtain such wondrous, magical armor increased his determination to become a Dominion Lord and gave him fortitude for the upcoming trial, which he judged would be the worst of the lot.

Lord Altura was Lord of Chivalry. Her armor was fashioned to honor the horse. Her helm, a stylized horse's head, was graced with a flowing mane of spun gold. Dagnarus wondered what animal the gods should choose for him. He hoped it might be the wolf, for whom he felt a special affinity.

The Hospitalers were waiting to welcome Dagnarus, who had never in his life been to the Halls of Healing and who had, before this, no intention of ever entering them. He inhaled fresh air deeply before he walked inside, for he expected to be assailed with all sorts of foul smells. He caught himself about to hesitate upon the broad steps, was startled and displeased to note all the physical sensations of fear: sweaty palms, shortness of breath, clenched stomach, griping bowels.

He had ridden in glorious charge upon the enemy, ridden so fast that his men had been left behind and he had attacked the enemy's front ranks alone. He had been surrounded, assaulted from all sides, before his men had managed to reach him and extricate him. And he had not then felt such terror as he now experienced. He had seen lepers in the street, seen their mutilated hands wrapped in rags, which did little to hide the ravages of the dread disease. He had seen faces no longer recognizable as such, with great holes where noses should have been. He envisioned himself – leprous, disfigured, pitied, forced to skulk about the streets ringing that damnable bell which said, 'Make way! Contagion comes! Make way!'

He stared with horror at the great double doors behind which such creatures lived, and, for a moment, he could not move. Fear paralyzed him. He saw himself disgraced by his very first trial, and that sent a shock to his system. Steely cold resolve shot through his veins. His head cleared, his fear became something he could manage. Jaw clenched, holding his head high and his body rigid, Dagnarus entered the Hall of the Hospitalers.

Once inside, he was pleasantly surprised and considerably relieved. The first rooms were the convalescent wards. These were light and airy and filled with patients in weakened condition, but who were recovering and were, therefore, on the whole, cheerful and not obnoxious to look upon.

'Come now, this isn't so bad,' Dagnarus said to himself. He walked among the patients, who sat in chairs, basking in the late-afternoon sunshine. Occasionally, he stopped and spoke kindly to a few, who were much honored by his attention. There was not a leper among the lot.

'You people do truly work miracles here,' said Dagnarus to one of the healers, a particularly sweet-looking and quite attractive young woman. 'I am glad I came. You may not believe this, Revered Magus,' he said confidentially, 'but I had a horror of this place. You have put my fears to rest.'

'I am glad we have been able to do so, Your Highness,' said the Revered Magus. 'Now, if you will come with me, I will show you the rest of the Hospital and then take you to where you will be ministering.'

'Am I not to be here?' Dagnarus glanced back at the cheerful room he had just visited.

'No, Your Highness,' said Lord Altura, in close attend-ance. 'These people do not need your ministrations. The sick and the incurably ill lie in a different wing of the building.'

Dagnarus ground his teeth in frustration, but there was no help for it. The Dominion Lords and the healers escorted him to another large room, this one not nearly so pleasant. Here were the sick, those with diseases at various stages – some of them feverish and delirious, some covered with pox, some vomiting into bowls held by the healers. Had he encountered any of these wretches on the street, Dagnarus would have hastily covered his mouth and nose with his handkerchief and walked past as quickly as possible.

He had no handkerchief, so this was not a temptation, though it was all he could do to keep from pressing the sleeve of his robe over his mouth. He breathed as little as possible, hoping to avoid sucking in the contagion.

'I wonder how you can stand it!' he said in low tones to the young woman at his side.

'You mean the sight of so much suffering?' she asked, looking at him with warmth in her eyes.

Well, no, that is not what he had meant – he had meant how could she stand the stench of vomit, the smell of sickness, the risk of catching some deadly illness. That was what he had meant. But he did not correct her mistake.

'It is difficult, especially in the beginning,' she admitted. 'But what is my discomfort compared to their pain? Nothing at all. And you cannot imagine the satisfaction one feels in helping people to throw off some dread disease, in watching them improve daily, in seeing a mother restored to her children, a child to her parents.'

'But sometimes you lose the battle,' Dagnarus said, trying to distract himself, fearful he might vomit just from the smell. Lavender and sage could do only so much.

'Yes, sometimes our patients die,' she answered steadfastly. 'And though their passings are sad, particularly for those left behind, their deaths are not as terrible as you might expect. We do all we can to make them comfortable, to make the end peaceful. Where they go, they will find freedom from their pain and their suffering. I have been with many who are able to see the afterlife from the shores of this life. All speak of the beauty, the feeling of being loved by a great and good entity. Sometimes those who draw near the far shore but who, for some reason, escape death and come back among the living, actually weep for sorrow at not being allowed to cross over.'

Dagnarus said nothing to destroy the young woman's pretty illusions. He had looked at death on the battlefield and seen nothing but an empty abyss, into which the soul tumbled and was swallowed by darkness. He wondered what sort of herb they fed the dying to induce such pleasant illusions.

'Well, then,' he said, nerving himself, hoping to find a patient who wasn't suffering from anything catching, 'hand me a rag and a basin of water and I will myself embark upon the task of easing suffering.'

'But you are not to work here, Your Highness,' said Lord Altura, looking grave. 'The incurables lie beyond.'

'Damn you to the Void,' muttered Dagnarus, who would, at that moment, have been glad to place Lord Altura among the incurables.

The solemn procession continued, passing down long corridors to a part of the building that was kept sealed off from the rest. The young woman remained behind, for, she said, she had not progressed far enough in her studies to have the right to enter this part of the Hospital. Dagnarus saw that she was disappointed by this and wondered at her sanity.

He used the time spent traversing the corridors – mostly empty, but with the occasional healer passing by him – to try to figure out how to escape this onerous and dangerous trial without doing irreparable harm to his cause. As they drew near, they could all hear screams – terrible screams – or wild and incoherent shouts. Dagnarus's stomach shriveled; he was having difficulty breathing. He considered for the first time quitting, abandoning his goal.

He permitted himself to imagine turning and fleeing. He would, he knew, be forever branded a coward. The soldiers who served under him and who admired him would sneer at him. They would say, and rightly, that his brother had undertaken this trial and had passed through it with grace and with courage. Dagnarus could do no less.

He gritted his teeth and walked on.

A door, barred and locked, opened to Lord Altura's knock. They were met by one of the healers, a man in his late thirties, a comely man with an engaging smile.

'Your Highness,' he said, 'we have been expecting you. Please enter and may the grace of the gods enter with you.'

Dagnarus could barely hear what the man said for the horrible screams coming from the room beyond the door. He had heard screams like those on the battlefield, from those with an arrow through their privates or a spear through the gut. But such screaming never lasted long.

The healer held the door open for Dagnarus. He entered, drawing on every bit of courage he possessed and resorting to some he did not even know existed. The three Dominion Lords, who were observing his actions, accompanied him. They had each spent their trials here and knew what to expect. None of them betrayed any emotion or hesitation.

Of course not, he thought bitterly. Undoubtedly their magical armor protects them from contagion.

He cursed them silently and heartily as he stepped into the hellish chamber. He noticed, as he passed through the door, that the hand of the healer was mottled with hideous patches of white – an early symptom of leprosy.

Dagnarus shuddered. Every instinct urged him to run. The smell of death and the screams of the tormented blended in a whirling haze of horror. The next thing he knew, he was being assisted to a wooden stool by the man with the mottled hand.

Seeing that diseased hand upon his arm, touching his robes, Dagnarus pulled away. Shamed at having nearly fainted, he was angry with himself, furious at the situation. He stood up so quickly that he overturned the stool, sent it clattering to the stone floor.

'Thank you, Healer,' he said through clenched teeth, casting a quick glance at the Dominion Lords, who regarded him impassively, 'but I do not require your aid.'

'Do not feel ashamed of a momentary weakness, Your Highness,' said the healer, with a cheerful smile. 'The fact that you are so sensitive to the suffering of others is much to your credit.'

Dagnarus barely heard the man's platitudes. 'What would you have me do, Healer?' he demanded, determined to get this onerous task over with as quickly as possible. 'Keep in mind that I am a warrior, my hands are callused from the sword, my touch is not gentle.'

'First, Your Highness, I will show you what we do here. Many people have misconceptions about our work.'

This part of the building was actually an entire wing, with different rooms devoted to different forms of incurable illness. The first area housed the lepers, who, except for the most seriously crippled, were able to move about, sit chatting to each other, perform certain small tasks, and lead almost normal lives.

Dagnarus and the Dominion Lords walked the chambers. The healer talked. Dagnarus, keeping fast hold of his courage and resolve, did not pay much attention to what the healer was saying. The healer did catch the prince's interest when he stated that in his opinion, leprosy was not as infectious as most people feared.

'Very few of us who work among the afflicted contract the disease,' he said. 'If it were highly contagious, you would expect that all of us would be infected. We have with us here only those who are in advanced stages of the disease, which affects the bones and so makes it difficult for them to get around. A combination of magic and the application of chaulmoogra oil, which we obtain from the orken realm – it comes from a tree that flourishes in the tropical regions – does much to ease their suffering and, in some cases, has actually helped to restore some of their damaged flesh.'

Dagnarus gave the lepers – their limbs and faces covered in bandages – a wide berth.

'Why is that man screaming?' he asked, interrupting the healer in some learned dialogue on the subject of madness, for they had left the lepers and were walking past several rooms where the insane who had been judged either harmful to others or to themselves were confined in private cells.

The madmen peered at Dagnarus as he passed, gibbering and hooting, reaching through the bars of their cell doors, trying to grab him. They passed one cell where a young girl sat on the floor, staring at the wall opposite. She rocked an imaginary baby in her arms. A healer sat beside her, talking to her in soft tones.

'Can you do nothing to stop that screaming?' Dagnarus asked.

He had heard the shrieks of this poor wretch ever since he entered. He had been waiting impatiently for them to end – probably in death. The screams continued on and on, however, and were wearing on his nerves.

'Alas, no, Your Highness,' said the healer sadly. 'The patient is in one of the rooms at the end of the hallway. He has a growth, a cancer, that is devouring his vital organs. Although we can sometimes cure these cancers if the growth is very small, this growth is quite advanced.

There is nothing we can do to stop it. As for the pain, we could ease it with our magic and the juice of the poppy, but he will not permit it. He is furious with us, you see, and flies into a rage whenever we come near.'

'Why? What did you do to him?'

'It is not what we did *to* him, Your Highness, but what we will not do *for* him,' said the healer. He glanced at Dagnarus speculatively. 'This man was a soldier. It is in my mind that perhaps you might be able to help persuade him to let us help him.'

At least, thought Dagnarus, this is better than rubbing oil into the sores of lepers.

'I should think all it would take would be a quick sock to the jaw,' he observed. 'He would then give you no further trouble.'

They were coming closer to the room. The pain-filled screams were horrible to hear. Dagnarus was beginning to reconsider. At least the lepers were quiet.

'We do not force our treatments upon patients unless they are either too young to be able to judge their condition for themselves or they have lost the ability to make known their will to us,' the healer replied. 'The wishes of the family are also taken into consideration. This poor man has no family, no one to care for him.'

They arrived at the man's room, a small stone cell with no window, for this part of the building was located inside the inner walls of the Hospital. The healer opened the door to the room and, with an inclination of his head, encouraged Dagnarus to enter.

Conscious of the Dominion Lords watching him, Dagnarus walked inside the room. Magical light lit the room with a soft and soothing glow. But nothing would soothe the tormented man, lying on sweat-soaked sheets, writhing in agony. Dagnarus looked at the patient more closely.

'I know this man. Sarof,' he called loudly, to be heard

410

over the man's screams. 'He was one of my lieutenants. Sarof,' he repeated, kneeling down beside the bed. 'I am sorry to see you like this.'

Sarof's eyes flared open; he stared at Dagnarus wildly, at first not knowing him. Then some sense of recognition came to the man. He cut off a scream with a sharp, indrawn breath, holding the pain at bay, distracted by the sight of the prince.

'Your Highness!' he gasped, and his pallid face was suffused with color. 'Thank the gods!' He reached out a shaking hand, grabbed hold of Dagnarus with a crushing grasp. 'You understand! You know how a soldier wants to die! Tell them, Your Highness! Tell these bastards to do what I want!'

'And what is that, Lieutenant?' Dagnarus asked, placing his hand over the hand that, for all it was weakened by illness, had the strength of desperation.

'Tell them to end it!' the man pleaded. Foam flecked his lips. He could bear the pain no longer, and, doubling over, he moaned and screamed again. 'I cannot stand this! I want to die! And they won't let me!'

Dagnarus looked up questioningly at the healer, who was slowly shaking his head. 'Our calling is to preserve life, not to end it. We cannot do as he asks. It is against our laws.'

Dagnarus turned again to the sick man. 'They are healers, Lieutenant. Not murderers. By law, they cannot do what you ask.'

'If this were a battlefield, you would not leave me in such misery,' Sarof said. Spittle drooled from his lips, his face was covered with perspiration. His breath came in painful gaspings.

'This is not a battlefield,' Dagnarus said sternly, rising to his feet. 'There is nothing I can do, Lieutenant. Let them give you something to ease the pain . . .'

'There is nothing!' Sarof snarled. 'Nothing in this world

that can ease my pain! Only in death! Only in death will I find rest! Bastards!' He moaned and screamed again, tossing from side to side.

And it was then Dagnarus saw that healers had tied the man to his bed, so that he would not hurl himself out of it in his spasms.

Dagnarus walked from the room, the screams dinning in his ears. Lieutenant Sarof had been a good soldier, a brave man. He had served well and honorably. He deserved a death better than this one – tied up like a criminal, suffering the torments of the damned. Stepping past the healer, who was doing nothing but shaking his head, Dagnarus grasped hold of the hilt of Lord Altura's sword and, before the astonished Dominion Lord could stop him, the prince yanked the sword free.

Dagnarus shoved aside the healer – who was making some feeble attempt to halt him. The prince returned to the room of the sick man. He lifted the sword above the lieutenant, looked down at him questioningly.

'This is your will, Sarof?'

'Yes, Your Highness!' the man gasped.

Dagnarus did not hesitate. Ignoring the horrified protests of the healer and the shocked cries of the Dominion Lords, Dagnarus thrust the sword's blade deep into the soldier's chest.

Sarof looked up at Dagnarus.

'The gods bless you . . .' he whispered. His eyes fixed, his head lolled to one side.

The screaming ceased.

Dagnarus yanked the sword free, wiped the blood on the blood-soaked sheets. Leaving the room, he handed the sword back to the astounded and shaken Lord Altura.

'Are there any other patients you would like me to treat?' Dagnarus asked mildly.

ELEVEN

The Votes Tallied

THE DEBATE OVER DAGNARUS'S ACCEPTANCE into the ranks of Dominion Lords was the longest ever held up to that time. As the Most Revered High Magus had stated in his speech at the beginning, the passing or failing of the trials was not as important as the means by which the candidate passed or failed. Means that would, presumably, show something about the nature of the candidate. As it happened, Dagnarus's trials revealed as much about the current Dominion Lords as they revealed about Dagnarus. Each person saw a different aspect of the prince.

'Almost as if there were four of me,' said Dagnarus, who was secretly listening, along with Silwyth, in a hidden alcove off the Council meeting room. The prince was supposed to be in his cell in the Temple, communing with the gods. 'And I standing in the center, looking at each.'

'Your Highness performed admirably, at least so I have been informed by my brethren,' Silwyth said, bowing.

'Ask *my* brother and he will tell you a far different story. Still, he will have difficulty swaying the vote to his side – as I make the count. Is that correct? What do you hear?'

'The count stands now very much as it stood when you

were first nominated, except perhaps that it is slightly better. As you commanded, I saw to it that word of your performance during the trials was leaked out to the populace, who were much taken by what they heard. Public opinion is strongly behind you. The Dominion Lords and the magi will face strong opposition should they vote you down. In addition, the Lord Altura – who had originally voted against your nomination – was much impressed by the merciful act you performed in the Halls of Healing. It seems that her mother had only recently succumbed to the same terrible illness and suffered greatly.'

'Yet my brother terms my actions "barbaric," a throwback to the days when men embraced the Void.'

Dagnarus and Silwyth exchanged significant looks. No more need be said on that subject.

'And, at any rate, killing the patient ended my tour of duty in that godsforsaken hospital. The healers couldn't get rid of me fast enough. What's happening now?'

The debate had raged for seven hours and appeared likely to go on for another seven. Silwyth had been in the alcove, eavesdropping, the entire time. The prince had just arrived. He had been celebrating his freedom from the Preparations in the hidden bedroom, making love to Valura, who was able to sneak away because her husband – a Dominion Lord – was attending the Council meeting to vote on her lover's acceptance.

Dagnarus could see into the room, but only by applying his eye to a small hole that had been drilled into the wall and that was concealed by a tapestry on the other side, a tapestry with a corresponding hole punched through the embroidered eye of a unicorn. Peering through the hole for any length of time made his eye water. There was nothing much to see, and so he took his ease upon a tall stool, refreshing himself with a goblet of wine, brought by Silwyth. The two could hear excellently well, particularly because voices had been raised to a fever pitch throughout most of the debate.

'What did they stop for?' Dagnarus asked. A sudden silence had fallen.

Silwyth applied his eye to the hole. 'Your royal father has entered, Your Highness. They rise to greet him. Now they are waiting for him to be seated. Your brother goes to attend him. Your father rebuffs him with an angry look.'

'If I've done nothing else, I've driven a wedge between those two,' Dagnarus said complacently, chewing strips of dried beef to take the edge off his hunger. 'The rumor is going around that my father might pass over Helmos and name me as his heir.'

'I have heard that rumor, Your Highness,' said Silwyth, 'and I regret to say that I do not put much stock in it.'

'No, I fancy you're right. My father would never do anything so completely opposed to the natural order of things. Still, it's given Helmos a few sleepless nights, I'll wager. Hush, my father is speaking . . .'

Both Silwyth and Dagnarus leaned nearer the wall to hear.

'What does he say?' Dagnarus asked. 'His voice is so low, I cannot hear.'

Elves can hear a wider range of pitches than humans, one reason it is difficult for humans to appreciate elven music.

'The King says that he has heard nothing but rumors about what happened during the trials. He asks to hear the true account. The Most Revered High Magus is now rising to speak.'

'Come, this should be entertaining,' said Dagnarus, drinking his wine and settling himself more comfortably.

'Your Majesty,' said the High Magus, 'by your leave, I will read you the report on the outcome of Prince Dagnarus's Seven Trials of Preparation. This report came from the Dominion Lords who assisted in his trials.

'The first trial – the Preparation of Compassion. The candidate entered the Hospital and killed the patient who had been assigned to his care.'

A growl from the King.

'Yes, Your Majesty, there were extenuating circumstances,' the High Magus admitted. 'The patient, who was in excruciating pain, begged the candidate to slay him. The patient gave his consent as the candidate held the sword over him. Four witnesses all testify to this. Two of the four maintain that the candidate acted with true compassion – more than has ever been previously exhibited by any other candidate. Two maintain that the candidate acted barbarously, usurping the role of the gods, whose province it is to take life.'

Loud voices interjected at this point; there was much shouting and confusion.

'What do they say?' Dagnarus asked.

'It is the orken Captain, Your Highness,' Silwyth replied. 'He is particularly incensed by the High Magus's words and demands that the last sentence be stricken from the record.'

'The orken practice ritual sacrifices, as I recall,' said Dagnarus. 'Both of their own kind and any others who happen along. They toss them into a volcano as offerings to some god, or so I have been told.'

'I have heard the same account, Your Highness, though I cannot swear as to its veracity.'

After some further argument, the Most Revered High Magus, with exemplary patience, agreed to modify the last sentence so that the part about the province of the gods was deleted and the offensive word 'barbarous' was changed to 'practical,' which the Captain found satisfactory.

'We then proceeded to the next test,' the Most Revered High Magus continued, first mopping his brow with a handkerchief. 'This was the Preparation of Strength. In this test, Your Majesty will recall, the candidate must

416

hold two buckets of sand in his hands, his arms extended outward, for as long as he can. This is difficult enough in itself, but further difficulty is added by allowing water to drip into the buckets, increasing their weight. The test not only shows physical strength, but the ability of the mind of the candidate to push his or her body beyond its limits. Thus length of time is not considered a primary factor.

'Lord Altura held the buckets for only fifteen minutes prior to dropping them, but this showed great fortitude and strength of will on her part, since she was not able to lift the buckets at all prior to her testing.'

'And how did Prince Dagnarus perform?' the King asked, his voice loud now and easily heard.

'The candidate held the buckets suspended for three hours,' said the Revered High Magus, adding, with a sigh, 'During this time, the candidate announced that he was bored and asked if we might not combine two of the Preparations. He would be willing to undergo the Preparation of Wisdom at the same time. This, of course, we had to refuse.'

'Has any other candidate shown such strength as the prince exhibited?' the King asked.

'No, Your Majesty,' said the Most Revered High Magus. 'None other has even come close.'

'Proceed,' said the King.

'Your Majesty, we come to the Preparation of Wisdom. In this trial, the candidate meets with the ten members of the Council of Magi, who ask the candidate to discourse on various questions, such as, "Why have the gods put evil into the world?" "What is the nature of the soul?" Of course, there are no right or wrong answers to these questions, but exploring them allows us to gain insight into the deep inner workings of the candidate. I recall with pleasure' – Reinholt's voice softened – 'the trial of Prince Helmos. We spent eighteen hours in discussion and could have spent longer but that we were constrained by the need to proceed with the testing.'

The voice of the Most Revered High Magus deepened with disapproval. 'We spent fifteen minutes in the Preparation of the candidate Prince Dagnarus, and ten of those minutes were spent waiting for the prince, who was late.'

'I had to take a crap,' Dagnarus said to Silwyth. 'I suppose even Dominion Lords take a crap now and then.'

The elf made no response, pretended he had not heard. The mention of bodily functions is not permitted among the elves, even among close family members, who resort to polite euphemisms if for some reason they are forced to refer to them at all.

'The first question asked was, "Why did the gods put evil in the world?" The candidate replied, "I do not know. I don't suppose anyone does."'

The Revered High Magus paused for effect.

'I see,' said the King testily. 'Is that true?'

'Well, yes, Your Majesty, but the point –'

'Do *you* know why the gods put evil into the world?' the King persisted.

'I could speculate –'

'I'm not asking for any of your damn philosophical speculations!' the King rasped. 'Do you know why the gods put evil into the world?'

'No, Your Majesty,' said the Most Revered High Magus stiffly. 'I do not.'

'Your Majesty,' Helmos intervened. 'Forgive me, but that is not the point. The point is –'

The King ignored him. 'And there are, as you said, no right and no wrong answers?'

'No, Your Majesty,' said the Most Revered High Magus, sighing again.

'So Prince Dagnarus's answer is perhaps the clearest, most honest answer to that question that exists.'

'True, Your Majesty.' Reinholt knew defeat when he saw it.

'Proceed.' The King was pleased.

'The next Preparations are those of Endurance and Leadership.' The Most Revered High Magus sounded resigned. 'In cases where there is no record of a candidate having been tested in either of these, we have trials that they must undergo. In the case of this candidate, however, his service in Your Majesty's army is well-known. Captain Argot and many of the men who served with Prince Dagnarus were summoned to testify. There is no doubting the candidate's ability to withstand extreme hardship, no doubting the candidate's ability to lead and inspire confidence – and indeed, I might almost go so far as to say adoration – in those who serve under him. We could devise no test that would be as difficult as those that he has already undergone. In view of this, with the consent of the Council of Dominion Lords, these two trials were abandoned.

'In the Preparation of Chivalry, the candidate demonstrated remarkable skill in riding –'

'He should. I taught him,' came a gruff voice.

'Is that Dunner?' asked Dagnarus, smiling.

Silwyth, peeking through the hole, nodded. 'Yes, Your Majesty.'

'– and in swordsmanship,' the Most Revered High Magus concluded. 'I doubt if there are any to match him. I know that *I* have never seen his like. Which brings us to the last trial, the Preparation of Understanding. In this trial, the candidate is taken into an empty room, whose walls are painted white. The candidate is left there for twenty-four hours without food or water, given a chance to commune with himself and the gods. When the time is up, the candidate is asked to describe his spiritual journey.'

'Twenty-four hours!' Dagnarus snorted. 'I swear the bastards left me in that damned room for twenty-four weeks! I was never so completely and utterly bored in my entire life! And you have no idea how thirsty you get when you know you cannot drink. I suppose I have gone for twenty-four hours during battles without water and not noticed the lack. In there, I was parched from almost the very first moment they shut that blasted door! If I had not slept through at least twelve of their fool hours, I should have gone mad.'

'Upon emerging,' the Most Revered High Magus was continuing, 'the candidate was asked what he saw upon his journey. He replied, "Nothing."'

'What did they expect me to see?' Dagnarus demanded. 'The room was empty, for gods' sakes!'

Silwyth concealed his smile from the prince by again applying his eye to the hole.

'You understand our problem, Your Majesty,' said the Revered High Magus, in rather hopeless tones.

'No, I do not,' the King returned bluntly. 'Prince Dagnarus undertook the trials and, if he did not pass them as others who have preceded him have passed them, he passed them according to his own nature. He was true to himself and it may be in the eyes of the gods that this is the best any of us can hope to achieve in our lives. But,' he added, 'I leave the Council to make its decision.'

'Your father is leaving,' Silwyth reported.

Dagnarus rose to his feet, stretched. 'And so must I. There is very little doubt now, I suppose, about which way the Council will vote. I have business to attend to. Remain here and let me know what hour they choose for the Transfiguration.'

'Yes, Your Highness.' Silwyth returned to his place at the spy hole but turned away a moment to halt the prince as he was leaving. 'Pardon, Your Highness, but I forgot to tell you that I received an answer this day from the Shield regarding your proposal.'

'Yes? And?'

'The Shield will be pleased to offer you his full backing and support. Not only that, but he has an army of five thousand men standing by, ready to cross the border as soon as you give the word.'

'Excellent!' Dagnarus rubbed his hands.

'The Shield did express concern about the border patrols, Your Highness.'

'It is a vast border, Silwyth,' said Dagnarus. 'There are areas that go for months without anyone keeping watch on them, particularly if the patrols are sent to train in another part of the kingdom. I will provide the Shield with a location on the border where it will be safe for an elven army to slip across.'

'Very good, Your Highness.'

'You should start practicing to call me "Your Majesty,"' said Dagnarus, with a wink.

'Touch wood, Your Highness!' Silwyth rebuked him. 'Quickly! It is wrong to tempt fate.'

'Bah!' said Dagnarus, laughing softly. 'You sound like an ork!'

But after the prince had departed, Silwyth, looking grave, rubbed his fingers on the seat of the wooden stool.

Disguised in the robes of one of the magi, heavily cloaked, his face concealed by his hood, Dagnarus returned to the Temple, but not to his cell. He would have to be there when the Dominion Lords came to tell him that his dearest wish had been granted. But that would not be for some time yet. The debate would last at least another several hours. Helmos was like his half brother in one respect – he would not give up without a fight.

Traveling by circuitous routes, Dagnarus made his way to the forgotten tombs and from there to the altar chamber dedicated to the Void. This would be his last visit. It was time to send the Vrykyl out into the world upon his master's business.

Dagnarus was extremely pleased with the Vrykyl. The prince had given Shakur several tests, and the Vrykyl had passed them all, had obeyed all the prince's orders without question. The Vrykyl's strength was impressive – triple that of an ordinary mortal. He was not a particularly pleasant companion – Dagnarus found it disconcerting to look into the Vrykyl's lifeless eyes. But Dagnarus had all the pleasant companionship he could ever want. What he needed now was a loyal and fearsome warrior.

Unlocking the door, the prince entered the chamber. He glanced toward the stone slab upon which the Vrykyl was accustomed to lie and saw – with shock – that Shakur was gone.

'Your Highness,' came a voice.

Dagnarus caught a glimpse – sidelong – of a man standing behind him. The prince turned, his hand on the hilt of his knife, the blade already sliding out of the sheath.

'Your Highness,' said the man. 'Don't you recognize me? It is I. Shakur.'

Dagnarus stared. He returned the knife to its place at his belt.

'I would not have recognized you,' said the prince. 'You are certainly *not* the Shakur I found in the death cell.'

The man was tall – taller than Shakur had been – his body better proportioned. The face was similar, though it lacked the terrible scar and was somewhat better-looking. His smile was almost engaging. The eyes were still dead, held no warmth, no laughter, no sorrow. To look into those eyes was to look into the Void. But, at first glance, most people would not notice. The man was well dressed, in fine clothes. Or what appeared to be fine clothes.

'It's all illusion,' said the Vrykyl. 'I can be whatever I want to be. Perhaps you would like me in this form.'

The Vrykyl's image began to shimmer and waver and then re-formed, coalesced into a new being. The prostitute with whom the real Shakur had spent his last remaining hours of life stood grinning wantonly in front of Dagnarus.

In an instant, the prostitute disappeared. The Vrykyl resumed his black-armored form.

'Excellent,' said Dagnarus, well pleased. 'This suits my needs admirably.'

'And my own,' the Vrykyl said, with a growl. He drew from his belt the Blood-knife, a knife he had made from his own bone. 'I will need to feed soon. I can take the form of any person I have ever known, so long as I can bring their image to mind. Thus, assuming a pleasing shape, I will be able to fool my victims and take them unaware.'

The Vrykyl cast a significant glance at the door. 'As I said, Your Highness, I will need to feed soon. I feel my strength waning.'

'And feed you shall,' said Dagnarus. He tossed the Vrykyl the key. 'I have a task for you to perform. Leave here when it is dark. Do not slay anyone in the city of Vinnengael. We have an active and astute sheriff, and I do not want him asking questions. When you are beyond the city's borders, you may do what you like.'

The Vrykyl bowed, to show he understood and would obey.

'Where do I go, Your Highness?'

'You will travel to the realm of Dunkarga. Can you ride a horse?' Dagnarus asked, suddenly struck by this detail, which he had not previously considered.

'Not without casting a spell over one,' the Vrykyl responded. 'Dumb animals are aware of my true nature and will not approach me. My magic will allow me to spellbind an animal, force it to serve me.'

'Then you will ride to the city of Karfa Kan. A minister of the King's awaits you there.'

King Olgaf had died, furious at the thought that Tamaros would outlive him. His son, the Queen's brother, had

423

ascended to the throne. King Reynard was not the scheming, meddling ruler his father had been. Reynard was coldly calculating. Reynard did not covet Vinnengael's wealth. He coveted Vinnengael.

'Deliver this missive the moment you arrive – day or night. If the King's messenger sleeps, awaken him.' Dagnarus held out a scroll. The handwriting was Gareth's, but the seal was the prince's own. 'You will wait for his reply and return to me at once when you have received it. This horse you ensorcel, I assume it will be fast?'

'Fast as night's shadows moving over the land, Your Highness. If it dies, I will find another. I could make the journey in a single night.'

'I give you then one night –'

'You forget, Your Highness,' the Vrykyl interrupted. 'I must feed first.'

'Do that then. But do not linger over your meal. I'll give you this night to journey there, an hour conferring with the King's minister, and the next day to journey back. I expect you, therefore, tomorrow at sunset. Do not enter Vinnengael, but wait for me outside the city gates. That will be the day of my Transfiguration. When you see me next, I will be a Dominion Lord.'

'Congratulations, Your Highness,' said the Vrykyl, tucking the missive into the belt from which hung the Blood-knife.

'The decision is not final yet, but there is little doubt. Remember, wait until dark before leaving. Take the form of one of the magi and you will have no difficulty passing through the Temple's environs. Here is a map showing you the way out of this chamber. Remember, do not kill while you are inside the city.'

'As you command, Your Highness,' said the Vrykyl. 'I look forward to being free of this place. I find the time passes slowly, especially when one has no need of sleep.'

'Since you have eons of time at your disposal, I suggest you grow used to it,' Dagnarus said.

Eons, Dagnarus reflected, as he walked the corridors, returning stealthily to his cell. I have Shakur's life essence now and I will gain others later, for I must have more of these Vrykyl. If I create forty Vrykyl, I shall have forty more lives, which will provide me how many more years? Close to forty hundred, if I have inherited my father's longevity. And if I keep creating Vrykyl, I will keep gaining lives. So, to all intents and purposes, I am ageless, and I still retain the advantage of being able to enjoy a good night's sleep!

Such reflections, though gratifying, were also fatiguing, particularly the mathematics, so on returning to his cell, Dagnarus lay down upon the bed and fell into a deep and peaceful slumber. He was aroused by a gentle tapping.

Dagnarus had been waiting for this signal. Even in his sleep, he was conscious of waiting for it and was awake instantly. Jumping from his bed, he entered the cupboard in haste and excitement.

'Yes?' he said softly.

'The vote has been cast, Your Highness,' said Gareth. 'You are to be a Dominion Lord.'

TWELVE

The Will of the Gods

S A CHILD, GARETH HAD MARCHED IN THE parade to honor the Transfiguration of Helmos. The memory of that day stood out among his other memories as a sparkling jewel on a necklace of wooden beads. He had been entranced and excited by the crowds, the colors, the joyous tumult. This day the crowds here to honor the Transfiguration oppressed him, the bright colors flaring in the sunlight jarred him, the tumult made his head ache.

Gareth was given a place of honor among Dagnarus's household, walking beside Silwyth and just ahead of the King. Unfortunately, this put him directly behind Helmos and his retinue. Helmos had paused on his way to take his place in line to speak a few kind words to Gareth, words that were lost in a sudden roar from the crowd when Dagnarus's standard was carried out of the castle. Gareth knew the words were kind, however, because of the expression on Helmos's face. Worn-out from a worried, sleepless night, burdened by the guilt of his culpability in hoodwinking the King and Council, Gareth could have thrown himself in the dust of the street at Helmos's feet and wept.

As it was, he only bowed and mumbled something incoherent in return as he felt the hot blood rush to his face. Helmos had given him a quick, concerned glance, but the King's chamberlain, who was ordering the line, hovered at the crown prince's elbow, politely urging Helmos to take his place so that the procession could begin.

Gareth gave a deep sigh and then jumped as long fingers pressed painfully into his forearm.

'This is a joyous occasion, Master Gareth,' said Silwyth, keeping his voice low, though there was not much danger that they could be heard over the shouts and singing of the populace. 'Look the part.'

'How can you say that? Dagnarus goes to his death this day,' Gareth returned in agony. 'And the fault will be mine.'

'The fault will be the prince's own. You did your best to warn him away,' Silwyth said, adding quietly, 'We are all in the hands of the gods, are we not?'

Gareth looked sharply at the elf to see if he was being funny or sarcastic, but Silwyth's face was smooth and opaque as a dish of milk.

'You know very well that two of us are not,' Gareth retorted softly, irritated at what he considered the elf's smug and uncaring complacency. 'Those who embrace the Void must necessarily deny the existence of the gods.'

'And yet the stars shine in the eternal darkness of the night,' Silwyth said.

Bowing to Gareth, the prince's chamberlain moved to take his place in line.

Gareth should have gone as well, but Silwyth's words struck him with penetrating force. He went cold to his fingertips. The words were meant to be comforting, perhaps, meaning that the gods would watch over Dagnarus whether he was worthy of their concern or not. Gareth understood that there must be a flip side to this pretty coin, however, and that the opposite was not so fair to look upon. It filled him with dread.

The chamberlain bullied and jostled people into line. The Queen's chair was carried into place. Her Majesty called out irritably, with loud shrillness to her ladies-in-waiting, who were gathered around her and who could do nothing right. Gareth's mother was among them, looking frayed, but pleased and excited. His father, who was suffering from gout, would not be in the parade. The King's chair was brought in next, the very last in the procession. His Majesty had been forced to give up riding horseback, though not until his ninetieth year and then only because his much-beloved horse had died of old age, a sign, the King said, that his own riding days were at an end.

Seeing that all was in readiness, the chamberlain gave the signal. The procession lurched forward. The day was fine, too fine. The sun beat down unmercifully upon those standing in line, waiting their turn. Clad in their heavy, ornate clothing, over which they wore ceremonial robes, the members of the court panted and gasped and plied feather fans. Several of the waggish younger lords among Dagnarus's retinue had placed large chunks of ice, taken from the cold-storage cellars, under their hats. Though the melting ice trickled down their faces, they were looked upon with envy by the rest of the sweltering crowd.

His own part of the household bunched together like herd animals. Gareth thought they would never start to move, that they would be standing in the broiling sun for all eternity. But when he did finally set out upon the journey from the castle to the Temple, he thought the pace much too fast, wished desperately that he could slow time, if not halt it altogether.

Silwyth elbowed him. 'You drag along as if you were marching in a funeral procession. Smile. Wave!'

Gareth did as he was told. Raising his head at that moment, he found himself staring into the face of his tutor, standing along the sidelines. Evaristo looked stern and disapproving. Seeing that Gareth noticed him, the tutor very pointedly shook his head, expressive of his concern. Gareth hastily averted his gaze, attempted to distract himself by paying attention to the rest of the crowd, and it was then he noticed the orken.

A memory of Helmos's procession came to mind with sudden clarity. Captain Argot asking his soldiers why the orken were not in attendance. He heard the conversation of ten years ago as well as if the men were standing beside him on this day.

'They're not plotting something, do you think?' Argot asked.

'No, Captain!' answered one of his lieutenants. 'Their shamans said that the omens were bad.'

'What was it – a flock of geese flying north from south, instead of south to north?'

'Something like that, Captain. Did you see the sunrise this morning, sir?'

'. . . remarkably beautiful, the gods shedding their blessing on the occasion.'

'Well, the orken thought it remarkably frightening . . .'

Gareth remembered the sunrise – he had never seen another to equal it, the sky itself had turned to fire. And he remembered that the omens had been right. Helmos had survived the Transfiguration but he had been named Lord of Sorrows and certainly his life after that had seemed to fulfill that dire prophecy. Gareth tried to think back on this morning's sunrise, but could not recall it. Nothing out of the ordinary apparently.

His heartbeat quickened. He gazed at the huge crowds of orken standing head and shoulders above everyone else, their human neighbors going out of their way to avoid contact with them, holding handkerchiefs over their noses to ward off the stench of fish. Gareth could have run over and hugged them.

The logical part of Gareth knew that believing in orken omens was tantamount to believing in such silly superstitions as avoiding black cats and expecting money when your palm itched. But the part of him that always tossed spilled salt over his left shoulder took hope. If the omens had been bad, the orken would not have come. Therefore, the omens for Dagnarus's Transfiguration must be good!

Lethargic from the heat, the procession crawled toward the temple. Gareth entered the shaded portico thankfully, mopping sweat from his face with the sleeve of his robe when no one was looking. He and the other members of the prince's household took seats of honor in the very front row of the vast and echoing auditorium. Silwyth left to go pay his homage at the elven altar.

Conscious of their importance, the nobility settled into their seats with quiet dignity. The chamberlain had asked them to maintain a proper and respectful silence, in the hope that this would influence the rest of the crowd. The hope was a forlorn one. Excited by the parade and the prospect of the ceremony, the common people – though somewhat subdued by the reverential atmosphere as they entered the Temple – took their seats in the gallery with much talking and the occasional smothered laugh.

Gareth was thankful that he wasn't obliged to speak to Silwyth or anyone. The faces of the gods represented above the altar seemed to stare down at him in reprobation. He told himself this was nonsense, as silly as believing in orken omens. He tried not to look at them, but his gaze was drawn in their direction, and every time he glanced up he found them staring sternly back. He squirmed in his chair until his neighbor – the prince's cupbearer – frowned at him and shook his head.

Silwyth returned and took his seat. The elf, whose face was generally expressionless, looked unusually grim.

'What?' Gareth whispered, plucking at the sleeve of Silwyth's ceremonial robes. 'What is wrong?'

Silwyth barely glanced at him.

'Tell me!' Gareth insisted, a prey now to wild terror.

Silwyth's lips compressed, as if he were bracing himself. Then he said, very softly, in elven, 'My offering was rejected.'

Gareth stared at the elf, appalled. He wanted to speak, to question further, but he lacked the power.

'It is not a bad sign for His Highness,' Silwyth said, his voice tight. 'The bad sign is for me. I must think what this means.'

'What does it mean?' Gareth demanded, but Silwyth had withdrawn into himself and would say no more.

Gareth huddled in his seat, dismayed; so frightened that he was physically ill. He looked up at the awful figures above the altar and cowered beneath them.

Bowing his head, hoping to avoid that terrible gaze, he prayed, the first prayer he had made to the gods from his heart since he was ten. 'If the prince dies, punish me as well, for I am as guilty as he!'

The crowd was eventually settled. The ten High Magi filed in, to take places of honor upon the stage in the ten high-backed wooden chairs provided.

It would not be long now.

Gareth's hands were icy cold; his fingers had lost all sensation. He chafed them and, as he did so, he felt the back of his neck along the upper part of his spine start to tingle with the feeling that someone was watching him. He turned around, searching behind him, and saw no one. Then he looked to his right and his eyes met the wide and frightened eyes of the Lady Valura.

She was seated on the other side of the aisle from him, but also in the front row, for her husband was a Dominion Lord and would be participating in the ceremony. She was extraordinarily pale, so pale that one of her servants was

431

gently fanning her. Valura's hand was wrapped tightly about the necklace she wore, the turquoise stone given her by Dagnarus. Oblivious to her ladies, to the crowd around her, to her husband, who was taking his place with the other Dominion Lords near the altar, Valura gazed intently at Gareth. So eloquent were her beautiful eyes that he understood her as well as if she had shouted. She was asking him for reassurance.

He had none to give. He tried to smile, but his smile must have been sickly, for it did not help her. Lady Valura sank back in her seat, her eyes now closed. Her maid plied the fan a little harder.

The crowd cheered the entrance of the Queen and her ladies. The cheer grew louder – a roar of affection – when the King entered. Clad in robes of velvet trimmed in ermine, he walked unassisted onto the stage. He had seemed feeble and frail during the procession, but perhaps that had been the effect of the heat. He shed the weight of old age inside the Temple. He stood taller than usual and walked with a firm stride.

Gareth stared straight ahead at the altar, but he did not see it. He saw nothing, felt nothing, not fear, not despair. The chill from his hands had spread throughout his body. People moved and spoke, but they were puppets performing at the fair, their wooden bodies small and grotesque and bound up with strings.

King Tamaros took his place on one side of the altar, opposite the High Magus. The crowd gave a final rustle, a final cough, and then fell silent. The High Magus rose to his feet. He bowed to the King, then pronounced the words that would begin the ceremony.

'Let the candidate be brought forward.'

Two Dominion Lords – one of them Valura's husband – left their posts, moved to the back alcove. A door opened. Gareth recalled with vivid clarity the Transfiguration ceremony of Helmos, and it seemed to him that he was watching two ceremonies at once – the one he had witnessed years before imprinted over the one happening now. Helmos had paused in the doorway, the light had streamed around him.

Dagnarus did not pause. Never noted for his patience, he must have been pressed against the door, for as soon as it started to move, he shouldered his way out, not even waiting for his ceremonial escort, but leaving them to catch up. He was in fine spirits, smiling triumphantly.

The Most Revered High Magus frowned, and even Tamaros looked grave and shook his head slightly, rebukingly.

Dagnarus realized instantly that his haste was unseemly, his exuberance misplaced. He slowed his pace, waited for his escort, and managed to contort his face into something more closely resembling humility and contrition. He came to stand before the altar.

A murmur swept through the crowd. Dagnarus had never appeared so regal, so handsome. His face was suffused with victory and joy; he was not in the least afraid. He made a low bow to the people, who loved him for it. There was scattered spontaneous applause, which drew a shocked and reprimanding look from the High Magus. Turning, Dagnarus walked over to his father, knelt before him.

'Father, I ask your blessing,' he said, his voice carrying clearly, echoing from the high-domed ceiling.

King Tamaros, touched and pleased, placed his hand upon his son's bowed head, stroked the auburn hair with its crisp curls. Only those in the front row could hear his reply, but all could feel it in their hearts.

'I grant my blessing, my son. You have made me very proud this day.'

Dagnarus rose to his feet and turned to face his brother.

Helmos, clad in the armor of a Dominion Lord, stood

beside his father. The Dominion Lords did not wear their helms, but Helmos might as well have had his on, for his face was hard and colder than steel. The Most Revered High Magus looked uneasy, the crowd tensed in nervous anticipation, expecting, fearing, hoping for an unpleasant scene.

Dagnarus knelt again. Lifting his head, he looked up at his half brother.

'Helmos, I ask your blessing. I will not go forward with this ceremony unless you grant it.'

Dagnarus was noble, beautiful, humble, earnest, solemn.

Helmos was moved; he could not help himself. He hesitated, as if he might truly refuse his blessing, gazed searchingly at Dagnarus as if he would plumb the very depths of his brother's soul. Dagnarus met his brother's gaze unflinching, unwavering.

Gareth, who knew it was all an act, who knew that Dagnarus was secretly laughing at Helmos, writhed in his seat and covered his eyes, unable to watch, unable to bear seeing Helmos made sport of, made the fool.

'Deny it!' Gareth prayed, but he knew Helmos would not, that he was charmed by Dagnarus as the mouse is charmed by the snake.

'I give you my blessing, brother,' said Helmos at last, his voice breaking with emotion.

'Thank you, brother,' Dagnarus said, and everyone in the crowd pulled out their handkerchiefs and dabbed their eyes.

Gareth sighed and lifted his head.

Last, Dagnarus went to his mother, who leapt from her seat and flung herself upon him, hugging him and weeping over him until he appeared somewhat put out and, disentangling her arms from around his neck, handed her back to her ladies.

He turned his gaze then, looked out into the crowd one last time. He looked straight at Valura, looked at her so long that Gareth knew that their love must be revealed to everyone in the building, and Silwyth murmured in elven, 'Do not do this to her, Your Highness!'

Gareth could not see the Lady Valura, who had shrunk into her seat, surrounded by her women.

Dagnarus at last broke off his gaze, stepped back to take his place by the altar.

'I am ready, Revered Magus,' he said, and his voice was a paean of victory.

The ceremony proceeded as it had with Helmos. The High Magus sat down in his chair. The vellum scroll was placed before him, along with the brush and the jar of lamb's blood. He was prepared to receive the will of the gods, write down the title Dagnarus would henceforth bear as Dominion Lord.

'Let the Miracle of the Transfiguration begin,' pronounced the High Magus.

Dagnarus knelt before the altar. King Tamaros came forward, rested both hands upon his son's bowed head, and called for the gods to grant to this candidate the wisdom and power accorded to a Dominion Lord.

'Are you willing, Dagnarus, son of Tamaros, to dedicate your life to the service of others? Will you be prepared to sacrifice that life, if need be, to save another?'

'The gods please, I am,' Dagnarus replied.

Tamaros stepped away from the altar.

Dagnarus turned and faced the audience. He crossed his hands over his breast, his expression confident, serene, certain. Gareth ceased breathing, waited for the expression of pain to cross Dagnarus's face, the expression that would signal the beginning of the transformation.

Dagnarus stood quite still, his head bowed.

Nothing happened.

He stood longer. Still nothing.

The ten magi in the back darted quick, uncertain glances at each other. The Dominion Lords stared straight ahead, faces stiff, though here and there a jaw muscle twitched. King Tamaros frowned. His hands tightened over the arms of his chair. He shot an angry glance at the Most Revered High Magus.

Reinholt repeated nervously, not with any certainty, 'The Miracle of the Armor commences.'

Only it did not. Nothing was commencing, nothing at all.

Dagnarus stood before the altar, before the people of Vinnengael, and nothing was happening to him. The lead actor in the play who has forgotten his lines. The lead actor who has been upstaged by the gods. The Transfiguration was going to be denied him.

A low muttering came from the audience. King Tamaros was livid with anger. Helmos gave his brother a pitying glance. Queen Emillia could be heard crying shrilly, 'What's going on? I don't understand!'

Dagnarus lifted his head. He was enraged. His rage flowed from him, twisting like a cyclone. Gareth felt the blast of that terrible rage strike him, press him back into his seat. He was not alone. People throughout the temple gasped, children began to cry, the lights on the altar candles wavered and flickered.

The Most Revered High Magus rose to his feet. His face was somber and stern. Nothing like this had ever before occurred. Reinholt looked at the King apologetically. Tamaros glared at the Most Revered High Magus, but there was nothing to be done, and the King knew it. The gods had spoken.

'I am deeply sorry, Prince Dagnarus,' the Most Revered High Magus said, 'but it seems that the gods have rejected your candidacy.'

Dagnarus's hands fell to his side. His fingers clenched into fists. He literally shook with anger and thwarted desire, his face flushed almost black with fury. He bit his lip through, in his rage; blood trickled down his chin.

Not only had he been denied his heart's dream, he had been humiliated before the entire kingdom, before his father and mother, before Valura, before his brother.

'No!' Dagnarus shouted, and his shout swelled to a shriek. 'No!' Turning, he smote his clenched fist upon the altar. 'The Void take the gods! I will have this!'

Shocked to the core of his being by the sacrilege, the High Magus extended his hand to the prince, endeavoring to remonstrate with him. Crying out in pain, Reinholt snatched back his hand as if it had been burned.

Dagnarus's body erupted in flame.

The Most Revered High Magus stumbled backward, horror-stricken. The Dominion Lords stared, appalled and shocked. Wild-eyed, King Tamaros started up out of his chair and ran toward his son, with some idea of trying to beat out the flames using his own frail hands.

'Stand back!' The High Magus cried in a terrible voice. 'This is the will of the gods! We may not interfere!'

Helmos caught hold of his father, restrained him. Tamaros collapsed in his son's arms like a broken toy, unable to move. Queen Emillia was screaming over and over on one note, like a rabbit being torn to pieces by the fox.

At Helmos's command, the Dominion Lords gathered to help the stricken King. They took him from Helmos's arms and, supporting the limp body, eased him back onto the throne.

Casting a grim, defiant glance at the High Magus, Helmos himself ran to Dagnarus, prepared to risk his life to try to save his brother. He could not come near enough to rescue him; the heat of the infernal fire consuming Dagnarus's body drove his brother back.

The flames whirled around Dagnarus. His flesh, blackened and charred, could be seen withering in the heat. Since that last defiant 'No!' he had not spoken. He had not screamed or cried out. His limbs curled in upon themselves in his excruciating agony, yet he made no sound.

A few people in the audience panicked, fled the building screaming. Others sat stunned, watching the terrible spectacle in awful fascination.

One heart-rending cry had come from Valura, but she had then fallen silent. From the sound of the scream, which seemed to have torn out her heart, she might well have died.

Gareth was stricken with horror, unable to move, to speak. He could not catch his breath and, recalling his vow, he thought that perhaps he would now die with his prince. He did not fight his fate; he did not want to live. The torment of his guilt and the knowledge that his complicity in this terrible tragedy must be revealed made death seem welcome by comparison.

The flames died suddenly, as if blown out by a blast of chill wind. A charred mass of blackened flesh, unrecognizable as a human being, lay before the altar. The magi and the Dominion Lords stared at it in horror. Reinholt snatched off the altar cloth, thinking to cover the body. He started forward, only to fall back in shock.

The charred mass had begun to move. Arms extended outward. The head lifted from the floor. The body that was twisted and burned began to straighten.

The magi gasped and cried upon the gods for mercy.

Blackness took shape and form: breastplate, leg guards, and bracers for the arms, hands gloved in black. The armor glistened in the light, a black carapace, with tendons and ligaments clearly visible against bone and muscle of black steel.

The ten High Magi huddled together like chicks in a storm. The Dominion Lords, recalling their duty, moved swiftly to guard the King and Helmos from this apparition. The audience might have been turned to stone, so silent were they as they watched this dread miracle.

The black-armored figure had now gained his full height. He gazed as if amazed at his hands and his arms, his face – covered with a black helm whose features were those of a ravening wolf – turned from left to right. His fingers flexed. He took a pace or two, testing his ability to move. He drew the shining black sword from its sheath and swung it experimentally, several times, testing his strength, his flexibility. And all the while, his mind must have been wondering, doubting, and at length understanding, accepting. Reveling.

He turned toward the audience and lifted the visor of his helm. The face of Dagnarus, pale, but handsome still, his eyes dark with the remembered pain, glittered with vindication. Gareth's eyes filled with tears. He did not know whether they were tears of joy or of bitter sorrow. He did not know whether to offer thanks to the gods or curse them. He dashed the tears away impatiently and jumped as a cold hand closed over his forearm.

'Be alert,' Silwyth whispered. 'Be ready. That is, if you are still loyal to him.'

Gareth understood. He would have a choice to make. There was no question. He had made the choice long ago, when he had chosen to remain in the playroom, the prince's whipping boy.

Dagnarus smiled, a mocking smile and, hand on his sword hilt, he turned to bow to his father.

Tamaros sat huddled in his chair. He did not move, he did not speak. His skin was ashen, his eyes wide and staring. The eyes were the only thing alive about him. The rest of him might have been a corpse. The right side of his mouth sagged, his right hand had slipped from the arm of the chair, dangled at his side.

'Father.' Dagnarus made a flourish with his black-gloved hand. 'It seems you have a son to rule the day, and now one to rule the night!'

Tamaros did not move. He tried to speak, but the only

439

sound that came from his shattered body was a guttural cry, like that of an animal pierced by an arrow.

Dagnarus cast him a disdainful glance, then turned to his mother. 'Well, Mother, this is what you always wanted. Are you proud of your son?'

Emillia stared at him, blinking. The shock had capsized a mind already adrift. She had no notion of what had transpired. All she knew was that she had seen her son die, and now he was alive. She gave a little twittering, gulping laugh and reached out a hand to touch the black armor.

'You are a Dominion Lord, my son. And someday you will be King. I always knew it. Oh, how elegant you look!'

Her ladies, gasping in horror, sought to hush her.

Dagnarus regarded his mother with contempt. He turned on his heel, turned his back upon his father and brother.

'And what do the gods have to say for themselves?' Dagnarus asked the Most Revered High Magus, with a slight, sneering smile. He pointed to the vellum. 'I am Lord. Lord of what?'

Reinholt stared at Dagnarus as if he were speaking a foreign tongue. Then, recollecting himself, the Magus looked down at the vellum on the altar. He reached out a shaking hand to lift it, exhibit it to the witnesses.

The vellum was drenched with blood.

When Dagnarus had struck the altar, he had caused the jar of lamb's blood to overturn, soaking the vellum. But those nearest could see that the vellum bore writing, letters of black, as if they had been scribed by flame.

'Lord of the Void,' read the Revered High Magus. He dropped the vellum to the altar as if it had burned his fingers.

Dagnarus's bravado failed him a moment. His face went nearly as white as his stricken father's, his hand clenched over the hilt of his sword. He stood in silence

440

for the time it takes to draw a shivering breath. For a fleeting instant he was the child Gareth remembered: unloved, bereft, lonesome, abandoned. Gareth would not have been surprised – he even half expected – to see Dagnarus suddenly collapse, fling himself at his father's feet, and beg forgiveness. Ambition, black as the armor, and pride, hard and cold as its shining surface, encased Dagnarus. He lifted his head, his eyes glittered.

'Be damned to you!' he said to the Magus. Gesturing with his hand, Dagnarus included all those in the Temple. 'Be damned to you all! And know this – one day I will be your master!'

Helmos had been tending his father, leaning over him, chafing the icy gray hands, asking if he was in pain. Helmos had paid little attention to Dagnarus, until this statement. He understood his brother's intent, he foresaw the danger with clarity given him by the gods.

'Seize him!' he cried. 'Hold him fast! Slay him, if need be!'

The Dominion Lords, led by Lord Mabreton, drew their swords and started to close in. Dagnarus placed his back against the altar. Strong and skilled though he was, he was weakened from his terrible trial and could not hope to withstand all ten, plus the battle magi who were also coming to add their skill in the apprehension of the avowed Lord of the Void.

'Hold!'

The voice was the King's, barely recognizable, but strong enough to be heard over the clash of metal and the stamping of feet.

Tamaros had managed, the gods alone knew how, to lift his crippled body from his chair. Balanced precariously, he reached out his left hand.

'Do not harm him!' he commanded, his voice a harsh croak. 'The fault is mine. Let him go.'

Tamaros collapsed, crumpled to the floor. His crown

rolled from his head, rolled across the stage and came to rest at Dagnarus's feet in a pool of lamb's blood.

Helmos did not see it, he was stooping over his father. The Dominion Lords saw it; so did the Revered Magi. No orken were needed to read that terrible omen. The Dominion Lords stood with swords at ready, but they did not strike. Tamaros was King still. He had issued a command and it must be obeyed.

Dagnarus picked up the crown. He held it sparkling in his hand. Walking past the Dominion Lords, not sparing them a glance, Dagnarus tossed the crown to Helmos.

'Keep it warm for me, brother,' Dagnarus said.

Jumping down from the stage, he landed with lupine grace upon the main floor of the amphitheater. Gareth and Silwyth joined him, Silwyth guarding the prince's back. The Dominion Lords remained standing, twitching like dogs who smell their prey and are kept at bay by their masters.

Dagnarus walked up to Valura. She had made no outcry beyond that one heart-rending scream when she thought she was watching her lover perish. She gazed up at him, pale and beautiful as a lily cut from its stem. Dagnarus stretched out his black-gloved hand.

'If I am to be Lord of the Void, will you be my Lady?' he asked.

Valura hesitated only an instant. She glanced past Dagnarus to her husband, then, ignoring the screams and cries of her women, Valura placed her hand in Dagnarus's hand. Turning her back upon her husband, she accompanied Dagnarus up the aisle. The two walked with strange and terrible majesty toward the huge double doors. Gareth and Silwyth came behind, the elf keeping constant watch at Dagnarus's back.

'Dagnarus!' Helmos cried. His voice carried throughout the Temple. 'Dagnarus, my brother, I give you a chance to yet redeem yourself. Renounce this evil that has seized

442

hold of you. Our father commands that we show you mercy and we will obey him. He loves you, Dagnarus. For our father's sake, turn back.'

Dagnarus turned, then, but only in defiance.

'The Void take you, brother,' he called out loudly. '*And our father.*'

THIRTEEN

The King is Dead.
Long Live the King.

D AGNARUS'S HORSE, IN CEREMONIAL TRAP-
pings, with roses braided into its mane and tail,
stood in front of the Temple. Held by one of
the Royal Guards, a man whose heroism in battle had won
him this honor, the horse was to carry the newly confirmed
Dominion Lord in triumph to the palace. The Royal
Guard formed a ring around the horse, protecting it from
the curious onlookers, who, unable to squeeze inside the
Temple, were waiting to cheer the new Dominion Lord.

The crowd was merry, and boisterous; they might have
been waiting for the fairgrounds to open. Many had
brought flasks of wine to quench their thirst. One group
sported its own minstrel, who had composed a song
in Dagnarus's honor and who was now singing it for
the sixteenth time to much applause and a continual
shower of coins. Some children began an impromptu
round dance, while groups of orken were teaching some
of the more gullible humans to play a dirt-simple gambling
game involving three shells and a pea.

Whispers that something had gone terribly wrong flew
from the Temple like great bat-winged birds, their shadows falling over the crowd, silencing the songster and

ending the dance. The Temple doors stood open, that as many might see and hear as possible. Now those clustered near the doors reported to those behind what was transpiring. Those behind passed the word to their neighbors.

'The Void . . . the Void . . . the Void . . .' was the whisper that brought shocked looks and gasps and protestations of disbelief.

The crowd surged forward, the same idea occurring to each person simultaneously, that he or she must push inside to see what was going on. The soldiers guarding the Temple door were quick to respond. They forced the mob back, but the soldiers, too, had heard the same rumors and were looking troubled and glancing often at their commanders.

'Find out what is happening!' Captain Argot ordered, but at that moment, he had his answer.

Dagnarus stood at the top of the Temple stairs. The sunlight struck the black armor, and it glistened with a thousand dark and eerie rainbow hues. His visor was raised, he looked swiftly about, pausing at the head of the steps to take in the situation. He ignored the buzzing crowd, ignored the appalled soldiers. They might have been so many insects. He could crush them if they annoyed him.

Turning, Dagnarus said something to Silwyth, made a gesture. The elf nodded. Satisfied that his order would be obeyed, Dagnarus proceeded to walk majestically down the stairs with Valura at his side, holding fast to his hand. No one made a move to stop them. The crowd and the soldiers fell back before him. Parents snatched up crying children, covered their eyes against the terror. The orken made the sign to ward off evil as Dagnarus passed by.

The guard holding Dagnarus's horse stood his ground until the black-armored apparition drew near him. Then he could stand it no longer. The guard ran, willing to accept punishment for failure to obey rather than to risk losing his soul to the demon prince.

The prince's horse was well trained and did not move. The color of its master's armor made no difference to the animal; the fear, excitement, and tension reminded it of the battlefield. The horse swiveled an eye at Dagnarus and shook its mane, as if to say impatiently, 'Let us get on with it, then!'

Dagnarus paused to rub the horse's neck. 'You, too, are loyal,' he said softly, touched. 'I will not forget.'

Lifting Valura in his arms, he swung her up to ride postillion. Moving easily and gracefully, as if the armor were a slick black coating on his skin and not heavy metal and mail, Dagnarus mounted his horse. Silwyth had commandeered one of the horses of the guard for himself and Gareth, who sat behind the elf, his arms clasped around Silwyth's slender body.

A wail came from the Temple and the cry, shouted from many throats, 'The King is dead!'

Captain Argot heard the cry. He looked first to the Temple, then back at Dagnarus, who was settling himself in the saddle. Argot spurred his horse forward. Reaching out, the captain caught hold of the bridle of the prince's horse.

Dagnarus gazed long at the man who had been his friend and mentor since childhood, loyal soldier and comrade. The captain gazed at the man he had admired above all others.

'Get down, my lord,' said Argot. 'You are under arrest.'

Dagnarus did not move. He placed a hand on the horse's neck, calming the beast, who was dancing impatiently, eager to be gone.

'Where do your loyalties lie, Captain?' Dagnarus asked.

'With my King,' said Argot, his face stern and pale.

'That would be Helmos now,' Dagnarus said dryly.

'Yes, my lord,' said Argot.

Dagnarus rested his hand on the hilt of his sword. 'You

taught me to use this, Captain. Do not force me to use it to slay you.'

'You will do what you must, my lord,' said Argot steadily. 'As will I.'

'Curse you for a disloyal bastard!' Dagnarus said angrily, drawing his sword and raising it.

Seeing their commander's bravery, his lieutenants and footmen were shamed into action and pressed forward to defend their captain. A ring of steel surrounded Dagnarus and his followers. Dagnarus, outnumbered a hundred to one, hesitated.

'Have no fear for me, my love!' Valura cried fiercely, withdrawing her arms from around Dagnarus's waist. 'Strike them down!'

'Let him go, Captain! That is an order.'

Argot looked up, astonished.

Helmos stood at the top of the Temple steps. 'Let them all go. Such was my father's dying command, and I will honor it. No one is to lay hands on my brother or those who choose to follow him so long as they leave the city of Vinnengael. But if they return to this city, as avowed worshipers of the Void, they will be considered outlaw and by law are subject to death.'

Argot did not take his eyes from Dagnarus, nor did he remove his hand from the bridle.

'Reconsider, Your Majesty!' Argot shouted. 'We should seize him now before his evil power grows!'

'You have your orders, Captain,' Helmos said, and his voice was stern and heavy with grief and regret. 'I am your King, and I will be obeyed.'

Slowly, Argot released his grip on the horse's bridle. 'Make way, men,' he ordered grimly.

Dagnarus sheathed his sword. With baleful looks, the soldiers fell back. Dagnarus spoke a word to his horse, touched the beast in the flank with his spurs. The horse leapt forward. People scrambled in terror to escape the animal's mad rush. Silwyth and Gareth rode behind; the elf graceful and at ease in the saddle; the magus bouncing and clinging to Silwyth in fear and desperation.

The sound of the horses' hooves drummed upon the cobblestones, drummed in hearts and heads. No one moved until the sound of that drumming had died away upon the hot, still air. And then the people, dazed and stupefied, looked at each other in disbelief and doubt.

For as long as any could remember, Tamaros had been King. He had been King for as long as their fathers and their grandfathers could remember. Some had come to think he would be King forever. Now he was gone, and it was as if a bully had kicked away the crutch upon which they, poor cripples, leaned. This morning, life had been safe, certain. Now nothing was certain anymore.

They looked toward the Temple stairs, toward their new King, but Helmos was not there. He had gone back inside to tend to the body of his father. Unhappy, anxious, bereft, the people began to disperse, hastening back to their homes, to lock up their valuables and take stock of their provisions, as in time of war.

'That was a mistake,' said Argot grimly. 'I pray the gods His Majesty will not come to regret it.'

'It was his father's dying command,' said one of the lieutenants, who had been on duty inside the Temple. 'I heard the King clearly. He ordered that no one harm Prince Dagnarus.'

'A command that the new king should have respectfully chosen to disobey. Tamaros is dead!' Argot said harshly, his expression dark. 'He is beyond the troubles of this world. But we live. And mark my words – we are the ones who will suffer.'

Helmos returned to the altar. A few people still sat huddled in their chairs inside the Temple, some too stunned by the calamities they had witnessed to move. A few others waited, watching, hoping for some miracle or at least reassurance. But most had departed, eager to tell friends and acquaintances all they had seen, to talk out their shock and their horror.

The healer had done what she could to compose the King's body, shutting the staring eyes and making a futile attempt to smooth out the unsightly grimace that twisted the mouth. The Dominion Lords formed a guard of honor around the body, looked to Helmos for orders.

His first were to dispose of the Queen, who was still present, insisting that someone tell Dagnarus she wanted to speak to him this instant. Upon being informed, gently, that the King was dead, the Queen said sharply, 'He is just having one of his fits. He will soon be brought round. Where is my son? Why doesn't he come to me?'

'She is overwhelmed with grief. Take her back to the castle,' Helmos said, regarding Emillia with pity. 'Give her some juice of poppy to help her sleep.'

'My lord,' said Anna, coming to stand by her husband's side. Her face was wet with tears. 'I am so sorry. So very sorry.'

He held her fast, finding comfort in her love. But he could not indulge in his grief long. He was King now. People were already hovering around him, waiting to pounce upon him with questions and demands. First, however, he would pay his final farewell to the dead.

Helmos and Anna knelt beside the body. Taking his father's hands, already chill with death, into his own, Helmos prayed aloud, asking the gods to bless his father, to take him to their beautiful dwelling place where he would be once again reunited with the woman he had never ceased to love. Helmos laid the still hands upon his father's breast.

Helmos then tried to ask a prayer of mercy and forgiveness for his brother, for he knew Tamaros would have wanted him to do so. The words would not pass the new

King's lips. He could not even speak them in his heart, and he understood then that it was the gods who were stopping his prayer. Not only would they refuse to grant it; they did not want to hear it.

His duty done to the dead, it was time for Helmos to start thinking about the living. Rising to his feet, he looked at the Dominion Lords, who stood in silent prayer around him.

'Where is Lord Mabreton?' Helmos asked.

'He is gone, Your Majesty.'

'Gone. Gone where?' Helmos demanded, though he could guess.

'Gone to avenge his honor, Your Majesty,' said the elf grimly.

Helmos looked grave. 'I commanded that my brother not be harmed.'

'Lord Mabreton is not bound to obey the law of a human King, my lord,' the elf replied. 'The only reason he did not challenge him in this hall is because it is a holy place in which blood may not be shed.'

Helmos felt a secret relief. He had been faced with an unpleasant dilemma. As a now avowed follower of the Void, his brother could not be allowed to live. Yet their father's last wish was that the prince should not be harmed. The problem, it seemed, would be taken out of his hands.

'What will become of Lady Valura?' he asked.

The elf's face hardened. 'She will be captured alive, if possible. If she has any sense of honor left, she will request death from the husband whom she has wronged. Her request will be granted, you may have no doubt. If she does not, Lord Mabreton will drag her back to her home, where she will be handed over to her parents, upon whose House she has brought disgrace and ruin. Her husband may lay claim to all her family's holdings and lands in reparation for the dishonor done to him. If she has borne him any children, he will have them put to death.'

450

'The gods have mercy!' Anna cried. 'The crime is their mother's! They are innocent.'

'That is true, Your Majesty,' said the elf lord, bowing. 'Yet the wronged husband could never be certain they were truly his children. He dare not trust the future of his line to a bastard. Now, if Your Majesty will excuse me, Lord Mabreton asked me to convey word to the Shield of the Divine of this sad occurrence. I must leave at once. The gods willing, I will return in time to attend your honored father's funeral.'

'And Silwyth, what of him?' Helmos asked, recalling that the elf had chosen to throw in his lot with Dagnarus.

'I am not certain, Your Majesty.' The elven lord was a loyal follower of the Shield. He knew that Silwyth and his family were favored of the Shield, and he suspected that Silwyth had been placed in the royal household as a spy by the Shield. He could not very well admit this to the new King, however.

The elven Dominion Lord was, in fact, sorely troubled. For the first time in over a hundred years, the human kingdoms of Vinnengael and its subject states were weak, vulnerable. The elven lord liked Helmos, but did not respect him as the elves had respected Tamaros. Helmos was a scholar, not a ruler. Spies kept the elves informed on human politics; he guessed that now that Tamaros was dead, the kingdom of Dunkarga, ruled by Dagnarus's uncle, had no reason to remain loyal and would split away. Perhaps even go to war. The elven lord would have bet all his considerable fortune that Dagnarus was probably headed in that direction right this moment.

The captain of the human armies had shown himself loyal to Helmos, but reports had it that the troops were much more likely to side with Dagnarus in a battle than with his brother. That might change now that Dagnarus had been shown to be a follower of the Void, but it might not. That would remain to be seen.

Much would also depend on whether or not Dagnarus escaped Lord Mabreton's wrath. If he did, and if he lived, there was no doubt in the elf's mind that the newly made Lord of the Void would carry out his promise and attempt to become ruler of Vinnengael.

If this happened, Vinnengael would be entering a period of civil war, and the Shield would be a fool if he did not act swiftly to take advantage of the turmoil to snap up disputed border towns, perhaps acquire some new territory.

As a Dominion Lord, the elf was pledged to peace. As a loyal follower of the Shield, the elf might be pledged to war. He wondered where he now stood.

Helmos could read the elf's thoughts as clearly as if they had been written in ink across his forehead. Helmos saw his danger and that of his people. Once again, he hoped the matter would be taken out of his hands.

'As for Silwyth,' the elf said, finally answering the question that had been asked of him, 'his crime will be judged by the Shield.'

'What crime?' Dunner demanded bluntly. The dwarf stumped over to stand before Helmos. 'Silwyth has committed no crime that I can see, except to remain loyal to a master he has served for over ten years! And what is Prince Dagnarus's crime? Nothing but to fall in love with a woman of such peerless beauty that *not* to fall in love with her would be a greater crime!'

'Dagnarus has shown himself to be a follower of the Void,' said Helmos.

'The Void!' Dunner snorted. 'What has that to do with anything?'

The dwarf was upset, shaken, troubled. He admired and loved Dagnarus, and could not come to grips with what had happened to the prince – a fate the dwarf only vaguely understood. Dunner wondered what all the furor was about. Dwarves do not view Void magic as evil, as do humans. They take a pragmatic view of Void magic, conceding that it has its uses and its place, as does the night, as does death.

'He should not be banished! His darkness makes the Dominion Lords shine that much brighter,' the dwarf insisted.

'By his darkness we are diminished,' said Helmos, coldly, rebuking him. 'And by taking his part, you are not worthy of the trust my father placed in you.'

Dunner was offended, deeply offended. Bowing once, stiffly, he turned and stalked away without another word.

Helmos did not realize the wound he had inflicted on the dwarf, and his unkind words were soon buried by other worries, by grief, by fear, by shame. The necromancers – those magi who tend to the dead – came to bear away his father's body, to ready it with various magicks, prepare the body for the lying-in-state and the funeral. Helmos watched them at their duties, his heart heavy and sore. He was ashamed at his emotions, ashamed that he could not feel pain over his beloved father's loss, but only anger. Anger at his father for having left his son to cope at such a time, anger at his father for having, in essence, created this new and dreadful Lord of the Void.

The necromancers concluded their work. Composing the body, they covered it with a cloth of golden silk. The body would, by custom, lie in state in the central hall of the palace, for all to come and pay their final respects. Lifting the body of the King to their shoulders, the necromancers bore him away with solemn, slow, and measured step. The human Dominion Lords formed an honor guard, and the procession wended its mournful way to the Halls of Necromancy.

The candle flames swelled suddenly in Helmos's vision, the stone altar seemed to dissolve. He closed his eyes and reached out a hand to steady himself. He could feel Anna's arms bracing him, hear her call out for help, but her voice was far away and seemed to be growing fainter and fainter.

He was assisted to a chair – the chair of the Most Revered High Magus next to the altar. Sinking into the seat, Helmos pressed his wife's hand, urging her not to worry about him. His vision seemed clouded with red, but then he saw that he was staring at the blood-soaked vellum, its words of fire burned black into the scroll.

Repulsed, Helmos averted his gaze. The High Magus hurriedly retrieved the document, handed it to a subordinate, who took it gingerly and with loathing. The document was borne away, to be placed in the archives of the Temple's Library.

'Healer!' Reinholt beckoned. 'Come attend to His Majesty!'

The King shook his head. 'No. It was a momentary weakness. I am already feeling better. And' – he sighed – 'there is much work to do. My dear,' he said to his wife, 'you should go to the Queen. See if there is anything we can do to ease her suffering.'

Anna regarded him, troubled. 'I do not want to leave you, my lord.'

'I will be fine. I want to speak a moment to the High Magus. Go to Emillia. Take the healer with you. Give the Queen our deepest sympathy.'

Anna left, not without several backward, anxious looks.

When she was gone, and the King and the magus were alone, Helmos asked quietly, 'Is it wrong, Revered Magus, for me to wish my brother dead?'

Reinholt was silent, thinking how to answer that question. He did not want to lie, yet he wanted to bring comfort. At last he said, 'The gods know what you must do, Your Majesty, and why it must be done.'

Helmos managed a weary smile. 'In other words, the gods may see fit to curse me, but I must bear it. For the sake of my people, my brother must die, and I must command his death.'

'Perhaps the elven lord –' the Revered High Magus began, but without much hope.

Helmos shook his head. 'My brother draws strength from the Void. With that help, he survived the immolation, the fire from heaven. It is my belief that a single lone Dominion Lord will not be able to slay him. Perhaps all of us together could not even do so. Yet, that must be our task, should he return.'

Reinholt made no reply. He had seen the elven Dominion Lords exchanging significant glances before they hurried off to return to their lands to report to the Shield. The High Magus had watched Dunner walk away, hurt and insulted. The ranks of the Dominion Lords were broken, split apart, even as Tamaros had split apart the Sovereign Stone. The Most Revered High Magus himself had seen the Void in the Stone's center. He had looked away, but another had not. Dagnarus had seen it and been drawn to it. His father's firm but loving hand might have saved his son, had he been there to advise him of the danger and pull him back. But that had not happened.

Still, perhaps some comfort could be offered, after all.

'Your father acted for the best, Your Majesty,' said Reinholt. 'He did what he believed was right. Do not think mistakenly that this tragedy is your father's fault. His only thought was to act nobly, generously by his younger son. Dagnarus took this noble, generous act and perverted it, defiled it. I have no doubt that young Gareth – the gods pity him – broke the vow of secrecy the magi take and revealed to Dagnarus the nature of the Seven Preparations. Thus he knew in advance how to answer, how to behave in order to impress us. He has forfeited his life, Your Majesty. The gods themselves have condemned him to death and, indeed, tried to destroy him with the fire. By the aid of the Void, he survived. If you kill him, you are as innocent of the deed as the executioner who carries out the King's law.'

A magus could be seen hovering in the shadows, not wanting to intrude upon the King's conversation.

On seeing the man, Reinholt beckoned him to come forward. 'Your Majesty, here is one I sent to gather some information for me. You may be interested in hearing what he has to report.'

'Let him approach,' said the King.

The brother bowed to the King. Looking exceedingly grave, he said, 'As you suspected, High Magus, the ancient chamber dedicated to the Void, which has been locked and abandoned for many years, has been recently reopened.'

Reinholt shook his head.

'High Magus, Your Majesty, I dread to tell you this, but . . . we found blood upon the altar.'

Helmos lifted his head, stared. 'Blood! Some animal . . .'

The High Magus sighed deeply. 'I think not, Your Majesty. If what I fear is true, this could explain how your brother survived the immolation. I do not want to say more now, before I have proof.'

'At least tell me what you suspect,' Helmos said.

Reinholt hesitated. 'I would not cause you more pain, Your Majesty. And what I fear may not have come to pass –'

'I must know now, High Magus,' Helmos said. 'If I am to deal with Dagnarus.' He smiled sadly. 'As for pain, I do not think it possible for you to inflict more upon me, even if you were to pierce me through with barbed arrows.'

'Very well. It is possible, Your Majesty, that Prince Dagnarus has come into possession of what is known as the Dagger of the Vrykyl, a terrible and evil artifact of the Void. This magical dagger, when used by a person whom the Void has embraced, has the power to steal the life essence of the victim and grant that essence to the one who wields the dagger.'

'May the gods have mercy!' Helmos cried, his face pale and ghastly.

'In addition, Your Majesty,' the High Magus continued relentlessly, 'the dagger that slays the victim also has the power to animate the corpse. There was once one among us, an old man named Zober. We suspected that he found such a dagger and took it away with him before we had a chance to stop him.'

'An artifact of the Void!' Helmos repeated. 'How would Dagnarus come by it? How would he even know of its existence?'

'We had assumed that Zober was dead or at least had traveled to some far distant land,' said the Most Revered High Magus. 'We should have done more to find him, to ascertain his whereabouts, but at the time, he was suspected only to be a worshiper of the Void. We had no proof. But now my guess is that Gareth must have run across Zober and obtained the dagger from him. As are all artifacts of the Void, the dagger would have been eager to be found.'

'How did this Zober get hold of such a dangerous weapon?' Helmos demanded. His eyes narrowed. 'How did he know about it?'

'He would have found references in the library, Your Majesty.'

'Knowledge like that should have been locked away, kept secret!'

'Knowledge is a two-edged sword, Your Majesty,' the Most Revered High Magus replied in gentle rebuke. 'Much that is used for good can be used also for ill. The juice of the poppy eases pain, but if taken in large quantities, it can send the person into a deep slumber from which he never rouses. Would you have us lock away all our books and manuscripts?'

'Not all,' Helmos said sharply. 'But it seems to me logical to destroy those dealing with such evil things.'

'But only in such books, Your Majesty, will we find how to counter the evil and fight against it. Evil exists in the world, Your Majesty, as does good. Destroying the books does not destroy the evil.'

'Well, well, that is neither here nor there now,' Helmos said with a touch of asperity. He rose to his feet, weary and dispirited.

'You should get some rest, Your Majesty,' said the Most Revered High Magus, laying a gentle hand upon Helmos's shoulder.

'I foresee very little rest for any of us, Reinholt,' said Helmos. 'I must make arrangements for both my father's funeral and for my brother's return at the head of an army. Let me know what more you discover about this accursed dagger.'

The Most Revered High Magus bowed low. 'The gods go with Your Majesty.'

'My poor father,' said Helmos softly. 'If he had known what evil my brother had done, he would never have ordered us to let Dagnarus escape unharmed.'

'Perhaps. Perhaps not, Your Majesty,' said the Most Revered High Magus. 'Your father was in the arms of Death when he found the strength to rise up and give his command. The gods alone are the only ones with the power to have restored him to life in order to issue that one last command.'

Helmos made no reply. There was nothing to say. One could only ask why the gods would have done such a thing, and to that there was no answer that any mortal knew or could ever hope to know. He was about to step down off the stage, when he was halted, confronted by the Captain of the orken and his companions.

'Yes, what is it, my lords?' Helmos forced himself to be patient.

'I offered to kill your brother when he was a pup,' said the Captain. 'The omens were very bad then. Your father should have listened to me.'

Helmos had nothing to say to this either. He was too

458

tired to try to explain, too tired for niceties that would be lost upon the orken anyway. Helmos was King now, with myriad burdens and responsibilities. He would have continued on past, but the orken took a step and blocked Helmos's path.

'My lord . . .' Helmos was starting to become angry.

'The omens this day were good for the orken,' said the Captain.

Helmos paused, regarded the ork closely. 'Does this mean that you will not assist me in fighting Prince Dagnarus?'

The Captain looked at the shaman, who shrugged her massive shoulders.

'We will see what future omens have to say,' the ork replied. 'But for now, the answer is no. We will be returning to our homeland.'

'As you choose, my lords,' said Helmos.

He left the stage, left the altar, and walked alone back to the palace.

FOURTEEN

The Lord of the Void

THE NEW-MADE LORD OF THE VOID MET UP with his Vrykyl outside the city gates. The guards permitted Dagnarus to pass through the gates, having no orders to do otherwise.

Shakur did not ask for explanation, seemed to know exactly what had transpired. Dagnarus had noticed before that he and the Vrykyl had some sort of strange mental link, that the Vrykyl would often answer a question before the prince had asked it or say something to indicate he had been following Dagnarus's thoughts. Dagnarus could also understand what Shakur was thinking and the prince had the impression that he could, with some effort, guide the thoughts of the being he had helped to create.

'What says the King's minister?' Dagnarus demanded, pausing a moment in their wild galloping, which had carried them out the gates in a rush.

'The King of Dunkarga supports you in your endeavor, Your Majesty. An army of ten thousand men will march upon your command.'

'Excellent. But, perhaps,' Dagnarus added, brooding, 'my uncle will not support me when he hears the lies that will be told about me. Already they are calling me "demon," and you can be assured that my dear brother, Helmos, will do what he can to encourage that belief.'

'From what I gathered in conversation with the minister, who is a trusted confidant, your uncle would not believe Helmos if he should make the claim that the sun shone in the sky. Not only that, but Reynard is ambitious, and ambition sees only what it wants to see.'

'Then I will return to Vinnengael,' Dagnarus said, looking up at the men-at-arms, who were staring down at him with astonishment. He raised his voice. 'Tell the King I will be back, and when I come it will be at the head of my army!'

'Oh, ride on, my lord!' Valura urged him desperately. 'We have spent too much time here already!'

Dagnarus scoffed. 'Helmos will not pursue us. He lacks the guts.'

'But my husband will, my lord,' Valura said, her voice low. 'I have brought him to shame and disgrace. He will not rest until he has caught us and avenged his honor.'

'That is true, Your Highness!' Silwyth called. He pointed. 'Look! Look there!'

The gates were being closed behind them. A cloud of dust rose from the streets. Dagnarus could hear and even feel the thundering gallop of hooves, possibly as many as a hundred elven horsemen, all of them highly skilled with bow and arrow.

It galled Dagnarus to have to run from his foes. Had he been alone, he might have stayed to fight. He felt strong enough to take on the gods themselves. But he had Valura to consider. She would be the primary target of her husband's rage and Dagnarus could not fight and protect her at the same time. Putting his spurs to his horse's flanks, he wheeled his steed and raced off down the road. Shakur and Silwyth followed, driving their horses hard. Gareth, pale and shaking, rode with his eyes squinched tight shut, more terrified of the horse than the possibility of battle. He hung on to Silwyth with a deathlike grip.

Lord Mabreton was shouting for the guards to keep the gate open, but Dagnarus knew that human soldiers would not be in a hurry to obey an order given them by an elf. There would be a delay at the gate, and this would gain him some time. He plotted his strategy as he rode.

His first goal must be to throw off pursuit. His second was to find a position he could defend and that would afford Valura protection. Risking a glance over his shoulder, he saw that the gates were starting to once again swing open, but very slowly. The elves were bottled up behind the gates. The highway Dagnarus rode curved, rounding a hill, and the city gate was lost to sight.

Dagnarus followed the highway for another few miles, then, finding the path he had sought, he wheeled, turned his horse off the road, and crashed into the forest. The others followed, their steeds slowing as they tried to break through what seemed an impassable tangle of scrub trees and thick undergrowth. The smell of sage, crushed beneath their horses' hooves, scented the air.

'Shakur! Cover our tracks!' Dagnarus ordered, slowing his mount but not stopping.

The Vrykyl, his face invisible beneath his black helm, nodded to show he understood. He slid from the saddle while the horse was still in motion and ran back to the road. Using his immense strength, the Vrykyl ripped out the underbrush and began arranging the limbs and small trees to conceal their passage.

Dagnarus pressed on, urging the horse as fast as possible along the path, which was overgrown and, in places, disappeared altogether. The trail was an ancient one that led to an old, tumbledown outpost, which the soldiers of ancient Vinnengael had once used to keep watch against her enemies.

Dagnarus was taking a calculated risk in turning off the

main road. His horse was swift and might have been able to outdistance those ridden by the elves. But the horse was carrying two people, as was Silwyth's mount, and would not be able to keep up a racing pace long. If his plan worked, and the elves were thrown off the trail, Dagnarus calculated that he and Valura had only to lie low for several days, until the elves gave up the chase, and then he would make good their escape.

The outpost was built on a cliff overlooking Lake Ildurel. There the watch had once lit huge bonfires, which could be seen from the village and which warned of enemy forces traveling up from the sea by boat. Made of stone dug out of the side of the mountain, the outpost had been abandoned for more than a hundred years, ever since Vinnengael had grown into a major city, whose strong walls would protect it from assault.

The outpost's small guardhouse was in disrepair, its walls crumbling, its roof long ago caved in. No shutters covered its windows, its single door, half-rotted away, hung precariously from rusted hinges. But the outpost would make an excellent hiding place. Few humans remembered the outpost's existence, and the elves would almost certainly not know of it. Dagnarus knew of it only because Captain Argot had brought the prince there as a youth, to illustrate a lesson on the importance of the outpost to the defense of what had then been a large fishing village.

In later years, Dagnarus had returned to the outpost, using it as an informal hunting lodge. He liked to sit on the cliff and look out over the vast lake, the surrounding lands, and down into the city of Vinnengael. An eagle could not have a better view. From the outpost, Dagnarus had been able to spot weaknesses in the city's defenses, weaknesses he planned on either shoring up – should he become King – or exploiting.

As his horse picked its way carefully up the steep trail, Dagnarus turned to make certain Valura was all right. He need not have worried. She reveled in the excitement. Her face was flushed, her lips parted in an ecstatic smile, her eyes glittered with pleasure. Once he heard her laugh, sparkling laughter that echoed over the rocks like splashing water.

Silwyth had been a soldier; he rode well and kept up with Dagnarus. Gareth had finally opened his eyes, only to see that they were climbing what appeared to him to be a vertical cliff face. He shut them again. Shakur had not yet returned. The Vrykyl waited behind to report on the elves.

The sun was setting on this strange and awful day when Dagnarus and his followers reached the outpost.

'I fear you will not find this place very comfortable, my love,' Dagnarus said, as he helped Valura from the horse. 'But I trust we need hide out here for only a few days, until your husband tires of seeking us.'

Valura looked grave. 'My husband will never tire of searching for us, my dear. Not if he were to live a thousand years.'

Dagnarus removed the black wolf-faced helm, shook out his sweat-damp hair. Silwyth was trying to persuade Gareth that they had arrived, they were safe, and he could dismount. Gareth opened his eyes, stared in shock at the river, which was only a ribbon of silver far, far beneath him. Shuddering, he looked hurriedly away. He tried to climb down off the horse, but he was so stiff and sore, his muscles so clenched with fear, that he slid off and fell heavily to the ground.

'The Shield of the Divine is my ally,' Dagnarus said, smiling in reassurance. 'He has agreed to provide me men and arms to overthrow my brother's rule. In return, he will have the border cities he wants. He will not allow the personal vendetta of one lord to imperil our alliance.'

Valura smiled sadly. 'How little you know of us, my own.' She kissed him tenderly. 'Silwyth will explain the situation. I am too tired to do so myself. No, my dearest, I can manage. All I need is a blanket to spread on the floor.'

'You do not even have a cloak,' Dagnarus chided gently. 'The night will be cold here in the mountains. Ah, my love,' he added, taking hold of her hands and drawing her close. 'What have I brought you to? Ruin, disgrace, danger. No food, nothing but a smelly horse blanket under which to sleep. You made a poor choice when you chose to come with me. You should have remained with your husband and denounced me along with all the others. At least you would be safe at home this night, warm in your bed with its silk sheets, eating peacock tongues and drinking mulled wine.'

'I long for those as the escaped prisoner longs for his iron manacles and his dark cell,' Valura replied. Her voice hardened. 'I have been a prisoner all my life – first in my father's house, then in the houses of my husbands. No chains bind me now except those of love, and those chains are made of forget-me-not and gossamer. Yet these chains are so strong, not even death can sunder them. If I die tomorrow, my love, my own, I shall die with a smile on my lips, for I have been happy this day. Happy to be free of our secret, happy to show the world how much I love you.'

He kissed the hands he held, kissed her fingers, and then kissed her lips. Against her protests, he accompanied her into the guardhouse, where he did what he could to make her comfortable. Silwyth went off to tend to the horses. A tumbledown stable located behind the guardhouse offered some shelter for the weary beasts.

Gareth was too shaken from his fall and drained from the day's cataclysmic events to be of much use to anyone. He sat forlornly on a portion of the crumbling stone wall that surrounded the guardhouse, staring out at the sky. Long streaks of red made it look as if the sinking sun was grasping at the clouds with bloody fingers, trying to save itself from sliding into night.

He glanced up dispiritedly as Dagnarus approached.

'Well, was it worth it?' Gareth asked bitterly.

'The pain?' Dagnarus's eyes darkened, his face blanched, his hand curled in upon itself in remembered agony. 'I did not believe I would survive,' he said, after a moment, his voice harsh. 'The pain of the fire was excruciating. I could see . . .' he paused, awed, ' . . . I could see the faces of the gods! They were not angry, only sad.' He smiled grimly. 'Odd, but I was reminded of Evaristo when he was beating you. The gods looked the same way as they punished me.'

He hesitated, as if he was loath to talk of it, but seemed to need to speak.

'It would have been easy to die. I *wanted* to die, to escape the terrible pain. But then I saw another face watching alongside the gods – my brother. And he was watching me suffer with a smile on his lips.'

'No, he wasn't!' Gareth protested, shocked. 'I saw Helmos quite clearly. He was horrified. He risked his life, trying to save you from the flames! The other lords had to pull him back, and even then he struggled to free himself.'

'Did he?' Dagnarus shrugged. 'Well, perhaps I was mistaken. At any rate, he *did* save my life, for it was the sight of that smug grin of his that gave me the will and the strength to battle the gods. In the midst of the fire, I sought the darkness. I entered the darkness, and in its vacuum, the flames died. And the darkness rewarded me! Made me stronger than a Dominion Lord. Better than even my father's creations.'

'Lord of the Void,' Gareth murmured.

'I feel its magical power inside me, much as a woman feels new life within her, or so I must imagine,' Dagnarus continued, ecstatic. 'The power is young yet, but it grows with every passing moment.'

'You will need it to escape Lord Mabreton,' Gareth observed darkly.

'Hah!' Dagnarus laughed. 'He's gone off on the wrong track. He and his men are probably halfway to Tinnafah by now!' He yawned, stretched. 'Gods! I am exhausted! I will go lie down with Valura for an hour or so.'

Dagnarus glanced down at his armored arms, the black breastplate. 'Speaking of sleep, what do I do with this strange armor? It is comfortable – I can hardly feel that I am wearing it. The armor seems to be a part of me, like my skin or fingernails. Yet I trust I am not expected to keep it on day and night.'

'Your brother Helmos and the other Dominion Lords wear a magical pendant given them by the gods, Your Highness,' Gareth said. He, too, was suddenly weary, but he was afraid to sleep. Every time he shut his eyes, he saw the prince withering in that holy fire. 'A touch on the pendant and a prayer to the gods causes their armor to appear.'

'I doubt if prayer to the gods will avail me much now,' Dagnarus said wryly. 'I don't suppose I pray to the Void?' he asked, doubtful.

Gareth sighed and shook his head. 'No, Your Highness. The Void does not give unconditionally, as do the gods. The Void takes first, then grants the request. You gave your soul. The Void accepted your sacrifice and rewarded you with renewed life, the armor, and the magical power it confers.'

Gareth studied the armor closely. The armor conformed to the body, re-created the body. He could see outlines of rib cage and muscle and sinew and bone. In the center of the breastplate, over the heart, an emblem was engraved. The emblem was simple – four mandalas, representing the four elements. In their center, a single black dot, darker than the armor itself, darker than night.

Gareth pointed his finger, careful not to touch the armor. 'That symbol, Your Highness. Look at it.'

Dagnarus peered down. 'I recognize it!' he said softly, awed. 'When I was . . . dying, I suppose, I saw it! Black amidst the flame, the wheel spun before my eyes. What does it mean?'

'It is a symbol for the Void, a very ancient one. The mandalas represent the other four elements. In the center is the Void. Place your palm over that symbol, Your Highness, and wish the armor away,' Gareth instructed.

Dagnarus did so. The armor disappeared, seeming, to their astonished gaze, to dissolve into the prince's skin, a drop of shining darkness draining into each pore, becoming part of his life's blood. Dagnarus stood in the clearing, clad in the white robes he had been wearing during the ceremony. Around his neck hung a round pendant. Cut from a single, large stone, the pendant glittered and sparkled in the sunlight with the radiance of a diamond, except that it was jet-black. At his side was the Dagger of the Vrykyl, held in place by his will, attached to him by the magic.

Dagnarus regarded the pendant and the dagger with satisfaction, the robes with disgust. 'A fine sight I shall look, riding over the countryside dressed like a virgin on her wedding day! Ah, here is the Vrykyl! What news of the elves?'

'They missed the trail completely, my Master,' said Shakur, bowing from horseback. 'I waited, hiding in the Void, and watched them gallop past. Not one thought to look off to the side, so intent were they upon catching you on the road ahead.'

'Fools!' Dagnarus dismissed them with a gesture of contempt. He looked with interest at Shakur's saddlebags. 'I don't suppose you have a change of clothes in there?'

'As it happens, I do, my Master,' Shakur replied. Opening the saddlebags, he drew out a leather tunic, a fine silk shirt, and woolen hose. He held them out to Dagnarus, who glanced at them disparagingly.

'A burgher's clothes. Still, I suppose that will have to do until I can buy something better. What is that brown stuff spattered all over them?'

'Blood, my Master,' said Shakur imperturbably. 'You ordered me to conceal the murder, and so I thought it best to leave no trace. I buried the body, but I brought the man's possessions with me, intending to sell them later.'

'Silwyth,' Dagnarus ordered, 'take these and wash them, see if you can make them fit for me to wear.'

Shakur lifted the visor, revealing the face with its dead eyes. The Vrykyl held out the soiled clothing to the elf.

Silwyth, his expression impassive, took a step backward.

'Drop them on the ground,' Silwyth commanded, making no move to touch them.

'Come take them from me, Elf,' said the Vrykyl, sneering.

Silwyth did not move. His nose wrinkled in disgust. 'I will not. I smell the stench of death and decay on you!'

'His name is Shakur, Silwyth,' Dagnarus said, watching the confrontation with some slight amusement. 'He is a Vrykyl, a creature of the Void who serves me – as do you,' he added, voice grating.

Silwyth bowed low. 'I serve Your Highness. I am loyal to Your Highness, as I believe I have proven. But I will not serve this corrupt mockery of sacred life.'

Dagnarus's face flushed in anger.

Gareth plucked at the prince's sleeve, whispered hurriedly, 'Don't force the issue, Your Highness! Not if you value Silwyth! The elves honor death, revere those who have died. The elves believe that their spirits leave this life to go on to another, better life. The idea of a spirit imprisoned in dead flesh is abhorrent to them.'

Dagnarus's anger simmered, but he said nothing to

Silwyth. A new and troubling thought had occurred to him.

'Will Valura feel this way, do you think?'

'I should imagine so, Your Highness,' Gareth said.

'Then I will send the Vrykyl away. He can precede us, rendezvous with my uncle's army. Shakur!' Dagnarus beckoned. 'I have new orders for you –'

'Too late, Your Highness!' Gareth said in a low voice.

Valura stood in the doorway of the building. Her face was livid, and she stared at Shakur with an expression of revulsion and horror.

'Death!' she whispered. 'Death is come for me!'

Her knees gave way. She sagged against the open door and would have fallen, but Dagnarus ran to her and caught her in his arms.

'No, my dear, my beloved!' the prince said. 'Not death, but life! I have found a way to defeat death. This body will not die!'

Valura's gaze shifted to the bloodstained clothing. 'He lives by feeding off the lives of others!' She shuddered, closed her eyes. 'I heard him say so.'

'In my cause,' Dagnarus emphasized. 'They die in my cause. By the gods, they should give thanks! That their petty little lives are now exalted, made worthwhile in my service. You do not doubt me, beloved,' he added, frowning, annoyed and displeased. 'You do not question my actions?'

'No, no!' Valura said, but she kept her face turned away from the Vrykyl and even lifted her hands to hide him from her sight. She pressed her head against Dagnarus's chest.

'I did what I felt compelled to do,' he said, his voice cool. His arm dropped from around her. 'Without this creature that so repulses you, we could not have escaped. Even now, we would most likely be at the mercy of your husband except for him. The Vrykyl's strength is ten times that of mortal men, he does not have the weaknesses of mortal men, he does not require sleep or food. He does not need rest. In his death, he gave me his life essence! Thus I survived the fire that would have killed me. We are bound together, he and I,' Dagnarus added, his voice softening in awe. 'His thoughts are mine. My thoughts are his. Should he travel to the far reaches of this world, I could still command him, and he would still obey me.'

Dagnarus gripped the Dagger of the Vrykyl, held it for Valura to see. He clasped her chin, when she would have turned her head away, forced her to look on the dagger, on him.

'Listen to me, my love,' Dagnarus continued, holding the dagger before her frightened gaze, 'with this weapon, I plan to create more of these Vrykyl, as many as my father made Dominion Lords. Each one will give me his life essence and so I will cheat death. I will have the life span of an elf or longer. Think of it! You and I will not be separated. I will not grow old and die while you remain young and beautiful. We will be together always, and it is the Vrykyl who makes this possible. Do not curse Shakur. You should instead be offering him your blessing.'

Valura turned to look upon the Vrykyl, but she did so very reluctantly, very unwillingly. Her eyes met the dead eyes of the animated corpse. She blenched and shuddered. But she did not avert her gaze.

'Forgive me for my silly weakness, my dear one,' she said, through lips so pale and stiff they could barely move.

Dagnarus kissed her tenderly. 'Come, love. This has been a trying day. You are exhausted.'

He assisted Valura back inside the outpost, only to return a few moments later.

'How is she?' Gareth asked anxiously. 'She did not look well.'

'The sight was shocking. My fault. I should have prepared her for it,' Dagnarus replied. 'She will soon come to accept the necessity, but for now, she needs time to adjust, and that will not happen while the Vrykyl is present. Shakur! Ride to Dunkarga. Tell them what has happened. Tell them I have need of the army now. Find out how soon they can be ready to move.'

'I am constrained to obey your command, my Master,' said Shakur. 'But I urge you to reconsider. Your Highness is not yet out of danger, and there are few of us to guard you as it is.'

'I have no need of any guards,' Dagnarus retorted. 'The elves are off on a wild-goose chase. You will do as I command, Shakur. The Dunkargans must be immediately apprised of the situation. Helmos knows that I will turn to Dunkarga for support. My brother may have already ordered his own army to march upon Dunkarga in an effort to forestall me! I gave you an order, Shakur. You will obey me.'

The Vrykyl bowed. Tossing the bloody clothes at Silwyth's feet, the Vrykyl lowered his visor, wheeled his horse, and galloped back through the woods.

'Well, what is the matter now?' Dagnarus demanded, rounding irritably upon Gareth.

'Nothing, Your Highness,' said Gareth.

'You think I acted wrongly to send the Vrykyl away?'

'I think he would have been useful, Your Highness,' Gareth said somberly. 'We must keep watch this night and we are all dropping from weariness.'

'There is nothing out there to watch for!' Dagnarus said angrily. 'But if it will make you happy, I will take the first watch while you and Silwyth sleep. And now make yourself useful. Draw water from the well and see if you can find something for us to eat. Silwyth, do what you can to wash the bloodstains from those clothes.'

Entering the outpost, Dagnarus slammed shut the door with such violent force that he nearly splintered it.

Twilight's afterglow still filled the sky, but night was already starting to creep through the woods. Gareth had no idea how he was supposed to find food. He could use his magic to start a fire, but such magical light – bright and white as the stars against the darkness – would be a beacon to anyone searching for them.

Gareth bent to help Silwyth pick up the clothes. 'Do you believe that Lord Mabreton has truly lost our trail?' he asked softly.

Silwyth gazed out into the gloaming, as if he could part the shadows and see what hid beneath them. Perhaps he did see more than Gareth. Elves have excellent eyesight, far better than humans. When Silwyth spoke, Gareth realized that the elf was not describing what he could see, but what he felt.

'Lord Mabreton has only one objective in life now – vengeance. He feels only one emotion – hatred. He is drawn to the object of his hatred and his vengeance like iron to lodestone. We must all of us keep careful watch this night.'

They kept careful watch that night. Dagnarus said testily that the growling of their stomachs would keep them all awake if nothing else. He had agreed, though with ill humor, that with Lord Mabreton searching for them, it would be folly to light a fire – magical or otherwise – on this high hilltop. Clouds covered the sky, the night was so very dark, darker than Gareth – who had never before spent a night outside of the comfortable walls of home or castle – had ever imagined possible. He dreaded leaving the ramshackle building for fear he should tumble down the well in the darkness or lose himself in the woods, never to find his way back again.

But the need to relieve himself drove him out of the building, searching for the privies in the blinding blackness. Fortunately, they had been built of the same whitish stone as the outpost. He found his way without falling into the well, which was a gaping black hole in the back courtyard.

Silwyth washed the clothes and laid them out to dry upon some large flat rocks that had been heated by the sun. Dagnarus stripped off the white robes, rolled them into a ball, and tossed them into a corner. The night was warm. He would make do with smallclothes until morning. The prince went out to keep the first watch. Valura accompanied him, loath to part from him, if only for a few hours. She had slept some, and was, she said, feeling much stronger.

Gareth lay down to try to sleep, but though he was nearly dropping with fatigue, the day's terrible events so disturbed him that he could not find the rest he desperately sought. He could hear Dagnarus and Valura talking and laughing softly together outdoors. The laughter gave way to harsh breathing and sighs of pleasure. Dagnarus was not keeping very good watch.

Gareth listened to their lovemaking with mingled repulsion, irritation, envy, and resentment. To make matters worse, Silwyth had fallen off to sleep the moment his head had touched the bundled cloak he was using for a pillow. Gareth tossed and turned and tried not to hear; tried not to imagine what was happening only a few feet away from him. But he was still awake when Dagnarus and Valura crept inside, their giggles smothered. He was still awake, though he pretended not to be, when Dagnarus touched his shoulder and told him it was time for him to take the second watch.

Gareth left without a word and took his place, perched uncomfortably on a hollowed-out portion of the outpost's small retaining wall. And then, of course, because he must not fall asleep, sleep came at last. He woke with a guilty start to find Silwyth standing over him.

'Among my people, any warrior who sleeps on guard

duty is not permitted to wake – ever. His throat is slit on the spot.'

'I am sorry,' Gareth said contritely, scrambling to his feet. He glanced about. 'I . . . I don't think I was asleep long.'

'You weren't.' Silwyth was grim. 'I was wakeful and when I heard you begin to mumble, I guessed that you had drifted off. Go inside. Return to your bed. I will take your watch. I rarely sleep more than a few hours at night anyway.'

Gareth made a feeble argument, which Silwyth cut short.

'Be quiet. Do not wake His Highness or the Lady Valura. Let them have one night of peace together, at least.' Silwyth settled himself on the wall, gazed out into the darkness.

Gareth lingered at the elf's side. 'You seem very sure that they will find us.'

'I am.'

'Well, shouldn't we be doing something?' Gareth asked helplessly.

'What war spells do you know, Magus?' Silwyth countered, his voice lilting, mocking.

'None,' Gareth admitted. 'I wasn't studying to be a war magus.'

'Then there is little for you to do except sleep.' Silwyth settled himself more comfortably upon the stone wall, turned his back to Gareth.

Chagrined, Gareth meekly accepted his dismissal and returned to the small fortification. He lay staring into the darkness until sleep rescued him from his fear at last.

FIFTEEN

The Sacrifice

DAGNARUS WOKE IN THE PREDAWN LIGHT. Valura nestled in his arms, her head upon his breast. Her long black hair spilled over his bare arm. Her eyes were closed, she breathed deeply and evenly, secure in his strength, comforted by his warmth. He did not like to disturb her, and so he lay long moments at her side without moving, guarding her sleep.

Outside, the birds' song was loud and cheerful, marking boundaries to their territories. Mating couples squabbled over nest-building. He smoothed the hair from Valura's face with a gentle touch. She had defied her husband for love of him. He was overwhelmed with love for her. Usually his energetic nature, an easy prey to boredom, had him up and out of bed the moment his eyes opened. This day, so peaceful and serene, he thought he might well lie alongside his lady all morning long.

'Your Highness!' Silwyth called softly through the window.

Dagnarus did not answer for fear of waking Valura. He was tempted to ignore the elf, feign sleep, but Silwyth's voice held a note of urgency. Carefully, gently, Dagnarus slid his arm from beneath Valura's head. She murmured in her sleep, her eyelids fluttered, but she did not awaken.

Tenderly, he cradled her head upon the white robes, which they had used for a pillow, and kissed her gently. Levering himself up quietly, he padded soft-footed to the open window.

'Well, what is it?' he demanded, in no very good humor.

'Keep down, Your Highness,' Silwyth cautioned. He was crouched on his haunches beneath the window, gazing intently out into the forest. 'Stay in the shadows.'

'What is it?' Dagnarus asked again. The prince followed his line of the sight. 'What have you seen?'

'Nothing, Your Highness,' Silwyth replied.

'Then why all the creeping and crouching?' Dagnarus demanded, exasperated. 'Listen! Birds are singing, busy and content. They are not spooked.' He pointed to two squirrels, playing a game of tag, jumping from branch to branch. 'Animals roam about freely.'

'And so they would, Your Highness, if an army of ten thousand elves was out there in those woods,' Silwyth said earnestly, his voice soft and low. 'You've fought elves before. You should know, Your Highness. We have an affinity for birds, who are creatures of the air and are pleased to do our bidding. Elven soldiers can move with the silence of ghosts; they could be all around us!'

Dagnarus left the outpost, walked outdoors. He still did not believe that anything was amiss, but as Silwyth said, he had fought elves before and respected them as a cunning and clever enemy. He kept to the shadows as Silwyth had advised.

'Have you seen anything? Heard anything?'

'No, Your Highness. But there is a taste on the air. A scent I do not like. It would be best if we all stayed within –'

'My lord?' Valura's voice, thick with sleep, came from the doorway. She could not see Dagnarus, crouched beneath the window, and she stepped out into the sunshine to search for him.

The arrow flew so swift, so silent that none of them saw it until it struck and soft flesh halted its flight. Valura gasped and sagged back against the door, staring in bewilderment at the feathered shaft buried deep in her thigh. Blood welled around the wound, soaked her silken gown.

Dagnarus gave a hoarse cry of outrage and sprang to his feet.

'No, Your Highness!' Silwyth shouted, attempting to seize hold of the prince and keep him out of danger.

Another arrow sped through the air, aimed at Dagnarus. The arrow would have pierced his heart, had he been an ordinary mortal. The Void, sensing its Lord's danger, acted to shield him. The black armor flowed over his body like dark water, protecting him from attack.

The arrow struck the black breastplate. The shaft vanished in a flash of fire, the arrowhead fell harmlessly to the ground. Dagnarus lifted the fainting Valura in his arms and carried her to safety inside the outpost.

Silwyth leapt through the open window, diving headfirst, amid an angry buzzing of arrows. Gareth, awakened by Dagnarus's cry, slammed shut the door. Arrows thunked into it or whistled eerily through the shutterless window, hitting the far wall.

'Down! Keep down!' Silwyth commanded, grabbing hold of Gareth and dragging him to the floor.

Dagnarus laid Valura upon the white robes. Blood soaked her clothing. She was ashen, her eyes wide and shocked, and she was quivering with the pain. Her breath came in quick, tight gasps. Her hand, sticky with blood, felt for the arrow.

Dagnarus gazed at her in grim despair, then reached for his sword.

'They will rush the building. How many would you estimate –'

'No, Your Highness,' Silwyth cried. 'That is not their plan. They will not attack us, so long as we are inside here.'

'Why? What can they hope to gain by skulking out there in the woods?' Dagnarus demanded, his voice shaking with fury.

'They will not attack because they fear they might kill the Lady Valura. They want her alive,' Silwyth said grimly. He looked at the wound. Blood pulsed from it, flowing fast. Silwyth lifted his gaze to the prince. 'But I fear that this was a poorly aimed shaft, my lord,' he said softly. 'The arrow has pierced a major artery. She cannot survive.'

'What do you know?' Dagnarus demanded angrily, and shoved Silwyth away. 'Are you a healer? My beloved.' He bent over her, took her cold hand in his. 'Beloved!'

'Prince Dagnarus,' cried a voice from outside the window.

'Lord Mabreton,' Silwyth muttered.

'Lord of the Void!' the elf shouted. 'There is no escape for you now. I challenge you to settle this in fair combat. If you are a man of honor, you will accept. First, however, you must give up the unfaithful, honorless, soulless woman who was once known as Lady Mabreton, but whose name is now Whore. I have a healer with me. The Whore will be well treated – better than she deserves. If she is wise, she will request death from me. That would not restore her honor, but it will save her family from disgrace. If not, I will take her back to her home, where her father will determine what is to be her fate.

'You can either send her out,' Lord Mabreton continued, his voice cold and hard, 'or you can watch her bleed to death. I will give you thirty minutes to make your decision.'

Valura thrust out her bloodstained hand, caught hold of Dagnarus's forearm. Her eyes were dark, shadowed with pain.

'No!' she begged him. 'Do not hand me over to him!' She sucked in a shivering breath, her eyes closed in agony. 'I . . . would die first . . .'

Dagnarus knelt beside her, bent to kiss her.

'I will never give you up!' he promised. 'Never! Do something!' he hissed.

Gareth was trying ineffectually to staunch the blood, which oozed out of the wound with the pulsing of the woman's heartbeat. He looked at the prince and shook his head. 'I am not a healer,' he said. 'And there are no healing spells in Void magic. Perhaps, if you could remove the arrow –'

'It's barbed!' Dagnarus said with a bitter curse. 'I have seen men hit with these cursed arrows. If I try to pull it out, I will rip the muscles of her leg out with it. The pain alone could kill her.'

Dagnarus gathered Valura in his arms, held her close. 'My love, my own love! You must not die! You must not leave me!'

Valura opened her eyes. Reaching up her hand, she touched Dagnarus's face through the open visor of the black helm. Her touch left streaks of blood upon his cheek. 'I see the shadows reaching for me,' she said weakly. 'But, there is a way. When I am gone, make me . . . one of them.' She reached out her hand and touched the Dagger of the Vrykyl. 'We will always . . . be together . . .'

'No!' Dagnarus cried, horrified. He laid her back down on the blood-soaked robes. 'No!' he said again, shuddering.

'Lady Valura . . .' Gareth admonished, shocked to the core of his being. 'You do not know what you are saying! These accursed dead have only a mockery of life! They are not truly alive! They feed off the living . . .'

Her fingers, slippery with her own blood, closed spasmodically over the dagger's hilt.

'Dagnarus . . .' Her eyes sought his eyes, met them, held them. 'I will not leave you . . . ever. I give my soul . . . to the Void.'

'Oh, gods! No!' Dagnarus moaned and fell to his knees at her side.

Valura said no word, made no sound. He could do nothing but watch her life ebb away. Her gaze remained on him for as long as she could see him, until death blotted him from her sight. Her hand, touching the dagger, went limp. Her eyes continued to stare at Dagnarus, but the stare was fixed, unseeing.

Dagnarus did not move. He said nothing, made no further outcry. He knelt beside her for so long that it seemed he might have turned to stone, been granted at last the Transfiguration that had been denied him. Gareth sat back, dazed and stunned by the tragedy, unable to react. Silwyth, with a deep sigh, leaned forward to shut the staring eyes.

'Don't touch her!' Dagnarus ordered savagely.

His lips compressed. After a moment's hesitation, he lifted the dagger.

'I will honor her last wish,' he said through clenched teeth. 'Is she an acceptable candidate?'

'I forbid it, Your Highness!' Silwyth cried, and tried to snatch the dagger.

Dagnarus backhanded the elf, striking him a blow that knocked him across the room. Silwyth slammed up against the wall and collapsed in a crumpled heap.

Dagnarus did not look to see if the elf was dead or alive. He laid the dagger on Valura's still breast.

'Your Highness,' said Gareth harshly. 'Are you certain this is what you want? Think! Think what she will become! A monster –'

The word died on his lips. He shrank from the prince's terrible fury.

'Tell me!' Dagnarus commanded. Foam flecked his lips. His eyes were dark and sunken in his head. 'Remind me of what I must do!'

'Her blood . . .' Gareth began hesitantly.

'Her life!' Dagnarus cried, and he bent and placed his lips upon the wound, sucking her blood as a child suckles at the breast of its mother.

'Put . . . put the dagger on her . . . breast,' Gareth said faintly, stricken with pity and horror. 'The dragon's head . . . toward her head. The crosspiece aligned . . .' He could not continue. Sick and dizzy, he feared he might faint.

Dagnarus's lips were stained with her blood. He arranged the dagger on Valura's breast, drew back his hand, and waited.

Slowly, the dagger began to rise into the air. The scales of the dragon, black and glistening, fell from the dagger, pierced Valura's flesh. Wherever the scales touched, they burrowed their way beneath the skin, flowed together until her body was encased in a hard, black shell of shining armor.

Dagnarus watched, his face like stone, implacable, immovable. A black helm, adorned with the wings of a bird, wings as black as those of a crow, covered Valura's face. Black-mailed gloves encased her hands. No part of her flesh remained visible. She was swallowed up by the darkness.

Valura's hand stirred, reached up, lifted the visor of the helm. Her eyes opened. They held no life, were dark and cold and fixed with a glassy stare. The eyes sought Dagnarus. Her gaze, with no life in it, rested on him.

'I am with you,' she said to him. 'Always.' She reached out her gloved hand.

He caught hold of her hand, pressed her fingers to his lips. 'Always,' he said. His words came from lips stained with her blood and were colder, more dead than hers, which spoke from the realm of death.

'Your time is up!' shouted Lord Mabreton. 'Send out the Whore or we will come in and drag her out.'

'Yes,' said Dagnarus softly. 'I will send you your wife.' He glanced carelessly behind him. 'Silwyth. Are you loyal to me, or do you now wish to be counted among my enemies?'

The elf had regained consciousness. He shook his head to clear it, felt his jaw. Blood oozed from a split and swollen lip. He cast one look at the new-made Vrykyl, a look of revulsion, and quickly averted his gaze.

'I am your servant, Your Highness, as always,' he said, wiping away blood. 'Forgive my recent failure.'

'You are forgiven,' said Dagnarus coolly. 'The Lady Valura is going to give herself up to her husband. You will accompany her.'

The Vrykyl had altered shape and form. Gone was the black armor and the bird-wing helm. Valura, as beautiful as she had been in life, wounded and seemingly helpless, languished on the blood-soaked robes. Her cold, dead gaze met Silwyth's. A shudder shook his frame. His face paled, but he did not falter.

'I will not fail you, Your Highness,' he said, and, bending down, he lifted the Vrykyl that had once been the Lady Valura in his arms.

Silwyth could feel the terrible cold of the Void and the smooth, brittle hardness of the black armor that the illusion hides, but never replaces. Silwyth's back was to Dagnarus. Only Gareth saw the struggle within the elf, a struggle so fierce he could not conceal it, as he was forced to touch the cursed corrupt creature of the Void.

'What are your orders, Your Highness?' Silwyth asked, a slight, very slight, catch in his voice.

'Carry the Lady Valura' – he did not call her Vrykyl, as he always did Shakur – 'to the clearing and set her down. Lord Mabreton will send his men to fetch her. You, my love, will deal with them.'

Valura nodded and smiled a terrible smile.

'I will answer Lord Mabreton's challenge,' Dagnarus said. His hand clenched over the hilt of his sword. 'I look forward to it. Gareth. The elven archers are hiding in these woods. At my signal, you will set the forest ablaze. Silwyth, when you have finished your task with the Lady Valura, you will run to the stables, lead the horses to a place of safety, away from the flames. We will join you shortly, when our work outside is finished.'

'They are bringing her out now, my lord,' reported one of the elven retainers.

Lord Mabreton watched in grief and bitter sorrow as the prince's servant, Silwyth, carried the wounded elf woman from the crumbling outpost. Lord Mabreton had truly loved his beautiful wife. Indeed, the lord had committed the very grave sin of loving her when she had been the wife of his brother. The lord had gallantly kept his illicit love hidden and would have carried it to his grave had not the untimely death of his brother made it possible for that love to be properly expressed.

He was aware that Valura did not return his love, but he had hoped to be able, through patience and kindness, to win her heart as he had won her hand in marriage. Their last months together had given him reason to hope that he was succeeding. For the first time in their marriage, Valura had been warm and responsive in their bed. She had seemed more cheerful, had ceased to complain about living among the humans. She had appeared to take an interest in her husband and what he did and said.

Now the lord knew the real reason for her sudden enjoyment of their lovemaking – she was acting a role, loving him in order to mask the stench of another man's love. Her sudden happiness could be attributed to the same cause. Lord Mabreton recalled her every move, every word, and wondered how he could have been so blind. The nights he had awakened to find her gone from their bed. She had been unable to sleep, she had told him, and had gone to walk in the cool air. The nights she spent in the castle, rather than in their home, claiming that the Queen had requested her to stay.

Lord Mabreton now hated the woman for the shame

she had brought to him and to his House. He had ordered the archers to shoot her in the leg, crippling her. The healers would keep her alive, but she would be subjected to agonizing torment that would end only in ignominious death, at his hands, if she had any scrap of honor left in her. Yet he could not look upon her, as the elf servant laid her gently on the ground, could not look upon her beauty that was still wondrous without feeling his love for her stir in his heart.

His eyes filled with tears. He turned from his men that they might not see his weakness. The prince's elven servant bowed in the direction of the unseen lord.

'My master, Prince Dagnarus, accepts the challenge of Lord Mabreton and will meet him in single combat upon this ground that is stained with the blood of the Lady Valura.'

'Excellent,' said Lord Mabreton. He wore the armor of the Dominion Lord, magical armor that shone silver in the sunlight. 'I will rid the world of this demon prince.'

'What of the prince's servant, Silwyth, my lord?' asked one of the archers, raising his bow, arrow nocked. 'He is a disgrace to our people. I have a clear shot at him.'

'Leave him be,' Lord Mabreton ordered tersely. 'The ancestors will deal with him.'

In truth, the lord knew that Silwyth was in the service of the Shield and that the Shield thought quite highly of the young elf. Lord Mabreton had no intention of being the one to kill the Shield's favorite spy.

'Two of you men, go fetch the female. Carry her to the healers. They are to treat her well and give her what ease they choose. She will have to ride at least part of the way back to the road, where she will then be placed in a litter for the journey home.'

The elves did as they were ordered. Two laid down their weapons and advanced into the compound, where Valura lay on a blanket, weak from loss of blood and fainting with pain. Yet, when the elven men came near her, she found the strength to lift her head and raise herself up on one arm.

'Do not touch me!' she ordered with a scathing glance. 'I will make my own way!'

Refusing their assistance, she pushed herself painfully off the ground, struggled to her feet. The arrow's shaft was still embedded in her thigh. She grimaced and gasped aloud when she was forced to put her weight upon her injured leg, almost fell. With great effort, she managed to remain standing, however. She limped forward, her lips compressed against the pain, her face ashen. Every step must have been agony for her, but she persevered, refusing all offers of aid.

Such courage and fortitude, even in one disgraced, is much admired. The elven soldiers murmured their approval. Lord Mabreton had to look away again, suppressing the urge to run forward and clasp her in his arms, to pardon her and take her back. Duty to his family would never permit such an act.

He waited until he could assure himself, by sneaking covert glances at her, that she was making her way to the healers. She moved slowly and painfully, leaning against tree trunks to aid her hobbling steps, but she continued to walk on her own. The guards came behind her, not offering to touch her, for every time one of them made a move toward her, she repelled him with a scornful, furious look.

'Lord Mabreton!' came a cold voice. 'I grow impatient.'

The Dominion Lord tore his gaze away from the woman who had once been his wife and focused on her demon lover.

Drawing his sword, Lord Mabreton went forward to meet the challenge.

*   *   *

'Remember, Your Highness,' Gareth warned Dagnarus, as the prince was about to set forth, 'the sword of a Dominion Lord is a blessed weapon, one that can be fatal to you.'

'But even then, Patch,' Dagnarus answered glibly, 'he will have to kill me twice.'

The two combatants, one clad all in silver and shining like the dawn, the other clad in black and dark as empty night, met on the field of honor. Visors lowered, the combatants could not see each other's faces, only the eyes through the eye slits. Each watched the eyes of his opponent, hoping to be able to judge where the next blow would fall.

They circled. Once Dagnarus lashed out with his sword, a slash easily parried by Lord Mabreton. The elf made a furious chop with his blade which was turned aside by Dagnarus. The two were measuring each other, each testing his opponent's strength and agility and skill. The opponents were evenly matched, that much was soon apparent.

Gareth turned from the window. He had to prepare for his magic, had to nerve himself to face the considerable pain casting such a powerful spell would cost him. He came to stand side by side with Silwyth in the open doorway to watch.

'For whom do you cheer?' the elf asked softly, his eyes on the combatants.

'For His Highness, of course,' Gareth answered.

The elf's gaze – dark and cynical – flicked to Gareth. Gareth tried to meet that gaze and found he couldn't. He looked back at the contest.

Dagnarus was a skilled warrior. He fought well in the tumult of battle, where the soldier has little time to think, but must react swiftly and instinctively to constantly changing conditions. Dagnarus lacked the patience of the skilled duelist, however. The elf lord's feints, dodges, and maneuverings soon angered the prince, who wanted to bring the contest to a swift end. Dagnarus began to make mistakes.

Silwyth clucked his tongue, exactly as he had done when the boys were young and the prince was being particularly obstinate and headstrong.

The sound took Gareth back to the playroom. He could not mourn lost innocence; he had left that behind the moment he had set foot in the castle. But he could mourn lost dreams. Shining silver and glistening black blurred in his vision. He lowered his head for a moment. Beside him, Silwyth caught his breath.

Fear rending his heart, Gareth look up swiftly to see Lord Mabreton thrust his sword into Dagnarus's chest. The blade of the Dominion Lord, blessed by the gods, pierced the black armor of the Lord of the Void with ease.

Lord Mabreton jerked his sword free. Blood followed it, washing over Dagnarus's black armor.

Dagnarus did not cry out. Letting his sword fall from his flaccid hand, he stared down at the gaping wound, at his blood flowing freely, and he seemed astonished. He sank to his knees. He pressed his hand over his chest.

As chivalry and honor commanded, Lord Mabreton would make no further attack on the dying man. The Dominion Lord handed his weapon to his squire to wipe off the blood. Arms folded across his chest, Lord Mabreton prepared to watch his enemy die.

Dagnarus made as if to fall forward. At the last moment, he seized his sword. Leaping to his feet, he lunged forward. Amazed and horrified, not believing what his senses told him was impossible, Lord Mabreton stood weaponless, helpless to halt the attack. Dagnarus plunged his blade into Lord Mabreton's throat.

The stroke was brutal, vicious. The black sword cut through the silver armor, severed the man's head from his body. Lord Mabreton was dead before his corpse keeled over. The squire made a desperate swipe at the attacker with his fallen lord's sword. Dagnarus bashed the squire in the face with his mailed fist, snapping the man's neck. Standing over the decapitated body of the elven Dominion Lord, Dagnarus raised his blood-slimed sword.

'Who is next?' he shouted, his voice echoing hideously from beneath his helm. 'Who will next challenge the Lord of the Void?'

From down the hill where the healers had carried Valura came fearful screams and cries – the fainting lady had transformed into a black avised bird of death, ripping apart the flesh of those who had murdered her.

'You must go now, Gareth,' said Silwyth. His voice was calm, revealed no emotion. 'You have your orders.'

Gareth did indeed have his orders. Cloaking himself in the darkness of the Void, he slipped out the door, unseen by the distracted elven archers, and ran around the back of the building. The thought came to his mind to keep running, run until he reached the edge of the cliff and keep running then – straight into blessed oblivion. He did not leap off the cliff, however. Not because he lacked the courage to kill himself – death would have been very easy for him now. He did not because inside he was already dead. Inside, he was as much a Vrykyl as Valura or Shakur. Only when Dagnarus died would the Vrykyl be freed from their cursed existence. Only when Dagnarus died would Gareth be freed of his.

As for Dagnarus, he had died already. His curse was to keep dying, over and over, over and over, over and over.

That night, the people of Vinnengael left their houses and gathered in the streets to watch a great fire burning on the top of Beacon Hill. All knew the outpost had long been abandoned; a hundred years had passed since a beacon fire had burned on that hilltop. This fire was obviously magical, for the white flames were green and purple at their heart. Their tongues leapt so high in the air that it seemed they might lick the stars.

The King and the Most Revered High Magus kept watch all night, observing the fire from the tower room.

'What do you think it is?' Helmos asked, after they had been watching, in silence, for an hour.

'I dread to speculate, Your Majesty,' Reinholt replied.

'Is it the magic of the Void?' Helmos stood before the window, staring at the silhouettes of distant trees, stark black skeletons against a backdrop of flame.

'Yes, Your Majesty,' answered the High Magus. 'It is the magic of the Void.'

The fire raged all night, eventually dying out in the morning. Thick smoke and ash roiled down the mountain, casting a pall over the city. Coughing and choking, people remained inside their houses, shut their windows and blocked the doors with blankets to keep the smoke out of their homes. The black smoke had a noxious odor, and the rumor spread that it was poisonous to breathe.

The orken left, every one of them, the shaman having reportedly told the Captain that the omens were among the worst she had ever witnessed in her life. Crowding aboard their ships, the orken set sail, taking advantage of the same wind that was carrying the cursed smoke down from the mountains.

The elves remained, to find out what had become of Lord Mabreton.

That day, they had their answer.

Captain Argot entered the palace, requested to see the King.

The King, the captain was told, was with his father.

Argot entered the hall where Tamaros lay in state. The body of the King, clad in red robes trimmed in gold, and covered with a blanket of purple cloth, lay upon a catafalque, with candles burning at his head and his feet. Around him, in the hallway, stood the empty suits of armor, keeping their dull and unending vigil over death.

Helmos sat on a chair at the King's side. The former King looked serene, calm, at peace. The new King's head was bowed with worry and doubt, their rising tide overwhelming his grief.

Captain Argot knelt in respect to the deceased King, then rose and advanced to make his report to the living one.

'What did you find?' Helmos asked.

In answer, Captain Argot held out a pendant. The pendant had once been shining silver, was now tarnished and blackened. Helmos took the pendant, stared at it. His eyes closed in anguish, his hand clenched over it.

'It is the pendant of a Dominion Lord. Lord Mabreton's, Your Majesty,' Captain Argot said. 'I recognize it.'

'No Dominion Lord ever removes his pendant,' Helmos replied, his voice heavy. 'Not unless he is dead.'

'We found the bodies of his men, Your Majesty. Most of the elves died in the blaze, which has completely blackened the hillside. Some did not, however. We found several . . .' Argot hesitated.

'Go on, Captain,' Helmos said.

'We found several elves who had not perished in the flames. Each of these – and they appeared to have been healers, Your Majesty, not soldiers – had been dismembered. We did not find Lord Mabreton's body at all. Only the pendant.'

'No trace of my bro –' Helmos halted, drew in a sharp breath. 'No trace of Dagnarus?'

'No, Your Majesty. Although we heard reports from the peasants who live between here and Dunkarga, rumors of demons riding steeds of darkness along the road toward Dunkarga. The peasants are ignorant, superstitious folk, Your Majesty . . .'

'Thank you, Captain.' Helmos turned away, turned to rest his hand upon his father's cold and lifeless hand.

'What are your orders, Your Majesty?' the captain asked. 'Forgive me for disturbing you, but the city is in an uproar –'

Helmos did not look around. He clasped his father's hand, sighed deeply.

'Prepare for war, Captain. Those are my orders. Prepare for war.'

PART
THREE

ONE

Split Apart

THE SHIELD OF THE DIVINE REVERENTIALLY approached the shrine dedicated to his Honored Ancestor. He wore his finest robes, for his mother had always maintained that she could judge a man's character by the quality of the silk he selected to clothe his body. The Shield carried in his own hands a honeyed oat cake – a favorite treat of the Honored Ancestor. Servants walked behind him, bowing every few feet as they approached the most sacred part of the house. They carried an ornate dragon pot filled with orange peel and black pepper tea and two small cups of porcelain so fine that one could almost see through them.

The Shield placed the oat cake in front of the shrine and directed the arrangement of the teacups. He dismissed the servants, poured the tea himself – the Honored Ancestor would appreciate the distinction. Then, sipping his tea, he waited until she should arrive.

The ghost of the old lady was not long in coming. Her watery image, accompanied by a faint fragrance of honeysuckle, appeared across the table from the Shield. Although the Honored Ancestor no longer had need of nourishment, nor could the Honored Ancestor drink the tea, she was pleased by the sentiment expressed with the offer.

After the formalities had been completed – after the Honored Ancestor had inquired anxiously about the state of health of every single member of the Shield's immediate family, including his fourteen children, and after the Shield had politely inquired after his other ancestors: great-grandfather and great-grandmother, great-aunts and great-uncles and even a favorite cousin, who had died untimely in battle, the two settled down to discuss business.

'The messenger from King Helmos arrived this morning, Honored Mother,' said the Shield, reaching into his robes and removing a scroll. He laid it down upon the table, rested his hand upon it. 'A Dominion Lord brought it, a Lord Altura. You see here the human King's request, which the Lord delivered with her own hands. The request is not what we expected.'

'Soldiers, gold, weapons,' said the lady, her eyes – the most solid part of her – bright as the eyes of a cardinal. She went through the motions of drinking tea, in order to keep her son from feeling embarrassment over drinking his tea when she could have none. 'He does not ask for any of those?'

'He does, of course, but only for form's sake,' the Shield replied. 'He has his spies, who tell him, no doubt, that elves comprise a goodly portion of Prince Dagnarus's forces. He knows that these troops entered human lands by my command or, if not that, at least with my knowledge.'

'He might think they came from the Divine,' the ghost observed, eyeing the honeyed oat cake wistfully.

'King Helmos understands that the Divine is my puppet and that he twitches only when I tug on his strings. I have maintained publicly that the elven forces fighting with Prince Dagnarus are renegades, but Helmos is no fool.'

'Send him an army, too,' the Honored Ancestor suggested. 'So long as we kill humans and gain our objectives, what does it matter whose side we're on?'

'I considered doing just that, but it is not an army he wants.'

The Shield shifted his gaze to an elaborate case made of gold and crystal, which stood in the most honored place on the household altar. Within the case, mounted upon a pedestal covered in purple velvet, was a singular jewel, formed in the shape of a triangle with smooth-planed sides. The diamond reflected the light of the altar candles, shimmered with myriad tiny rainbows.

'The Sovereign Stone!' said the ghost suddenly, sharply.

'Yes, Honored Mother.' The Shield bowed. 'That is why I thought it best to remove the stone from the garden where it was kept and bring it here to our house. King Helmos requests the stone's return. One might almost say – demands.'

'Ah!' The Honored Ancestor frowned and forgot her imaginary tea. The birdlike eyes glinted, narrowed. 'That presents a difficulty. Is he then in such dire need? Does he truly think the demon prince can seize the crown?' She shook her ghostly head. 'Even if the Lord of the Void were to lay siege to the city, Vinnengael is a mighty fortress. Their stockpiles of food could last for months. They have an unending supply of water. What has King Helmos to fear? It is not' – the ghost sniffed – 'not like *we* elves were pitting our might against him. Then the human King might indeed have cause to worry.'

'Yet we do not send our might against Vinnengael for those very reasons,' the Shield said, and poured himself another cup of tea. 'That and the fact that we make far more money by trading with the humans than we ever could subjugating them. No, it seems to me that it would be best if we left the humans to slit each other's throats and when they have drained each other of blood, we seize the borderlands we want and then grow rich by selling them the wood and other raw materials they will need in order to rebuild their lives.

'That is my plan, and I think it is a good one. However' – the Shield set down his cup, looked concerned – 'I did not anticipate that the King would ask for the return of the Sovereign Stone.'

'And why is this a problem?' asked the Honored Ancestor. 'Simply tell him that it is ours, and we intend to keep it.'

'The matter is not that simple, Honored Mother. When I accepted the stone, I swore an oath to the gods. We all swore it. If one of the four who each holds a portion of the stone should ever be in dire need, the other three would return their portions of the stone, so that it may be joined together.'

'And what happens when the stone is joined together?' the ghostly lady asked, a shrewd gleam in her eyes.

The Shield reflected. 'I do not know,' he said at last. 'Its magical power will be increased fourfold, I should imagine.'

'And all that power in the hands of the human king.' The ghost pursed her lips.

'True, Honored Mother,' said the Shield, nodding. 'I had thought of that.'

'You see his plan, of course, my son,' the Honored Ancestor said. 'Helmos does not really need the power of the stone to fight a civil war with his brother. No! King Helmos is using this war as an excuse to regain the stone, which his father heedlessly gave away. I have heard it said that there were those among his own advisors who counseled King Tamaros that the stone should not be split at all. When King Helmos has the stone intact, he will use its power to defeat his brother. But he will not stop there. He will then turn his greedy gaze upon us. We would defeat him, of course,' the Honored Ancestor said with sublime unconcern. 'But the battle would cost many elven lives.'

'You are wise, Honored Mother,' said the Shield, bowing from the waist. 'It is small wonder that I come to you for counsel.'

The ghost smiled, well pleased.

'But,' continued the Shield, 'I swore an oath to the gods. I would not be foresworn. To do so would be to lose face and plunge our family into disgrace. The Divine would be certain to find out, and he would claim, and rightly so, that having broken one oath, I could not be trusted to keep any oath.'

'When will Prince Dagnarus launch his attack?' the Honored Ancestor asked.

'According to Silwyth, my spy in the prince's household, the prince moves slowly. He has gathered his forces. He could be ready to advance with the rising of the new moon, although that is not certain. He enjoys seeing his brother sweat.'

The ghostly lady smiled sweetly. 'This is what you do, my son. You will tell this Dominion Lord that you must know the will of the Father and Mother in regard to the Sovereign Stone. This will require prayer, fasting, solemn ceremony, the gathering of all the priests in the realm, the intercession of the Divine . . .'

'In this, I can guarantee that for once the Divine and I will be in agreement, Honored Mother,' the Shield interjected. 'He is as loath to part with the Sovereign Stone as I.'

'Excellent. It will take at least six months to bring together the priests, some of whom must travel from their holy shrines in the high mountaintops. After that, the ceremonial games to honor the gods and the offering of the proper sacrifices will take another two months and then there is the interpretation of the gods' answer. That can sometimes take a full year or more . . .'

The Shield rose respectfully to his feet and bowed deeply three times. 'May this House always rely upon you for wisdom, Honored Mother,' he said earnestly. 'And may you always be here to guide us.'

Seating himself again, he moved on to discuss family

matters, which took up some time. Then they played a game of mah-jongg.

There was, after all, no need for haste.

The Captain of Captains was happily ensconced in his favorite tavern in the coastal city of Quash'Gaat, enjoying his two favorite pastimes: drinking his favorite liquor and endeavoring to solve a tangram. The liquor's orken name is 'cha-gow' which roughly translates as 'breast milk' or 'mother's milk.' Few humans can stand to smell cha-gow, much less stomach the stuff, which is reputed to be made from fish oil mixed with fermented pineapple.

The tangram is a puzzle consisting of a square piece of wood divided into seven parts: five triangles, a square, and a rhomboid. These parts can be combined to form two equal squares – child's play. The pieces can also be used to create hundreds of figures from boats to bottles, beasts to men. The Captain had been challenged to make the tangram into an albatross, a puzzle that might have been fairly simple for him had he not been under a time constraint of sixty-seven foot thumps.

The time was being counted out loud with the enthusiastic and rhythmic stomping of many booted orken feet, for the tavern was filled to capacity that day. A storm had kept the fishing boats in port and prevented the ships from setting out to sea. The floor of the tavern shook with the stamping, as did the table on which the Captain was endeavoring to sort out the tangram, causing the puzzle to jiggle violently and throwing off his concentration.

'Fifty-six, fifty-seven . . .' chanted the orken, now slamming the flats of their hands upon the tables or banging the tables with their mugs.

The Captain had just about got it, was moving the rhomboid into position, when a commotion broke out in the vicinity of the tavern's entrance.

'In the King's name!' called a human voice. 'Let me pass!'

'King of what?' the orken roared back. 'What *is* his name?' 'No kings around here, thanks, come back another day' and other witticisms greeted the speaker.

The Captain shifted his head to see what was going on and inadvertently moved his hand from the pieces of the puzzle.

'You lose!' shouted the shaman, seated at the table across from him.

'Sixty-one, sixty-two.' Some voices were still counting, though most – on hearing the game had ended – had petered out.

The Captain, swiveling, glared at the shaman with a baleful expression. 'I still have time!'

'You took your hand away,' the shaman pointed out. 'That means you are finished and that' – she gazed with disdain at the puzzle pieces – 'is no albatross that I ever saw!'

'I haven't put on the beak yet!' the Captain roared.

'In the King's name!' The human voice sounded angry. 'I have a message for the Captain!'

'You owe for this round,' said the shaman, gulping down her cha-gow with satisfaction.

Glowering, the Captain paid up, then turned, in no very good humor, to confront the human who had been the cause of his losing.

The human, who was wearing shining silver armor, had not been able to make his way around the doorway, where the orken were entertaining themselves by sticking out their feet when he tried to move past them, tripping him, or 'accidentally' bumping him back out the door.

'Let him come to me,' the Captain ordered, recognizing one of the Dominion Lords.

The Captain's commands were always carried out with the utmost alacrity, for the Captain was known to demand a high order of discipline on his ship. The human was seized upon by several orken and hustled through the crowd so fast that the man's feet never touched the floor until the orken plopped him down, with his dignity much affronted, in front of the Captain.

'The human, as ordered, sir!' one of the orken reported, touching his forehead in salute.

The Captain raised his hand for quiet. The tavern was immediately plunged into a silence so deep they might have all been on the ocean floor.

'I have been sent by . . . King Helmos of Vinnengael,' said the lord, catching his breath. 'I bear an urgent message to you, the Captain, from His Majesty the King.'

The Dominion Lord paused, seeming to expect some sort of reply.

'You wouldn't be much of a messenger if you didn't bear a message,' observed the Captain obligingly.

His Lordship tried again. 'The message is from King Helmos. It is very urgent.'

'Then spit it out, man!' the Captain ordered irritably. 'I know who it's from. No need to keep repeating it.'

Lowering his voice, the lord leaned forward. 'The message is private, Captain. For you alone.'

A murmur of displeasure rumbled through the bar, once again shaking the floor. The Captain snorted and waved his hand. 'This concerns the orken people, does it not?'

'Well, my lord . . .' The messenger hesitated.

'Speak it out for all to hear,' the Captain insisted. 'I have no secrets from my people.'

The Dominion Lord couldn't make himself heard for a few minutes because of the table thumping and thigh-slapping which marked the orken's approval of their Captain's words.

When silence was once more restored, the lord said, 'Reliable information leads King Helmos to believe that the city of Vinnengael will shortly come under attack from

Dagnarus, the Lord of the Void. In order that the people of Vinnengael may fend off this unwarranted and most unjust attack, King Helmos requests that the orken return their portion of the Sovereign Stone to Vinnengael, thus fulfilling the oath the Captain made to King Tamaros and his heirs in perpetuity.'

The Captain kept his gaze on the human throughout this recital. At the end, the Captain blinked once and asked him to repeat it. The messenger did so and proffered the request in writing, which the ork took out of politeness. He looked at the flowing script with some admiration and not a little distrust and dropped it onto the table, where it began to soak up spilled cha-gow.

The Captain gave the matter due consideration and then said, with a dismissive gesture, 'Tell King Helmos no.'

Apparently this was not the answer the Dominion Lord expected. 'But, Captain, you swore an oath before the gods to return the stone when it was needed! Surely you will not break your sacred vow?'

The Captain looked to his shaman. 'What was the day on which I swore that oath?'

'Third day,' said the shaman. The orken name their days by the order of their appearance within an eleven-day span of time.

'Third day,' the Captain repeated. 'All know that third day is the most unlucky day of the week and that all vows sworn or all promises made on a third day are only good until the next third day.'

The orken around him nodded sagely.

'I doubt that King Tamaros knew that,' said the Dominion Lord, an angry flush starting to rise in his face.

'That is his fault then,' said the Captain dourly. 'Not mine.'

'But to break your oath to the gods –'

'The gods know that third day is unlucky,' the Captain said. 'They will not be offended.'

The Dominion Lord lowered his voice. 'Sir, King Helmos's need is dire. The Lord of the Void has many foul magicks at his hand that he will hurl against us. He has created more demons of the Void known as Vrykyl to lead his army. If you do not return the Sovereign Stone, there is a possibility that Vinnengael will fall!'

'And if we send our part of the rock to Vinnengael and if Vinnengael falls and if Dagnarus wins, he will acquire our portion of the Sovereign Stone as well as the humans' portion and the elven and the dwarven portion. And then what?' the Captain demanded.

'I . . . I don't . . .' The Dominion Lord was taken aback.

'I'll tell you. Dagnarus will then be powerful enough to rule the orken and the elves and the dwarves and the humans and possibly the gods themselves into the bargain,' the Captain stated succinctly. 'The orken part of the Sovereign Stone remains with us to protect us should Vinnengael fall, which you say now seems likely.'

'But, if you send the stone as you promised, Vinnengael will *not* fall!' The Dominion Lord pleaded his cause. 'The elves and the dwarves are going to send theirs!'

'Are you sure of that?' The Captain eyed the human with amusement. 'Does your King have their stones now in his possession?'

'Not when I left,' the Dominion Lord admitted. 'Three of us set out at the same time, each bound for a different realm. It took me longer to find you than I had expected and thus –'

'None will send them,' said the Captain, and turned back to his tangram.

'I hope and pray and trust that you are wrong, sir,' said the lord.

'I will make you a wager,' offered the Captain, not looking up from the puzzle pieces. 'If the other two parts of the Sovereign Stone are returned, I will send mine. But not until then. Tell your King that.'

504

'I doubt your stone would arrive in time,' said the Dominion Lord bitterly. 'Dagnarus is forming his army even as we speak. But I thank you for that much at least.'

Bowing, he left the tavern. The orken, at a glance and a raised eyebrow from their Captain, stood aside to let the King's messenger pass by unmolested.

'Give him an escort to the Portal,' said the Captain, looking after the human with a sad shake of his head. 'Someone that feeble-minded shouldn't be allowed to wander around loose.'

The messenger to the dwarves had a difficult task finding Dunner, the sole dwarven Dominion Lord. The messenger located Dunner's dwelling – a modest structure made of clay, built low to the ground. The Dominion Lord peered inside the house, even entered and wandered through it, searching for the dwarf. He found no sign of him, no sign that the dwelling was currently occupied. However, most dwellings of the Unhorsed do not look occupied to the casual observer. The dwarves do not adorn their dwellings with knickknacks. They own no cherished treasures. There are no comfortable chairs in which to take one's ease, no carved bedsteads hung with velvet curtains, no chests filled with clothing or cabinets filled with crockery.

The dwellings of the Unhorsed are furnished as sparsely as those of their nomadic kinsmen. Any one of the households in the City of the Unhorsed could be packed up and ready to transport on horseback in the space of a few moments. Since many of their occupants are housebound, unable to walk, much less ride, such impermanence gives the permanent dwellings a rather wistful air. The occupants will never depart until they leave behind their crippled bodies and enter the Wolf's body to roam forever over grassy plains – a time most eagerly await.

Dunner's furnishing contained a bundle of blankets spread over a straw mattress; a plate, a dish, a spoon, and a mug; and a finely woven rug meant for sitting. The only difference between Dunner's dwelling and those of the other Unhorsed was a great stack of books in a corner and sheaves of vellum, together with pen and ink, placed under the books to keep the vellum flat and clean. The walls of the dwelling were bare. The only chair was a chair on wheels, and this seemed to be more of a relic than useful, for it was covered with dust.

The Dominion Lord asked a neighbor if Dunner had left the city, but the dwarven woman only shrugged her shoulders. She had no idea where Dunner was, did not want to know. Her own sorrows occupied all her time. She had no need of those that burdened her neighbors.

'Where will I find the Sovereign Stone, then?' asked the Dominion Lord. 'I ask out of the greatest urgency, Madam.'

The dwarven woman eyed him sullenly. 'I never heard of any "sovering stone." There is some sort of a rock that came from the human kingdom and that Dunner seems to fancy. If that is what you mean, you will find it in that tent, not far from here.'

She snorted derisively and hobbled away before the Dominion Lord could recover from his shock at hearing the most precious and sacred Sovereign Stone referred to as 'some sort of a rock.'

The Dominion Lord set off in search of the 'sovering stone.' He was in a bit of a quandary. By rights, Dunner was the stone's official guardian, and his permission was required in order to transport the dwarven portion of the stone back to Vinnengael. But there was every possibility that Dunner had wandered off somewhere as dwarves were known to do. He might be a hundred, even a thousand miles from here. The Dominion Lord could search for years and not find the dwarf.

Yet, here was the Sovereign Stone seemingly. Undoubtedly Dunner had left someone to guard the stone in his absence. The Dominion Lord decided that if he could gain the guardian's permission, he would be free to honorably remove the Sovereign Stone without Dunner's consent. The Dominion Lord was relieved to think that the stone might be in other hands, hands that had not shaken in friendship the hand of the Lord of the Void.

The Dominion Lord touched his pendant, prayed to the gods to bless his errand. His magical armor flowed over him as cooling as water on a hot day. He did not plan to intimidate these dwarven guardians, but he did hope to impress them, as he hoped to impress upon them the urgency and importance of his cause. Stooping low to enter the doorway, which was built to dwarven height, the Dominion Lord halted in the shadows and stared.

The Sovereign Stone was there, the diamond sparkling from atop a wooden box covered with a horse blanket. The blanket was finely woven and extremely beautiful but there was no doubting it was a horse blanket. And there were no guards around it. The only people in the building were six or seven dwarven children, who were – or so it seemed – using the sacred Sovereign Stone for a plaything!

As the Dominion Lord watched, too shocked to be able to speak, one of the children – a girl with a withered arm – took hold of the Sovereign Stone and removed it from its place upon the horse blanket. The stone was attached to a thong made of braided horsehair. The girl placed the sacred Sovereign Stone around her neck.

The other children bowed to the girl and reached out to touch her, as if for luck. They seemed to be serious about their play – the Dominion Lord had to credit them with that much. They weren't giggling. They weren't making a mockery of the stone. But the Sovereign Stone was not a toy!

The Dominion Lord now felt no qualms at all about removing the stone from dwarven hands. It would not be returned until the dwarves could assure the Council that the stone would be honored and treated with respect.

He stepped out of the shadows and into a pool of sunlight streaming through an opening in the tent roof.

'What is the meaning of this?' he demanded, speaking dwarven, his voice quite stern.

The children were startled, both at the unexpected voice and the amazing appearance of the silver-clad lord, who had to stand with bowed head and shoulders else his helm would have punched through the canvas. But the children weren't awed or frightened. Standing their ground, they regarded him suspiciously. Four of them placed themselves between him and the girl wearing the stone. He considered that part of the game, and as such it irritated him.

'Hand that to me!' he ordered the children. 'The Sovereign Stone is not a toy! It is a holy artifact, given to us by the gods.'

'Who are you, human?' asked the girl wearing the stone around her neck. Dwarves with their deep, gruff voices, would have considered her child's voice shrill, but she sounded like a human adult to the Dominion Lord. 'And what right do you have to enter our holy temple?'

'Temple,' he murmured. It had not occurred to him before now that this tent could be a temple, the wooden box and the horse blanket a dwarven notion of an altar.

If that was true, he had committed a grave error. The children were right, and he was in the wrong. He had entered their 'temple' without permission, and he had not introduced himself as would any true chivalrous lord.

'I am Gregor,' he said. 'A Dominion Lord of Vinnengael. My allegiance is to King Helmos. I apologize for my

508

rudeness. I was deeply offended to see the Sovereign Stone being used as a toy, however.'

'We, too, would be offended by such a sight,' the dwarven child said gravely. 'But you need not worry. We are the Guardians of the Sovereign Stone, and we would not permit anyone to make sport of it.'

The guardians! Lord Gregor stared, aghast. These children, the stone's guardians! Dunner had much to answer for, and the dwarf would do so. Lord Gregor would bring him up before the Council.

'I do not mean to offend you, but you are children. Children should not be guarding the Sovereign Stone. Great warriors should be guarding it. And you should not be wearing it as a frivolous adornment,' Lord Gregor added, gesturing.

'Indeed I do not!' The girl was indignant.

'The stone sat here for many cycles of the moon,' said a boy. He had assumed what Lord Gregor now saw to be a defensive posture to protect the stone. 'It was alone. No one came to see it. No one came to do it honor. It was neglected, abandoned.'

Like these children, Lord Gregor thought. Orphans all of them. Abandoned by their parents, neglected by those forced to care for them.

'We came here to see the stone one day,' said the girl. 'It shone brightly in the sun and sent rainbows dancing all around. It was the most beautiful thing we'd ever seen.'

'We dusted it and swept the floor and made its dwelling clean and neat,' said another boy.

'And every day one of us takes it up and wears it against our heart' – the girl placed her hand upon her small chest – 'to do it honor and to make the stone know that it belongs here. That it is one of us.'

The Dominion Lord knelt on one knee. He did so in part because he was growing stiff from the continued stooping but mostly because he felt that these children had earned his respect.

'I most humbly beg your pardon,' he said. 'I did not understand and was quick to judge. Accept my apology, Guardians of the Sovereign Stone.'

'We accept it, Lord Gregor,' said the girl with a quaint gravity that might have suited King Helmos himself. 'And now tell us why you have come to the City of the Unhorsed.'

'I came seeking Lord Dunner,' Lord Gregor replied. 'He accepted the Sovereign Stone from my King to hold in trust for your people. When he did so, Lord Dunner swore an oath that if my King required the stone to aid us in battle, the dwarves would return the stone. My King's need is great,' the Lord continued simply, 'and he sent me to ask for its return in fulfillment of the oath. I had hoped to speak to Lord Dunner.'

The children looked at each other. They seemed to reach some sort of consensus in that look. 'We know Lord Dunner,' said the girl. 'He is the only one besides us who comes to pay honor to the stone. But we do not know where he is.'

· 'If he had word of your coming,' added the boy, 'he would be here to meet you.'

'I sent no word,' Lord Gregor said, feeling more and more that he had completely bungled this matter. 'I traveled in haste. Our kingdom is in dire peril.'

'Who started this war?' the girl asked.

Lord Gregor explained as best he could, telling them how Prince Dagnarus had turned to evil; how he sought to be King when, by rights, he had no claim to the throne.

'A war between human brothers,' the girl said, clarifying the situation in her mind.

'Yes, that is true,' Lord Gregor confirmed.

'My father is the leader of his clan,' said the girl. 'If he and my uncle were to fight, would the humans send us their part of the Sovereign Stone to help one win over the other?'

'I . . . well . . .' The Dominion Lord could not lie. The very idea was ludicrous, of course. He fumbled for a way to make these children understand that a family feud among the dwarves was far different from a war between the King of Vinnengael and his demon-brother.

'And how would the humans know which brother was in the right?' asked a boy. 'Perhaps the clan chief is a bad leader. Perhaps his brother would be a better leader. Perhaps the brother deserves to be the leader. You humans would not know this. You might send the stone to the wrong one.'

'You humans would not send the stone at all,' another boy said, regarding Lord Gregor with a penetrating gaze. 'Would you?'

'There is a vast difference,' Lord Gregor tried to explain. 'Vinnengael is an immense kingdom; the most powerful kingdom on the continent. What happens in Vinnengael will affect everyone – dwarves included. Whereas what happens in a single dwarven clan is . . . is . . . not as important,' he finished lamely.

'It is to us,' said the girl. 'For those in the clan, that clan is their continent. It is the most powerful force in their world. This realm of Vinnengael of which you speak is far away from us.'

'Just as one clan will not meddle in the affairs of another,' said the boy, 'so we dwarves should not meddle in the affairs of you humans.'

'We will keep our part of the Sovereign Stone with us,' the girl concluded. 'Where we know it is safe and that someone will come every day to do it honor.'

Removing the stone from around her neck, the girl placed the stone with much reverence back upon its place on the horse blanket. The dwarven children gathered around the stone and bowed before it. Then, forming a line around the stone with their small bodies, they turned and looked steadily at Lord Gregor.

He could seize the stone. He could snatch it from its place, take it by force. These children could not stop him, though probably they would attempt to do so, and he would have no choice but to hurt them.

Lord Gregor guessed that if he did that, the stone would cease to make rainbows in the sunshine. Its luster would dim. As a Dominion Lord, he had sworn an oath to protect the innocent and the weak, to protect children like these. He could argue that the dwarves were breaking their sworn oath and that thus they had forfeited the right to the stone, but he had the feeling the gods would not accept that argument. If Lord Dunner had been here, that would have been different. Dunner had sworn the oath, and Dunner would have to take responsibility for breaking it. But Dunner was not here and the Dominion Lord would not steal the stone from children.

Lord Gregor pondered what to do. He eventually decided that the only option was to return immediately to Vinnengael, explain the situation, and ask for counsel. If King Helmos demanded that he come back and seize the Sovereign Stone by force, Lord Gregor would do so. But only if his King and fellow Dominion Lords demanded it.

And Lord Gregor did not think King Helmos would.

Bowing to the children and to the Sovereign Stone, Lord Gregor left the temple.

The children bid farewell to the stone, promising to return tomorrow, and then they left the temple to take up their dreary lives. Lives that for a moment or two every day were filled with rainbows.

Not until that night, long after Lord Gregor had entered the Portal and was safely on his way back to Vinnengael did Dunner enter the tent. The temple was dark, except for the Sovereign Stone, which seemed to shine with a faint radiance. The radiance might have been conjured up by wishful thinking, or perhaps the stone really did have its own inner light. Dunner could never make up his mind.

He knelt before the stone, but he did not touch it tonight, as he did sometimes, delighting in the warmth that entered his body and eased his spirit. He was there to bid farewell to it, for he would never see it again. He had broken his oath, for he had been a secretive, silent witness to the proceedings in the tent. He would be punished for oath-breaking; he knew that. He would take his curse as far from the stone as possible.

Far from the stone and its guardians.

Dunner left the city on foot, walking into the desolate plains.

He did not ride, for he was one of the Unhorsed.

TWO

—◆◆◆◆◆—

The Keepers of Time

NORTH OF VINNENGAEL, CLOUD HEIGHT IN the Dragon Mountain, stands the great monastery of the Keepers of Time. The distance from Vinnengael to the monastery does not seem far if one looks at a map, but in actuality a journey to the monastery takes many, many days. There is a trail, but it is little more than a donkey path, and it is twisted and torturous as it winds its way back and forth like a lazy old snake basking in the sun on the side of the mountain.

The monastery is an immense structure, made of huge blocks of granite, its walls seeming to rise up out of the bones of the mountain. It is old, its origins mysterious. Not even the Keepers know how their monastery came to be built or who built it, for, according to legend, the monastery was already there when they were brought to the mountain at the beginning of time.

The Keepers themselves believe that the monastery was built by the Ancients, a race said to have existed on Loerem long before elves or man or dwarves or orken; a race that presumably died out, but not before they had left intriguing traces of their existence. The monastery was perhaps the greatest and most extensive of their works, though there are some who say that the Ancients were responsible for diverting the flow of the river, carving out cliffs, and creating the seven waterfalls that were later to surround the palace of Vinnengael.

Paintings of extraordinary beauty, which are often found in odd places – on the side of a sheer rock face or the ceiling of a grotto – are said to be the work of the Ancients. Why a society that had the capability of producing such monumental architectural wonders as the great monastery, creating such scientific wonders as waterfalls, and such artistic wonders as these exquisite paintings should have disappeared was inexplicable. Many legends are told of the Ancients, who are universally agreed to be a tall people – taller than the orken, of slender build – more slender than the elves, of wondrous beauty – more beautiful than the most beautiful human, and skilled at riding – more skilled than any dwarf. Indeed, the dwarves have a legend telling how the Ancients captured and tamed the first wild horses.

There was once a shipload of orken, blown off course by a terrible storm, who made landfall on an unknown continent and who claimed to have there met the Ancients, whom they described as small, wizened, timid folk who lived in mud huts. This story was generally discounted, since orken are known to be notorious liars. Those who have heard it maintain that the orken had run across dwarves, who might seem small and wizened to those who had been subsisting for weeks on a diet of the intoxicating cha-gow.

The monastery is simple in design, with large square columns, smooth walls, and spacious rooms that are open to the sun and wind, rain and snow. There are many windows but no panes of glass, no iron bars to repel invaders, no arrow slits in the walls. The monastery is a house of peace, tranquillity, and serenity. It is not a fortress. Admittedly by the time any invading army made its way up the mountainside, those who had not tumbled over the edge of the cliffs would have been too exhausted from the climb to do more than lie down and gasp for breath in the thin air.

The monastery is entirely self-subsistent; the monks live on what they raise in their gardens and the food offerings made by those who make the torturous journey up the mountain to seek counsel. The monks drink nothing but the water from the mountain springs, the taste of which is said to rival the finest wine, and the rare and special tea that only grows there. The tea not only extends their lives, but preserves their bodies after death. The preservation of the bodies is most important, since the history of time is recorded on the monk's skin. The monks' corpses are saved and cataloged, much like the books in the Royal Library. To take a walk in the tombs of the monastery – and they are not referred to as tombs, but as the Catalog – is to take a walk back into the past.

Though people often make the long trek up the mountain seeking counsel, the monks never give advice. They never say a man should do such or so. They do not have the art of divination. They cannot see into the future. But they see all of the past and thus they have come to know much about the workings of the hearts and minds of mankind, which also includes elvenkind, dwarvenkind, and orkenkind. The monks will tell a supplicant how his problem relates to the very same problem faced by a man seventy years earlier and how he had solved it using X or how he had discovered that he could not solve it at all, but that another man thirty years after had run across something similar and succeeded by trying Y. Since most people are convinced that their problems are unique to themselves, such information is often not welcome nor considered particularly helpful. For this reason and because of the rigors of the trip up the mountain, the number of people who seek advice of the monks is small.

As for the monks, they are constantly coming and going up and down the side of the mountain, riding their stalwart, surefooted donkeys, who are not very fast, but who can guarantee that their riders will arrive safely at their destination. Accompanying the monks on their journeys into the world to record history as it occurs are their bodyguards.

These guards come from a tribe of people known as the Omarah, who have long lived in the mountains and worship and revere the monks. No greater honor may be accorded to a member of the Omarah than to be chosen by the monks as one of the select few who travel the world with them and whose responsibility it is to guard the monk's person both in life and in death. For should a monk die upon the road, it is the sacred duty of the Omarah bodyguard to return the body to the monastery, where it may take its proper place in the Catalog. The Omarah are human in origin, but as tall and as strong as orken. Indeed, if it were not impossible to crossbreed among the races, one might think that the Omarah are a cross of orken and humans.

The bodyguards are the tallest and strongest of their kind, men and women. Each serves ten years, starting from age twenty to age thirty, when they retire. Upon retirement the bodyguards are rewarded by a gift of a plot of land, a small flock of sheep or goats, and a house. The guards are ever after honored by members of their tribe and often sit upon tribal councils or became tribal leaders.

It is odd indeed to see a procession as it wends its way out of the mountains – the monk, small and shrunken, his skin turned a rich brown color from the tea and covered all over with intricate tattoo marks, trotting along on his sedate donkey, surrounded by gigantic men and women over seven feet tall, clad in leather armor and armed with massive spears that seem the size of oak trees.

517

The persons of the monks are sacred. Any who assault one of the monks or one of the bodyguard are said to be cursed not only by the gods but by the Void, as well. The monastery itself is ruled by five dragons, who are rarely seen. The five dragons will exact awful vengeance upon any city or village, group or individual responsible for the untimely death of one of the monks.

Such is their knowledge of and insight into the past that the monks can predict events with an uncanny regularity that often makes it seem as if they can see into the future. Whenever any event of historical importance is about to happen, one of the monks will almost certainly arrive to record it. The same is true of events that at the time seem to be of no importance, but that will later turn out to play a pivotal role in history.

Almost a year had passed since Dagnarus became Lord of the Void, and its events had been recorded in the monastery. Almost six months of that year had passed since Helmos had sent out the Dominion Lords to retrieve the three missing parts of the Sovereign Stone. Two of the requests had been flatly denied. The elves were still in prayer, still making offerings, still holding games to honor the gods over the matter, but Helmos knew a denial when he smelled one.

At that time, four monks who were the leaders of the Order of the Keepers of Time summoned one of their number into their presence. There were in reality five monks who headed the Order, for the fifth was seen only on rare occasions and only when there was dire trouble in the world. In fact, the four monks had expected the arrival of the fifth to this meeting. When the fifth did not show, they delayed the start of their proceedings for as long as they possibly could, looked continually at the fifth chair in the chamber, expecting that at any moment it might be filled. The fifth monk did not make an appearance, however, and his absence was duly noted with a tattoo mark on the arm of the monk summoned into the exalted presence.

This monk's name was Tabita, a spry old lady of about one hundred and eighty. She was a human, as are all the monks at the monastery. Although the monks place no stricture on race, and they accept any who are serious about dedicating their lives to the pursuit of history, few members of the other races choose such a life. All races, even those who are most prejudiced against humans, honor the monks and treat them with great respect. The elves find, however, that the tea that extends the lives of a human shortens the life span of an elf to a considerable degree, cutting off some two hundred years. The dwarves, though they like the notion of traveling the world, dislike the idea that they have to take time to write it all down. The orken, with their reliance on omens and signs and portents, are far too unpredictable to make good historians. Thus most of the monks are human.

Tabita had nearly reached the end of her life span. She was the eldest of the monks currently living and the most honored. Her body was covered with tattoos, recounting all the important events she had witnessed. Among them was the birth of King Tamaros, which had been recorded on the shin of her left leg. Tattoos covered all her body, including her face, which was so seamed with wrinkles as to make most of the tattoos almost unreadable. In death, the skin would be drawn taut and smooth over the bones – an effect of the tea, which prevented the body's decay.

The crown of Tabita's shaved head was still bare as that of a baby's. On that portion of the body the monk records what he or she considers the most momentous event of a lifetime, and Tabita had yet to record hers. Many of the younger monks whispered that only when this event was finally set down would she consider her life's work complete and so be able to die in peace.

Perhaps these whispers had reached the head of the

Order, or perhaps they guessed what was coming and had saved her to record it.

'Tabita,' said Fire, for each head was known only by the name of the god he or she served. Fire was clad in a cloth of orange-red. 'It is time for you to travel to Vinnengael.'

Tabita bowed her bare head to each of the four and to the vacant chair, for the fifth – though absent – was never forgotten. She had been expecting this summons. 'I will leave immediately, Honored One. And I thank you,' she added.

Tabita had not been a tall woman, and the tea and her vast age had shrunken her still more. Standing before the four, she seemed as fragile, as brittle and dry as a corn-husk doll. She wore only the simplest of clothing – a long piece of fabric bound around her body, rather like a winding cloth. The monks never wear cloaks or heavier robes, no matter how bitter cold or inclement the weather. The tea provides the body all the warmth it requires.

'The army of Dagnarus is on the move,' said Air, whose winding cloth was sky-blue in color. 'It is a vast army comprising elves and humans, among them the fierce barbarian warriors, the Trevinici. Because the army is so large, their progress is slow. You should have ample time to reach Vinnengael ahead of them.'

'The gates of Vinnengael are closed and guarded,' said Water, who wore green. 'The Portals are sealed, no one may enter from any of the lands of the other races. Since they refused to give up their parts of the Sovereign Stone, King Helmos no longer trusts those who were once his allies and has not asked for further assistance from them. No one in Vinnengael is allowed to leave by the Portals now, for King Helmos fears that they might be captured by elves or dwarves or orken and turned over to Dagnarus.'

'Those people living on farms around the city have already abandoned their homes and fled inside the city walls for protection,' said Earth, dressed in brown. 'King

Helmos is expecting your arrival, however, and the gates will be opened for you and your retinue.'

The four monks and Tabita glanced at the vacant chair, as if assuming now it must be filled, but it remained empty. Tabita bowed to each in turn, to indicate she understood and accepted their information.

'It is likely that you will be embroiled in a bitter battle, the likes of which have never before been seen on Loerem,' said Fire gravely. 'The danger to yourself cannot be overstated.'

'I understand,' said Tabita calmly. 'And I am prepared. The gods willing, I will have time to record whatever may transpire before I die.'

'We have chosen the best and strongest of the Omarah to accompany you. Both armies have promised to provide you safe passage through their ranks, but there is no telling what may happen in the chaos of war.'

'I am aware of that,' Tabita said. 'To be quite honest, I grow very weary of this life and would gladly take my place in the Catalog.'

'The gods' blessing be with you,' said the four simultaneously, and bowed to Tabita, who bowed to the four in turn.

A clanking of metal and heavy, heavy footfalls indicated that the Omarah bodyguard was forming in the monastery's courtyard. Tabita had no need to pack for her journey, for the monks have no possessions of their own. When the monks travel, they live off the land – the bodyguards do the hunting and cooking – or they are fed by those they meet along the way.

Leaving the four, Tabita headed for the stables to choose a donkey. There was a small, gentle gray – a favorite of the old woman's – and Tabita hoped that the gray had not already been appropriated by some other traveling monk.

She entered an alleyway that separates the main building

521

from the stables. The alley is cloaked in perpetual shadow, cast either by the top of the mountain that looms over the monastery or by the main building itself. Sunlight never reaches the alley. Snow that falls in the winter remains all the year long there, though flowers bloom in the sunshine of the monastery's gardens.

Tabita had reached the end of the alley, the stables were in sight, when a shadow blocked her way. The old woman lifted her head, fixed the shadow with a shrewd gaze.

A monk stood before her. The figure was tall and gaunt and, unlike the others, was shrouded in black, which covered every single portion of the body; even the hands were wrapped in strips of black. The face was not visible, only two eyes, which peered out of the darkness and yet seemed such a part of the darkness that Tabita almost didn't recognize them as eyes at all, simply darker bits of darkness.

She had never in all her one hundred and seventy years in the monastery (she had entered as a child of ten) seen the fifth monk. She knew well that was whom she faced, however, and her bow was very deep and very reverent.

The fifth monk spoke no word, which would have been muffled by the black cloth covering the lower portion of the face. Reaching out a black-wrapped hand, the fifth monk laid that hand upon Tabita's bare head.

The touch of that hand was cold even to tea-warmed blood. Tabita was chilled, and shivered. She kept her head bowed, too humbled to look up. The touch was withdrawn. She remained standing, head bowed, for several long moments and only when the shadow, too, was withdrawn and she could again see sunlight at the end of the alley did she realize she was alone.

She had received the blessing of the fifth monk. She had been embraced by the Void. Awed and profoundly moved, Tabita continued on her way to the stable, where she found, to her great joy, that those who tended the stable had received advance word of her need and the gray donkey was saddled and patiently waiting.

The army of Dagnarus, Lord of the Void, was on the march. The army was thirty thousand strong, formed of warriors from Dunkarga, led by their King, Dagnarus's uncle; elven warriors under the leadership of one of their own generals, sent by the Shield; Trevinici warriors, always happy to fight no matter what the cause, but now hoping to firmly establish their claim to certain disputed lands; and a host of mercenary soldiers who had been lured to Dagnarus's banner by money and the promise of rich looting.

The mercenaries were led by Shakur, a commander so fell that even the most callous and cruel warrior, who fought only for love of gold, and generally cared not a hang about orders, the type who would just as soon stab a commander in the back as salute him, cringed and knuckled their foreheads respectfully whenever the Vrykyl approached.

The army had spent the year camped on the vast open grassy plains outside the city of Dalon'Ren, on the eastern border of Dunkarga. Dagnarus made no move to conceal his might; rather, he flaunted it, well knowing the value of demoralizing the enemy. He knew Helmos's spies were watching him, and he welcomed them. Let them return and describe the vast host assembled to attack Vinnengael. Let the people worry and fret and gnaw at their hearts. Let the merchants quit coming, the trade fall to nothing, the economy falter. Let the city weaken from within, so that it would fall more readily when attacked from without.

Thus did Dagnarus deliberately delay his attack. When all in Vinnengael expected him to come roaring down upon them soon after he had escaped Lord Mabreton, Dagnarus let them sweat upon the battlements, while he trained his warriors at his leisure. Occasionally he would assemble his army, gather in supplies, load up the wagons, and appear to be on the verge of marching. He would receive reports from his own spies that the inhabitants of Vinnengael, hearing Dagnarus was on the move, were laying in supplies, preparing for a siege. He heard reports of farmers fleeing their fields, reports of the soldiers manning the walls. At the last moment, he would announce to his troops that this had all been an exercise. The next morning, they were back to drilling in the grassy fields as usual.

Twice more, he made this feint. His soldiers had found it amusing at first, though now they were starting to chafe and champ at the bit. Dagnarus could not hold them much longer, but he didn't need to hold them much longer. He knew – everyone in the world knew – that Vinnengael's so-called allies had refused to give up their portions of the Sovereign Stone.

Vinnengael was on its own, left to watch the horizon to the west in fear that slowly gave way to weariness and weariness that slowly began to give way to despair – a city under siege and not an enemy within one hundred miles.

With the end of summer, when the harvest had been gathered in, so that all his troops had to do was take what they wanted from full granaries and storehouses, he gave the order for his army to prepare to march. This time, everyone knew he meant it.

'We launch a two-pronged assault,' he told his generals, gathered together in the black-bannered command tent. 'Here and here.' He pointed to a map, spread out on a large table.

He wore his black, shining, bestial armor, though not the helm, so that his commanders could see his face and be aware of his determination, his fierce resolution. Valura stood at his side, armored and helmed. Few ever saw her face, and those who did regretted it, for they would see that beautiful and terrible visage in their dreams ever after. She was always at Dagnarus's side, his bodyguard.

Silwyth was now his lord's aide-de-camp and liaison between Dagnarus and his elven troops, helping to smooth out many little difficulties and misunderstandings natural between two cultures. Silwyth was present this day as translator.

Gareth was also in attendance. He had gathered about him sorcerers, those who had embraced the Void. Shunned and persecuted by people who either knew or suspected what they were, the sorcerers found not only refuge in Dagnarus's army, but monetary reward and respect for their talents. Though Gareth was among the youngest in years, he was one of the eldest in Void magic, for he had been studying it since he was a child, while most of the others had come to it in their adult years. For the first time in his life, people regarded Gareth with respect – including Dagnarus.

'Part of our forces will attack the city from the north. That is the direction from which they expect us to come, and we do not want to disappoint them. Their main defenses will be concentrated there.'

'That is because that is the only direction from which we *can* attack, Your Highness,' stated the elven general, not bothering to conceal his scorn. 'The remainder of the city is guarded by sheer cliffs and waterfalls. The Portals have been sealed off by the magi, their magic no longer works. And, therefore, I am completely opposed to splitting our forces! We will need every man we have and probably wish we had twice the number to breach their defenses at the north wall.'

'A two-pronged attack,' Dagnarus repeated, his voice grating. His cold, dark eyes never wavered, never blinked. 'We hit here at the north wall. We let them think that is the main thrust of our assault. But the real attack will come from here.' He laid his finger upon the line that marked the winding path of the broad and swift-flowing River Hammerclaw.

'You're mad!' the elf scoffed, nothing daunted by Dagnarus's baleful gaze. 'Do you plan to have us plunge down the waterfalls? Are we to capture the city by dashing ourselves to pieces on the rocks below? Or perhaps you plan to drink up the river,' he added, mocking. The elven officers accompanying him laughed dutifully at their commander's wit.

'That is exactly what I plan to do,' Dagnarus replied gravely, with a glance at Gareth, who bowed. The elves ceased their laughter, looked grim.

'I will have nothing to do with Void magic,' their commander stated.

'I would not ask you to,' Dagnarus returned. 'Your forces, along with Shakur's, will attack the north wall, draw their attention, and keep it.'

The elven general continued to cavil and finally left without committing himself or his forces. Nominally, the elves were fighting for the Shield, not for Dagnarus, as the elves were constantly reminding him, leading him to wonder more than once if their alliance was worth the trouble and causing Silwyth to spend much time in negotiations.

In this instance, Silwyth came back to Dagnarus's tent several hours after the initial meeting. 'General Urul has agreed to the plan, Your Highness,' Silwyth reported. 'He was mainly quibbling in order to save face before his men. I made a few meaningless concessions to him, concessions that may easily be withdrawn if you so choose. He no longer opposes you.'

'The Void take him and all elves,' Dagnarus muttered, drinking off a glass of wine. 'Present company excluded, of course.'

Silwyth bowed and silently poured His Highness another cup.

Dagnarus was drinking a great deal of wine these days. He began when he woke and continued to his final cupful to lure the sleep that would not come to him sober. The wine had no effect on him that anyone could tell, no matter how much he drank, and he drank enough to have sent an ordinary human to an early grave. The wine never cheered him, never brought a spark of light to his shadowed eyes, never brought a smile to his lips. He did not even seem to relish the taste, but drank it down uncaring.

It was as if he were pouring the wine into the Void, Gareth often thought to himself. Pouring it into the Void that had become Dagnarus.

'Are the sorcerers ready?' Dagnarus asked, emptying his cup and holding it out for more.

'Yes, Your Highness,' Gareth replied, biting his tongue, knowing that to remonstrate with the prince about his overindulgence in wine was less than useless. Such remonstrations in the past had brought down on him either a furious tirade or a sullen refusal to speak at all. 'I must tell Your Highness that a spell of this magnitude has never, to my knowledge, been cast before. I have no idea what its effects will be, nor its long-term ramifications. Its casting will demand every bit of magical energy each of us possesses. We will all of us be weakened after the casting to the extent that I doubt if any of us will be able to cast another spell for a long period of time. There is a possibility that some of us may die –'

'There's a possibility that all of us may die,' Dagnarus returned. 'A hazard of war, in case you hadn't noticed.' He looked up, his dark eyes flashing with a spark not even the wine could drown. 'Are your precious sorcerers a bunch of damn cowards?'

Gareth sighed. 'I only wished to apprise you of the situation and to let you know that if you use us to cast this one large spell, we will be of no further use to you afterward.'

'So long as you cast that one spell and you cast it well and it *works*' – Dagnarus laid emphasis upon the word – 'the Void may take all your sorcerers and welcome. Victory will be mine.'

Gareth knew the next request was hopeless and that he risked incurring the prince's ire, but he owed it to Helmos to at least try.

'Your Highness, may I suggest that it would be only fair to warn your brother of what we intend to do, give him a chance to surrender the city. You'll save thousands of lives –'

Dagnarus laughed. The laughter, soaked in wine, was mirthless and grating and terrible to hear. The prince's anger would have been far easier to bear than that unearthly laugh.

'Do you honestly think that my dear brother would surrender to me? Allow a "demon of the Void" to rule in his stead? What a chump you are, Patch! It is no wonder I keep you around. You are the only one who can amuse me anymore. I should make you my fool, not my whipping boy.'

Gareth bowed and left the tent, so angry he dared not trust himself to speak. He knew quite well that Dagnarus was right, Helmos would never surrender, and Gareth did not know which brother angered him the most. Dagnarus for speaking the truth, or Helmos for refusing to see it.

That night, the night before the army marched out, Gareth lay in his bed, listening to Dagnarus and Valura talking in low voices, making plans for how they would rule Vinnengael as King and Queen.

At length Dagnarus's voice died away. Gareth knew what he would find if he walked into the prince's tent, and the knowledge did nothing to contribute to his peace of mind. He would find the Vrykyl, encased in her black and shining armor, standing over the bed of her lover, guarding his wine-sodden, troubled sleep.

*　　*　　*

Captain Argot sought out Helmos in the tower room that had once been King Tamaros's favorite place and that had now become a refuge for his son.

'The army of the Lord of the Void is on the march at last, Your Majesty.'

'Is that certain?' Helmos looked up. He might have been his father, sitting there, surrounded by books and papers. Helmos had aged much in the last few months and looked, in his thirties, very much as Tamaros had looked in his seventies.

'Yes, Your Majesty.'

Helmos smiled wanly. 'I might almost say that I am glad, were it not wicked to be glad for war and its inevitable death and destruction. Yet' – he sighed deeply – 'I will be relieved when this is over. We must summon the other Dominion Lords.'

'I have taken the liberty of doing so, Your Majesty.'

'We will meet and make final plans, then, this night. What is the disposition of the prince's march?'

'That is what I find odd, Your Majesty,' said Argot. He gestured to an aide, who stepped forward and, at the King's nod, cleared away a stack of books and spread a map out upon the table. 'Our reports indicate that the main body of his forces – including the elven army – are taking the route we expected them to take, along the Vinnengael Road, intending to hit us at the north wall. This army is led by the Vrykyl, who we now believe to be a former army deserter turned assassin – a man named Shakur. According to the gaoler, Prince Dagnarus and the magus, Gareth, freed Shakur from prison only a short while prior to the prince's Transfiguration. The prince kept Shakur locked up in a room for a few days, then that was the last anyone saw of Shakur alive.'

Helmos shuddered. He had turned very pale. 'Poor wretch,' he said in a low voice. 'I have been reading what information there is on the Vrykyl. Whatever heinous crimes he had committed, he did not deserve such a dreadful fate. But you said there was something odd about this, Captain. Surely, from what you have previously explained to me, we expected the Lord of the Void to attack Vinnengael from the north. Indeed, as you said, it is the only direction from which he could possibly attack us. You will therefore concentrate your forces at the north wall.'

'I know I said that, Your Majesty,' Argot said, frowning at the map. 'But now I begin to wonder. Prince Dagnarus was the best, the most gifted commander under whom I have ever served. He knows – he has to know – that a frontal assault on the north wall has very little chance of succeeding. As for putting the city under siege, we have food stores enough to hold out for months, throughout the winter if we are careful. We have water in abundance. Out there in the open, with no shelter from the winter winds, he and his troops would suffer far more than we during a prolonged siege. He could not sustain it. So what is his plan?'

Captain Argot's frown deepened. He seemed to expect the map to tell him and was annoyed when it did not. He glowered at the map almost as if it were a prisoner, withholding valuable information. 'What is his plan?' he muttered to himself.

'I think you overestimate him, Captain,' said Helmos. 'Once, yes, Dagnarus was an able commander, but that was before the Void sucked whatever was good and best out of him and left his soul dark and empty. I have been thinking long on this, and it seems to me that Dagnarus does not even want to capture Vinnengael, at all. He wants nothing more than to inflict whatever terrible punishment he can upon us, never mind the cost to himself or those who follow him.'

Captain Argot and his aide exchanged glances – both had served under Dagnarus, both respected him, if they no longer admired him.

'There could be something in what you say, Your Majesty,' said the captain, unwilling to contradict directly his King. 'And yet . . .'

'Speak plainly, Captain. I am no military expert. I rely on you for advice on these matters.'

'Yes, Your Majesty,' said the captain somberly. 'According to our scouts, the Lord of the Void does not ride with his army. He has disappeared, and so has a considerable portion of his forces. At least that is what we believe.'

'You believe?' Helmos looked grave. 'Can't you tell?'

'Not with any certainty, Your Majesty. The prince is very clever. He did not bother to hide from us the fact that he was building an army, but he did manage to conceal its numbers from us. Soldiers were constantly marching in and out of the prince's encampment. Their uniforms and their banners changed continuously. Our spies may well have counted the same man six different times, or there may be six men for every one we counted. The only force we are certain of is the elven force. Also, Your Majesty, it is said that the prince has gathered together a large number of sorcerers, magi dedicated to the Void. There has been inclement weather in the mountains – strange, thick fogs, unusual for this time of year. It could be that this weather is magical and has been devised to conceal the prince's movements.'

'But if he and an army are marching through the mountains, what can they hope to accomplish?' Helmos demanded. 'They will still end up at the north wall. The city is surrounded by sheer cliffs on two sides and the river on the third. Even though he has every sorcerer in the world dedicated to the Void, they could not give his army wings like the birds who fly over the walls or gills like the fish who swim in the river!'

'No, but they could find a way to scale the cliffs and breach the walls with their magicks. I would like to hold a force in reserve, prepared to move to counter an attack from wherever it may come. Should it turn out that they are needed at the north wall, we can always send them there.'

'I will discuss this with the Dominion Lords,' Helmos said. 'I leave this to their judgment.'

'Very good, Your Majesty.' Argot hesitated, then asked, 'And where will Your Majesty and the other members of His Majesty's family be during the battle?'

'The Queen remains here in Vinnengael. I tried to persuade her to take refuge in her family's castle, which is located on the river, but she will not leave.'

'Her Majesty's courage is well-known,' said Argot, bowing.

'Yes.' Helmos smiled, and this time his smile was warm, as always when he thought of or spoke of his beloved wife. 'As to the Dowager Emillia, we had hoped to be able to accede to her wishes and give her escort back to her homeland, but she is not well enough for travel.'

The rumor was all over the city that the dowager had gone melancholy mad and had to be watched day and night or she would do herself or someone else some harm.

'And Your Majesty?' Argot asked. 'Where will Your Majesty be during the battle?'

Helmos looked surprised. 'In the Temple, of course. Praying to the gods to preserve us.'

'Very good, Your Majesty,' Argot said, but to himself he thought, You would be much better advised to be out on the walls alongside those of us who are going to die to preserve you, rather than with the gods, who probably care not one whit about this battle.

Helmos seemed to hear the unspoken words. A faint flush overspread his cheeks. 'Though I wear the armor of a Dominion Lord, I am no warrior, Captain, as you well know. I would only be in the soldiers' way, were I to try to take my place upon the battlements. But I will be fighting, though my sword is made of faith, not steel.

I will be fighting to protect the Sovereign Stone,' the King said, gently touching the diamond pendant that he wore on a braided chain of silver and gold around his neck. He wore it always, now, so it was said. Even when he slept.

'I had not forgotten the Sovereign Stone, Your Majesty,' Captain Argot replied. 'I was going to suggest that the sacred stone be sent away under guard to some safe place –'

'You've been speaking to the High Magus,' Helmos interrupted.

'Reinholt speaks with wisdom, Your Majesty. If – the gods forbid – Vinnengael should fall, the Sovereign Stone must be preserved. At least, it should be hidden in the Temple, in a secret place, kept safe by wizard locks –'

'And what good would it do any of us there? I have heard of misers possessed of sacks of gold who, though starving and clad in rags against the cold, refuse to spend one penny of their hoard, not even to feed or warm themselves! I will not make that mistake. I will use the power of the Sovereign Stone to save the city.'

'Then at least allow me to place guards around you –'

Helmos shook his head. 'That would make it look as if I lacked faith.'

'The Dominion Lords, then. Forgive me for pressing, Your Majesty, but I feel it is my duty –'

'No need to ask my pardon, Captain. You and the Dominion Lords may do what you like about protecting the city. In this, however, I hold sway. I took the burden and the joy of the Sovereign Stone upon myself. None other but myself may bear it. I have faith in the gods. They will keep it safe from falling into the Void. They will see to it that the stone that is now divided will once more be whole. That is all, Captain,' Helmos added, returning to his studies. 'Let me know when the Dominion Lords have arrived.'

Captain Argot accepted his dismissal. He could do

nothing else. But he planned to bring up the matter of protecting the Sovereign Stone before the Dominion Lords.

It was all very well to talk of wielding a shining sword of faith. But, to the captain's mind, such a sword would be stronger if the blade were tempered with the alloy of common sense.

THREE

Command the Darkness

THE ARMY OF PRINCE DAGNARUS, LORD OF the Void, marched along the old Vinnengael Road, thousands strong, their gaily colored banners whipping in the wind blowing from the ocean, bringing with it the sharp tang of salt and winter. They were led by a figure wearing shining black armor, but that figure – so the Vinnengalean scouts reported, creeping through the brush, close as they dared – was not Prince Dagnarus.

Where was he? No one knew. He did not march with his army, that much was certain. The hearts of the people of Vinnengael were cheered; rumor spread that the prince was dead, that the gods – through the intercession of King Helmos – had struck down the evil demon before he could attack Vinnengael. His army was coming to lay down its arms and surrender. People built bonfires and began dancing in the streets. Captain Argot ordered his men to go into the city and quell the nonsense, tell the dancers to return to their homes or else find a place upon the wall with the rest of the city's defenders. The army had not come to surrender. It had come to conquer.

As for the whereabouts of Prince Dagnarus, Captain

Argot asked that question of himself a hundred times a day until he heard it hammering at him even in his sleep. Argot had fought alongside the prince. Argot had seen Dagnarus ride in the forefront of the charge, lead the troops over the wall himself, be the first to reach the enemy lines. He was not the type of general to lead from the rear. He was out there somewhere, and if Argot knew where, he might have some idea of the prince's strategy.

Not a single scout reported seeing the prince, but then the weather in the mountains was terrible. Hard-driven rain slanted down like arrows. Devastating lightning set trees to blazing. Thunderclaps started rockslides. Finally, a blinding fog enveloped the mountains, fog so thick that the entire dwarven nation mounted on horseback might have ridden through those mountains and no one would have been the wiser.

Argot held a force in reserve, ready to send it at a moment's notice to wherever it was Dagnarus planned to try to make a breakthrough. This meant that the north wall was defended only adequately. If its defenders began to falter, he would have to send in the reserve force there. The Dominion Lords had elected to remain with the defenders on the north wall, adding their powerful magicks to those of the war magi.

King Helmos stood upon the walls with the Dominion Lords gathered around him – the human Dominion Lords only. The Shield of the Divine had sent word that the elven Dominion Lords, fearing that the Lord of the Void might turn his wrath upon the elven homelands, had elected to remain with their own people. The orken Dominion Lords sent word that because of bad omens the entire population had taken to the sea – the only place they considered themselves safe. As for the single dwarven Dominion Lord, Dunner sent no word at all.

Helmos watched the valleys to the north of Vinnengael fill with enemy troops setting up camp, preparing for the attack. They took their time, allowed the people of Vinnengael to get a good look at the size and might of their army. Let them tremble at the sight of the enormous siege engines, like no siege engines anyone had ever before seen. Great monstrous affairs built of wood covered over with armor plate. A platform built on the top housed what looked for all the world like a large water pump. The warriors on the walls pointed at these and laughed and wondered if Dagnarus meant to provide them with a shower bath.

'Still no sign of the prince?' Helmos asked.

'No, Your Majesty,' Argot replied. 'He is not among the forces gathered out there, I would swear it. Not unless he is skulking about in disguise, and that is not his way. Prince Dagnarus is no coward, whatever else he may be. Our scouts who were outside the city have either all returned or we have lost contact with them. Those who came back reported that they had seen no sign of him, but that the strange weather in the mountains kept them from seeing much of anything.'

Helmos sighed deeply.

'Your Majesty!' One of the Dominion Lords pointed. The sun was dipping toward the horizon. Its red flame glinted off the spear tips of a small force of soldiers advancing along the road. The enemy troops allowed them to pass, appearing to afford them considerable respect, for wagons loaded with supplies imperiled their cargo as their drivers hastened to steer to the side, leave the road clear.

'Dagnarus?' Helmos asked, leaning over the wall, trying to see.

'No, I do not think so, Your Majesty,' said Lord Altura, her eyesight keen as that of an eagle. 'It is the Keeper of Time, here to record the battle.'

The enormous Omarah bodyguards paced along slowly, not in the least discomfited or intimidated by the vast army through which they marched, nor yet by the opposing army that lined the city's walls. In their midst rode a small brown woman mounted upon a small gray donkey.

'Let the gates be opened,' Helmos commanded. 'Give the Keeper escort to the Temple and there let her every wish be granted.'

Argot relayed the order. The gates, which had been shored up against attack, were opened with much trouble. But no one murmured a word of complaint as the Keeper of Time, smiling benignly, trotted through them.

The sun vanished. Night marched with the invading army, or so it seemed. As the numbers of troops increased, so did the darkness. Campfires sparkled, as thick or thicker than stars.

'When will they attack?' Helmos asked quietly.

'With the dawn, Your Majesty,' Argot replied.

'Get what sleep you can. Tell the men to do the same,' Helmos said.

'Yes, Your Majesty,' Argot replied.

He and the King both knew there would be no sleep for anyone in Vinnengael that night.

Helmos returned to the palace, where his chamberlain captured him and tried to entice him to supper. The very smell of the food made the King nauseous. He waved the plate away.

'Where is the Queen?'

'She is with the Dowager, Your Majesty,' said the chamberlain, adding, in a low voice, 'The Dowager is very bad this evening. Worse than I have ever known.'

Guards opened the door to the Dowager's chambers for His Majesty. Helmos entered Emillia's presence silently, subdued by an odd mixture of loathing and pity. Gone were all the ornaments and knickknacks that had once cluttered her chamber. Emillia had either broken them, when one of her mad fits was on her, or they had been removed out of fear for her safety. Gone were the numerous ladies-in-waiting. Most had fled Vinnengael for the safety of their own noble houses. Those who remained had been sent by Queen Anna to assist in the Halls of Healing, which would soon be filled with wartime casualties.

An elderly servant, who had been with the Queen's own personal household, was all that remained to wait upon her, along with one of the healers, who watched over her constantly.

The Dowager sat preening before the empty wall where her mirror had once hung. The mirror had long ago been broken; she had attacked one of the servants with the jagged pieces. Helmos tried to be as silent as he could, hoping to attract his wife's attention without disturbing the Dowager, but at the sound of his footfall, Emillia looked quickly around.

She was a pathetic sight, her hair flying about in crazy wisps, for she was constantly fussing with it, ordering it to be put up, then taken down, then put up again a hundred times a day. Her body was shriveled and shrunken. They had to force her to eat, feed her like a baby. Her eyes stared at him from out of a cadaverous face.

She looked, Helmos thought, as her son had looked, withering in the holy fire.

'Dagnarus?' she called, peering through the gloom. 'Dagnarus? Where is that boy? It is high time he visited his mother! I have sent for him and sent for him and he chooses to ignore me. We shall have to teach him a lesson. Where is that whipping boy?' The Dowager straightened herself with a jerk. 'You there!' She had caught sight of Helmos. 'Send in the whipping boy! I shall have him flogged within an inch of his life. That will teach my son manners, I am sure.'

'Yes, Your Majesty,' said Helmos. The only way to handle Emillia was to humor her madness, according to the healers. The least little ray of reality slipping in through the chinks in her walled-up mind was unbearable for her. Only time and patience would bring about a cure, lead her out of the cell into which she had escaped to protect herself from the pain. 'The whipping boy shall be sent, as you command.'

Helmos beckoned to his wife, who was seated beside the Dowager, a task she took upon herself for hours every day; catering to Emillia's mad whims and listening with patience to her pitiful prattle. Anna rested her hand sympathetically upon Emillia's withered hand. Rising, she bowed, as if Emillia were still Queen and Anna just another lady-in-waiting. The healer took Anna's place.

'You should drink some water, Your Majesty,' the healer said, holding out a wooden cup.

Emillia struck it away, splashing water over her gown.

Patiently, the healer picked up the cup, refilled it, and offered it again.

'I had no idea she had grown this bad,' Helmos said to his wife in a low voice.

Anna nodded. 'It seems to me she grows a little worse every day. The healers have stopped saying that time will effect a cure. They want to move her to the Halls of Healing, but I fear the sudden change would kill her.'

'Her care is a great burden upon you, my dear,' Helmos said, drawing his wife near.

'Not so bad,' Anna said, smiling with feigned cheerfulness. 'She is docile when I am there. The healers say that I am a good influence upon her. I am the only one who can persuade her to eat.'

'You must leave her for the moment,' Helmos said. 'I need you now.'

'Yes, of course,' said Anna, worried and anxious. 'What is it? I heard . . .' She faltered a moment, then said, striving to sound calm, 'I heard that Dagnarus's army is taking up position outside the north wall.'

'Yes,' Helmos answered. 'Captain Argot says that the attack will come with the dawn.'

The two walked down the long corridor in silence, her

arm entwined with his, their steps pacing together, strides equal and matched. The empty stands of armor formed a silent honor guard for the King and Queen until, about halfway down the corridor, one of the spears suddenly slipped from its knight's rusted grasp and fell to the floor with an ungodly clanging and clattering, almost at the King's feet.

Helmos halted, staring, pale as if the spear had struck him. At his side, Anna gasped and pressed her hand against her wildly beating heart.

The clatter echoed loudly through the palace, causing servants and guards to come running.

'Your Majesty!' Guards had their swords drawn, were searching for some enemy. 'Are you all right? Where is the attacker?'

'Here,' said Helmos, with a strained smile. 'You see how we are blessed! The spirits of these knights long dead have returned and are eager for battle to be joined!'

The guards nodded appreciatively, pleased with the King's fancy. A servant lifted the spear and attempted to replace it, but the metal hand was so badly rusted that it would not hold. At a sign from the Queen, the servant propped the spear up to one side and hurriedly withdrew.

Anna had witnessed her husband's alarming pallor. 'My love, what is it?'

'If I were an ork,' Helmos said, his gaze fixed upon the fallen spear, 'I would be heading for the sea about now.'

'But you are not an ork,' said Anna practically. 'You know that the glove was rusty and that our footfalls as we approached caused a vibration that resulted in the spear falling to the floor.'

She hoped to see him smile and laugh at himself in self-deprecation, but he remained somber and grave.

'A strange heaviness hangs on my heart,' Helmos said softly. 'I have walked the palace halls this day and it is as if I

541

am walking them for the last time. No, no, my dear. Let me speak. They say a man's life passes before his eyes before he dies. I have seen my life this day. I saw my mother, Anna,' he said, his voice tender and filled with pain. 'I saw her standing by a window. She turned and smiled at me, but when I would have spoken, she was gone. I walked past the playroom and something compelled me to look inside, and I was there – a boy again, with my tutor among my books. And then Dagnarus was there, with that wretched whipping boy, Gareth. I could hear their laughter and see Dagnarus moving his toy soldiers about in the old sandbox.

'And my father. My father has been with me all this day. He looks at me so sadly, as if he wanted to say something or explain something. It is odd, but I have the feeling he seeks my forgiveness. As if there was ever anything he did that required it! And you, my own, my heart's dearest.' He halted in the hall, turned to face her, clasped her hands, and brushed away the silent tears that fell from her eyes. 'You are the blessed dream and the blessed reality.'

He kissed her on the forehead, as if in benediction.

She could not speak for long moments, then she said, swallowing her fear, 'You have not slept these past three nights, my lord. Nor have you touched more than a mouthful of food. It is no wonder you are plagued with these strange fantasies. I'll wager,' she said, with a tremulous little laugh, 'that a good beefsteak would send them all packing!'

Helmos did smile then, his love for her welling up in his heart and lighting the terrible darkness. He held her close. 'I am on my way to the Temple, to prepare for my holy vigil. I wanted to bid you farewell and to urge you, once more, to leave the city.' He held her face in both his hands, so that she was forced to look into his eyes. 'It is not too late. There is the tunnel, of which you know, that leads to the secret place up in the mountains. A band of retainers, chosen men, stand waiting to escort you –'

Anna was shaking her head. 'I will not leave,' she said firmly. 'You know I will not, so don't badger me. I will stay with poor Emillia. She may be disturbed by the unusual noise and clamor. I place my faith in the gods, my husband, and in you.'

They clung to each other, loath to part, though hard duty called to each. Helmos, stroking his wife's hair, looked down the hallway. The servants were lighting the torches, and by their wavering light, Helmos saw every one of the empty knights lift his visor, and the darkness of the Void pour from them like a black river.

The army led by Dagnarus marched through the mountains, concealed by the storms of his sorcerers' creation. Their path was lit by vivid lightning, which struck all around them, yet never in their midst. Their march was accompanied by the drumbeat of thunder, their progress shrouded in fog so thick they could not see the boles of the trees on either side of the narrow mountain trail, yet the way they walked was clear, for the fog lifted with their coming and fell with their passing. Rain like spears and sleet like arrows landed all around them, but they remained untouched by the elements. The roads they traveled were smooth and dry.

They marched hard and fast. These warriors were hand-picked by Dagnarus himself, after months of observing them in training. These were the best, the elite of the army. No one dropped out of the line of march, though the trek up and down the sides of the mountains was long and difficult and wearing. No one uttered a word of complaint. Dagnarus marched with them. He shared their hardship, did not ask of them anything he did not ask of himself. He slept upon the rocky ground, he forded the icy streams, he ate the cold food, for they dared not light a fire. Valura walked at his side, never tiring, rarely speaking, always watching him and him alone.

The soldiers admired their commander, but they did not like the Vrykyl. Her fell beauty, visible on those rare occasions when she removed her helm, haunted their dreams. They knew that she fed upon the living and though it was reported that Dagnarus had forbidden the Vrykyl to slay any of his troops, the soldiers did not trust this creature of the Void. They divided their night watch between looking out for the enemy and looking out for the Vrykyl.

The sorcerers of the Void marched with the army, as well. They, too, were not trusted by the soldiers, though Void magic was keeping them hidden from enemy eyes. The sorcerers had trained for months alongside the soldiers and now the magi not only kept up with the rapid pace of the forced march, but several did so while drawing on their own energy to work the magic of the storm. Only a few were detailed to perform this task. Gareth had ordered the majority to conserve their strength in preparation for the immense and difficult feat of magic they would have to perform at the journey's end.

Dagnarus's magical connection with Shakur and the other Vrykyl made him a party to their thoughts and thus the prince knew the precise moment when his army had arrived outside the walls of Vinnengael. Dagnarus's army emerged from the mountains that same evening, the troops weary but triumphant. The soldiers would have the night to rest along the riverbank. There would be no sleep for the sorcerers.

Gareth saw to it that his people were well fed, appropriating rather more than their share of the army's victuals, for the magi would need all their strength and more for the upcoming trial. The magi sat apart, shunned by the ordinary foot soldier, who gave them a wide berth when he was forced by duty or necessity to go near them at all.

While the sorcerers were eating and discussing their night's work in low, eager voices, Gareth sought out Dagnarus.

The prince squatted on a flat rock, eating supper – a small amount of dried and stringy beef, some hard-as-rock bread, dipped in wine to make it palatable, and more wine to wash it all down. They lit no fire, but now that the magical storms had lifted, the night was clear and filled with the pale cold light of moon and stars. Valura stood near him, her hand on his shoulder – the pale hand of love, cold and dead; its fingers locked forever around the prince's heart. Silwyth stood in the shadows, a wineskin in his hand.

Gareth bowed.

Dagnarus regarded him with a glint in his eyes. 'Well, are your sorcerers ready to begin?'

'Yes, Your Highness. I –'

'Then begin.' Dagnarus motioned for Silwyth to pour more wine.

'Begging your pardon, Your Highness,' Gareth said, 'but I need to know that you are completely and unalterably committed to this undertaking, that you are aware of the possible consequences, both to your sorcerers and to yourself.'

'To the magi?' Dagnarus shrugged. 'Some will die. The loss is acceptable. To myself?' The emerald eyes flickered with displeasure. 'What will be the consequence to myself? You never spoke of this.'

'I did, Your Highness,' Gareth said patiently, 'when first you proposed this stratagem. The spell you require is so powerful that your assistance will be needed to perform it. The Void magic will drain you of your life's energy, not much, not like it will drain the rest of us, for Your Highness has lives to spare now,' he added with a bitter irony that he could not conceal. 'But you will perhaps feel a weakness, a certain light-headedness –'

Dagnarus scowled. 'You know that I lead my troops into battle on the morrow?'

'Yes, Your Highness. That is why I wanted to make sure you knew that you would experience some weakening effect and to determine if you wanted us to go ahead –'

'It is rather late to back out now, Patch,' Dagnarus stated. 'I do *not* recall you speaking to me of this. Did he, Silwyth?'

'Yes, Your Highness,' said the elf softly, again refilling the wine cup.

Dagnarus flashed Silwyth a look of anger, which the elf pretended he did not see. 'Well, perhaps you did. I am launching the largest assault the world has ever witnessed against the strongest, best-fortified city in the world. I cannot be expected to remember every little trivial detail that may arise.' He waved a negligent hand. 'I will be ready when I am needed for your spell-casting. I doubt it will bother me much at that.'

'You will be needed close to the time when the spell is ready, which will be near dawn,' said Gareth. 'Might I suggest that Your Highness try to sleep, to be at the peak of your strength?'

'You may suggest anything you damn well like,' Dagnarus returned sullenly. 'Go back to your hedge-wizards, Patch. I have a meeting with my commanders.' He dismissed Gareth with a wave and bent over a map of Vinnengael he had spread out upon the ground.

Gareth cast a meaningful glance at Silwyth, who indicated, by a slight lifting of his shoulders and a slight lowering of his head that he would do what he could. Gareth was turning away, when Dagnarus said, without looking up, 'You will not be involved in this deadly spell-casting, will you, Patch?'

'Yes, Your Highness,' Gareth replied. 'I am their commander, as you command your troops. I will not ask my people to do anything I will not do myself.'

'I forbid it, Patch,' Dagnarus said, continuing to study his map. 'I will need your help to deal with my brother.'

Hearing no response, Dagnarus raised his head, frowning. 'Well? Answer me!'

'Do not ask me to do this, Your Highness,' Gareth said softly. 'I beg of you.'

Dagnarus's face flushed with anger and the wine. 'I do not *ask* you to do anything, Patch! I command you!'

Gareth could say nothing. What he might have said, he should have said a long, long time ago. He was like the Vrykyl, though he had never felt the stinging pain of the dagger. Dagnarus had drunk of Gareth's soul, fed off it, and made it a part of himself. Gareth bowed silently and returned to his command. The sorcerers rose as he approached, indicating their respect for the young man and also their readiness to begin.

'You know what is required of you,' Gareth said, addressing the group, which was made up of men and women, mostly older than himself. All human, they came from various parts of Vinnengael, from villages as far north as Myammar, as far south as Lu'keshrah. 'You know the sacrifice you will be called upon to make.'

'We know,' said one woman calmly, 'and we welcome it!'

Gareth understood. Most of the sorcerers had come to Void magic like himself – by accident. They were magi who, from ambition or greed or pride, were discontented with the slow and methodical process of elemental magic, wanted magic that was faster, more powerful. Though Void magic was painful and oftentimes debilitating, though they were forced to wrap their hands and faces in cloth to hide the pustules and ulcerations, though their neighbors whispered about them and they were often persecuted, killed outright, or driven from their homes to roam the world, the sorcerers believed that the end result was worth it. And now they would prove it. They would demonstrate their power to the world. They would win the respect for which they hungered. At last they could stop fleeing, turn to face their detractors and their tormentors, and say to them proudly, 'This is who we are! This is what we can do! Look on us and tremble!'

No sacrifice – not even that of their lives – was too great.

'I am not going to be taking part as I had intended,' Gareth said, his voice harsh to mask his frustration. 'The prince has commanded that I accompany him when we enter the city. You, Tiumum, will take my place as leader.'

The sorcerers were not surprised, nor were they upset. It was only logical that His Highness should want his most skilled sorcerer at his side. Looking within himself, Gareth understood why he was so terribly disappointed. He had been hoping to lose himself in the Void – if not to die, then at least to lose consciousness. He had hoped, coward that he was, to know nothing of what was happening until all had ended.

The sorcerers came together in a circle on the edge of the riverbank, fifty of them, the largest gathering of Void magi in the history of the world. Tiumum, the eldest of them all, lifted her voice and began to call upon the Void, exhorting it to embrace them, to encompass them, to exalt them. One by one, the other sorcerers joined her, adding their voices – deep bass, high-pitched treble. All except Gareth, who sat in silence, watching.

When each had recited the chant nine times, they began to walk the circle, each following one behind the other, feet shuffling as they disturbed the brown pine needles that littered the side of the riverbank. Round and round they moved, the chant rising and falling. Each was careful to walk in the others' footsteps, careful not to stray out of the path or to break the circle.

The soldiers who had been in the vicinity of the riverbank left it the moment the chanting started. Considering it bad luck to watch a Void sorcerer casting a spell, the soldiers ran deep into the woods, as far from the sorcerers as they dared, to escape the sound and the sight of the spell-casting. Crouching in the darkness, the soldiers fingered charms they had purchased or made and now wore around their necks, charms that presumably protected them from any splatterings of Void magic that might slosh over the sides.

Gareth watched with disdain the soldiers' departure. He wondered cynically how they managed to separate their distrust and hatred of Void wizards from their loyalty to their commander, the avowed Lord of the Void. Probably because they had never seen him perform any magic. They had seen him wield shield and sword as did any warrior. Well, they would see him perform magic with the dawning. Make of it what they liked.

The night deepened. Hour after hour, the wizards walked the circle until their feet had stamped out a round path in the mud. Gareth sat on a tree stump and watched. He watched when he should have been sleeping, to conserve his energy for the morrow. The chant thrummed through him, tingled in his fingertips, burned a circle in his brain like the one in the mud. Had he tried to sleep, he would have seen that circle – a dark hole surrounded by fire – wheeling round and round. Better to stay awake.

Late in the night, he had company. Silwyth came to stand beside him. The elf frowned at the chant and at the sorcerers, but at least he did not avert his gaze or rub a chicken's foot.

'His Highness is asleep,' the elf said to Gareth. 'When do you want me to awaken him?'

'An hour before dawn. And try to keep him from the wineskin, will you?'

'And how am I to do that, Master Whipping Boy?' Silwyth asked mockingly. 'He is my prince. I do what I am told.'

'You'll find a way,' Gareth retorted. 'You always do.

Say that it sprang a leak or that bears ran off with it. His victory depends upon his ability to concentrate and focus his energy. Our lives – all our lives – depend upon him.'

'The wine eases his pain,' Silwyth said quietly. 'He told me, once, that when he dreams, he feels the terrible heat of the flames and sees his own flesh withering and turning black in the fire . . .'

Gareth shrugged. Once he might have found it in his heart to pity. No longer.

'I will see to it that he is sober in the morning,' Silwyth said, and departed.

Gareth kept watch throughout the night. The sorcerers continued their chant until some could barely speak for the rawness of their throats, while others lost their voices completely, and could only whisper or mouth the words. They walked and walked, round and round, weariness seizing hold of their limbs, stumbling, catching on to and supporting each other. Once, however, one of the magi fell to the ground and did not rise up. Horrible ulcerations covered his body. His skin ran with blood. The other sorcerers continued to walk, stepping over the body of their fallen comrade.

Gareth walked over to the magus – a man not many years older than himself. Placing his hand upon the man's pulse, Gareth felt it weak and faltering. He dragged the man to the side, away from the circle, and summoned one of the healers recruited from Dunkarga. The healer looked at the young man, looked at the sorcerers, and said coldly that she doubted she could do much for him, but she would try. Gareth was not surprised to hear later that the young man was dead.

Hour after hour passed. Gareth could see no sign that the spell was working, and fear seized him. Dagnarus would be furious. He had staked everything upon this plan succeeding. Gareth was nearing the point of panic when finally he saw what he had been waiting to see.

He cautioned himself against hope, tamped down the sudden elation. Telling himself his eyes were tired and playing tricks, he looked away and looked back. The result was the same. The sorcerers walking the circle could now see the magic beginning to work, as well. Their voices strengthened. Their bodies, slumping with fatigue, straightened. The pace of their walking increased. Round and round they traversed the circle and within that circle the darkness of the Void – darker far than the darkest part of the darkest night – began to form.

Once Gareth had been able to see by the lambent light of stars and moon the full circle of sorcerers. Now he could see only those on the side nearest him. The others entered darkness as they circled around, emerged again on the other side. It was as though a thick pillar of jet had formed in their midst.

The spell was working.

It was now an hour before dawn. The sky to the east turned pale blue, though beneath the trees all was black. The river flowed swift and dark. There was no doubt in Gareth's mind. The sorcerers encircled a portion of the Void, a dark hole cut into the dawn.

Heavy, crashing footfalls broke the silence. Gareth looked over his shoulder to see Dagnarus, his hair tousled, clad only in his shirt and breeches, stockings and boots, stomping through the forest. He was in a very bad temper, his face grim and glowering. Valura walked behind him, her own footfalls unheard on the rotting leaves.

Thrilled with his achievement, Gareth was in far too good a mood himself to let his prince's ill humor bother him. Dagnarus would cheer up shortly. When he saw the miracle they were about to perform, he would cheer up immensely.

'Good morning, Your Highness,' said Gareth. 'Did you sleep well?'

'No, I did not, damn your eyes!' Dagnarus retorted.

'And never a drop to drink this morning, either. Silwyth, that clown, has allowed bears to run off with the wine! I shall have him hanged. What is this you are doing – some child's game?'

He glowered at the circling wizards.

'Indeed, no, Your Highness,' said Gareth. 'This is the spell. It has worked. Your wizards have summoned the Void and brought it here for you to command.'

'By the gods!' Dagnarus stared, awed, his thirst and the pain assuaged, both forgotten. 'You have done it!'

'Say rather, *they* have done it, Your Highness,' Gareth said with quiet pride in his people. 'I took no part, per your orders.'

'What happens now?' Dagnarus demanded.

'Now it is your turn, Your Highness. Now we need your magic, the power that the Void has granted you.'

'You shall have it and welcome!' Dagnarus's eyes gleamed and this time it was not the wine that illuminated them. 'Instruct me. Tell me what to do. Will it be dangerous?' he asked, offhand, more for information than out of fear.

'Not to you, Your Highness,' Gareth said, his voice low. 'Invoke the power. Become the Lord of the Void.'

Dagnarus placed his hand upon the pendant he wore on his breast. The black armor erupted from his skin. Like drops of oil, the armor flowed glistening over his limbs. The black bestial helm covered his head, mailed gloves sheathed his hands.

The chanting of the sorcerers increased in pitch and in intensity. Another fell from the circle; no one paid her any attention. They kicked her limp and bloody body to one side that it might not impede their spell-casting.

'Your Highness, the Void is yours to command!' Gareth shouted above the chanting voices.

Dagnarus walked toward the wheeling circle of sorcerers. As he drew near, their leader gave a great shout and brought them all to a halt with a loud clapping of his hands. They stood quite still, pale and trembling with fatigue and the concentration required to hold the spell in place.

Dagnarus reached past them, reached beyond them, thrust his hand into the darkness. He shuddered and cried out in pain, as if he had plunged his hand into icy water, except that this darkness was far colder than any ice, colder than the final cold that grips the living and can never be warmed. Valura made a sound, a gasp, a hiss of alarm, and took a step toward him.

Not thinking what he was doing, only concerned that she might disrupt the spell, Gareth reached out and grabbed hold of the Vrykyl's black armor. A jolt like lightning numbed his arm to the shoulder. She rounded on him, fury in her contorted features, if there was none in the cold, dead eyes.

'Do not interfere!' Gareth told her, holding on to her, though his arm tingled painfully. 'If you thwart him in this, he will denounce you, cast you from his side. He's only looking for an excuse. He already loathes you, as you well know.'

Gareth could bear the pain no longer. Releasing his grip, he began to massage his aching arm. Valura looked back to Dagnarus, but she made no move now to stop him. Her head lowered. Had Gareth believed it possible, he could have sworn she wept. She had died for love of Dagnarus, died to protect him. She had doomed herself to the life of the damned to be with him, and she, too, had often seen the look of revulsion on his face when she returned to him after a kill, with blood on her lips and her hands.

She could not give him up. She could not leave him, as he could not give her up. The Dagger of the Vrykyl bound them together, made each a party to the other's thoughts and perhaps, with Dagnarus, there lingered some faint and desolate hope that one day he would look into those dead eyes, which now held nothing but darkness, and once more see himself.

Gareth's heart was wrung with pity for her, even as he recoiled from her. He could not take time to comfort her, had there been any comfort he could offer. They had to cast the spell now, or there would be no casting. The prince's arm and hand were no longer visible. His limb had been swallowed by the darkness. The Void was his.

'Command it, Your Highness!' Gareth urged. 'Use the magic as you will! Quickly!'

Dagnarus raised his arm, and the pillar of opaque darkness rose with it.

'The river!' he shouted in a voice terrible to hear, a voice that brought the sleeping soldiers to their feet, their hands grappling for weapons, thinking they were under attack. 'I command you to swallow the river!'

The darkness vanished. The sorcerers were left staring at each other until their strength gave way and they sank to the ground, panting and gasping, or simply collapsed. Some lay quite still. Dagnarus stood on the shore, watching, with Gareth at his side. Valura kept to the shadows behind him, avoiding the first rays of the morning light that gilded the ripples of the swift-flowing river.

Nothing happened, and again fear and doubt shriveled Gareth's stomach, though he knew with cold logic that the spell had worked perfectly and that they had only to wait. Still, the relief he felt when he saw the ripples on the river start to alter, to swirl around a central point in the middle of the swift-flowing water was indescribable. He leaned back against the bole of a tree and watched his handiwork with pride.

As Dagnarus had commanded, the Void swallowed the River Hammerclaw, as if a plug had been yanked from the bunghole at the bottom of a cask of wine. The river water began to swirl downward, falling faster and faster into an enormous maw of blackness that grew wider and wider until it stretched from bank to bank. The river water swirled into the vortex, slid over the lip of the enormous hole, a maelstrom eerie in its silence. All sound of the water's cascade was absorbed by the blackness. The sun rose, but its light could not penetrate the darkness. No rainbows danced across this dread waterfall.

Beyond the Void, the riverbed was laid bare as the water dried up, its rock-strewn floor glistened in the morning light. Fish flopped about on the wet rocks, gasping and dying. The riverbed would be slippery and treacherous to walk. Here and there stood pools of water and large patches of oozing, clinging mud. But the army did not have far to travel. In the light, Gareth could see the walls of the castle dead ahead, walls where no guard stood, for they trusted the river to guard their backs. Walls easily breached by Dagnarus's army, who would enter by way of the aqueducts that carried fresh water from the river into the castle.

Vinnengael, kept alive by her waterfalls, would die by them.

'You must hurry, Your Highness,' Gareth cried. 'The spell will last only from sun's rising to sun's setting! Then the water will return!'

'That is all the time we need,' Dagnarus said. 'Shakur launched his assault on the north wall with the dawn. While my brother's forces grapple with the enemy before them, we will slip in behind and seize them by the throat.'

He gave a great shout. The trumpets sounded, drums beat. The soldiers formed into the order of battle and, with a cheer for Dagnarus, his troops surged down into the riverbed and marched on Vinnengael.

FOUR

The Battle of Vinnengael

IN THE SMALL CELL THAT WAS THE PORTAL OF
the Gods, Helmos fought his own lonely battle, fought
to gain the attention of the gods, fought to make them
understand his need for help in order to save his city and
its people. No soldier on the wall, battling fiercely with
sword and knife to drive back the enemy, who time and
again managed to gain the battlements, fought harder than
his King. His foes were not beating on him with cold steel
or hacking at him with battle-axes. He could have wished
they were. His foes were more insidious, attacking him
from within, destroying hope and confidence and thus
they were more punishing by far.

The gods had turned from him, ignored him, refused to
answer him. He blamed himself. His faith was not perfect,
as had been his father's. Helmos's nature was a more questioning nature. He had questioned the gods' ways more than
once, questioned where his father had accepted. Even now,
Helmos knew rebellion and resentment in his heart, when he
should have known nothing but submission and humility.

Questioning is not wrong, he thought. The gods' ways
are not always clear to man. How are we to understand
unless we ask right out: Why?

Why kill my mother in her youth? Why did you take her from us when we most needed her? Why create Dominion Lords and put into the world their dark opposites? Why not force the other races to obey their own gods-sworn oaths? Why tempt a willful child to fall to evil? Why permit that child to grow to manhood and grant him the power to become a thing of evil? Why bring so many unwanted children into the world and deny my wife and me a child of our own? Why harden the hearts of our allies so that they do not come to our aid? Why bring death and misery to a city of beauty and light? Why do you seem to abandon us at our time of greatest need?

His heart repeated the questions as his lips prayed for help. He prayed as sincerely as he could, but his prayers were whispers, never loud enough to be heard, apparently, for he did not believe anyone was listening to them. The questions of his heart, wrung from him, wet with his heart's blood, clanged and clambered like enormous iron bells, ringing throughout the heavens.

He prayed to the gods, not kneeling, but standing before them, shouting, pleading to be heard. He prayed until his throat was raw and his voice hoarse and he was parched with thirst, but he had vowed that he would endure the same hardships as his troops. No water should ease him, no food nourish him until the battle was ended and his city saved.

At length, weary with a weariness that was more of the heart and spirit than it was of the body, Helmos sat down upon the bed, the same bed where his father had often rested.

Exhausted, he slept, though he did not mean to.

He was a little child again, barely able to walk, his hand clutching the skirts of a gown in front of him. He could not see, from his low vantage point, who wore the gown, but he knew it was an adult of enormous size and proportion. He toddled as fast as he was able, hanging on to the skirt to keep from falling, and he could hear his own small voice prattling, 'Why? Why? Why? I want, I want, I want. Why? Why? Why? I want, I want, I want. Why? Why? Why?'

A gentle voice sounded above him, far above him. 'You will see when your eyes close. You will hear when you are deaf. You will understand when you are past understanding. Take hope from this: the four can never be one but, in time, the one may be four.'

They held out to him a bright and shiny bauble. He released the hem of the gown to seize it . . .

Helmos clutched the Sovereign Stone in his hand.

'I am on my own. You speak in riddles. You do not care. You have probably never cared. If I had been blessed with children, I would have taken them into my arms and answered their questions, every one. I would have cherished them and loved them if I had been father to a thousand!'

'You are loved,' said the gentle voice, 'and our children number as the stars.'

Tears crept from his clenched shut eyes, bitter tears that stung his throat and choked him with their bile. He became aware, eventually, of a tapping at the door, a tapping that had been going on for some time, for he seemed to have heard it throughout his dream.

He woke suddenly, alarmed.

The need must be dire for someone to disturb him in the Portal of the Gods. He rose stiffly to his feet and walked to the small door, unlatched it, opened it.

The Most Revered High Magus stood without, the only one who dared to interrupt the King at his prayers. One look at the man's pallid and haggard face and Helmos knew that his prayers would go unanswered.

'Forgive me, Your Majesty –'

'Yes, what is it, High Magus?' Helmos asked, calm with despair.

'The river . . . the river has vanished!' The man's white hair seemed to stand on end with horror.

'Vanished?' Helmos stared. 'Make sense! What do you mean "vanished"?'

'Just that!' Reinholt said, licking dry lips. 'Some dread magic, undoubtedly the magic of the Void, has sucked the river dry. Drained it! Water no longer flows into the city. Fires are breaking out all over. Those siege towers at which we laughed . . .' He wrung his hands. 'No one is laughing now. The pumps spew forth a demonic substance – black fire. It rains down on us like jelly and bursts into flame upon impact! People turn to living torches, houses are burning all over the city, and now we have no water with which to douse them.'

Helmos could not comprehend. His mind stumbled along, clutching at the words of the High Magus, asking, 'Why? Why? Why?'

'And there is worse, Your Majesty. A river of darkness flows in place of the River Hammerclaw. A vast army marches down the empty riverbed, an army led by your brother, Prince Dagnarus. There is nothing to stop him from entering Vinnengael.'

Reinholt drew in a deep breath, sought to calm himself. 'Your Majesty. You must take the Sovereign Stone and flee the city, while there is yet time. No matter if Vinnengael falls, it will never truly fall so long as the Sovereign Stone escapes.'

'I will not leave.'

'Your Majesty –'

'The Sovereign Stone is our only chance for salvation. If not ours, then those who come after. It must remain in the Portal of the Gods.' Helmos closed his hand over the stone with such force that the sharp edges pierced his flesh. He felt the sting, felt the blood, warm and sticky, and was careful not to open his hand, not to let the High Magus see. Then Helmos thought of his wife, of Anna

559

trapped in the palace, of Dagnarus's troops invading the palace . . .

'The Queen!' he said, his heart misgiving him. 'I must go to her.'

'Rest easy, Your Majesty,' said the High Magus. 'I have already dispatched war magi to protect her. If I may say so, she is safer away from you than she would be in your presence. Dagnarus's quarrel is with you, Helmos. Once again, I urge you to take the Sovereign Stone and flee to safety. Not only for yourself, but for the sake of us all!'

'And be branded a coward.' Helmos was angry. 'The King who ran from his kingdom at the first sign of trouble! My people would lose all respect for me. Our allies would rejoice in our weakness and move in to snap up what pieces are left over when my brother has finished carving us. If I could ever return and claim my throne, how could I expect the meanest beggar in the street to show me respect? No, High Magus,' he concluded with decision. 'What you ask is impossible.'

The High Magus sighed deeply. 'I understand, Your Majesty. And what you say is true. It is a dreadful dilemma and one that you alone can resolve. We will support you in your decision, of course.'

'I will do what my father would want me to do,' Helmos said simply. 'I will remain here in the Portal of the Gods, where he received the Sovereign Stone. I will remain here, and keep faith with the gods.'

'May the gods hear your prayers, Your Majesty,' the High Magus said, and, backing out of the doorway, he softly and gently shut the door behind him.

Helmos sat upon the bed. He wiped the blood from his hand upon the pillow, which was wet from his tears.

The first words Dagnarus said on entering the palace, the first command he gave was: 'Find my brother. Find Helmos and bring him and the Sovereign Stone to me.'

'I will go, Your Highness,' Gareth offered. This was one order he was glad to obey. He hoped desperately to be the one to find Helmos and to help him escape, to hide him, to somehow save him from Dagnarus's wrath.

Dagnarus cast Gareth a suspicious glance. The prince knew that Gareth held Helmos in high regard. But Dagnarus also knew that Gareth was the only one of his forces, besides Silwyth, who knew his way around the maze of palace corridors. The prince could not go himself, not yet. He was busy with the thousand responsibilities of a commander, dividing his forces, sending some to search and some to secure the palace. Already fighting could be heard in the lower hallways, where the guard had been keeping watch to prevent the enemy from coming in the front. He would have to make certain that the palace was his first, before he set out to resolve personal matters.

'Go with Patch,' Dagnarus ordered Silwyth, and then the prince was called away by his commanders and the sound of battle.

Gareth hastened through the corridors, familiar to him, but not to most of the army. He headed straight for the King's royal chambers. He did not believe he would find Helmos there, but Gareth hoped to find Queen Anna, hoped to be able to persuade her that he had her husband's interests at heart. Hoped to be able to convince her to tel him where Helmos might be found.

Gareth had been raised in the palace, he knew his around here better than around his family's own smaller house. But he discovered, to his dismay, halls looked strange and unfamiliar to him. He v why and realized suddenly it was because he in from the back. He was seeing everythin wrong angle. The smoke from burning build through the windows, borne by the wild sea, swirled through the hallways. Th past in ragged tatters, sometimes obs sometimes setting him coughing, other times clearing completely.

Gareth ran through corridors with only a vague idea where he was going, guessing it was the right way, but not truly certain. He might have asked Silwyth, who accompanied him, but his mind was intent upon how he was going to deal with Silwyth. The last thing he wanted to do was to ask the elf for help, show weakness.

At length, Gareth entered a corridor and there, in front of him, was the playroom. Memories flooded in on him – memories of a child lost in the palace, memories of a prince's warm and welcoming smile. Now Gareth knew where he was. He halted and turned to face the elf.

'Leave me, Silwyth. Leave me to do this on my own. If you don't . . .' Gareth paused, steeled himself. 'If you don't, I shall use my magic against you. You may be quick with a knife' – he recalled the time he had watched Silwyth stab Lord Mabreton in the back – 'but the magic of the Void is faster.'

'What do you intend to do, Master Gareth?' Silwyth ̵sked coolly. 'Urge Helmos to escape? Take him to a ̵ of safety? Conceal him from his brother?'

̵looked blank, pretended he didn't understand.

̵with you. He is not a coward, nor is ̵ay die, that which he is and that ̵hrough time. He knows this. ̵ay have need of a hero. ̵d and if Dagnarus

̵oldly stubborn, 'or

̵ on his lips was a rare ̵ion Gareth had ever seen ̵ not because you threaten ̵ I am leaving His Highness.

My time here is finished. My time with *Dagnarus* is finished.' He spit the word from his mouth.

Gareth stared, amazed and suspicious. He coughed in the smoke, but hurriedly cleared his throat, that he should not miss anything of this startling revelation.

'You thought, the lot of you humans, that I served His Highness out of loyalty or love or some other misguided emotion. Indeed I did not. I did not truly serve Dagnarus at all. I have another master.'

'The Shield,' Gareth said. 'We knew that. It was by his command that you killed Lord Mabreton. We knew you were nothing but a spy.'

'Spy,' Silwyth repeated calmly. 'Yes, for all these years I have been a spy in the palace, a spy on all you humans did and said. I reported it all dutifully to my master. I have been well rewarded. But all that has come to an end.'

Gareth was skeptical. 'Why? There is little doubt but that Dagnarus's forces will be victorious. He will be King of Vinnengael. He thinks highly of you. He trusts you. You would be ideally placed –'

'You are not telling me anything I do not already know,' Silwyth interrupted. 'You are not telling me anything my master does not already know and plans for me. But I cannot obey the Shield this time. I won't obey. I have a duty to the Shield, that is true, but I have a higher duty to the honor of our people. The moment His Highness took the blood of Lady Valura upon his lips, the moment he chose to turn her into a creature damned and accursed, a monster that brings shame and dishonor upon all her people, that is the moment I swore I would disobey my master and leave my post.

'I would avenge her death upon Dagnarus,' Silwyth added, his dark smile twisting bitterly, 'but that is impossible. He is invincible, at least now. I will take my vengeance in other ways. There are more ways to die than by death. I will destroy his credibility with the elves. Once I tell the Divine about Lady Valura, the entire elven nation will rise against him. He will win this war, only to face another. And the next he might not win so easily.'

'But what will happen to you?' Gareth asked. 'I know something of elven ways. By disobeying the Shield, your life is forfeit –'

'Perhaps. Perhaps not. When the Divine discovers that the Shield has been plotting against him, has secretly supported a Lord of the Void, the Shield may find that he has all he can do to keep himself from tumbling down the cliff, much less trying to pull me down with him. I will be considered a turncoat. I will be disgraced and dishonored. But I will have my revenge.'

'Why tell me?' Gareth demanded. 'You know I will tell him.'

Silwyth regarded Gareth with disdain and loathing. 'I want you to tell him. Tell him I will have my revenge on him. It may be tomorrow. It may be a hundred years from tomorrow. I am patient. I can wait. The waiting for me will be easier for knowing that he will, from now on, live every day in fear. He has many lives, it is true, but that many will I take from him. Is the wine poisoned? What is that strange taste in his food? Is that the flash of a dagger in the moonlight? Is that someone creeping up behind him? The answer to all those is *yes*! The answer is Silwyth! Tell him.'

The elf turned on his heel and vanished into the smoke-heavy darkness.

Gareth stood a moment in the hallway, confused and afraid, torn in two and cursing the elf. Should I continue on, search for Helmos? Or should I return to Dagnarus, warn him to beware of Silwyth? The elf claimed he was fleeing Vinnengael, but Gareth saw that to trust anything Silwyth said was to trust the roused serpent not to strike.

In the end, Gareth determined, quite logically, that Dagnarus could take care of himself. A Lord of the Void, protected by the magical armor of the Void, with many life spans at his disposal, the prince was certainly not about to fall victim to an elf with a knife. Not this day, at least. Gareth continued his search, heading for the King's tower room, where he hoped he might find Helmos overseeing the battle from that advantageous position.

Some inner part of Gareth wished Silwyth success, wished that the elf might do what Gareth, with his dead soul, could not do. He acknowledged that dreadful wish and went on.

Vinnengael was on the verge of defeat. Its defenders continued to hold the north wall, though the black fire and the vicious and prolonged assault by Dagnarus's troops – mercenaries eager for the looting and rapine promised them if they took Vinnengael – had decimated the defenders' numbers and was wearing down their morale. But behind them, the city was in flames.

Captain Argot had been forced to use his reserve troops to help fight the fires, which were burning out of control, consuming businesses and houses. The citizens were in a panic, trying in vain to save their homes, clogging the streets and impeding efforts to help douse the flames. And then the river dried up, strangely, inexplicably.

The moment he heard that report, Argot saw Dagnarus's strategy, saw it clearly. Though it meant almost certain defeat, the captain was soldier enough to appreciate the brilliance.

'What a general!' he said to himself in grudging admiration. 'What a fine –'

That was his last word, his last thought. An arrow struck him, pierced his eye. He was dead before his body tumbled from the wall.

Word that the Lord of the Void had used his powerful magic to drain the river – Vinnengael's heart's blood – was a blow to her defenders. The second blow fell when they heard that the prince's troops had entered the palace from the rear, had taken the palace with ease, and were marching to crush the defenders on the north wall between the anvil of Shakur below and the hammer of Dagnarus behind.

The soldiers remained at their posts, determined to die where they stood, preferring that to perishing in the flames racing through the streets below or being trampled to death by the panic-stricken mob.

High in one of the towers of the palace, Anna kept her lonely watch over poor mad Emillia. The Dowager was in a pitiful state, trembling and sobbing or, what was worse, horribly laughing. Anna did her best to assuage the madwoman's terrors, both real and imaginary, terrors brought on by the smoke, the tension of those around her, the strange sounds echoing through the palace – sounds of tramping feet and shouted orders, the clash of steel.

The sounds of battle did not last very long. An ominous silence settled over them, choking, like the smoke.

'What . . . what does it mean, Your Majesty?' asked the healer, who had chosen to remain with Emillia. 'Have we won?'

Anna turned from the open window where she had been watching the fires blaze up, one after the other, all over Vinnengael.

'Yes, I'm sure that is what it means,' she lied. 'Soon all will be over, and we will be at peace at last.' That much, at least, was the truth.

Screams were audible, even this far away. A child, screaming, perhaps trapped in a burning building, unable to escape . . .

'What is that?' Emillia cried. 'I heard my baby cry! Bring him to me, this instant!'

Anna closed the curtains.

'No, no,' she said, trying to smile with lips so stiff that she feared the smile would make them crack and bleed. 'No, no, Your Majesty. Your baby sleeps soundly. And you must try to sleep yourself.' Tears slid down her cheeks.

The rhythmic tramp of booted feet thundered in the hallway. The healer pressed her hand over her mouth, stifling her cries so as not to alarm her patient. Anna reached out, caught hold of the young healer's hand. Outside the door, war magi stood guard, but their guard could not hold for long. Not against the force that bore down on them.

Light – magical, awful – flashed from beneath the closed and locked door. Voices cried out in agony, blasts and the ringing of swords echoed through the halls. One voice, harsh and cold and horribly familiar to Anna, issued a single command. The door burst asunder, the wizard lock that held it shattered.

Dagnarus strode inside, followed by a Vrykyl and his troops. He paused, his eyes adjusting to the room's dimness after the flaring torchlight in the corridor.

'Where is he?' he demanded, his helmed head turning, seeking. 'Where is Helmos? I know he is here. He might as well face me. His guards are dead . . .'

'Hush!' Anna commanded. She rose to confront him, pale and cold with anger. 'Lower your voice! Don't you see how you frighten her?'

Emillia was gasping and crying, trembling all over. Her eyes started from her head, her face writhed, her mouth gabbled. She stared at Dagnarus in the black armor, the horned helm, in a paroxysm of fear.

Dagnarus removed his helm, shook back his sweat-damp hair from his eyes. Motioning his men to remain where they were, he stepped forward, to see better in the wavering light. His face registered nothing at the sight of the madwoman, neither pity nor revulsion. Dagnarus did not recognize Emillia. Not at first.

A line puckered his brows. He walked forward another step.

'Mother . . .'

He spoke the word so softly that it was barely audible. Anna heard it but only because she saw it on his lips.

Emillia straightened, her hands patted her wispy hair. 'You there. Chamberlain.' She spoke to Dagnarus, made a gesture that would have once been imperious but, with her withered hand, was only pathetic. 'Tell my son that he must come to see his mother. I sent for him yesterday and the day before and still he does not come to see me. He is a wicked, ungrateful child.'

Dagnarus turned his shadowed gaze to Anna. 'How long has she been like this?'

'Ever since . . .' Anna paused, not quite certain what to say or how to say it. 'Ever since you left,' she finished softly.

Dagnarus's gaze went back to his mother. He stared at her and his face set, grim and expressionless. His gaze left his mother, never to go back to her. He fixed his eyes upon Anna.

'Madam, where is your husband?'

'Where he needs to be,' Anna replied steadily.

Dagnarus regarded her long, considering. Then he bowed to her, low and respectful, and turned to his men. 'Helmos is not here. Move out. Search the rest of the palace. Quietly,' he added. 'Quietly.'

Pausing in the shattered doorway, he turned back. 'I thank you for your care of her, Madam. I am sorry to have troubled you. I will leave my own guards posted at the door. You will not be harmed.'

Bowing again, he left the room.

Anna's strength gave way. She sank into a chair, her teeth clamping down hard on her lip so that she would not weep, not when he might be able to still hear her.

'The gods keep my husband safe!' She prayed in her heart. 'The gods keep and bless him!'

*   *   *

'Well?' Dagnarus demanded abruptly, coming across Gareth. 'Have you found him?'

'The King is not in the palace,' Gareth reported.

Dagnarus eyed his friend. 'He's not? Then where is he?' He glanced around. 'And where is Silwyth?'

'He has fled,' said Valura, and there was a hint of emotion in her usually lifeless voice, a hint of dark triumph, as of an enemy vanquished. 'The elf has betrayed you, my beloved. Think no more of him.'

Dagnarus looked astonished, dubious.

'What she says is true,' Gareth admitted. 'Silwyth is gone. He said to tell you –'

'I don't give a damn what that traitor says!' Dagnarus snarled savagely. 'Where is the King?'

Gareth lowered his eyes. 'The servants – those who have not fled – think he might be on the wall with his troops.'

'Helmos anywhere near a battle?' Dagnarus snorted derisively. 'I doubt it. You are lying. You would do or say anything to protect him. But no matter. For now I myself know where to find him. "Where he needs to be" his wife said. Of course. He is in the Temple. My brother has run, sniveling, to the gods.'

The smoke was thicker by far outside the palace. Red-hot cinders rose on the draughts created by the firestorms sweeping through the city. Warriors fought and died by the blazing light. A booming sound, irregular and loud, like the beating of an unquiet heart, sent shudders through the ground.

'What is that?' Gareth asked fearfully, covering his mouth and nose with his cloak.

'The battering ram,' said Dagnarus with satisfaction. 'Shakur is breaking through the main city gate.'

People swirled around them, soldiers running from the battle, soldiers running to the battle and stopping to argue with or exhort those who were fleeing; mothers crying out for someone to find their lost children; husbands searching frantically for entire families that had disappeared. They bumped into Gareth, shoved him, pushed, caromed off him.

One soldier, wild with battle rage, sought to attack Valura. She did not even draw her sword, but crushed the man's skull, through his steel helm, with a blow from her fist. But even in their panic, no one came near Dagnarus. The Void surrounded him, created an island of calm on which he stood dry-shod as wave after wave of chaos burst on the shores.

He strode on eagerly toward the Temple, silhouetted against the fire, seeming carved out of blackness. Dagnarus did not cover his nose against the smoke, but breathed in the smell of death and destruction, as though it were holy incense.

'We shall have to rebuild Vinnengael, of course,' he said as he walked. 'It will rise from the ashes, newborn, ten times more beautiful. I will build a city to make my father proud!'

'Not this way!' Gareth cried, pointing, for Dagnarus had been so bold as to walk straight up the front of the Temple steps. 'Look!'

The front doors to the Temple were ringed round with war magi. They stood in a semicircle, some twenty of them. A magical shield radiated out from them, illuminated them with a soft white light, as if the moon shone in the midst of the garish flaming bursts of a dying sun. The sight of the war magi gave Dagnarus pause.

'Not even you can fight them all!' Gareth shouted, to be heard above the screams of the mob.

'No, you're right,' Dagnarus said, eyeing them coolly. 'Trust those idiots to waste their energy guarding the Temple when they are needed on the walls. But things will change when I am King! We will enter from the back. I'll lay wager no one has thought to guard the rear.'

The buttery was guarded, but only by a few magi, who had been sent to ward off looters, those who would take advantage of any type of suffering and turmoil to make off with what they could carry. Those few magi could not stand against the Lord of the Void nor against a Vrykyl. Gareth tried not to look too closely at the crumpled bodies over which he stepped. He was afraid that he might recognize them and, indeed, he thought he saw their former tutor, Evaristo.

Gareth refused to let himself think about that. His soul was in such turmoil, such anxiety and worry over the coming confrontation of brother against brother, prince against King, that he could spare no thought or regret for anything else.

They entered the Temple storage room. Located underground and windowless, it was relatively free of the asphyxiating smoke.

Dagnarus halted. 'Do you know where this Portal is?' he asked, glancing around, as if he thought the Portal of the Gods might be among the wine casks and cheeses, dead chickens, and bloody slabs of meat. He turned to Gareth, who had known the question was coming and had been dreading it.

'Where is the Portal?' he repeated angrily.

How easy to claim ignorance! And yet Dagnarus would not believe him. Anyone who had spent years of his life in the Temple, as had Gareth, would know where to find the Portal of the Gods.

'Yes, Your Highness. I know.'

'What?' Dagnarus demanded sharply, irritably. 'Don't mumble!'

'I know.'

'Then you will take me there.'

Gareth hesitated. Dagnarus's eyes narrowed dangerously.

'Promise me . . . promise me that you will not kill

him,' Gareth said finally, the words coming out in a gasp.

'Kill him! Of course, I won't kill him!' Dagnarus cried, exasperated. 'I am not a monster! He is my brother. Besides, I intend for him to witness my triumph, my victory! I shall make good use of him. Perhaps even let him remain a Dominion Lord. They will all come under my control, of course, and he might be useful to me. No, Patch. Helmos has but to hand over the Sovereign Stone, and I will kiss him on both cheeks and take him to my bosom.'

'You know he would sooner die than do that,' Gareth said.

'Listen to me, Patch!' Dagnarus caught hold of Gareth, squeezing his arms painfully, dragged him close. The helm's wolfish visor cut into Gareth's face, the points pricked his flesh. 'I will find this Portal. I will search the Temple from top to bottom, tear it down stone by stone if necessary. But I will find it. And know this. Right now, I am pleased with my success and in a merciful mood. But if you thwart me, if I have to rip apart this Temple to locate my brother, I will not be in a good humor at all. My anger and frustration will grow with every door I open in vain, and by the time I do find him, I will be inclined to simply throttle him and have done with it.

'Now, what will it be, Patch? Will you take me to my brother?'

'I will take you to him,' Gareth agreed.

After all, this might be best, he thought. At least I will be present at the interview, whereas otherwise Dagnarus would most certainly leave me behind in a fury, if he did not kill me outright.

Gareth had not yet used his magic, there had been no need. His strength was holding up well. He knew Helmos would never give up the Sovereign Stone, but there might be a possibility Gareth could save one brother from himself and save the other in spite of himself.

He led the way, swiftly and surely, through the Temple to the very center.

He led Dagnarus to the Portal of the Gods.

FIVE

The Portal of the Gods

HELMOS SAT UPON THE BED IN THE CELL that was the Portal of the Gods, the Sovereign Stone clasped tightly in his hand. He no longer prayed to the gods for intercession. They would not come. They would not storm the walls of Vinnengael and drive away the enemy with their flaming swords and golden trumpets.

And why, he thought suddenly, should they?

His own question took him completely by surprise. He pondered on it.

Well, of course, they should. He reasoned first. Why? Because I ask them to. Because it is mine and I want to keep it.

But the gods did not build the walls. The gods did not farm the land or gather in the crops. The gods did not put the books in the library or the beds in the hospital. Yes, the gods gave us the magic to try to heal those in the Hospital, just as the gods provided the stone for the walls and the eyes to read the books. And who is responsible for the walls, the books, the beds? Those who gave us the means to use them, or we, who produced them?

The gods gave us the Portals, so that we should travel

to the lands of our brethren and come to know them better. And what have we done? In our fear, we sealed them shut!

He opened his hand and gazed at the Sovereign Stone. He called to mind the ceremony, saw the stone in his father's hands – a perfect diamond, flawless, smooth. He saw it split into four parts and then Helmos saw what his brother had seen – the emptiness in the center, the Void left when the pieces were separated. Helmos stared into the Void, aghast, appalled, and for a moment it seemed that the emptiness would empty the world of light and beauty and truth.

'No,' he said aloud. 'I will not allow it.'

He stared straight into the darkness, unafraid, and though the darkness was very great and very terrible to look upon, he saw, on the outer fringes, four tiny points of light. Four points of light that would continue to burn.

Like the stars, the deeper the darkness, the brighter the lights shine.

The gods could not save him, could not save Vinnengael. Man must save himself or lose himself, as he chooses. The parents teach the child to walk. They watch it fall, bump its head. They listen to it cry in fear and see it reach to be picked up and carried. The parents refuse, though it pains them.

The child must walk alone.

Helmos knew then with absolute certainty that the gods had indeed answered his prayer. They had not answered it the way he wanted. They had not snatched him up from the hard floor to be kissed and cuddled, cradled and protected. He must walk alone and though the darkness would overtake him, just as night overtakes the day, the gods had given him the means to live through the night and look forward to the dawn.

'Forgive me, Father,' Helmos said softly, tears welling in his eyes. 'Forgive me for doubting you. Only by splitting the stone apart, only by accepting and understanding and honoring our differences can we hope to bring the stone back together again. For you saw that if we do, if we succeed, the sundered stone will be stronger than the whole.'

He drew the chain that held the Sovereign Stone from around his neck. He placed his lips against the stone, kissed it reverently, and then set the stone upon the altar.

He left it there and walked toward the door, the door that would take him back into the world, into the darkness.

He walked alone but he knew that somewhere fond parents watched his steps through their own tears.

The Revered High Magus had heard that animals can predict devastating earthquakes. Dogs are said to become extremely agitated. They cannot rest in one place but must pace endlessly and, if shut indoors, will whine and paw at the door, trying to escape outside. Flocks of birds will fly up suddenly into the air right before the ground begins to tremble. If this was true, then the Most Revered High Magus knew well what they felt.

Not an earthquake, per se. At least not within the earth. The very fabric of magic, however, was unstable. He had sensed tiny rents and cracks and tremors at the very start of the battle, and it seemed to him that they grew in magnitude and severity. Though he was in his study, his thoughts were in another part of the Temple, in the Portal of the Gods with Helmos. Reinholt glanced often at his study door, thinking that at any time the King must enter with the word that all was well. The gods would vanquish their foes and cast Dagnarus back into the Void.

But hours passed and Helmos did not come to bring him this news and the Most Revered High Magus was now profoundly worried. He had not liked the expression on the King's face the last time he had spoken to Helmos. It was a look of one who has lost his faith, a look of hopelessness and despair. Was it the gods' anger the Most Revered High Magus was experiencing? Anger against their enemies? Or anger against those who had chosen to ignore their warnings?

Reinholt paced like the nervous dog around the study. Though here alone, he was not isolated or cut off from what was happening in the city. He received reports from couriers almost every minute and undoubtedly these reports were contributing to his agitation. The condition of couriers spoke eloquently, they had no need for words – their robes torn and covered with blood, their faces black with soot and cinders, their tears ploughing tracks through the grime. He grew to dread the knock upon his door and when another fell, his first impulse was to tell them to go away. His sense of duty and responsibility prevailed. He opened the door.

Nine men and women, clad in furs and iron, armed with spears like trees, their expressions calm, stood in the doorway. The warriors surrounded a shriveled, shrunken little brown bird of a woman, her body all covered with tattoos.

The Revered Magus stared, recovered, and made a low and belated bow. 'Keeper Tabita! I am honored by your presence. Please, come inside.'

Yet even as he invited her to cross the threshold, his spirits were in turmoil, now despairing, now fluttering with wild hope. He had met Tabita upon her arrival, had seen the bare spot on her head. That spot was now almost entirely filled in with tattoos telling the tragic story of the battle for Vinnengael. Only one small area remained unmarked, an area at the very crown of her head. The end was fast approaching. And she had come here to witness it.

Tabita toddled inside the study. Her face was cheerful, even ecstatic. She was nearing the culmination of her life's work. An observer of life, a recorder of events, she was not moved by the horrendous sights she must have witnessed. Seating herself in a chair, with the assistance of the High Magus, who had practically to lift her into it, she gazed out calmly upon the end.

Her feet swung over the edge of the chair, coming nowhere near the floor. She accepted some biscuits and a glass of wine in which to soak them, sat eating and drinking and looking about her with her sharp, bright eyes. She wore slung about her shoulder a bag carrying the tools of her trade. When her repast was finished, she removed the special indelible ink and the magic stylus from the bag, placed them upon the table in readiness. The stylus would pierce her flesh, inscribe there the whorls and lines and dots, markings that could be read only by those trained to the art, the knowledge of which was a closely guarded secret of the Keepers.

The nine Omarah bodyguards entered the High Magus's study and ranged themselves around the walls, wherever there was space, their spearpoints gouging holes in the woodwork. They stood silently, their heads bowed beneath the low ceiling, their eyes fixed upon one object – the Keeper.

The Most Revered High Magus completely failed in his duties as host. His fear and anxiety, wound up with his hope, had tied him into knots. He could not pace his room anymore, not without tripping over the feet of the bodyguard, and he was quite incapable of making polite conversation. He sat fidgeting nervously, tapping on the table with his fingertips. Tabita inked her stylus.

Minutes passed. The Revered High Magus could not endure the waiting another moment. The fabric of magic seemed to twist tighter and tighter. The magic was taut as a rope in a tug-of-war between monumental forces. Neither force would let go, neither dare let go now for fear the rope would snap back and destroy them. It was the rope itself that must break, unable to bear the strain.

'An apt analogy,' said Tabita, though the High Magus had not spoken it aloud.

'Keeper,' said Reinholt, desperate, 'is there . . . is there anything we can do? . . .'

'I only see. I only record.' She patted her head and swung her feet back and forth. 'But I like your analogy.'

The High Magus sank back into gloomy foreboding. He was roused moments later by the sounds of footfalls outside the antechamber door. He leapt to his feet and flung it open.

'Yes?' He strode into the corridor. 'What is it, Roderick?' he demanded, recognizing the head of the war magi. 'What news?'

'Dagnarus is here, High Magus! He is inside the Temple! He has gone straight to the Portal of the Gods!'

'Of course.' Reinholt breathed a sigh in understanding. 'That is why the magic is being pulled and twisted and tugged, almost to the breaking point. The confrontation between the two must come. There is nothing I can do, nothing anyone can do to stop it. The Lord of Sorrows, the gods have named Helmos. This is his fate. He has taken it upon himself. To try to free him from it would be to rob him of his triumph.'

'We are preparing to attack, High Magus. I –'

'No! Do not attack!'

'But, High Magus!' The war magus was appalled. 'We cannot permit . . .'

'It is out of our hands!' Reinholt gasped for air, wiped his sweating forehead. 'We have other, greater responsibilities. We must evacuate the city!'

The war magus stared, his mouth gaping wide.

'Go forth! You and the other war magi and anyone else you can find. Go into the city and warn the people to flee! Tell them to escape by any means they can! Evacuate the Hospital! Hurry, hurry! We do not have much time!'

The Most Revered High Magus turned back to his

study. He started to warn the Keeper, started to urge her to flee, but he saw that her eyes were closed. The stylus was in her hand, she was lifting her hand to the bare spot upon her head.

'I fear that this place . . . may be deadly,' the Magus said softly, speaking to the Omarah, not daring to disturb the Keeper.

The Omarah nodded implacably, unperturbed.

The Keeper began to write.

'This,' said Gareth, coming to a halt before a small door set inside a nondescript wall. 'This is the Portal of the Gods.'

Dagnarus glanced at it disparagingly. 'This is nothing more than a novice's cell.'

'Nonetheless,' said Gareth gravely. 'It is the Portal.' He was very pale, haggard and trembling. 'Your brother is within.'

Dagnarus eyed the cell door grimly. He could now begin to feel the emanations, the magic shiver in his hand.

'Leave me,' he said abruptly.

'Your Highness! It is too dangerous –'

'Leave me!' Dagnarus shouted, rounding on Gareth. His eyes were dark, and Gareth recoiled from them.

'This is between my brother and me,' Dagnarus said. 'And if you must know, Patch, friend of my youth, I do not altogether trust you. I believe that you would save my brother, if you could.'

The truth spoke from Gareth's heart.

'If I could . . .' he said softly.

'At least you are an honest traitor,' Dagnarus muttered. 'Not like that bastard Silwyth. Valura, take Master Whipping Boy out of my sight.'

'I could kill him,' she offered, and there was an odd warmth in the dead voice, a flicker of hatred, of jealousy.

'No, he has his uses. You hear that uproar? The war

magi saw us. They are probably now marching to attack us. The two of you return to the end of the hall and there stand guard. Fight them if you must. Let no one pass.'

'I do not want to leave you.' Valura reached out her black-gloved hand in a touch, a caress.

He drew back, out of her reach.

'You will obey me,' he ordered coldly. 'I am your master.'

Valura's hand hung motionless in the air. And then, more lifeless than the day she had first died, her hand drew back, sank down.

She turned away from him and walked into the smoke-filled corridor. Dagnarus looked after her, his gaze dark and lowering. Then he turned to stare – grim and hard – at the door to the Portal.

'The gods curse your father!' Gareth cried suddenly, passionately, vehemently. 'And my curse fall upon the gods! This is their fault. You should never have looked inside the Sovereign Stone!'

Dagnarus smiled then. He seemed to soften with the smile, and then the smile twisted. 'You know, Patch, I don't think it happened quite that way.' The emerald eyes were clear and empty, emptier even than the dead eyes of the Vrykyl. 'I think the Sovereign Stone looked inside me.'

He fell silent. From the Portal came the sound of Helmos's voice. The words were inaudible, but the voice itself was strong and resolute, with no tremulous quaver, no crack of fear.

'Go on,' Dagnarus commanded. 'Leave me. I must finish what I've begun.'

Half-blinded by tears, Gareth turned and stumbled down the hallway. He stopped only when he realized, with deep shame, that he was glad to have been ordered away, that at least he was absolved of all responsibility.

Understanding this, he halted and, wiping the tears,

glanced at Valura. If she knew what he intended, she would try to stop him. The Vrykyl had taken up her post, was standing guard, as she had been ordered. She paid no attention to him.

Gareth hesitated only a moment, then broke into a run.

The distance he had to cover was not far, but, as in a nightmarish dream when the hall one walks seems short, yet grows longer with every frantic step, this hallway seemed to lengthen and stretch away from him.

Still he ran.

Dagnarus waited until he was certain he was alone, waited until he had banished from him the last two who loved him. Free of them, free of all constraints, he smote his fist upon the closed door.

'Helmos! The gods cannot help you now. They have abandoned you. Come out and treat with me, if you would save yourself and your city.'

The door to the Portal of the Gods opened. Helmos stood within, the armor of the Dominion Lord shining silver, reflecting a brilliant white light emanating from the Portal.

Dagnarus, staring past his brother, stared in awe.

The Portal was no longer a small and cramped cell. The Portal was an enormous chamber, its walls not visible to him, its ceiling the dome of heaven. The dome was empty, yet the emptiness was filled with light, not darkness. In the very center, the Sovereign Stone – the quarter piece of the Sovereign Stone – sparkled bright against the radiant light, as the evening star shines at sunset.

Dagnarus's view shifted from the Portal to the prize – unguarded, alone. Only his brother stood between him and his greatest desire. His brother stood alone.

The King's expression was grave, serious, but the light

that shone in the Portal behind him shone also in his eyes.

'You know why I have come,' Dagnarus said, regarding his brother with hatred, hatred tinged with envy. 'You know what I want. My armies are victorious, the city of Vinnengael is mine. The Sovereign Stone will be mine as well. Stand aside.'

Helmos said nothing, but he did not move.

'Stand aside, Helmos!' Dagnarus repeated, his gloved hand resting upon the hilt of his black sword. 'I do not want to hurt you – you are my brother, our father's blood runs in both of us.' His expression hardened. 'But I will cut you down without a qualm unless you move from that doorway.'

'It is for our father's sake, as well as your own, that I say this to you,' Helmos answered, his voice calm. 'Do not enter the Portal of the Gods, Dagnarus. The Sovereign Stone can never be yours. The gods will surely destroy you if you try to take it.'

'The gods destroy me?' Dagnarus laughed. 'Why, dear brother, I am practically a god myself! I wield the Dagger of the Vrykyl. I have drunk the blood of those I gave to the Void. I have more lives than the proverbial cat!'

Dagnarus moved a step closer. 'Step aside, Helmos. Or else your dear wife, whom I left just now in care of my troops, will be a widow.'

Helmos paled at this, but his resolve did not waver. 'The gods keep her,' he said softly. 'And bring her safe to me when this is all done.' He looked at his brother almost tenderly. 'Our father's last thoughts were of you. His last earthly concern was for you. I tell you this in his name. If you enter the Portal, you do so at your own peril. And you not only endanger yourself, you endanger all of Vinnengael.'

'Do you dare threaten me?' Dagnarus sneered.

'No,' said Helmos. 'I am trying to warn you.' He drew

his sword, not skillfully, for he was a scholar, not a warrior. 'For your own sake and the sake of my people, I will stop you.'

'You can try, brother,' said Dagnarus, drawing his sword in his turn. 'I need only kill you once, Helmos. You, on the other hand, must kill me many times over. That's something not even the gods could do!'

Dagnarus thrust the blade forward, his movement swift and skilled. Helmos moved clumsily to block the thrust and Dagnarus struck the King's blade aside, sent the sword flying from his brother's hands. Dagnarus lifted his sword, intending to cleave between helm and breastplate, sever Helmos's neck.

Strong hands seized Dagnarus's arm, halted the killing stroke. Dagnarus turned in fury that changed to astonishment.

Gareth had hold of the prince. The whipping boy's skin was a mass of oozing pustules. Gareth gasped, 'Metal to ice!' and touched the sword.

The blade shattered. Numbing cold paralyzed Dagnarus's hands.

'Damn you!' he cried in outrage, and turned on Gareth. He would have killed him then and there, but he heard movement behind him.

Helmos made a dive to regain his sword. Dagnarus kicked it away, sent it slithering into the Portal. Helmos could not retrieve it without abandoning his post at the door.

'Hand to hand then,' said Dagnarus, his breath coming heavily. He flung aside the useless hilt of the broken sword. 'As I guess it was always meant to be.'

He leapt at his brother, his hands grappling for Helmos's throat. Helmos met the charge, his hands closing over Dagnarus's wrists. The two struggled, locked in desperate combat upon the threshold of the Portal of the Gods. The armor of the Dominion Lord protected Helmos from Dagnarus's attack. The armor of the Void shielded Dagnarus.

Dagnarus was the younger, the stronger, the more skilled. But he was overconfident, overeager. He had expected to strike down his brother – his weak and bookish brother – with ease. That had not happened, and now, frustrated, his will thwarted, the prince lost his head. He tried to overbear Helmos with his strength. Helmos used Dagnarus's own strength against him, upended him.

Dagnarus lay on his back on the floor, dazed and stunned by the heavy fall, unable to move. It was as if the gods held him pinned down.

Helmos grabbed his sword. Grasping it, he raised it over Dagnarus.

'The gods and our father forgive me!' he prayed.

A ball of darkness, formed of the Void, as big as a man's fist, molded and shaped by Gareth's bloodstained hands and hurled with the force of his magic, struck Helmos full in the chest. Not even the might of the Void could penetrate the armor of a Dominion Lord, but the ball struck Helmos a terrible blow, wrenched the sword from his hands. Helmos fell backward and lay unmoving.

Dagnarus regained his feet. He drew his dagger, the Dagger of the Vrykyl, and stood over his unconscious brother.

'Dagnarus, don't!' Gareth cried. His energy was drained. He could barely stand. With strength born of desperation, he clawed at Dagnarus. 'I stopped him! You must not kill him! He is . . . your brother.'

'You did indeed stop him, Patch,' Dagnarus said. 'I thank you for that. You will be rewarded.'

He tried to shake Gareth off.

'All my life, I have borne your punishment,' Gareth said, clinging to him with uncharacteristic tenacity. 'I will bear this! Accuse me! Say it is my fault! Only do not do this dreadful crime!'

Inside the Portal of the Gods, the Sovereign Stone shone with a rainbow light.

'Yes, you will be punished!' Dagnarus cried. Seizing hold of Gareth by the neck, he slammed the whipping boy's head against the stone wall, cracking his skull. 'I am sorry, Patch,' he said to the pain-filled eyes that stared at him, still pleading, their light already dimming. 'I warned you in the beginning. "I will do what I want to do, though they kill you for it."'

He struck Gareth's head against the rock a second time, then let loose his grasp. The body slid down the wall, leaving a bloody smear on the white stone.

Turning, the Lord of the Void plunged the dagger of the Vrykyl into his brother's throat.

Helmos died without a cry. His body lay across the threshold, one arm stretched out as if, even in death, he would try to prevent his brother from entering.

Dagnarus kicked aside his brother's warding arm. The prince stepped over the body and entered the Portal of the Gods.

He reached out his hand, his fingers touched the jewel, his prize, his reward. He felt it, cool and beautiful. Its light was painful to him, though. He couldn't look at it directly. He grasped the stone, his black gloves closing around it, trying to douse the light that lanced through him like spears of flame.

In that moment, the magic snapped, whipping around, recoiled back upon him.

He could not die, but he could wish to die. He moaned in agony and curled in upon himself and sank to the ground, tried to crawl into the ground, anything to escape the torment.

He heard the magic's concussive blast, felt the ground shake. He saw, through eyelids closed against the searing pain, the Temple fall, the walls of the city crumble. Attacker and defender plunged headlong into the rubble, their war forever ended. The river, freed of the Void, surged down its bed in a raging torrent.

Dagnarus howled in rage and cursed the gods, the mean-spirited gods, so jealous of his victory that they would destroy Vinnengael rather than permit him to win it.

He could not die. They could not kill him. He would defeat them yet. His hand clenched the Sovereign Stone, clasped it in a deathlike grip.

Though he had lost all else, this was his. They would not take it from him.

The light gave way, diminished, died.

Darkness, soothing and restful, came to claim him, Lord of the Void.

SIX

The Well of Darkness

I T SEEMED THE WORLD FELL ON HER.

Valura saw Gareth racing back down the hall. She tried to stop him, was within arm's reach of him when he cast his black spell, the spell that toppled Helmos and gave Dagnarus victory. Gareth's own death mattered not at all to Valura, who hated him as she hated all who were close to Dagnarus. Especially the living.

She watched Dagnarus step into the Portal. Its awful light blinded her, filled her with such pain that she could have plucked out her eyes rather than stare into it.

She waited for him to return to her, waited for him to emerge triumphant, and then she heard him cry out, a hoarse, agonized scream of rage and anger.

She tried to defy the light, tried to steel herself to brave it, though it seemed as if it must consume the dark tendrils of magic that held her lifeless body together. With great effort, she reached the door of the Portal, and the light exploded.

She cried out to him, fought to save him, but the blast lifted her as if she were dust and hurled her far, far from him. The world fell down upon her, burying her under the gigantic blocks that had once been the Temple but were now tossed about like discarded toys.

She did not lose consciousness. She could not lose consciousness, more was the pity. She heard the voices of the living crying out in pain and in dying, but they were nothing to her, the twittering of birds, the natterings of insects. The one voice she listened for, the voice she longed to hear, the only voice that mattered did not call out. His voice was still and silent.

The rocks settled atop her. The darkness closed over her. Dust drifted down around her, water or perhaps blood dripped and splattered in her face. She struggled to rise, discovered that her body was pinned beneath a huge broken column and mounds of debris on top of that.

The silence reverberated horribly in her head. Frantic to hear the voice, she lifted the column, tossed it aside. Crawling on hands and knees, she fought her way out from under the rubble, shoving aside the enormous blocks of marble, setting off small avalanches in the mountain of broken rock that had once been the Temple.

Her struggle took long hours, maybe days. She had to find him. By the time she had clawed her way to the surface, night was gone. Dawn's gray light was spreading over Vinnengael like a blanket of ashes. But what dawn? How many dawns after how many nights?

She stood atop the destruction and stared around, and though the Vrykyl rarely feel emotion and then only strong emotion – remembered from when they were alive – Valura was amazed and appalled and awed by what she saw.

The beautiful city of Vinnengael, wealthy and prosperous, envied and admired, lay in ruins. The palace still stood, but only parts of it. Turrets had fallen in upon themselves, portions of walls collapsed. The waterfalls had returned with the rushing of the river, but their water was dark and turgid and had a reddish tinge to it. Smoke hung in the air, fires burned on all the levels of the city. Falling ash and cinders had turned the lovely blue of Lake Ildurel black.

A few survivors crawled out from the rubble, some calling frantically for loved ones and pawing through the ruins; others dazed and shocked, wandering the blasted city like lost children waiting for someone to find them and take them home.

A shadow slid over them and they cried out and scurried away. The shadow slid over Valura, dark enough to penetrate her darkness, its chill cold enough to cause her decaying flesh to shiver. She crouched involuntarily, staring upward.

A dragon, an enormous creature, dark against the gray dawn, circled Vinnengael like a great carrion crow. Its red eyes searched for something, and it appeared to find what it sought, for the dragon swooped, diving downward with clawed feet splayed and wings extended.

Valura thought at first the dragon was coming for her, and she knew real fear, for the sword of a Dominion Lord and the claws of a dragon are two weapons mortal to a Vrykyl. The dragon paid no attention to her, however, and, as it neared, Valura's fear eased. This dragon was kin to her. This dragon was of the Void.

The dragon landed atop a portion of the ruined Temple. Delicately, the dragon picked through the rubble.

Valura knew fear again, another type of fear. Perhaps the dragon was searching for Dagnarus! She crept from under the cover of the broken building to gain a better view.

The dragon picked up and tossed aside chunks of debris, until it had dug a large hole – the size of a small building – in the rubble. Reaching down with a front foreclaw, the dragon brought forth, with careful tenderness, a body.

The body was not Dagnarus. This body was small, small as a child's, and brown and covered with odd markings. A Keeper. That would explain the presence of the dragon, one of the five dragons who guarded Time's Fortress, and who wanted nothing more than to know how the story ended.

Clutching the tiny form in its huge clawed foot, the Dragon of the Void spread its wings and soared into the sky, its lashing tail sending a mountain of rubble clattering and thundering to the street.

Valura turned away. She had only one objective and that was to find him. The Temple was in such ruin she had no idea where to begin to look. She felt despair and hopelessness – two oft-remembered emotions. Banishing them now as she had banished them before, she set about her work.

She was weak, she discovered, weak from the effects of the blast, weak from having to dig her way out from under what remained of the Temple. Fortunately, there was no lack of the dying upon which to feed. She ended the life of an injured woman sobbing over her dead lover, and considered that she had done the woman a favor.

Her thirst slaked, her strength returned, Valura went back to the Temple and started moving aside the broken stones, one by one.

'You waste your time,' said a voice, a cold voice, one that did not speak aloud but through the Blood-knife she wore at her waist. 'He's dead.'

Valura did not respond, did not halt her work. Shakur walked over to confront her.

She raised her head. His dead eyes stared at her. Behind him, the dead eyes of the other Vrykyl stared at her. Behind them, the dead eyes of the city of Vinnengael stared at her.

'He is here somewhere,' Valura told Shakur. 'He was inside the Portal. Its magic will protect him.'

'The Portal!' Shakur was disdainful. 'The Portals cannot protect anyone. The Portals are gone.'

'Gone!' Valura halted in her work. She had no choice

but to believe him. Those connected by the Blood-knife cannot lie to each other. 'Gone! What do you mean?'

Shakur stood atop the ruin, gazing around, his black-helmed head seeming to sniff the swirling, drifting smoke.

'Victory was ours,' he said. 'We pushed them off the walls. The gates opened to our might. Our soldiers surged inside. Many of their troops broke and ran, but some did not. The Dominion Lords fought on, and they rallied the brave to their side. Yet, we would have been victorious, of that I have little doubt.

'And then the bells began to ring. The magi poured into the street, shouting that doom was come upon us all and that all should flee the city to save their lives. I felt the truth of what they said. I felt the magic torn loose, lashing through the air like whips. The living felt it, too. Our soldiers had no more thought of winning, but ran for their lives. Friend and foe dropped swords and joined hands, to help each other flee.'

'And you?' Valura asked coolly. She hated him more than all the rest. 'What did you do, Shakur? Did you run as well?'

'I did not run. I took advantage of the turmoil to refresh myself, as I see you have done.' Shakur's dead gaze focused on the blood on Valura's lips and hands. 'And then a shaft of light so bright it seared my eyes blazed out of the Temple. It lit the night like day. Then came the blast. I watched Vinnengael die, and then I knew that he was dead. The master was dead and we were free.'

Valura turned away from him, went back to her work.

'It was in my mind to enter one of the Portals,' Shakur continued. Kicking at a smoldering beam with his booted foot, he sent cinders sparking into the death-tinged air. 'I planned to make my way to the elven lands. The feeding would be good there. The elves do not know us. I could raise my own army, become my own king . . .'

'And what happened?' Valura asked, glancing at him from out the eye slits of her helm. 'Why didn't you?'

'I told you. The Portals are no longer there.'

'Then where did they go?'

Shakur shrugged. 'Disappeared? Perhaps. Moved? That's a possibility. All I know is that you may walk into the entryway, the part that has not been knocked down, but beyond that is nothing. The magic is dissipated. You can no longer feel it.' He glanced around. 'Just as you can no longer feel it here.'

Valura continued working.

'Come with us, Valura,' Shakur said. He motioned to the other Vrykyl. 'We will carve out our own kingdom, be our own masters. There are cities ripe for the taking. You are powerful and strong, your beauty lures men easily to their deaths. I can make good use of you.'

Valura ceased her work. Shakur was right. The magic was gone. The Portal of the Gods was no longer here. But it was somewhere, and Dagnarus was with it. She could hear his voice now, hear it faintly, hear it in the Blood-knife.

'You will form an army, Shakur,' she said. 'A mighty army. But not for yourself, not for your own glory and ambition. You will form the army of Dagnarus.'

The Vrykyl laughed derisively.

'The story is not ended. He lives, Shakur,' Valura said with such conviction that Shakur's laughter ceased. 'Our lord is weak and he is wounded. The magic flung him far, far from here. But it could not kill him. He is alive. And though I must search a hundred, hundred years, I will find him.

'And when he returns, his army will scour the world.'

EPILOGUE

T HE BAHK WAS AN ADULT MALE, A YOUNG
one, not yet fully grown, his body – and his brain
– still developing. This fact – that he was quite
young – explains how he came to be wandering about the
wilderness of this strange and unfamiliar world, lost and
hungry.

An older, more mature bahk would have never entered
the strange cavelike hole that appeared so very suddenly
in the forest. Though drawn to the hole by the smell of
magic – bahks adore magic, as humans adore chocolate –
an elder bahk would have sensed that this was not bright
and shining wizard-magic, not the magic that pleasantly
tickles the fingers and sends a thrilling sensation throughout the body, not the magic that glitters and sparkles in the
sunshine, warms the hands and heart at night. This hole
was god-magic, and therefore dangerous, if not downright
deadly.

An elder bahk might well have entered the hole, but only
after days of watching it and examining it and tossing rocks
inside it to see if Something tossed them right back out and
making offerings of dead taan or dead humans or whatever
other prey the bahk happened to have on hand.

But there were no elder bahk around when the youngster
stumbled upon the hole. No elders to bash the dull-witted
youth over the head and drive him away. His unfinished

brain could not detect the scent of the gods. All he smelled was the magic, and so he ran inside. He thought he was entering a cave.

The cave proved to be extremely different from most caves with which the young bahk was familiar. Its floor and walls were perfectly smooth, made of what appeared to be gray rock. The scent of magic was quite strong inside the cave. The bahk imagined a treasure trove of wondrous arcane artifacts hidden within. He walked and walked, searching for the treasure room, but all he found was more gray rock. He walked until he was starting to grow discouraged and frustrated, tired and footsore and extremely angry.

At that point, he bashed his fist against the gray rock, or what he thought was gray rock. It was as if he'd bashed his fist against the smooth surface of clear water. His fist went right through the rock. He could see his fingers wiggling at him from the other side.

Now the bahk was scared. He realized he'd made a dreadful mistake. He turned to flee, to leave this terrible place, only to find that the way back looked exactly like the way forward. He turned again, to look back the way he'd been going, turned around again to see if he'd got it right and, by this time, was hopelessly confused.

Panicked, the young bahk howled dismally, hoping one of the elders would come find him and take him out of this horrible gray place. No one came, and, after a time, the bahk's throat hurt and so he quit. He sat down and wept a little, lost and lonely and scared and now hungry.

Hunger prompted him to get up and continue walking, the idea having finally struggled into his brain that only by moving did he have some chance of escape.

The bahk's intelligence was rewarded. Light – sunlight – shone ahead of him. The bahk gave a hoarse raw squeal of pleasure and dashed forward, emerging from the gray hole into a forest. The bahk was so thankful to be free of the terrible hole that he did a little dance, a dance whose foot-thumping enthusiasm caused several small trees in the vicinity to shake loose from the ground.

Only when he was finally tired of dancing and starting to think that it was way past time for supper did the bahk actually look around. He realized, in cold terror, that this was not his homeland. This was a forest, and he did not live in a forest. He lived in a desert. A warm and friendly desert with vast expanses of sand. A desert where a bahk could see in all directions, see if his enemies were approaching.

The bahk tried to sort out in his mind what had happened. The only answer was that, in his absence, these trees had moved in and taken over his desert.

Trees. The bahk had seen a few trees in his lifetime, and he didn't particularly like them. The elder bahk taught that trees were good. The elder bahk made weapons out of the trees, weapons they gave the younger bahk when they came of age and taught them to use. But it would be many years yet before this young bahk was deemed to have sense enough to wield a weapon.

The bahk glowered at the trees and twisted his face into a ferocious scowl, to show them that he wasn't scared. He flexed his arms and stomped his feet to intimidate them, and, when they didn't respond, he gained confidence and bashed a few of them with his enormous fist.

The trees waved their arms and shuddered at the blows, but they didn't fight back. Feeling pleased with himself, the bahk moved on to his next problem – his shrunken and empty belly. He needed food, the bahk's favorite food, their only food – the succulent fruit of the obabwi cactus, which grows plentifully in the bahks' desert homeland.

In order to find the cacti, the bahk would have to get past these nasty trees. He started walking, sniffing the air for cactus. A scent came to him, but it was not the juicy scent of obabwi fruit. It was the foul scent of those who feed off animals, the scent of humans. Mingled with this repulsive scent was another smell, much more pleasant and far more exciting – the scent of magic.

It occurred dimly to the bahk that he'd had magic enough to last him a lifetime. But the terror he had experienced was rapidly fading from his mind, having been overtaken and beaten down by hunger. The bahk would certainly never enter the dread hole again, but he blamed the hole itself for having caused his problems, not the magic.

Humans use magic. Humans make magic work for them. Humans are repositories of lovely magical things. The bahks don't use the magic. They don't want the magic to serve them. They love the magic for its own sake. They like to carry magic around, like to pull it out and admire it twenty times a day. They like to adorn their bodies with magic, like to sleep with it at night, tucked beneath their heads.

The bahk ripped a sapling out of the ground to use as a club, one of the very few weapons with which a young bahk is ever trusted. Humans were almost always unwilling to part with their magical artifacts and would generally fight to keep them. The bahk wasn't afraid. Even though he was only half-grown – about the size of two tall human males laid end to end – humans had few weapons that could hurt him. He would be much taller when he was full-grown, about the height of four humans standing atop each other, his body solid as a mountain with a hide so tough that it would easily deflect razor-sharp arrow points and turn aside the best steel sword blades.

The bahk crashed through the trees, which refused to move out of his way, though he yelled and hollered at them and eventually starting shoving them over. The magic scent was strong, filled his nostrils with its promise of excitement. He lumbered forward, snuffling the air, like a cat to catnip.

Not far from the hole, he found the human and the magic.

The human lay on the ground. His eyes were closed, his breathing harsh and ragged and gasping. He was wearing armor. The bahk recognized it as armor, though it was shining black. The human's helm lay on the ground at his side. The black armor was itself magical, and the bahk started to seize it, to rip it off the human. But the armor burned his fingers when he touched it, burned them painfully. Snarling in outrage, the bahk snatched back his burned hand and thrust the fingers in his mouth, sucking on them. He bashed the human a few times with his club in a fit of temper.

The human moaned. His head rolled in agony. His eyelids opened, fixed upon the bahk. He stared at the creature looming over him in horror and astonishment. The bahk paid no attention to the human, who was certainly not a threat. The bahk had found the source of the magic, held fast in the human's hand – a bright and shining diamond.

This magic was gentle. This magic wouldn't hurt the bahk. This jewel, which was smooth-sided and triangular in shape, was the most wonderful thing the bahk had ever seen. Entranced by its beauty, the bahk reached down to seize it.

The human cried out and struggled and tried to stand. He was too weak. He fell back, gasping in pain. The bahk seized hold of the human's hand, which was clasped tightly around the magical diamond. The human, wounded though he was, fought to keep the jewel. He clasped his fingers around it so tightly that it cut into his flesh. Blood ran from his hand, but he would not let loose.

The bahk crouched down beside the human. Lifting the human's hand to his mouth, the bahk crunched the hand between his teeth. Bone cracked, the human screamed. A terrible taste flooded the bahk's mouth. He spit out blood and bits of bone and flesh, peered down at the hand, and grinned in triumph. Amidst what was left of the human's broken and mangled fingers shone the wondrous diamond, the loveliest thing the bahk had ever seen.

He plucked the diamond free, dropped the human's arm carelessly to the ground, and stood up to his full height.

The human actually tried to rise, seemed intent on trying to take back the jewel. The bahk struck the human with the club a couple of times and the human – his face covered with blood – sank to the ground and did not stir.

The bahk stood gazing with elation and awe at his prize and then, urged on by the rumblings of his stomach, he wandered off through the trees in search of food.

Quicksilver Rising

Book One of the Quicksilver Trilogy

Stan Nicholls

Spectacular magic, adventure and intrigue.

Reeth Caldason is the last remaining member of a tribe of warriors who were brutally massacred decades ago. Cursed with episodes of blind rage than endanger anyone near him, he is forced to wander the world seeking revenge for his people and a cure for his magical affliction.

But the spell that binds Reeth is an esoteric one, and his search has so far been fruitless. Only when a young sorcerer's apprentice named Kutch tells him of the mysterious Covenant does he regain a glimmer of hope. Forming an uneasy alliance the two head for the capital city in search of this secretive magical society, unaware that they are about to be drawn into a dangerous world of conspiracy and sedition.

'Gripping … has all the ingredients to become a classic'
DAVID GEMMELL

'Easily as much fun as you'd expect'
JON COURTENAY GRIMWOOD, *Guardian*

'A hugely entertaining read'
JAMES BARCLAY

ISBN 0 00 714150 5